NIGHT AND DAY

JACOB'S ROOM

Night and Day

Jacob's Room

VIRGINIA WOOLF

with Introductions and Notes by
DORINDA GUEST

WORDSWORTH CLASSICS

For my husband
ANTHONY JOHN RANSON
with love from your wife, the publisher.
Eternally grateful for your unconditional love.

Readers who are interested in other titles from
Wordsworth Editions are invited to visit our website at
www.wordsworth-editions.com

First published in 2012 by Wordsworth Editions Limited
8B East Street, Ware, Hertfordshire SG12 9HJ

ISBN 978 1 84022 680 5

Wordsworth Editions
is the company founded in 1987 by
MICHAEL TRAYLER

Typeset in Great Britain by Antony Gray
Printed and bound by Clays Ltd, St Ives plc

CONTENTS

GENERAL INTRODUCTION

Wordsworth Classics are inexpensive editions designed to appeal to the general reader and students. We commission teachers and specialists to write wide-ranging, jargon-free introductions and in some cases to provide notes that will assist the understanding of our readers rather than interpret the stories for them. In the same spirit, because the pleasures of reading are inseparable from the surprises, secrets and revelations that all narratives contain, we strongly advise you to enjoy this book before turning to the Introduction.

General Adviser: KEITH CARABINE
Rutherford College, University of Kent at Canterbury

NIGHT AND DAY

Night and Day

VIRGINIA WOOLF

A novel by
VIRGINIA WOOLF
first published in 1919

INTRODUCTION

> Why, she reflected, should there be this perpetual disparity
> between the thought and the action, between the life of solitude
> and the life of society, this astonishing precipice on one side of
> which the soul was active and in broad daylight, on the other
> side of which it was contemplative and dark as night?
>
> (*Night and Day*, p. 261)

The second of Virginia Woolf's novels, *Night and Day*, as its title implies,
employs an oppositional symbolism: the private and the social, the silent
and the communicable, the solid and the ethereal; a contradictory world,
as Woolf recorded in her Diary: 'Now is life very solid, or very shifting?
I am haunted by the two contradictions' (*Diary*, Vol. III, 4 January 1929,
p. 218). It is both a daylight comedy and a melancholy exploration of the
mind's search for an intangible vision, at the same time encouraging the
hope that some link can be forged between its silent and communicable
worlds. *Night and Day* is fairly conventional in structure in comparison
with her later, more experimental novels, and yet in this novel there is
much focus on introspection and shifting states of being, capturing the
ins and outs of consciousness in all its hues and ambiguities. The novel
as a whole calls into question the values on which the rationale and
substance for traditional fiction had been based: 'civilisation' and the
existing structures of society, especially love, marriage and the family.

Composition and contemporary criticism

Comparatively little is known about the gestation of *Night and Day* and
of Woolf's progress in its composition. In July 1916 Woolf remarked
to her sister Vanessa that she was considering writing a novel 'about'
her and, given that Katharine Hilbery in many ways resembles Vanessa,
she was certainly beginning to formulate the novel (*Letters*, II, p 109).
In a letter to her Latin teacher, Janet Case, she hinted: ' . . . try thinking
of Katharine as Vanessa, not me; and suppose her concealing a passion

for painting and forced to go into society by George [Duckworth]'
(*Letters*, II, p. 400). Woolf identified strongly with her sister's dilemma.
She completed the first draft of the novel on Armistice Day, 11
November 1918 (*Letters*, II, p. 290). Spending the following months
revising and typing the manuscript, she passed it to Leonard Woolf
to read at the end of March, and took it to her publisher, Gerald
Duckworth, on 1 April 1919 (*Diary*, I, pp. 259, 261). It was subsequently
published on 20 October 1919, to mixed reviews. Ford Madox Ford
called it a 'moral-less but very entertaining . . . ado about nothing'.[1] Yet
this is precisely the point; *Night and Day* was intended to include the
parts of our life that barely speak to us, apparently insignificant events,
random 'moments of being', the 'little daily miracles', the 'matches
struck unexpectedly in the dark',[2] the experience of enhanced present-
ness, and exhilarating flights into the life of the mind, the imagination.
A sense of unspoken, submerged meanings resonates in this novel; it
fluctuates between the outer and inner life, between social comedy and
alienation, between the solid houses and streets of London and the
ceaseless flux of the river.

Katherine Mansfield saw *Night and Day* as a ship returning from a
long voyage, unaware of recent turmoil, and surprisingly lacking any
'scars';[3] ostensibly she was referring both to the turmoil of literary
representation and to the turmoil of the First World War. Mansfield's
review stung Woolf deeply. Winifred Holtby was also well aware of the
limitations in Woolf's early novels, and was unafraid to point them out,
albeit with quiet tact. Discussing *Night and Day*, she claimed that it is
'this straining towards some larger life, some more liberal standard of
values, which disturbs the quiet and enclosed perfection of the comedy',
and that Woolf's characters were 'too big for her plot'.[4]

In her critique of *Night and Day*, Mansfield demanded a literature
that recognised the demise of the Victorian world, vanished for ever; a
literature that expressed the influence of the trauma of war on human
character, not merely on subject matter, but in style and form. The

---

1 Ford Madox Ford, *Piccadilly Review* (23 October 1919), reprinted in *Virginia
   Woolf: The Critical Heritage*, pp. 72–5
2 Virginia Woolf, *To the Lighthouse*, Stella McNichol (ed.), Penguin, London
   1992, p. 175
3 Clare Hanson (ed.), *The Critical Writings of Katherine Mansfield*, Macmillan,
   London, 1987, pp. 56–7
4 See Winifred Holtby, *Virginia Woolf: A Critical Memoir*, Continuum,
   London, 2007.

social and psychological conditions of the post-war period, she argued, posed a challenge to the conventions of representation that it was the obligation of art to meet. *Night and Day* was in many ways a novel Woolf had to write before she could embark on that change of perspective she had foreseen the war entailed, its conventional style part of a necessary therapeutic process, and a way in which to work through her intensely ambivalent relationship with her Victorian inheritance. When her husband Leonard described the novel as 'melancholy', she wrote in her diary that 'the process of discarding the old, when one is by no means certain what to put in their place, is a sad one', implying at once the recognition of the end of the Victorian era and the struggle to relinquish its potent influence (*Diary*, I, 27 March 1919, p. 259). *Night and Day* mimics nineteenth-century realism even as it outlines the passing of all things Victorian.

Woolf wrote a large part of *Night and Day* while convalescing from a bout of depression, restricted to writing for 'only one half-hour a day' (*Letters*, IV, p. 231). Looking back on it in the 1930s she felt it had taught her 'certain elements of composition which I should not have had the patience to learn had I been in the full flush of health always' (*Letters*, IV, p. 231). By 1932 she had come to think of *Night and Day* as 'dead'; indeed, in the *Times Literary Supplement* it was described as 'only a love story', one that 'left politics, and war, and sociology and things like that, alone'.[5] However, as recent critics have shown, the novel does in fact address politics and war, albeit elliptically.[6] Though there is no direct mention of war, it is none the less shaped by it and the sense of crisis it produced. And, in order for this novel to be 'dead' as characterised by Woolf, it suggests that it also gave life.

Night and Day has often been seen as an anomaly in Woolf oeuvre, in agreement with Mansfield's view, a regression to a conservative form of novel before the great advances of the 1920s. However, *Night and Day* is closer to *Jacob's Room* than is usually recognised; it is an anti-novel parodying the conventions of romance just as *Jacob's Room* parodies those of the *Bildungsroman*. *Night and Day* is full of scenes of ridiculous confusion, abrupt exits and entrances, coincidental meetings, secrets, conversations at cross purposes and unwelcome interruptions from absurd figures in the form of Katharine's aunts. Such dramatic

5   as cited in *Virginia Woolf: The Critical Heritage*, Robin Majumdar and Allen McLaurin (eds), Routledge, London, 1997, p. 76
6   See Jane Goldman, *The Cambridge Introduction to Virginia Woolf*, Cambridge University Press, Cambridge, 2006, p. 50.

techniques permeate the novel. By placing sceptical rationalists in a genre that requires spontaneous passionate types, Woolf undermines the genre's central assumptions. Moreover, in the novel's questioning of what it is 'to do' something, and its reassessment of women's professions, it anticipates *To the Lighthouse*.

The trajectory of *Night and Day* is, on the surface, a simple one. The novel begins with the quintessentially English action of pouring tea. Yet Katharine's role as hostess at a Sunday-evening tea-party holds little of her interest. Trapped in a stultifying drawing-room where she must observe social propriety and fulfil the role of 'angel in the house',[7] Katharine gives veiled public voice to her private anxiety: that she may never find someone of the opposite sex with whom she can speak of her true feelings, rather than the customary banalities of teatime gossip. Yet, there is a man present who can perceive the underlying current beneath her social manner. Ralph Denham's ability to intuit the truth of her inattention establishes, from the beginning, the psychic tie between these two, albeit at times one of antipathy.

The elements of this initial scene resonate beyond the drawing-room to reveal the anxieties Woolf faced as she struggled to write *Night and Day* and the strategies she used to allay her fears. By adopting, transforming and transcending her traditional literary model she was able to address the question of women's struggle to work while avoiding direct self-expression. If the novel originates in that struggle to find the time and place to do serious work, it speaks of a similar endeavour on the part of many women in the Victorian and modern eras: to resist the duty to serve as 'angel in the house' in order to do the work one has chosen. Katherine's desire for power and independence remains largely unrecognised, operating at a subliminal level; a desire vicariously fulfilled through the figure of Mary Datchet. While the novel indicates that there is a significant difference between men's work, which is respected and properly paid, and Mary's voluntary work, it nevertheless confers on her a sustaining sense of her own value. If work is a burden for the men in the novel, for the women it is an aspiration and a privilege. Mary initially works for an organisation devoted to 'general suffrage'. Early in 1918 the right to vote was granted to women of property over thirty. 'I don't feel much more important – perhaps

---

7   In her essay 'Professions for Women' (1931), Woolf insisted on the woman writer's necessary suppression of the traditionally submissive and domestic feminine role encapsulated in Coventry Patmore's *The Angel in the House*.

slightly so' (*Diary*, I, 12 March 1918, p. 127), Woolf observed. This step, though important, did not mark the end of a fifty-year struggle, but rather the opening of a new chapter in the struggle for social, political and economic equality.

The contrast between Mary Datchet, efficient, practical, hard-working, dedicated to her cause, and the discourse of romance, dream and the imagination intrinsic to Katharine is fundamental to the way the novel conceptualises modernity and the nineteenth-century legacy. The gap between Katharine's mythologised envious perception of Mary's life and the complex lived reality of it is a deep one. In mediating between past and present, *Night and Day* tends towards a prioritisation of the claims of the imagination and of a figurative engagement with the world. The description of Mary Datchet's daily routine imbues her with a persistent self-consciousness concerning the life she leads. As she leaves her apartment 'she said to herself she was very glad' not to be leading a life of leisure; in the street she 'liked to think herself one of the workers', and she 'liked to pretend that she was indistinguishable from the rest' (pp. 70–1). The root of her self-consciousness lies some-what in her dependency on a private income and the voluntary nature of her work set against the predominately male world of 'formal' work. It is the self-consciousness of anyone deliberately adopting an unusual and unprecedented lifestyle. Woolf's engagement with suffrage aesthetics, and her fictional representation of suffragists and suffragettes (in *Night and Day* and *The Years*), may be understood in relation to, and underpinning, a broader continuum of feminist aesthetics,[8] and a spectrum of fictional representations of feminist women.

Night and Day demonstrates in embryonic form ideas which would be developed further in *A Room of One's Own*. Woolf may be said to think back through the legacies of women writers (in her allusions to Jane Austen and George Eliot for example) and to critique the tradition she had inherited. By layering her parody of them with references to Shakespearian comedy she anticipates her later attempt to lay claim, by means of the concept of androgyny, to a subversive feminist agenda. A retrospective analogy may be drawn between Katharine's emancipation as a woman and Woolf's development as a writer. Unwieldy though the

8 Woolf's entire oeuvre is a formidable challenge to patriarchy, but she was hesitant about definition by critics: 'The difficulty about criticism is that it is so superficial. The writer has gone so much deeper [. . .] Our criticism is only a bird's eye view of the pinnacle of an iceberg. The rest under water' (16 August 1933, *Diary*, IV, p. 173).

form of *Night and Day* might be, it is appropriate that Katharine's story of escape from nineteenth-century traditions should be described in the kind of novel which was in its turn to be escaped from. By posing the limits of setting as a problem endemic to traditional literary forms, Woolf marks in her own way the transition between traditional and experimental forms.

Dreams and Reality

'Dreams and Realities' served as the draft title for *Night and Day*, indicating a satirical approach to the dominant ideological model of courtship and the lived reality of it; traditional gender roles are explored and subtly undermined. Note the satire: when Mrs Hilbery speaks of poetry as a refuge, Woolf trusts us to see through rather than with the character:

> 'Lovely, lovely Ophelia!' she exclaimed. 'What a wonder power it is – poetry! I wake up in the morning all bedraggled; there's a yellow fog outside; little Emily turns on the electric light when she brings me my tea, and says, "Oh, ma' am, the water's frozen in the cistern, and cook's cut her finger to the bone." And then I open a little green book, and the birds are singing, the stars shining, the flowers twinkling.
>
> [p. 268]

The satirist need only aim the spotlight; their own mouths condemn. Woolf regarded this romantic comedy, her longest novel, as a means of 'learning what to leave out by putting it all in' (*Letters*, VI, p. 216). It is something which Mrs Hilbery has yet to learn: 'Her mother refused, also, to face the radical questions of what to leave in and what to leave out' (p. 44). For all her eccentricity, however, Mrs Hilbery acts as the *dea ex machina* in the novel, inspired as she was by Woolf's aunt (through Leslie Stephen's first marriage), Thackeray's daughter Anne Ritchie (*Letters*, II, p. 406). Anne Ritchie had much of Mrs Hilbery's randomness, her inconsequentiality, her spontaneity. As such, Mrs Hilbery serves a crucial function, flitting between the fictive world of Shakespeare's comedies and the complications of the lives of those in her family. By drawing on a pseudo aunt Woolf avoids the 'great men', and endorses women and their affections as a fruitful source of inspiration and continuity.

Ralph Denham, raising Katharine to the eminence of a goddess, often views her in a purely fantastic atmosphere:

> For ever since he had visited the Hilberys he had been much at the mercy of a phantom Katharine, who came to him when he sat alone, and answered him as he would have her answer, and was always beside him to crown those varying triumphs which were transacted almost every night, in imaginary scenes, as he walked through the lamplit streets home from the office.   [p. 82]

Ralph, like Katharine, constructs a fantastic image that, because of its grandiose dimensions, inevitably creates conflict whenever confronted with reality. Just as Katharine's 'magnanimous hero' defends against any anxiety and guilt pursuant to her attaining the love she craves, so Ralph's dream image of Katharine safely distances him from the real woman. While both see each other as foreign in nature they delay their union by disfiguring reality with their respective dreams and halos of illusion.

Daydreams play a crucial role in the novel, coexisting with yet transfiguring everyday life and providing the chief means of representing inner life, the life of the mind. Whereas dreams are eventually lost with time, reality has the inimitable characteristic of transforming itself, and reasserting its influence in another direction. Dreams dissipate while reality changes direction. Katharine's fantasies reveal her longing for a degree of power and control more often achieved by men, largely withheld from women and quite at odds with her society's conception of marriage. Wishing to free herself from her engagement to William Rodney, she encourages William to establish an intimate relationship with her cousin Cassandra. Unable to reconcile her hidden desire for domination with being a woman, her idealism with everyday life, her inner passions with love or marriage, these unbridgeable gaps are the source of her silences which the novel articulates as 'dreams', the 'things one doesn't say' (*Letters*, II, p. 400).

Just as Rachel Vinrace in Woolf's first novel, *The Voyage Out*, must struggle to speak for herself when others endlessly seek to educate and speak for her, Katharine's life in *Night and Day* is 'so hemmed in with the progress of other lives that the sound of its own advance [is] inaudible' (p. 92). *Jacob's Room* subsequently abandons the project of developing its protagonists voice altogether, instead experimenting with the project of others speaking in his place, even down to the creaking of his empty chair.

Katharine's wish to escape from the constraints of society is no death wish like that of Rachel in *The Voyage Out*, or longing for annihilation in war as in *Jacob's Room*, yet her escape routes resemble death in providing a way out of immediate existence. Katharine allows herself to become preoccupied with the past, the assistance she affords her mother on the biography of Richard Alardyce supplying the occasion and the materials:

> The glorious past, in which men and women grew to unexampled size, intruded too much upon the present, and dwarfed it too consistently, to be altogether encouraging to one forced to make her experiment in living when the great age was dead.   [p. 43]

The immersion in past grandeur offers a relationship with her grandfather resembling the one those 'intermittent young men' have with her father, lessening her envy and exercising her mind in the detailed work on the biography, applying order to her mother's diffuse and disorganised manner. Katharine's secondary escape from reality entails her work on mathematics, a love which she hides from others, not wishing to incur their disapprobation. It is a love which distinguishes her from her mother, 'the last person she wished to resemble, much though she admired her' (p. 48). At the same time, Katharine is at risk of being stifled by the work on her ancestor, feeling 'half crushed' (p. 46) as well as being cast in an unfavourable light in relation to him: 'perhaps the conclusiveness of a great ancestor is a little discouraging to those who run the risk of comparison with him' (p. 43). Woolf herself, daughter of Leslie Stephen, a well-known man of letters and editor of the *Dictionary of National Biography*, wrote on her late father's birthday, had he lived 'his life would have entirely ended mine' (*Diary*, II, 28 November 1928, p. 208). Woolf's frank statement of conflict between a woman's achievement and the internalisation of patriarchal authority, even after such authority is lessened, is echoed in Katharine's wish to be liberated from the burden of the past.

Despite her stultifying surroundings, Katharine displays self-awareness in relation to love. Receiving a love letter and sonnet from William Rodney, Katharine 'could see in what direction her feelings ought to flow, supposing they revealed themselves' (p. 92). She is conscious of traditional courtship narratives, and can conceive herself as a character in one, but does not personally experience those feelings. She is conscious of love as a social convention, a theatrical performance, a pageant, an illusion, or a convenient fiction. When she does think of romantic love, it assumes the form of parody, 'a magnanimous hero, riding a great horse by the shore of the sea' (p. 93). While her upbringing overburdens her with demands to act as a 'proper woman', she, perhaps subconsciously, compensates with defence mechanisms that keep her more natural inclinations safe from the onslaught. Her self-consciousness and self-control are echoed in Ralph Denham: when they finally reach an understanding they retain a sense of their fundamental isolation; Katharine 'had now to get used to the fact that someone shared her loneliness' (p. 374).

Katharine and Ralph intensely resent the familial pressures that curtail their freedom. By the end of the novel they are in open conflict with Katharine's father, who sees his formerly tractable daughter looking 'like a wild animal caged in a civilised dwelling-place' (p. 342). But her revolution is short lived and the rebels are quickly reintegrated into family and society. Yet Woolf's sense of the dividedness of human nature will not allow her to simplify feelings along the lines dictated by ideological imperatives. Though Ralph rages against the pressure of his home, Katharine's visit to it releases a very different but equally genuine feeling: 'All that brotherhood and sisterhood and a common childhood in a common past mean, all the stability, the unambitious comradeship, and tacit understanding of family life at its best, came to his mind' (p. 291).

Woolf's focus on her characters' self-consciousness creates in the reader an awareness that the roles those characters occupy are socially created, that they might have made other choices, and that they might yet create entirely new roles. If Katharine's self-discovery involves an element of inauthenticity, it is because her society does not give a name to her 'profession' (p. 47) of living at home, or acknowledge its worth.

Sexuality and the 'blot fringed with flame'

Sexuality is precisely a point of silence in the novel, its absence made more noticeably apparent by the novels written before and after *Night and Day*. *The Voyage Out* and *Jacob's Room* both treat sexuality with comparative directness, while acknowledging its disturbing or disruptive nature, and the difficulty of accommodating it within social rules and familial relationships. There is little physical contact in *Night and Day*, with the lovers seemingly scarcely conscious of each other's bodies; it is only between the women one finds greater physical intimacy, hinting at a subtext of lesbian eroticism, with Mary patting Katharine's knee affectionately (p. 141) or fingering the fur on the hem of her skirt (pp. 214, 217).

The image of the 'blot fringed with flame' which Ralph inadvertently draws in his attempt to communicate with Katharine, suggests the transformation of the world and its phenomena which love engenders.

This is also an early instance of Woolf's ability to evoke, through an image, sensations which resist verbal explanation. Silence has an authority; there is a feeling or intuition about reality that cannot be conveyed in words, it must be suggested and, by repeated images, be brought slowly before the reader to penetrate the barrier between the sayable and the unsayable, infusing silence with a new psychic and narrative life. It is only when words fail that Ralph finds himself drawing the 'blot fringed with flame', and when Katharine sees it, it tells her far more than anything Ralph could say. It becomes the focus of a cathexis, a concentration of psychic energy, seemingly unwarranted by its simplicity. The lovers move beyond words to 'a state of clear-sightedness where the lifting of a finger had effect, and one word spoke more than a sentence' (p. 383). Language gives way to silence as they travel 'the dark paths of thought side by side towards something discerned in the distance which gradually possessed them both' (p. 383). However, the continuous contradictions and reverberations of the text make it difficult to accept that there can be any real conclusion to, or final naming of, Katharine and Ralph's feelings. By placing two such characters at the centre of a courtship novel, Woolf undermines the central idea of romantic fiction, the idea of spontaneous and authentic self-expression. The end of the novel it may be, but it is not the end of uncertainties and the unspoken thoughts that have driven it. They are groping in a 'difficult region, where the unfinished, the unfulfilled, the unwritten, the unreturned, came together in their ghostly way and wore the semblance of the complete and the satisfactory' (p. 384). For all their fantasies of communion, Ralph and Katharine speak to one another from the separate depth of their own selves: 'From the heart of his darkness he spoke his thanksgiving; from a region as far, as hidden, she answered him' (p. 385). In their moment of deepest communion, each speaks, paradoxically, from an unknown and hidden region. Present in *Night and Day* largely as an absence, as a space of possibilities that cannot be spoken or given a precise form, the alternative subjectivity fleetingly envisioned becomes a viable, though still largely unspeakable, mode of being in the later novels.

Woolf explores in her fiction fundamental questions concerning the nature of identity. To what degree is it predetermined or conditioned? To what degree do we deliberately assume or construct an identity? Do we consist of multiple selves? Where do the boundaries of self overlap or merge with those of others? She is interested in those moments when the individual transcends the confines of his or her identity to partake of a broader identity or to merge mystically with the universe.

In this way Woolf's poetic vision elevates the ordinary and the everyday. The reader can relish the way in which Woolf captures the fleeting moods and emotions of her characters, their struggle to know themselves when the 'selves' they are exploring are constantly shifting, and her portrayal of the dynamics among men and women in a time when women were close to gaining the vote.

Katharine's emancipation from the nineteenth century in all its forms – her parents, the house, William's idea of marriage, the family tea kettle, is the result of her emotion for Ralph. Though she has to undergo a private and difficult struggle in order to understand her feelings, the struggle takes her towards a mutual experience. However, the obscure and melancholy tone of the last chapter results from the great difficulty the lovers have in expressing their vision of an 'orderly' world: 'She felt him trying to piece together in a laborious and elementary fashion fragments of belief, unsoldered and separate, lacking the unity of phrases fashioned by the old believers' (p. 384). Yet the truth is hard to retain, appearing only in '[m]oments, fragments, a second of vision, and then the flying waters, the winds dissipating and dissolving' (p. 385). The struggle to sustain the moment of vision against the external elements, to throw the lighthouse beam against the formidable darkness, will culminate in the later novels.

DORINDA GUEST

Bibliography

Emily Blair, *Virginia Woolf and the Nineteenth-Century Domestic Novel*, State University of New York Press, Albany, 2007

Julia Briggs, *Reading Virginia Woolf*, Edinburgh University Press, Edinburgh 2006

Patricia Clements and Isobel Grundy (eds), *Virginia Woolf: New Critical Essays*, Vision Press, 1983. (See especially Virginia Blain's 'Narrative Voice and the Female Perspective in Virginia Woolf's Early Novels' and Susan Dick's 'The Tunnelling Process: Some Aspects of Virginia Woolf's Use of Memory and the Past'.)

Margaret Comstock, ' "The current answers don't do": The Comic Form of *Night and Day*', in *Women's Studies*, Vol. 4, pp. 153–71

Melinda Feldt Cummings, '*Night and Day*; Virginia Woolf's Visionary Synthesis of Reality', in *Modern Fiction Studies*, Vol. 18/3, pp. 339–49

Jane De Gay, *Virginia Woolf's Novels and the Literary Past*, Edinburgh University Press, Edinburgh, 2006

Avrom Fleishman, *Virginia Woolf: A Critical Reading*, Johns Hopkins University Press, 1975

Jane Goldman, *The Cambridge Introduction to Virginia Woolf*, Cambridge University Press, Cambridge, 2006

Winifred Holtby, *Virginia Woolf: A Critical Memoir*, Continuum, London, 2007

Hermione Lee, *The Novels of Virginia Woolf*, Methuen, London, 1977

Susan J. Leonardi, 'Bare Places and Ancient Blemishes: Virginia Woolf's Search for New Language in *Night and Day*', in *Novel*, Vol. 19, pp. 150–63

Robin Majumdar and Allen McLaurin (eds), *Virginia Woolf: The Critical Heritage*, Routledge, London, 1997

Randy Malamud, 'Splitting the Husks: Virginia Woolf's Modernist Language in *Night and Day*', in *South Central Review*, Vol. 6/1, pp. 32–45

Jane Marcus, 'Enchanted Organ, Magic Bells: *Night and Day* as a Comic Opera', in *Virginia Woolf and the Languages of Patriarchy*, Indiana University Press, Bloomington, 1987, pp. 18–35

Allen McLaurin, *Virginia Woolf: The Echoes Enslaved*, Cambridge University Press, Cambridge, 1973. (See especially 'Verisimilitude and Illusion: *The Voyage Out* and *Night and Day*'.)

Sue Roe, Susan Sellers (eds), *The Cambridge Companion to Virginia Woolf*, Cambridge University Press, Cambridge, 2000

Jeanne Schulkind (ed.), *Moments of Being*, Chatto & Windus, London, 1976

Susan M. Squier, *Virginia Woolf and London: The Sexual Politics of the City*, University of North Carolina Press, 1985. (See especially Chapter 4, 'Tradition and Revision: The Classic City Novel and Virginia Woolf's *Night and Day*'.)

Virginia Woolf, *A Passionate Apprentice: The Early Journals 1897–1909*, edited by Mitchell A. Leaska, Hogarth Press, London, 1990

Virginia Woolf, *The Diary of Virginia Woolf*, 5 volumes, edited by Anne Olivier Bell, Hogarth Press, London, 1977

Virginia Woolf, *The Letters of Virginia Woolf*, 6 volumes, edited by Nigel Nicholson and Joanne Trautmann, Hogarth Press, London, 1975–80

Andrea P. Zemgulys, ' "*Night and Day* is Dead": Virginia Woolf in London "Literary and Historic" ', in *Twentieth-Century Literature*, Vol. 46/1, pp. 56–77

Joanne P. Zuckerman, 'Anne Thackeray Ritchie as the Model for Mrs Hilbery in Virginia Woolf's *Night and Day*', in *Virginia Woolf Quarterly*, Vol. 1, pp. 32–46

NIGHT AND DAY

TO

VANESSA BELL

but, looking for a phrase,
I found none to stand
beside your name

Chapter 1

It was a Sunday evening in October, and in common with many other young ladies of her class, Katharine Hilbery was pouring out tea. Perhaps a fifth part of her mind was thus occupied, and the remaining parts leapt over the little barrier of day which interposed between Monday morning and this rather subdued moment, and played with the things one does voluntarily and normally in the daylight. But although she was silent, she was evidently mistress of a situation which was familiar enough to her, and inclined to let it take its way for the six hundredth time, perhaps, without bringing into play any of her unoccupied faculties. A single glance was enough to show that Mrs Hilbery was so rich in the gifts which make tea-parties of elderly distinguished people successful that she scarcely needed any help from her daughter, provided that the tiresome business of teacups and bread and butter was discharged for her.

Considering that the little party had been seated round the tea-table for less than twenty minutes, the animation observable on their faces, and the amount of sound they were producing collectively, were very creditable to the hostess. It suddenly came into Katharine's mind that if someone opened the door at this moment he would think that they were enjoying themselves; he would think, 'What an extremely nice house to come into!' and instinctively she laughed, and said something to increase the noise, for the credit of the house presumably, since she herself had not been feeling exhilarated. At the very same moment, rather to her amusement, the door was flung open, and a young man entered the room. Katharine, as she shook hands with him, asked him, in her own mind, 'Now, do you think we're enjoying ourselves enormously?' . . . 'Mr Denham, mother,' she said aloud, for she saw that her mother had forgotten his name.

That fact was perceptible to Mr Denham also, and increased the awkwardness which inevitably attends the entrance of a stranger into a room full of people much at their ease and all launched upon sentences. At the same time, it seemed to Mr Denham as if a thousand softly padded doors had closed between him and the street outside. A fine mist, the etherealised essence of the fog, hung visibly in the wide and rather empty space of the drawing-room, all silver where the candles were grouped on the tea-table, and ruddy again in the firelight. With the omnibuses and cabs still running in his head, and his body still tingling with his quick walk along the streets and in and out of traffic and foot-passengers, this drawing-room seemed very remote and still; and the faces of the elderly people were mellowed, at some distance from each other, and had a bloom on them owing to the fact that the air in the drawing-room was thickened by blue grains of mist. Mr Denham had come in as Mr Fortescue, the eminent novelist,[1] reached the middle of a very long sentence. He kept this suspended while the newcomer sat down, and Mrs Hilbery deftly joined the severed parts by leaning towards him and remarking: 'Now, what would you do if you were married to an engineer, and had to live in Manchester, Mr Denham?'

'Surely she could learn Persian,' broke in a thin, elderly gentleman. 'Is there no retired schoolmaster or man of letters in Manchester with whom she could read Persian?'

'A cousin of ours has married and gone to live in Manchester,' Katharine explained. Mr Denham muttered something, which was indeed all that was required of him, and the novelist went on where he had left off. Privately, Mr Denham cursed himself very sharply for having exchanged the freedom of the street for this sophisticated drawing-room, where, among other disagreeables, he certainly would not appear at his best. He glanced round him, and saw that, save for Katharine, they were all over forty, the only consolation being that Mr Fortescue was a considerable celebrity, so that tomorrow one might be glad to have met him.

'Have you ever been to Manchester?' he asked Katharine.

'Never,' she replied.

'Why do you object to it, then?'

Katharine stirred her tea, and seemed to speculate, so Denham thought, upon the duty of filling somebody else's cup, but she was really wondering how she was going to keep this strange young man in harmony with the rest. She observed that he was compressing his teacup, so that there was danger lest the thin china might cave inwards. She could see that he was nervous; one would expect a bony young man with his face slightly reddened by the wind, and his hair not altogether smooth, to be nervous in such a party. Further, he probably disliked this kind of thing, and had come out of curiosity, or because her father had invited him – anyhow, he would not be easily combined with the rest.

'I should think there would be no one to talk to in Manchester,' she replied at random. Mr Fortescue had been observing her for a moment or two, as novelists are inclined to observe, and at this remark he smiled, and made it the text for a little further speculation.

'In spite of a slight tendency to exaggeration, Katharine decidedly hits the mark,' he said, and lying back in his chair, with his opaque contemplative eyes fixed on the ceiling, and the tips of his fingers pressed together, he depicted, first the horrors of the streets of Manchester, and then the bare, immense moors on the outskirts of the town, and then the scrubby little house in which the girl would live, and then the professors and the miserable young students devoted to the more strenuous works of our younger dramatists who would visit her, and how her appearance would change by degrees, and how she would fly to London, and how Katharine would have to lead her about, as one leads an eager dog on a chain, past rows of clamorous butchers' shops, poor dear creature.

'Oh, Mr Fortescue,' exclaimed Mrs Hilbery, as he finished, 'I had just written to say how I envied her! I was thinking of the big gardens and the dear old ladies in mittens, who read nothing but the *Spectator*, and snuff the candles. Have they *all* disappeared? I told her she would find the nice things of London without the horrid streets that depress one so.'

'There is the university,' said the thin gentleman, who had previously insisted upon the existence of people knowing Persian.

'I know there are moors there, because I read about them in a book the other day,' said Katharine.

'I am grieved and amazed at the ignorance of my family,' Mr Hilbery remarked. He was an elderly man, with a pair of oval, hazel eyes which were rather bright for his time of life, and relieved the heaviness of his face. He played constantly with a little green stone attached to his watch-chain, thus displaying long and very sensitive fingers, and had a habit of moving his head hither and thither very quickly without altering the position of his large and rather corpulent body, so that he seemed to be providing himself incessantly with food for amusement and reflection with the least possible expenditure of energy. One might suppose that he had passed the time of life when his ambitions were personal, or that he had gratified them as far as he was likely to do, and now employed his considerable acuteness rather to observe and reflect than to attain any result.[2]

Katharine, so Denham decided, while Mr Fortescue built up another rounded structure of words, had a likeness to each of her parents, but these elements were rather oddly blended. She had the quick, impulsive movements of her mother, the lips parting often to speak, and closing again; and the dark oval eyes of her father brimming with light upon a

basis of sadness, or, since she was too young to have acquired a sorrowful
point of view, one might say that the basis was not sadness so much as a
spirit given to contemplation and self-control. Judging by her hair, her
colouring and the shape of her features, she was striking, if not actually
beautiful. Decision and composure stamped her, a combination of
qualities that produced a very marked character, and one that was not
calculated to put a young man, who scarcely knew her, at his ease. For
the rest, she was tall; her dress was of some quiet colour, with old
yellow-tinted lace for ornament, to which the spark of an ancient jewel
gave its one red gleam. Denham noticed that, although silent, she kept
sufficient control of the situation to answer immediately her mother
appealed to her for help, and yet it was obvious to him that she attended
only with the surface skin of her mind. It struck him that her position
at the tea-table, among all these elderly people, was not without its
difficulties, and he checked his inclination to find her, or her attitude,
generally antipathetic to him. The talk had passed over Manchester,
after dealing with it very generously.

'Would it be the Battle of Trafalgar or the Spanish Armada,
Katharine?' her mother demanded.

'Trafalgar, mother.'

'Trafalgar, of course! How stupid of me! Another cup of tea, with a
thin slice of lemon in it, and then, dear Mr Fortescue, please explain my
absurd little puzzle. One can't help believing gentlemen with Roman
noses, even if one meets them in omnibuses.'

Mr Hilbery here interposed so far as Denham was concerned, and
talked a great deal of sense about the solicitors' profession, and the
changes which he had seen in his lifetime. Indeed, Denham properly
fell to his lot, owing to the fact that an article by Denham upon some
legal matter, published by Mr Hilbery in his *Review*, had brought
them acquainted. But when a moment later Mrs Sutton Bailey was
announced, he turned to her, and Mr Denham found himself sitting
silent, rejecting possible things to say, beside Katharine, who was silent
too. Being much about the same age and both under thirty, they were
prohibited from the use of a great many convenient phrases which
launch conversation into smooth waters. They were further silenced by
Katharine's rather malicious determination not to help this young man,
in whose upright and resolute bearing she detected something hostile
to her surroundings, by any of the usual feminine amenities. They
therefore sat silent, Denham controlling his desire to say something
abrupt and explosive, which should shock her into life. But Mrs Hilbery
was immediately sensitive to any silence in the drawing-room, as of

a dumb note in a sonorous scale, and leaning across the table she observed, in the curiously tentative detached manner which always gave her phrases the likeness of butterflies flaunting from one sunny spot to another, 'D'you know, Mr Denham, you remind me so much of dear Mr Ruskin[3] . . . Is it his tie, Katharine, or his hair, or the way he sits in his chair? Do tell me, Mr Denham, are you an admirer of Ruskin? Someone, the other day, said to me, "Oh, no, we don't read Ruskin, Mrs Hilbery." What *do* you read, I wonder? – for you can't spend all your time going up in aeroplanes and burrowing into the bowels of the earth.'

She looked benevolently at Denham, who said nothing articulate, and then at Katharine, who smiled but said nothing either, upon which Mrs Hilbery seemed possessed by a brilliant idea, and exclaimed: 'I'm sure Mr Denham would like to see our things, Katharine. I'm sure he's not like that dreadful young man, Mr Ponting, who told me that he considered it our duty to live exclusively in the present. After all, what *is* the present? Half of it's the past, and the better half, too, I should say,' she added, turning to Mr Fortescue.

Denham rose, half meaning to go, and thinking that he had seen all that there was to see, but Katharine rose at the same moment, and saying, 'Perhaps you would like to see the pictures,' led the way across the drawing-room to a smaller room opening out of it.

The smaller room was something like a chapel in a cathedral, or a grotto in a cave, for the booming sound of the traffic in the distance suggested the soft surge of waters, and the oval mirrors, with their silver surface, were like deep pools trembling beneath starlight. But the comparison to a religious temple of some kind was the more apt of the two, for the little room was crowded with relics.

As Katharine touched different spots, lights sprang here and there and revealed a square mass of red-and-gold books, and then a long skirt in blue-and-white paint lustrous behind glass, and then a mahogany writing-table, with its orderly equipment, and, finally, a picture above the table, to which special illumination was accorded. When Katharine had touched these last lights, she stood back, as much as to say, 'There!' Denham found himself looked down upon by the eyes of the great poet, Richard Alardyce,[4] and suffered a little shock which would have led him, had he been wearing a hat, to remove it. The eyes looked at him out of the mellow pinks and yellows of the paint with divine friendliness, which embraced him and passed on to contemplate the entire world. The paint had so faded that very little but the beautiful large eyes were left, dark in the surrounding dimness.

Katharine waited as though for him to receive a full impression, and then she said: 'This is his writing-table. He used this pen,' and she lifted a quill pen and laid it down again. The writing-table was splashed with old ink, and the pen dishevelled in service. There lay the gigantic gold-rimmed spectacles, ready to his hand, and beneath the table was a pair of large, worn slippers, one of which Katharine picked up, remarking: 'I think my grandfather must have been at least twice as large as anyone is nowadays. This,' she went on, as if she knew what she had to say by heart, 'is the original manuscript of the "Ode to Winter". The early poems are far less corrected than the later. Would you like to look at it?'

While Mr Denham examined the manuscript, she glanced up at her grandfather, and, for the thousandth time, fell into a pleasant dreamy state in which she seemed to be the companion of those giant men, of their own lineage, at any rate, and the insignificant present moment was put to shame. That magnificent ghostly head on the canvas, surely, never beheld all the trivialities of a Sunday afternoon, and it did not seem to matter what she and this young man said to each other, for they were only small people.

'This is a copy of the first edition of the poems,' she continued, without considering the fact that Mr Denham was still occupied with the manuscript, 'which contains several poems that have not been reprinted, as well as corrections.' She paused for a minute, and then went on, as if these spaces had all been calculated. 'That lady in blue is my great-grandmother, by Millington. Here is my uncle's walking-stick – he was Sir Richard Warburton, you know, and rode with Havelock to the Relief of Lucknow.[5] And then, let me see – oh, that's the original Alardyce, 1697, the founder of the family fortunes, with his wife. Someone gave us this bowl the other day because it has their crest and initials. We think it must have been given them to celebrate their silver wedding-day.'

Here she stopped for a moment, wondering why it was that Mr Denham said nothing. Her feeling that he was antagonistic to her, which had lapsed while she thought of her family possessions, returned so keenly that she stopped in the middle of her catalogue and looked at him. Her mother, wishing to connect him reputably with the great dead, had compared him with Mr Ruskin; and the comparison was in Katharine's mind, and led her to be more critical of the young man than was fair, for a young man paying a call in a tail-coat is in a different element altogether from a head seized at its climax of expressiveness, gazing immutably from behind a sheet of glass, which was all that remained to her of Mr Ruskin. He had a singular face – a face built for swiftness and decision rather than for massive contemplation; the fore-head broad, the nose long and formidable, the lips clean-shaven and at once dogged and sensitive, the cheeks lean, with a deeply running tide of red blood in them. His eyes, expressive now of the usual masculine impersonality and authority, might reveal more subtle emotions under favourable circumstances, for they were large, and of a clear, brown colour; they seemed unexpectedly to hesitate and speculate; but Katharine only looked at him to wonder whether his face would not have come nearer the standard of her dead heroes if it had been adorned with side-whiskers. In his spare build and thin, though healthy, cheeks, she saw tokens of an angular and acrid soul. His voice, she noticed, had a slight vibrating or creaking sound in it, as he laid down the manuscript and said: 'You must be very proud of your family, Miss Hilbery.'

'Yes, I am,' Katharine answered; and she added, 'Do you think there's anything wrong in that?'

'Wrong? How should it be wrong? It must be a bore, though, showing your things to visitors,' he added reflectively.

'Not if the visitors like them.'

'Isn't it difficult to live up to your ancestors?' he proceeded.

'I dare say I shouldn't try to write poetry,' Katharine replied.

'No. And that's what I should hate. I couldn't bear my grandfather to cut me out. And, after all,' Denham went on, glancing round him satirically, as Katharine thought, 'it's not your grandfather only. You're cut out all the way round. I suppose you come of one of the most distinguished families in England. There are the Warburtons and the Mannings – and you're related to the Otways, aren't you? I read it all in some magazine,' he added.

'The Otways are my cousins,' Katharine replied.

'Well,' said Denham, in a final tone of voice, as if his argument were proved.

'Well,' said Katharine, 'I don't see that you've proved anything.'

Denham smiled, in a peculiarly provoking way. He was amused and gratified to find that he had the power to annoy his oblivious, super-cilious hostess, if he could not impress her; though he would have preferred to impress her.

He sat silent, holding the precious little book of poems unopened in his hands, and Katharine watched him, the melancholy or contemplative expression deepening in her eyes as her annoyance faded. She appeared to be considering many things. She had forgotten her duties.

'Well,' said Denham again, suddenly opening the little book of poems, as though he had said all that he meant to say or could, with propriety, say. He turned over the pages with great decision, as if he were judging the book in its entirety, the printing and paper and binding, as well as the poetry, and then, having satisfied himself of its good or bad quality, he placed it on the writing-table, and examined the malacca cane with the gold knob which had belonged to the soldier.

'But aren't you proud of your family?' Katharine demanded.

'No,' said Denham. 'We've never done anything to be proud of – unless you count paying one's bills a matter for pride.'

'That sounds rather dull,' Katharine remarked.

'You would think us horribly dull,' Denham agreed.

'Yes, I might find you dull, but I don't think I should find you ridiculous,' Katharine added, as if Denham had actually brought that charge against her family.

'No – because we're not in the least ridiculous. We're a respectable middle-class family, living at Highgate.'

'We don't live at Highgate, but we're middle class too, I suppose.'

Denham merely smiled, and replacing the malacca cane on the rack, he drew a sword from its ornamental sheath.

'That belonged to Clive, so we say,' said Katharine, taking up her duties as hostess again automatically.

'Is it a lie?' Denham enquired.

'It's a family tradition. I don't know that we can prove it.'

'You see, we don't have traditions in our family,' said Denham.

'You sound very dull,' Katharine remarked, for the second time.

'Merely middle class,' Denham replied.

'You pay your bills, and you speak the truth. I don't see why you should despise us.'

Mr Denham carefully sheathed the sword which the Hilberys said belonged to Clive.

'I shouldn't like to be you; that's all I said,' he replied, as if he were saying what he thought as accurately as he could.

'No, but one never would like to be anyone else.'

'I should. I should like to be lots of other people.'

'Then why not us?' Katharine asked.

Denham looked at her as she sat in her grandfather's armchair, drawing her great-uncle's malacca cane smoothly through her fingers, while her background was made up equally of lustrous blue-and-white paint, and crimson books with gilt lines on them. The vitality and composure of her attitude, as of a bright-plumed bird poised easily before further flights, roused him to show her the limitations of her lot. So soon, so easily, would he be forgotten.

'You'll never know anything at first hand,' he began, almost savagely. 'It's all been done for you. You'll never know the pleasure of buying things after saving up for them, or reading books for the first time, or making discoveries.'

'Go on,' Katharine observed, as he paused, suddenly doubtful, when he heard his voice proclaiming aloud these facts, whether there was any truth in them.

'Of course, I don't know how you spend your time,' he continued, a little stiffly, 'but I suppose you have to show people round. You are writing a life of your grandfather, aren't you? And this kind of thing' – he nodded towards the other room, where they could hear bursts of cultivated laughter – 'must take up a lot of time.'

She looked at him expectantly, as if between them they were decorating a small figure of herself, and she saw him hesitating in the disposition of some bow or sash.

'You've got it very nearly right,' she said, 'but I only help my mother. I don't write myself.'

'Do you do anything yourself?' he demanded.

'What do you mean?' she asked. 'I don't leave the house at ten and come back at six.'

'I don't mean that.'

Mr Denham had recovered his self-control; he spoke with a quietness which made Katharine rather anxious that he should explain himself, but at the same time she wished to annoy him, to waft him away from her on some light current of ridicule or satire, as she was wont to do with these intermittent young men of her father's.

'Nobody ever does do anything worth doing nowadays,' she remarked. 'You see' – she tapped the volume of her grandfather's poems – 'we don't even print as well as they did, and as for poets or painters or novelists – there are none; so, at any rate, I'm not singular.'

'No, we haven't any great men,' Denham replied. 'I'm very glad that we haven't. I hate great men. The worship of greatness in the nineteenth century seems to me to explain the worthlessness of that generation.'

Katharine opened her lips and drew in her breath, as if to reply with equal vigour, when the shutting of a door in the next room withdrew her attention, and they both became conscious that the voices, which had been rising and falling round the tea-table, had fallen silent; the light, even, seemed to have sunk lower. A moment later Mrs Hilbery appeared in the doorway of the ante-room. She stood looking at them with a smile of expectancy on her face, as if a scene from the drama of the younger generation were being played for her benefit. She was a remarkable-looking woman, well advanced in the sixties, but owing to the lightness of her frame and the brightness of her eyes she seemed to have been wafted over the surface of the years without taking much harm in the passage. Her face was shrunken and aquiline, but any hint of sharpness was dispelled by the large blue eyes, at once sagacious and innocent, which seemed to regard the world with an enormous desire that it should behave itself nobly, and an entire confidence that it could do so, if it would only take the pains.

Certain lines on the broad forehead and about the lips might be taken to suggest that she had known moments of some difficulty and perplexity in the course of her career, but these had not destroyed her trustfulness, and she was clearly still prepared to give everyone any number of fresh chances and the whole system the benefit of the doubt. She wore a great resemblance to her father, and suggested, as he did, the fresh airs and open spaces of a younger world.

'Well,' she said, 'how do you like our things, Mr Denham?'

Mr Denham rose, put his book down, opened his mouth, but said nothing, as Katharine observed, with some amusement.

Mrs Hilbery handled the book he had laid down.

'There are some books that *live*,' she mused. 'They are young with us, and they grow old with us. Are you fond of poetry, Mr Denham? But what an absurd question to ask! The truth is, dear Mr Fortescue has almost tired me out. He is so eloquent and so witty, so searching and so profound that, after half an hour or so, I feel inclined to turn out all the lights. But perhaps he'd be more wonderful than ever in the dark. What d'you think, Katharine? Shall we give a little party in complete darkness? There'd have to be bright rooms for the bores . . . '

Here Mr Denham held out his hand.

'But we've any number of things to show you!' Mrs Hilbery exclaimed, taking no notice of it. 'Books, pictures, china, manuscripts, and the very chair that Mary Queen of Scots sat in when she heard of Darnley's murder. I must lie down for a little, and Katharine must change her dress (though she's wearing a very pretty one), but if you don't mind being left alone, supper will be at eight. I dare say you'll write a poem of your own while you're waiting. Ah, how I love the firelight! Doesn't our room look charming?'

She stepped back and bade them contemplate the empty drawing-room, with its rich, irregular lights, as the flames leapt and wavered.

'Dear things!' she exclaimed. 'Dear chairs and tables! How like old friends they are – faithful, silent friends. Which reminds me, Katharine, little Mr Anning is coming tonight, and Tite Street, and Cadogan

Square . . . Do remember to get that drawing of your great-uncle glazed. Aunt Millicent remarked it last time she was here, and I know how it would hurt me to see *my* father in a broken glass.'

It was like tearing through a maze of diamond-glittering spiders' webs to say goodbye and escape, for at each movement Mrs Hilbery remembered something further about the villainies of picture-framers or the delights of poetry, and at one time it seemed to the young man that he would be hypnotised into doing what she pretended to want him to do, for he could not suppose that she attached any value whatever to his presence. Katharine, however, made an opportunity for him to leave, and for that he was grateful to her, as one young person is grateful for the understanding of another.

Chapter 2

The young man shut the door with a sharper slam than any visitor had used that afternoon, and walked up the street at a great pace, cutting the air with his walking-stick. He was glad to find himself outside that drawing-room, breathing raw fog, and in contact with unpolished people who only wanted their share of the pavement allowed them. He thought that if he had had Mr or Mrs or Miss Hilbery out here he would have made them, somehow, feel his superiority, for he was chafed by the memory of halting awkward sentences which had failed to give even the young woman with the sad but inwardly ironical eyes a hint of his force. He tried to recall the actual words of his little outburst, and unconsciously supplemented them by so many words of greater expressiveness that the irritation of his failure was somewhat assuaged. Sudden stabs of the unmitigated truth assailed him now and then, for he was not inclined by nature to take a rosy view of his conduct, but what with the beat of his foot upon the pavement, and the glimpse which half-drawn curtains offered him of kitchens, dining-rooms and drawing-rooms, illustrating with mute power different scenes from different lives, his own experience lost its sharpness.

His own experience underwent a curious change. His speed slackened, his head sank a little towards his breast, and the lamplight shone now and again upon a face grown strangely tranquil. His thought was so absorbing that when it became necessary to verify the name of a street, he looked at it for a time before he read it; when he came to a crossing, he seemed to have to reassure himself by two or three taps, such as a blind man gives, upon the curb; and, reaching the Underground station, he blinked in the bright circle of light, glanced at his watch, decided that he might still indulge himself in darkness, and walked straight on.

And yet the thought was the thought with which he had started. He was still thinking about the people in the house which he had left; but instead of remembering, with whatever accuracy he could, their looks and sayings, he had consciously taken leave of the literal truth. A turn of the street, a firelit room, something monumental in the procession of the lamp-posts, who shall say what accident of light or shape had suddenly changed the prospect within his mind, and led him to murmur aloud: 'She'll do . . . Yes, Katharine Hilbery'll do . . . I'll take Katharine Hilbery.'

As soon as he had said this, his pace slackened, his head fell, his eyes became fixed. The desire to justify himself, which had been so urgent, ceased to torment him, and, as if released from constraint, so that they worked without friction or bidding, his faculties leapt forward and fixed, as a matter of course, upon the form of Katharine Hilbery. It was marvellous how much they found to feed upon, considering the destructive nature of Denham's criticism in her presence. The charm, which he had tried to disown, when under the effect of it, the beauty, the character, the aloofness, which he had been determined not to feel, now possessed him wholly; and when, as happened by the nature of things, he had exhausted his memory, he went on with his imagination. He was conscious of what he was about, for in thus dwelling upon Miss Hilbery's qualities, he showed a kind of method, as if he required this vision of her for a particular purpose. He increased her height, he darkened her hair; but physically there was not much to change in her. His most daring liberty was taken with her mind, which, for reasons of his own, he desired to be exalted and infallible, and of such independence that it was only in the case of Ralph Denham that it swerved from its high, swift flight, but where he was concerned, though fastidious at first, she finally swooped from her eminence to crown him with her approval. These delicious details, however, were to be worked out in all their ramifications at his leisure; the main point was that Katharine Hilbery would do; she would do for weeks, perhaps for months. In taking her he had provided himself with something the lack of which had left a bare place in his mind for a considerable time. He gave a sigh of satisfaction; his consciousness of his actual position somewhere in the neighbourhood of Knightsbridge returned to him, and he was soon speeding in the train towards Highgate.

Although thus supported by the knowledge of his new possession of considerable value, he was not proof against the familiar thoughts which the suburban streets and the damp shrubs growing in front gardens and the absurd names painted in white upon the gates of those gardens suggested to him. His walk was uphill, and his mind dwelt gloomily upon the house which he approached, where he would find six or seven brothers and sisters, a widowed mother, and, probably, some aunt or uncle sitting down to an unpleasant meal under a very bright light. Should he put in force the threat which, two weeks ago, some such gathering had wrung from him – the terrible threat that if visitors came on Sunday he should dine alone in his room? A glance in the direction of Miss Hilbery determined him to make his stand this very night, and accordingly, having let himself in, having verified the presence of Uncle Joseph by means of a bowler hat and a very large umbrella, he gave his orders to the maid, and went upstairs to his room.

He went up a great many flights of stairs, and he noticed, as he had very seldom noticed, how the carpet became steadily shabbier, until it ceased altogether, how the walls were discoloured, sometimes by cascades of damp and sometimes by the outlines of picture-frames since removed, how the paper flapped loose at the corners and a great flake of plaster had fallen from the ceiling. The room itself was a cheerless one to return to at this inauspicious hour. A flattened sofa would, later in the evening, become a bed; one of the tables concealed a washing apparatus; his clothes and boots were disagreeably mixed with books which bore the gilt of college arms; and, for decoration, there hung upon the wall photographs of bridges and cathedrals and large, unprepossessing groups of insufficiently clothed young men,[6] sitting in rows one above another upon stone steps. There was a look of meanness and shabbiness in the furniture and curtains, and nowhere any sign of luxury or even of a cultivated taste, unless the cheap classics in the bookcase were a sign of an effort in that direction. The only object that threw any light upon the character of the room's owner was a large perch, placed in the window to catch the air and sun, upon which a tame and, apparently, decrepit rook hopped dryly from side to side. The bird, encouraged by a scratch behind the ear, settled upon Denham's shoulder. He lit his gas-fire and settled down in gloomy patience to await his dinner.

After he had been sitting thus for some minutes a small girl popped her head in to say, 'Mother says, aren't you coming down, Ralph? Uncle Joseph – '

'They're to bring my dinner up here,' said Ralph, peremptorily; whereupon she vanished, leaving the door ajar in her haste to be gone.

After Denham had waited some minutes, in the course of which neither he nor the rook took their eyes off the fire, he muttered a curse, ran downstairs, intercepted the parlour-maid, and cut himself a slice of bread and cold meat. As he did so, the dining-room door sprang open and a voice exclaimed 'Ralph!' but Ralph paid no attention to the voice, and made off upstairs with his plate. He set it down in a chair opposite him, and ate with a ferocity that was due partly to anger and partly to hunger. His mother, then, was determined not to respect his wishes; he was a person of no importance in his own family; he was sent for and treated as a child. He reflected, with a growing sense of injury, that almost every one of his actions since opening the door of his room had been won from the grasp of the family system. By rights, he should have been sitting downstairs in the drawing-room describing his afternoon's adventures, or listening to the afternoon's adventures of other people; the room itself, the gas-fire, the armchair – all had been fought for; the wretched bird, with half its feathers out and one leg lamed by a cat, had been rescued under protest; but what his family most resented, he reflected, was his wish for privacy. To dine alone, or to sit alone after dinner, was flat rebellion, to be fought with every weapon of underhand stealth or of open appeal. Which did he dislike most – deception or tears? But, at any rate, they could not rob him of his thoughts; they could not make him say where he had been or whom he had seen. That was his own affair; that, indeed, was a step entirely in the right direction, and, lighting his pipe, and cutting up the remains of his meal for the benefit of the rook, Ralph calmed his rather excessive irritation and settled down to think over his prospects.

This particular afternoon was a step in the right direction, because it was part of his plan to get to know people beyond the family circuit, just as it was part of his plan to learn German this autumn, and to review legal books for Mr Hilbery's *Critical Review*. He had always made plans since he was a small boy; for poverty, and the fact that he was the eldest son of a large family, had given him the habit of thinking of spring and summer, autumn and winter, as so many stages in a prolonged campaign. Although he was still under thirty, this forecasting habit had marked two semicircular lines above his eyebrows, which threatened, at this moment, to crease into their wonted shapes. But instead of settling down to think, he rose, took a small piece of cardboard marked in large letters with the word OUT, and hung it upon the handle of his door. This done, he sharpened a pencil, lit a reading-lamp and opened his book. But still he hesitated to take his seat. He scratched the rook; he walked to the window; he parted the curtains, and looked down upon the city which lay, hazily luminous, beneath him. He looked across the vapours in the direction of Chelsea; looked fixedly for a moment, and then returned to his chair. But the whole thickness of some learned counsel's treatise upon torts did not screen him satisfactorily. Through the pages he saw a drawing-room, very empty and spacious; he heard low voices, he saw women's figures, he could even smell the scent of the cedar log which flamed in the grate. His mind relaxed its tension, and seemed to be giving out now what it had taken in unconsciously at the time. He could remember Mr Fortescue's exact words, and the rolling emphasis with which he delivered them, and he began to repeat what Mr Fortescue had said, in Mr Fortescue's own manner, about Manchester. His mind then began to wander about the house, and he wondered whether there were other rooms like the drawing-room, and he thought, inconsequently, how beautiful the bathroom must be, and how leisurely it was – the life of these well-kept people, who were, no doubt, still sitting in the same room, only they had changed their clothes, and little Mr Anning was there, and the aunt who would mind if the glass of her father's picture was broken. Miss Hilbery had changed her dress ('although she's wearing such a pretty one,' he heard her mother say), and she was talking to Mr Anning, who was well over forty, and bald into the bargain, about books. How peaceful and spacious it was; and the peace possessed him so completely that his muscles slackened, his book drooped from his hand, and he forgot that the hour of work was wasting minute by minute.

He was roused by a creak upon the stair. With a guilty start he composed himself, frowned and looked intently at the fifty-sixth page of his volume. A step paused outside his door, and he knew that the person, whoever it might be, was considering the placard, and debating whether to honour its decree or not. Certainly, policy advised him to sit still in autocratic silence, for no custom can take root in a family unless every breach of it is punished severely for the first six months or so. But Ralph was conscious of a distinct wish to be interrupted, and his disappointment was perceptible when he heard the creaking sound rather farther down the stairs, as if his visitor had decided to withdraw. He rose, opened the door with unnecessary abruptness, and waited on the landing. The person stopped simultaneously half a flight downstairs.

'Ralph?' said a voice, enquiringly.

'Joan?'

'I was coming up, but I saw your notice.'

'Well, come along in, then.' He concealed his desire beneath a tone as grudging as he could make it.

Joan came in, but she was careful to show, by standing upright with one hand upon the mantelpiece, that she was only there for a definite purpose, which discharged, she would go.

She was older than Ralph by some three or four years. Her face was round but worn and expressed that tolerant but anxious good humour which is the special attribute of elder sisters in large families. Her pleasant brown eyes resembled Ralph's, save in expression, for whereas he seemed to look straightly and keenly at one object, she appeared to be in the habit of considering everything from many different points of view. This made her appear his elder by more years than existed in fact between them. Her gaze rested for a moment or two upon the rook. She then said, without any preface: 'It's about Charles and Uncle John's offer . . . Mother's been talking to me. She says she can't afford to pay for him after this term. She says she'll have to ask for an overdraft as it is.'

'That's simply not true,' said Ralph.

'No. I thought not. But she won't believe me when I say it.'

Ralph, as if he could foresee the length of this familiar argument, drew up a chair for his sister and sat down himself.

'I'm not interrupting?' she enquired.

Ralph shook his head, and for a time they sat silent. The lines curved themselves in semicircles above their eyes.

'She doesn't understand that one's got to take risks,' he observed, finally.

'I believe mother would take risks if she knew that Charles was the sort of boy to profit by it.'

'He's got brains, hasn't he?' said Ralph. His tone had taken on that shade of pugnacity which suggested to his sister that some personal grievance drove him to take the line he did. She wondered what it might be, but at once recalled her mind, and assented.

'In some ways he's fearfully backward, though, compared with what you were at his age. And he's difficult at home, too. He makes Molly slave for him.'

Ralph made a sound which belittled this particular argument. It was plain to Joan that she had struck one of her brother's perverse moods, and he was going to oppose whatever his mother said. He called her 'she', which was a proof of it. She sighed involuntarily, and the sigh annoyed Ralph, and he exclaimed with irritation: 'It's pretty hard lines to stick a boy into an office at seventeen!'

'Nobody *wants* to stick him into an office,' she said.

She, too, was becoming annoyed. She had spent the whole of the afternoon discussing wearisome details of education and expense with her mother, and she had come to her brother for help, encouraged, rather irrationally, to expect help by the fact that he had been out somewhere, she didn't know and didn't mean to ask where, all the afternoon.

Ralph was fond of his sister, and her irritation made him think how unfair it was that all these burdens should be laid on her shoulders.

'The truth is,' he observed gloomily, 'that I ought to have accepted Uncle John's offer. I should have been making six hundred a year by this time.'

'I don't think that for a moment,' Joan replied quickly, repenting of her annoyance. 'The question, to my mind, is whether we couldn't cut down our expenses in some way.'

'A smaller house?'

'Fewer servants, perhaps.'

Neither brother nor sister spoke with much conviction, and after reflecting for a moment what these proposed reforms in a strictly economical household meant, Ralph announced very decidedly: 'It's out of the question.'

It was out of the question that she should put any more household work upon herself. No, the hardship must fall on him, for he was determined that his family should have as many chances of distinguishing themselves as other families had – as the Hilberys had, for example. He believed secretly and rather defiantly, for it was a fact not capable of proof, that there was something very remarkable about his family.

'If mother won't run risks – '

'You really can't expect her to sell out again.'

'She ought to look upon it as an investment; but if she won't, we must find some other way, that's all.'

A threat was contained in this sentence, and Joan knew, without asking, what the threat was. In the course of his professional life, which now extended over six or seven years, Ralph had saved, perhaps, three or four hundred pounds. Considering the sacrifices he had made in order to put by this sum it always amazed Joan to find that he used it to gamble with, buying shares and selling them again, increasing it sometimes, sometimes diminishing it, and always running the risk of losing every penny of it in a day's disaster. But although she wondered, she could not help loving him the better for his odd combination of Spartan self-control and what appeared to her romantic and childish folly. Ralph interested her more than anyone else in the world, and she often broke off in the middle of one of these economic discussions, in spite of their gravity, to consider some fresh aspect of his character.

'I think you'd be foolish to risk your money on poor old Charles,' she observed. 'Fond as I am of him, he doesn't seem to me exactly brilliant . . . Besides, why should you be sacrificed?'

'My dear Joan,' Ralph exclaimed, stretching himself out with a gesture of impatience, 'don't you see that we've all got to be sacrificed? What's the use of denying it? What's the use of struggling against it? So it always has been, so it always will be. We've got no money and we never shall have any money. We shall just turn round in the mill every day of our lives until we drop and die, worn out, as most people do, when one comes to think of it.'

Joan looked at him, opened her lips as if to speak, and closed them again. Then she said, very tentatively: 'Aren't you happy, Ralph?'

'No. Are you? Perhaps I'm as happy as most people, though. God knows whether I'm happy or not. What is happiness?'[7]

He glanced with half a smile, in spite of his gloomy irritation, at his sister. She looked, as usual, as if she were weighing one thing with another, and balancing them together before she made up her mind.

'Happiness,' she remarked at length enigmatically, rather as if she were sampling the word, and then she paused. She paused for a considerable space, as if she were considering happiness in all its bearings. 'Hilda was here today,' she suddenly resumed, as if they had never mentioned happiness. 'She brought Bobbie – he's a fine boy now.' Ralph observed, with an amusement that had a tinge of irony in it, that she was now going to sidle away quickly from this dangerous approach to intimacy on to topics of general and family interest. Nevertheless, he reflected, she was the only one of his family with whom he found it possible to discuss happiness, although he might very well have discussed happiness with Miss Hilbery at their first meeting. He looked critically at Joan, and wished that she did not look so provincial or suburban in her high green dress with the faded trimming, so patient, and almost resigned. He began to wish to tell her about the Hilberys in order to abuse them, for in the miniature battle which so often rages between two quickly following impressions of life, the life of the Hilberys was getting the better of the life of the Denhams in his mind, and he wanted to assure himself that there was some quality in which Joan infinitely surpassed Miss Hilbery. He should have felt that his own sister was more original, and had greater vitality than Miss Hilbery had; but his main impression of Katharine now was of a person of great vitality and composure; and at the moment he could not perceive what poor dear Joan had gained from the fact that she was the granddaughter of a man who kept a shop, and herself earned her own living. The infinite dreariness and sordidness of their life oppressed him in spite of his fundamental belief that, as a family, they were somehow remarkable.

'Shall you talk to mother?' Joan enquired. 'Because, you see, the thing's got to be settled, one way or another. Charles must write to Uncle John if he's going there.'

Ralph sighed impatiently.

'I suppose it doesn't much matter either way,' he exclaimed. 'He's doomed to misery in the long run.'

A slight flush came into Joan's cheek.

'You know you're talking nonsense,' she said. 'It doesn't hurt anyone to have to earn their own living. I'm very glad I have to earn mine.'

Ralph was pleased that she should feel this, and wished her to continue, but he went on, perversely enough.

'Isn't that only because you've forgotten how to enjoy yourself? You never have time for anything decent – '

'As for instance?'

'Well, going for walks, or music, or books, or seeing interesting people. You never do anything that's really worth doing any more than I do.'

'I always think you could make this room much nicer, if you liked,' she observed.

'What does it matter what sort of room I have when I'm forced to spend all the best years of my life drawing up deeds in an office?'

'You said two days ago that you found the law so interesting.'

'So it is if one could afford to know anything about it.'

('That's Herbert only just going to bed now,' Joan interposed, as a door on the landing slammed vigorously. 'And then he won't get up in the morning.')

Ralph looked at the ceiling, and shut his lips closely together. Why, he wondered, could Joan never for one moment detach her mind from the details of domestic life? It seemed to him that she was getting more and more enmeshed in them, and capable of shorter and less frequent flights into the outer world, and yet she was only thirty-three.

'D'you ever pay calls now?' he asked abruptly.

'I don't often have the time. Why do you ask?'

'It might be a good thing, to get to know new people, that's all.'

'Poor Ralph!' said Joan suddenly, with a smile. 'You think your sister's getting very old and very dull – that's it, isn't it?'

'I don't think anything of the kind,' he said stoutly, but he flushed.

'But you lead a dog's life, Joan. When you're not working in an office, you're worrying over the rest of us. And I'm not much good to you, I'm afraid.'

Joan rose, and stood for a moment warming her hands, and, apparently, meditating as to whether she should say anything more or not. A feeling of great intimacy united the brother and sister, and the semicircular lines above their eyebrows disappeared. No, there was nothing more to be said on either side. Joan brushed her brother's head with her hand as she passed him, murmured good-night, and left the room. For some minutes after she had gone Ralph lay quiescent, resting his head on his hand, but gradually his eyes filled with thought, and the lines reappeared on his brow, as the pleasant impression of companionship and ancient sympathy waned, and he was left to think on alone.

After a time he opened his book, and read on steadily, glancing once or twice at his watch, as if he had set himself a task to be accomplished in a certain measure of time. Now and then he heard voices in the house, and the closing of bedroom doors, which showed that the building, at the top of which he sat, was inhabited in every one of its cells. When midnight struck, Ralph shut his book, and with a candle in his hand, descended to the ground floor, to ascertain that all lights were extinct and all doors locked. It was a threadbare, well-worn house that he thus examined, as if the inmates had grazed down all luxuriance and plenty to the verge of decency; and in the night, bereft of life, bare places and ancient blemishes were unpleasantly visible. Katharine Hilbery, he thought, would condemn it off-hand.

Chapter 3

Denham had accused Katharine Hilbery of belonging to one of the most distinguished families in England, and if anyone will take the trouble to consult Mr Galton's *Hereditary Genius*,[8] he will find that this assertion is not far from the truth. The Alardyces, the Hilberys, the Millingtons and the Otways seem to prove that intellect is a possession which can be tossed from one member of a certain group to another almost indefinitely, and with apparent certainty that the brilliant gift will be safely caught and held by nine out of ten of the privileged race. They had been conspicuous judges and admirals, lawyers and servants of the state for some years before the richness of the soil culminated in the rarest flower that any family can boast, a great writer, a poet eminent among the poets of England, a Richard Alardyce; and having produced him, they proved once more the amazing virtues of their race by proceeding unconcernedly again with their usual task of breeding distinguished men. They had sailed with Sir John Franklin to the North Pole, and ridden with Havelock to the Relief of Lucknow, and when they were not lighthouses firmly based on rock for the guidance of their generation, they were steady, serviceable candles, illuminating the ordinary chambers of daily life. Whatever profession you looked at, there was a Warburton or an Alardyce, a Millington or a Hilbery somewhere in authority and prominence.

It may be said, indeed, that English society being what it is, no very great merit is required, once you bear a well-known name, to put you into a position where it is easier on the whole to be eminent than obscure. And if this is true of the sons, even the daughters, even in the nineteenth century, are apt to become people of importance – philanthropists and educationalists if they are spinsters, and the wives of distinguished men if they marry. It is true that there were several lamentable exceptions to this rule in the Alardyce group, which seems to indicate that the cadets of such houses go more rapidly to the bad than the children of ordinary fathers and mothers, as if it were somehow a relief to them. But, on the whole, in these first years of the twentieth century, the Alardyces and their relations were keeping their heads well above water. One finds them at the tops of professions, with letters after their names; they sit in luxurious public offices, with private secretaries attached to them; they write solid books in dark covers, issued by the presses of the two great universities, and when one of them dies the chances are that another of them writes his biography.

Now the source of this nobility was, of course, the poet, and his immediate descendants, therefore, were invested with greater lustre than the collateral branches. Mrs Hilbery, in virtue of her position as the only child of the poet, was spiritually the head of the family, and Katharine, her daughter, had some superior rank among all the cousins and connections, the more so because she was an only child. The Alardyces had married and intermarried, and their offspring were generally profuse, and had a way of meeting regularly in each other's houses for meals and family celebrations which had acquired a semi-sacred character and were as regularly observed as days of feasting and fasting in the Church.

In times gone by, Mrs Hilbery had known all the poets, all the novelists, all the beautiful women and distinguished men of her time. These being now either dead or secluded in their infirm glory, she made her house a meeting-place for her own relations, to whom she would lament the passing of the great days of the nineteenth century, when every department of letters and art was represented in England by two or three illustrious names. Where are their successors? she would ask, and the absence of any poet or painter or novelist of the true calibre at the present day was a text upon which she liked to ruminate, in a sunset mood of benignant reminiscence, which it would have been hard to disturb had there been need. But she was far from visiting their inferiority upon the younger generation. She welcomed them very heartily to her house, told them her stories, gave them sovereigns and ices and good advice, and weaved round them romances which had generally no likeness to the truth.

The quality of her birth oozed into Katharine's consciousness from a dozen different sources as soon as she was able to perceive anything. Above her nursery fireplace hung a photograph of her grandfather's tomb in Poets' Corner,[9] and she was told, in one of those moments of grown-up confidence which are so tremendously impressive to the child's mind, that he was buried there because he was a 'good and great man'. Later, on an anniversary, she was taken by her mother through the fog in a hansom cab, and given a large bunch of bright, sweet-scented flowers to lay upon his tomb. The candles in the church, the singing and the booming of the organ, were all, she thought, in his honour. Again and again she was brought down into the drawing-room to receive the blessing of some awful distinguished old man, who sat, even to her childish eye, somewhat apart, all gathered together and clutching a stick, unlike an ordinary visitor in her father's own armchair, and her father himself was there, unlike himself, too, a little excited and very polite. These formidable old creatures used to take her in their arms, look very keenly in her eyes, and then bless her and tell her that she must mind and be a good girl, or else detect a look in her face something like Richard's as a small boy. That drew down upon her her mother's fervent embrace, and she was sent back to the nursery very proud, and with a mysterious sense of an important and unexplained state of things, which time, by degrees, unveiled to her.

There were always visitors – uncles and aunts and cousins 'from India', to be reverenced for their relationship alone, and others of the solitary and formidable class, whom she was enjoined by her parents to 'remember all your life'. By these means, and from hearing constant talk of great men and their works, her earliest conceptions of the world included an august circle of beings to whom she gave the names of Shakespeare, Milton, Wordsworth, Shelley, and so on, who were, for some reason, much more nearly akin to the Hilberys than to other people. They made a kind of boundary to her vision of life, and played a considerable part in determining her scale of good and bad in her own small affairs. Her descent from one of these gods was no surprise to her, but matter for satisfaction, until, as the years wore on, the privileges of her lot were taken for granted, and certain drawbacks made themselves very manifest. Perhaps it is a little depressing to inherit not lands but an example of intellectual and spiritual virtue; perhaps the conclusiveness of a great ancestor is a little discouraging to those who run the risk of comparison with him. It seems as if, having flowered so splendidly, nothing now remained possible but a steady growth of good, green stalk and leaf. For these reasons, and for others, Katharine had her moments of despondency. The glorious past, in which men and women grew to unexampled size, intruded too much upon the present, and dwarfed it too consistently, to be altogether encouraging to one forced to make her experiment in living when the great age was dead.

She was drawn to dwell upon these matters more than was natural, in the first place owing to her mother's absorption in them, and in the second because a great part of her time was spent in imagination with the dead, since she was helping her mother to produce a life of the great poet. When Katharine was seventeen or eighteen – that is to say, some ten years ago – her mother had enthusiastically announced that now, with a daughter to help her, the biography would soon be published. Notices to this effect found their way into the literary papers, and for some time Katharine worked with a sense of great pride and achievement.

Lately, however, it had seemed to her that they were making no way at all, and this was the more tantalising because no one with the ghost of a literary temperament could doubt but that they had materials for one of the greatest biographies that has ever been written. Shelves and boxes bulged with the precious stuff. The most private lives of the most interesting people lay furled in yellow bundles of close-written manuscript. In addition to this Mrs Hilbery had in her own head as bright a vision of that time as now remained to the living, and could give those flashes and thrills to the old words which gave them almost the substance of flesh. She had no difficulty in writing, and covered a page every morning as instinctively as a thrush sings, but nevertheless, with all this to urge and inspire, and the most devout intention to accomplish the work, the book still remained unwritten. Papers accumulated without much furthering their task, and in dull moments Katharine had her doubts whether they would ever produce anything at all fit to lay before the public. Where did the difficulty lie? Not in their materials, alas! nor in their ambitions, but in something more profound, in her own inaptitude, and above all, in her mother's temperament. Katharine would calculate that she had never known her write for more than ten minutes at a time. Ideas came to her chiefly when she was in motion. She liked to perambulate the room with a duster in her hand, with which she stopped to polish the backs of already lustrous books, musing and romancing as she did so. Suddenly the right phrase or the penetrating point of view would suggest itself, and she would drop her duster and write ecstatically for a few breathless moments; and then the mood would pass away, and the duster would be sought for, and the old books polished again. These spells of in-spiration never burnt steadily, but flickered over the gigantic mass of the subject as capriciously as a will-o'-the-wisp, lighting now on this point, now on that. It was as much as Katharine could do to keep the pages of her mother's manuscript in order, but to sort them so that the sixteenth year of Richard Alardyce's life succeeded the fifteenth was beyond her skill. And yet they were so brilliant, these paragraphs, so nobly phrased, so lightning-like in their illumination, that the dead seemed to crowd the very room. Read continuously, they produced a sort of vertigo, and set her asking herself in despair what on earth she was to do with them? Her mother refused, also, to face the radical questions of what to leave in and what to leave out. She could not decide how far the public was to be told the truth about the poet's separation from his wife. She drafted passages to suit either case, and then liked each so well that she could not decide upon the rejection of either.

But the book must be written. It was a duty that they owed the world, and to Katharine, at least, it meant more than that, for if they could not between them get this one book accomplished they had no right to their privileged position. Their increment became yearly more and more unearned. Besides, it must be established indisputably that her grandfather was a very great man.

By the time she was twenty-seven, these thoughts had become very familiar to her. They trod their way through her mind as she sat opposite her mother of a morning at a table heaped with bundles of old letters and well supplied with pencils, scissors, bottles of gum, india-rubber bands, large envelopes, and other appliances for the manufacture of books. Shortly before Ralph Denham's visit, Katharine had resolved to try the effect of strict rules upon her mother's habits of literary composition. They were to be seated at their tables every morning at ten o'clock, with a clean-swept morning of empty, secluded hours before them. They were to keep their eyes fast upon the paper, and nothing was to tempt them to speech, save at the stroke of the hour when ten minutes for relaxation were to be allowed them. If these rules were observed for a year, she made out on a sheet of paper that the completion of the book was certain, and she laid her scheme before her mother with a feeling that much of the task was already accomplished. Mrs Hilbery examined the sheet of paper very carefully. Then she clapped her hands and exclaimed enthusiastically: 'Well done, Katharine! What a wonderful head for business you've got! Now I shall keep this before me, and every day I shall make a little mark in my pocketbook, and on the last day of all – let me think, what shall we do to celebrate the last day of all? If it weren't the winter we could take a jaunt to Italy. They say Switzerland's very lovely in the snow, except for the cold. But, as you say, the great thing is to finish the book. Now let me see – '

When they inspected her manuscripts, which Katharine had put in order, they found a state of things well calculated to dash their spirits, if they had not just resolved on reform. They found, to begin with, a great variety of very imposing paragraphs with which the biography was to open; many of these, it is true, were unfinished, and resembled triumphal arches standing upon one leg, but, as Mrs Hilbery observed, they could be patched up in ten minutes, if she gave her mind to it. Next, there was an account of the ancient home of the Alardyces, or rather, of spring in Suffolk, which was very beautifully written, although not essential to the story. However, Katharine had put together a string of names and dates, so that the poet was capably brought into the world, and his ninth year was reached without further mishap. After that, Mrs Hilbery wished, for sentimental reasons, to introduce the recollections of a very fluent old lady, who had been brought up in the same village, but these Katharine decided must go. It might be advisable to introduce here a sketch of contemporary poetry contributed by Mr Hilbery, and thus terse and learned and altogether out of keeping with the rest, but Mrs Hilbery was of opinion that it was too bare, and made one feel altogether like a good little girl in a lecture-room, which was not at all in keeping with her father. It was put on one side. Now came the period of his early manhood, when various affairs of the heart must either be concealed or revealed; here again Mrs Hilbery was of two minds, and a thick packet of manuscript was shelved for further consideration.

Several years were now altogether omitted, because Mrs Hilbery had found something distasteful to her in that period, and had preferred to dwell upon her own recollections as a child. After this, it seemed to Katharine that the book became a wild dance of will-o'-the-wisps, without form or continuity, without coherence even, or any attempt to make a narrative. Here were twenty pages upon her grandfather's taste in hats, an essay upon contemporary china, a long account of a summer day's expedition into the country, when they had missed their train, together with fragmentary visions of all sorts of famous men and women, which seemed to be partly imaginary and partly authentic. There were, moreover, thousands of letters, and a mass of faithful recollections contributed by old friends, which had grown yellow now in their envelopes, but must be placed somewhere or their feelings would be hurt. So many volumes had been written about the poet since his death that she had also to dispose of a great number of misstatements, which involved minute researches and much correspondence. Sometimes Katharine brooded, half crushed, among her papers; sometimes she felt that it was necessary for her very existence that she should free herself from the past; at others, that the past had completely displaced the present, which, when one resumed life after a morning among the dead, proved to be of an utterly thin and inferior composition.

The worst of it was that she had no aptitude for literature. She did not like phrases. She had even some natural antipathy to that process of self-examination, that perpetual effort to understand one's own feeling, and express it beautifully, fitly, or energetically in language, which constituted so great a part of her mother's existence. She was, on the contrary, inclined to be silent; she shrank from expressing herself even in talk, let alone in writing. As this disposition was highly convenient in a family much given to the manufacture of phrases, and seemed to argue a corresponding capacity for action, she was, from her childhood even, put in charge of household affairs. She had the reputation, which nothing in her manner contradicted, of being the most practical of people. Ordering meals, directing servants, paying bills, and so contriving that every clock ticked more or less accurately in time and a number of vases were always full of fresh flowers, was supposed to be a natural endowment of hers, and, indeed, Mrs Hilbery often observed that it was poetry the wrong side out. From a very early age, too, she had to exert herself in another capacity; she had to counsel and help and generally sustain her mother. Mrs Hilbery would have been perfectly well able to sustain herself if the world had been what the world is not. She was beautifully adapted for life on another planet. But the natural genius she had for conducting affairs there was of no real use to her here. Her watch, for example, was a constant source of surprise to her, and at the age of sixty-five she was still amazed at the ascendancy which rules and reasons exerted over the lives of other people. She had never learnt her lesson, and had constantly to be punished for her ignorance. But as that ignorance was combined with a fine natural insight which saw deep whenever it saw at all, it was not possible to write Mrs Hilbery off among the dunces; on the contrary, she had a way of seeming the wisest person in the room. But, on the whole, she found it very necessary to seek support in her daughter.

Katharine, thus, was a member of a very great profession which has, as yet, no title and very little recognition, although the labour of mill and factory is, perhaps, no more severe and the results of less benefit to the world. She lived at home. She did it very well, too. Anyone coming to the house in Cheyne Walk felt that here was an orderly place, shapely, controlled – a place where life had been trained to show to the best advantage, and, though composed of different elements, made to appear harmonious and with a character of its own. Perhaps it was the chief triumph of Katharine's art that Mrs Hilbery's character predominated. She and Mr Hilbery appeared to be a rich background for her mother's more striking qualities.

Silence being, thus, both natural to her and imposed upon her, the only other remark that her mother's friends were in the habit of making about it was that it was neither a stupid silence nor an indifferent silence. But to what quality it owed its character, since character of some sort it had, no one troubled themselves to enquire. It was understood that she was helping her mother to produce a great book. She was known to manage the household. She was certainly beautiful. That accounted for her satisfactorily. But it would have been a surprise, not only to other people but to Katharine herself, if some magic watch could have taken count of the moments spent in an entirely different occupation from her ostensible one. Sitting with faded papers before her, she took part in a series of scenes such as the taming of wild ponies upon the American prairies, or the conduct of a vast ship in a hurricane round a black promontory of rock, or in others more peaceful, but marked by her complete emancipation from her present surroundings and, needless to say, by her surpassing ability in her new vocation. When she was rid of the pretence of paper and pen, phrase-making and biography, she turned her attention in a more legitimate direction, though, strangely enough, she would rather have confessed her wildest dreams of hurricane and prairie than the fact that, upstairs, alone in her room, she rose early in the morning or sat up late at night to . . . work at mathematics. No force on earth would have made her confess that. Her actions when thus engaged were furtive and secretive, like those of some nocturnal animal. Steps had only to sound on the staircase, and she slipped her paper between the leaves of a great Greek dictionary which she had purloined from her father's room for this purpose. It was only at night, indeed, that she felt secure enough from surprise to concentrate her mind to the utmost.

Perhaps the unwomanly nature of the science made her instinctively wish to conceal her love of it. But the more profound reason was that in her mind mathematics were directly opposed to literature. She would not have cared to confess how infinitely she preferred the exactitude, the starlike impersonality, of figures to the confusion, agitation and vagueness of the finest prose. There was something a little unseemly in thus opposing the tradition of her family; something that made her feel wrong-headed, and thus more than ever disposed to shut her desires away from view and cherish them with extraordinary fondness. Again and again she was thinking of some problem when she should have been thinking of her grandfather. Waking from these trances, she would see that her mother, too, had lapsed into some dream almost as visionary as her own, for the people who played their parts in it had long been numbered among the dead. But, seeing her own state mirrored in her mother's face, Katharine would shake herself awake with a sense of irritation. Her mother was the last person she wished to resemble, much though she admired her. Her common sense would assert itself almost brutally, and Mrs Hilbery, looking at her with her odd sidelong glance, that was half malicious and half tender, would liken her to 'your wicked old uncle Judge Peter, who used to be heard delivering sentence of death in the bathroom. Thank heaven, Katharine, I've not a drop of *him* in me!'

Chapter 4

At about nine o'clock at night, on every alternate Wednesday, Miss Mary Datchet made the same resolve, that she would never again lend her rooms for any purposes whatsoever. Being, as they were, rather large and conveniently situated in a street mostly dedicated to offices off the Strand, people who wished to meet, either for purposes of enjoyment, or to discuss art, or to reform the state, had a way of suggesting that Mary had better be asked to lend them her rooms.

She always met the request with the same frown of well-simulated annoyance, which presently dissolved in a kind of half-humorous, half-surly shrug, as of a large dog tormented by children who shakes his ears. She would lend her rooms, but only on condition that all the arrangements were made by her. This fortnightly meeting of a society for the free discussion of everything entailed a great deal of moving, and pulling, and ranging of furniture against the wall, and placing of breakable and precious things in safe places. Miss Datchet was quite capable of lifting a kitchen table on her back, if need were, for although well-proportioned and dressed becomingly, she had the appearance of unusual strength and determination.

She was some twenty-five years of age, but looked older because she earned, or intended to earn, her own living, and had already lost the look of the irresponsible spectator, and taken on that of the private in the army of workers.[10] Her gestures seemed to have a certain purpose, the muscles round eyes and lips were set rather firmly, as though the senses had undergone some discipline, and were held ready for a call on them. She had contracted two faint lines between her eyebrows, not from anxiety but from thought, and it was quite evident that all the feminine instincts of pleasing, soothing and charming were crossed by others in no way peculiar to her sex. For the rest she was brown-eyed, a little clumsy in movement, and suggested country birth and a descent from respectable hard-working ancestors, who had been men of faith and integrity rather than doubters or fanatics.

At the end of a fairly hard day's work it was certainly something of an effort to clear one's room, to pull the mattress off one's bed, and lay it on the floor, to fill a pitcher with cold coffee, and to sweep a long table clear for plates and cups and saucers, with pyramids of little pink biscuits between them; but when these alterations were effected, Mary felt a lightness of spirit come to her, as if she had put off the stout stuff of her working hours and slipped over her entire being some vesture of thin, bright silk. She knelt before the fire and looked out into the room. The light fell softly, but with clear radiance, through shades of yellow and blue paper, and the room, which was set with one or two sofas resembling grassy mounds in their lack of shape, looked unusually large and quiet. Mary was led to think of the heights of a Sussex down,[11] and the swelling green circle of some camp of ancient warriors. The moonlight would be falling there so peacefully now, and she could fancy the rough pathway of silver upon the wrinkled skin of the sea.

'And here we are,' she said, half aloud, half satirically, yet with evident pride, 'talking about art.'

She pulled a basket containing balls of differently coloured wools and a pair of stockings which needed darning towards her, and began to set her fingers to work; while her mind, reflecting the lassitude of her body, went on perversely, conjuring up visions of solitude and quiet, and she pictured herself laying aside her knitting and walking out on to the down, and hearing nothing but the sheep cropping the grass close to the roots, while the shadows of the little trees moved very slightly this way and that in the moonlight as the breeze went through them. But she was perfectly conscious of her present situation, and derived some pleasure from the reflection that she could rejoice equally in solitude, and in the presence of the many very different people who were now making their way, by divers paths, across London to the spot where she was sitting.

As she ran her needle in and out of the wool, she thought of the various stages in her own life which made her present position seem the culmination of successive miracles. She thought of her clerical father in his country parsonage, and of her mother's death, and of her own determination to obtain education, and of her college life, which had merged, not so very long ago, in the wonderful maze of London, which still seemed to her, in spite of her constitutional level-headedness, like a vast electric light, casting radiance upon the myriads of men and women who crowded round it. And here she was at the very centre of it all, that centre which was constantly in the minds of people in remote Canadian forests and on the plains of India, when their thoughts turned to England. The nine mellow strokes, by which she was now apprised of the hour, were a message from the great clock at Westminster itself.[12] As the last of them died away, there was a firm knocking on her own door, and she rose and opened it. She returned to the room, with a look of steady pleasure in her eyes, and she was talking to Ralph Denham, who followed her.

'Alone?' he said, as if he were pleasantly surprised by that fact.

'I am sometimes alone,' she replied.

'But you expect a great many people,' he added, looking round him. 'It's like a room on the stage. Who is it tonight?'

'William Rodney, upon the Elizabethan use of metaphor. I expect a good solid paper, with plenty of quotations from the classics.'

Ralph warmed his hands at the fire, which was flapping bravely in the grate, while Mary took up her stocking again.

'I suppose you are the only woman in London who darns her own stockings,' he observed.

'I'm only one of a great many thousands really,' she replied, 'though I must admit that I was thinking myself very remarkable when you came in. And now that you're here I don't think myself remarkable at all. How horrid of you! But I'm afraid you're much more remarkable than I am. You've done much more than I've done.'

'If that's your standard, you've nothing to be proud of,' said Ralph grimly.

'Well, I must reflect with Emerson that it's being and not doing that matters,'[13] she continued.

'Emerson?' Ralph exclaimed, with derision. 'You don't mean to say you read Emerson?'

'Perhaps it wasn't Emerson; but why shouldn't I read Emerson?' she asked, with a tinge of anxiety.

'There's no reason that I know of. It's the combination that's odd – books and stockings. The combination is very odd.' But it seemed to recommend itself to him. Mary gave a little laugh, expressive of happiness, and the particular stitches that she was now putting into her work appeared to her to be done with singular grace and felicity. She held out the stocking and looked at it approvingly.

'You always say that,' she said. 'I assure you it's a common "combination", as you call it, in the houses of the clergy. The only thing that's odd about me is that I enjoy them both – Emerson and the stocking.'

A knock was heard, and Ralph exclaimed: 'Damn those people! I wish they weren't coming!'

'It's only Mr Turner, on the floor below,' said Mary, and she felt grateful to Mr Turner for having alarmed Ralph, and for having given a false alarm.

'Will there be a crowd?' Ralph asked, after a pause.

'There'll be the Morrises and the Crashaws, and Dick Osborne, and Septimus, and all that set. Katharine Hilbery is coming, by the way, so William Rodney told me.'

'Katharine Hilbery!' Ralph exclaimed.

'You know her?' Mary asked, with some surprise.

'I went to a tea-party at her house.'

Mary pressed him to tell her all about it, and Ralph was not at all unwilling to exhibit proofs of the extent of his knowledge. He described the scene with certain additions and exaggerations which interested Mary very much.

'But, in spite of what you say, I do admire her,' she said. 'I've only seen her once or twice, but she seems to me to be what one calls a "personality".'

'I didn't mean to abuse her. I only felt that she wasn't very sympathetic to me.'

'They say she's going to marry that queer creature Rodney.'

'Marry Rodney? Then she must be more deluded than I thought her.'

'Now that's my door, all right,' Mary exclaimed, carefully putting her wools away, as a succession of knocks reverberated unnecessarily, accompanied by a sound of people stamping their feet and laughing. A moment later the room was full of young men and women, who came in with a peculiar look of expectation, exclaimed 'Oh!' when they saw Denham, and then stood still, gaping rather foolishly.

The room very soon contained between twenty and thirty people, who found seats for the most part upon the floor, occupying the mattresses, and hunching themselves together into triangular shapes. They were all young and some of them seemed to make a protest by their hair and dress, and something sombre and truculent in the expression of their faces, against the more normal type, who would have passed unnoticed in an omnibus or an underground railway. It was notable that the talk was confined to groups, and was, at first, entirely spasmodic in character, and muttered in undertones as if the speakers were suspicious of their fellow-guests.

Katharine Hilbery came in rather late, and took up a position on the floor, with her back against the wall. She looked round quickly, recognised about half a dozen people, to whom she nodded, but failed to see Ralph, or, if so, had already forgotten to attach any name to him. But in a second these heterogeneous elements were all united by the voice of Mr Rodney, who suddenly strode up to the table and began very rapidly in high-strained tones: 'In undertaking to speak of the Elizabethan use of metaphor in poetry – '

All the different heads swung slightly or steadied themselves into a position in which they could gaze straight at the speaker's face, and the same rather solemn expression was visible on all of them. But, at the same time, even the faces that were most exposed to view, and therefore most tautly under control, disclosed a sudden impulsive tremor which, unless directly checked, would have developed into an outburst of laughter. The first sight of Mr Rodney was irresistibly ludicrous. He was very red in the face, whether from the cool November night or nervousness, and every movement, from the way he wrung his hands to the way he jerked his head to right and left, as though a vision drew him now to the door, now to the window, bespoke his horrible discomfort under the stare of so many eyes. He was scrupulously well dressed, and a pearl in the centre of his tie seemed to give him a touch of aristocratic opulence. But the rather prominent eyes and the impulsive stammering manner, which seemed to indicate a torrent of ideas intermittently pressing for utterance and always checked in their course by a clutch of nervousness, drew no pity, as in the case of a more imposing personage, but a desire to laugh, which was, however, entirely lacking in malice. Mr Rodney was evidently so painfully conscious of the oddity of his appearance, and his very redness and the starts to which his body was liable gave such proof of his own discomfort, that there was something endearing in this ridiculous susceptibility, although most people would probably have echoed Denham's private exclamation, 'Fancy marrying a creature like that!'

His paper was carefully written out, but in spite of this precaution Mr Rodney managed to turn over two sheets instead of one, to choose the wrong sentence where two were written together, and to discover his own handwriting suddenly illegible. When he found himself possessed of a coherent passage, he shook it at his audience almost aggressively, and then fumbled for another. After a distressing search a fresh discovery would be made, and produced in the same way, until, by means of repeated attacks, he had stirred his audience to a degree of animation quite remarkable in these gatherings. Whether they were stirred by his enthusiasm for poetry or by the contortions which a human being was going through for their benefit, it would be hard to say. At length Mr Rodney sat down impulsively in the middle of a sentence, and, after a pause of bewilderment, the audience expressed its relief at being able to laugh aloud in a decided outburst of applause.

Mr Rodney acknowledged this with a wild glance round him, and, instead of waiting to answer questions, he jumped up, thrust himself through the seated bodies into the corner where Katharine was sitting, and exclaimed, very audibly: 'Well, Katharine, I hope I've made a big enough fool of myself even for you! It was terrible! terrible! terrible!'

'Hush! You must answer their questions,' Katharine whispered, desiring, at all costs, to keep him quiet. Oddly enough, when the speaker was no longer in front of them, there seemed to be much that was suggestive in what he had said. At any rate, a pale-faced young man with sad eyes was already on his feet, delivering an accurately worded speech with perfect composure. William Rodney listened with a curious lifting of his upper lip, although his face was still quivering slightly with emotion.

'Idiot!' he whispered. 'He's misunderstood every word I said!'

'Well then, answer him,' Katharine whispered back.

'No, I shan't! They'd only laugh at me. Why did I let you persuade me that these sort of people care for literature?' he continued.

There was much to be said both for and against Mr Rodney's paper. It had been crammed with assertions that such-and-such passages, taken liberally from English, French and Italian, are the supreme pearls of literature. Further, he was fond of using metaphors which, compounded in the study, were apt to sound either cramped or out of place as he delivered them in fragments. Literature was a fresh garland of spring flowers, he said, in which yew berries and the purple night-shade mingled with the various tints of the anemone; and somehow or other this garland encircled marble brows. He had read very badly some very beautiful quotations. But through his manner and his con-fusion of language there had emerged some passion of feeling which, as he spoke, formed in the majority of the audience a little picture or an idea which each now was eager to give expression to. Most of the people there proposed to spend their lives in the practice either of writing or painting, and merely by looking at them it could be seen that, as they listened to Mr Purvis first, and then to Mr Greenhalgh, they were seeing something done by these gentlemen to a possession which they thought to be their own. One person after another rose, and, as with an ill-balanced axe, attempted to hew out his conception of art a little more clearly, and sat down with the feeling that, for some reason which he could not grasp, his strokes had gone awry. As they sat down they turned almost invariably to the person sitting next them, and rectified and continued what they had just said in public. Before long, therefore, the groups on the mattresses and the groups on the chairs were all in communication with each other, and Mary Datchet, who had begun to darn stockings again, stooped down and remarked to Ralph: 'That was what I call a first-rate paper.'

Both of them instinctively turned their eyes in the direction of the reader of the paper. He was lying back against the wall, with his eyes apparently shut, and his chin sunk upon his collar. Katharine was turning over the pages of his manuscript as if she were looking for some passage that had particularly struck her, and had difficulty in finding it.

'Let's go and tell him how much we liked it,' said Mary, thus suggesting an action which Ralph was anxious to take, though without her he would have been too proud to do it, for he suspected that he had more interest in Katharine than she had in him.

'That was a very interesting paper,' Mary began, without any shyness, seating herself on the floor opposite to Rodney and Katharine. 'Will you lend me the manuscript to read in peace?'

Rodney, who had opened his eyes on their approach, regarded her for a moment in suspicious silence. 'Do you say that merely to disguise the fact of my ridiculous failure?' he asked.

Katharine looked up from her reading with a smile.

'He says he doesn't mind what we think of him,' she remarked. 'He says we don't care a rap for art of any kind.'

'I asked her to pity me, and she teases me!' Rodney exclaimed.

'I don't intend to pity you, Mr Rodney,' Mary remarked, kindly, but firmly. 'When a paper's a failure, nobody says anything, whereas now, just listen to them!'

The sound, which filled the room, with its hurry of short syllables, its sudden pauses, and its sudden attacks, might be compared to some animal hubbub, frantic and inarticulate.

'D'you think that's all about my paper?' Rodney enquired, after a moment's attention, with a distinct brightening of expression.

'Of course it is,' said Mary. 'It was a very suggestive paper.'

She turned to Denham for confirmation, and he corroborated her.

'It's the ten minutes after a paper is read that proves whether it's been a success or not,' he said. 'If I were you, Rodney, I should be very pleased with myself.'

This commendation seemed to comfort Mr Rodney completely, and he began to bethink him of all the passages in his paper which deserved to be called 'suggestive'.

'Did you agree at all, Denham, with what I said about Shakespeare's later use of imagery? I'm afraid I didn't altogether make my meaning plain.'

Here he gathered himself together, and by means of a series of frog-like jerks, succeeded in bringing himself close to Denham.

Denham answered him with the brevity which is the result of having another sentence in the mind to be addressed to another person. He wished to say to Katharine: 'Did you remember to get that picture glazed before your aunt came to dinner?' but, besides having to answer Rodney, he was not sure that the remark, with its assertion of intimacy, would not strike Katharine as impertinent. She was listening to what someone in another group was saying. Rodney, meanwhile, was talking about the Elizabethan dramatists.

He was a curious-looking man since, upon first sight, especially if he chanced to be talking with animation, he appeared, in some way, ridiculous; but, next moment, in repose, his face, with its large nose, thin cheeks and lips expressing the utmost sensibility, somehow recalled a Roman head bound with laurel, cut upon a circle of semi-transparent reddish stone. It had dignity and character. By profession a clerk in a government office, he was one of those martyred spirits to whom literature is at once a source of divine joy and of almost intolerable irritation. Not content to rest in their love of it, they must attempt to practise it themselves, and they are generally endowed with very little facility in composition. They condemn whatever they produce. Moreover, the violence of their feelings is such that they seldom meet with adequate sympathy, and being rendered very sensitive by their cultivated perceptions, suffer constant slights both to their own persons and to the thing they worship. But Rodney could never resist making trial of the sympathies of anyone who seemed favourably disposed, and Denham's praise had stimulated his very susceptible vanity.

'You remember the passage just before the death of the Duchess?'[14] he continued, edging still closer to Denham, and adjusting his elbow and knee in an incredibly angular combination. Here, Katharine, who had been cut off by these manoeuvres from all communication with the outer world, rose, and seated herself upon the window-sill, where she was joined by Mary Datchet. The two young women could thus survey the whole party. Denham looked after them, and made as if he were tearing handfuls of grass up by the roots from the carpet. But as it fell in accurately with his conception of life that all one's desires were bound to be frustrated, he concentrated his mind upon literature, and determined, philosophically, to get what he could out of that.

Katharine was pleasantly excited. A variety of courses was open to her. She knew several people slightly, and at any moment one of them might rise from the floor and come and speak to her; on the other hand, she might select somebody for herself, or she might strike into Rodney's discourse, to which she was intermittently attentive. She was conscious of Mary's body beside her, but, at the same time, the consciousness of being both of them women made it unnecessary to speak to her. But Mary, feeling, as she had said, that Katharine was a 'personality', wished so much to speak to her that in a few moments she did.

'They're exactly like a flock of sheep, aren't they?' she said, referring to the noise that rose from the scattered bodies beneath her.

Katharine turned and smiled.

'I wonder what they're making such a noise about?' she said.

'The Elizabethans, I suppose.'

'No, I don't think it's got anything to do with the Elizabethans. There! Didn't you hear them say, "Insurance Bill"?'[15]

'I wonder why men always talk about politics?' Mary speculated. 'I suppose, if we had votes,[16] we should, too.'

'I dare say we should. And you spend your life in getting us votes, don't you?'

'I do,' said Mary, stoutly. 'From ten to six every day I'm at it.'

Katharine looked at Ralph Denham, who was now pounding his way through the metaphysics of metaphor with Rodney, and was reminded of his talk that Sunday afternoon. She connected him vaguely with Mary.

'I suppose you're one of the people who think we should all have professions,' she said, rather distantly, as if feeling her way among the phantoms of an unknown world.

'Oh dear no,' said Mary at once.

'Well, I think I do,' Katharine continued, with half a sigh. 'You will always be able to say that you've done something, whereas, in a crowd like this, I feel rather melancholy.'

'In a crowd? Why in a crowd?' Mary asked, deepening the two lines between her eyes and hoisting herself nearer to Katharine upon the window-sill.

'Don't you see how many different things these people care about? And I want to beat them down – I only mean,' she corrected herself, 'that I want to assert myself, and it's difficult, if one hasn't a profession.'

Mary smiled, thinking that to beat people down was a process that should present no difficulty to Miss Katharine Hilbery. They knew each other so slightly that the beginning of intimacy, which Katharine seemed to initiate by talking about herself, had something solemn in it, and they were silent, as if to decide whether to proceed or not. They tested the ground.

'Ah, but I want to trample upon their prostrate bodies!' Katharine announced, a moment later, with a laugh, as if at the train of thought which had led her to this conclusion.

'One doesn't necessarily trample upon people's bodies because one runs an office,' Mary remarked.

'No. Perhaps not,' Katharine replied. The conversation lapsed, and Mary saw Katharine looking out into the room rather moodily with closed lips, the desire to talk about herself or to initiate a friendship having, apparently, left her. Mary was struck by her capacity for being thus easily silent, and occupied with her own thoughts. It was a habit that spoke of loneliness and a mind thinking for itself. When Katharine remained silent Mary was slightly embarrassed.

'Yes, they're very like sheep,' she repeated, foolishly.

'And yet they are very clever – at least,' Katharine added, 'I suppose they have all read Webster.'

'Surely you don't think that a proof of cleverness? I've read Webster,

I've read Ben Jonson, but I don't think myself clever – not exactly, at least.'

'I think you must be very clever,' Katharine observed.

'Why? Because I run an office?'

'I wasn't thinking of that. I was thinking how you live alone in this room, and have parties.'

Mary reflected for a second.

'It means, chiefly, a power of being disagreeable to one's own family, I think. I have that, perhaps. I didn't want to live at home, and I told my father. He didn't like it . . . But then I have a sister, and you haven't, have you?'

'No, I haven't any sisters.'

'You are writing a life of your grandfather?' Mary pursued.

Katharine seemed instantly to be confronted by some familiar thought from which she wished to escape. She replied, 'Yes, I am helping my mother,' in such a way that Mary felt herself baffled, and put back again into the position in which she had been at the beginning of their talk. It seemed to her that Katharine possessed a curious power of drawing near and receding, which sent alternate emotions through her far more quickly than was usual, and kept her in a condition of curious alertness. Desiring to classify her, Mary bethought her of the convenient term 'egoist'.

'She's an egoist,' she said to herself, and stored that word up to give to Ralph one day when, as it would certainly fall out, they were discussing Miss Hilbery.

'Heavens, what a mess there'll be tomorrow morning!' Katharine exclaimed. 'I hope you don't sleep in this room, Miss Datchet?'

Mary laughed.

'What are you laughing at?' Katharine demanded.

'I won't tell you.'

'Let me guess. You were laughing because you thought I'd changed the conversation?'

'No.'

'Because you think – ' She paused.

'If you want to know, I was laughing at the way you said Miss Datchet.'

'Mary, then. Mary, Mary, Mary.'

So saying, Katharine drew back the curtain in order, perhaps, to conceal the momentary flush of pleasure which is caused by coming perceptibly nearer to another person.

'Mary Datchet,' said Mary. 'It's not such an imposing name as Katharine Hilbery, I'm afraid.'

They both looked out of the window, first up at the hard silver moon, stationary among a hurry of little grey-blue clouds, and then down upon the roofs of London, with all their upright chimneys, and then below them at the empty moonlit pavement of the street, upon which the joint of each paving-stone was clearly marked out. Mary then saw Katharine raise her eyes again to the moon, with a contemplative look in them, as though she were setting that moon against the moon of other nights, held in memory. Someone in the room behind them made a joke about star-gazing, which destroyed their pleasure in it, and they looked back into the room again.

Ralph had been watching for this moment, and he instantly produced his sentence.

'I wonder, Miss Hilbery, whether you remembered to get that picture glazed?' His voice showed that the question was one that had been prepared.

'Oh, you idiot!' Mary exclaimed, very nearly aloud, with a sense that Ralph had said something very stupid. So, after three lessons in Latin grammar, one might correct a fellow student, whose knowledge did not embrace the ablative of 'mensa'.[17]

'Picture – what picture?' Katharine asked. 'Oh, at home, you mean – that Sunday afternoon. Was it the day Mr Fortescue came? Yes, I think I remembered it.'

The three of them stood for a moment awkwardly silent, and then Mary left them in order to see that the great pitcher of coffee was properly handled, for beneath all her education she preserved the anxieties of one who owns china.

Ralph could think of nothing further to say; but could one have stripped off his mask of flesh, one would have seen that his will-power was rigidly set upon a single object – that Miss Hilbery should obey him. He wished her to stay there until, by some measures not yet apparent to him, he had conquered her interest. These states of mind transmit themselves very often without the use of language, and it was evident to Katharine that this young man had fixed his mind upon her. She instantly recalled her first impressions of him, and saw herself again proffering family relics. She reverted to the state of mind in which he had left her that Sunday afternoon. She supposed that he judged her very severely. She argued naturally that, if this were the case, the burden of the conversation should rest with him. But she submitted so far as to stand perfectly still, her eyes upon the opposite wall, and her lips very nearly closed, though the desire to laugh stirred them slightly.

'You know the names of the stars, I suppose?' Denham remarked, and from the tone of his voice one might have thought that he grudged Katharine the knowledge he attributed to her.

She kept her voice steady with some difficulty.

'I know how to find the Pole star if I'm lost.'

'I don't suppose that often happens to you.'

'No. Nothing interesting ever happens to me,' she said.

'I think you make a system of saying disagreeable things, Miss Hilbery,' he broke out, again going further than he meant to. 'I suppose it's one of the characteristics of your class. They never talk seriously to their inferiors.'

Whether it was that they were meeting on neutral ground tonight, or whether the carelessness of an old grey coat that Denham wore gave an ease to his bearing that he lacked in conventional dress, Katharine certainly felt no impulse to consider him outside the particular set in which she lived.

'In what sense are you my inferior?' she asked, looking at him gravely, as though honestly searching for his meaning. The look gave him great pleasure. For the first time he felt himself on perfectly equal terms with a woman whom he wished to think well of him, although he could not have explained why her opinion of him mattered one way or another. Perhaps, after all, he only wanted to have something of her to take home to think about. But he was not destined to profit by his advantage.

'I don't think I understand what you mean,' Katharine repeated, and then she was obliged to stop and answer someone who wished to know whether she would buy a ticket for an opera from them, at a reduction. Indeed, the temper of the meeting was now unfavourable to separate conversation; it had become rather debauched and hilarious, and people who scarcely knew each other were making use of Christian names with apparent cordiality, and had reached that kind of gay tolerance and general friendliness which human beings in England only attain after sitting together for three hours or so, and the first cold blast in the air of the street freezes them into isolation once more. Cloaks were being flung round the shoulders, hats swiftly pinned to the head; and Denham had the mortification of seeing Katharine helped to prepare herself by the ridiculous Rodney. It was not the convention of the meeting to say goodbye, or necessarily even to nod to the person with whom one was talking; but, nevertheless, Denham was disappointed by the completeness with which Katharine parted from him, without any attempt to finish her sentence. She left with Rodney.

Chapter 5

Denham had no conscious intention of following Katharine, but, seeing her depart, he took his hat and ran rather more quickly down the stairs than he would have done if Katharine had not been in front of him. He overtook a friend of his, by name Harry Sandys, who was going the same way, and they walked together a few paces behind Katharine and Rodney.

The night was very still, and on such nights, when the traffic thins away, the walker becomes conscious of the moon in the street, as if the curtains of the sky had been drawn apart, and the heaven lay bare, as it does in the country. The air was softly cool, so that people who had been sitting talking in a crowd found it pleasant to walk a little before deciding to stop an omnibus or encounter light again in an underground railway. Sandys, who was a barrister with a philosophic tendency, took out his pipe, lit it, murmured 'hum' and 'ha', and was silent. The couple in front of them kept their distance accurately, and appeared, so far as Denham could judge by the way they turned towards each other, to be talking very constantly. He observed that when a pedestrian going the opposite way forced them to part they came together again directly afterwards. Without intending to watch them he never quite lost sight of the yellow scarf twisted round Katharine's head, or the light overcoat which made Rodney look fashionable among the crowd. At the Strand he supposed that they would separate, but instead they crossed the road, and took their way down one of the narrow passages which lead through ancient courts to the river. Among the crowd of people in the big thoroughfares Rodney seemed merely to be lending Katharine his escort, but now, when passengers were rare and the footsteps of the couple were distinctly heard in the silence, Denham could not help picturing to himself some change in their conversation. The effect of the light and shadow, which seemed to increase their height, was to make them mysterious and significant, so that Denham had no feeling of irritation with Katharine, but rather a half-dreamy acquiescence in the course of the world. Yes, she did very well to dream about – but Sandys had suddenly begun to talk. He was a solitary man who had made his friends at college and always addressed them as if they were still undergraduates arguing in his room, though many months or even years had passed in some cases between the last sentence and the present one. The method was a little singular, but very restful, for it seemed to ignore completely all accidents of human life, and to span very deep abysses with a few simple words.

On this occasion he began, while they waited for a minute on the edge of the Strand: 'I hear that Bennett has given up his theory of truth.'

Denham returned a suitable answer, and he proceeded to explain how this decision had been arrived at, and what changes it involved in the philosophy which they both accepted. Meanwhile Katharine and Rodney drew farther ahead, and Denham kept, if that is the right expression for an involuntary action, one filament of his mind upon them, while with the rest of his intelligence he sought to understand what Sandys was saying.

As they passed through the courts thus talking, Sandys laid the tip of his stick upon one of the stones forming a time-worn arch, and struck it meditatively two or three times in order to illustrate something very obscure about the complex nature of one's apprehension of facts. During the pause which this necessitated, Katharine and Rodney turned the corner and disappeared. For a moment Denham stopped involuntarily in his sentence, and continued it with a sense of having lost something.

Unconscious that they were observed, Katharine and Rodney had come out on the Embankment. When they had crossed the road, Rodney slapped his hand upon the stone parapet above the river and exclaimed: 'I promise I won't say another word about it, Katharine! But do stop a minute and look at the moon upon the water.'

Katharine paused, looked up and down the river, and snuffed the air.

'I'm sure one can smell the sea, with the wind blowing this way,' she said.

They stood silent for a few moments while the river shifted in its bed, and the silver and red lights which were laid upon it were torn by the current and joined together again. Very far off up the river a steamer hooted with its hollow voice of unspeakable melancholy, as if from the heart of lonely mist-shrouded voyagings.

'Ah!' Rodney cried, striking his hand once more upon the balustrade, 'why can't one say how beautiful it all is? Why am I condemned for ever, Katharine, to feel what I can't express? And the things I can give there's no use in my giving. Trust me, Katharine,' he added hastily, 'I won't speak of it again. But in the presence of beauty – look at the iridescence round the moon! – one feels – one feels – Perhaps if you married me – I'm half a poet, you see, and I can't pretend not to feel what I do feel. If I could write – ah, that would be another matter. I shouldn't bother you to marry me then, Katharine.'

He spoke these disconnected sentences rather abruptly, with his eyes alternately upon the moon and upon the stream.

'But for me I suppose you would recommend marriage?' said Katharine, with her eyes fixed on the moon.

'Certainly I should. Not for you only, but for all women. Why, you're nothing at all without it; you're only half alive; using only half your faculties; you must feel that for yourself. That is why – ' Here he stopped himself, and they began to walk slowly along the Embankment, the moon fronting them.

' "With how sad steps she climbs the sky, how silently and with how wan a face",[18] Rodney quoted.

'I've been told a great many unpleasant things about myself tonight,' Katharine stated, without attending to him. 'Mr Denham seems to think it his mission to lecture me, though I hardly know him. By the way, William, you know him; tell me, what is he like?'

William drew a deep sigh.

'We may lecture you till we're blue in the face – '

'Yes – but what's he like?'

'And we write sonnets to your eyebrows, you cruel practical creature. Denham?' he added, as Katharine remained silent. 'A good fellow, I should think. He cares, naturally, for the right sort of things, I expect. But you mustn't marry him, though. He scolded you, did he – what did he say?'

'What happens with Mr Denham is this: He comes to tea. I do all I can to put him at his ease. He merely sits and scowls at me. Then I show him our manuscripts. At this he becomes really angry, and tells me I've no business to call myself a middle-class woman. So we part in a huff; and next time we meet, which was tonight, he walks straight up to me, and says, "Go to the Devil!" That's the sort of behaviour my mother complains of. I want to know, what does it mean?'

She paused and, slackening her steps, looked at the lighted train drawing itself smoothly over Hungerford Bridge.

'It means, I should say, that he finds you chilly and unsympathetic.'

Katharine laughed with round, separate notes of genuine amusement.

'It's time I jumped into a cab and hid myself in my own house,' she exclaimed.

'Would your mother object to my being seen with you? No one could possibly recognise us, could they?' Rodney enquired, with some solicitude.

Katharine looked at him, and perceiving that his solicitude was genuine, she laughed again, but with an ironical note in her laughter.

'You may laugh, Katharine, but I can tell you that if any of your friends saw us together at this time of night they would talk about it, and I should find that very disagreeable. But why do you laugh?'

'I don't know. Because you're such a queer mixture, I think. You're half poet and half old maid.'

'I know I always seem to you highly ridiculous. But I can't help having inherited certain traditions and trying to put them into practice.'

'Nonsense, William. You may come of the oldest family in Devonshire, but that's no reason why you should mind being seen alone with me on the Embankment.'

'I'm ten years older than you are, Katharine, and I know more of the world than you do.'

'Very well. Leave me and go home.'

Rodney looked back over his shoulder and perceived that they were being followed at a short distance by a taxicab, which evidently awaited his summons. Katharine saw it, too, and exclaimed: 'Don't call that cab for me, William. I shall walk.'

'Nonsense, Katharine; you'll do nothing of the kind. It's nearly twelve o'clock, and we've walked too far as it is.'

Katharine laughed and walked on so quickly that both Rodney and the taxicab had to increase their pace to keep up with her.

'Now, William,' she said, 'if people see me racing along the Embankment like this they *will* talk. You had far better say good-night, if you don't want people to talk.'

At this William beckoned, with a despotic gesture, to the cab with one hand, and with the other he brought Katharine to a standstill.

'Don't let the man see us struggling, for God's sake!' he murmured. Katharine stood for a moment quite still.

'There's more of the old maid in you than the poet,' she observed briefly.

William shut the door sharply, gave the address to the driver, and turned away, lifting his hat punctiliously high in farewell to the invisible lady.

He looked back after the cab twice, suspiciously, half expecting that she would stop it and dismount; but it bore her swiftly on, and was soon out of sight. William felt in the mood for a short soliloquy of indignation, for Katharine had contrived to exasperate him in more ways than one.

'Of all the unreasonable, inconsiderate creatures I've ever known, she's the worst!' he exclaimed to himself, striding back along the Embankment. 'Heaven forbid that I should ever make a fool of myself with her again. Why, I'd sooner marry the daughter of my landlady than Katharine Hilbery! She'd leave me not a moment's peace – and she'd never understand me – never, never, never!'

Uttered aloud and with vehemence so that the stars of heaven might hear, for there was no human being at hand, these sentiments sounded satisfactorily irrefutable. Rodney quieted down, and walked on in silence, until he perceived someone approaching him who had some-thing, either in his walk or his dress, which proclaimed that he was one of William's acquaintances before it was possible to tell which of them he was. It was Denham who, having parted from Sandys at the bottom of his staircase, was now walking to the Tube at Charing Cross, deep in the thoughts which his talk with Sandys had suggested. He had forgotten the meeting at Mary Datchet's rooms, he had forgotten Rodney, and metaphors and Elizabethan drama, and could have sworn that he had forgotten Katharine Hilbery, too, although that was more disputable. His mind was scaling the highest pinnacles of its alps, where there was only starlight and the untrodden snow. He cast strange eyes upon Rodney, as they encountered each other beneath a lamp-post.

'Ha!' Rodney exclaimed.

If he had been in full possession of his mind, Denham would probably have passed on with a salutation. But the shock of the interruption made him stand still, and before he knew what he was doing, he had turned and was walking with Rodney in obedience to Rodney's invitation to come to his rooms and have something to drink. Denham had no wish to drink with Rodney, but he followed him passively enough. Rodney was gratified by this obedience. He felt inclined to be communicative with this silent man, who possessed so obviously all the good masculine qualities in which Katharine now seemed lamentably deficient.

'You do well, Denham,' he began impulsively, 'to have nothing to do with young women. I offer you my experience – if one trusts them one invariably has cause to repent. Not that I have any reason at this moment,' he added hastily, 'to complain of them. It's a subject that crops up now and again for no particular reason. Miss Datchet, I dare say, is one of the exceptions. Do you like Miss Datchet?'

These remarks indicated clearly enough that Rodney's nerves were in a state of irritation, and Denham speedily woke to the situation of the world as it had been one hour ago. He had last seen Rodney walking with Katharine. He could not help regretting the eagerness with which his mind returned to these interests and fretted him with the old trivial anxieties. He sank in his own esteem. Reason bade him break from Rodney, who clearly tended to become confidential, before he had utterly lost touch with the problems of high philosophy. He looked along the road, and marked a lamp-post at a distance of some hundred yards, and decided that he would part from Rodney when they reached this point.

'Yes, I like Mary; I don't see how one could help liking her,' he remarked cautiously, with his eye on the lamp-post.

'Ah, Denham, you're so different from me. You never give yourself away. I watched you this evening with Katharine Hilbery. My instinct is to trust the person I'm talking to. That's why I'm always being taken in, I suppose.'

Denham seemed to be pondering this statement of Rodney's, but, as a matter of fact, he was hardly conscious of Rodney and his revelations, and was only concerned to make him mention Katharine again before they reached the lamp-post.

'Who's taken you in now?' he asked. 'Katharine Hilbery?'

Rodney stopped and once more began beating a kind of rhythm, as if he were marking a phrase in a symphony, upon the smooth stone balustrade of the Embankment.

'Katharine Hilbery,' he repeated, with a curious little chuckle. 'No, Denham, I have no illusions about that young woman. I think I made that plain to her tonight. But don't run away with a false impression,' he continued eagerly, turning and linking his arm through Denham's, as though to prevent him from escaping; and, thus compelled, Denham passed the monitory lamp-post, to which, in passing, he breathed an excuse, for how could he break away when Rodney's arm was actually linked in his? 'You must not think that I have any bitterness against her – far from it. It's not altogether her fault, poor girl. She lives, you know, one of those odious, self-centered lives – at least, I think them odious for a woman – feeding her wits upon everything, having control of everything, getting far too much her own way at home – spoilt, in a sense, feeling that everyone is at her feet, and so not realising how she hurts – that is, how rudely she behaves to people who haven't all her advantages. Still, to do her justice, she's no fool,' he added, as if to warn Denham not to take any liberties. 'She has taste. She has sense. She can understand you when you talk to her. But she's a woman, and there's an end of it,' he added, with another little chuckle, and dropped Denham's arm.

'And did you tell her all this tonight?' Denham asked.

'Oh dear me, no. I should never think of telling Katharine the truth about herself. That wouldn't do at all. One has to be in an attitude of adoration in order to get on with Katharine.

'Now I've learnt that she's refused to marry him why don't I go home?' Denham thought to himself. But he went on walking beside Rodney, and for a time they did not speak, though Rodney hummed snatches of a tune out of an opera by Mozart. A feeling of contempt and liking combine very naturally in the mind of one to whom another has just spoken unpremeditatedly, revealing rather more of his private feelings than he intended to reveal. Denham began to wonder what sort of person Rodney was, and at the same time Rodney began to think about Denham.

'You're a slave like me, I suppose?' he asked.

'A solicitor, yes.'

'I sometimes wonder why we don't chuck it. Why don't you emigrate, Denham? I should have thought that would suit you.'

'I've a family.'

'I'm often on the point of going myself. And then I know I couldn't live without this' – and he waved his hand towards the City of London, which wore, at this moment, the appearance of a town cut out of grey-blue cardboard, and pasted flat against the sky, which was of a deeper blue.

'There are one or two people I'm fond of, and there's a little good music, and a few pictures, now and then – just enough to keep one dangling about here. Ah, but I couldn't live with savages! Are you fond of books? Music? Pictures? D'you care at all for first editions? I've got a few nice things up here, things I pick up cheap, for I can't afford to give what they ask.'

They had reached a small court of high eighteenth-century houses, in one of which Rodney had his rooms. They climbed a very steep staircase, through whose uncurtained windows the moonlight fell, illuminating the banisters with their twisted pillars, and the piles of plates set on the window-sills, and jars half-full of milk. Rodney's rooms were small, but the sitting-room window looked out into a courtyard, with its flagged pavement, and its single tree, and across to the flat red-brick fronts of the opposite houses, which would not have surprised Dr Johnson,[19] if he had come out of his grave for a turn in the moonlight. Rodney lit his lamp, pulled his curtains, offered Denham a chair, and, flinging the manuscript of his paper on the Elizabethan use of metaphor on to the table, exclaimed: 'Oh dear me, what a waste of time! But it's over now, and so we may think no more about it.'

He then busied himself very dexterously in lighting a fire, producing glasses, whisky, a cake, and cups and saucers. He put on a faded crimson dressing-gown, and a pair of red slippers, and advanced to Denham with a tumbler in one hand and a well-burnished book in the other.

'The Baskerville Congreve,'[20] said Rodney, offering it to his guest. 'I couldn't read him in a cheap edition.'

When he was seen thus among his books and his valuables, amiably anxious to make his visitor comfortable, and moving about with something of the dexterity and grace of a Persian cat, Denham relaxed his critical attitude, and felt more at home with Rodney than he would have done with many men better known to him. Rodney's room was the room of a person who cherishes a great many personal tastes, guarding them from the rough blasts of the public with scrupulous attention. His papers and his books rose in jagged mounds on table and floor, round which he skirted with nervous care lest his dressing-gown might disarrange them ever so slightly. On a chair stood a stack of photographs of statues and pictures, which it was his habit to exhibit, one by one, for the space of a day or two. The books on his shelves were as orderly as regiments of soldiers, and the backs of them shone like so many bronze beetle-wings; though, if you took one from its place you saw a shabbier volume behind it, since space was limited. An oval Venetian mirror stood above the fireplace, and reflected duskily in its spotted depths the faint yellow and crimson of a jarful of tulips which stood among the letters and pipes and cigarettes upon the mantelpiece. A small piano occupied a corner of the room, with the score of *Don Giovanni* open upon the bracket.

'Well, Rodney,' said Denham, as he filled his pipe and looked about him, 'this is all very nice and comfortable.'

Rodney turned his head half round and smiled, with the pride of a proprietor, and then prevented himself from smiling.

'Tolerable,' he muttered.

'But I dare say it's just as well that you have to earn your own living.'

'If you mean that I shouldn't do anything good with leisure if I had it, I dare say you're right. But I should be ten times as happy with my whole day to spend as I liked.'

'I doubt that,' Denham replied.

They sat silent, and the smoke from their pipes joined amicably in a blue vapour above their heads.

'I could spend three hours every day reading Shakespeare,' Rodney remarked. 'And there's music and pictures, let alone the society of the people one likes.'

'You'd be bored to death in a year's time.'

'Oh, I grant you I should be bored if I did nothing. But I should write plays.'

'H'm!'

'I should write plays,' he repeated. 'I've written three-quarters of one already, and I'm only waiting for a holiday to finish it. And it's not bad – no, some of it's really rather nice.'

The question arose in Denham's mind whether he should ask to see this play, as, no doubt, he was expected to do. He looked rather stealthily at Rodney, who was tapping the coal nervously with a poker, and quivering almost physically, so Denham thought, with desire to talk about this play of his, and vanity unrequited and urgent. He seemed very much at Denham's mercy, and Denham could not help liking him, partly on that account.

'Well, . . . will you let me see the play?' Denham asked, and Rodney looked immediately appeased, but, nevertheless, he sat silent for a moment, holding the poker perfectly upright in the air, regarding it with his rather prominent eyes, and opening his lips and shutting them again.

'Do you really care for this kind of thing?' he asked at length, in a different tone of voice from that in which he had been speaking. And, without waiting for an answer, he went on, rather querulously: 'Very few people care for poetry. I dare say it bores you.'

'Perhaps,' Denham remarked.

'Well, I'll lend it you,' Rodney announced, putting down the poker.

As he moved to fetch the play, Denham stretched a hand to the bookcase beside him, and took down the first volume which his fingers touched. It happened to be a small and very lovely edition of Sir Thomas Browne,[21] containing the 'Urn Burial', the 'Hydriotaphia', and the 'Garden of Cyrus', and, opening it at a passage which he knew very nearly by heart, Denham began to read and, for some time, continued to read.

Rodney resumed his seat, with his manuscript on his knee, and from time to time he glanced at Denham, and then joined his fingertips and crossed his thin legs over the fender, as if he experienced a good deal of pleasure. At length Denham shut the book, and stood, with his back to the fireplace, occasionally making an inarticulate humming sound which seemed to refer to Sir Thomas Browne. He put his hat on his head, and stood over Rodney, who still lay stretched back in his chair, with his toes within the fender.

'I shall look in again some time,' Denham remarked, upon which

Rodney held up his hand, containing his manuscript, without saying anything except – 'If you like.'

Denham took the manuscript and went. Two days later he was much surprised to find a thin parcel on his breakfast plate, which, on being opened, revealed the very copy of Sir Thomas Browne which he had studied so intently in Rodney's rooms. From sheer laziness he returned no thanks, but he thought of Rodney from time to time with interest, disconnecting him from Katharine, and meant to go round one evening and smoke a pipe with him. It pleased Rodney thus to give away whatever his friends genuinely admired. His library was constantly being diminished.

Chapter 6

Of all the hours of an ordinary working weekday, which are the pleasantest to look forward to and to look back upon? If a single instance is of use in framing a theory, it may be said that the minutes between nine-twenty-five and nine-thirty in the morning had a singular charm for Mary Datchet. She spent them in a very enviable frame of mind; her contentment was almost unalloyed. High in the air as her flat was, some beams from the morning sun reached her even in November, striking straight at curtain, chair and carpet, and painting there three bright, true spaces of green, blue and purple, upon which the eye rested with a pleasure which gave physical warmth to the body.

There were few mornings when Mary did not look up, as she bent to lace her boots, and as she followed the yellow rod from curtain to breakfast-table she usually breathed some sigh of thankfulness that her life provided her with such moments of pure enjoyment. She was robbing no one of anything, and yet, to get so much pleasure from simple things, such as eating one's breakfast alone in a room which had nice colours in it, clean from the skirting of the boards to the corners of the ceiling, seemed to suit her so thoroughly that she used at first to hunt about for someone to apologise to, or for some flaw in the situation. She had now been six months in London, and she could find no flaw, but that, as she invariably concluded by the time her boots were laced, was solely and entirely due to the fact that she had her work. Every day, as she stood with her dispatch-box in her hand at the door of her flat, and gave one look back into the room to see that everything was straight before she left, she said to herself that she was very glad that she was going to leave it all, that to have sat there all day long, in the enjoyment of leisure, would have been intolerable.

Out in the street she liked to think herself one of the workers who, at this hour, take their way in rapid single file along all the broad pavements of the City, with their heads slightly lowered, as if all their effort were to follow each other as closely as might be; so that Mary used to figure to herself a straight rabbit-run worn by their unswerving feet upon the pavement. But she liked to pretend that she was indistinguishable from the rest, and that when a wet day drove her to the Underground or omnibus, she gave and took her share of crowd and wet with clerks and typists and commercial men, and shared with them the serious business of winding-up the world to tick for another four-and-twenty hours.

Thus thinking, on the particular morning in question, she made her away across Lincoln's Inn Fields and up Kingsway, and so through Southampton Row until she reached her office in Russell Square. Now and then she would pause and look into the window of some bookseller or flower shop, where, at this early hour, the goods were being arranged, and empty gaps behind the plate glass revealed a state of undress. Mary felt kindly disposed towards the shopkeepers, and hoped that they would trick the midday public into purchasing, for at this hour of the morning she ranged herself entirely on the side of the shopkeepers and bank clerks, and regarded all who slept late and had money to spend as her enemy and natural prey. And directly she had crossed the road at Holborn, her thoughts all came naturally and regularly to roost upon her work, and she forgot that she was, properly speaking, an amateur worker, whose services were unpaid, and could hardly be said to wind the world up for its daily task, since the world, so far, had shown very little desire to take the boons which Mary's society for woman's suffrage had offered it.

She was thinking all the way up Southampton Row of notepaper and foolscap, and how an economy in the use of paper might be effected (without, of course, hurting Mrs Seal's feelings), for she was certain that the great organisers always pounce, to begin with, upon trifles like these, and build up their triumphant reforms upon a basis of absolute solidity; and, without acknowledging it for a moment, Mary Datchet was determined to be a great organiser, and had already doomed her society to reconstruction of the most radical kind. Once or twice lately, it is true, she had started, broad awake, before turning into Russell Square, and denounced herself rather sharply for being already in a groove, capable, that is, of thinking the same thoughts every morning at the same hour, so that the chestnut-coloured brick of the Russell Square houses had some curious connection with her thoughts about office economy, and served also as a sign that she should get into trim for meeting Mr Clacton, or Mrs Seal, or whoever might be beforehand with her at the office. Having no religious belief, she was the more conscientious about her life, examining her position from time to time very seriously, and nothing annoyed her more than to find one of these bad habits nibbling away unheeded at the precious substance. What was the good, after all, of being a woman if one didn't keep fresh, and cram one's life with all sorts of views and experiments? Thus she always gave herself a little shake, as she turned the corner, and, as often as not, reached her own door whistling a snatch of a Somersetshire ballad.

The Suffrage office was at the top of one of the large Russell Square houses, which had once been lived in by a great City merchant and his family, and was now let out in slices to a number of societies which displayed assorted initials upon doors of ground glass, and kept, each of them, a typewriter which clicked busily all day long. The old house, with its great stone staircase, echoed hollowly to the sound of typewriters and of errand-boys from ten to six. The noise of different typewriters already at work, disseminating their views upon the protection of native races, or the value of cereals as foodstuffs, quickened Mary's steps, and she always ran up the last flight of steps which led to her own landing, at whatever hour she came, so as to get her typewriter to take its place in competition with the rest.

She sat herself down to her letters, and very soon all these speculations were forgotten, and the two lines drew themselves between her eyebrows as the contents of the letters, the office furniture and the sounds of activity in the next room gradually asserted their sway upon her. By eleven o'clock the atmosphere of concentration was running so strongly in one direction that any thought of a different order could hardly have survived its birth more than a moment or so. The task which lay before her was to organise a series of entertainments, the profits of which were to benefit the society, which drooped for want of funds. It was her first attempt at organisation on a large scale, and she meant to achieve something remarkable. She meant to use the cumbrous machine to pick out this, that and the other interesting person from the muddle of the world, and to set them for a week in a pattern which must catch the eyes of cabinet ministers, and the eyes once caught, the old arguments were to be delivered with unexampled originality. Such was the scheme as a whole; and in contemplation of it she would become quite flushed and excited, and have to remind herself of all the details that intervened between her and success.

The door would open, and Mr Clacton would come in to search for a certain leaflet buried beneath a pyramid of leaflets. He was a thin, sandy-haired man of about thirty-five, spoke with a cockney accent, and had about him a frugal look, as if nature had not dealt generously with him in any way, which, naturally, prevented him from dealing generously with other people. When he had found his leaflet, and offered a few jocular hints upon keeping papers in order, the typewriting would stop abruptly, and Mrs Seal would burst into the room with a letter which needed explanation in her hand. This was a more serious interruption than the other, because she never knew exactly what she wanted, and half a dozen requests would bolt from her, no one of which was clearly stated. Dressed in plum-coloured velveteen, with short, grey hair, and a face that seemed permanently flushed with philanthropic enthusiasm, she was always in a hurry and always in some disorder. She wore two crucifixes, which got themselves entangled in a heavy gold chain upon her breast, and seemed to Mary expressive of her mental ambiguity. Only her vast enthusiasm and her worship of Miss Markham, one of the pioneers of the society, kept her in her place, for which she had no sound qualification.

So the morning wore on, and the pile of letters grew, and Mary felt, at last, that she was the centre ganglion of a very fine network of nerves which fell over England and one of these days, when she touched the heart of the system, would begin feeling and rushing together and emitting their splendid blaze of revolutionary fireworks – for some such metaphor represents what she felt about her work, when her brain had been heated by three hours of application.

Shortly before one o'clock Mr Clacton and Mrs Seal desisted from their labours, and the old joke about luncheon, which came out regularly at this hour, was repeated with scarcely any variation of words. Mr Clacton patronised a vegetarian restaurant; Mrs Seal brought sandwiches, which she ate beneath the plane trees in Russell Square; while Mary generally went to a gaudy establishment, upholstered in red plush, near by, where, much to the vegetarian's disapproval, you could buy steak, two inches thick, or a roast section of fowl, swimming in a pewter dish.

'The bare branches against the sky do one so much *good*,' Mrs Seal asserted, looking out into the square.

'But one can't lunch off trees, Sally,' said Mary.

'I confess I don't know how you manage it, Miss Datchet,' Mr Clacton remarked. 'I should sleep all the afternoon, I know, if I took a heavy meal in the middle of the day.'

'What's the very latest thing in literature?' Mary asked, good-humouredly pointing to the yellow-covered volume beneath Mr Clacton's arm, for he invariably read some new French author at lunchtime, or squeezed in a visit to a picture gallery, balancing his social work with an ardent culture of which he was secretly proud, as Mary had very soon divined.

So they parted and Mary walked away, wondering if they guessed that she really wanted to get away from them, and supposing that they had not quite reached that degree of subtlety. She bought herself an evening paper, which she read as she ate, looking over the top of it again and again at the queer people who were buying cakes or imparting their secrets, until some young woman whom she knew came in, and she called out, 'Eleanor, come and sit by me,' and they finished their lunch together, parting on the strip of pavement among the different lines of traffic with a pleasant feeling that they were stepping once more into their separate places in the great and eternally moving pattern of human life.

But, instead of going straight back to the office today, Mary turned into the British Museum, and strolled down the gallery with the shapes of stone until she found an empty seat directly beneath the gaze of the Elgin Marbles. She looked at them, and seemed, as usual, borne up on some wave of exaltation and emotion, by which her life at once became solemn and beautiful – an impression which was due as much, perhaps, to the solitude and chill and silence of the gallery as to the actual beauty of the statues. One must suppose, at least, that her emotions were not purely aesthetic, because, after she had gazed at the Ulysses[22] for a minute or two, she began to think about Ralph Denham. So secure did she feel with these silent shapes that she almost yielded to an impulse to say, 'I am in love with you,' aloud. The presence of this immense and enduring beauty made her almost alarmingly conscious of her desire, and at the same time proud of a feeling which did not display anything like the same proportions when she was going about her daily work.

She repressed her impulse to speak aloud, and rose and wandered about rather aimlessly among the statues until she found herself in another gallery devoted to engraved obelisks and winged Assyrian bulls, and her emotion took another turn. She began to picture herself travelling with Ralph in a land where these monsters were couchant in the sand. 'For,' she thought to herself, as she gazed fixedly at some information printed behind a piece of glass, 'the wonderful thing about you is that you're ready for anything; you're not in the least conventional, like most clever men.'

And she conjured up a scene of herself on a camel's back, in the desert, while Ralph commanded a whole tribe of natives.

'That is what you can do,' she went on, moving on to the next statue. 'You always make people do what you want.'

A glow spread over her spirit, and filled her eyes with brightness. Nevertheless, before she left the Museum she was very far from saying, even in the privacy of her own mind, 'I am in love with you,' and that sentence might very well never have framed itself. She was, indeed, rather annoyed with herself for having allowed such an ill-considered breach of her reserve, weakening her powers of resistance, she felt, should this impulse return again. For, as she walked along the street to her office, the force of all her customary objections to being in love with anyone overcame her. She did not want to marry at all. It seemed to her that there was something amateurish in bringing love into touch with a perfectly straightforward friendship, such as hers was with Ralph, which, for two years now, had based itself upon common interests in impersonal topics, such as the housing of the poor, or the taxation of land values.[23]

But the afternoon spirit differed intrinsically from the morning spirit. Mary found herself watching the flight of a bird, or making drawings of the branches of the plane trees upon her blotting-paper. People came in to see Mr Clacton on business, and a seductive smell of cigarette smoke issued from his room. Mrs Seal wandered about with newspaper cuttings, which seemed to her either 'quite splendid' or 'really too bad for words'. She used to paste these into books, or send them to her friends, having first drawn a broad bar in blue pencil down the margin, a proceeding which signified equally and indistinguishably the depths of her reprobation or the heights of her approval.

About four o'clock on that same afternoon Katharine Hilbery was walking up Kingsway. The question of tea presented itself. The street lamps were being lit already, and as she stood still for a moment beneath one of them, she tried to think of some neighbouring drawing-room where there would be firelight and talk congenial to her mood. That mood, owing to the spinning traffic and the evening veil of unreality, was ill-adapted to her home surroundings. Perhaps, on the whole, a shop was the best place in which to preserve this queer sense of heightened existence. At the same time she wished to talk. Remembering Mary Datchet and her repeated invitations, she crossed the road, turned into Russell Square, and peered about, seeking for numbers with a sense of adventure that was out of all proportion to the deed itself. She found herself in a dimly lighted hall, unguarded by a porter, and pushed open the first swing door. But the office-boy had never heard of Miss Datchet. Did she belong to the SRFR? Katharine shook her head with a smile of dismay. A voice from within shouted, 'No. The SGS[24] – top floor.'

Katharine mounted past innumerable glass doors, with initials on them, and became steadily more and more doubtful of the wisdom of her venture. At the top she paused for a moment to breathe and collect herself. She heard the typewriter and formal professional voices inside, not belonging, she thought, to anyone she had ever spoken to. She touched the bell, and the door was opened almost immediately by Mary herself. Her face had to change its expression entirely when she saw Katharine.

'You!' she exclaimed. 'We thought you were the printer.' Still holding the door open, she called back, 'No, Mr Clacton, it's not Penningtons. I should ring them up again – double three double eight, Central. Well, this is a surprise. Come in,' she added. 'You're just in time for tea.'

The light of relief shone in Mary's eyes. The boredom of the afternoon was dissipated at once, and she was glad that Katharine had found them in a momentary press of activity, owing to the failure of the printer to send back certain proofs.

The unshaded electric light shining upon the table covered with papers dazed Katharine for a moment. After the confusion of her twilight walk, and her random thoughts, life in this small room appeared extremely concentrated and bright. She turned instinctively to look out of the window, which was uncurtained, but Mary immediately recalled her.

'It was very clever of you to find your way,' she said, and Katharine wondered, as she stood there, feeling, for the moment, entirely detached and unabsorbed, why she had come. She looked, indeed, to Mary's eyes strangely out of place in the office. Her figure in the long cloak, which took deep folds, and her face, which was composed into a mask of sensitive apprehension, disturbed Mary for a moment with a sense of the presence of someone who was of another world, and, therefore, subversive of her world. She became immediately anxious that Katharine should be impressed by the importance of her world, and hoped that neither Mrs Seal nor Mr Clacton would appear until the impression of importance had been received. But in this she was disappointed. Mrs Seal burst into the room holding a kettle in her hand, which she set upon the stove, and then, with inefficient haste, she set light to the gas, which flared up, exploded, and went out.

'Always the way, always the way,' she muttered. 'Kit Markham is the only person who knows how to deal with the thing.'

Mary had to go to her help, and together they spread the table, and apologised for the disparity between the cups and the plainness of the food.

'If we had known Miss Hilbery was coming, we should have bought a cake,' said Mary, upon which Mrs Seal looked at Katharine for the first time, suspiciously, because she was a person who needed cake.

Here Mr Clacton opened the door, and came in, holding a typewritten letter in his hand, which he was reading aloud.

'Salford's affiliated,'[25] he said.

'Well done, Salford!' Mrs Seal exclaimed enthusiastically, thumping the teapot which she held upon the table, in token of applause.

'Yes, these provincial centres seem to be coming into line at last,' said Mr Clacton, and then Mary introduced him to Miss Hilbery, and he asked her, in a very formal manner, if she were interested 'in our work'.

'And the proofs still not come?' said Mrs Seal, putting both her elbows on the table, and propping her chin on her hands, as Mary began to pour out tea. 'It's too bad – too bad. At this rate we shall miss the country post. Which reminds me, Mr Clacton, don't you think we should circularise the provinces with Partridge's last speech? What? You've not read it? Oh, it's the best thing they've had in the House this Session.[26] Even the Prime Minister – '

But Mary cut her short.

'We don't allow shop at tea, Sally,' she said firmly. 'We fine her a penny each time she forgets, and the fines go to buying a plum cake,' she explained, seeking to draw Katharine into the community. She had given up all hope of impressing her.

'I'm sorry, I'm sorry,' Mrs Seal apologised. 'It's my misfortune to be an enthusiast,' she said, turning to Katharine. 'My father's daughter could hardly be anything else. I think I've been on as many committees as most people. Waifs and Strays, Rescue Work, Church Work, COS[27] – local branch – besides the usual civic duties which fall to one as a householder. But I've given them all up for our work here, and I don't regret it for a second,' she added. 'This is the root question, I feel; until women have votes – '

'It'll be sixpence, at least, Sally,' said Mary, bringing her fist down on the table. 'And we're all sick to death of women and their votes.'

Mrs Seal looked for a moment as though she could hardly believe her ears, and made a deprecating 'tut-tut-tut' in her throat, looking alternately at Katharine and Mary, and shaking her head as she did so.

Then she remarked, rather confidentially to Katharine, with a little nod in Mary's direction: 'She's doing more for the cause than any of us. She's giving her youth – for, alas! when I was young there were domestic circumstances – ' she sighed, and stopped short.

Mr Clacton hastily reverted to the joke about luncheon, and explained how Mrs Seal fed on a bag of biscuits under the trees, whatever the weather might be, rather, Katharine thought, as though Mrs Seal were a pet dog who had convenient tricks.

'Yes, I took my little bag into the square,' said Mrs Seal, with the self-conscious guilt of a child owning some fault to its elders. 'It was really very sustaining, and the bare boughs against the sky do one so much *good*. But I shall have to give up going into the square,' she proceeded, wrinkling her forehead. 'The injustice of it! Why should I have a beautiful square all to myself, when poor women who need rest have nowhere at all to sit?' She looked fiercely at Katharine, giving her short locks a little shake. 'It's dreadful what a tyrant one still is, in spite of all one's efforts. One tries to lead a decent life, but one can't. Of course, directly one thinks of it, one sees that *all* squares should be open to *everyone*. Is there any society with that object, Mr Clacton? If not, there should be, surely.'

'A most excellent object,' said Mr Clacton in his professional manner. 'At the same time, one must deplore the ramification of organisations, Mrs Seal. So much excellent effort thrown away, not to speak of pounds, shillings and pence. Now how many organisations of a philanthropic nature do you suppose there are in the City of London itself, Miss Hilbery?' he added, screwing his mouth into a queer little smile, as if to show that the question had its frivolous side.

Katharine smiled, too. Her unlikeness to the rest of them had, by this time, penetrated to Mr Clacton, who was not naturally observant, and he was wondering who she was; this same unlikeness had subtly stimulated Mrs Seal to try and make a convert of her. Mary, too, looked at her almost as if she begged her to make things easy. For Katharine had shown no disposition to make things easy. She had scarcely spoken, and her silence, though grave and even thoughtful, seemed to Mary the silence of one who criticises.

'Well, there are more in this house than I'd any notion of,' she said. 'On the ground floor you protect natives, on the next you emigrate women and tell people to eat nuts – '

'Why do you say that "*we*" do these things?' Mary interposed, rather sharply. 'We're not responsible for all the cranks who choose to lodge in the same house with us.'

Mr Clacton cleared his throat and looked at each of the young ladies in turn. He was a good deal struck by the appearance and manner of Miss Hilbery, which seemed to him to place her among those cultivated and luxurious people of whom he used to dream. Mary, on the other hand, was more of his own sort, and a little too much inclined to order him about. He picked up crumbs of dry biscuit and put them into his mouth with incredible rapidity.

'You don't belong to our society, then?' said Mrs Seal.

'No, I'm afraid I don't,' said Katharine, with such ready candour that Mrs Seal was nonplussed, and stared at her with a puzzled expression, as if she could not classify her among the varieties of human beings known to her.

'But surely – ' she began.

'Mrs Seal is an enthusiast in these matters,' said Mr Clacton, almost apologetically. 'We have to remind her sometimes that others have a right to their views even if they differ from our own . . . *Punch*[28] has a very funny picture this week, about a suffragist and an agricultural labourer. Have you seen this week's *Punch*, Miss Datchet?'

Mary laughed, and said, 'No.'

Mr Clacton then told them the substance of the joke, which, however, depended a good deal for its success upon the expression which the artist had put into the people's faces. Mrs Seal sat all the time perfectly grave. Directly he had done speaking she burst out: 'But surely, if you care about the welfare of your sex at all, you must wish them to have the vote?'

'I never said I didn't wish them to have the vote,' Katharine protested.

'Then why aren't you a member of our society?' Mrs Seal demanded.

Katharine stirred her spoon round and round, stared into the swirl of the tea, and remained silent. Mr Clacton, meanwhile, framed a question which, after a moment's hesitation, he put to Katharine.

'Are you in any way related, I wonder, to the poet Alardyce? His daughter, I believe, married a Mr Hilbery.'

'Yes; I'm the poet's granddaughter,' said Katharine, with a little sigh, after a pause; and for a moment they were all silent.

'The poet's granddaughter!' Mrs Seal repeated, half to herself, with a shake of her head, as if that explained what was otherwise inexplicable.

The light kindled in Mr Clacton's eye.

'Ah, indeed. That interests me very much,' he said. 'I owe a great debt to your grandfather, Miss Hilbery. At one time I could have repeated the greater part of him by heart. But one gets out of the way of reading poetry, unfortunately. You don't remember him, I suppose?'

A sharp rap at the door made Katharine's answer inaudible. Mrs Seal looked up with renewed hope in her eyes, and exclaiming: 'The proofs at last!' ran to open the door. 'Oh, it's only Mr Denham!' she cried, without any attempt to conceal her disappointment. Ralph, Katharine supposed, was a frequent visitor, for the only person he thought it necessary to greet was herself, and Mary at once explained the strange fact of her being there by saying: 'Katharine has come to see how one runs an office.'

Ralph felt himself stiffen uncomfortably, as he said: 'I hope Mary hasn't persuaded you that she knows how to run an office?'

'What, doesn't she?' said Katharine, looking from one to the other.

At these remarks Mrs Seal began to exhibit signs of discomposure, which displayed themselves by a tossing movement of her head, and, as Ralph took a letter from his pocket and placed his finger upon a certain sentence, she forestalled him by exclaiming in confusion: 'Now, I know what you're going to say, Mr Denham! But it was the day Kit Markham was here, and she upsets one so – with her wonderful vitality, always thinking of something new that we ought to be doing and aren't – and I was conscious at the time that my dates were mixed. It had nothing to do with Mary at all, I assure you.'

'My dear Sally, don't apologise,' said Mary, laughing. 'Men are such pedants – they don't know what things matter, and what things don't.'

'Now, Denham, speak up for our sex,' said Mr Clacton, in a jocular manner, indeed, but like most insignificant men he was very quick to resent being found fault with by a woman, in argument with whom he was fond of calling himself 'a mere man'. He wished, however, to enter into a literary conservation with Miss Hilbery, and thus let the matter drop.

'Doesn't it seem strange to you, Miss Hilbery,' he said, 'that the French, with all their wealth of illustrious names, have no poet who can compare with your grandfather? Let me see. There's Chénier and Hugo and Alfred de Musset[29] – wonderful men, but, at the same time, there's a richness, a freshness about Alardyce – '

Here the telephone bell rang, and he had to absent himself with a smile and a bow which signified that, although literature is delightful, it is not work. Mrs Seal rose at the same time, but remained hovering over the table, delivering herself of a tirade against party government. 'For if I were to tell you what I know of backstairs intrigue, and what can be done by the power of the purse, you wouldn't credit me, Mr Denham, you wouldn't, indeed. Which is why I feel that the only work for my father's daughter – for he was one of the pioneers, Mr Denham, and on his tombstone I had that verse from the Psalms put, about the sowers and the seed[30] . . . And what wouldn't I give that he should be alive now, seeing what we're going to see – ' but reflecting that the glories of the future depended in part upon the activity of her typewriter, she bobbed her head and hurried back to the seclusion of her little room, from which immediately issued sounds of enthusiastic, but obviously erratic, composition.

Mary made it clear at once, by starting a fresh topic of general interest, that though she saw the humour of her colleague, she did not intend to have her laughed at.

'The standard of morality seems to me frightfully low,' she observed reflectively, pouring out a second cup of tea, 'especially among women who aren't well educated. They don't see that small things matter, and that's where the leakage begins, and then we find ourselves in difficulties – I very nearly lost my temper yesterday,' she went on, looking at Ralph with a little smile, as though he knew what happened when she lost her temper. 'It makes me very angry when people tell me lies – doesn't it make you angry?' she asked Katharine.

'But considering that everyone tells lies,' Katharine remarked, looking about the room to see where she had put down her umbrella and her parcel, for there was an intimacy in the way in which Mary and Ralph addressed each other which made her wish to leave them. Mary, on the other hand, was anxious, superficially at least, that Katharine should stay and so fortify her in her determination not to be in love with Ralph.

Ralph, while lifting his cup from his lips to the table, had made up his mind that if Miss Hilbery left, he would go with her.

'I don't think that I tell lies, and I don't think that Ralph tells lies, do you, Ralph?' Mary continued.

Katharine laughed, with more gaiety, as it seemed to Mary, than she could properly account for. What was she laughing at? At them, presumably. Katharine had risen, and was glancing hither and thither, at the presses and the cupboards, and all the machinery of the office, as if she included them all in her rather malicious amusement, which caused Mary to keep her eyes on her straightly and rather fiercely, as if she were a gay-plumed, mischievous bird, who might light on the topmost bough and pick off the ruddiest cherry, without any warning. Two women less like each other could scarcely be imagined, Ralph thought, looking from one to the other. Next moment, he too rose, and nodding to Mary, as Katharine said goodbye, opened the door for her, and followed her out.

Mary sat still and made no attempt to prevent them from going. For a second or two after the door had shut on them her eyes rested on the door with a straightforward fierceness in which, for a moment, a certain degree of bewilderment seemed to enter; but, after a brief hesitation, she put down her cup and proceeded to clear away the tea-things.

The impulse which had driven Ralph to take this action was the result of a very swift little piece of reasoning, and thus, perhaps, was not quite so much of an impulse as it seemed. It passed through his mind that if he missed this chance of talking to Katharine, he would have to face an enraged ghost, when he was alone in his room again, demanding an explanation of his cowardly indecision. It was better, on the whole, to risk present discomfiture than to waste an evening bandying excuses and constructing impossible scenes with this uncompromising section of himself. For ever since he had visited the Hilberys he had been much at the mercy of a phantom Katharine, who came to him when he sat alone, and answered him as he would have her answer, and was always beside him to crown those varying triumphs which were transacted almost every night, in imaginary scenes, as he walked through the lamplit streets home from the office. To walk with Katharine in the flesh would either feed that phantom with fresh food, which, as all who nourish dreams are aware, is a process that becomes necessary from time to time, or refine it to such a degree of thinness that it was scarcely serviceable any longer; and that, too, is sometimes a welcome change to a dreamer. And all the time Ralph was well aware that the bulk of Katharine was not represented in his dreams at all, so that when he met her he was bewildered by the fact that she had nothing to do with his dream of her.

When, on reaching the street, Katharine found that Mr Denham proceeded to keep pace by her side, she was surprised and, perhaps, a little annoyed. She, too, had her margin of imagination, and tonight her activity in this obscure region of the mind required solitude. If she had had her way, she would have walked very fast down the Tottenham Court Road, and then sprung into a cab and raced swiftly home. The view she had had of the inside of an office was of the nature of a dream to her. Shut off up there, she compared Mrs Seal and Mary Datchet and Mr Clacton to enchanted people in a bewitched tower, with the spiders' webs looping across the corners of the room, and all the tools of the necromancer's craft at hand; for so aloof and unreal and apart from the normal world did they seem to her, in the house of in-numerable typewriters, murmuring their incantations and concocting their drugs, and flinging their frail spiders' webs over the torrent of life which rushed down the streets outside.

She may have been conscious that there was some exaggeration in this fancy of hers, for she certainly did not wish to share it with Ralph. To him, she supposed, Mary Datchet, composing leaflets for cabinet ministers among her typewriters, represented all that was interesting and genuine; and, accordingly, she shut them both out from all share in the crowded street, with its pendant necklace of lamps, its lighted windows, and its throng of men and women, which exhilarated her to such an extent that she very nearly forgot her companion. She walked very fast, and the effect of people passing in the opposite direction was to produce a queer dizziness both in her head and in Ralph's, which set their bodies far apart. But she did her duty by her companion almost unconsciously.

'Mary Datchet does that sort of work very well . . . She's responsible for it, I suppose?'

'Yes. The others don't help at all . . . Has she made a convert of you?'

'Oh no. That is, I'm a convert already.'

'But she hasn't persuaded you to work for them?'

'Oh dear no – that wouldn't do at all.'

So they walked on down the Tottenham Court Road, parting and coming together again, and Ralph felt much as though he were addressing the summit of a poplar in a high gale of wind.

'Suppose we get on to that omnibus?' he suggested.

Katharine acquiesced, and they climbed up, and found themselves alone on top of it.

'But which way are you going?' Katharine asked, waking a little from the trance into which movement among moving things had thrown her.

'I'm going to the Temple,'[31] Ralph replied, inventing a destination on the spur of the moment. He felt the change come over her as they sat down and the omnibus began to move forward. He imagined her contemplating the avenue in front of them with those honest sad eyes which seemed to set him at such a distance from them. But the breeze was blowing in their faces; it lifted her hat for a second, and she drew out a pin and stuck it in again – a little action which seemed, for some reason, to make her rather more fallible. Ah, if only her hat would blow off, and leave her altogether dishevelled, accepting it from his hands!

'This is like Venice,' she observed, raising her hand. 'The motor cars, I mean, shooting about so quickly, with their lights.'

'I've never seen Venice,' he replied. 'I keep that and some other things for my old age.'

'What are the other things?' she asked.

'There's Venice and India and, I think, Dante, too.'

She laughed.

'Think of providing for one's old age! And would you refuse to see Venice if you had the chance?'

Instead of answering her, he wondered whether he should tell her something that was quite true about himself; and as he wondered, he told her.

'I've planned out my life in sections ever since I was a child, to make it last longer. You see, I'm always afraid that I'm missing something – '

'And so am I!' Katharine exclaimed. 'But, after all,' she added, 'why should you miss anything?'

'Why? Because I'm poor, for one thing,' Ralph rejoined. 'You, I suppose, can have Venice and India and Dante every day of your life.'

She said nothing for a moment, but rested one hand, which was bare of glove, upon the rail in front of her, meditating upon a variety of things, of which one was that this strange young man pronounced Dante as she was used to hearing it pronounced, and another, that he had, most unexpectedly, a feeling about life that was familiar to her. Perhaps, then, he was the sort of person she might take an interest in, if she came to know him better, and as she had placed him among those whom she would never want to know better, this was enough to make her silent. She hastily recalled her first view of him, in the little room where the relics were kept, and ran a bar through half her impressions, as one cancels a badly written sentence, having found the right one.

'But to know that one might have things doesn't alter the fact that one hasn't got them,' she said, in some confusion. 'How could I go to India, for example? Besides,' she began impulsively, and stopped herself. Here the conductor came round, and interrupted them. Ralph waited for her to resume her sentence, but she said no more.

'I have a message to give your father,' he remarked. 'Perhaps you would give it him, or I could come – '

'Yes, do come,' Katharine replied.

'Still, I don't see why you shouldn't go to India,' Ralph began, in order to keep her from rising, as she threatened to do.

But she got up in spite of him, and said goodbye with her usual air of decision, and left him with a quickness which Ralph connected now with all her movements. He looked down and saw her standing on the pavement edge, an alert, commanding figure, which waited its season to cross, and then walked boldly and swiftly to the other side. That gesture and action would be added to the picture he had of her, but at present the real woman completely routed the phantom one.

Chapter 7

'And little Augustus Pelham said to me, "It's the younger generation knocking at the door," and I said to him, "Oh, but the younger generation comes in without knocking, Mr Pelham." Such a feeble little joke, wasn't it, but down it went into his notebook all the same.'

'Let us congratulate ourselves that we shall be in the grave before that work is published,' said Mr Hilbery.

The elderly couple were waiting for the dinner-bell to ring and for their daughter to come into the room. Their armchairs were drawn up on either side of the fire, and each sat in the same slightly crouched position, looking into the coals, with the expressions of people who have had their share of experiences and wait, rather passively, for something to happen. Mr Hilbery now gave all his attention to a piece of coal which had fallen out of the grate, and to selecting a favourable position for it among the lumps that were burning already. Mrs Hilbery watched him in silence, and the smile changed on her lips as if her mind still played with the events of the afternoon.

When Mr Hilbery had accomplished his task, he resumed his crouching position again, and began to toy with the little green stone attached to his watch-chain. His deep, oval-shaped eyes were fixed upon the flames, but behind the superficial glaze seemed to brood an observant and whimsical spirit, which kept the brown of the eye still unusually vivid. But a look of indolence, the result of scepticism or of a taste too fastidious to be satisfied by the prizes and conclusions so easily within his grasp, lent him an expression almost of melancholy. After sitting thus for a time, he seemed to reach some point in his thinking which demonstrated its futility, upon which he sighed and stretched his hand for a book lying on the table by his side.

Directly the door opened he closed the book, and the eyes of father and mother both rested on Katharine as she came towards them. The sight seemed at once to give them a motive which they had not had before. To them she appeared, as she walked towards them in her light evening dress, extremely young, and the sight of her refreshed them, were it only because her youth and ignorance made their knowledge of the world of some value.

'The only excuse for you, Katharine, is that dinner is still later than you are,' said Mr Hilbery, putting down his spectacles.

'I don't mind her being late when the result is so charming,' said Mrs Hilbery, looking with pride at her daughter. 'Still, I don't know that I *like* your being out so late, Katharine,' she continued. 'You took a cab, I hope?'

Here dinner was announced, and Mr Hilbery formally led his wife downstairs on his arm. They were all dressed for dinner, and, indeed, the prettiness of the dinner-table merited that compliment. There was no cloth upon the table, and the china made regular circles of deep blue upon the shining brown wood. In the middle there was a bowl of tawny red and yellow chrysanthemums, and one of pure white, so fresh that the narrow petals were curved backwards into a firm white ball. From the surrounding walls the heads of three famous Victorian writers surveyed this entertainment, and slips of paper pasted beneath them testified in the great man's own handwriting that he was yours sincerely or affectionately or for ever. The father and daughter would have been quite content, apparently, to eat their dinner in silence, or with a few cryptic remarks expressed in a shorthand which could not be understood by the servants. But silence depressed Mrs Hilbery, and far from minding the presence of maids, she would often address herself to them, and was never altogether unconscious of their approval or disapproval of her remarks. In the first place she called them to witness that the room was darker than usual, and had all the lights turned on.

'That's more cheerful,' she exclaimed. 'D'you know, Katharine, that ridiculous goose came to tea with me? Oh, how I wanted you! He tried to make epigrams all the time, and I got so nervous, expecting them, you know, that I spilt the tea – and he made an epigram about that!'

'Which ridiculous goose?' Katharine asked her father.

'Only one of my geese, happily, makes epigrams – Augustus Pelham, of course,' said Mrs Hilbery.

'I'm not sorry that I was out,' said Katharine.

'Poor Augustus!' Mrs Hilbery exclaimed. 'But we're all too hard on him. Remember how devoted he is to his tiresome old mother.'

'That's only because she is his mother. Anyone connected with himself – '

'No, no, Katharine – that's too bad. That's – what's the word I mean, Trevor, something long and Latin – the sort of word you and Katharine know – '

Mr Hilbery suggested 'cynical'.

'Well, that'll do. I don't believe in sending girls to college, but I should teach them that sort of thing. It makes one feel so dignified, bringing out these little allusions, and passing on gracefully to the next topic. But I don't know what's come over me – I actually had to ask Augustus the name of the lady Hamlet was in love with,[32] as you were out, Katharine, and heaven knows what he mayn't put down about me in his diary.'

'I wish,' Katharine started, with great impetuosity, and checked herself. Her mother always stirred her to feel and think quickly, and then she remembered that her father was there, listening with attention.

'What is it you wish?' he asked, as she paused.

He often surprised her, thus, into telling him what she had not meant to tell him; and then they argued, while Mrs Hilbery went on with her own thoughts.

'I wish mother wasn't famous. I was out at tea, and they would talk to me about poetry.'

'Thinking you must be poetical, I see – and aren't you?'

'Who's been talking to you about poetry, Katharine?' Mrs Hilbery demanded, and Katharine was committed to giving her parents an account of her visit to the Suffrage office.

'They have an office at the top of one of the old houses in Russell Square. I never saw such queer-looking people. And the man discovered I was related to the poet, and talked to me about poetry. Even Mary Datchet seems different in that atmosphere.'

'Yes, the office atmosphere is very bad for the soul,' said Mr Hilbery.

'I don't remember any offices in Russell Square in the old days, when mama lived there,' Mrs Hilbery mused, 'and I can't fancy turning one of those noble great rooms into a stuffy little Suffrage office. Still, if the clerks read poetry there must be something nice about them.'

'No, because they don't read it as we read it,' Katharine insisted.

'But it's nice to think of them reading your grandfather, and not filling up those dreadful little forms all day long,' Mrs Hilbery persisted, her notion of office life being derived from some chance view of a scene behind the counter at her bank, as she slipped the sovereigns into her purse.

'At any rate, they haven't made a convert of Katharine, which was what I was afraid of,' Mr Hilbery remarked.

'Oh no,' said Katharine very decidedly, 'I wouldn't work with them for anything.'

'It's curious,' Mr Hilbery continued, agreeing with his daughter, 'how the sight of one's fellow-enthusiasts always chokes one off. They show up the faults of one's cause so much more plainly than one's antagonists. One can be enthusiastic in one's study, but directly one comes into touch with the people who agree with one, all the glamour goes. So I've always found,' and he proceeded to tell them, as he peeled his apple, how he committed himself once, in his youthful days, to make a speech at a political meeting, and went there ablaze with enthusiasm for the ideals of his own side; but while his leaders spoke, he became gradually converted to the other way of thinking, if thinking it could be called, and had to feign illness in order to avoid making a fool of himself – an experience which had sickened him of public meetings.

Katharine listened and felt as she generally did when her father, and to some extent her mother, described their feelings, that she quite understood and agreed with them, but, at the same time, saw something which they did not see, and always felt some disappointment when they fell short of her vision, as they always did. The plates succeeded each other swiftly and noiselessly in front of her, and the table was decked for dessert, and as the talk murmured on in familiar grooves, she sat there, rather like a judge, listening to her parents, who did, indeed, feel it very pleasant when they made her laugh.

Daily life in a house where there are young and old is full of curious little ceremonies and pieties, which are discharged quite punctually, though the meaning of them is obscure, and a mystery has come to brood over them which lends even a superstitious charm to their performance. Such was the nightly ceremony of the cigar and the glass of port, which were placed on the right hand and on the left hand of Mr Hilbery, and simultaneously Mrs Hilbery and Katharine left the room. All the years they had lived together they had never seen Mr Hilbery smoke his cigar or drink his port, and they would have felt it unseemly if, by chance, they had surprised him as he sat there. These short, but clearly marked, periods of separation between the sexes were always used for an intimate postscript to what had been said at dinner, the sense of being women together coming out most strongly when the male sex was, as if by some religious rite, secluded from the female. Katharine knew by heart the sort of mood that possessed her as she walked upstairs to the drawing-room, her mother's arm in hers; and she could anticipate the pleasure with which, when she had turned on the lights, they both regarded the drawing-room, fresh swept and set in order for the last section of the day, with the red parrots swinging on the chintz curtains, and the armchairs warming in the blaze. Mrs Hilbery stood over the fire, with one foot on the fender, and her skirts slightly raised.

'Oh, Katharine,' she exclaimed, 'how you've made me think of mama and the old days in Russell Square! I can see the chandeliers, and the green silk of the piano, and mama sitting in her cashmere shawl by the window, singing till the little ragamuffin boys outside stopped to listen. Papa sent me in with a bunch of violets while he waited round the corner. It must have been a summer evening. That was before things were hopeless . . .'

As she spoke an expression of regret, which must have come frequently to cause the lines which now grew deep round the lips and eyes, settled on her face. The poet's marriage had not been a happy one. He had left his wife, and after some years of a rather reckless existence, she had died, before her time. This disaster had led to great irregularities of education, and, indeed, Mrs Hilbery might be said to have escaped education altogether. But she had been her father's companion at the season when he wrote the finest of his poems. She had sat on his knee in taverns and other haunts of drunken poets, and it was for her sake, so people said, that he had cured himself of his dissipation, and become the irreproachable literary character that the world knows, whose inspiration had deserted him. As Mrs Hilbery grew old she thought more and more of the past, and this ancient disaster seemed at times almost to prey upon her mind, as if she could not pass out of life herself without laying the ghost of her parent's sorrow to rest.

Katharine wished to comfort her mother, but it was difficult to do this satisfactorily when the facts themselves were so much of a legend. The house in Russell Square, for example, with its noble rooms, and the magnolia tree in the garden, and the sweet-voiced piano, and the sound of feet coming down the corridors, and other properties of size and romance – had they any existence? Yet why should Mrs Alardyce live all alone in this gigantic mansion, and, if she did not live alone, with whom did she live? For its own sake, Katharine rather liked this tragic story, and would have been glad to hear the details of it, and to have been able to discuss them frankly. But this it became less and less possible to do, for though Mrs Hilbery was constantly reverting to the story, it was always in this tentative and restless fashion, as though by a touch here and there she could set things straight which had been crooked these sixty years. Perhaps, indeed, she no longer knew what the truth was.

'If they'd lived now,' she concluded, 'I feel it wouldn't have happened. People aren't so set upon tragedy as they were then. If my father had been able to go round the world, or if she'd had a rest cure, everything would have come right. But what could I do? And then they had bad friends, both of them, who made mischief. Ah, Katharine, when you marry, be quite, quite sure that you love your husband!'

The tears stood in Mrs Hilbery's eyes.

While comforting her, Katharine thought to herself, 'Now this is what Mary Datchet and Mr Denham don't understand. This is the sort of position I'm always getting into. How simple it must be to live as they do!' for all the evening she had been comparing her home and her father and mother with the Suffrage office and the people there.

'But, Katharine,' Mrs Hilbery continued, with one of her sudden changes of mood, 'though, heaven knows, I don't want to see you married, surely if ever a man loved a woman, William loves you. And it's a nice, rich-sounding name too – Katharine Rodney, which, unfortunately, doesn't mean that he's got any money, because he hasn't.'

The alteration of her name annoyed Katharine, and she observed, rather sharply, that she didn't want to marry anyone.

'It's very dull that you can only marry one husband, certainly,' Mrs Hilbery reflected. 'I always wish that you could marry everybody who wants to marry you. Perhaps they'll come to that in time, but meanwhile I confess that dear William – ' But here Mr Hilbery came in, and the more solid part of the evening began. This consisted in the reading aloud by Katharine from some prose work or other, while her mother knitted scarves intermittently on a little circular frame, and her father read the newspaper, not so attentively but that he could comment humorously now and again upon the fortunes of the hero and the heroine. The Hilberys subscribed to a library, which delivered books on Tuesdays and Fridays, and Katharine did her best to interest her parents in the works of living and highly respectable authors; but Mrs Hilbery was perturbed by the very look of the light, gold-wreathed volumes, and would make little faces as if she tasted something bitter as the reading went on; while Mr Hilbery would treat the moderns with a curious elaborate banter such as one might apply to the antics of a promising child. So this evening, after five pages or so of one of these masters, Mrs Hilbery protested that it was all too clever and cheap and nasty for words.

'Please, Katharine, read us something *real*.'

Katharine had to go to the bookcase and choose a portly volume in sleek, yellow calf, which had directly a sedative effect upon both her parents. But the delivery of the evening post broke in upon the periods of Henry Fielding,[33] and Katharine found that her letters needed all her attention.

Chapter 8

She took her letters up to her room with her, having persuaded her mother to go to bed directly Mr Hilbery left them, for so long as she sat in the same room as her mother, Mrs Hilbery might, at any moment, ask for a sight of the post. A very hasty glance through many sheets had shown Katharine that, by some coincidence, her attention had to be directed to many different anxieties simultaneously. In the first place, Rodney had written a very full account of his state of mind, which was illustrated by a sonnet, and he demanded a reconsideration of their position, which agitated Katharine more than she liked. Then there were two letters which had to be laid side by side and compared before she could make out the truth of their story, and even when she knew the facts she could not decide what to make of them; and finally she had to reflect upon a great many pages from a cousin who found himself in financial difficulties, which forced him to the uncongenial occupation of teaching the young ladies of Bungay[34] to play upon the violin.

But the two letters which each told the same story differently were the chief source of her perplexity. She was really rather shocked to find it definitely established that her own second cousin, Cyril Alardyce, had lived for the last four years with a woman who was not his wife, who had borne him two children, and was now about to bear him another. This state of things had been discovered by Mrs Milvain, her Aunt Celia, a zealous enquirer into such matters, whose letter was also under consideration. Cyril, she said, must be made to marry the woman at once; and Cyril, rightly or wrongly, was indignant with such interference with his affairs, and would not own that he had any cause to be ashamed of himself. Had he any cause to be ashamed of himself? Katharine wondered; and she turned to her aunt again.

'Remember,' she wrote, in her profuse, emphatic statement, 'that he bears your grandfather's name, and so will the child that is to be born. The poor boy is not so much to blame as the woman who deluded him, thinking him a gentleman, which he *is*, and having money, which he has *not*.'

'What would Ralph Denham say to this?' thought Katharine, beginning to pace up and down her bedroom. She twitched aside the curtains, so that, on turning, she was faced by darkness, and looking

out, could just distinguish the branches of a plane tree and the yellow
lights of someone else's windows.

'What would Mary Datchet and Ralph Denham say?' she reflected,
pausing by the window, which, as the night was warm, she raised, in
order to feel the air upon her face, and to lose herself in the nothingness
of night. But with the air the distant humming sound of far-off crowded
thoroughfares was admitted to the room. The incessant and tumultuous
hum of the distant traffic seemed, as she stood there, to represent the
thick texture of her life, for her life was so hemmed in with the progress
of other lives that the sound of its own advance was inaudible. People
like Ralph and Mary, she thought, had it all their own way, and an
empty space before them, and, as she envied them, she cast her mind
out to imagine an empty land where all this petty intercourse of men
and women, this life made up of the dense crossings and entanglements
of men and women, had no existence whatever. Even now, alone, at
night, looking out into the shapeless mass of London, she was forced to
remember that there was one point and here another with which she
had some connection. William Rodney, at this very moment, was seated
in a minute speck of light somewhere to the east of her, and his mind
was occupied, not with his book, but with her. She wished that no one
in the whole world would think of her. However, there was no way of
escaping from one's fellow-beings, she concluded, and shut the window
with a sigh, and returned once more to her letters.

She could not doubt but that William's letter was the most genuine
she had yet received from him. He had come to the conclusion that he
could not live without her, he wrote. He believed that he knew her, and
could give her happiness, and that their marriage would be unlike other
marriages. Nor was the sonnet, in spite of its accomplishment, lacking
in passion, and Katharine, as she read the pages through again, could
see in what direction her feelings ought to flow, supposing they revealed
themselves. She would come to feel a humorous sort of tenderness for
him, a zealous care for his susceptibilities, and, after all, she considered,
thinking of her father and mother, what is love?

Naturally, with her face, position and background, she had experience
of young men who wished to marry her, and made protestations of love,
but, perhaps because she did not return the feeling, it remained something of a pageant to her. Not having experience of it herself, her mind
had unconsciously occupied itself for some years in dressing up an
image of love, and the marriage that was the outcome of love, and the
man who inspired love, which naturally dwarfed any examples that
came her way. Easily, and without correction by reason, her imagination

made pictures, superb backgrounds casting a rich though phantom light upon the facts in the foreground. Splendid as the waters that drop with resounding thunder from high ledges of rock, and plunge downwards into the blue depths of night, was the presence of love she dreamt, drawing into it every drop of the force of life, and dashing them all asunder in the superb catastrophe in which everything was surrendered, and nothing might be reclaimed. The man, too, was some magnanimous hero, riding a great horse by the shore of the sea. They rode through forests together, they galloped by the rim of the sea. But waking, she was able to contemplate a perfectly loveless marriage, as the thing one did actually in real life, for possibly the people who dream thus are those who do the most prosaic things.

At this moment she was much inclined to sit on into the night, spinning her light fabric of thoughts until she tired of their futility, and went to her mathematics; but, as she knew very well, it was necessary that she should see her father before he went to bed. The case of Cyril Alardyce must be discussed, her mother's illusions and the rights of the family attended to. Being vague herself as to what all this amounted to, she had to take counsel with her father. She took her letters in her hand and went downstairs. It was past eleven, and the clocks had come into their reign, the grandfather's clock in the hall ticking in competition with the small clock on the landing. Mr Hilbery's study ran out behind the rest of the house, on the ground floor, and was a very silent, subterranean place, the sun in daytime casting a mere abstract of light through a skylight upon his books and the large table, with its spread of white papers, now illumined by a green reading-lamp. Here Mr Hilbery sat editing his review, or placing together documents by means of which it could be proved that Shelley had written 'of' instead of 'and', or that the inn in which Byron had slept was called the 'Nag's Head' and not the 'Turkish Knight', or that the Christian name of Keats's uncle had been John rather than Richard, for he knew more minute details about these poets than any man in England, probably, and was preparing an edition of Shelley which scrupulously observed the poet's system of punctuation. He saw the humour of these researches, but that did not prevent him from carrying them out with the utmost scrupulosity.

He was lying back comfortably in a deep armchair smoking a cigar, and ruminating the fruitful question as to whether Coleridge had wished to marry Dorothy Wordsworth,[35] and what, if he had done so, would have been the consequences to him in particular, and to literature in general. When Katharine came in he reflected that he knew what she had come for, and he made a pencil note before he spoke to her. Having done this, he saw that she was reading, and he watched her for a moment without saying anything. She was reading *Isabella and the Pot of Basil*'[36] and her mind was full of the Italian hills and the blue daylight, and the hedges set with little rosettes of red and white roses. Feeling that her father waited for her, she sighed and said, shutting her book: 'I've had a letter from Aunt Celia about Cyril, father . . . It seems to be true – about his marriage. What are we to do?'

'Cyril seems to have been behaving in a very foolish manner,' said Mr Hilbery, in his pleasant and deliberate tones.

Katharine found some difficulty in carrying on the conversation, while her father balanced his fingertips so judiciously, and seemed to reserve so many of his thoughts for himself.

'He's about done for himself, I should say,' he continued.

Without saying anything, he took Katharine's letters out of her hand, adjusted his eyeglasses, and read them through.

At length he said, 'Humph!' and gave the letters back to her.

'Mother knows nothing about it,' Katharine remarked. 'Will you tell her?'

'I shall tell your mother. But I shall tell her that there is nothing whatever for us to do.'

'But the marriage?' Katharine asked, with some diffidence.

Mr Hilbery said nothing, and stared into the fire.

'What in the name of conscience did he do it for?' he speculated at last, rather to himself than to her.

Katharine had begun to read her aunt's letter over again, and she now quoted a sentence. ' "Ibsen and Butler[37] . . . He has sent me a letter full of quotations – nonsense, though clever nonsense." '

'Well, if the younger generation want to carry on its life on those lines, it's none of our affair,' he remarked.

'But isn't it our affair, perhaps, to make them get married?' Katharine asked rather wearily.

'Why the dickens should they apply to me?' her father demanded with sudden irritation.

'Only as the head of the family – '

'But I'm not the head of the family. Alfred's the head of the family. Let them apply to Alfred,' said Mr Hilbery, relapsing again into his armchair. Katharine was aware that she had touched a sensitive spot, however, in mentioning the family.

'I think, perhaps, the best thing would be for me to go and see them,' she observed.

'I won't have you going anywhere near them,' Mr Hilbery replied with unwonted decision and authority. 'Indeed, I don't understand why they've dragged you into the business at all – I don't see that it's got anything to do with you.'

'I've always been friends with Cyril,' Katharine observed.

'But did he ever tell you anything about this?' Mr Hilbery asked rather sharply.

Katharine shook her head. She was, indeed, a good deal hurt that Cyril had not confided in her – did he think, as Ralph Denham or Mary Datchet might think, that she was, for some reason, unsympathetic – hostile even?

'As to your mother,' said Mr Hilbery, after a pause, in which he seemed to be considering the colour of the flames, 'you had better tell her the facts. She'd better know the facts before everyone begins to talk about it, though why Aunt Celia thinks it necessary to come, I'm sure I don't know. And the less talk there is the better.'

Granting the assumption that gentlemen of sixty who are highly cultivated, and have had much experience of life, probably think of many things which they do not say, Katharine could not help feeling rather puzzled by her father's attitude, as she went back to her room. What a distance he was from it all! How superficially he smoothed these events into a semblance of decency which harmonised with his own view of life! He never wondered what Cyril had felt, nor did the hidden aspects of the case tempt him to examine into them. He merely seemed to realise, rather languidly, that Cyril had behaved in a way which was foolish, because other people did not behave in that way. He seemed to be looking through a telescope at little figures hundreds of miles in the distance.

Her selfish anxiety not to have to tell Mrs Hilbery what had happened made her follow her father into the hall after breakfast the next morning in order to question him.

'Have you told mother?' she asked. Her manner to her father was almost stern, and she seemed to hold endless depths of reflection in the dark of her eyes.

Mr Hilbery sighed.

'My dear child, it went out of my head.' He smoothed his silk hat energetically, and at once affected an air of hurry. 'I'll send a note round from the office . . . I'm late this morning, and I've any amount of proofs to get through.'

'That wouldn't do at all,' Katharine said decidedly. 'She must be told – you or I must tell her. We ought to have told her at first.'

Mr Hilbery had now placed his hat on his head, and his hand was on the doorknob. An expression which Katharine knew well from her childhood, when he asked her to shield him in some neglect of duty, came into his eyes: malice, humour and irresponsibility were blended in it. He nodded his head to and fro significantly, opened the door with an adroit movement, and stepped out with a lightness unexpected at his age. He waved his hand once to his daughter, and was gone. Left alone, Katharine could not help laughing to find herself cheated as usual in domestic bargainings with her father, and left to do the disagreeable work which belonged, by rights, to him.

Chapter 9

Katharine disliked telling her mother about Cyril's misbehaviour quite as much as her father did, and for much the same reasons. They both shrank, nervously, as people fear the report of a gun on the stage, from all that would have to be said on this occasion. Katharine, moreover, was unable to decide what she thought of Cyril's misbehaviour. As usual, she saw something which her father and mother did not see, and the effect of that something was to suspend Cyril's behaviour in her mind without any qualification at all. They would think whether it was good or bad; to her it was merely a thing that had happened.

When Katharine reached the study, Mrs Hilbery had already dipped her pen in the ink.

'Katharine,' she said, lifting it in the air, 'I've just made out such a queer, strange thing about your grandfather. I'm three years and six months older than he was when he died. I couldn't very well have been his mother, but I might have been his elder sister, and that seems to me such a pleasant fancy. I'm going to start quite fresh this morning, and get a lot done.'

She began her sentence, at any rate, and Katharine sat down at her own table, untied the bundle of old letters upon which she was working, smoothed them out absent-mindedly, and began to decipher the faded script. In a minute she looked across at her mother, to judge her mood. Peace and happiness had relaxed every muscle in her face; her lips were parted very slightly, and her breath came in smooth, controlled inspirations like those of a child who is surrounding itself with a building of bricks, and increasing in ecstasy as each brick is placed in position. So Mrs Hilbery was raising round her the skies and trees of the past with every stroke of her pen, and recalling the voices of the dead. Quiet as the room was, and undisturbed by the sounds of the present moment, Katharine could fancy that here was a deep pool of past time, and that she and her mother were bathed in the light of sixty years ago. What could the present give, she wondered, to compare with the rich crowd of gifts bestowed by the past? Here was a Thursday morning in process of manufacture; each second was minted fresh by the clock upon the mantelpiece. She strained her ears and could just hear, far off, the hoot of a motor car and the rush of wheels coming nearer and dying away again, and the voices of men crying old iron and vegetables in one of the poorer streets at the back of the house. Rooms, of course, accumulate their suggestions, and any room in which one has been used to carry on any particular occupation gives off memories of moods, of ideas, of postures that have been seen in it; so that to attempt any different kind of work there is almost impossible.

Katharine was unconsciously affected, each time she entered her mother's room, by all these influences, which had had their birth years ago, when she was a child, and had something sweet and solemn about them, and connected themselves with early memories of the cavernous glooms and sonorous echoes of the Abbey[38] where her grandfather lay buried. All the books and pictures, even the chairs and tables, had belonged to him, or had reference to him; even the china dogs on the mantelpiece and the little shepherdesses with their sheep had been bought by him for a penny a piece from a man who used to stand with a tray of toys in Kensington High Street, as Katharine had often heard her mother tell. Often she had sat in this room, with her mind fixed so firmly on those vanished figures that she could almost see the muscles round their eyes and lips, and had given to each his own voice, with its tricks of accent, and his coat and his cravat. Often she had seemed to herself to be moving among them, an invisible ghost among the living, better acquainted with them than with her own friends, because she knew their secrets and possessed a divine foreknowledge of their destiny. They had been so unhappy, such muddlers, so wrong-headed, it seemed to her. She could have told them what to do, and what not to do. It was a melancholy fact that they would pay no heed to her, and were bound to come to grief in their own antiquated way. Their behaviour was often grotesquely irrational; their conventions monstrously absurd; and yet, as she brooded upon them, she felt so closely attached to them that it was useless to try to pass judgement upon them. She very nearly lost consciousness that she was a separate being, with a future of her own. On a morning of slight depression, such as this, she would try to find some sort of clue to the muddle which their old letters presented; some reason which seemed to make it worth while to them; some aim which they kept steadily in view – but she was interrupted.

Mrs Hilbery had risen from her table, and was standing looking out of the window at a string of barges swimming up the river.

Katharine watched her. Suddenly Mrs Hilbery turned abruptly, and exclaimed: 'I really believe I'm bewitched! I only want three sentences, you see, something quite straightforward and commonplace, and I can't find 'em.'

She began to pace up and down the room, snatching up her duster; but she was too much annoyed to find any relief, as yet, in polishing the backs of books.

'Besides,' she said, giving the sheet she had written to Katharine, 'I don't believe this'll do. Did your grandfather ever visit the Hebrides, Katharine?' She looked in a strangely beseeching way at her daughter. 'My mind got running on the Hebrides, and I couldn't help writing a little description of them. Perhaps it would do at the beginning of a chapter. Chapters often begin quite differently from the way they go on, you know.' Katharine read what her mother had written. She might have been a schoolmaster criticising a child's essay. Her face gave Mrs Hilbery, who watched it anxiously, no ground for hope.

'It's very beautiful,' she stated, 'but, you see, mother, we ought to go from point to point – '

'Oh, I know,' Mrs Hilbery exclaimed. 'And that's just what I can't do. Things keep coming into my head. It isn't that I don't know everything and feel everything (who did know him, if I didn't?), but I can't put it down, you see. There's a kind of blind spot,' she said, touching her forehead, 'there. And when I can't sleep o' nights, I fancy I shall die without having done it.'

From exultation she had passed to the depths of depression which the imagination of her death aroused. The depression communicated itself to Katharine. How impotent they were, fiddling about all day long with papers! And the clock was striking eleven and nothing done! She watched her mother, now rummaging in a great brass-bound box which stood by her table, but she did not go to her help. Of course, Katharine reflected, her mother had now lost some paper, and they would waste the rest of the morning looking for it. She cast her eyes down in irritation, and read again her mother's musical sentences about the silver gulls, and the roots of little pink flowers washed by pellucid streams, and the blue mists of hyacinths, until she was struck by her mother's silence. She raised her eyes. Mrs Hilbery had emptied a portfolio containing old photographs over her table, and was looking from one to another.

'Surely, Katharine,' she said, 'the men were far handsomer in those days than they are now, in spite of their odious whiskers? Look at old John Graham, in his white waistcoat – look at Uncle Harley. That's Peter the manservant, I suppose. Uncle John brought him back from India.'

Katharine looked at her mother, but did not stir or answer. She had suddenly become very angry, with a rage which their relationship made silent, and therefore doubly powerful and critical. She felt all the unfairness of the claim which her mother tacitly made to her time and sympathy, and what Mrs Hilbery took, Katharine thought bitterly, she wasted. Then, in a flash, she remembered that she had still to tell her about Cyril's misbehaviour. Her anger immediately dissipated itself; it broke like some wave that has gathered itself high above the rest; the waters were resumed into the sea again, and Katharine felt once more full of peace and solicitude, and anxious only that her mother should be protected from pain. She crossed the room instinctively, and sat on the arm of her mother's chair. Mrs Hilbery leant her head against her daughter's body.

'What is nobler,' she mused, turning over the photographs, 'than to be a woman to whom everyone turns, in sorrow or difficulty? How have the young women of your generation improved upon that, Katharine? I can see them now, sweeping over the lawns at Melbury House, in their flounces and furbelows, so calm and stately and imperial (and the monkey and the little black dwarf following behind), as if nothing mattered in the world but to be beautiful and kind. But they did more than we do, I sometimes think. They *were*, and that's better than doing. They seem to me like ships, like majestic ships, holding on their way, not shoving or pushing, not fretted by little things, as we are, but taking their way, like ships with white sails.'

Katharine tried to interrupt this discourse, but the opportunity did not come, and she could not forbear to turn over the pages of the album in which the old photographs were stored. The faces of these men and women shone forth wonderfully after the hubbub of living faces, and seemed, as her mother had said, to wear a marvellous dignity and calm, as if they had ruled their kingdoms justly and deserved great love. Some were of almost incredible beauty, others were ugly enough in a forcible way, but none were dull or bored or insignificant. The superb stiff folds of the crinolines suited the women; the cloaks and hats of the gentlemen seemed full of character. Once more Katharine felt the serene air all round her, and seemed far off to hear the solemn beating of the sea upon the shore. But she knew that she must join the present on to this past.

Mrs Hilbery was rambling on, from story to story.

'That's Janie Mannering,' she said, pointing to a superb, white-haired dame, whose satin robes seemed strung with pearls. 'I must have told you how she found her cook drunk under the kitchen table when the Empress[39] was coming to dinner, and tucked up her velvet sleeves (she always dressed like an empress herself), cooked the whole meal, and appeared in the drawing-room as if she'd been sleeping on a bank of roses all day. She could do anything with her hands – they all could – make a cottage or embroider a petticoat.

'And that's Queenie Colquhoun,' she went on, turning the pages, 'who took her coffin out with her to Jamaica, packed with lovely shawls and bonnets, because you couldn't get coffins in Jamaica, and she had a horror of dying there (as she did), and being devoured by the white ants. And there's Sabine, the loveliest of them all; ah! it was like a star rising when she came into the room. And that's Miriam, in her coach-man's cloak, with all the little capes on, and she wore great top-boots underneath. You young people may say you're unconventional, but you're nothing compared with her.'

Turning the page, she came upon the picture of a very masculine, handsome lady, whose head the photographer had adorned with an imperial crown.

'Ah, you wretch!' Mrs Hilbery exclaimed, 'what a wicked old despot you were, in your day! How we all bowed down before you! "Maggie," she used to say, "if it hadn't been for me, where would you be now?" And it was true; she brought them together, you know. She said to my father, "Marry her," and he did; and she said to poor little Clara, "Fall down and worship him," and she did; but she got up again, of course. What else could one expect? She was a mere child – eighteen – and half dead with fright, too. But that old tyrant never repented. She used to say that she had given them three perfect months, and no one had a right to more; and I sometimes think, Katharine, that's true, you know. It's more than most of us have, only we have to pretend, which was a thing neither of them could ever do. I fancy,' Mrs Hilbery mused, 'that there was a kind of sincerity in those days between men and women which, with all your outspokenness, you haven't got.'

Katharine again tried to interrupt. But Mrs Hilbery had been gathering impetus from her recollections, and was now in high spirits.

'They must have been good friends at heart,' she resumed, 'because she used to sing his songs. Ah, how did it go?' and Mrs Hilbery, who had a very sweet voice, trolled out a famous lyric of her father's which had been set to an absurdly and charmingly sentimental air by some early Victorian composer.

'It's the vitality of them!' she concluded, striking her fist against the table. 'That's what we haven't got! We're virtuous, we're earnest, we go to meetings, we pay the poor their wages, but we don't live as they lived. As often as not, my father wasn't in bed three nights out of the seven, but always fresh as paint in the morning. I hear him now, come singing up the stairs to the nursery, and tossing the loaf for breakfast on his sword-stick, and then off we went for a day's pleasuring – Richmond, Hampton Court, the Surrey Hills. Why shouldn't we go, Katharine? It's going to be a fine day.'

At this moment, just as Mrs Hilbery was examining the weather from the window, there was a knock at the door. A slight, elderly lady came in, and was saluted by Katharine, with very evident dismay, as 'Aunt Celia!' She was dismayed because she guessed why Aunt Celia had come. It was certainly in order to discuss the case of Cyril and the woman who was not his wife, and owing to her procrastination Mrs Hilbery was quite unprepared. Who could be more unprepared? Here she was, suggesting that all three of them should go on a jaunt to Blackfriars to inspect the site of Shakespeare's theatre, for the weather was hardly settled enough for the country.

To this proposal Mrs Milvain listened with a patient smile, which indicated that for many years she had accepted such eccentricities in her sister-in-law with bland philosophy. Katharine took up her position at some distance, standing with her foot on the fender, as though by so doing she could get a better view of the matter. But, in spite of her aunt's presence, how unreal the whole question of Cyril and his morality appeared! The difficulty, it now seemed, was not to break the news gently to Mrs Hilbery, but to make her understand it. How was one to lasso her mind, and tether it to this minute, unimportant spot? A matter-of-fact statement seemed best.

'I think Aunt Celia has come to talk about Cyril, mother,' she said rather brutally. 'Aunt Celia has discovered that Cyril is married. He has a wife and children.'

'No, he is *not* married,' Mrs Milvain interposed, in low tones, addressing herself to Mrs Hilbery. 'He has two children, and another on the way.'

Mrs Hilbery looked from one to the other in bewilderment.

'We thought it better to wait until it was proved before we told you,' Katharine added.

'But I met Cyril only a fortnight ago at the National Gallery!' Mrs Hilbery exclaimed. 'I don't believe a word of it,' and she tossed her head with a smile on her lips at Mrs Milvain, as though she could quite understand her mistake, which was a very natural mistake, in the case of a childless woman, whose husband was something very dull in the Board of Trade.

'I didn't *wish* to believe it, Maggie,' said Mrs Milvain. 'For a long time I *couldn't* believe it. But now I've seen, and I *have* to believe it.'

'Katharine,' Mrs Hilbery demanded, 'does your father know of this?' Katharine nodded.

'Cyril married!' Mrs Hilbery repeated. 'And never telling us a word, though we've had him in our house since he was a child – noble William's son! I can't believe my ears!'

Feeling that the burden of proof was laid upon her, Mrs Milvain now proceeded with her story. She was elderly and fragile, but her childlessness seemed always to impose these painful duties on her, and to revere the family, and to keep it in repair, had now become the chief object of her life. She told her story in a low, spasmodic, and somewhat broken voice.

'I have suspected for some time that he was not happy. There were new lines on his face. So I went to his rooms, when I knew he was engaged at the poor men's college. He lectures there – Roman law, you know, or it may be Greek. The landlady said Mr Alardyce only slept there about once a fortnight now. He looked so ill, she said. She had seen him with a young person. I suspected something directly. I went to his room, and there was an envelope on the mantelpiece, and a letter with an address in Seton Street, off the Kennington Road.'40

Mrs Hilbery fidgeted rather restlessly, and hummed fragments of her tune, as if to interrupt.

'I went to Seton Street,' Aunt Celia continued firmly. 'A very low place – lodging-houses, you know, with canaries in the windows. Number seven just like all the others. I rang, I knocked; no one came. I went down the area. I am certain I saw someone inside – children – a cradle. But no reply – no reply.' She sighed, and looked straight in front of her with a glazed expression in her half-veiled blue eyes.

'I stood in the street,' she resumed, 'in case I could catch a sight of one of them. It seemed a very long time. There were rough men singing in the public-house round the corner. At last the door opened, and someone – it must have been the woman herself – came right past me. There was only the pillar-box between us.'

'And what did she look like?' Mrs Hilbery demanded.

'One could see how the poor boy had been deluded,' was all that Mrs Milvain vouchsafed by way of description.

'Poor thing!' Mrs Hilbery exclaimed.

'Poor Cyril!' Mrs Milvain said, laying a slight emphasis upon Cyril.

'But they've got nothing to live upon,' Mrs Hilbery continued. 'If he'd come to us like a man,' she went on, 'and said, "I've been a fool," one would have pitied him; one would have tried to help him. There's nothing so disgraceful after all – But he's been going about all these years, pretending, letting one take it for granted, that he was single. And the poor deserted little wife – '

'She is *not* his wife,' Aunt Celia interrupted.

'I've never heard anything so detestable!' Mrs Hilbery wound up, striking her fist on the arm of her chair. As she realised the facts she became thoroughly disgusted, although, perhaps, she was more hurt by the concealment of the sin than by the sin itself. She looked splendidly roused and indignant; and Katharine felt an immense relief and pride in her mother. It was plain that her indignation was very genuine, and that her mind was as perfectly focused upon the facts as anyone could wish – more so, by a long way, than Aunt Celia's mind, which seemed to be timidly circling, with a morbid pleasure, in these unpleasant shades. She and her mother together would take the situation in hand, visit Cyril, and see the whole thing through.

'We must realise Cyril's point of view first,' she said, speaking directly to her mother, as if to a contemporary, but before the words were out of her mouth, there was more confusion outside, and cousin Caroline, Mrs Hilbery's maiden cousin, entered the room. Although she was by birth an Alardyce, and Aunt Celia a Hilbery, the complexities of the family relationship were such that each was at once first and second cousin to the other, and thus aunt and cousin to the culprit Cyril, so that his misbehaviour was almost as much cousin Caroline's affair as Aunt Celia's. Cousin Caroline was a lady of very imposing height and circumference, but in spite of her size and her handsome trappings, there was something exposed and unsheltered in her expression, as if for many summers her thin red skin and hooked nose and reduplication of chins, so much resembling the profile of a cockatoo, had been bared to the weather; she was, indeed, a single lady; but she had, it was the habit to say, 'made a life for herself', and was thus entitled to be heard with respect.

'This unhappy business,' she began, out of breath as she was. 'If the train had not gone out of the station just as I arrived, I should have been with you before. Celia has doubtless told you. You will agree with me, Maggie. He must be made to marry her at once for the sake of the children – '

'But does he refuse to marry her?' Mrs Hilbery enquired, with a return of her bewilderment.

'He has written an absurd perverted letter, all quotations,' cousin Caroline puffed. 'He thinks he's doing a very fine thing, where we only see the folly of it . . . The girl's every bit as infatuated as he is – for which I blame him.'

'She entangled him,' Aunt Celia intervened, with a very curious smoothness of intonation, which seemed to convey a vision of threads weaving and interweaving a close, white mesh round their victim.

'It's no use going into the rights and wrongs of the affair now, Celia,' said cousin Caroline with some acerbity, for she believed herself the only practical one of the family, and regretted that, owing to the slowness of the kitchen clock, Mrs Milvain had already confused poor dear Maggie with her own incomplete version of the facts. 'The mischief's done, and very ugly mischief too. Are we to allow the third child to be born out of wedlock? (I am sorry to have to say these things before you, Katharine.) He will bear your name, Maggie – your father's name, remember.'

'But let us hope it will be a girl,' said Mrs Hilbery.

Katharine, who had been looking at her mother constantly while the chatter of tongues held sway, perceived that the look of straightforward indignation had already vanished; her mother was evidently casting about in her mind for some method of escape, or bright spot, or sudden illumination which should show to the satisfaction of everybody that all had happened, miraculously but incontestably, for the best.

'It's detestable – quite detestable!' she repeated, but in tones of no great assurance; and then her face lit up with a smile which, tentative at first, soon became almost assured. 'Nowadays, people don't think so badly of these things as they used to do,' she began. 'It will be horribly uncomfortable for them sometimes, but if they are brave, clever children, as they will be, I dare say it'll make remarkable people of them in the end. Robert Browning used to say that every great man has Jewish blood in him, and we must try to look at it in that light. And, after all, Cyril has acted on principle. One may disagree with his principle, but, at least, one can respect it – like the French Revolution, or Cromwell cutting the king's head off. Some of the most terrible things in history have been done on principle,' she concluded.

'I'm afraid I take a very different view of principle,' cousin Caroline remarked tartly.

'Principle!' Aunt Celia repeated, with an air of deprecating such a word in such a connection. 'I will go tomorrow and see him,' she added.

'But why should you take these disagreeable things upon yourself, Celia?' Mrs Hilbery interposed, and cousin Caroline thereupon protested with some further plan involving sacrifice of herself.

Growing weary of it all, Katharine turned to the window, and stood among the folds of the curtain, pressing close to the window-pane, and gazing disconsolately at the river much in the attitude of a child depressed by the meaningless talk of its elders. She was much disappointed in her mother – and in herself too. The little tug which she gave to the blind, letting it fly up to the top with a snap, signified her annoyance. She was very angry, and yet impotent to give expression to her anger, or know with whom she was angry. How they talked and moralised and made up stories to suit their own version of the becoming, and secretly praised their own devotion and tact! No; they had their dwelling in a mist, she decided; hundreds of miles away – away from what? 'Perhaps it would be better if I married William,' she thought suddenly, and the thought appeared to loom through the mist like solid ground. She stood there, thinking of her own destiny, and the elder ladies talked on, until they had talked themselves into a decision to ask the young woman to luncheon, and tell her, very friendlily, how such behaviour appeared to women like themselves, who knew the world. And then Mrs Hilbery was struck by a better idea.

Chapter 10

Messrs Grateley and Hooper, the solicitors in whose firm Ralph Denham was clerk, had their office in Lincoln's Inn Fields, and there Ralph Denham appeared every morning very punctually at ten o'clock. His punctuality, together with other qualities, marked him out among the clerks for success, and indeed it would have been safe to wager that in ten years' time or so one would find him at the head of his profession, had it not been for a peculiarity which sometimes seemed to make everything about him uncertain and perilous. His sister Joan had already been disturbed by his love of gambling with his savings. Scrutinising him constantly with the eye of affection, she had become aware of a curious perversity in his temperament which caused her much anxiety, and would have caused her still more if she had not recognised the germs of it in her own nature. She could fancy Ralph suddenly sacrificing his entire career for some fantastic imagination; some cause or idea or even (so her fancy ran) for some woman seen from a railway train, hanging up clothes in a back yard. When he had found this beauty or this cause, no force, she knew, would avail to restrain him from pursuit of it. She suspected the East also, and always fidgeted herself when she saw him with a book of Indian travels in his hand, as though he were sucking contagion from the page. On the other hand, no common love affair, had there been such a thing, would have caused her a moment's uneasiness where Ralph was concerned. He was destined in her fancy for something splendid in the way of success or failure, she knew not which.

And yet nobody could have worked harder or done better in all the recognised stages of a young man's life than Ralph had done, and Joan had to gather materials for her fears from trifles in her brother's behaviour which would have escaped any other eye. It was natural that she should be anxious. Life had been so arduous for all of them from the start that she could not help dreading any sudden relaxation of his grasp upon what he held, though, as she knew from inspection of her own life, such sudden impulse to let go and make away from the discipline and the drudgery was sometimes almost irresistible. But with Ralph, if he broke away, she knew that it would be only to put himself under harsher constraint; she figured him toiling through sandy deserts under a tropical sun to find the source of some river or the haunt of some fly; she figured him living by the labour of his hands in some city slum, the victim of one of those terrible theories of right and wrong which were current at the time; she figured him prisoner for life in the house of a woman who had seduced him by her misfortunes. Half proudly, and wholly anxiously, she framed such thoughts, as they sat, late at night, talking together over the gas-stove in Ralph's bedroom.

It is likely that Ralph would not have recognised his own dream of a future in the forecasts which disturbed his sister's peace of mind. Certainly, if any one of them had been put before him he would have rejected it, with a laugh, as the sort of life that held no attractions for him. He could not have said how it was that he had put these absurd notions into his sister's head. Indeed, he prided himself upon being well broken into a life of hard work, about which he had no sort of illusions. His vision of his own future, unlike many such forecasts, could have been made public at any moment without a blush; he attributed to himself a strong brain, and conferred on himself a seat in the House of Commons at the age of fifty, a moderate fortune, and, with luck, an unimportant office in a Liberal government. There was nothing extravagant in a forecast of that kind, and certainly nothing dishonourable. Nevertheless, as his sister guessed, it needed all Ralph's strength of will, together with the pressure of circumstances, to keep his feet moving in the path which led that way. It needed, in particular, a constant repetition of a phrase to the effect that he shared the common fate, found it best of all, and wished for no other; and by repeating such phrases he acquired punctuality and habits of work, and could very plausibly demonstrate that to be a clerk in a solicitor's office was the best of all possible lives, and that other ambitions were vain.

But, like all beliefs not genuinely held, this one depended very much upon the amount of acceptance it received from other people, and in private, when the pressure of public opinion was removed, Ralph let himself swing very rapidly away from his actual circumstances upon strange voyages which, indeed, he would have been ashamed to describe. In these dreams, of course, he figured in noble and romantic parts, but self-glorification was not the only motive of them. They gave outlet to some spirit which found no work to do in real life, for, with the pessimism which his lot forced upon him, Ralph had made up his mind that there was no use for what, contemptuously enough, he called dreams, in the world which we inhabit. It sometimes seemed to him that this spirit was the most valuable possession he had; he thought that by means of it he could set flowering waste tracts of the earth, cure many ills or raise up beauty where none now existed; it was, too, a fierce and potent spirit which would devour the dusty books and parchments on the office wall with one lick of its tongue, and leave him in a minute standing in nakedness, if he gave way to it. His endeavour, for many years, had been to control the spirit, and at the age of twenty-nine he thought he could pride himself upon a life rigidly divided into the hours of work and those of dreams; the two lived side by side without harming each other. As a matter of fact, this effort at discipline had been helped by the interests of a difficult profession, but the old conclusion to which Ralph had come when he left college still held sway in his mind, and tinged his views with the melancholy belief that life for most people compels the exercise of the lower gifts and wastes the precious ones, until it forces us to agree that there is little virtue, as well as little profit, in what once seemed to us the noblest part of our inheritance.

Denham was not altogether popular either in his office or among his family. He was too positive, at this stage of his career, as to what was right and what wrong, too proud of his self-control, and, as is natural in the case of persons not altogether happy or well suited in their conditions, too apt to prove the folly of contentment, if he found anyone who confessed to that weakness. In the office his rather ostentatious efficiency annoyed those who took their own work more lightly, and, if they foretold his advancement, it was not altogether sympathetically.

Indeed, he appeared to be rather a hard and self-sufficient young man, with a queer temper, and manners that were uncompromisingly abrupt, who was consumed with a desire to get on in the world, which was natural, these critics thought, in a man of no means, but not engaging.

The young men in the office had a perfect right to these opinions, because Denham showed no particular desire for their friendship. He liked them well enough, but shut them up in that compartment of life which was devoted to work. Hitherto, indeed, he had found little difficulty in arranging his life as methodically as he arranged his expenditure, but about this time he began to encounter experiences which were not so easy to classify. Mary Datchet had begun this confusion two years ago by bursting into laughter at some remark of his, almost the first time they met. She could not explain why it was. She thought him quite astonishingly odd. When he knew her well enough to tell her how he spent Monday and Wednesday and Saturday, she was still more amused; she laughed till he laughed, too, without knowing why. It seemed to her very odd that he should know as much about breeding bulldogs as any man in England; that he had a collection of wild flowers found near London; and his weekly visit to old Miss Trotter at Ealing, who was an authority upon the science of heraldry, never failed to excite her laughter. She wanted to know everything, even the kind of cake which the old lady supplied on these occasions; and their summer excursions to churches in the neighbourhood of London for the purpose of taking rubbings of the brasses became most important festivals, from the interest she took in them. In six months she knew more about his odd friends and hobbies than his own brothers and sisters knew, after living with him all his life; and Ralph found this very pleasant, though disordering, for his own view of himself had always been profoundly serious.

Certainly it was very pleasant to be with Mary Datchet and to become, directly the door was shut, quite a different sort of person, eccentric and lovable, with scarcely any likeness to the self most people knew. He became less serious, and rather less dictatorial at home, for he was apt to hear Mary laughing at him, and telling him, as she was fond of doing, that he knew nothing at all about anything. She made him, also, take an interest in public questions, for which she had a natural liking; and was in process of turning him from Tory to Radical,[41] after a course of public meetings, which began by boring him acutely, and ended by exciting him even more than they excited her.

But he was reserved; when ideas started up in his mind, he divided them automatically into those he could discuss with Mary, and those he must keep to himself. She knew this and it interested her, for she was accustomed to find young men very ready to talk about themselves, and had come to listen to them as one listens to children, without any thought of herself. But with Ralph, she had very little of this maternal feeling, and, in consequence, a much keener sense of her own individuality.

Late one afternoon Ralph stepped along the Strand to an interview with a lawyer upon business. The afternoon light was almost over, and already streams of greenish and yellowish artificial light were being poured into an atmosphere which, in country lanes, would now have been soft with the smoke of wood fires; and on both sides of the road the shop windows were full of sparkling chains and highly polished leather cases, which stood upon shelves made of thick plate-glass. None of these different objects was seen separately by Denham, but from all of them he drew an impression of stir and cheerfulness. Thus it came about that he saw Katharine Hilbery coming towards him, and looked straight at her, as if she were only an illustration of the argument that was going forward in his mind. In this spirit he noticed the rather set expression in her eyes, and the slight, half-conscious movement of her lips, which, together with her height and the distinction of her dress, made her look as if the scurrying crowd impeded her, and her direction were different from theirs. He noticed this calmly; but suddenly, as he passed her, his hands and knees began to tremble, and his heart beat painfully. She did not see him, and went on repeating to herself some lines which had stuck to her memory: 'It's life that matters, nothing but life – the process of discovering – the everlasting and perpetual process, not the discovery itself at all.'[42] Thus occupied, she did not see Denham, and he had not the courage to stop her. But immediately the whole scene in the Strand wore that curious look of order and purpose which is imparted to the most heterogeneous things when music sounds; and so pleasant was this impression that he was very glad that he had not stopped her, after all. It grew slowly fainter, but lasted until he stood outside the barrister's chambers.

When his interview with the barrister was over, it was too late to go back to the office. His sight of Katharine had put him queerly out of tune for a domestic evening. Where should he go? To walk through the streets of London until he came to Katharine's house, to look up at the windows and fancy her within, seemed to him possible for a moment; and then he rejected the plan almost with a blush as, with a curious division of consciousness, one plucks a flower sentimentally and throws it away, with a blush, when it is actually picked. No, he would go and see Mary Datchet. By this time she would be back from her work.

To see Ralph appear unexpectedly in her room threw Mary for a
second off her balance. She had been cleaning knives in her little
scullery, and when she had let him in she went back again, and turned
on the cold-water tap to its fullest volume, and then turned it off again.
'Now,' she thought to herself, as she screwed it tight, 'I'm not going to
let these silly ideas come into my head . . . Don't you think Mr Asquith
deserves to be hanged?' she called back into the sitting-room, and when
she joined him, drying her hands, she began to tell him about the latest
evasion on the part of the government with respect to the Women's
Suffrage Bill.[43] Ralph did not want to talk about politics, but he could
not help respecting Mary for taking such an interest in public questions.
He looked at her as she leant forward, poking the fire, and expressing
herself very clearly in phrases which bore distantly the taint of the
platform, and he thought, 'How absurd Mary would think me if she
knew that I almost made up my mind to walk all the way to Chelsea in
order to look at Katharine's windows. She wouldn't understand it, but I
like her very much as she is.'

For some time they discussed what the women had better do; and as
Ralph became genuinely interested in the question, Mary unconsciously
let her attention wander, and a great desire came over her to talk to
Ralph about her own feelings; or, at any rate, about something personal,
so that she might see what he felt for her; but she resisted this wish. But
she could not prevent him from feeling her lack of interest in what he
was saying, and gradually they both became silent. One thought after
another came up in Ralph's mind, but they were all, in some way,
connected with Katharine, or with vague feelings of romance and
adventure such as she inspired. But he could not talk to Mary about
such thoughts; and he pitied her for knowing nothing of what he was
feeling. 'Here,' he thought, 'is where we differ from women; they have
no sense of romance.'

'Well, Mary,' he said at length, 'why don't you say something
amusing?'

His tone was certainly provoking, but, as a general rule, Mary was not
easily provoked. This evening, however, she replied rather sharply:
'Because I've got nothing amusing to say, I suppose.'

Ralph thought for a moment, and then remarked: 'You work too
hard. I don't mean your health,' he added, as she laughed scornfully, 'I
mean that you seem to me to be getting wrapped up in your work.'

'And is that a bad thing?' she asked, shading her eyes with her hand.
'I think it is,' he returned abruptly.

'But only a week ago you were saying the opposite.' Her tone was defiant, but she became curiously depressed. Ralph did not perceive it, and took this opportunity of lecturing her, and expressing his latest views upon the proper conduct of life. She listened, but her main impression was that he had been meeting someone who had influenced him. He was telling her that she ought to read more, and to see that there were other points of view as deserving of attention as her own. Naturally, having last seen him as he left the office in company with Katharine, she attributed the change to her; it was likely that Katharine, on leaving the scene which she had so clearly despised, had pronounced some such criticism, or suggested it by her own attitude. But she knew that Ralph would never admit that he had been influenced by anybody.

'You don't read enough, Mary,' he was saying. 'You ought to read more poetry.'

It was true that Mary's reading had been rather limited to such works as she needed to know for the sake of examinations; and her time for reading in London was very little. For some reason, no one likes to be told that they do not read enough poetry, but her resentment was only visible in the way she changed the position of her hands, and in the fixed look in her eyes. And then she thought to herself, 'I'm behaving exactly as I said I wouldn't behave,' whereupon she relaxed all her muscles and said, in her reasonable way: 'Tell me what I ought to read, then.'

Ralph had unconsciously been irritated by Mary, and he now delivered himself of a few names of great poets which were the text for a discourse upon the imperfection of Mary's character and way of life.

'You live with your inferiors,' he said, warming unreasonably, as he knew, to his text. 'And you get into a groove because, on the whole, it's rather a pleasant groove. And you tend to forget what you're there for. You've the feminine habit of making much of details. You don't see when things matter and when they don't. And that's what's the ruin of all these organisations. That's why the suffragists have never done anything all these years. What's the point of drawing-room meetings and bazaars? You want to have ideas, Mary; get hold of something big; never mind making mistakes, but don't niggle. Why don't you throw it all up for a year, and travel? – see something of the world. Don't be content to live with half a dozen people in a backwater all your life. But you won't,' he concluded.

'I've rather come to that way of thinking myself – about myself, I mean,' said Mary, surprising him by her acquiescence. 'I should like to go somewhere far away.'

For a moment they were both silent. Ralph then said: 'But look here, Mary, you haven't been taking this seriously, have you?' His irritation was spent, and the depression, which she could not keep out of her voice, made him feel suddenly with remorse that he had been hurting her.

'You won't go away, will you?' he asked. And as she said nothing, he added, 'Oh no, don't go away.'

'I don't know exactly what I mean to do,' she replied. She hovered on the verge of some discussion of her plans, but she received no encouragement. He fell into one of his queer silences, which seemed to Mary, in spite of all her precautions, to have reference to what she also could not prevent herself from thinking about – their feeling for each other and their relationship. She felt that the two lines of thought bored their way in long, parallel tunnels which came very close indeed, but never ran into each other.

When he had gone, and he left her without breaking his silence more than was needed to wish her good-night, she sat on for a time, reviewing what he had said. If love is a devastating fire which melts the whole being into one mountain torrent, Mary was no more in love with Denham than she was in love with her poker or her tongs. But probably these extreme passions are very rare, and the state of mind thus depicted belongs to the very last stages of love, when the power to resist has been eaten away, week by week or day by day. Like most intelligent people, Mary was something of an egoist, to the extent, that is, of attaching great importance to what she felt, and she was by nature enough of a moralist to like to make certain, from time to time, that her feelings were creditable to her. When Ralph left her she thought over her state of mind, and came to the conclusion that it would be a good thing to learn a language – say Italian or German. She then went to a drawer, which she had to unlock, and took from it certain deeply scored manuscript pages. She read them through, looking up from her reading every now and then and thinking very intently for a few seconds about Ralph. She did her best to verify all the qualities in him which gave rise to emotions in her; and persuaded herself that she accounted reasonably for them all. Then she looked back again at her manuscript, and decided that to write grammatical English prose is the hardest thing in the world. But she thought about herself a great deal more than she thought about grammatical English prose or about Ralph Denham, and it may therefore be disputed whether she was in love, or, if so, to which branch of the family her passion belonged.

Chapter 11

'It's life that matters, nothing but life – the process of discovering, the everlasting and perpetual process,' said Katharine, as she passed under the archway, and so into the wide space of King's Bench Walk, 'not the discovery itself at all.' She spoke the last words looking up at Rodney's windows, which were a semilucent red colour, in her honour, as she knew. He had asked her to tea with him. But she was in a mood when it is almost physically disagreeable to interrupt the stride of one's thought, and she walked up and down two or three times under the trees before approaching his staircase. She liked getting hold of some book which neither her father or mother had read, and keeping it to herself, and gnawing its contents in privacy, and pondering the meaning without sharing her thoughts with anyone, or having to decide whether the book was a good one or a bad one. This evening she had twisted the words of Dostoevsky to suit her mood – a fatalistic mood – to proclaim that the process of discovery was life, and that, presumably, the nature of one's goal mattered not at all. She sat down for a moment upon one of the seats; felt herself carried along in the swirl of many things; decided, in her sudden way, that it was time to heave all this thinking overboard, and rose, leaving a fishmonger's basket on the seat behind her. Two minutes later her rap sounded with authority upon Rodney's door.

'Well, William,' she said, 'I'm afraid I'm late.'

It was true, but he was so glad to see her that he forgot his annoyance. He had been occupied for over an hour in making things ready for her, and he now had his reward in seeing her look right and left, as she slipped her cloak from her shoulders, with evident satisfaction, although she said nothing. He had seen that the fire burnt well; jam-pots were on the table, tin covers shone in the fender, and the shabby comfort of the room was extreme. He was dressed in his old crimson dressing-gown, which was faded irregularly, and had bright new patches on it, like the paler grass which one finds on lifting a stone. He made the tea, and Katharine drew off her gloves, and crossed her legs with a gesture that was rather masculine in its ease. Nor did they talk much until they were smoking cigarettes over the fire, having placed their teacups upon the floor between them.

They had not met since they had exchanged letters about their relationship. Katharine's answer to his protestation had been short and sensible. Half a sheet of notepaper contained the whole of it, for she merely had to say that she was not in love with him, and so could not marry him, but their friendship would continue, she hoped, unchanged. She had added a postscript in which she stated, 'I like your sonnet very much.'

So far as William was concerned, this appearance of ease was assumed. Three times that afternoon he had dressed himself in a tail-coat, and three times he had discarded it for an old dressing-gown; three times he had placed his pearl tie-pin in position, and three times he had removed it again, the little looking-glass in his room being the witness of these changes of mind. The question was, which would Katharine prefer on this particular afternoon in December? He read her note once more, and the postscript about the sonnet settled the matter. Evidently she admired most the poet in him; and as this, on the whole, agreed with his own opinion, he decided to err, if anything, on the side of shabbiness. His demeanour was also regulated with premeditation; he spoke little, and only on impersonal matters; he wished her to realise that in visiting him for the first time alone she was doing nothing remarkable, although, in fact, that was a point about which he was not at all sure.

Certainly Katharine seemed quite unmoved by any disturbing thoughts; and if he had been completely master of himself, he might, indeed, have complained that she was a trifle absent-minded. The ease, the familiarity of the situation alone with Rodney, among teacups and candles, had more effect upon her than was apparent. She asked to look at his books, and then at his pictures. It was while she held a photograph from the Greek in her hands that she exclaimed, impulsively, if incongruously: 'My oysters! I had a basket,' she explained, 'and I've left it somewhere. Uncle Dudley dines with us tonight. What in the world have I done with them?'

She rose and began to wander about the room. William rose also, and stood in front of the fire, muttering, 'Oysters, oysters – your basket of oysters!' but though he looked vaguely here and there, as if the oysters might be on the top of the bookshelf, his eyes returned always to Katharine. She drew the curtain and looked out among the scanty leaves of the plane trees.

'I had them,' she calculated, 'in the Strand; I sat on a seat. Well, never mind,' she concluded, turning back into the room abruptly, 'I dare say some old creature is enjoying them by this time.'

'I should have thought that you never forgot anything,' William remarked, as they settled down again.

'That's part of the myth about me, I know,' Katharine replied.

'And I wonder,' William proceeded, with some caution, 'what the truth about you is? But I know this sort of thing doesn't interest you,' he added hastily, with a touch of peevishness.

'No; it doesn't interest me very much,' she replied candidly.

'What shall we talk about then?' he asked.

She looked rather whimsically round the walls of the room.

'However we start, we end by talking about the same thing – about poetry, I mean. I wonder if you realise, William, that I've never read even Shakespeare? It's rather wonderful how I've kept it up all these years.'

'You've kept it up for ten years very beautifully, as far as I'm concerned,' he said.

'Ten years? So long as that?'

'And I don't think it's always bored you,' he added.

She looked into the fire silently. She could not deny that the surface of her feeling was absolutely unruffled by anything in William's character; on the contrary, she felt certain that she could deal with whatever turned up. He gave her peace, in which she could think of things that were far removed from what they talked about. Even now, when he sat within a yard of her, how easily her mind ranged hither and thither! Suddenly a picture presented itself before her, without any effort on her part as pictures will, of herself in these very rooms; she had come in from a lecture, and she held a pile of books in her hand, scientific books, and books about mathematics and astronomy which she had mastered. She put them down on the table over there. It was a picture plucked from her life two or three years hence, when she was married to William; but here she checked herself abruptly.

She could not entirely forget William's presence, because, in spite of his efforts to control himself, his nervousness was apparent. On such occasions his eyes protruded more than ever, and his face had more than ever the appearance of being covered with a thin crackling skin, through which every flush of his volatile blood showed itself instantly. By this time he had shaped so many sentences and rejected them, felt so many impulses and subdued them, that he was a uniform scarlet.

'You may say you don't read books,' he remarked, 'but, all the same, you know about them. Besides, who wants you to be learned? Leave that to the poor devils who've got nothing better to do. You – you – ahem! – '

'Well, then, why don't you read me something before I go?' said Katharine, looking at her watch.

'Katharine, you've only just come! Let me see now, what have I got to show you?' He rose, and stirred about the papers on his table, as if in doubt; he then picked up a manuscript, and after spreading it smoothly upon his knee, he looked up at Katharine suspiciously. He caught her smiling.

'I believe you only ask me to read out of kindness,' he burst out. 'Let's find something else to talk about. Who have you been seeing?'

'I don't generally ask things out of kindness,' Katharine observed; 'however, if you don't want to read, you needn't.'

William gave a queer snort of exasperation, and opened his manuscript once more, though he kept his eyes upon her face as he did so. No face could have been graver or more judicial.

'One can trust you, certainly, to say unpleasant things,' he said, smoothing out the page, clearing his throat, and reading half a stanza to himself. 'Ahem! The Princess is lost in the wood, and she hears the sound of a horn. (This would all be very pretty on the stage, but I can't get the effect here.) Anyhow, Sylvano enters, accompanied by the rest of the gentlemen of Gratian's court. I begin where he soliloquises.' He jerked his head and began to read.

Although Katharine had just disclaimed any knowledge of literature, she listened attentively. At least, she listened to the first twenty-five lines attentively, and then she frowned. Her attention was only aroused again when Rodney raised his finger – a sign, she knew, that the meter was about to change.

His theory was that every mood has its meter. His mastery of meters was very great; and, if the beauty of a drama depended upon the variety of measures in which the personages speak, Rodney's plays must have challenged the works of Shakespeare. Katharine's ignorance of Shakespeare did not prevent her from feeling fairly certain that plays should not produce a sense of chill stupor in the audience, such as overcame her as the lines flowed on, sometimes long and sometimes short, but always delivered with the same lilt of voice, which seemed to nail each line firmly on to the same spot in the hearer's brain. Still, she reflected, these sorts of skill are almost exclusively masculine; women neither practise them nor know how to value them; and one's husband's proficiency in this direction might legitimately increase one's respect for him, since mystification is no bad basis for respect. No one could doubt that William was a scholar. The reading ended with the finish of the act; Katharine had prepared a little speech.

'That seems to me extremely well written, William; although, of course, I don't know enough to criticise in detail.'

'But it's the skill that strikes you – not the emotion?'

'In a fragment like that, of course, the skill strikes one most.'

'But perhaps – have you time to listen to one more short piece? the scene between the lovers? There's some real feeling in that, I think. Denham agrees that it's the best thing I've done.'

'You've read it to Ralph Denham?' Katharine enquired, with surprise. 'He's a better judge than I am. What did he say?'

'My dear Katharine,' Rodney exclaimed, 'I don't ask you for criticism, as I should ask a scholar. I dare say there are only five men in England whose opinion of my work matters a straw to me. But I trust you where feeling is concerned. I had you in my mind often when I was writing those scenes. I kept asking myself, "Now is this the sort of thing Katharine would like?" I always think of you when I'm writing, Katharine, even when it's the sort of thing you wouldn't know about. And I'd rather – yes, I really believe I'd rather – you thought well of my writing than anyone in the world.'

This was so genuine a tribute to his trust in her that Katharine was touched.

'You think too much of me altogether, William,' she said, forgetting that she had not meant to speak in this way.

'No, Katharine, I don't,' he replied, replacing his manuscript in the drawer. 'It does me good to think of you.'

So quiet an answer, followed as it was by no expression of love, but merely by the statement that if she must go he would take her to the Strand, and would, if she could wait a moment, change his dressing-gown for a coat, moved her to the warmest feeling of affection for him that she had yet experienced. While he changed in the next room, she stood by the bookcase, taking down books and opening them, but reading nothing on their pages.

She felt certain that she would marry Rodney. How could one avoid it? How could one find fault with it? Here she sighed, and, putting the thought of marriage away, fell into a dream state, in which she became another person, and the whole world seemed changed. Being a frequent visitor to that world, she could find her way there unhesitatingly. If she had tried to analyse her impressions, she would have said that there dwelt the realities of the appearances which figure in our world; so direct, powerful and unimpeded were her sensations there, compared with those called forth in actual life. There dwelt the things one might have felt, had there been cause; the perfect happiness of which here we taste the fragment; the beauty seen here in flying glimpses only. No doubt much of the furniture of this world was drawn directly from the past, and even from the England of the Elizabethan age. However the embellishment of this imaginary world might change, two qualities were constant in it. It was a place where feelings were liberated from the constraint which the real world puts upon them; and the process of awakenment was always marked by resignation and a kind of stoical acceptance of facts. She met no acquaintance there, as Denham did, miraculously transfigured; she played no heroic part. But there certainly she loved some magnanimous hero, and as they swept together among the leaf-hung trees of an unknown world, they shared the feelings which came fresh and fast as the waves on the shore. But the sands of her liberation were running fast; even through the forest branches came sounds of Rodney moving things on his dressing-table; and Katharine woke herself from this excursion by shutting the cover of the book she was holding, and replacing it in the bookshelf.

'William,' she said, speaking rather faintly at first, like one sending a voice from sleep to reach the living. 'William,' she repeated firmly, 'if you still want me to marry you, I will.'

Perhaps it was that no man could expect to have the most momentous question of his life settled in a voice so level, so toneless, so devoid of joy or energy. At any rate William made no answer. She waited stoically. A moment later he stepped briskly from his dressing-room, and observed that if she wanted to buy more oysters he thought he knew where they could find a fishmonger's shop still open. She breathed deeply a sigh of relief.

Extract from a letter sent a few days later by Mrs Hilbery to her sister-in-law, Mrs Milvain:

. . . How stupid of me to forget the name in my telegram. Such a nice, rich, English name, too, and, in addition, he has all the graces of intellect; he has read literally *everything*. I tell Katharine, I shall always put him on my right side at dinner, so as to have him by me when people begin talking about characters in Shakespeare. They won't be rich, but they'll be very, very happy. I was sitting in my room late one night, feeling that nothing nice would ever happen to me again, when I heard Katharine outside in the passage, and I thought to myself, 'Shall I call her in?' and then I thought (in that hopeless, dreary way one does think, with the fire going out and one's birthday just over), 'Why should I lay my troubles on *her*?' But my little self-control had its reward, for next moment she tapped at the door and came in, and sat on the rug, and though we neither of us said anything, I felt so happy all of a second that I couldn't help crying, 'Oh, Katharine, when you come to my age, how I hope you'll have a daughter, too!'

You know how silent Katharine is. She was so silent, for such a long time, that in my foolish, nervous state I dreaded something, I don't quite know what. And then she told me how, after all, she had made up her mind. She had written. She expected him tomorrow. At first I wasn't glad at all. I didn't want her to marry anyone; but when she said, 'It will make no difference. I shall always care for you and father most,' then I saw how selfish I was, and I told her she must give him everything, everything, everything! I told her I should be thankful to come second. But why, when everything's turned out just as one always hoped it would turn out, why then can one do nothing but cry, nothing but feel a desolate old woman whose life's been a failure, and now is nearly over, and age is so cruel? But Katharine said to me, 'I am happy. I'm very happy.' And then I thought, though it all seemed so desperately dismal at the time, Katharine had said she was happy, and I should have a son, and it would all turn out so much more wonderfully than I could possibly imagine, for though the sermons don't say so, I do believe the world is meant for us to be happy in. She told me that they would live quite near us, and see us every day; and she would go on with the *Life*, and we should finish it as we had meant to. And, after all, it would be far more horrid if she didn't marry – or suppose she married someone we couldn't endure? Suppose she had fallen in love with someone who was married already?

And though one never thinks anyone good enough for the people one's fond of, he has the kindest, truest instincts, I'm sure, and though he seems nervous and his manner is not commanding, I only think these things because it's Katharine. And now I've written this, it comes over me that, of course, all the time, Katharine has what he hasn't. She does command, she isn't nervous; it comes naturally to her to rule and control. It's time that she should give all this to someone who will need her when we aren't there, save in our spirits, for whatever people say, I'm sure I shall come back to this wonderful world where one's been so happy and so miserable, where, even now, I seem to see myself stretching out my hands for another present from the great Fairy Tree whose boughs are still hung with enchanting toys, though they are rarer now, perhaps, and between the branches one sees no longer the blue sky, but the stars and the tops of the mountains.

One doesn't know any more, does one? One hasn't any advice to give one's children. One can only hope that they will have the same vision and the same power to believe, without which life would be so meaningless. That is what I ask for Katharine and her husband.

Chapter 12

'Is Mr Hilbery at home, or Mrs Hilbery?' Denham asked, of the parlour-maid in Chelsea, a week later.

'No, sir. But Miss Hilbery is at home,' the girl answered.

Ralph had anticipated many answers, but not this one, and now it was unexpectedly made plain to him that it was the chance of seeing Katharine that had brought him all the way to Chelsea on pretence of seeing her father.

He made some show of considering the matter, and was taken upstairs to the drawing-room. As upon that first occasion, some weeks ago, the door closed as if it were a thousand doors softly excluding the world; and once more Ralph received an impression of a room full of deep shadows, firelight, unwavering silver candle flames, and empty spaces to be crossed before reaching the round table in the middle of the room, with its frail burden of silver trays and china teacups. But this time Katharine was there by herself; the volume in her hand showed that she expected no visitors.

Ralph said something about hoping to find her father.

'My father is out,' she replied. 'But if you can wait, I expect him soon.'

It might have been due merely to politeness, but Ralph felt that she received him almost with cordiality. Perhaps she was bored by drinking tea and reading a book all alone; at any rate, she tossed the book on to a sofa with a gesture of relief.

'Is that one of the moderns whom you despise?' he asked, smiling at the carelessness of her gesture.

'Yes,' she replied. 'I think even you would despise him.'

'Even I?' he repeated. 'Why even I?'

'You said you liked modern things; I said I hated them.'

This was not a very accurate report of their conversation among the relics, perhaps, but Ralph was flattered to think that she remembered anything about it.

'Or did I confess that I hated all books?' she went on, seeing him look up with an air of enquiry. 'I forget – '

'Do you hate all books?' he asked.

'It would be absurd to say that I hate all books when I've only read ten, perhaps; but – ' Here she pulled herself up short.

'Well?'

'Yes, I do hate books,' she continued. 'Why do you want to be forever talking about your feelings? That's what I can't make out. And poetry's all about feelings – novels are all about feelings.'

She cut a cake vigorously into slices, and providing a tray with bread and butter for Mrs Hilbery, who was in her room with a cold, she rose to go upstairs.

Ralph held the door open for her, and then stood with clasped hands in the middle of the room. His eyes were bright, and, indeed, he scarcely knew whether they beheld dreams or realities. All down the street and on the doorstep, and while he mounted the stairs, his dream of Katharine possessed him; on the threshold of the room he had dismissed it, in order to prevent too painful a collision between what he dreamt of her and what she was. And in five minutes she had filled the shell of the old dream with the flesh of life; looked with fire out of phantom eyes. He glanced about him with bewilderment at finding himself among her chairs and tables; they were solid, for he grasped the back of the chair in which Katharine had sat; and yet they were unreal; the atmosphere was that of a dream. He summoned all the faculties of his spirit to seize what the minutes had to give him; and from the depths of his mind there rose unchecked a joyful recognition of the truth that human nature surpasses, in its beauty, all that our wildest dreams bring us hints of.

Katharine came into the room a moment later. He stood watching her come towards him, and thought her more beautiful and strange than his dream of her; for the real Katharine could speak the words which seemed to crowd behind the forehead and in the depths of the eyes, and the commonest sentence would be flashed on by this immortal light. And she overflowed the edges of the dream; he remarked that her softness was like that of some vast snowy owl; she wore a ruby on her finger.

'My mother wants me to tell you,' she said, 'that she hopes you have begun your poem. She says everyone ought to write poetry . . . All my relations write poetry,' she went on. 'I can't bear to think of it sometimes – because, of course, it's none of it any good. But then one needn't read it – '

'You don't encourage me to write a poem,' said Ralph.

'But you're not a poet, too, are you?' she enquired, turning upon him with a laugh.

'Should I tell you if I were?'

'Yes. Because I think you speak the truth,' she said, searching him for proof of this apparently, with eyes now almost impersonally direct. It would be easy, Ralph thought, to worship one so far removed, and yet of so straight a nature; easy to submit recklessly to her, without thought of future pain.

'Are you a poet?' she demanded. He felt that her question had an unexplained weight of meaning behind it, as if she sought an answer to a question that she did not ask.

'No. I haven't written any poetry for years,' he replied. 'But all the same, I don't agree with you. I think it's the only thing worth doing.'

'Why do you say that?' she asked, almost with impatience, tapping her spoon two or three times against the side of her cup.

'Why?' Ralph laid hands on the first words that came to mind. 'Because, I suppose, it keeps an ideal alive which might die otherwise.'

A curious change came over her face, as if the flame of her mind were subdued; and she looked at him ironically and with the expression which he had called sad before, for want of a better name for it.

'I don't know that there's much sense in having ideals,' she said.

'But you have them,' he replied energetically. 'Why do we call them ideals? It's a stupid word. Dreams, I mean – '

She followed his words with parted lips, as though to answer eagerly when he had done; but as he said, 'Dreams, I mean,' the door of the drawing-room swung open, and so remained for a perceptible instant. They both held themselves silent, her lips still parted.

Far off, they heard the rustle of skirts. Then the owner of the skirts appeared in the doorway, which she almost filled, nearly concealing the figure of a very much smaller lady who accompanied her.

'My aunts!' Katharine murmured, under her breath. Her tone had a hint of tragedy in it, but no less, Ralph thought, than the situation required. She addressed the larger lady as Aunt Millicent; the smaller was Aunt Celia, Mrs Milvain, who had lately undertaken the task of marrying Cyril to his wife. Both ladies, but Mrs Cosham (Aunt Millicent) in particular, had that look of heightened, smoothed, incarnadined existence which is proper to elderly ladies paying calls in London about five o'clock in the afternoon. Portraits by Romney,[44] seen through glass, have something of their pink, mellow look, their blooming softness, as of apricots hanging upon a red wall in the afternoon sun. Mrs Cosham was so apparelled with hanging muffs, chains and swinging draperies that it was impossible to detect the shape of a human being in the mass of brown and black which filled the armchair. Mrs Milvain was a much slighter figure; but the same doubt as to the precise lines of her contour filled Ralph, as he regarded them, with dismal foreboding. What remark of his would ever reach these fabulous and fantastic characters? – for there was something fantastically unreal in the curious swayings and noddings of Mrs Cosham, as if her equipment included a large wire spring. Her voice had a high-pitched, cooing note, which prolonged words and cut them short until the English language seemed no longer fit for common purposes. In a moment of nervousness, so Ralph thought, Katharine had turned on innumerable electric lights. But Mrs Cosham had gained impetus (perhaps her swaying movements had that end in view) for sustained speech; and she now addressed Ralph deliberately and elaborately.

'I come from Woking,[45] Mr Popham. You may well ask me, why Woking? and to that I answer, for perhaps the hundredth time, because of the sunsets. We went there for the sunsets, but that was five-and-twenty years ago. Where are the sunsets now? Alas! There is no sunset now nearer than the South Coast.' Her rich and romantic notes were accompanied by a wave of a long white hand, which, when waved, gave off a flash of diamonds, rubies and emeralds. Ralph wondered whether she more resembled an elephant, with a jewelled head-dress, or a superb cockatoo, balanced insecurely upon its perch, and pecking capriciously at a lump of sugar.

'Where are the sunsets now?' she repeated. 'Do you find sunsets now, Mr Popham?'

'I live at Highgate,' he replied.

'At Highgate? Yes, Highgate has its charms; your Uncle John lived at Highgate,' she jerked in the direction of Katharine. She sank her head upon her breast, as if for a moment's meditation, which past, she looked up and observed: 'I dare say there are very pretty lanes in Highgate. I can recollect walking with your mother, Katharine, through lanes blossoming with wild hawthorn. But where is the hawthorn now? You remember that exquisite description in De Quincey,[46] Mr Popham? – but I forget, you, in your generation, with all your activity and enlightenment, at which I can only marvel' – here she displayed both her beautiful white hands – 'do not read De Quincey. You have your Belloc, your Chesterton, your Bernard Shaw [47] – why should you read De Quincey?'

'But I do read De Quincey,' Ralph protested, 'more than Belloc and Chesterton, anyhow.'

'Indeed!' exclaimed Mrs Cosham, with a gesture of surprise and relief mingled. 'You are, then, a *rara avis* in your generation. I am delighted to meet anyone who reads De Quincey.'

Here she hollowed her hand into a screen, and, leaning towards Katharine, enquired, in a very audible whisper, 'Does your friend *write*?'

'Mr Denham,' said Katharine, with more than her usual clearness and firmness, 'writes for the *Review*. He is a lawyer.'

'The clean-shaved lips, showing the expression of the mouth! I recognise them at once. I always feel at home with lawyers, Mr Denham –'

'They used to come about so much in the old days,' Mrs Milvain interposed, the frail, silvery notes of her voice falling with the sweet tone of an old bell.

'You say you live at Highgate,' she continued. 'I wonder whether you happen to know if there is an old house called Tempest Lodge still in existence – an old white house in a garden?'

Ralph shook his head, and she sighed.

'Ah, no; it must have been pulled down by this time, with all the other old houses. There were such pretty lanes in those days. That was how your uncle met your Aunt Emily, you know,' she addressed Katharine. 'They walked home through the lanes.'

'A sprig of May in her bonnet,' Mrs Cosham ejaculated, reminiscently.

'And next Sunday he had violets in his buttonhole. And that was how we guessed.'

Katharine laughed. She looked at Ralph. His eyes were meditative, and she wondered what he found in this old gossip to make him ponder so contentedly. She felt, she hardly knew why, a curious pity for him.

'Uncle John – yes, "poor John", you always called him. Why was that?' she asked, to make them go on talking, which, indeed, they needed little invitation to do.

'That was what his father, old Sir Richard, always called him. Poor John, or the fool of the family,' Mrs Milvain hastened to inform them. 'The other boys were so brilliant, and he could never pass his examinations, so they sent him to India – a long voyage in those days, poor fellow. You had your own room, you know, and you did it up. But he will get his knighthood and a pension, I believe,' she said, turning to Ralph, 'only it is not England.'

'No,' Mrs Cosham confirmed her, 'it is not England. In those days we thought an Indian judgeship about equal to a county-court judgeship at home. His Honour – a pretty title, but still, not at the top of the tree. However,' she sighed, 'if you have a wife and seven children, and people nowadays very quickly forget your father's name – well, you have to take what you can get,' she concluded.

'And I fancy,' Mrs Milvain resumed, lowering her voice rather confidentially, 'that John would have done more if it hadn't been for his wife, your Aunt Emily. She was a very good woman, devoted to him, of course, but she was not ambitious for him, and if a wife isn't ambitious for her husband, especially in a profession like the law, clients soon get to know of it. In our young days, Mr Denham, we used to say that we knew which of our friends would become judges, by looking at the girls they married. And so it was, and so, I fancy, it always will be. I don't think,' she added, summing up these scattered remarks, 'that any man is really happy unless he succeeds in his profession.'

Mrs Cosham approved of this sentiment with more ponderous sagacity from her side of the tea-table, in the first place by swaying her head, and in the second by remarking: 'No, men are not the same as women. I fancy Alfred Tennyson spoke the truth about that as about many other things. How I wish he'd lived to write "The Prince" – a sequel to *The Princess*![48] I confess I'm almost tired of princesses. We want someone to show us what a good man can be. We have Laura and Beatrice, Antigone and Cordelia,[49] but we have no heroic man. How do you, as a poet, account for that, Mr Denham?'

'I'm not a poet,' said Ralph good-humouredly. 'I'm only a solicitor.'

'But you write, too?' Mrs Cosham demanded, afraid lest she should be balked of her priceless discovery, a young man truly devoted to literature.

'In my spare time,' Denham reassured her.

'In your spare time!' Mrs Cosham echoed. 'That is a proof of devotion, indeed.' She half closed her eyes, and indulged herself in a fascinating picture of a briefless barrister lodged in a garret, writing immortal novels by the light of a farthing dip. But the romance which fell upon the figures of great writers and illumined their pages was no false radiance in her case. She carried her pocket Shakespeare about with her, and met life fortified by the words of the poets. How far she saw Denham, and how far she confused him with some hero of fiction, it would be hard to say. Literature had taken possession even of her memories. She was matching him, presumably, with certain characters in the old novels, for she came out, after a pause, with: 'Um – um – Pendennis – Warrington – I could never forgive Laura,'[50] she pronounced energetically, 'for not marrying George, in spite of everything. George Eliot did the very same thing; and Lewes[51] was a little frog-faced man, with the manner of a dancing master. But Warrington, now, had everything in his favour: intellect, passion, romance, distinction, and the connection was a mere piece of undergraduate folly. Arthur, I confess, has always seemed to me a bit of a fop; I can't imagine how Laura married him. But you say you're a solicitor, Mr Denham. Now there are one or two things I should like to ask you – about Shakespeare – ' She drew out her small, worn volume with some difficulty, opened it, and shook it in the air. 'They say, nowadays, that

Shakespeare was a lawyer. They say, that accounts for his knowledge of human nature. There's a fine example for you, Mr Denham. Study your clients, young man, and the world will be the richer one of these days, I have no doubt. Tell me, how do we come out of it, now; better or worse than you expected?'

Thus called upon to sum up the worth of human nature in a few words, Ralph answered unhesitatingly: 'Worse, Mrs Cosham, a good deal worse. I'm afraid the ordinary man is a bit of a rascal – '

'And the ordinary woman?'

'No, I don't like the ordinary woman either – '

'Ah, dear me, I've no doubt that's very true, very true.' Mrs Cosham sighed. 'Swift[52] would have agreed with you, anyhow – ' She looked at him, and thought that there were signs of distinct power in his brow. He would do well, she thought, to devote himself to satire.

'Charles Lavington, you remember, was a solicitor,' Mrs Milvain interposed, rather resenting the waste of time involved in talking about fictitious people when you might be talking about real people. 'But you wouldn't remember him, Katharine.'

'Mr Lavington? Oh, yes, I do,' said Katharine, waking from other thoughts with her little start. 'The summer we had a house near Tenby. I remember the field and the pond with the tadpoles, and making haystacks with Mr Lavington.'

'She is right. There *was* a pond with tadpoles,' Mrs Cosham corroborated. 'Millais made studies of it for *Ophelia*.[53] Some say that is the best picture he ever painted – '

'And I remember the dog chained up in the yard, and the dead snakes hanging in the toolhouse.'

'It was at Tenby that you were chased by the bull,' Mrs Milvain continued. 'But that you couldn't remember, though it's true you were a wonderful child. Such eyes she had, Mr Denham! I used to say to her father, "She's watching us, and summing us all up in her little mind." And they had a nurse in those days,' she went on, telling her story with charming solemnity to Ralph, 'who was a good woman, but engaged to a sailor. When she ought to have been attending to the baby, her eyes were on the sea. And Mrs Hilbery allowed this girl – Susan her name was – to have him to stay in the village. They abused her goodness, I'm sorry to say, and while they walked in the lanes, they stood the perambulator alone in a field where there was a bull. The animal became enraged by the red blanket in the perambulator, and heaven knows what might have happened if a gentleman had not been walking by in the nick of time, and rescued Katharine in his arms!'

'I think the bull was only a cow, Aunt Celia,' said Katharine.

'My darling, it was a great red Devonshire bull, and not long after it gored a man to death and had to be destroyed. And your mother forgave Susan – a thing I could never have done.'

'Maggie's sympathies were entirely with Susan and the sailor, I am sure,' said Mrs Cosham, rather tartly. 'My sister-in-law,' she continued, 'has laid her burdens upon providence at every crisis in her life, and providence, I must confess, has responded nobly, so far – '

'Yes,' said Katharine, with a laugh, for she liked the rashness which irritated the rest of the family. 'My mother's bulls always turn into cows at the critical moment.'

'Well,' said Mrs Milvain, 'I'm glad you have someone to protect you from bulls now.'

'I can't imagine William protecting anyone from bulls,' said Katharine.

It happened that Mrs Cosham had once more produced her pocket volume of Shakespeare, and was consulting Ralph upon an obscure passage in *Measure for Measure*. He did not at once seize the meaning of what Katharine and her aunt were saying; William, he supposed, referred to some small cousin, for he now saw Katharine as a child in a pinafore; but, nevertheless, he was so much distracted that his eye could hardly follow the words on the paper. A moment later he heard them speak distinctly of an engagement ring.

'I like rubies,' he heard Katharine say.

> 'To be imprison'd in the viewless winds,
> And blown with restless violence round about
> The pendant world . . . '[54]

Mrs Cosham intoned; at the same instant 'Rodney' fitted itself to 'William' in Ralph's mind. He felt convinced that Katharine was engaged to Rodney. His first sensation was one of violent rage with her for having deceived him throughout the visit, fed him with pleasant old wives' tales, let him see her as a child playing in a meadow, shared her youth with him, while all the time she was a stranger entirely, and engaged to marry Rodney.

But was it possible? Surely it was not possible. For in his eyes she was still a child. He paused so long over the book that Mrs Cosham had time to look over his shoulder and ask her niece: 'And have you settled upon a house yet, Katharine?'

This convinced him of the truth of the monstrous idea. He looked up at once and said: 'Yes, it's a difficult passage.'

His voice had changed so much, he spoke with such curtness and even with such contempt, that Mrs Cosham looked at him fairly puzzled. Happily she belonged to a generation which expected uncouthness in its men, and she merely felt convinced that this Mr Denham was very, very clever. She took back her Shakespeare, as Denham seemed to have no more to say, and secreted it once more about her person with the infinitely pathetic resignation of the old.

'Katharine's engaged to William Rodney,' she said, by way of filling in the pause; 'a very old friend of ours. He has a wonderful knowledge of literature, too – wonderful.' She nodded her head rather vaguely. 'You should meet each other.'

Denham's one wish was to leave the house as soon as he could; but the elderly ladies had risen, and were proposing to visit Mrs Hilbery in her bedroom, so that any move on his part was impossible. At the same time, he wished to say something, but he knew not what, to Katharine alone. She took her aunts upstairs, and returned, coming towards him once more with an air of innocence and friendliness that amazed him.

'My father will be back,' she said. 'Won't you sit down?' and she laughed, as if now they might share a perfectly friendly laugh at the tea-party.

But Ralph made no attempt to seat himself.

'I must congratulate you,' he said. 'It was news to me.' He saw her face change, but only to become graver than before.

'My engagement?' she asked. 'Yes, I am going to marry William Rodney.'

Ralph remained standing with his hand on the back of a chair in absolute silence. Abysses seemed to plunge into darkness between them. He looked at her, but her face showed that she was not thinking of him. No regret or consciousness of wrong disturbed her.

'Well, I must go,' he said at length.

She seemed about to say something, then changed her mind and said merely: 'You will come again, I hope. We always seem' – she hesitated – 'to be interrupted.'

He bowed and left the room.

Ralph strode with extreme swiftness along the Embankment. Every muscle was taut and braced as if to resist some sudden attack from outside. For the moment it seemed as if the attack were about to be directed against his body, and his brain thus was on the alert, but without understanding. Finding himself, after a few minutes, no longer under observation, and no attack delivered, he slackened his pace; the pain spread all through him, took possession of every governing seat, and met with scarcely any resistance from powers exhausted by their first effort at defence. He took his way languidly along the river embankment, away from home rather than towards it. The world had him at its mercy. He made no pattern out of the sights he saw. He felt himself now, as he had often fancied other people, adrift on the stream, and far removed from control of it, a man with no grasp upon circumstances any longer. Old battered men loafing at the doors of public-houses now seemed to be his fellows, and he felt, as he supposed them to feel, a mingling of envy and hatred towards those who passed quickly and certainly to a goal of their own. They, too, saw things very thin and shadowy, and were wafted about by the lightest breath of wind. For the substantial world, with its prospect of avenues leading on and on to the invisible distance, had slipped from him, since Katharine was engaged. Now all his life was visible, and the straight, meagre path had its ending soon enough. Katharine was engaged, and she had deceived him, too. He felt for corners of his being untouched by his disaster; but there was no limit to the flood of damage; not one of his possessions was safe now. Katharine had deceived him; she had mixed herself with every thought of his, and reft of her they seemed false thoughts which he would blush to think again. His life seemed immeasurably impoverished.

He sat himself down, in spite of the chilly fog which obscured the farther bank and left its lights suspended upon a blank surface, upon one of the riverside seats, and let the tide of disillusionment sweep through him. For the time being all bright points in his life were blotted out; all prominences levelled. At first he made himself believe that Katharine had treated him badly, and drew comfort from the thought that, left alone, she would recollect this, and think of him and tender him, in silence, at any rate, an apology. But this grain of comfort failed him after a second or two, for, upon reflection, he had to admit that Katharine owed him nothing. Katharine had promised nothing, taken nothing; to her his dreams had meant nothing. This, indeed, was the lowest pitch of his despair. If the best of one's feelings mean nothing to the person most concerned in those feelings, what reality is left us? The old romance which had warmed his days for him, the thoughts of Katharine which had painted every hour, were now made to appear foolish and enfeebled. He rose, and looked into the river, whose swift race of dun-coloured waters seemed the very spirit of futility and oblivion.

'In what can one trust, then?' he thought, as he leant there. So feeble and insubstantial did he feel himself that he repeated the word aloud. 'In what can one trust? Not in men and women. Not in one's dreams about them. There's nothing – nothing, nothing left at all.'

Now Denham had reason to know that he could bring to birth and keep alive a fine anger when he chose. Rodney provided a good target for that emotion. And yet at the moment, Rodney and Katharine herself seemed disembodied ghosts. He could scarcely remember the look of them. His mind plunged lower and lower. Their marriage seemed of no importance to him. All things had turned to ghosts; the whole mass of the world was insubstantial vapour, surrounding the solitary spark in his mind, whose burning point he could remember, for it burnt no more. He had once cherished a belief, and Katharine had embodied this belief, and she did so no longer. He did not blame her; he blamed nothing, nobody; he saw the truth. He saw the dun-coloured race of waters and the blank shore. But life is vigorous; the body lives, and the body, no doubt, dictated the reflection, which now urged him to movement, that one may cast away the forms of human beings, and yet retain the passion which seemed inseparable from their existence in the flesh. Now this passion burnt on his horizon, as the winter sun makes a greenish pane in the west through thinning clouds. His eyes were set on something infinitely far and remote; by that light he felt he could walk, and would, in future, have to find his way. But that was all there was left to him of a populous and teeming world.

Chapter 13

The lunch hour in the office was only partly spent by Denham in the consumption of food. Whether fine or wet, he passed most of it pacing the gravel paths in Lincoln's Inn Fields. The children got to know his figure, and the sparrows expected their daily scattering of breadcrumbs. No doubt, since he often gave a copper and almost always a handful of bread, he was not as blind to his surroundings as he thought himself.

He thought that these winter days were spent in long hours before white papers radiant in electric light; and in short passages through fog-dimmed streets. When he came back to his work after lunch he carried in his head a picture of the Strand, scattered with omnibuses, and of the purple shapes of leaves pressed flat upon the gravel, as if his eyes had always been bent upon the ground. His brain worked incessantly, but his thought was attended with so little joy that he did not willingly recall it; but drove ahead, now in this direction, now in that; and came home laden with dark books borrowed from a library.

Mary Datchet, coming from the Strand at lunchtime, saw him one day taking his turn, closely buttoned in an overcoat, and so lost in thought that he might have been sitting in his own room.

She was overcome by something very like awe by the sight of him; then she felt much inclined to laugh, although her pulse beat faster. She passed him, and he never saw her. She came back and touched him on the shoulder.

'Gracious, Mary!' he exclaimed. 'How you startled me!'

'Yes. You looked as if you were walking in your sleep,' she said. 'Are you arranging some terrible love affair? Have you got to reconcile a desperate couple?'

'I wasn't thinking about my work,' Ralph replied, rather hastily. 'And, besides, that sort of thing's not in my line,' he added, rather grimly.

The morning was fine, and they had still some minutes of leisure to spend. They had not met for two or three weeks, and Mary had much to say to Ralph; but she was not certain how far he wished for her company. However, after a turn or two, in which a few facts were communicated, he suggested sitting down, and she took the seat beside him. The sparrows came fluttering about them, and Ralph produced from his pocket the half of a roll saved from his luncheon. He threw a few crumbs among them.

'I've never seen sparrows so tame,' Mary observed, by way of saying something.

'No,' said Ralph. 'The sparrows in Hyde Park aren't as tame as this. If we keep perfectly still, I'll get one to settle on my arm.'

Mary felt that she could have forgone this display of animal good temper, but seeing that Ralph, for some curious reason, took a pride in the sparrows, she bet him sixpence that he would not succeed.

'Done!' he said; and his eye, which had been gloomy, showed a spark of light. His conversation was now addressed entirely to a bald cock-sparrow, who seemed bolder than the rest; and Mary took the opportunity of looking at him. She was not satisfied; his face was worn, and his expression stern. A child came bowling its hoop through the concourse of birds, and Ralph threw his last crumbs of bread into the bushes with a snort of impatience.

'That's what always happens – just as I've almost got him,' he said. 'Here's your sixpence, Mary. But you've only got it thanks to that brute of a boy. They oughtn't to be allowed to bowl hoops here – '

'Oughtn't to be allowed to bowl hoops! My dear Ralph, what nonsense!'

'You always say that,' he complained; 'and it isn't nonsense. What's the point of having a garden if one can't watch birds in it? The street does all right for hoops. And if children can't be trusted in the streets, their mothers should keep them at home.'

Mary made no answer to this remark, but frowned.

She leant back on the seat and looked about her at the great houses breaking the soft grey-blue sky with their chimneys.

'Ah, well,' she said, 'London's a fine place to live in. I believe I could sit and watch people all day long. I like my fellow-creatures . . . '

Ralph sighed impatiently.

'Yes, I think so, when you come to know them,' she added, as if his disagreement had been spoken.

'That's just when I don't like them,' he replied. 'Still, I don't see why you shouldn't cherish that illusion, if it pleases you.' He spoke without much vehemence of agreement or disagreement. He seemed chilled.

'Wake up, Ralph! You're half asleep!' Mary cried, turning and pinching his sleeve. 'What have you been doing with yourself? Moping? Working? Despising the world, as usual?'

As he merely shook his head, and filled his pipe, she went on: 'It's a bit of a pose, isn't it?'

'Not more than most things,' he said.

'Well,' Mary remarked, 'I've a great deal to say to you, but I must go on – we have a committee.' She rose, but hesitated, looking down upon him rather gravely. 'You don't look happy, Ralph,' she said. 'Is it anything, or is it nothing?'

He did not immediately answer her, but rose, too, and walked with her towards the gate. As usual, he did not speak to her without considering whether what he was about to say was the sort of thing that he could say to her.

'I've been bothered,' he said at length. 'Partly by work, and partly by family troubles. Charles has been behaving like a fool. He wants to go out to Canada as a farmer – '

'Well, there's something to be said for that,' said Mary; and they passed the gate, and walked slowly round the Fields again, discussing difficulties which, as a matter of fact, were more or less chronic in the Denham family, and only now brought forward to appease Mary's sympathy, which, however, soothed Ralph more than he was aware of. She made him at least dwell upon problems which were real in the sense that they were capable of solution; and the true cause of his melancholy, which was not susceptible to such treatment, sank rather more deeply into the shades of his mind.

Mary was attentive; she was helpful. Ralph could not help feeling grateful to her, the more so, perhaps, because he had not told her the truth about his state; and when they reached the gate again he wished to make some affectionate objection to her leaving him. But his affection took the rather uncouth form of expostulating with her about her work.

'What d'you want to sit on a committee for?' he asked. 'It's waste of your time, Mary.'

'I agree with you that a country walk would benefit the world more,' she said. 'Look here,' she added suddenly, 'why don't you come to us at Christmas? It's almost the best time of year.'

'Come to you at Disham?' Ralph repeated.

'Yes. We won't interfere with you. But you can tell me later,' she said, rather hastily, and then started off in the direction of Russell Square. She had invited him on the impulse of the moment, as a vision of the country came before her; and now she was annoyed with herself for having done so, and then she was annoyed at being annoyed.

'If I can't face a walk in a field alone with Ralph,' she reasoned, 'I'd better buy a cat and live in a lodging at Ealing, like Sally Seal – and he won't come. Or did he mean that he *would* come?'

She shook her head. She really did not know what he had meant. She never felt quite certain; but now she was more than usually baffled. Was he concealing something from her? His manner had been odd; his deep absorption had impressed her; there was something in him that she had not fathomed, and the mystery of his nature laid more of a spell upon her than she liked. Moreover, she could not prevent herself from doing now what she had often blamed others of her sex for doing – from endowing her friend with a kind of heavenly fire, and passing her life before it for his sanction.

Under this process, the committee rather dwindled in importance; the Suffrage shrank; she vowed she would work harder at the Italian language; she thought she would take up the study of birds. But this programme for a perfect life threatened to become so absurd that she very soon caught herself out in the evil habit, and was rehearsing her speech to the committee by the time the chestnut-coloured bricks of Russell Square came in sight. Indeed, she never noticed them. She ran upstairs as usual, and was completely awakened to reality by the sight of Mrs Seal, on the landing outside the office, inducing a very large dog to drink water out of a tumbler.

'Miss Markham has already arrived,' Mrs Seal remarked, with due solemnity, 'and this is her dog.'

'A very fine dog, too,' said Mary, patting him on the head.

'Yes. A magnificent fellow,' Mrs Seal agreed. 'A kind of St Bernard, she tells me – so like Kit to have a St Bernard. And you guard your mistress well, don't you, Sailor? You see that wicked men don't break into her larder when she's out at *her* work – helping poor souls who have lost their way . . . But we're late – we must begin!' and scattering the rest of the water indiscriminately over the floor, she hurried Mary into the committee-room.

Chapter 14

Mr Clacton was in his glory. The machinery which he had perfected and controlled was now about to turn out its bi-monthly product, a committee meeting; and his pride in the perfect structure of these assemblies was great. He loved the jargon of committee-rooms; he loved the way in which the door kept opening as the clock struck the hour, in obedience to a few strokes of his pen on a piece of paper; and when it had opened sufficiently often, he loved to issue from his inner chamber with documents in his hands, visibly important, with a pre-occupied expression on his face that might have suited a prime minister advancing to meet his cabinet. By his orders the table had been decorated beforehand with six sheets of blotting-paper, with six pens, six ink-pots, a tumbler and a jug of water, a bell, and, in deference to the taste of the lady members, a vase of hardy chrysanthemums. He had already surreptitiously straightened the sheets of blotting-paper in relation to the ink-pots, and now stood in front of the fire engaged in conversation with Miss Markham. But his eye was on the door, and when Mary and Mrs Seal entered, he gave a little laugh and observed to the assembly which was scattered about the room: 'I fancy, ladies and gentlemen, that we are ready to commence.'

So speaking, he took his seat at the head of the table, and arranging one bundle of papers upon his right and another upon his left, called upon Miss Datchet to read the minutes of the previous meeting. Mary obeyed. A keen observer might have wondered why it was necessary for the secretary to knit her brows so closely over the tolerably matter-of-fact statement before her. Could there be any doubt in her mind that it had been resolved to circularise the provinces with Leaflet No. 3, or to issue a statistical diagram showing the proportion of married women to spinsters in New Zealand; or that the net profits of Mrs Hipsley's Bazaar had reached a total of five pounds eight shillings and twopence halfpenny?

Could any doubt as to the perfect sense and propriety of these statements be disturbing her? No one could have guessed, from the look of her, that she was disturbed at all. A pleasanter and saner woman than Mary Datchet was never seen within a committee-room. She seemed a compound of the autumn leaves and the winter sunshine; less poetically speaking, she showed both gentleness and strength, an indefinable promise of soft maternity blending with her evident fitness for honest labour. Nevertheless, she had great difficulty in reducing her mind to obedience; and her reading lacked conviction, as if, as was indeed the case, she had lost the power of visualising what she read. And directly the list was completed, her mind floated to Lincoln's Inn Fields and the fluttering wings of innumerable sparrows. Was Ralph still enticing the bald-headed cock-sparrow to sit upon his hand? Had he succeeded? Would he ever succeed? She had meant to ask him why it is that the sparrows in Lincoln's Inn Fields are tamer than the sparrows in Hyde Park – perhaps it is that the passers-by are rarer, and they come to recognise their benefactors. For the first half-hour of the committee meeting, Mary had thus to do battle with the sceptical presence of Ralph Denham, who threatened to have it all his own way. Mary tried half a dozen methods of ousting him. She raised her voice, she articulated distinctly, she looked firmly at Mr Clacton's bald head, she began to write a note. To her annoyance, her pencil drew a little round figure on the blotting-paper, which, she could not deny, was really a bald-headed cock-sparrow. She looked again at Mr Clacton; yes, he was bald, and so are cock-sparrows. Never was a secretary tormented by so many unsuitable suggestions, and they all came, alas! with something ludicrously grotesque about them, which might, at any moment, provoke her to such flippancy as would shock her colleagues for ever. The thought of what she might say made her bite her lips, as if her lips would protect her.

But all these suggestions were but flotsam and jetsam cast to the surface by a more profound disturbance, which, as she could not consider it at present, manifested its existence by these grotesque nods and beckonings. Consider it, she must, when the committee was over. Meanwhile, she was behaving scandalously; she was looking out of the window, and thinking of the colour of the sky, and of the decorations on the Imperial Hotel, when she ought to have been shepherding her colleagues, and pinning them down to the matter in hand. She could not bring herself to attach more weight to one project than to another. Ralph had said – she could not stop to consider what he had said, but he had somehow divested the proceedings of all reality. And then, without conscious effort, by some trick of the brain, she found herself becoming interested in some scheme for organising a newspaper campaign. Certain articles were to be written; certain editors approached. What line was it advisable to take? She found herself strongly disapproving of what Mr Clacton was saying. She committed herself to the opinion that now was the time to strike hard. Directly she had said this, she felt that she had turned upon Ralph's ghost; and she became more and more in earnest, and anxious to bring the others round to her point of view. Once more, she knew exactly and indisputably what is right and what is wrong. As if emerging from a mist, the old foes of the public good loomed ahead of her – capitalists, newspaper proprietors, anti-suffragists, and, in some ways most pernicious of all, the masses who take no interest one way or another – among whom, for the time being, she certainly discerned the features of Ralph Denham. Indeed, when Miss Markham asked her to suggest the names of a few friends of hers, she expressed herself with unusual bitterness: 'My friends think all this kind of thing useless.' She felt that she was really saying that to Ralph himself.

'Oh, they're that sort, are they?' said Miss Markham, with a little laugh; and with renewed vigour their legions charged the foe.

Mary's spirits had been low when she entered the committee-room; but now they were considerably improved. She knew the ways of this world; it was a shapely, orderly place; she felt convinced of its right and its wrong; and the feeling that she was fit to deal a heavy blow against her enemies warmed her heart and kindled her eye. In one of those flights of fancy, not characteristic of her but tiresomely frequent this afternoon, she envisaged herself battered with rotten eggs upon a platform, from which Ralph vainly begged her to descend. But –

'What do I matter compared with the cause?' she said, and so on. Much to her credit, however teased by foolish fancies, she kept the surface of her brain moderate and vigilant, and subdued Mrs Seal very tactfully more than once when she demanded, 'Action! – everywhere! – at once!' as became her father's daughter.

The other members of the committee, who were all rather elderly people, were a good deal impressed by Mary, and inclined to side with her and against each other, partly, perhaps, because of her youth. The feeling that she controlled them all filled Mary with a sense of power; and she felt that no work can equal in importance, or be so exciting as, the work of making other people do what you want them to do. Indeed, when she had won her point she felt a slight degree of contempt for the people who had yielded to her.

The committee now rose, gathered together their papers, shook them straight, placed them in their attaché-cases, snapped the locks firmly together, and hurried away, having, for the most part, to catch trains, in order to keep other appointments with other committees, for they were all busy people. Mary, Mrs Seal and Mr Clacton were left alone; the room was hot and untidy, the pieces of pink blotting-paper were lying at different angles upon the table, and the tumbler was half full of water, which someone had poured out and forgotten to drink.

Mrs Seal began preparing the tea, while Mr Clacton retired to his room to file the fresh accumulation of documents. Mary was too much excited even to help Mrs Seal with the cups and saucers. She flung up the window and stood by it, looking out. The street lamps were already lit; and through the mist in the square one could see little figures hurrying across the road and along the pavement on the farther side. In her absurd mood of lustful arrogance, Mary looked at the little figures and thought, 'If I liked I could make you go in there or stop short; I could make you walk in single file or in double file; I could do what I liked with you.' Then Mrs Seal came and stood by her.

'Oughtn't you to put something round your shoulders, Sally?' Mary asked, in rather a condescending tone of voice, feeling a sort of pity for the enthusiastic ineffective little woman. But Mrs Seal paid no attention to the suggestion.

'Well, did you enjoy yourself?' Mary asked, with a little laugh.

Mrs Seal drew a deep breath, restrained herself, and then burst out, looking out, too, upon Russell Square and Southampton Row, and at the passers-by, 'Ah, if only one could get every one of those people into this room, and make them understand for five minutes! But they *must* see the truth someday . . . If only one could *make* them see it . . . '

Mary knew herself to be very much wiser than Mrs Seal, and when Mrs Seal said anything, even if it was what Mary herself was feeling, she automatically thought of all that there was to be said against it. On this occasion her arrogant feeling that she could direct everybody dwindled away.

'Let's have our tea,' she said, turning back from the window and pulling down the blind. 'It was a good meeting – didn't you think so, Sally?' she let fall, casually, as she sat down at the table. Surely Mrs Seal must realise that Mary had been extraordinarily efficient?

'But we go at such a snail's pace,' said Sally, shaking her head impatiently.

At this Mary burst out laughing, and all her arrogance was dissipated.

'You can afford to laugh,' said Sally, with another shake of her head, 'but I can't. I'm fifty-five, and I dare say I shall be in my grave by the time we get it – if we ever do.'

'Oh, no, you won't be in your grave,' said Mary, kindly.

'It'll be such a great day,' said Mrs Seal, with a toss of her locks. 'A great day, not only for us, but for civilisation. That's what I feel, you know, about these meetings. Each one of them is a step onwards in the great march – humanity, you know. We do want the people after us to have a better time of it – and so many don't see it. I wonder how it is that they don't see it?'

She was carrying plates and cups from the cupboard as she spoke, so that her sentences were more than usually broken apart. Mary could not help looking at the odd little priestess of humanity with something like admiration. While she had been thinking about herself, Mrs Seal had thought of nothing but her vision.

'You mustn't wear yourself out, Sally, if you want to see the great day,' she said, rising and trying to take a plate of biscuits from Mrs Seal's hands.

'My dear child, what else is my old body good for?' she exclaimed, clinging more tightly than before to her plate of biscuits. 'Shouldn't I be proud to give everything I have to the cause? – for I'm not an intelligence like you. There were domestic circumstances – I'd like to tell you one of these days – so I say foolish things. I lose my head, you know. You don't. Mr Clacton doesn't. It's a great mistake, to lose one's head. But my heart's in the right place. And I'm so glad Kit has a big dog, for I didn't think her looking well.'

They had their tea, and went over many of the points that had been raised in the committee rather more intimately than had been possible then; and they all felt an agreeable sense of being in some way behind the scenes; of having their hands upon strings which, when pulled, would completely change the pageant exhibited daily to those who read the newspapers. Although their views were very different, this sense united them and made them almost cordial in their manners to each other.

Mary, however, left the tea-party rather early, desiring both to be alone, and then to hear some music at the Queen's Hall.[55] She fully intended to use her loneliness to think out her position with regard to Ralph; but although she walked back to the Strand with this end in view, she found her mind uncomfortably full of different trains of thought. She started one and then another. They seemed even to take their colour from the street she happened to be in. Thus the vision of humanity appeared to be in some way connected with Bloomsbury, and faded distinctly by the time she crossed the main road; then a belated organ-grinder in Holborn set her thoughts dancing incongruously; and by the time she was crossing the great misty square of Lincoln's Inn Fields, she was cold and depressed again, and horribly clear-sighted. The dark removed the stimulus of human companionship, and a tear actually slid down her cheek, accompanying a sudden conviction within her that she loved Ralph, and that he didn't love her. All dark and empty now was the path where they had walked that morning, and the sparrows silent in the bare trees. But the lights in her own building soon cheered her; all these different states of mind were submerged in the deep flood of desires, thoughts, perceptions, antagonisms, which washed perpetually at the base of her being, to rise into prominence in turn when the conditions of the upper world were favourable. She put off the hour of clear thought until Christmas, saying to herself, as she lit her fire, that it is impossible to think anything out in London; and, no doubt, Ralph wouldn't come at Christmas, and she would take long walks into the heart of the country, and decide this question and all the others that puzzled her. Meanwhile, she thought, drawing her feet up on to the fender, life was full of complexity; life was a thing one must love to the last fibre of it.

She had sat there for five minutes or so, and her thoughts had had time to grow dim, when there came a ring at her bell. Her eye brightened; she felt immediately convinced that Ralph had come to visit her. Accordingly, she waited a moment before opening the door; she wanted to feel her hands secure upon the reins of all the troublesome emotions which the sight of Ralph would certainly arouse. She composed herself unnecessarily, however, for she had to admit, not Ralph, but Katharine and William Rodney. Her first impression was that they were both extremely well dressed. She felt herself shabby and slovenly beside them, and did not know how she should entertain them, nor could she guess why they had come. She had heard nothing of their engagement. But after the first disappointment, she was pleased, for she felt instantly that Katharine was a personality, and, moreover, she need not now exercise her self-control.

'We were passing and saw a light in your window, so we came up,' Katharine explained, standing and looking very tall and distinguished and rather absent-minded.

'We have been to see some pictures,' said William. 'Oh, dear,' he exclaimed, looking about him, 'this room reminds me of one of the worst hours in my existence – when I read a paper, and you all sat round and jeered at me. Katharine was the worst. I could feel her gloating over every mistake I made. Miss Datchet was kind. Miss Datchet just made it possible for me to get through, I remember.'

Sitting down, he drew off his light yellow gloves, and began slapping his knees with them. His vitality was pleasant, Mary thought, although he made her laugh. The very look of him was inclined to make her laugh. His rather prominent eyes passed from one young woman to the other, and his lips perpetually formed words which remained unspoken.

'We have been seeing old masters at the Grafton Gallery,' said Katharine, apparently paying no attention to William, and accepting a cigarette which Mary offered her. She leant back in her chair, and the smoke which hung about her face seemed to withdraw her still further from the others.

'Would you believe it, Miss Datchet,' William continued, 'Katharine doesn't like Titian.[56] She doesn't like apricots, she doesn't like peaches, she doesn't like green peas. She likes the Elgin Marbles, and grey days without any sun. She's a typical example of the cold northern nature. I come from Devonshire – '

Had they been quarrelling, Mary wondered, and had they, for that reason, sought refuge in her room, or were they engaged, or had Katharine just refused him? She was completely baffled.

Katharine now reappeared from her veil of smoke, knocked the ash from her cigarette into the fireplace, and looked, with an odd expression of solicitude, at the irritable man.

'Perhaps, Mary,' she said tentatively, 'you wouldn't mind giving us some tea? We did try to get some, but the shop was so crowded, and in the next one there was a band playing; and most of the pictures, at any rate, were very dull, whatever you may say, William.' She spoke with a kind of guarded gentleness.

Mary, accordingly, retired to make preparations in the pantry.

'What in the world are they after?' she asked of her own reflection in the little looking-glass which hung there. She was not left to doubt much longer, for, on her coming back into the sitting-room with the tea-things, Katharine informed her, apparently having been instructed so to do by William, of their engagement.

'William,' she said, 'thinks that perhaps you don't know. We are going to be married.'

Mary found herself shaking William's hand, and addressing her congratulations to him, as if Katharine were inaccessible; she had, indeed, taken hold of the tea-kettle.

'Let me see,' Katharine said, 'one puts hot water into the cups first, doesn't one? You have some dodge of your own, haven't you, William, about making tea?'

Mary was half inclined to suspect that this was said in order to conceal nervousness, but if so, the concealment was unusually perfect. Talk of marriage was dismissed. Katharine might have been seated in her own drawing-room, controlling a situation which presented no sort of difficulty to her trained mind. Rather to her surprise, Mary found herself making conversation with William about old Italian pictures, while Katharine poured out tea, cut cake and kept William's plate supplied, without joining more than was necessary in the conversation. She seemed to have taken possession of Mary's room, and to handle the cups as if they belonged to her. But it was done so naturally that it bred no resentment in Mary; on the contrary, she found herself putting her hand on Katharine's knee, affectionately, for an instant. Was there something maternal in this assumption of control? And thinking of Katharine as one who would soon be married, these maternal airs filled Mary's mind with a new tenderness, and even with awe. Katharine seemed very much older and more experienced than she was.

Meanwhile Rodney talked. If his appearance was superficially against him, it had the advantage of making his solid merits something of a surprise. He had kept notebooks; he knew a great deal about pictures. He could compare different examples in different galleries, and his authoritative answers to intelligent questions gained not a little, Mary felt, from the smart taps which he dealt, as he delivered them, upon the lumps of coal. She was impressed.

'Your tea, William,' said Katharine gently.

He paused, gulped it down, obediently, and continued.

And then it struck Mary that Katharine, in the shade of her broad-brimmed hat, and in the midst of the smoke, and in the obscurity of her character, was, perhaps, smiling to herself, not altogether in the maternal spirit. What she said was very simple, but her words, even, 'Your tea, William,' were set down as gently and cautiously and exactly as the feet of a Persian cat stepping among china ornaments. For the second time that day Mary felt herself baffled by something inscrutable in the character of a person to whom she felt herself much attracted. She thought that if she were engaged to Katharine, she, too, would find herself very soon using those fretful questions with which William evidently teased his bride. And yet Katharine's voice was humble.

'I wonder how you find the time to know all about pictures as well as books?' she asked.

'How do I find the time?' William answered, delighted, Mary guessed, at this little compliment. 'Why, I always travel with a notebook. And I ask my way to the picture gallery the very first thing in the morning. And then I meet men, and talk to them. There's a man in my office who knows all about the Flemish school.[57] I was telling Miss Datchet about the Flemish school. I picked up a lot of it from him – it's a way men have – Gibbons, his name is. You must meet him. We'll ask him to lunch. And this not caring about art,' he explained, turning to Mary, 'it's one of Katharine's poses, Miss Datchet. Did you know she posed? She pretends that she's never read Shakespeare. And why should she read Shakespeare, since she *is* Shakespeare – Rosalind,[58] you know,' and he gave his queer little chuckle. Somehow this compliment appeared very old-fashioned and almost in bad taste. Mary actually felt herself blush, as if he had said 'the sex' or 'the ladies'. Constrained, perhaps, by nervousness, Rodney continued in the same vein.

'She knows enough – enough for all decent purposes. What do you women want with learning, when you have so much else – everything, I should say – everything. Leave us something, eh, Katharine?'

'Leave you something?' said Katharine, apparently waking from a brown study. 'I was thinking we must be going – '

'Is it tonight that Lady Ferrilby dines with us? No, we mustn't be late,' said Rodney, rising. 'D'you know the Ferrilbys, Miss Datchet? They own Trantem Abbey,' he added, for her information, as she looked doubtful. 'And if Katharine makes herself very charming tonight, perhaps'll lend it to us for the honeymoon.'

'I agree that may be a reason. Otherwise she's a dull woman,' said Katharine. 'At least,' she added, as if to qualify her abruptness, 'I find it difficult to talk to her.'

'Because you expect everyone else to take all the trouble. I've seen her sit silent a whole evening,' he said, turning to Mary, as he had frequently done already. 'Don't you find that, too? Sometimes when we're alone, I've counted the time on my watch' – here he took out a large gold watch, and tapped the glass – 'the time between one remark and the next. And once I counted ten minutes and twenty seconds, and then, if you'll believe me, she only said "Um!"'

'I'm sure I'm sorry,' Katharine apologised. 'I know it's a bad habit, but then, you see, at home – '

The rest of her excuse was cut short, so far as Mary was concerned, by the closing of the door. She fancied she could hear William finding fresh fault on the stairs. A moment later, the doorbell rang again, and Katharine reappeared, having left her purse on a chair. She soon found it, and said, pausing for a moment at the door, and speaking differently as they were alone: 'I think being engaged is very bad for the character.' She shook her purse in her hand until the coins jingled, as if she alluded merely to this example of her forgetfulness. But the remark puzzled Mary; it seemed to refer to something else; and her manner had changed so strangely, now that William was out of hearing, that she could not help looking at her for an explanation. She looked almost stern, so that Mary, trying to smile at her, only succeeded in producing a silent stare of interrogation.

As the door shut for the second time, she sank on to the floor in front of the fire, trying, now that their bodies were not there to distract her, to piece together her impressions of them as a whole. And, though priding herself, with all other men and women, upon an infallible eye for character, she could not feel at all certain that she knew what motives inspired Katharine Hilbery in life. There was something that carried her on smoothly, out of reach – something, yes, but what? – something that reminded Mary of Ralph. Oddly enough, he gave her the same feeling, too, and with him, too, she felt baffled. Oddly enough, for no two people, she hastily concluded, were more unlike. And yet both had this hidden impulse, this incalculable force – this thing they cared for and didn't talk about – oh, what was it?

Chapter 15

The village of Disham[59] lies somewhere on the rolling piece of cultivated ground in the neighbourhood of Lincoln, not so far inland but that a sound, bringing rumours of the sea, can be heard on summer nights or when the winter storms fling the waves upon the long beach. So large is the church, and in particular the church tower, in comparison with the little street of cottages which compose the village, that the traveller is apt to cast his mind back to the Middle Ages as the only time when so much piety could have been kept alive. So great a trust in the Church can surely not belong to our day, and he goes on to conjecture that every one of the villagers has reached the extreme limit of human life. Such are the reflections of the superficial stranger, and his sight of the population, as it is represented by two or three men hoeing in a turnip-field, a small child carrying a jug and a young woman shaking a piece of carpet outside her cottage door, will not lead him to see anything very much out of keeping with the Middle Ages in the village of Disham as it is today. These people, though they seem young enough, look so angular and so crude that they remind him of the little pictures painted by monks in the capital letters of their manuscripts. He only half understands what they say, and speaks very loud and clearly, as though, indeed, his voice had to carry through a hundred years or more before it reached them. He would have a far better chance of understanding some dweller in Paris or Rome, Berlin or Madrid, than these countrymen of his who have lived for the last two thousand years not two hundred miles from the City of London.

The Rectory stands about half a mile beyond the village. It is a large house, and has been growing steadily for some centuries round the great kitchen, with its narrow red tiles, as the rector would point out to his guests on the first night of their arrival, taking his brass candlestick, and bidding them mind the steps up and the steps down, and notice the immense thickness of the walls, the old beams across the ceiling, the staircases as steep as ladders, and the attics, with their deep, tent-like roofs, in which swallows bred, and once a white owl. But nothing very interesting or very beautiful had resulted from the different additions made by the different rectors.

The house, however, was surrounded by a garden, in which the rector took considerable pride. The lawn, which fronted the drawing-room windows, was a rich and uniform green, unspotted by a single daisy, and on the other side of it two straight paths led past beds of tall, standing flowers to a charming grassy walk, where the Reverend Wyndham Datchet would pace up and down at the same hour every morning, with a sundial to measure the time for him. As often as not, he carried a book in his hand, into which he would glance, then shut it up, and repeat the rest of the ode from memory. He had most of Horace by heart, and had got into the habit of connecting this particular walk with certain odes which he repeated duly, at the same time noting the condition of his flowers, and stooping now and again to pick any that were withered or overblown. On wet days, such was the power of habit over him, he rose from his chair at the same hour, and paced his study for the same length of time, pausing now and then to straighten some book in the bookcase, or alter the position of the two brass crucifixes standing upon cairns of serpentine stone upon the mantelpiece. His children had a great respect for him, credited him with far more learning than he actually possessed, and saw that his habits were not interfered with, if possible. Like most people who do things methodically, the rector himself had more strength of purpose and power of self-sacrifice than of intellect or of originality. On cold and windy nights he rode off to visit sick people, who might need him, without a murmur; and by virtue of doing dull duties punctually, he was much employed upon committees and local boards and councils; and at this period of his life (he was sixty-eight) he was beginning to be commiserated by tender old ladies for the extreme leanness of his person, which, they said, was worn out upon the roads when it should have been resting before a comfortable fire. His elder daughter, Elizabeth, lived with him and managed the house, and already much resembled him in dry sincerity and methodical habit of mind; of the two sons one, Richard, was an estate agent, the other, Christopher, was reading for the Bar. At Christmas, naturally, they met together; and for a month past the arrangement of the Christmas week had been much in the mind of mistress and maid, who prided themselves every year more confidently upon the excellence of their equipment. The late Mrs Datchet had left an excellent cupboard of linen, to which Elizabeth had succeeded at the age of nineteen, when her mother died, and the charge of the family rested upon the shoulders of the eldest daughter. She kept a fine flock of yellow chickens, sketched a little, certain rose trees in the garden were committed specially to her care; and what with the care of the house, the care of the chickens, and the care of the poor, she scarcely knew what it was to have an idle minute. An extreme rectitude of mind, rather than any gift, gave her weight in the family. When Mary wrote to say that she had asked Ralph Denham to stay with them, she added, out of deference to Elizabeth's character, that he was very nice, though rather queer, and had been over-working himself in London. No doubt Elizabeth would conclude that Ralph was in love with her, but there could be no doubt either that not a word of this would be spoken by either of them, unless, indeed, some catastrophe made mention of it unavoidable.

Mary went down to Disham without knowing whether Ralph intended to come; but two or three days before Christmas she received a telegram from Ralph, asking her to take a room for him in the village. This was followed by a letter explaining that he hoped he might have his meals with them; but quiet, essential for his work, made it necessary to sleep out.

Mary was walking in the garden with Elizabeth, and inspecting the roses, when the letter arrived.

'But that's absurd,' said Elizabeth decidedly, when the plan was explained to her. 'There are five spare rooms, even when the boys are here. Besides, he wouldn't get a room in the village. And he oughtn't to work if he's overworked.'

'But perhaps he doesn't want to see so much of us,' Mary thought to herself, although outwardly she assented, and felt grateful to Elizabeth for supporting her in what was, of course, her desire. They were cutting roses at the time, and laying them, head by head, in a shallow basket.

'If Ralph were here, he'd find this very dull,' Mary thought, with a little shiver of irritation, which led her to place her rose the wrong way in the basket. Meanwhile, they had come to the end of the path, and while Elizabeth straightened some flowers, and made them stand upright within their fence of string, Mary looked at her father, who was pacing up and down, with his hand behind his back and his head bowed in meditation. Obeying an impulse which sprang from some desire to interrupt this methodical marching, Mary stepped on to the grass walk and put her hand on his arm.

'A flower for your buttonhole, father,' she said, presenting a rose.

'Eh, dear?' said Mr Datchet, taking the flower, and holding it at an angle which suited his bad eyesight, without pausing in his walk.

'Where does this fellow come from? One of Elizabeth's roses – I hope you asked her leave. Elizabeth doesn't like having her roses picked without her leave, and quite right, too.'

He had a habit, Mary remarked, and she had never noticed it so clearly before, of letting his sentences tail away in a continuous murmur, whereupon he passed into a state of abstraction, presumed by his children to indicate some train of thought too profound for utterance.

'What?' said Mary, interrupting, for the first time in her life, perhaps, when the murmur ceased. He made no reply. She knew very well that he wished to be left alone, but she stuck to his side much as she might have stuck to some sleepwalker, whom she thought it right gradually to awaken. She could think of nothing to rouse him with except: 'The garden's looking very nice, father.'

'Yes, yes, yes,' said Mr Datchet, running his words together in the same abstracted manner, and sinking his head yet lower upon his breast. And suddenly, as they turned their steps to retrace their way, he jerked out: 'The traffic's very much increased, you know. More rolling-stock needed already. Forty trucks went down yesterday by the 12.15 – counted them myself. They've taken off the 9.03, and given us an 8.30 instead – suits the businessmen, you know. You came by the old 3.10 yesterday, I suppose?'

She said, 'Yes,' as he seemed to wish for a reply, and then he looked at his watch, and made off down the path towards the house, holding the rose at the same angle in front of him. Elizabeth had gone round to the side of the house, where the chickens lived, so that Mary found herself alone, holding Ralph's letter in her hand. She was uneasy. She had put off the season for thinking things out very successfully, and now that

Ralph was actually coming, the next day, she could only wonder how her family would impress him. She thought it likely that her father would discuss the train service with him; Elizabeth would be bright and sensible and always leaving the room to give messages to the servants. Her brothers had already said that they would give him a day's shooting. She was content to leave the problem of Ralph's relations to the young men obscure, trusting that they would find some common ground of masculine agreement. But what would he think of *her*? Would he see that she was different from the rest of the family? She devised a plan for taking him to her sitting-room, and artfully leading the talk towards the English poets, who now occupied prominent places in her little book-case. Moreover, she might give him to understand, privately, that she, too, thought her family a queer one – queer, yes, but not dull. That was the rock past which she was bent on steering him. And she thought how she would draw his attention to Edward's passion for Jorrocks,[60] and the enthusiasm which led Christopher to collect moths and butterflies though he was now twenty-two. Perhaps Elizabeth's sketching, if the fruits were invisible, might lend colour to the general effect which she wished to produce of a family, eccentric and limited, perhaps, but not dull. Edward, she perceived, was rolling the lawn, for the sake of exercise; and the sight of him, with pink cheeks, bright little brown eyes and a general resemblance to a clumsy young cart-horse in its winter coat of dusty brown hair, made Mary violently ashamed of her ambitious scheming. She loved him precisely as he was; she loved them all; and as she walked by his side, up and down, and down and up, her strong moral sense administered a sound drubbing to the vain and romantic element aroused in her by the mere thought of Ralph. She felt quite certain that, for good or for bad, she was very like the rest of her family.

Sitting in the corner of a third-class railway carriage, on the afternoon of the following day, Ralph made several enquiries of a commercial traveller in the opposite corner. They centered round a village called Lampsher, not three miles, he understood, from Lincoln; was there a big house in Lampsher, he asked, inhabited by a gentleman of the name of Otway?

The traveller knew nothing, but rolled the name of Otway on his tongue, reflectively, and the sound of it gratified Ralph amazingly. It gave him an excuse to take a letter from his pocket in order to verify the address.

'Stogdon House, Lampsher, Lincoln,' he read out.

'You'll find somebody to direct you at Lincoln,' said the man; and Ralph had to confess that he was not bound there this very evening.

'I've got to walk over from Disham,' he said, and in the heart of him could not help marvelling at the pleasure which he derived from making a bagman in a train believe what he himself did not believe. For the letter, though signed by Katharine's father, contained no invitation or warrant for thinking that Katharine herself was there; the only fact it disclosed was that for a fortnight this address would be Mr Hilbery's address. But when he looked out of the window, it was of her he thought; she, too, had seen these grey fields, and, perhaps, she was there where the trees ran up a slope, and one yellow light shone now, and then went out again, at the foot of the hill. The light shone in the windows of an old grey house, he thought. He lay back in his corner and forgot the commercial traveller altogether. The process of visualising Katharine stopped short at the old grey manor-house; instinct warned him that if he went much further with this process reality would soon force itself in; he could not altogether neglect the figure of William Rodney. Since the day when he had heard from Katharine's lips of her engagement, he had refrained from investing his dream of her with the details of real life. But the light of the late afternoon glowed green behind the straight trees, and became a symbol of her. The light seemed to expand his heart. She brooded over the grey fields, and was with him now in the railway carriage, thoughtful, silent, and infinitely tender; but the vision pressed too close, and must be dismissed, for the train was slackening. Its abrupt jerks shook him wide awake, and he saw Mary Datchet, a sturdy russet figure, with a dash of scarlet about it, as the carriage slid down the platform. A tall youth who accompanied her shook him by the hand, took his bag, and led the way without uttering one articulate word.

Never are voices so beautiful as on a winter's evening, when dusk almost hides the body, and they seem to issue from nothingness with a note of intimacy seldom heard by day. Such an edge was there in Mary's voice when she greeted him. About her seemed to hang the mist of the winter hedges and the clear red of the bramble leaves. He felt himself at once stepping on to the firm ground of an entirely different world, but he did not allow himself to yield to the pleasure of it directly. They gave him his choice of driving with Edward or of walking home across the fields with Mary – not a shorter way, they explained, but Mary thought it a nicer way. He decided to walk with her, being conscious, indeed, that he got comfort from her presence. What could be the cause of her cheerfulness, he wondered, half ironically and half enviously, as the pony-cart started briskly away, and the dusk swam between their eyes and the tall form of Edward, standing up to drive, with the reins in one hand and the whip in the other. People from the village, who had been to the market town, were climbing into their gigs or setting off home down the road together in little parties. Many salutations were addressed to Mary, who shouted back, with the addition of the speaker's name. But soon she led the way over a stile, and along a path worn slightly darker than the dim green surrounding it. In front of them the sky now showed itself of a reddish-yellow, like a slice of some semilucent stone behind which a lamp burnt, while a fringe of black trees with distinct branches stood against the light, which was obscured in one direction by a hump of earth, in all other directions the land lying flat to the very verge of the sky. One of the swift and noiseless birds of the winter's night seemed to follow them across the field, circling a few feet in front of them, disappearing and returning again and again.

Mary had gone this walk many hundred times in the course of her life, generally alone, and at different stages the ghosts of past moods would flood her mind with a whole scene or train of thought merely at the sight of three trees from a particular angle, or at the sound of the pheasant clucking in the ditch. But tonight the circumstances were strong enough to oust all other scenes; and she looked at the field and the trees with an involuntary intensity as if they had no such associations for her.

'Well, Ralph,' she said, 'this is better than Lincoln's Inn Fields, isn't it? Look, there's a bird for you! Oh, you've brought glasses, have you? Edward and Christopher mean to make you shoot. Can you shoot? I shouldn't think so – '

'Look here, you must explain,' said Ralph. 'Who are these young men? Where am I staying?'

'You are staying with us, of course,' she said boldly. 'Of course, you're staying with us – you don't mind coming, do you?'

'If I had, I shouldn't have come,' he said sturdily. They walked on in silence; Mary took care not to break it for a time. She wished Ralph to feel, as she thought he would, all the fresh delights of the earth and air. She was right. In a moment he expressed his pleasure, much to her comfort.

'This is the sort of country I thought you'd live in, Mary,' he said, pushing his hat back on his head, and looking about him. 'Real country. No gentlemen's seats.'

He snuffed the air, and felt more keenly than he had done for many weeks the pleasure of owning a body.

'Now we have to find our way through a hedge,' said Mary. In the gap of the hedge Ralph tore up a poacher's wire, set across a hole to trap a rabbit.

'It's quite right that they should poach,' said Mary, watching him tugging at the wire. 'I wonder whether it was Alfred Duggins or Sid Rankin? How can one expect them not to, when they only make fifteen shillings a week? Fifteen shillings a week,' she repeated, coming out on the other side of the hedge, and running her fingers through her hair to rid herself of a bramble which had attached itself to her. 'I could live on fifteen shillings a week – easily.'

'Could you?' said Ralph. 'I don't believe you could,' he added.

'Oh yes. They have a cottage thrown in, and a garden where one can grow vegetables. It wouldn't be half bad,' said Mary, with a soberness which impressed Ralph very much.

'But you'd get tired of it,' he urged.

'I sometimes think it's the only thing one would never get tired of,' she replied.

The idea of a cottage where one grew one's own vegetables and lived on fifteen shillings a week, filled Ralph with an extraordinary sense of rest and satisfaction.

'But wouldn't it be on the main road, or next door to a woman with six squalling children, who'd always be hanging her washing out to dry across your garden?'

'The cottage I'm thinking of stands by itself in a little orchard.'

'And what about the Suffrage?' he asked, attempting sarcasm.

'Oh, there are other things in the world besides the Suffrage,' she replied, in an off-hand manner which was slightly mysterious.

Ralph fell silent. It annoyed him that she should have plans of which he knew nothing; but he felt that he had no right to press her further. His mind settled upon the idea of life in a country cottage. Conceivably, for he could not examine into it now, here lay a tremendous possibility; a solution of many problems. He struck his stick upon the earth, and stared through the dusk at the shape of the country.

'D'you know the points of the compass?' he asked.

'Well, of course,' said Mary. 'What d'you take me for? – a cockney like you?' She then told him exactly where the north lay, and where the south.

'It's my native land, this,' she said. 'I could smell my way about it blindfold.'

As if to prove this boast, she walked a little quicker, so that Ralph found it difficult to keep pace with her. At the same time, he felt drawn to her as he had never been before; partly, no doubt, because she was more independent of him than in London, and seemed to be attached firmly to a world where he had no place at all. Now the dusk had fallen to such an extent that he had to follow her implicitly, and even lean his hand on her shoulder when they jumped a bank into a very narrow lane. And he felt curiously shy of her when she began to shout through her hands at a spot of light which swung upon the mist in a neighbouring field. He shouted, too, and the light stood still.

'That's Christopher, come in already, and gone to feed his chickens,' she said.

She introduced him to Ralph, who could see only a tall figure in gaiters, rising from a fluttering circle of soft feathery bodies, upon whom the light fell in wavering discs, calling out now a bright spot of yellow, now one of greenish-black and scarlet. Mary dipped her hand in the bucket he carried, and was at once the centre of a circle also; and as she cast her grain she talked alternately to the birds and to her brother, in the same clucking, half-inarticulate voice, as it sounded to Ralph, standing on the outskirts of the fluttering feathers in his black overcoat.

He had removed his overcoat by the time they sat round the dinner-table, but nevertheless he looked very strange among the others. A country life and breeding had preserved in them all a look which Mary hesitated to call either innocent or youthful, as she compared them, now sitting round in an oval, softly illuminated by candlelight; and yet it was something of the kind, yes, even in the case of the rector himself. Though superficially marked with lines, his face was a clear pink, and his blue eyes had the long-sighted, peaceful expression of eyes seeking the turn of the road, or a distant light through rain, or the darkness of winter. She looked at Ralph. He had never appeared to her more concentrated and full of purpose; as if behind his forehead were massed so much experience that he could choose for himself which part of it he would display and which part he would keep to himself. Compared with that dark and stern countenance, her brothers' faces, bending low over their soup-plates, were mere circles of pink, unmolded flesh.

'You came by the 3.10, Mr Denham?' said the Reverend Wyndham Datchet, tucking his napkin into his collar, so that almost the whole of his body was concealed by a large white diamond. 'They treat us very well, on the whole. Considering the increase of traffic, they treat us very well indeed. I have the curiosity sometimes to count the trucks on the goods' trains, and they're well over fifty – well over fifty, at this season of the year.'

The old gentleman had been roused agreeably by the presence of this attentive and well-informed young man, as was evident by the care with which he finished the last words in his sentences, and his slight exaggeration in the number of trucks on the trains. Indeed, the chief burden of the talk fell upon him, and he sustained it tonight in a manner which caused his sons to look at him admiringly now and then; for they felt shy of Denham, and were glad not to have to talk themselves. The store of information about the present and past of this particular corner of Lincolnshire which old Mr Datchet produced really surprised his children, for though they knew of its existence, they had forgotten its extent, as they might have forgotten the amount of family plate stored in the plate-chest, until some rare celebration brought it forth.

After dinner, parish business took the rector to his study, and Mary proposed that they should sit in the kitchen.

'It's not the kitchen really,' Elizabeth hastened to explain to her guest, 'but we call it so – '

'It's the nicest room in the house,' said Edward.

'It's got the old rests by the side of the fireplace, where the men hung their guns,' said Elizabeth, leading the way, with a tall brass candlestick in her hand, down a passage. 'Show Mr Denham the steps, Christopher . . . When the Ecclesiastical Commissioners were here two years ago they said this was the most interesting part of the house. These narrow bricks prove that it is five hundred years old – five hundred years, I think – they may have said six.' She, too, felt an impulse to exaggerate the age of the bricks, as her father had exaggerated the number of trucks. A big lamp hung down from the centre of the ceiling and, together with a fine log fire, illuminated a large and lofty room, with rafters running from wall to wall, a floor of red tiles, and a substantial fireplace built up of those narrow red bricks which were said to be five hundred years old. A few rugs and a sprinkling of armchairs had made this ancient kitchen into a sitting-room. Elizabeth, after pointing out the gun-racks, and the hooks for smoking hams, and other evidence of incontestable age, and explaining that Mary had had the idea of turning the room into a sitting-room – otherwise it was used for hanging out the wash and for the men to change in after shooting – considered that she had done her duty as hostess, and sat down in an upright chair directly beneath the lamp, beside a very long and narrow oak table. She placed a pair of horn spectacles upon her nose, and drew towards her a basketful of threads and wools. In a few minutes a smile came to her face, and remained there for the rest of the evening.

'Will you come out shooting with us tomorrow?' said Christopher, who had, on the whole, formed a favourable impression of his sister's friend.

'I won't shoot, but I'll come with you,' said Ralph.

'Don't you care about shooting?' asked Edward, whose suspicions were not yet laid to rest.

'I've never shot in my life,' said Ralph, turning and looking him in the face, because he was not sure how this confession would be received.

'You wouldn't have much chance in London, I suppose,' said Christopher. 'But won't you find it rather dull – just watching us?'

'I shall watch birds,' Ralph replied, with a smile.

'I can show you the place for watching birds,' said Edward, 'if that's what you like doing. I know a fellow who comes down from London about this time every year to watch them. It's a great place for the wild geese and the ducks. I've heard this man say that it's one of the best places for birds in the country.'

'It's about the best place in England,' Ralph replied. They were all gratified by this praise of their native county; and Mary now had the pleasure of hearing these short questions and answers lose their undertone of suspicious inspection, so far as her brothers were concerned, and develop into a genuine conversation about the habits of birds which afterwards turned to a discussion as to the habits of solicitors, in which it was scarcely necessary for her to take part. She was pleased to see that her brothers liked Ralph, to the extent, that is, of wishing to secure his good opinion. Whether or not he liked them it was impossible to tell from his kind but experienced manner. Now and then she fed the fire with a fresh log, and as the room filled with the fine, dry heat of burning wood, they all, with the exception of Elizabeth, who was outside the range of the fire, felt less and less anxious about the effect they were making, and more and more inclined for sleep. At this moment a vehement scratching was heard on the door.

'Piper! – oh, damn! – I shall have to get up,' murmured Christopher.

'It's not Piper, it's Pitch,' Edward grunted.

'All the same, I shall have to get up,' Christopher grumbled. He let in the dog, and stood for a moment by the door, which opened into the garden, to revive himself with a draught of the black, starlit air.

'Do come in and shut the door!' Mary cried, half turning in her chair.

'We shall have a fine day tomorrow,' said Christopher with complacency, and he sat himself on the floor at her feet, and leant his back against her knees, and stretched out his long stockinged legs to the fire – all signs that he felt no longer any restraint at the presence of the stranger. He was the youngest of the family, and Mary's favourite, partly because his character resembled hers, as Edward's character resembled Elizabeth's. She made her knees a comfortable rest for his head, and ran her fingers through his hair.

'I should like Mary to stroke my head like that,' Ralph thought to himself suddenly, and he looked at Christopher, almost affectionately, for calling forth his sister's caresses. Instantly he thought of Katharine, the thought of her being surrounded by the spaces of night and the open air; and Mary, watching him, saw the lines upon his forehead suddenly deepen. He stretched out an arm and placed a log upon the fire, constraining himself to fit it carefully into the frail red scaffolding, and also to limit his thoughts to this one room.

Mary had ceased to stroke her brother's head; he moved it impatiently between her knees, and, much as though he were a child, she began once more to part the thick, reddish-coloured locks this way and that. But a far stronger passion had taken possession of her soul than any her brother could inspire in her, and, seeing Ralph's change of expression, her hand almost automatically continued its movements, while her mind plunged desperately for some hold upon slippery banks.

Chapter 16

Into that same black night, almost, indeed, into the very same layer of starlit air, Katharine Hilbery was now gazing, although not with a view to the prospects of a fine day for duck shooting on the morrow. She was walking up and down a gravel path in the garden of Stogdon House, her sight of the heavens being partially intercepted by the light leafless hoops of a pergola. Thus a spray of clematis would completely obscure Cassiopeia, or blot out with its black pattern myriads of miles of the Milky Way. At the end of the pergola, however, there was a stone seat, from which the sky could be seen completely swept clear of any earthly interruption, save to the right, indeed, where a line of elm trees was beautifully sprinkled with stars, and a low stable building had a full drop of quivering silver just issuing from the mouth of the chimney. It was a moonless night, but the light of the stars was sufficient to show the outline of the young woman's form, and the shape of her face gazing gravely, indeed almost sternly, into the sky. She had come out into the winter's night, which was mild enough, not so much to look with scientific eyes upon the stars, as to shake herself free from certain purely terrestrial discontents. Much as a literary person in like circumstances would begin, absent-mindedly, pulling out volume after volume, so she stepped into the garden in order to have the stars at hand, even though she did not look at them. Not to be happy, when she was supposed to be happier than she would ever be again – that, as far as she could see, was the origin of a discontent which had begun almost as soon as she arrived, two days before, and seemed now so intolerable that she had left the family party, and come out here to consider it by herself. It was not she who thought herself unhappy, but her cousins, who thought it for her. The house was full of cousins, much of her age, or even younger, and among them they had some terribly bright eyes. They seemed always on the search for something between her and Rodney which they expected to find and yet did not find; and when they searched, Katharine became aware of wanting what she had not been conscious of wanting in London, alone with William and her parents. Or, if she did not want it, she missed it. And this state of mind depressed her, because she had been accustomed always to give complete satisfaction, and her self-love was now a little ruffled. She would have liked to break through the reserve habitual to her in order to justify her engagement to someone whose opinion she valued. No one had spoken a word of criticism, but they left her alone with William; not that that would have mattered, if they had not left her alone so politely; and, perhaps, that would not have mattered if they had not seemed so queerly silent, almost respectful, in her presence, which gave way to criticism, she felt, out of it.

Looking now and then at the sky, she went through the list of her cousins' names: Eleanor, Humphrey, Marmaduke, Silvia, Henry, Cassandra, Gilbert and Mostyn – Henry, the cousin who taught the young ladies of Bungay to play upon the violin, was the only one in whom she could confide, and as she walked up and down beneath the hoops of the pergola, she did begin a little speech to him, which ran something like this: 'To begin with, I'm very fond of William. You can't deny that. I know him better than anyone, almost. But why I'm marrying him is, partly, I admit – I'm being quite honest with you, and you mustn't tell anyone – partly because I want to get married. I want to have a house of my own. It isn't possible at home. It's all very well for you, Henry; you can go your own way. I have to be there always. Besides, you know what our house is. You wouldn't be happy either, if you didn't do something. It isn't that I haven't the time at home – it's the atmosphere.' Here, presumably, she imagined that her cousin, who had listened with his usual intelligent sympathy, raised his eyebrows a little, and interposed: 'Well, but what do you want to do?'

Even in this purely imaginary dialogue, Katharine found it difficult to confide her ambition to an imaginary companion.

'I should like,' she began, and hesitated quite a long time before she forced herself to add, with a change of voice, 'to study mathematics – to know about the stars.'

Henry was clearly amazed, but too kind to express all his doubts; he only said something about the difficulties of mathematics, and remarked that very little was known about the stars.

Katharine thereupon went on with the statement of her case.

'I don't care much whether I ever get to know anything – but I want to work out something in figures – something that hasn't got to do with human beings. I don't want people particularly. In some ways, Henry, I'm a humbug – I mean, I'm not what you all take me for. I'm not domestic, or very practical or sensible, really. And if I could calculate things, and use a telescope, and have to work out figures, and know to a fraction where I was wrong, I should be perfectly happy, and I believe I should give William all he wants.'

Having reached this point, instinct told her that she had passed beyond the region in which Henry's advice could be of any good; and, having rid her mind of its superficial annoyance, she sat herself upon the stone seat, raised her eyes unconsciously and thought about the deeper questions which she had to decide, she knew, for herself. Would she, indeed, give William all he wanted? In order to decide the question, she ran her mind rapidly over her little collection of significant sayings, looks, compliments, gestures, which had marked their intercourse during the last day or two. He had been annoyed because a box, containing some clothes specially chosen by him for her to wear, had been taken to the wrong station, owing to her neglect in the matter of labels. The box had arrived in the nick of time, and he had remarked, as she came downstairs on the first night, that he had never seen her look more beautiful. She outshone all her cousins. He had discovered that she never made an ugly movement; he also said that the shape of her head made it possible for her, unlike most women, to wear her hair low. He had twice reproved her for being silent at dinner; and once for never attending to what he said. He had been surprised at the excellence of her French accent, but he thought it was selfish of her not to go with her mother to call upon the Middletons, because they were old family friends and very nice people. On the whole, the balance was nearly even; and, writing down a kind of conclusion in her mind which finished the sum for the present, at least, she changed the focus of her eyes, and saw nothing but the stars.

Tonight they seemed fixed with unusual firmness in the blue, and flashed back such a ripple of light into her eyes that she found herself thinking that tonight the stars were happy. Without knowing or caring more for Church practices than most people of her age, Katharine could not look into the sky at Christmas-time without feeling that, at this one season, the heavens bend over the earth with sympathy, and signal with immortal radiance that they, too, take part in her festival. Somehow, it seemed to her that they were even now beholding the procession of kings and wise men upon some road on a distant part of the earth. And yet, after gazing for another second, she found the stars did their usual work upon the mind, froze to cinders the whole of our short human history, and reduced the human body to an apelike, furry form, crouching amid the brushwood of a barbarous clod of mud.[61] This stage was soon succeeded by another, in which there was nothing in the universe save stars and the light of stars; as she looked up the pupils of her eyes so dilated with starlight that the whole of her seemed dissolved in silver and spilt over the ledges of the stars for ever and ever indefinitely through space. Somehow simultaneously, though incongruously, she was riding with the magnanimous hero upon the shore or under forest trees, and so might have continued were it not for the rebuke forcibly administered by the body, which, content with the normal conditions of life, in no way furthers any attempt on the part of the mind to alter them. She grew cold, shook herself, rose and walked towards the house.

By the light of the stars, Stogdon House looked pale and romantic, and about twice its natural size. Built by a retired admiral in the early years of the nineteenth century, the curving bow windows of the front, now filled with reddish-yellow light, suggested a portly three-decker, sailing seas where those dolphins and narwhals who disport themselves upon the edges of old maps were scattered with an impartial hand. A semicircular flight of shallow steps led to a very large door, which Katharine had left ajar. She hesitated, cast her eyes over the front of the house, marked that a light burnt in one small window upon an upper floor, and pushed the door open. For a moment she stood in the square hall, among many horned skulls, sallow globes, cracked oil-paintings and stuffed owls, hesitating, it seemed, whether she should open the door on her right, through which the stir of life reached her ears. Listening for a moment, she heard a sound which decided her, apparently, not to enter; her uncle, Sir Francis, was playing his nightly game of whist; it appeared probable that he was losing.

She went up the curving stairway, which represented the one attempt at ceremony in the otherwise rather dilapidated mansion, and down a narrow passage until she came to the room whose light she had seen from the garden. Knocking, she was told to come in. A young man, Henry Otway, was reading, with his feet on the fender. He had a fine head, the brow arched in the Elizabethan manner, but the gentle, honest eyes were rather sceptical than glowing with the Elizabethan vigour. He gave the impression that he had not yet found the cause which suited his temperament.

He turned, put down his book, and looked at her. He noticed her rather pale, dew-drenched look, as of one whose mind is not altogether settled in the body. He had often laid his difficulties before her, and guessed, in some ways hoped, that perhaps she now had need of him. At the same time, she carried on her life with such independence that he scarcely expected any confidence to be expressed in words.

'You have fled, too, then?' he said, looking at her cloak. Katharine had forgotten to remove this token of her star-gazing.

'Fled?' she asked. 'From whom d'you mean? Oh, the family party. Yes, it was hot down there, so I went into the garden.'

'And aren't you very cold?' Henry enquired, placing coal on the fire, drawing a chair up to the grate, and laying aside her cloak. Her indifference to such details often forced Henry to act the part generally taken by women in such dealings. It was one of the ties between them.

'Thank you, Henry,' she said. 'I'm not disturbing you?'

'I'm not here. I'm at Bungay,' he replied. 'I'm giving a music lesson to Harold and Julia. That was why I had to leave the table with the ladies – I'm spending the night there, and I shan't be back till late on Christmas Eve.'

'How I wish – ' Katharine began, and stopped short. 'I think these parties are a great mistake,' she added briefly, and sighed.

'Oh, horrible!' he agreed; and they both fell silent.

Her sigh made him look at her. Should he venture to ask her why she sighed? Was her reticence about her own affairs as inviolable as it had often been convenient for rather an egoistical young man to think it? But since her engagement to Rodney, Henry's feeling towards her had become rather complex: equally divided between an impulse to hurt her and an impulse to be tender to her; and all the time he suffered a curious irritation from the sense that she was drifting away from him for ever upon unknown seas. On her side, directly Katharine got into his presence, and the sense of the stars dropped from her, she knew that any intercourse between people is extremely partial; from the whole mass of her feelings, only one or two could be selected for Henry's inspection, and therefore she sighed. Then she looked at him, and their eyes meeting, much more seemed to be in common between them than had appeared possible. At any rate they had a grandfather in common; at any rate there was a kind of loyalty between them sometimes found between relations who have no other cause to like each other, as these two had.

'Well, what's the date of the wedding?' said Henry, the malicious mood now predominating.

'I think some time in March,' she replied.

'And afterwards?' he asked.

'We take a house, I suppose, somewhere in Chelsea.'

'It's very interesting,' he observed, stealing another look at her.

She lay back in her armchair, her feet high upon the side of the grate, and in front of her, presumably to screen her eyes, she held a newspaper from which she picked up a sentence or two now and again. Observing this, Henry remarked: 'Perhaps marriage will make you more human.'

At this she lowered the newspaper an inch or two, but said nothing. Indeed, she sat quite silent for over a minute.

'When you consider things like the stars, our affairs don't seem to matter very much, do they?' she said suddenly.

'I don't think I ever do consider things like the stars,' Henry replied. 'I'm not sure that that's not the explanation, though,' he added, now observing her steadily.

'I doubt whether there is an explanation,' she replied rather hurriedly, not clearly understanding what he meant.

'What? No explanation of anything?' he enquired, with a smile.

'Oh, things happen. That's about all,' she let drop in her casual, decided way.

'That certainly seems to explain some of your actions,' Henry thought to himself.

'One thing's about as good as another, and one's got to do something,' he said aloud, expressing what he supposed to be her attitude, much in her accent.

Perhaps she detected the imitation, for looking gently at him, she said, with ironical composure: 'Well, if you believe that your life must be simple, Henry.'

'But I don't believe it,' he said shortly.

'No more do I,' she replied.

'What about the stars?' he asked a moment later. 'I understand that you rule your life by the stars?'

She let this pass, either because she did not attend to it, or because the tone was not to her liking.

Once more she paused, and then she enquired: 'But do you always understand why you do everything? Ought one to understand? People like my mother understand,' she reflected. 'Now I must go down to them, I suppose, and see what's happening.'

'What could be happening?' Henry protested.

'Oh, they may want to settle something,' she replied vaguely, putting her feet on the ground, resting her chin on her hands, and looking out of her large dark eyes contemplatively at the fire.

'And then there's William,' she added, as if by an afterthought.

Henry very nearly laughed, but restrained himself.

'Do they know what coals are made of, Henry?' she asked, a moment later.

'Mares' tails, I believe,' he hazarded.

'Have you ever been down a coal-mine?' she went on.

'Don't let's talk about coal-mines, Katharine,' he protested. 'We shall probably never see each other again. When you're married – '

Tremendously to his surprise, he saw the tears stand in her eyes.

'Why do you all tease me?' she said. 'It isn't kind.'

Henry could not pretend that he was altogether ignorant of her meaning, though, certainly, he had never guessed that she minded the teasing. But before he knew what to say, her eyes were clear again, and the sudden crack in the surface was almost filled up.

'Things aren't easy, anyhow,' she stated.

Obeying an impulse of genuine affection, Henry spoke.

'Promise me, Katharine, that if I can ever help you, you will let me.'

She seemed to consider, looking once more into the red of the fire, and decided to refrain from any explanation.

'Yes, I promise that,' she said at length, and Henry felt himself gratified by her complete sincerity, and began to tell her now about the coal-mine, in obedience to her love of facts.

They were, indeed, descending the shaft in a small cage, and could hear the picks of the miners, something like the gnawing of rats, in the earth beneath them, when the door was burst open, without any knocking.

'Well, here you are!' Rodney exclaimed. Both Katharine and Henry turned round very quickly and rather guiltily. Rodney was in evening dress. It was clear that his temper was ruffled.

'That's where you've been all the time,' he repeated, looking at Katharine.

'I've only been here about ten minutes,' she replied.

'My dear Katharine, you left the drawing-room over an hour ago.'

She said nothing.

'Does it very much matter?' Henry asked.

Rodney found it hard to be unreasonable in the presence of another man, and did not answer him.

'They don't like it,' he said. 'It isn't kind to old people to leave them alone – although I've no doubt it's much more amusing to sit up here and talk to Henry.'

'We were discussing coal-mines,' said Henry urbanely.

'Yes. But we were talking about much more interesting things before that,' said Katharine.

From the apparent determination to hurt him with which she spoke, Henry thought that some sort of explosion on Rodney's part was about to take place.

'I can quite understand that,' said Rodney, with his little chuckle, leaning over the back of his chair and tapping the woodwork lightly with his fingers. They were all silent, and the silence was acutely uncomfortable to Henry, at least.

'Was it very dull, William?' Katharine suddenly asked, with a complete change of tone and a little gesture of her hand.

'Of course it was dull,' William said sulkily.

'Well, you stay and talk to Henry, and I'll go down,' she replied.

She rose as she spoke, and as she turned to leave the room, she laid her hand, with a curiously caressing gesture, upon Rodney's shoulder. Instantly Rodney clasped her hand in his, with such an impulse of emotion that Henry was annoyed, and rather ostentatiously opened a book.

'I shall come down with you,' said William, as she drew back her hand, and made as if to pass him.

'Oh no,' she said hastily. 'You stay here and talk to Henry.'

'Yes, do,' said Henry, shutting up his book again. His invitation was polite, without being precisely cordial. Rodney evidently hesitated as to the course he should pursue, but seeing Katharine at the door, he exclaimed: 'No. I want to come with you.'

She looked back, and said in a very commanding tone, and with an expression of authority upon her face: 'It's useless for you to come. I shall go to bed in ten minutes. Good-night.'

She nodded to them both, but Henry could not help noticing that her last nod was in his direction. Rodney sat down rather heavily.

His mortification was so obvious that Henry scarcely liked to open the conversation with some remark of a literary character. On the other hand, unless he checked him, Rodney might begin to talk about his feelings, and irreticence is apt to be extremely painful, at any rate in prospect. He therefore adopted a middle course; that is to say, he wrote a note upon the fly-leaf of his book, which ran, 'The situation is becoming most uncomfortable.' This he decorated with those flourishes and decorative borders which grow of themselves upon these occasions; and as he did so, he thought to himself that whatever Katharine's difficulties might be, they did not justify her behaviour. She had spoken with a kind of brutality which suggested that, whether it is natural or assumed, women have a peculiar blindness to the feelings of men.

The pencilling of this note gave Rodney time to recover himself. Perhaps, for he was a very vain man, he was more hurt that Henry had seen him rebuffed than by the rebuff itself. He was in love with Katharine, and vanity is not decreased but increased by love; especially, one may hazard, in the presence of one's own sex. But Rodney enjoyed the courage which springs from that laughable and lovable defect, and when he had mastered his first impulse, in some way to make a fool of himself, he drew inspiration from the perfect fit of his evening dress. He chose a cigarette, tapped it on the back of his hand, displayed his exquisite pumps on the edge of the fender, and summoned his self-respect.

'You've several big estates round here, Otway,' he began. 'Any good hunting? Let me see, what pack would it be? Who's your great man?'

'Sir William Budge, the sugar king, has the biggest estate. He bought out poor Stanham, who went bankrupt.'

'Which Stanham would that be? Verney or Alfred?'

'Alfred . . . I don't hunt myself. You're a great huntsman, aren't you? You have a great reputation as a horseman, anyhow,' he added, desiring to help Rodney in his effort to recover his complacency.

'Oh, I love riding,' Rodney replied. 'Could I get a horse down here? Stupid of me! I forgot to bring any clothes. I can't imagine, though, who told you I was anything of a rider?'

To tell the truth, Henry laboured under the same difficulty; he did not wish to introduce Katharine's name, and, therefore, he replied vaguely that he had always heard that Rodney was a great rider. In truth, he had heard very little about him, one way or another, accepting him as a figure often to be found in the background at his aunt's house, and inevitably, though inexplicably, engaged to his cousin.

'I don't care much for shooting,' Rodney continued; 'but one has to do it, unless one wants to be altogether out of things. I dare say there's some very pretty country round here. I stayed once at Bolham Hall.

Young Cranthorpe was up with you, wasn't he? He married old Lord Bolham's daughter. Very nice people – in their way.'

'I don't mix in that society,' Henry remarked, rather shortly. But Rodney, now started on an agreeable current of reflection, could not resist the temptation of pursuing it a little further. He appeared to himself as a man who moved easily in very good society, and knew enough about the true values of life to be himself above it.

'Oh, but you should,' he went on. 'It's well worth staying there, anyhow, once a year. They make one very comfortable, and the women are ravishing.'

'The women?' Henry thought to himself, with disgust. 'What could any woman see in you?' His tolerance was rapidly becoming exhausted, but he could not help liking Rodney nevertheless, and this appeared to him strange, for he was fastidious, and such words in another mouth would have condemned the speaker irreparably. He began, in short, to wonder what kind of creature this man who was to marry his cousin might be. Could anyone, except a rather singular character, afford to be so ridiculously vain?

'I don't think I should get on in that society,' he replied. 'I don't think I should know what to say to Lady Rose if I met her.'

'I don't find any difficulty,' Rodney chuckled. 'You talk to them about their children, if they have any, or their accomplishments – painting, gardening, poetry – they're so delightfully sympathetic. Seriously, you know I think a woman's opinion of one's poetry is always worth having. Don't ask them for their reasons. Just ask them for their feelings. Katharine, for example – '

'Katharine,' said Henry, with an emphasis upon the name, almost as if he resented Rodney's use of it, 'Katharine is very unlike most women.'

'Quite,' Rodney agreed. 'She is – ' He seemed about to describe her, and he hesitated for a long time. 'She's looking very well,' he stated, or rather almost enquired, in a different tone from that in which he had been speaking.

Henry bent his head.

'But, as a family, you're given to moods, eh?'

'Not Katharine,' said Henry, with decision.

'Not Katharine,' Rodney repeated, as if he weighed the meaning of the words. 'No, perhaps you're right. But her engagement has changed her. Naturally,' he added, 'one would expect that to be so.' He waited for Henry to confirm this statement, but Henry remained silent.

'Katharine has had a difficult life, in some ways,' he continued. 'I expect that marriage will be good for her. She has great powers.'

'Great,' said Henry, with decision.

'Yes – but now what direction d'you think they take?'

Rodney had completely dropped his pose as a man of the world, and seemed to be asking Henry to help him in a difficulty.

'I don't know,' Henry hesitated cautiously.

'D'you think children – a household – that sort of thing – d'you think that'll satisfy her? Mind, I'm out all day.'

'She would certainly be very competent,' Henry stated.

'Oh, she's wonderfully competent,' said Rodney. 'But – I get absorbed in my poetry. Well, Katharine hasn't got that. She admires my poetry, you know, but that wouldn't be enough for her?'

'No,' said Henry. He paused. 'I think you're right,' he added, as if he were summing up his thoughts. 'Katharine hasn't found herself yet. Life isn't altogether real to her yet – I sometimes think – '

'Yes?' Rodney enquired, as if he were eager for Henry to continue. 'That is what I – ' he was going on, as Henry remained silent, but the sentence was not finished, for the door opened, and they were interrupted by Henry's younger brother Gilbert, much to Henry's relief, for he had already said more than he liked.

Chapter 17

When the sun shone, as it did with unusual brightness that Christmas week, it revealed much that was faded and not altogether well kept up in Stogdon House and its grounds. In truth, Sir Francis had retired from service under the Government of India with a pension that was not adequate, in his opinion, to his services, as it certainly was not adequate to his ambitions. His career had not come up to his expectations, and although he was a very fine, white-whiskered, mahogany-coloured old man to look at, and had laid down a very choice cellar of good reading and good stories, you could not long remain ignorant of the fact that some thunderstorm had soured them; he had a grievance. This grievance dated back to the middle years of the last century, when, owing to some official intrigue, his merits had been passed over in a disgraceful manner in favour of another, his junior.

The rights and wrongs of the story, presuming that they had some existence in fact, were no longer clearly known to his wife and children; but this disappointment had played a very large part in their lives, and had poisoned the life of Sir Francis much as a disappointment in love is said to poison the whole life of a woman. Long brooding on his failure, continual arrangement and rearrangement of his deserts and rebuffs, had made Sir Francis much of an egoist, and in his retirement his temper became increasingly difficult and exacting.

His wife now offered so little resistance to his moods that she was practically useless to him. He made his daughter Eleanor into his chief confidante, and the prime of her life was being rapidly consumed by her father. To her he dictated the memoirs which were to avenge his memory, and she had to assure him constantly that his treatment had been a disgrace. Already, at the age of thirty-five, her cheeks were whitening as her mother's had whitened, but for her there would be no memories of Indian suns and Indian rivers, and clamour of children in a nursery; she would have very little of substance to think about when she sat, as Lady Otway now sat, knitting white wool, with her eyes fixed almost perpetually upon the same embroidered bird upon the same fire-screen. But then Lady Otway was one of the people for whom the great make-believe game of English social life has been invented; she spent most of her time in pretending to herself and her neighbours that she was a dignified, important, much-occupied person, of considerable social standing and sufficient wealth. In view of the actual state of things this game needed a great deal of skill; and, perhaps, at the age she had reached – she was over sixty – she played far more to deceive herself than to deceive anyone else. Moreover, the armour was wearing thin; she forgot to keep up appearances more and more.

The worn patches in the carpets, and the pallor of the drawing-room, where no chair or cover had been renewed for some years, were due not only to the miserable pension, but to the wear and tear of twelve children, eight of whom were sons. As often happens in these large families, a distinct dividing-line could be traced, about halfway in the succession, where the money for educational purposes had run short, and the six younger children had grown up far more economically than the elder. If the boys were clever, they won scholarships, and went to school; if they were not clever, they took what the family connection had to offer them. The girls accepted situations occasionally, but there were always one or two at home, nursing sick animals, tending silk-worms, or playing the flute in their bedrooms. The distinction between the elder children and the younger corresponded almost to the dis-tinction between a higher class and a lower one, for with only a haphazard education and insufficient allowances, the younger children had picked up accomplishments, friends and points of view which were not to be found within the walls of a public school or of a government office. Between the two divisions there was considerable hostility, the elder trying to patronise the younger, the younger refusing to respect the elder; but one feeling united them and instantly closed any risk of a breach – their common belief in the superiority of their own family to all others. Henry was the eldest of the younger group, and their leader; he bought strange books and joined odd societies; he went without a tie for a whole year, and had six shirts made of black flannel. He had long refused to take a seat either in a shipping office or in a tea-merchant's warehouse; and persisted, in spite of the disapproval of uncles and aunts, in practising both violin and piano, with the result that he could not perform professionally upon either. Indeed, for thirty-two years of life he had nothing more substantial to show than a manuscript book containing the score of half an opera. In this protest of his, Katharine had always given him her support, and as she was generally held to be an extremely sensible person, who dressed too well to be eccentric, he had found her support of some use. Indeed, when she came down at Christmas she usually spent a great part of her time in private conferences with Henry and with Cassandra, the youngest girl, to whom the silkworms belonged. With the younger section she had a great reputation for common sense, and for something that they despised but inwardly respected and called knowledge of the world – that is to say, of the way in which respectable elderly people, going to their clubs and dining out with ministers, think and behave. She had more than once played the part of ambassador between Lady Otway and her children. That poor lady, for instance, consulted her for advice when, one day, she opened Cassandra's bedroom door on a mission of discovery, and found the ceiling hung with mulberry-leaves, the windows blocked with cages, and the tables stacked with home-made machines for the manufacture of silk dresses.

'I wish you could help her to take an interest in something that other people are interested in, Katharine,' she observed, rather plaintively, detailing her grievances. 'It's all Henry's doing, you know, giving up her parties and taking to these nasty insects. It doesn't follow that if a man can do a thing a woman may too.'

The morning was sufficiently bright to make the chairs and sofas in Lady Otway's private sitting-room appear more than usually shabby, and the gallant gentlemen, her brothers and cousins, who had defended the Empire and left their bones on many frontiers, looked at the world through a film of yellow which the morning light seemed to have drawn across their photographs. Lady Otway sighed, it may be at the faded relics, and turned, with resignation, to her balls of wool, which, curiously and characteristically, were not an ivory-white, but rather a tarnished yellow-white. She had called her niece in for a little chat. She had always trusted her, and now more than ever, since her engagement to Rodney, which seemed to Lady Otway extremely suitable, and just what one would wish for one's own daughter. Katharine unwittingly increased her reputation for wisdom by asking to be given knitting-needles too.

'It's so very pleasant,' said Lady Otway, 'to knit while one's talking. And now, my dear Katharine, tell me about your plans.'

The emotions of the night before, which she had suppressed in such a way as to keep her awake till dawn, had left Katharine a little jaded, and thus more matter-of-fact than usual. She was quite ready to discuss her plans – houses and rents, servants and economy – without feeling that they concerned her very much. As she spoke, knitting methodically meanwhile, Lady Otway noted, with approval, the upright, responsible bearing of her niece, to whom the prospect of marriage had brought some gravity most becoming in a bride, and yet, in these days, most rare. Yes, Katharine's engagement had changed her a little.

'What a perfect daughter, or daughter-in-law!' she thought to herself, and could not help contrasting her with Cassandra, surrounded by innumerable silkworms in her bedroom.

'Yes,' she continued, glancing at Katharine with the round, greenish eyes which were as inexpressive as moist marbles, 'Katharine is like the girls of my youth. We took the serious things of life seriously.' But just as she was deriving satisfaction from this thought, and was producing some of the hoarded wisdom which none of her own daughters, alas! seemed now to need, the door opened, and Mrs Hilbery came in, or rather, did not come in, but stood in the doorway and smiled, having evidently mistaken the room.

'I never *shall* know my way about this house!' she exclaimed. 'I'm on my way to the library, and I don't want to interrupt. You and Katharine were having a little chat?'

The presence of her sister-in-law made Lady Otway slightly uneasy. How could she go on with what she was saying in Maggie's presence? for she was saying something that she had never said, all these years, to Maggie herself.

'I was telling Katharine a few little commonplaces about marriage,' she said, with a little laugh. 'Are none of my children looking after you, Maggie?'

'Marriage,' said Mrs Hilbery, coming into the room, and nodding her head once or twice, 'I always say marriage is a school. And you don't

get the prizes unless you go to school. Charlotte has won all the prizes,'
she added, giving her sister-in-law a little pat, which made Lady Otway
more uncomfortable still. She half laughed, muttered something, and
ended on a sigh.

'Aunt Charlotte was saying that it's no good being married unless you
submit to your husband,' said Katharine, framing her aunt's words into
a far more definite shape than they had really worn; and when she spoke
thus she did not appear at all old-fashioned. Lady Otway looked at her
and paused for a moment.

'Well, I really don't advise a woman who wants to have things her own
way to get married,' she said, beginning a fresh row rather elaborately.

Mrs Hilbery knew something of the circumstances which, as she
thought, had inspired this remark. In a moment her face was clouded
with sympathy which she did not quite know how to express.

'What a shame it was!' she exclaimed, forgetting that her train of
thought might not be obvious to her listeners. 'But, Charlotte, it would
have been much worse if Frank had disgraced himself in any way. And it
isn't what our husbands *get*, but what they *are*. I used to dream of white
horses and palanquins,[62] too; but still, I like the ink-pots best. And who
knows?' she concluded, looking at Katharine, 'your father may be made
a baronet tomorrow.'

Lady Otway, who was Mr Hilbery's sister, knew quite well that, in
private, the Hilberys called Sir Francis 'that old Turk', and though she
did not follow the drift of Mrs Hilbery's remarks, she knew what
prompted them.

'But if you can give way to your husband,' she said, speaking to
Katharine, as if there were a separate understanding between them, 'a
happy marriage is the happiest thing in the world.'

'Yes,' said Katharine, 'but – ' She did not mean to finish her sentence,
she merely wished to induce her mother and her aunt to go on talking
about marriage, for she was in the mood to feel that other people could
help her if they would. She went on knitting, but her fingers worked
with a decision that was oddly unlike the smooth and contemplative
sweep of Lady Otway's plump hand. Now and then she looked swiftly
at her mother, then at her aunt. Mrs Hilbery held a book in her hand,
and was on her way, as Katharine guessed, to the library, where another
paragraph was to be added to that varied assortment of paragraphs, the
Life of Richard Alardyce. Normally, Katharine would have hurried her
mother downstairs, and seen that no excuse for distraction came her
way. Her attitude towards the poet's life, however, had changed with
other changes; and she was content to forget all about her scheme of

hours. Mrs Hilbery was secretly delighted. Her relief at finding herself excused manifested itself in a series of sidelong glances of sly humour in her daughter's direction, and the indulgence put her in the best of spirits. Was she to be allowed merely to sit and talk? It was so much pleasanter to sit in a nice room filled with all sorts of interesting odds and ends which she hadn't looked at for a year, at least, than to seek out one date which contradicted another in a dictionary.

'We've all had perfect husbands,' she concluded, generously forgiving Sir Francis all his faults in a lump. 'Not that I think a bad temper is really a fault in a man. I don't mean a bad temper,' she corrected herself, with a glance obviously in the direction of Sir Francis. 'I should say a quick, impatient temper. Most, in fact *all* great men have had bad tempers – except your grandfather, Katharine,' and here she sighed, and suggested that, perhaps, she ought to go down to the library.

'But in the ordinary marriage, is it necessary to give way to one's husband?' said Katharine, taking no notice of her mother's suggestion, blind even to the depression which had now taken possession of her at the thought of her own inevitable death.

'I should say yes, certainly,' said Lady Otway, with a decision most unusual for her.

'Then one ought to make up one's mind to that before one is married,' Katharine mused, seeming to address herself.

Mrs Hilbery was not much interested in these remarks, which seemed to have a melancholy tendency, and to revive her spirits she had recourse to an infallible remedy – she looked out of the window.

'Do look at that lovely little blue bird!' she exclaimed, and her eye looked with extreme pleasure at the soft sky, at the trees, at the green fields visible behind those trees, and at the leafless branches which surrounded the body of the small blue tit. Her sympathy with nature was exquisite.

'Most women know by instinct whether they can give it or not,' Lady Otway slipped in quickly, in rather a low voice, as if she wanted to get this said while her sister-in-law's attention was diverted. 'And if not – well then, my advice would be – don't marry.'

'Oh, but marriage is the happiest life for a woman,' said Mrs Hilbery, catching the word marriage, as she brought her eyes back to the room again. Then she turned her mind to what she had said.

'It's the most *interesting* life,' she corrected herself. She looked at her daughter with a look of vague alarm. It was the kind of maternal scrutiny which suggests that in looking at her daughter a mother is really looking at herself. She was not altogether satisfied; but she purposely made no attempt to break down the reserve which, as a matter of fact, was a quality she particularly admired and depended upon in her daughter. But when her mother said that marriage was the most interesting life, Katharine felt, as she was apt to do suddenly, for no definite reason, that they understood each other, in spite of differing in every possible way. Yet the wisdom of the old seems to apply more to feelings which we have in common with the rest of the human race than to our feelings as individuals, and Katharine knew that only someone of her own age could follow her meaning. Both these elderly women seemed to her to have been content with so little happiness, and at the moment she had not sufficient force to feel certain that their version of marriage was the wrong one. In London, certainly, this temperate attitude towards her own marriage had seemed to her just. Why had she now changed? Why did it now depress her? It never occurred to her that her own conduct could be anything of a puzzle to her mother, or that elder people are as much affected by the young as the young are by them. And yet it was true that love – passion – whatever one chose to call it, had played far less part in Mrs Hilbery's life than might have seemed likely, judging from her enthusiastic and imaginative temperament. She had always been more interested by other things. Lady Otway, strange though it seemed, guessed more accurately at Katharine's state of mind than her mother did.

'Why don't we all live in the country?' exclaimed Mrs Hilbery, once more looking out of the window. 'I'm sure one would think such beautiful things if one lived in the country. No horrid slum houses to depress one, no trams or motor cars; and the people all looking so plump and cheerful. Isn't there some little cottage near you, Charlotte, which would do for us, with a spare room, perhaps, in case we asked a friend down? And we should save so much money that we should be able to travel – '

'Yes. You would find it very nice for a week or two, no doubt,' said Lady Otway. 'But what hour would you like the carriage this morning?' she continued, touching the bell.

'Katharine shall decide,' said Mrs Hilbery, feeling herself unable to prefer one hour to another. 'And I was just going to tell you, Katharine, how, when I woke this morning, everything seemed so clear in my head that if I'd had a pencil I believe I could have written quite a long chapter. When we're out on our drive I shall find us a house. A few trees round it, and a little garden, a pond with a Chinese duck, a study for your father, a study for me, and a sitting room for Katharine, because then she'll be a married lady.'

At this Katharine shivered a little, drew up to the fire, and warmed her hands by spreading them over the topmost peak of the coal. She wished to bring the talk back to marriage again, in order to hear Aunt Charlotte's views, but she did not know how to do this.

'Let me look at your engagement ring, Aunt Charlotte,' she said, noticing her own.

She took the cluster of green stones and turned it round and round, but she did not know what to say next.

'That poor old ring was a sad disappointment to me when I first had it,' Lady Otway mused. 'I'd set my heart on a diamond ring, but I never liked to tell Frank, naturally. He bought it at Simla.'[63]

Katharine turned the ring round once more, and gave it back to her aunt without speaking. And while she turned it round her lips set themselves firmly together, and it seemed to her that she could satisfy William as these women had satisfied their husbands; she could pretend to like emeralds when she preferred diamonds. Having replaced her ring, Lady Otway remarked that it was chilly, though not more so than one must expect at this time of year. Indeed, one ought to be thankful to see the sun at all, and she advised them both to dress warmly for their drive. Her aunt's stock of commonplaces, Katharine sometimes suspected, had been laid in on purpose to fill silences with, and had little to do with her private thoughts. But at this moment they seemed terribly in keeping with her own conclusions, so that she took up her knitting again and listened, chiefly with a view to confirming herself in the belief that to be engaged to marry someone with whom you are not in love is an inevitable step in a world where the existence of passion is only a traveller's story brought from the heart of deep forests and told so rarely that wise people doubt whether the story can be true. She did her best to listen to her mother asking for news of John, and to her aunt replying with the authentic history of Hilda's engagement to an officer in the Indian Army, but she cast her mind alternately towards forest paths and starry blossoms, and towards pages of neatly written mathematical signs. When her mind took this turn her marriage seemed no more than an archway through which it was necessary to pass in order to have her desire. At such times the current of her nature ran in its deep narrow channel with great force and with an alarming lack of consideration for the feelings of others. Just as the two elder ladies had finished their survey of the family prospects, and Lady Otway was nervously anticipating some general statement as to life and death from her sister-in-law, Cassandra burst into the room with the news that the carriage was at the door.

'Why didn't Andrews tell me himself?' said Lady Otway, peevishly, blaming her servants for not living up to her ideals.

When Mrs Hilbery and Katharine arrived in the hall, ready dressed for their drive, they found that the usual discussion was going forward as to the plans of the rest of the family. In token of this, a great many doors were opening and shutting, two or three people stood irresolutely on the stairs, now going a few steps up, and now a few steps down, and Sir Francis himself had come out from his study, with *The Times* under his arm, and a complaint about noise and draughts from the open door which, at least, had the effect of bundling the people who did not want to go into the carriage, and sending those who did not want to stay back to their rooms. It was decided that Mrs Hilbery, Katharine, Rodney, and Henry should drive to Lincoln, and anyone else who wished to go should follow on bicycles or in the pony-cart. Everyone who stayed at Stogdon House had to make this expedition to Lincoln in obedience to Lady Otway's conception of the right way to entertain her guests, which she had imbibed from reading in fashionable papers of the behaviour of Christmas parties in ducal houses. The carriage horses were both fat and aged, still they matched; the carriage was shaky and uncomfortable, but the Otway arms were visible on the panels. Lady Otway stood on the topmost step, wrapped in a white shawl, and waved her hand almost mechanically until they had turned the corner under the laurel bushes, when she retired indoors with a sense that she had played her part, and a sigh at the thought that none of her children felt it necessary to play theirs.

The carriage bowled along smoothly over the gently curving road. Mrs Hilbery dropped into a pleasant, inattentive state of mind, in which she was conscious of the running green lines of the hedges, of the swelling ploughland and of the mild blue sky, which served her, after the first five minutes, for a pastoral background to the drama of human life; and then she thought of a cottage garden, with the flash of yellow daffodils against blue water; and what with the arrangement of these different prospects, and the shaping of two or three lovely phrases, she did not notice that the young people in the carriage were almost silent. Henry, indeed, had been included against his wish, and revenged himself by observing Katharine and Rodney with disillusioned eyes; while Katharine was in a state of gloomy self-suppression which resulted in complete apathy. When Rodney spoke to her she either said, 'Hum!' or assented so listlessly that he addressed his next remark to her mother. His deference was agreeable to her, his manners were exemplary; and when the church towers and factory chimneys of the town came into sight, she roused herself, and recalled memories of the fair summer of 1853, which fitted in harmoniously with what she was dreaming of the future.

Chapter 18

But other passengers were approaching Lincoln meanwhile by other roads on foot. A county town draws the inhabitants of all vicarages, farms, country houses and wayside cottages, within a radius of ten miles at least, once or twice a week to its streets; and among them, on this occasion, were Ralph Denham and Mary Datchet. They despised the roads, and took their way across the fields; and yet, from their appearance, it did not seem as if they cared much where they walked so long as the way did not actually trip them up. When they left the vicarage, they had begun an argument which swung their feet along so rhythmically in time with it that they covered the ground at over four miles an hour, and saw nothing of the hedgerows, the swelling ploughland or the mild blue sky. What they saw were the Houses of Parliament and the Government Offices in Whitehall. They both belonged to the class which is conscious of having lost its birthright in these great structures and is seeking to build another kind of lodging for its own notion of law and government. Purposely, perhaps, Mary did not agree with Ralph; she loved to feel her mind in conflict with his, and to be certain that he spared her female judgement no ounce of his male muscularity. He seemed to argue as fiercely with her as if she were his brother. They were alike, however, in believing that it behoved them to take in hand the repair and reconstruction of the fabric of England. They agreed in thinking that nature has not been generous in the endowment of our councillors. They agreed, unconsciously, in a mute love for the muddy field through which they tramped, with eyes narrowed close by the concentration of their minds. At length they drew breath, let the argument fly away into the limbo of other good arguments, and, leaning over a gate, opened their eyes for the first time and looked about them. Their feet tingled with warm blood and their breath rose in steam around them. The bodily exercise made them both feel more direct and less self-conscious than usual, and Mary, indeed, was overcome by a sort of light-headedness which made it seem to her that it mattered very little what happened next. It mattered so little, indeed, that she felt herself on the point of saying to Ralph: 'I love you; I shall never love anybody else. Marry me or leave me; think what you like of me – I don't care a straw.' At the moment, however, speech or silence seemed immaterial, and she merely clapped her hands together and looked at the distant woods, with the rust-like bloom on their brown, and the green and blue landscape through the steam of her own breath. It seemed a mere toss-up whether she said, 'I love you,' or whether she said, 'I love the beech trees,' or only, 'I love – I love.'

'Do you know, Mary,' Ralph suddenly interrupted her, 'I've made up my mind.'

Her indifference must have been superficial, for it disappeared at once. Indeed, she lost sight of the trees, and saw her own hand upon the topmost bar of the gate with extreme distinctness, while he went on: 'I've made up my mind to chuck my work and live down here. I want you to tell me about that cottage you spoke of. However, I suppose there'll be no difficulty about getting a cottage, will there?' He spoke with an assumption of carelessness as if expecting her to dissuade him.

She still waited, as if for him to continue; she was convinced that in some roundabout way he approached the subject of their marriage.

'I can't stand the office any longer,' he proceeded. 'I don't know what my family will say; but I'm sure I'm right. Don't you think so?'

'Live down here by yourself?' she asked.

'Some old woman would do for me, I suppose,' he replied. 'I'm sick of the whole thing,' he went on, and opened the gate with a jerk. They began to cross the next field walking side by side.

'I tell you, Mary, it's utter destruction, working away, day after day, at stuff that doesn't matter a damn to anyone. I've stood eight years of it, and I'm not going to stand it any longer. I suppose this all seems to you mad, though?'

By this time Mary had recovered her self-control.

'No. I thought you weren't happy,' she said.

'Why did you think that?' he asked, with some surprise.

'Don't you remember that morning in Lincoln's Inn Fields?' she asked.

'Yes,' said Ralph, slackening his pace and remembering Katharine and her engagement, the purple leaves stamped into the path, the white paper radiant under the electric light, and the hopelessness which seemed to surround all these things.

'You're right, Mary,' he said, with something of an effort, 'though I don't know how you guessed it.'

She was silent, hoping that he might tell her the reason of his unhappiness, for his excuses had not deceived her.

'I was unhappy – very unhappy,' he repeated. Some six weeks separated him from that afternoon when he had sat upon the Embankment watching his visions dissolve in mist as the waters swam past and the sense of his desolation still made him shiver. He had not recovered in the least from that depression. Here was an opportunity for making himself face it, as he felt that he ought to; for, by this time, no doubt, it was only a sentimental ghost, better exorcised by ruthless exposure to such an eye as Mary's, than allowed to underlie all his actions and thoughts as had been the case ever since he first saw Katharine Hilbery pouring out tea. He must begin, however, by mentioning her name, and this he found it impossible to do. He persuaded himself that he could make an honest statement without speaking her name; he persuaded himself that his feeling had very little to do with her.

'Unhappiness is a state of mind,' he said, 'by which I mean that it is not necessarily the result of any particular cause.'

This rather stilted beginning did not please him, and it became more and more obvious to him that, whatever he might say, his unhappiness had been directly caused by Katharine.

'I began to find my life unsatisfactory,' he started afresh. 'It seemed to me meaningless.' He paused again, but felt that this, at any rate, was true, and that on these lines he could go on.

'All this money-making and working ten hours a day in an office, what's it *for*? When one's a boy, you see, one's head is so full of dreams that it doesn't seem to matter what one does. And if you're ambitious, you're all right; you've got a reason for going on. Now my reasons ceased to satisfy me. Perhaps I never had any. That's very likely now I come to think of it. (What reason is there for anything, though?) Still, it's impossible, after a certain age, to take oneself in satisfactorily. And I know what carried me on' – for a good reason now occurred to him – 'I wanted to be the saviour of my family and all that kind of thing. I wanted them to get on in the world. That was a lie, of course – a kind of self-glorification, too. Like most people, I suppose, I've lived almost entirely among delusions, and now I'm at the awkward stage of finding it out. I want another delusion to go on with. That's what my unhappiness amounts to, Mary.'

There were two reasons that kept Mary very silent during this speech, and drew curiously straight lines upon her face. In the first place, Ralph made no mention of marriage; in the second, he was not speaking the truth.

'I don't think it will be difficult to find a cottage,' she said, with cheerful hardness, ignoring the whole of this statement. 'You've got a little money, haven't you? Yes,' she concluded, 'I don't see why it shouldn't be a very good plan.'

They crossed the field in complete silence. Ralph was surprised by her remark and a little hurt, and yet, on the whole, rather pleased. He had convinced himself that it was impossible to lay his case truthfully before Mary, and, secretly, he was relieved to find that he had not parted with his dream to her. She was, as he had always found her, the sensible, loyal friend, the woman he trusted; whose sympathy he could count upon, provided he kept within certain limits. He was not displeased to find that those limits were very clearly marked. When they had crossed the next hedge she said to him: 'Yes, Ralph, it's time you made a break. I've come to the same conclusion myself. Only it won't be a country cottage in my case; it'll be America. America!' she cried. 'That's the place for me! They'll teach me something about organising a movement there, and I'll come back and show you how to do it.'

If she meant consciously or unconsciously to belittle the seclusion and security of a country cottage, she did not succeed; for Ralph's determination was genuine. But she made him visualise her in her own character, so that he looked quickly at her, as she walked a little in front of him across the ploughed field; for the first time that morning he saw her independently of him or of his preoccupation with Katharine. He seemed to see her marching ahead, a rather clumsy but powerful and independent figure, for whose courage he felt the greatest respect.

'Don't go away, Mary!' he exclaimed, and stopped.

'That's what you said before, Ralph,' she returned, without looking at him. 'You want to go away yourself and you don't want me to go away. That's not very sensible, is it?'

'Mary,' he cried, stung by the remembrance of his exacting and dictatorial ways with her, 'what a brute I've been to you!'

It took all her strength to keep the tears from springing, and to thrust back her assurance that she would forgive him till Doomsday if he chose. She was preserved from doing so only by a stubborn kind of respect for herself which lay at the root of her nature and forbade surrender, even in moments of almost overwhelming passion. Now, when all was tempest and high-running waves, she knew of a land where the sun shone clear upon Italian grammars and files of docketed papers. Nevertheless, from the skeleton pallor of that land and the rocks that broke its surface, she knew that her life there would be harsh and lonely almost beyond endurance. She walked steadily a little in front of him across the ploughed field. Their way took them round the verge of a wood of thin trees standing at the edge of a steep fold in the land. Looking between the tree-trunks, Ralph saw laid out on the perfectly flat and richly green meadow at the bottom of the hill a small grey manor-house, with ponds, terraces and clipped hedges in front of it, a farm building or so at the side, and a screen of fir trees rising behind, all perfectly sheltered and self-sufficient. Behind the house the hill rose again, and the trees on the farther summit stood upright against the sky, which appeared of a more intense blue between their trunks. His mind at once was filled with a sense of the actual presence of Katharine; the grey house and the intense blue sky gave him the feeling of her presence close by. He leant against a tree, forming her name beneath his breath: 'Katharine. Katharine,' he said aloud, and then, looking round, saw Mary walking slowly away from him, tearing a long spray of ivy from the trees as she passed them. She seemed so definitely opposed to the vision he held in his mind that he returned to it with a gesture of impatience.

'Katharine, Katharine,' he repeated, and seemed to himself to be with her. He lost his sense of all that surrounded him; all substantial things – the hour of the day, what we have done and are about to do, the presence of other people and the support we derive from seeing their belief in a common reality – all this slipped from him. So he might have felt if the earth had dropped from his feet, and the empty blue had hung all round him, and the air had been steeped in the presence of one woman. The chirp of a robin on the bough above his head awakened him, and his awakenment was accompanied by a sigh. Here was the world in which he had lived; here the ploughed field, the high road yonder, and Mary, stripping ivy from the trees. When he came up with her he linked his arm through hers and said: 'Now, Mary, what's all this about America?'

There was a brotherly kindness in his voice which seemed to her magnanimous, when she reflected that she had cut short his explanations and shown little interest in his change of plan. She gave him her reasons for thinking that she might profit by such a journey, omitting the one reason which had set all the rest in motion. He listened attentively, and made no attempt to dissuade her. In truth, he found himself curiously eager to make certain of her good sense, and accepted each fresh proof of it with satisfaction, as though it helped him to make up his mind about something. She forgot the pain he had caused her, and in place of it she became conscious of a steady tide of well-being which harmonised very aptly with the tramp of their feet upon the dry road and the support of his arm. The comfort was the more glowing in that it seemed to be the reward of her determination to behave to him simply and without attempting to be other than she was. Instead of making out an interest in the poets, she avoided them instinctively, and dwelt rather insistently upon the practical nature of her gifts.

In a practical way she asked for particulars of his cottage, which hardly existed in his mind, and corrected his vagueness.

'You must see that there's water,' she insisted, with an exaggeration of interest. She avoided asking him what he meant to do in this cottage, and, at last, when all the practical details had been thrashed out as much as possible, he rewarded her by a more intimate statement.

'One of the rooms,' he said, 'must be my study, for, you see, Mary, I'm going to write a book.' Here he withdrew his arm from hers, lit his pipe, and they tramped on in a sagacious kind of comradeship, the most complete they had attained in all their friendship.

'And what's your book to be about?' she said, as boldly as if she had never come to grief with Ralph in talking about books. He told her unhesitatingly that he meant to write the history of the English village from Saxon days to the present time. Some such plan had lain as a seed in his mind for many years; and now that he had decided, in a flash, to give up his profession, the seed grew in the space of twenty minutes both tall and lusty. He was surprised himself at the positive way in which he spoke. It was the same with the question of his cottage. That had come into existence, too, in an unromantic shape – a square white house standing just off the high road, no doubt, with a neighbour who kept a pig and a dozen squalling children; for these plans were shorn of all romance in his mind, and the pleasure he derived from thinking of them was checked directly it passed a very sober limit. So a sensible man who has lost his chance of some beautiful inheritance might tread out the narrow bounds of his actual dwelling-place, and assure himself that life is supportable within its demesne, only one must grow turnips and cabbages, not melons and pomegranates. Certainly Ralph took some pride in the resources of his mind, and was insensibly helped to right himself by Mary's trust in him. She wound her ivy spray round her ash plant, and for the first time for many days, when alone with Ralph, set no spies upon her motives, sayings and feelings, but surrendered herself to complete happiness.

Thus talking, with easy silences and some pauses to look at the view over the hedge and to decide upon the species of a little grey-brown bird slipping among the twigs, they walked into Lincoln, and after strolling up and down the main street, decided upon an inn where the rounded window suggested substantial fare, nor were they mistaken. For over a hundred and fifty years hot joints, potatoes, greens and apple puddings had been served to generations of country gentlemen, and now, sitting at a table in the hollow of the bow window, Ralph and Mary took their share of this perennial feast. Looking across the joint, halfway through the meal, Mary wondered whether Ralph would ever come to look quite like the other people in the room. Would he be absorbed among the round pink faces, pricked with little white bristles, the calves fitted in shiny brown leather, the black-and-white check suits, which were sprinkled about in the same room with them? She half hoped so; she thought that it was only in his mind that he was different. She did not wish him to be too different from other people. The walk had given him a ruddy colour, too, and his eyes were lit up by a steady, honest light, which could not make the simplest farmer feel ill at ease, or suggest to the most devout of clergymen a disposition to sneer at his faith. She loved the steep cliff of his forehead, and compared it to the brow of a young Greek horseman, who reins his horse back so sharply that it half falls on its haunches. He always seemed to her like a rider on a spirited horse. And there was an exaltation to her in being with him, because there was a risk that he would not be able to keep to the right pace among other people. Sitting opposite him at the little table in the window, she came back to that state of careless exaltation which had overcome her when they halted by the gate, but now it was accompanied by a sense of sanity and security, for she felt that they had a feeling in common which scarcely needed embodiment in words. How silent he was! leaning his forehead on his hand, now and then, and again looking steadily and gravely at the backs of the two men at the next table, with so little self-consciousness that she could almost watch his mind placing one thought solidly upon the top of another; she thought that she could feel him thinking, through the shade of her fingers, and she could anticipate the exact moment when he would put an end to his thought and turn a little in his chair and say: 'Well, Mary – ?' inviting her to take up the thread of thought where he had dropped it.

And at that very moment he turned just so, and said: 'Well, Mary?' with the curious touch of diffidence which she loved in him.

She laughed, and she explained her laugh on the spur of the moment by the look of the people in the street below. There was a motor car, with an old lady swathed in blue veils, and a lady's maid on the seat opposite, holding a King Charles's spaniel; there was a country-woman wheeling a perambulator full of sticks down the middle of the road; there was a bailiff in gaiters discussing the state of the cattle market with a dissenting minister – so she defined them.

She ran over this list without any fear that her companion would think her trivial. Indeed, whether it was due to the warmth of the room or to the good roast beef, or whether Ralph had achieved the process which is called making up one's mind, certainly he had given up testing

the good sense, the independent character, the intelligence shown in
her remarks. He had been building one of those piles of thought, as
ramshackle and fantastic as a Chinese pagoda, half from words let fall
by gentlemen in gaiters, half from the litter in his own mind, about
duck shooting and legal history, about the Roman occupation of
Lincoln and the relations of country gentlemen with their wives, when,
from all this disconnected rambling, there suddenly formed itself in
his mind the idea that he would ask Mary to marry him. The idea was
so spontaneous that it seemed to shape itself of its own accord before
his eyes. It was then that he turned round and made use of his old,
instinctive phrase: 'Well, Mary – ?'

As it presented itself to him at first, the idea was so new and interesting
that he was half inclined to address it, without more ado, to Mary
herself. His natural instinct to divide his thoughts carefully into two
different classes before he expressed them to her prevailed. But as he
watched her looking out of the window and describing the old lady, the
woman with the perambulator, the bailiff and the dissenting minister,
his eyes filled involuntarily with tears. He would have liked to lay his
head on her shoulder and sob, while she parted his hair with her fingers
and soothed him and said: 'There, there. Don't cry! Tell me why you're
crying – '; and they would clasp each other tight, and her arms would
hold him like his mother's. He felt that he was very lonely, and that he
was afraid of the other people in the room.

'How damnable this all is!' he exclaimed abruptly.

'What are you talking about?' she replied, rather vaguely, still looking
out of the window.

He resented this divided attention more than, perhaps, he knew, and
he thought how Mary would soon be on her way to America.

'Mary,' he said, 'I want to talk to you. Haven't we nearly done? Why
don't they take away these plates?'

Mary felt his agitation without looking at him; she felt convinced that
she knew what it was that he wished to say to her.

'They'll come all in good time,' she said; and felt it necessary to
display her extreme calmness by lifting a salt-cellar and sweeping up a
little heap of breadcrumbs.

'I want to apologise,' Ralph continued, not quite knowing what he
was about to say, but feeling some curious instinct which urged him to
commit himself irrevocably, and to prevent the moment of intimacy
from passing.

'I think I've treated you very badly. That is, I've told you lies. Did you
guess that I was lying to you? Once in Lincoln's Inn Fields and again

today on our walk. I am a liar, Mary. Did you know that? Do you think you do know me?'

'I think I do,' she said.

At this point the waiter changed their plates.

'It's true I don't want you to go to America,' he said, looking fixedly at the tablecloth. 'In fact, my feelings towards you seem to be utterly and damnably bad,' he said energetically, although forced to keep his voice low.

'If I weren't a selfish beast I should tell you to have nothing more to do with me. And yet, Mary, in spite of the fact that I believe what I'm saying, I also believe that it's good we should know each other – the world being what it is, you see – ' and by a nod of his head he indicated the other occupants of the room, 'for, of course, in an ideal state of things, in a decent community even, there's no doubt you shouldn't have anything to do with me – seriously, that is.'

'You forget that I'm not an ideal character, either,' said Mary, in the same low and very earnest tones, which, in spite of being almost inaudible, surrounded their table with an atmosphere of concentration which was quite perceptible to the other diners, who glanced at them now and then with a queer mixture of kindness, amusement and curiosity.

'I'm much more selfish than I let on, and I'm worldly a little – more than you think, anyhow. I like bossing things – perhaps that's my greatest fault. I've none of your passion for – ' here she hesitated, and glanced at him, as if to ascertain what his passion was for – 'for the truth,' she added, as if she had found what she sought indisputably.

'I've told you I'm a liar,' Ralph repeated obstinately.

'Oh, in little things, I dare say,' she said impatiently. 'But not in real ones, and that's what matters. I dare say I'm more truthful than you are in small ways. But I could never care' – she was surprised to find herself speaking the word, and had to force herself to speak it out – 'for anyone who was a liar in that way. I love the truth a certain amount – a considerable amount – but not in the way you love it.' Her voice sank, became inaudible, and wavered as if she could scarcely keep herself from tears.

'Good heavens!' Ralph exclaimed to himself. 'She loves me! Why did I never see it before? She's going to cry; no, but she can't speak.'

The certainty overwhelmed him so that he scarcely knew what he was doing; the blood rushed to his cheeks, and although he had quite made up his mind to ask her to marry him, the certainty that she loved him seemed to change the situation so completely that he could not do it. He did not dare to look at her. If she cried, he did not know what he should do. It seemed to him that something of a terrible and devastating nature had happened. The waiter changed their plates once more.

In his agitation Ralph rose, turned his back upon Mary, and looked out of the window. The people in the street seemed to him only a dissolving and combining pattern of black particles; which, for the moment, represented very well the involuntary procession of feelings and thoughts which formed and dissolved in rapid succession in his own mind. At one moment he exulted in the thought that Mary loved him; at the next, it seemed that he was without feeling for her; her love was repulsive to him. Now he felt urged to marry her at once; now to disappear and never see her again. In order to control this disorderly race of thought he forced himself to read the name on the chemist's shop directly opposite him; then to examine the objects in the shop windows, and then to focus his eyes exactly upon a little group of women looking in at the great windows of a large draper's shop. This discipline having given him at least a superficial control of himself, he was about to turn and ask the waiter to bring the bill, when his eye was caught by a tall figure walking quickly along the opposite pavement – a tall figure, upright, dark and commanding, much detached from her surroundings. She held her gloves in her left hand, and the left hand was bare. All this Ralph noticed and enumerated and recognised before he put a name to the whole – Katharine Hilbery. She seemed to be looking for somebody. Her eyes, in fact, scanned both sides of the street, and for one second were raised directly to the bow window in which Ralph stood; but she looked away again instantly without giving any sign that she had seen him. This sudden apparition had an extra-ordinary effect upon him. It was as if he had thought of her so intensely that his mind had formed the shape of her, rather than that he had seen her in the flesh outside in the street. And yet he had not been thinking of her at all. The impression was so intense that he could not dismiss it, nor even think whether he had seen her or merely imagined her. He sat down at once, and said, briefly and strangely, rather to himself than to Mary: 'That was Katharine Hilbery.'

'Katharine Hilbery? What do you mean?' she asked, hardly under-standing from his manner whether he had seen her or not.

'Katharine Hilbery,' he repeated. 'But she's gone now.'

'Katharine Hilbery!' Mary thought, in an instant of blinding revelation; 'I've always known it was Katharine Hilbery!' She knew it all now.

After a moment of downcast stupor, she raised her eyes, looked steadily at Ralph, and caught his fixed and dreamy gaze levelled at a point far beyond their surroundings, a point that she had never reached in all the time that she had known him. She noticed the lips just parted, the fingers loosely clenched, the whole attitude of rapt contemplation, which fell like a veil between them. She noticed everything about him; if there had been other signs of his utter alienation she would have sought them out, too, for she felt that it was only by heaping one truth upon another that she could keep herself sitting there, upright. The truth seemed to support her; it struck her, even as she looked at his face, that the light of truth was shining far away beyond him; the light of truth, she seemed to frame the words as she rose to go, shines on a world not to be shaken by our personal calamities.

Ralph handed her her coat and her stick. She took them, fastened the coat securely, grasped the stick firmly. The ivy spray was still twisted about the handle; this one sacrifice, she thought, she might make to sentimentality and personality, and she picked two leaves from the ivy and put them in her pocket before she disencumbered her stick of the rest of it. She grasped the stick in the middle, and settled her fur cap closely upon her head, as if she must be in trim for a long and stormy walk. Next, standing in the middle of the road, she took a slip of paper from her purse, and read out loud a list of commissions entrusted to her – fruit, butter, string, and so on; and all the time she never spoke directly to Ralph or looked at him.

Ralph heard her giving orders to attentive, rosy-cheeked men in white aprons, and in spite of his own preoccupation, he commented upon the determination with which she made her wishes known. Once more he began, automatically, to take stock of her characteristics. Standing thus, superficially observant and stirring the sawdust on the floor meditatively with the toe of his boot, he was roused by a musical and familiar voice behind him, accompanied by a light touch upon his shoulder.

'I'm not mistaken? Surely Mr Denham? I caught a glimpse of your coat through the window, and I felt sure that I knew your coat. Have you seen Katharine or William? I'm wandering about Lincoln looking for the ruins.'[64]

It was Mrs Hilbery; her entrance created some stir in the shop; many people looked at her.

'First of all, tell me where I am,' she demanded, but, catching sight of the attentive shopman, she appealed to him. 'The ruins – my party is waiting for me at the ruins. The Roman ruins – or Greek, Mr Denham? Your town has a great many beautiful things in it, but I wish it hadn't so many ruins. I never saw such delightful little pots of honey in my life –

are they made by your own bees? Please give me one of those little pots, and tell me how I shall find my way to the ruins.'

'And now,' she continued, having received the information and the pot of honey, having been introduced to Mary, and having insisted that they should accompany her back to the ruins, since in a town with so many turnings, such prospects, such delightful little half-naked boys dabbling in pools, such Venetian canals, such old blue china in the curiosity shops, it was impossible for one person all alone to find her way to the ruins. 'Now,' she exclaimed, 'please tell me what you're doing here, Mr Denham – for you *are* Mr Denham, aren't you?' she enquired, gazing at him with a sudden suspicion of her own accuracy. 'The brilliant young man who writes for the *Review*, I mean? Only yesterday my husband was telling me he thought you one of the cleverest young men he knew. Certainly, you've been the messenger of providence to me, for unless I'd seen you I'm sure I should never have found the ruins at all.'

They had reached the Roman arch when Mrs Hilbery caught sight of her own party, standing like sentinels facing up and down the road so as to intercept her if, as they expected, she had got lodged in some shop.

'I've found something much better than ruins!' she exclaimed. 'I've found two friends who told me how to find you, which I could never have done without them. They must come and have tea with us. What a pity that we've just had luncheon.' Could they not somehow revoke that meal?

Katharine, who had gone a few steps by herself down the road, and was investigating the window of an ironmonger, as if her mother might have got herself concealed among mowing-machines and garden-shears, turned sharply on hearing her voice, and came towards them. She was a great deal surprised to see Denham and Mary Datchet. Whether the cordiality with which she greeted them was merely that which is natural to a surprise meeting in the country, or whether she was really glad to see them both, at any rate she exclaimed with unusual pleasure as she shook hands: 'I never knew you lived here. Why didn't you say so, and we could have met? And are you staying with Mary?' she continued, turning to Ralph. 'What a pity we didn't meet before.'

Thus confronted at a distance of only a few feet by the real body of the woman about whom he had dreamt so many million dreams, Ralph stammered; he made a clutch at his self-control; the colour either came to his cheeks or left them, he knew not which; but he was determined to face her and track down in the cold light of day whatever vestige of truth there might be in his persistent imaginations. He did not succeed in saying anything. It was Mary who spoke for both of them. He was struck dumb by finding that Katharine was quite different, in some strange way, from his memory, so that he had to dismiss his old view in order to accept the new one. The wind was blowing her crimson scarf across her face; the wind had already loosened her hair, which looped across the corner of one of the large, dark eyes which, so he used to think, looked sad; now they looked bright with the brightness of the sea struck by an unclouded ray; everything about her seemed rapid, fragmentary, and full of a kind of racing speed. He realised suddenly that he had never seen her in the daylight before.

Meanwhile, it was decided that it was too late to go in search of ruins as they had intended; and the whole party began to walk towards the stables where the carriage had been put up.

'Do you know,' said Katharine, keeping slightly in advance of the rest with Ralph, 'I thought I saw you this morning, standing at a window. But I decided that it couldn't be you. And it must have been you all the same.'

'Yes, I thought I saw you – but it wasn't you,' he replied.

This remark, and the rough strain in his voice, recalled to her memory so many difficult speeches and abortive meetings that she was jerked directly back to the London drawing-room, the family relics and the tea-table; and at the same time recalled some half-finished or interrupted remark which she had wanted to make herself or to hear from him – she could not remember what it was.

'I expect it was me,' she said. 'I was looking for my mother. It happens every time we come to Lincoln. In fact, there never was a family so unable to take care of itself as ours is. Not that it very much matters, because someone always turns up in the nick of time to help us out of our scrapes. Once I was left in a field with a bull when I was a baby – but where did we leave the carriage? Down that street or the next? The next, I think.' She glanced back and saw that the others were following obediently, listening to certain memories of Lincoln upon which Mrs Hilbery had started. 'But what are you doing here?' she asked.

'I'm buying a cottage. I'm going to live here – as soon as I can find a cottage, and Mary tells me there'll be no difficulty about that.'

'But,' she exclaimed, almost standing still in her surprise, 'you will give up the Bar, then?' It flashed across her mind that he must already be engaged to Mary.

'The solicitor's office? Yes. I'm giving that up.'

'But why?' she asked. She answered herself at once, with a curious change from rapid speech to an almost melancholy tone. 'I think you're very wise to give it up. You will be much happier.'

At this very moment, when her words seemed to be striking a path into the future for him, they stepped into the yard of an inn, and there beheld the family coach of the Otways, to which one sleek horse was already attached, while the second was being led out of the stable door by the ostler.

'I don't know what one means by happiness,' he said briefly, having to step aside in order to avoid a groom with a bucket. 'Why do you think I shall be happy? I don't expect to be anything of the kind. I expect to be rather less unhappy. I shall write a book and curse my charwoman – if happiness consists in that. What do you think?'

She could not answer because they were immediately surrounded by other members of the party – by Mrs Hilbery and Mary, Henry Otway and William.

Rodney went up to Katharine immediately and said to her: 'Henry is going to drive home with your mother, and I suggest that they should put us down halfway and let us walk back.'

Katharine nodded her head. She glanced at him with an oddly furtive expression.

'Unfortunately we go in opposite directions, or we might have given you a lift,' he continued to Denham. His manner was unusually peremptory; he seemed anxious to hasten the departure, and Katharine looked at him from time to time, as Denham noticed, with an expression half of enquiry, half of annoyance. She at once helped her mother into her cloak, and said to Mary: 'I want to see you. Are you going back to London at once? I will write.' She half smiled at Ralph, but her look was a little overcast by something she was thinking, and in a very few minutes the Otway carriage rolled out of the stable yard and turned down the high road leading to the village of Lampsher.

The return drive was almost as silent as the drive from home had been in the morning; indeed, Mrs Hilbery leant back with closed eyes in her corner, and either slept or feigned sleep, as her habit was in the intervals between the seasons of active exertion, or continued the story which she had begun to tell herself that morning.

About two miles from Lampsher the road ran over the rounded summit of the heath, a lonely spot marked by an obelisk of granite, setting forth the gratitude of some great lady of the eighteenth century who had been set upon by highwaymen at this spot and delivered from death just as hope seemed lost. In summer it was a pleasant place, for the deep woods on either side murmured, and the heather, which grew thick round the granite pedestal, made the light breeze taste sweetly; in winter the sighing of the trees was deepened to a hollow sound, and the heath was as grey and almost as solitary as the empty sweep of the clouds above it.

Here Rodney stopped the carriage and helped Katharine to alight. Henry, too, gave her his hand, and fancied that she pressed it very slightly in parting as if she sent him a message. But the carriage rolled on immediately, without wakening Mrs Hilbery, and left the couple standing by the obelisk. That Rodney was angry with her and had made this opportunity for speaking to her, Katharine knew very well; she was neither glad nor sorry that the time had come, nor, indeed, knew what to expect, and thus remained silent. The carriage grew smaller and smaller upon the dusky road, and still Rodney did not speak. Perhaps, she thought, he waited until the last sign of the carriage had disappeared beneath the curve of the road and they were left entirely alone. To cloak their silence she read the writing on the obelisk, to do which she had to walk completely round it. She was murmuring a word to two of the pious lady's thanks above her breath when Rodney joined her. In silence they set out along the cart-track which skirted the verge of the trees.

To break the silence was exactly what Rodney wished to do, and yet could not do to his own satisfaction. In company it was far easier to approach Katharine; alone with her, the aloofness and force of her character checked all his natural methods of attack. He believed that she had behaved very badly to him, but each separate instance of unkindness seemed too petty to be advanced when they were alone together.

'There's no need for us to race,' he complained at last; upon which she immediately slackened her pace, and walked too slowly to suit him. In desperation he said the first thing he thought of, very peevishly and without the dignified prelude which he had intended.

'I've not enjoyed my holiday.'

'No?'

'No. I shall be glad to get back to work again.'

'Saturday, Sunday, Monday – there are only three days more,' she counted.

'No one enjoys being made a fool of before other people,' he blurted out, for his irritation rose as she spoke, and got the better of his awe of her, and was inflamed by that awe.

'That refers to me, I suppose,' she said calmly.

'Every day since we've been here you've done something to make me appear ridiculous,' he went on. 'Of course, so long as it amuses you, you're welcome; but we have to remember that we are going to spend our lives together. I asked you, only this morning, for example, to come out and take a turn with me in the garden. I was waiting for you ten minutes, and you never came. Everyone saw me waiting. The stable-boys saw me. I was so ashamed that I went in. Then, on the drive you hardly spoke to me. Henry noticed it. Everyone notices it . . . You find no difficulty in talking to Henry, though.'

She noted these various complaints and determined philosophically to answer none of them, although the last stung her to considerable irritation. She wished to find out how deep his grievance lay.

'None of these things seem to me to matter,' she said.

'Very well, then. I may as well hold my tongue,' he replied.

'In themselves they don't seem to me to matter; if they hurt you, of course they matter,' she corrected herself scrupulously. Her tone of consideration touched him, and he walked on in silence for a space.

'And we might be so happy, Katharine!' he exclaimed impulsively, and drew her arm through his. She withdrew it directly.

'As long as you let yourself feel like this we shall never be happy,' she said.

The harshness, which Henry had noticed, was again unmistakable in her manner. William flinched and was silent. Such severity, accompanied by something indescribably cold and impersonal in her manner, had constantly been meted out to him during the last few days, always in the company of others. He had recouped himself by some ridiculous display of vanity which, as he knew, put him still more at her mercy. Now that he was alone with her there was no stimulus from outside to draw his attention from his injury. By a considerable effort of self-control he forced himself to remain silent, and to make himself distinguish what part of his pain was due to vanity, what part to the certainty that no woman really loving him could speak thus.

'What do I feel about Katharine?' he thought to himself. It was clear that she had been a very desirable and distinguished figure, the mistress of her little section of the world; but more than that, she was the person of all others who seemed to him the arbitress of life, the woman whose judgement was naturally right and steady, as his had never been in spite of all his culture. And then he could not see her come into a room without a sense of the flowing of robes, of the flowering of blossoms, of the purple waves of the sea, of all things that are lovely and mutable on the surface but still and passionate in their heart.

'If she were callous all the time and had only led me on to laugh at me I couldn't have felt that about her,' he thought. 'I'm not a fool, after all. I can't have been utterly mistaken all these years. And yet, when she speaks to me like that! The truth of it is,' he thought, 'that I've got such despicable faults that no one could help speaking to me like that. Katharine is quite right. And yet those are not my serious feelings, as she knows quite well. How can I change myself? What would make her care for me?' He was terribly tempted here to break the silence by asking Katharine in what respects he could change himself to suit her; but he sought consolation instead by running over the list of his gifts and acquirements, his knowledge of Greek and Latin, his knowledge of art and literature, his skill in the management of meters, and his ancient west-country blood. But the feeling that underlay all these feelings and puzzled him profoundly and kept him silent was the certainty that he loved Katharine as sincerely as he had it in him to love anyone. And yet she could speak to him like that! In a sort of bewilderment he lost all desire to speak, and would quite readily have taken up some different topic of conversation if Katharine had started one. This, however, she did not do.

He glanced at her, in case her expression might help him to understand her behaviour. As usual, she had quickened her pace unconsciously, and was now walking a little in front of him; but he could gain little information from her eyes, which looked steadily at the brown heather, or from the lines drawn seriously upon her forehead. Thus to lose touch with her, for he had no idea what she was thinking, was so unpleasant to him that he began to talk about his grievances again, without, however, much conviction in his voice.

'If you have no feeling for me, wouldn't it be kinder to say so to me in private?'

'Oh, William,' she burst out, as if he had interrupted some absorbing train of thought, 'how you go on about feelings! Isn't it better not to talk so much, not to be worrying always about small things that don't really matter?'

'That's the question precisely,' he exclaimed. 'I only want you to tell me that they don't matter. There are times when you seem indifferent to everything. I'm vain, I've a thousand faults; but you know they're not everything; you know I care for you.'

'And if I say that I care for you, don't you believe me?'

'Say it, Katharine! Say it as if you meant it! Make me feel that you care for me!'

She could not force herself to speak a word. The heather was growing dim around them, and the horizon was blotted out by white mist. To ask her for passion or for certainty seemed like asking that damp prospect for fierce blades of fire or the faded sky for the intense blue vault of June.

He went on now to tell her of his love for her, in words which bore, even to her critical senses, the stamp of truth; but none of this touched her, until, coming to a gate whose hinge was rusty, he heaved it open with his shoulder, still talking and taking no account of his effort. The virility of this deed impressed her; and yet, normally, she attached no value to the power of opening gates. The strength of muscles has nothing to do on the face of it with the strength of affections; nevertheless, she felt a sudden concern for this power running to waste on her account, which, combined with a desire to keep possession of that strangely attractive masculine power, made her rouse herself from her torpor.

Why should she not simply tell him the truth – which was that she had accepted him in a misty state of mind when nothing had its right shape or size? that it was deplorable, but that with clearer eyesight marriage was out of the question? She did not want to marry anyone. She wanted to go away by herself, preferably to some bleak northern moor, and there study mathematics and the science of astronomy. Twenty words would explain the whole situation to him. He had ceased to speak; he had told her once more how he loved her and why. She summoned her courage, fixed her eyes upon a lightning-splintered ash tree, and, almost as if she were reading a writing fixed to the trunk, began: 'I was wrong to get engaged to you. I shall never make you happy. I have never loved you.'

'Katharine!' he protested.

'No, never,' she repeated obstinately. 'Not rightly. Don't you see, I didn't know what I was doing?'

'You love someone else?' he cut her short.

'Absolutely no one.'

'Henry?' he demanded.

'Henry? I should have thought, William, even you – '

'There is someone,' he persisted. 'There has been a change in the last few weeks. You owe it to me to be honest, Katharine.'

'If I could, I would,' she replied.

'Why did you tell me you would marry me, then?' he demanded.

Why, indeed? A moment of pessimism, a sudden conviction of the undeniable prose of life, a lapse of the illusion which sustains youth midway between heaven and earth, a desperate attempt to reconcile herself with facts – she could only recall a moment, as of waking from a dream, which now seemed to her a moment of surrender. But who could give reasons such as these for doing what she had done? She shook her head very sadly.

'But you're not a child – you're not a woman of moods,' Rodney persisted. 'You couldn't have accepted me if you hadn't loved me!' he cried.

A sense of her own misbehaviour, which she had succeeded in keeping from her by sharpening her consciousness of Rodney's faults, now swept over her and almost overwhelmed her. What were his faults in comparison with the fact that he cared for her? What were her virtues in comparison with the fact that she did not care for him? In a flash the conviction that not to care is the uttermost sin of all stamped itself upon her inmost thought; and she felt herself branded for ever.

He had taken her arm, and held her hand firmly in his, nor had she the force to resist what now seemed to her his enormously superior strength. Very well; she would submit, as her mother and her aunt and most women, perhaps, had submitted; and yet she knew that every second of such submission to his strength was a second of treachery to him.

'I did say I would marry you, but it was wrong,' she forced herself to say, and she stiffened her arm as if to annul even the seeming submission of that separate part of her; 'for I don't love you, William; you've noticed it, everyone's noticed it; why should we go on pretending? When I told you I loved you, I was wrong. I said what I knew to be untrue.'

As none of her words seemed to her at all adequate to represent what she felt, she repeated them, and emphasised them without realising the effect that they might have upon a man who cared for her. She was completely taken aback by finding her arm suddenly dropped; then she saw his face most strangely contorted; was he laughing, it flashed across her? In another moment she saw that he was in tears. In her bewilderment at this apparition she stood aghast for a second. With a desperate sense that this horror must, at all costs, be stopped, she then put her arms about him, drew his head for a moment upon her shoulder, and led him on, murmuring words of consolation, until he heaved a great sigh. They held fast to each other; her tears, too, ran down her cheeks; and were both quite silent. Noticing the difficulty with which he walked, and feeling the same extreme lassitude in her own limbs, she proposed that they should rest for a moment where the bracken was brown and shrivelled beneath an oak tree. He assented. Once more he gave a great sigh, and wiped his eyes with a childlike unconsciousness, and began to speak without a trace of his previous anger. The idea came to her that they were like the children in the fairy tale[65] who were lost in a wood, and with this in her mind she noticed the scattering of dead leaves all round them which had been blown by the wind into heaps, a foot or two deep, here and there.

'When did you begin to feel this, Katharine?' he said; 'for it isn't true to say that you've always felt it. I admit I was unreasonable the first night when you found that your clothes had been left behind. Still, where's the fault in that? I could promise you never to interfere with your clothes again. I admit I was cross when I found you upstairs with Henry. Perhaps I showed it too openly. But that's not unreasonable either when one's engaged. Ask your mother. And now this terrible thing – ' He broke off, unable for the moment to proceed any further. 'This decision you say you've come to – have you discussed it with anyone? Your mother, for example, or Henry?'

'No, no, of course not,' she said, stirring the leaves with her hand. 'But you don't understand me, William – '

'Help me to understand you – '

'You don't understand, I mean, my real feelings; how could you? I've only now faced them myself. But I haven't got the sort of feeling – love, I mean – I don't know what to call it – ' she looked vaguely towards the horizon sunk under mist – 'but, anyhow, without it our marriage would be a farce – '

'How a farce?' he asked. 'But this kind of analysis is disastrous!' he exclaimed.

'I should have done it before,' she said gloomily.

'You make yourself think things you don't think,' he continued, becoming demonstrative with his hands, as his manner was. 'Believe me, Katharine, before we came here we were perfectly happy. You were full of plans for our house – the chair-covers, don't you remember? – like any other woman who is about to be married. Now, for no reason whatever, you begin to fret about your feeling and about my feeling, with the usual result. I assure you, Katharine, I've been through it all myself. At one time I was always asking myself absurd questions which came to nothing either. What you want, if I may say so, is some occupation to take you out of yourself when this morbid mood comes on. If it hadn't been for my poetry, I assure you, I should often have been very much in the same state myself. To let you into a secret,' he continued, with his little chuckle, which now sounded almost assured, 'I've often gone home from seeing you in such a state of nerves that I had to force myself to write a page or two before I could get you out of my head. Ask Denham; he'll tell you how he met me one night; he'll tell you what a state he found me in.'

Katharine started with displeasure at the mention of Ralph's name.

The thought of the conversation in which her conduct had been made a subject for discussion with Denham roused her anger; but, as she instantly felt, she had scarcely the right to grudge William any use of her name, seeing what her fault against him had been from first to last. And yet Denham! She had a view of him as a judge. She figured him sternly weighing instances of her levity in this masculine court of enquiry into feminine morality and gruffly dismissing both her and her family with some half-sarcastic, half-tolerant phrase which sealed her doom, as far as he was concerned, for ever. Having met him so lately, the sense of his character was strong in her. The thought was not a pleasant one for a proud woman, but she had yet to learn the art of subduing her expression. Her eyes fixed upon the ground, her brows drawn together, gave William a very fair picture of the resentment that she was forcing herself to control. A certain degree of apprehension, occasionally culminating in a kind of fear, had always entered into his love for her, and had increased, rather to his surprise, in the greater intimacy of their engagement. Beneath her steady, exemplary surface ran a vein of passion which seemed to him now perverse, now completely irrational, for it never took the normal channel of glorification of him and his doings; and, indeed, he almost preferred the steady good sense, which had always marked their relationship, to a more romantic bond. But passion she had, he could not deny it, and hitherto he had tried to see it employed in his thoughts upon the lives of the children who were to be born to them.

'She will make a perfect mother – a mother of sons,' he thought; but seeing her sitting there, gloomy and silent, he began to have his doubts on this point. 'A farce, a farce,' he thought to himself. 'She said that our marriage would be a farce,' and he became suddenly aware of their situation, sitting upon the ground, among the dead leaves, not fifty yards from the main road, so that it was quite possible for someone passing to see and recognise them. He brushed off his face any trace that might remain of that unseemly exhibition of emotion. But he was more troubled by Katharine's appearance, as she sat rapt in thought upon the ground, than by his own; there was something improper to him in her self-forgetfulness. A man naturally alive to the conventions of society, he was strictly conventional where women were concerned, and especially if the women happened to be in any way connected with him. He noticed with distress the long strand of dark hair touching her shoulder and two or three dead beech leaves attached to her dress; but to recall her mind in their present circumstances to a sense of these details was impossible. She sat there, seeming unconscious of everything.

He suspected that in her silence she was reproaching herself; but he wished that she would think of her hair and of the dead beech leaves, which were of more immediate importance to him than anything else. Indeed, these trifles drew his attention strangely from his own doubtful and uneasy state of mind; for relief, mixing itself with pain, stirred up a most curious hurry and tumult in his breast, almost concealing his first sharp sense of bleak and overwhelming disappointment. In order to relieve this restlessness and close a distressingly ill-ordered scene, he rose abruptly and helped Katharine to her feet. She smiled a little at the minute care with which he tidied her and yet, when he brushed the dead leaves from his own coat, she flinched, seeing in that action the gesture of a lonely man.

'William,' she said, 'I will marry you. I will try to make you happy.'

Chapter 19

The afternoon was already growing dark when the two other wayfarers, Mary and Ralph Denham, came out on the high road beyond the outskirts of Lincoln. The high road, as they both felt, was better suited to this return journey than the open country, and for the first mile or so of the way they spoke little. In his own mind Ralph was following the passage of the Otway carriage over the heath; he then went back to the five or ten minutes that he had spent with Katharine, and examined each word with the care that a scholar displays upon the irregularities of an ancient text. He was determined that the glow, the romance, the atmosphere of this meeting should not paint what he must in future regard as sober facts. On her side Mary was silent, not because her thoughts took much handling, but because her mind seemed empty of thought as her heart of feeling. Only Ralph's presence, as she knew, preserved this numbness, for she could foresee a time of loneliness when many varieties of pain would beset her. At the present moment her effort was to preserve what she could of the wreck of her self-respect, for such she deemed that momentary glimpse of her love so involuntarily revealed to Ralph. In the light of reason it did not much matter, perhaps, but it was her instinct to be careful of that vision of herself which keeps pace so evenly beside every one of us, and had been damaged by her confession. The grey night coming down over the country was kind to her; and she thought that one of these days she would find comfort in sitting upon the earth, alone, beneath a tree.

Looking through the darkness, she marked the swelling ground and the tree. Ralph made her start by saying abruptly: 'What I was going to say when we were interrupted at lunch was that if you go to America I shall come, too. It can't be harder to earn a living there than it is here. However, that's not the point. The point is, Mary, that I want to marry you. Well, what do you say?' He spoke firmly, waited for no answer, and took her arm in his. 'You know me by this time, the good and the bad,' he went on. 'You know my tempers. I've tried to let you know my faults. Well, what do you say, Mary?'

She said nothing, but this did not seem to strike him.

'In most ways, at least in the important ways, as you said, we know each other and we think alike. I believe you are the only person in the world I could live with happily. And if you feel the same about me – as you do, don't you, Mary? – we should make each other happy.' Here he paused, and seemed to be in no hurry for an answer; he seemed, indeed, to be continuing his own thoughts.

'Yes, but I'm afraid I couldn't do it,' Mary said at last. The casual and rather hurried way in which she spoke, together with the fact that she was saying the exact opposite of what he expected her to say, baffled him so much that he instinctively loosened his clasp upon her arm and she withdrew it quietly.

'You couldn't do it?' he asked.

'No, I couldn't marry you,' she replied.

'You don't care for me?'

She made no answer.

'Well, Mary,' he said, with a curious laugh, 'I must be an arrant fool, for I thought you did.' They walked for a minute or two in silence, and suddenly he turned to her, looked at her, and exclaimed: 'I don't believe you, Mary. You're not telling me the truth.'

'I'm too tired to argue, Ralph,' she replied, turning her head away from him. 'I ask you to believe what I say. I can't marry you; I don't want to marry you.'

The voice in which she stated this was so evidently the voice of one in some extremity of anguish that Ralph had no course but to obey her. And as soon as the tone of her voice had died out, and the surprise faded from his mind, he found himself believing that she had spoken the truth, for he had but little vanity, and soon her refusal seemed a natural thing to him. He slipped through all the grades of despondency until he reached a bottom of absolute gloom. Failure seemed to mark the whole of his life; he had failed with Katharine, and now he had failed with Mary. Up at once sprang the thought of Katharine, and with it a sense of exulting freedom, but this he checked instantly. No good had ever come to him from Katharine; his whole relationship with her had been made up of dreams; and as he thought of the little substance there had been in his dreams he began to lay the blame of the present catastrophe upon his dreams.

'Haven't I always been thinking of Katharine while I was with Mary? I might have loved Mary if it hadn't been for that idiocy of mine. She cared for me once, I'm certain of that, but I tormented her so with my humours that I let my chances slip, and now she won't risk marrying me. And this is what I've made of my life – nothing, nothing, nothing.'

The tramp of their boots upon the dry road seemed to asseverate nothing, nothing, nothing. Mary thought that this silence was the silence of relief; his depression she ascribed to the fact that he had seen Katharine and parted from her, leaving her in the company of William Rodney. She could not blame him for loving Katharine, but that, when he loved another, he should ask her to marry him – that seemed to her the cruellest treachery. Their old friendship and its firm base upon indestructible qualities of character crumbled, and her whole past seemed foolish, herself weak and credulous, and Ralph merely the shell of an honest man. Oh, the past – so much made up of Ralph; and now, as she saw, made up of something strange and false and other than she had thought it. She tried to recapture a saying she had made to help herself that morning, as Ralph paid the bill for luncheon; but she could see him paying the bill more vividly than she could remember the phrase. Something about truth was in it; how to see the truth is our great chance in this world.

'If you don't want to marry me,' Ralph now began again, without abruptness, with diffidence rather, 'there is no need why we should cease to see each other, is there? Or would you rather that we should keep apart for the present?'

'Keep apart? I don't know – I must think about it.'

'Tell me one thing, Mary,' he resumed; 'have I done anything to make you change your mind about me?'

She was immensely tempted to give way to her natural trust in him, revived by the deep and now melancholy tones of his voice, and to tell him of her love, and of what had changed it. But although it seemed likely that she would soon control her anger with him, the certainty that he did not love her, confirmed by every word of his proposal, forbade any freedom of speech. To hear him speak and to feel herself unable to reply, or constrained in her replies, was so painful that she longed for the time when she should be alone. A more pliant woman would have taken this chance of an explanation, whatever risks attached to it; but to one of Mary's firm and resolute temperament there was degradation in the idea of self-abandonment; let the waves of emotion rise ever so high, she could not shut her eyes to what she conceived to be the truth. Her silence puzzled Ralph. He searched his memory for words or deeds that might have made her think badly of him. In his present mood instances came but too quickly, and on top of them this culminating proof of his baseness – that he had asked her to marry him when his reasons for such a proposal were selfish and half-hearted.

'You needn't answer,' he said grimly. 'There are reasons enough, I know. But must they kill our friendship, Mary? Let me keep that, at least.'

'Oh,' she thought to herself, with a sudden rush of anguish which threatened disaster to her self-respect, 'it has come to this – to this – when I could have given him everything!'

'Yes, we can still be friends,' she said, with what firmness she could muster.

'I shall want your friendship,' he said. He added, 'If you find it possible, let me see you as often as you can. The oftener the better. I shall want your help.'

She promised this, and they went on to talk calmly of things that had no reference to their feelings – a talk which, in its constraint, was infinitely sad to both of them.

One more reference was made to the state of things between them late that night, when Elizabeth had gone to her room and the two young men had stumbled off to bed in such a state of sleep that they hardly felt the floor beneath their feet after a day's shooting.

Mary drew her chair a little nearer to the fire, for the logs were burning low, and at this time of night it was hardly worth while to replenish them. Ralph was reading, but she had noticed for some time that his eyes instead of following the print were fixed rather above the page with an intensity of gloom that came to weigh upon her mind. She had not weakened in her resolve not to give way, for reflection had only made her more bitterly certain that, if she gave way, it would be to her own wish and not to his. But she had determined that there was no reason why he should suffer if her reticence were the cause of his suffering. Therefore, although she found it painful, she spoke: 'You asked me if I had changed my mind about you, Ralph,' she said. 'I think there's only one thing. When you asked me to marry you, I don't think you meant it. That made me angry – for the moment. Before, you'd always spoken the truth.'

Ralph's book slid down upon his knee and fell upon the floor. He rested his forehead on his hand and looked into the fire. He was trying to recall the exact words in which he had made his proposal to Mary.

'I never said I loved you,' he said at last.

She winced; but she respected him for saying what he did, for this, after all, was a fragment of the truth which she had vowed to live by.

'And to me marriage without love doesn't seem worth while,' she said.

'Well, Mary, I'm not going to press you,' he said. 'I see you don't want to marry me. But love – don't we all talk a great deal of nonsense about it? What does one mean? I believe I care for you more genuinely than nine men out of ten care for the women they're in love with. It's only a story one makes up in one's mind about another person, and one knows all the time it isn't true. Of course one knows; why, one's always taking care not to destroy the illusion. One takes care not to see them too often, or to be alone with them for too long together. It's a pleasant illusion, but if you're thinking of the risks of marriage, it seems to me that the risk of marrying a person you're in love with is something colossal.'

'I don't believe a word of that, and what's more you don't, either,' she replied with anger. 'However, we don't agree; I only wanted you to understand.' She shifted her position, as if she were about to go. An instinctive desire to prevent her from leaving the room made Ralph rise at this point and begin pacing up and down the nearly empty kitchen, checking his desire, each time he reached the door, to open it and step out into the garden. A moralist might have said that at this point his mind should have been full of self-reproach for the suffering he had caused. On the contrary, he was extremely angry, with the confused impotent anger of one who finds himself unreasonably but efficiently frustrated. He was trapped by the illogicality of human life. The obstacles in the way of his desire seemed to him purely artificial, and yet he could see no way of removing them. Mary's words, the tone of her voice even, angered him, for she would not help him. She was part of the insanely jumbled muddle of a world which impedes the sensible life. He would have liked to slam the door or break the hind legs of a chair, for the obstacles had taken some such curiously substantial shape in his mind.

'I doubt that one human being ever understands another,' he said, stopping in his march and confronting Mary at a distance of a few feet. 'Such damned liars as we all are, how can we? But we can try. If you don't want to marry me, don't; but the position you take up about love, and not seeing each other – isn't that mere sentimentality? You think I've behaved very badly,' he continued, as she did not speak. 'Of course I behave badly; but you can't judge people by what they do. You can't go through life measuring right and wrong with a foot-rule. That's what you're always doing, Mary; that's what you're doing now.'

She saw herself in the Suffrage office, delivering judgement, meting out right and wrong, and there seemed to her to be some justice in the charge, although it did not affect her main position.

'I'm not angry with you,' she said slowly. 'I will go on seeing you, as I said I would.'

It was true that she had promised that much already, and it was difficult for him to say what more it was that he wanted – some intimacy, some help against the ghost of Katharine, perhaps, something that he knew he had no right to ask; and yet, as he sank into his chair and looked once more at the dying fire it seemed to him that he had been defeated, not so much by Mary as by life itself. He felt himself thrown back to the beginning of life again, where everything has yet to be won; but in extreme youth one has an ignorant hope. He was no longer certain that he would triumph.

Chapter 20

Happily for Mary Datchet she returned to the office to find that by some obscure Parliamentary manoeuvre the vote had once more slipped beyond the attainment of women. Mrs Seal was in a condition bordering upon frenzy. The duplicity of ministers, the treachery of mankind, the insult to womanhood, the setback to civilisation, the ruin of her life's work, the feelings of her father's daughter – all these topics were discussed in turn, and the office was littered with newspaper cuttings branded with the blue, if ambiguous, marks of her displeasure. She confessed herself at fault in her estimate of human nature.

'The simple elementary acts of justice,' she said, waving her hand towards the window, and indicating the foot-passengers and omnibuses then passing down the far side of Russell Square, 'are as far beyond them as they ever were. We can only look upon ourselves, Mary, as pioneers in a wilderness. We can only go on patiently putting the truth before them. It isn't *them*,' she continued, taking heart from her sight of the traffic, 'it's their leaders. It's those gentlemen sitting in Parliament and drawing four hundred a year of the people's money. If we had to put our case to the people, we should soon have justice done to us. I have always believed in the people, and I do so still. But – ' She shook her head and implied that she would give them one more chance, and if they didn't take advantage of that she couldn't answer for the consequences.

Mr Clacton's attitude was more philosophical and better supported by statistics. He came into the room after Mrs Seal's outburst and pointed out, with historical illustrations, that such reverses had happened in every political campaign of any importance. If anything, his spirits were improved by the disaster. The enemy, he said, had taken the offensive; and it was now up to the society to outwit the enemy. He gave Mary to understand that he had taken the measure of their cunning, and had already bent his mind to the task which, so far as she could make out, depended solely upon him. It depended, so she came to think, when invited into his room for a private conference, upon a systematic revision of the card-index, upon the issue of certain new lemon-coloured leaflets, in which the facts were marshalled once more in a very striking way, and upon a large-scale map of England dotted with little pins tufted with differently coloured plumes of hair according to their geographical position. Each district, under the new system, had its flag, its bottle of ink, its sheaf of documents tabulated and filed for reference in a drawer, so that by looking under M or S, as the case might be, you had all the facts with respect to the Suffrage organisations of that county at your fingers' ends. This would require a great deal of work, of course.

'We must try to consider ourselves rather in the light of a telephone exchange – for the exchange of ideas, Miss Datchet,' he said; and taking pleasure in his image, he continued it. 'We should consider ourselves the centre of an enormous system of wires, connecting us up with every district of the country. We must have our fingers upon the pulse of the community; we want to know what people all over England are thinking; we want to put them in the way of thinking rightly.' The system, of course, was only roughly sketched so far – jotted down, in fact, during the Christmas holidays.

'When you ought to have been taking a rest, Mr Clacton,' said Mary dutifully, but her tone was flat and tired.

'We learn to do without holidays, Miss Datchet,' said Mr Clacton, with a spark of satisfaction in his eye.

He wished particularly to have her opinion of the lemon-coloured leaflet. According to his plan, it was to be distributed in immense quantities immediately, in order to stimulate and generate, 'to generate and stimulate,' he repeated, 'right thoughts in the country before the meeting of Parliament.'

'We have to take the enemy by surprise,' he said. 'They don't let the grass grow under their feet. Have you seen Bingham's address to his constituents? That's a hint of the sort of thing we've got to meet, Miss Datchet.'

He handed her a great bundle of newspaper cuttings, and, begging her to give him her views upon the yellow leaflet before lunchtime, he turned with alacrity to his different sheets of paper and his different bottles of ink.

Mary shut the door, laid the documents upon her table and sank her head on her hands. Her brain was curiously empty of any thought. She listened, as if, perhaps, by listening she would become merged again in the atmosphere of the office. From the next room came the rapid spasmodic sounds of Mrs Seal's erratic typewriting; she, doubtless, was already hard at work helping the people of England, as Mr Clacton put it, to think rightly; 'generating and stimulating', those were his words. She was striking a blow against the enemy, no doubt, who didn't let the grass grow beneath their feet. Mr Clacton's words repeated themselves accurately in her brain. She pushed the papers wearily over to the farther side of the table. It was no use, though; something or other had happened to her brain – a change of focus so that near things were indistinct again. The same thing had happened to her once before, she remembered, after she had met Ralph in the gardens of Lincoln's Inn Fields; she had spent the whole of a committee meeting in thinking about sparrows and colours, until, almost at the end of the meeting, her old convictions had all come back to her. But they had only come back, she thought with scorn at her feebleness, because she wanted to use them to fight against Ralph. They weren't, rightly speaking, convictions at all. She could not see the world divided into separate compartments of good people and bad people, any more than she could believe so implicitly in the rightness of her own thought as to wish to bring the population of the British Isles into agreement with it. She looked at the lemon-coloured leaflet, and thought almost enviously of the faith which could find comfort in the issue of such documents; for herself she would be content to remain silent for ever if a share of personal happiness were granted her. She read Mr Clacton's statement with a curious division of judgement, noting its weak and pompous verbosity on the one hand, and, at the same time, feeling that faith, faith in an illusion, perhaps, but, at any rate, faith in something, was of all gifts the most to be envied. An illusion it was, no doubt. She looked curiously round her at the furniture of the office, at the machinery in which she had taken so much pride, and marvelled to think that once the copying-presses, the card-index, the files of documents, had all been shrouded, wrapped in some mist which gave them a unity and a general dignity and purpose independently of their separate significance. The ugly cumbersomeness of the furniture alone impressed her now. Her attitude had become very lax and despondent when the typewriter stopped in the next room. Mary immediately drew up to the table, laid hands on an unopened envelope, and adopted an expression which might hide her state of mind from Mrs Seal. Some instinct of decency required that she should not allow Mrs Seal to see her face. Shading her eyes with her fingers, she watched Mrs Seal pull out one drawer after another in her search for some envelope or leaflet. She was tempted to drop her fingers and exclaim: 'Do sit down, Sally, and tell me how you manage it – how you manage, that is, to bustle about with perfect confidence in the necessity of your own activities, which to me seem as futile as the buzzing of a belated bluebottle.' She said nothing of the kind, however, and the presence of industry which she preserved so long as Mrs Seal was in the room served to set her brain in motion, so that she dispatched her morning's work much as usual. At one o'clock she was surprised to find how efficiently she had dealt with the morning. As she put her hat on she determined to lunch at a shop in the Strand, so as to set that other piece of mechanism, her body, into action. With a brain working and a body working one could keep step with the crowd and never be found out for the hollow machine, lacking the essential thing, that one was conscious of being.

She considered her case as she walked down the Charing Cross Road. She put to herself a series of questions. Would she mind, for example, if the wheels of that motor-omnibus passed over her and crushed her to death? No, not in the least; or an adventure with that disagreeable-looking man hanging about the entrance of the Tube station? No; she could not conceive fear or excitement. Did suffering in any form appal her? No, suffering was neither good nor bad. And this essential thing? In the eyes of every single person she detected a flame; as if a spark in the brain ignited spontaneously at contact with the things they met and drove them on. The young women looking into the milliners' windows had that look in their eyes; and elderly men turning over books in the second-hand bookshops, and eagerly waiting to hear what the price was – the very lowest price – they had it, too. But she cared nothing at all for clothes or for money either. Books she shrank from, for they were connected too closely with Ralph. She kept on her way resolutely through the crowd of people, among whom she was so much of an alien, feeling them cleave and give way before her.

Strange thoughts are bred in passing through crowded streets should the passenger, by chance, have no exact destination in front of him, much as the mind shapes all kinds of forms, solutions, images when listening inattentively to music. From an acute consciousness of herself as an individual, Mary passed to a conception of the scheme of things in which, as a human being, she must have her share. She half held a vision; the vision shaped and dwindled. She wished she had a pencil and a piece of paper to help her to give a form to this conception which composed itself as she walked down the Charing Cross Road. But if she talked to anyone, the conception might escape her. Her vision seemed to lay out the lines of her life until death in a way which satisfied her sense of harmony. It only needed a persistent effort of thought, stimulated in this strange way by the crowd and the noise, to climb the crest of existence and see it all laid out once and for ever. Already her suffering as an individual was left behind her. Of this process, which was to her so full of effort, which comprised infinitely swift and full passages of thought, leading from one crest to another, as she shaped her conception of life in this world, only two articulate words escaped her, muttered beneath her breath – 'Not happiness – not happiness.'

She sat down on a seat opposite the statue of one of London's heroes upon the Embankment,[66] and spoke the words aloud. To her they represented the rare flower or splinter of rock brought down by a climber in proof that he has stood for a moment, at least, upon the highest peak of the mountain. She had been up there and seen the world spread to the horizon. It was now necessary to alter her course to some extent, according to her new resolve. Her post should be in one of those exposed and desolate stations which are shunned naturally by happy people. She arranged the details of the new plan in her mind, not without a grim satisfaction.

'Now,' she said to herself, rising from her seat, 'I'll think of Ralph.'

Where was he to be placed in the new scale of life? Her exalted mood seemed to make it safe to handle the question. But she was dismayed to find how quickly her passions leapt forward the moment she sanctioned this line of thought. Now she was identified with him and rethought his thoughts with complete self-surrender; now, with a sudden cleavage of spirit, she turned upon him and denounced him for his cruelty.

'But I refuse – I refuse to hate anyone,' she said aloud; chose the moment to cross the road with circumspection; and ten minutes later lunched in the Strand, cutting her meat firmly into small pieces, but giving her fellow-diners no further cause to judge her eccentric. Her soliloquy crystallised itself into little fragmentary phrases emerging suddenly from the turbulence of her thought, particularly when she had to exert herself in any way, either to move, to count money or to choose a turning. 'To know the truth – to accept without bitterness' – those, perhaps, were the most articulate of her utterances, for no one could have made head or tail of the queer gibberish murmured in front of the statue of Francis, Duke of Bedford,[67] save that the name of Ralph occurred frequently in very strange connections, as if, having spoken it, she wished, superstitiously, to cancel it by adding some other word that robbed the sentence with his name in it of any meaning.

Those champions of the cause of women, Mr Clacton and Mrs Seal, did not perceive anything strange in Mary's behaviour, save that she was almost half an hour later than usual in coming back to the office. Happily, their own affairs kept them busy, and she was free from their inspection. If they had surprised her they would have found her lost, apparently, in admiration of the large hotel across the square, for, after writing a few words, her pen rested upon the paper, and her mind pursued its own journey among the sun-blazoned windows and the drifts of purplish smoke which formed her view. And, indeed, this background was by no means out of keeping with her thoughts. She saw to the remote spaces behind the strife of the foreground, enabled now to gaze there, since she had renounced her own demands, privileged to see the larger view, to share the vast desires and sufferings of the mass of mankind. She had been too lately and too roughly mastered by facts to take an easy pleasure in the relief of renunciation; such satisfaction as she felt came only from the discovery that, having renounced everything that made life happy, easy, splendid, individual, there remained a hard reality, unimpaired by one's personal adventures, remote as the stars, unquenchable as they are.

While Mary Datchet was undergoing this curious transformation from the particular to the universal, Mrs Seal remembered her duties with regard to the kettle and the gas-fire. She was a little surprised to find that Mary had drawn her chair to the window, and, having lit the gas, she raised herself from a stooping posture and looked at her. The most obvious reason for such an attitude in a secretary was some kind of indisposition. But Mary, rousing herself with an effort, denied that she was indisposed.

'I'm frightfully lazy this afternoon,' she added, with a glance at her table. 'You must really get another secretary, Sally.'

The words were meant to be taken lightly, but something in the tone of them roused a jealous fear which was always dormant in Mrs Seal's breast. She was terribly afraid that one of these days Mary, the young woman who typified so many rather sentimental and enthusiastic ideas, who had some sort of visionary existence in white with a sheaf of lilies in her hand, would announce, in a jaunty way, that she was about to be married.

'You don't mean that you're going to leave us?' she said.

'I've not made up my mind about anything,' said Mary – a remark which could be taken as a generalisation.

Mrs Seal got the teacups out of the cupboard and set them on the table. 'You're not going to be married, are you?' she asked, pronouncing the words with nervous speed.

'Why are you asking such absurd questions this afternoon, Sally?' Mary asked, not very steadily. 'Must we all get married?'

Mrs Seal emitted a most peculiar chuckle. She seemed for one moment to acknowledge the terrible side of life which is concerned with the emotions, the private lives, of the sexes, and then to sheer off from it with all possible speed into the shades of her own shivering virginity. She was made so uncomfortable by the turn the conversation had taken, that she plunged her head into the cupboard, and endeavoured to abstract some very obscure piece of china.

'We have our work,' she said, withdrawing her head, displaying cheeks more than usually crimson, and placing a jam-pot emphatically upon the table. But, for the moment, she was unable to launch herself upon one of those enthusiastic, but inconsequent, tirades upon liberty, democracy, the rights of the people and the iniquities of the government in which she delighted. Some memory from her own past or from the past of her sex rose to her mind and kept her abashed. She glanced furtively at Mary, who still sat by the window with her arm upon the sill. She noticed how young she was and full of the promise of womanhood. The sight made her so uneasy that she fidgeted the cups upon their saucers.

'Yes – enough work to last a lifetime,' said Mary, as if concluding some passage of thought.

Mrs Seal brightened at once. She lamented her lack of scientific training, and her deficiency in the processes of logic, but she set her mind to work at once to make the prospects of the cause appear as alluring and important as she could. She delivered herself of an harangue in which she asked a great many rhetorical questions and answered them with a little bang of one fist upon another.

'To last a lifetime? My dear child, it will last all our lifetimes. As one falls another steps into the breach. My father, in his generation, a pioneer – I, coming after him, do my little best. What, alas! can one do more? And now it's you young women – we look to you – the future looks to you. Ah, my dear, if I'd a thousand lives, I'd give them all to our cause. The cause of women, d'you say? I say the cause of humanity. And there are some' – she glanced fiercely at the window – 'who don't see it! There are some who are satisfied to go on, year after year, refusing to admit the truth. And we who have the vision – the kettle boiling over? No, no, let me see to it – we who know the truth,' she continued, gesticulating with the kettle and the teapot. Owing to these encumbrances, perhaps, she lost the thread of her discourse, and concluded, rather wistfully, 'It's all so *simple*.' She referred to a matter that was a perpetual source of bewilderment to her – the extraordinary incapacity of the human race, in a world where the good is so unmistakably divided from the bad, of distinguishing one from the other, and embodying what ought to be done in a few large, simple Acts of Parliament, which would, in a very short time, completely change the lot of humanity.

'One would have thought,' she said, 'that men of university training, like Mr Asquith – one would have thought that an appeal to reason would not be unheard by them. But reason,' she reflected, 'what is reason without reality?'

Doing homage to the phrase, she repeated it once more, and caught the ear of Mr Clacton, as he issued from his room; and he repeated it a third time, giving it, as he was in the habit of doing with Mrs Seal's phrases, a dryly humorous intonation. He was well pleased with the world, however, and he remarked, in a flattering manner, that he would like to see that phrase in large letters at the head of a leaflet.

'But, Mrs Seal, we have to aim at a judicious combination of the two,' he added in his magisterial way to check the unbalanced enthusiasm of the women. 'Reality has to be voiced by reason before it can make itself felt. The weak point of all these movements, Miss Datchet,' he continued, taking his place at the table and turning to Mary as usual when about to deliver his more profound cogitations, 'is that they are not based upon sufficiently intellectual grounds. A mistake, in my opinion. The British public likes a pellet of reason in its jam of eloquence – a pill of reason in its pudding of sentiment,' he said, sharpening the phrase to a satisfactory degree of literary precision.

His eyes rested, with something of the vanity of an author, upon the yellow leaflet which Mary held in her hand. She rose, took her seat at the head of the table, poured out tea for her colleagues, and gave her opinion upon the leaflet. So she had poured out tea, so she had criticised

Mr Clacton's leaflets a hundred times already; but now it seemed to her that she was doing it in a different spirit; she had enlisted in the army, and was a volunteer no longer. She had renounced something and was now – how could she express it? – not quite 'in the running' for life. She had always known that Mr Clacton and Mrs Seal were not in the running, and across the gulf that separated them she had seen them in the guise of shadow people, flitting in and out of the ranks of the living – eccentrics, undeveloped human beings, from whose substance some essential part had been cut away. All this had never struck her so clearly as it did this afternoon, when she felt that her lot was cast with them for ever. One view of the world plunged in darkness, so a more volatile temperament might have argued after a season of despair, let the world turn again and show another, more splendid, perhaps. No, Mary thought, with unflinching loyalty to what appeared to her to be the true view, having lost what is best, I do not mean to pretend that any other view does instead. Whatever happens, I mean to have no presences in my life. Her very words had a sort of distinctness which is sometimes produced by sharp, bodily pain. To Mrs Seal's secret jubilation the rule which forbade discussion of shop at teatime was overlooked. Mary and Mr Clacton argued with a cogency and a ferocity which made the little woman feel that something very important – she hardly knew what – was taking place. She became much excited; one crucifix became entangled with another, and she dug a considerable hole in the table with the point of her pencil in order to emphasise the most striking heads of the discourse; and how any combination of cabinet ministers could resist such discourse she really did not know.

She could hardly bring herself to remember her own private instrument of justice – the typewriter. The telephone-bell rang, and as she hurried off to answer a voice which always seemed a proof of importance by itself, she felt that it was at this exact spot on the surface of the globe that all the subterranean wires of thought and progress came together. When she returned, with a message from the printer, she found that Mary was putting on her hat firmly; there was something imperious and dominating in her attitude altogether.

'Look, Sally,' she said, 'these letters want copying. These I've not looked at. The question of the new census will have to be gone into carefully. But I'm going home now. Good-night, Mr Clacton; good-night, Sally.'

'We are very fortunate in our secretary, Mr Clacton,' said Mrs Seal, pausing with her hand on the papers, as the door shut behind Mary. Mr Clacton himself had been vaguely impressed by something in

Mary's behaviour towards him. He envisaged a time even when it would become necessary to tell her that there could not be two masters in one office – but she was certainly able, very able, and in touch with a group of very clever young men. No doubt they had suggested to her some of her new ideas.

He signified his assent to Mrs Seal's remark, but observed, with a glance at the clock, which showed only half an hour past five: 'If she takes the work seriously, Mrs Seal – but that's just what some of your clever young ladies don't do.' So saying he returned to his room, and Mrs Seal, after a moment's hesitation, hurried back to her labours.

Chapter 21

Mary walked to the nearest station and reached home in an incredibly short space of time, just so much, indeed, as was needed for the intelligent understanding of the news of the world as the *Westminster Gazette*[68] reported it. Within a few minutes of opening her door, she was in trim for a hard evening's work. She unlocked a drawer and took out a manuscript, which consisted of a very few pages, entitled, in a forcible hand, 'Some Aspects of the Democratic State'. The aspects dwindled out in a cries-cross of blotted lines in the very middle of a sentence, and suggested that the author had been interrupted, or convinced of the futility of proceeding, with her pen in the air . . . Oh, yes, Ralph had come in at that point. She scored that sheet very effectively, and, choosing a fresh one, began at a great rate with a generalisation upon the structure of human society, which was a good deal bolder than her custom. Ralph had told her once that she couldn't write English, which accounted for those frequent blots and insertions; but she put all that behind her, and drove ahead with such words as came her way, until she had accomplished half a page of generalisation and might legitimately draw breath. Directly her hand stopped her brain stopped too, and she began to listen. A paper-boy shouted down the street; an omnibus ceased and lurched on again with the heave of duty once more shouldered; the dullness of the sounds suggested that a fog had risen since her return, if, indeed, a fog has power to deaden sound, of which fact she could not be sure at the present moment. It was the sort of fact Ralph Denham knew. At any rate, it was no concern of hers, and she was about to dip a pen when her ear was caught by the sound of a step upon the stone staircase. She followed it past Mr Chippen's chambers; past Mr Gibson's; past Mr Turner's; after which it became her sound. A postman, a washerwoman, a circular, a bill – she presented herself with each of these perfectly natural possibilities; but, to her surprise, her mind rejected each one of them impatiently, even apprehensively. The step became slow, as it was apt to do at the end of the steep climb, and Mary, listening for the regular sound, was filled with an intolerable nervousness. Leaning against the table, she felt the knock of her heart push her body perceptibly backwards and forwards – a state of nerves astonishing and reprehensible in a stable woman. Grotesque fancies took shape. Alone, at the top of the house, an unknown person approaching nearer and nearer – how could she escape? There was no way of escape. She did not even know whether that oblong mark on the ceiling was a trap-door to the roof or not. And if she got on to the roof – well, there was a drop of sixty feet or so on to the pavement. But she sat perfectly still, and when the knock sounded, she got up directly and opened the door without hesitation. She saw a tall figure outside, with something ominous to her eyes in the look of it.

'What do you want?' she said, not recognising the face in the fitful light of the staircase.

'Mary? I'm Katharine Hilbery!'

Mary's self-possession returned almost excessively, and her welcome was decidedly cold, as if she must recoup herself for this ridiculous waste of emotion. She moved her green-shaded lamp to another table, and covered 'Some Aspects of the Democratic State' with a sheet of blotting-paper.

'Why can't they leave me alone?' she thought bitterly, connecting Katharine and Ralph in a conspiracy to take from her even this hour of solitary study, even this poor little defence against the world. And, as she smoothed down the sheet of blotting-paper over the manuscript, she braced herself to resist Katharine, whose presence struck her, not merely by its force, as usual, but as something in the nature of a menace.

'You're working?' said Katharine, with hesitation, perceiving that she was not welcome.

'Nothing that matters,' Mary replied, drawing forward the best of the chairs and poking the fire.

'I didn't know you had to work after you had left the office,' said Katharine, in a tone which gave the impression that she was thinking of something else, as was, indeed, the case.

She had been paying calls with her mother, and in between the calls Mrs Hilbery had rushed into shops and bought pillow-cases and blotting-books on no perceptible method for the furnishing of Katharine's house. Katharine had a sense of impedimenta accumulating on all sides of her. She had left her at length, and had come on to keep an engagement to dine with Rodney at his rooms. But she did not mean to get to him before seven o'clock, and so had plenty of time to walk all the way from Bond Street to the Temple if she wished it. The flow of faces streaming on either side of her had hypnotised her into a mood of profound despondency, to which her expectation of an evening alone with Rodney contributed. They were very good friends again, better friends, they both said, than ever before. So far as she was concerned this was true. There were many more things in him than she had guessed until emotion brought them forth – strength, affection, sympathy. And she thought of them and looked at the faces passing, and thought how much alike they were, and how distant, nobody feeling anything as she felt nothing, and distance, she thought, lay inevitably between the closest, and their intimacy was the worst pretence of all. For, 'Oh dear,' she thought, looking into a tobacconist's window, 'I don't care for any of them, and I don't care for William, and people say this is the thing that matters most, and I can't see what they mean by it.'

She looked desperately at the smooth-bowled pipes, and wondered – should she walk on by the Strand or by the Embankment? It was not a simple question, for it concerned not different streets so much as different streams of thought. If she went by the Strand she would force herself to think out the problem of the future, or some mathematical problem; if she went by the river she would certainly begin to think about things that didn't exist – the forest, the ocean beach, the leafy solitudes, the magnanimous hero. No, no, no! A thousand times no! – it wouldn't do; there was something repulsive in such thoughts at present; she must take something else; she was out of that mood at present. And then she thought of Mary; the thought gave her confidence, even pleasure of a sad sort, as if the triumph of Ralph and Mary proved that the fault of her failure lay with herself and not with life. An indistinct idea that the sight of Mary might be of help, combined with her natural trust in her, suggested a visit; for, surely, her liking was of a kind that implied liking upon Mary's side also. After a moment's hesitation she decided, although she seldom acted upon impulse, to act upon this one, and turned down a side street and found Mary's door. But her reception was not encouraging; clearly Mary didn't want to see her, had no help to impart, and the half-formed desire to confide in her was quenched immediately. She was slightly amused at her own delusion, looked rather absent-minded, and swung her gloves to and fro, as if doling out the few minutes accurately before she could say goodbye.

Those few minutes might very well be spent in asking for information as to the exact position of the Suffrage Bill, or in expounding her own very sensible view of the situation. But there was a tone in her voice, or a shade in her opinions, or a swing of her gloves which served to irritate Mary Datchet, whose manner became increasingly direct, abrupt, and even antagonistic. She became conscious of a wish to make Katharine realise the importance of this work, which she discussed so coolly, as though she, too, had sacrificed what Mary herself had sacrificed. The swinging of the gloves ceased, and Katharine, after ten minutes, began to make movements preliminary to departure. At the sight of this, Mary was aware – she was abnormally aware of things tonight – of another very strong desire; Katharine was not to be allowed to go, to disappear into the free, happy world of irresponsible individuals. She must be made to realise – to feel.

'I don't quite see,' she said, as if Katharine had challenged her explicitly, 'how, things being as they are, anyone can help trying, at least, to do something.'

'No. But how *are* things?'

Mary pressed her lips, and smiled ironically; she had Katharine at her mercy; she could, if she liked, discharge upon her head wagonloads of revolting proof of the state of things ignored by the casual, the amateur, the looker-on, the cynical observer of life at a distance. And yet she hesitated. As usual, when she found herself in talk with Katharine, she began to feel rapid alternations of opinion about her, arrows of sensation striking strangely through the envelope of personality, which shelters us so conveniently from our fellows. What an egoist, how aloof she was! And yet, not in her words, perhaps, but in her voice, in her face, in her attitude, there were signs of a soft brooding spirit, of a sensibility unblunted and profound, playing over her thoughts and deeds, and investing her manner with an habitual gentleness. The arguments and phrases of Mr Clacton fell flat against such armour.

'You'll be married, and you'll have other things to think of,' she said inconsequently, and with an accent of condescension. She was not going to make Katharine understand in a second, as she would, all she herself had learnt at the cost of such pain. No. Katharine was to be happy; Katharine was to be ignorant; Mary was to keep this knowledge of the impersonal life for herself. The thought of her morning's renunciation stung her conscience, and she tried to expand once more into that impersonal condition which was so lofty and so painless. She must check this desire to be an individual again, whose wishes were in conflict with those of other people. She repented of her bitterness.

Katharine now renewed her signs of leave-taking; she had drawn on one of her gloves, and looked about her as if in search of some trivial saying to end with. Wasn't there some picture, or clock, or chest of drawers which might be singled out for notice? something peaceable and friendly to end the uncomfortable interview? The green-shaded lamp burnt in the corner, and illumined books and pens and blotting-paper. The whole aspect of the place started another train of thought and struck her as enviably free; in such a room one could work – one could have a life of one's own.

'I think you're very lucky,' she observed. 'I envy you, living alone and having your own things' – and engaged in this exalted way, which had no recognition or engagement-ring, she added in her own mind.

Mary's lips parted slightly. She could not conceive in what respects Katharine, who spoke sincerely, could envy her.

'I don't think you've got any reason to envy me,' she said.

'Perhaps one always envies other people,' Katharine observed vaguely.

'Well, but you've got everything that anyone can want.'

Katharine remained silent. She gazed into the fire quietly, and without a trace of self-consciousness. The hostility which she had divined in Mary's tone had completely disappeared, and she forgot that she had been upon the point of going.

'Well, I suppose I have,' she said at length. 'And yet I sometimes think – ' She paused; she did not know how to express what she meant.

'It came over me in the Tube the other day,' she resumed, with a smile; 'what is it that makes these people go one way rather than the other? It's not love; it's not reason; I think it must be some idea. Perhaps, Mary, our affections are the shadow of an idea. Perhaps there isn't any such thing as affection in itself . . . ' She spoke half-mockingly, asking her question, which she scarcely troubled to frame, not of Mary, or of anyone in particular.

But the words seemed to Mary Datchet shallow, supercilious, cold-blooded and cynical all in one. All her natural instincts were roused in revolt against them.

'I'm the opposite way of thinking, you see,' she said.

'Yes; I know you are,' Katharine replied, looking at her as if now she were about, perhaps, to explain something very important.

Mary could not help feeling the simplicity and good faith that lay behind Katharine's words.

'I think affection is the only reality,' she said.

'Yes,' said Katharine, almost sadly. She understood that Mary was
thinking of Ralph, and she felt it impossible to press her to reveal more
of this exalted condition; she could only respect the fact that, in some
few cases, life arranged itself thus satisfactorily and pass on. She rose to
her feet accordingly. But Mary exclaimed, with unmistakable earnestness, that she must not go; that they met so seldom; that she wanted to
talk to her so much . . . Katharine was surprised at the earnestness with
which she spoke. It seemed to her that there could be no indiscretion in
mentioning Ralph by name.

Seating herself 'for ten minutes', she said: 'By the way, Mr Denham
told me he was going to give up the Bar and live in the country. Has he
gone? He was beginning to tell me about it, when we were interrupted.'

'He thinks of it,' said Mary briefly. The colour at once came to her
face.

'It would be a very good plan,' said Katharine in her decided way.

'You think so?'

'Yes, because he would do something worth while; he would write a
book. My father always says that he's the most remarkable of the young
men who write for him.'

Mary bent low over the fire and stirred the coal between the bars
with a poker. Katharine's mention of Ralph had roused within her an
almost irresistible desire to explain to her the true state of the case
between herself and Ralph. She knew, from the tone of her voice, that
in speaking of Ralph she had no desire to probe Mary's secrets, or to
insinuate any of her own. Moreover, she liked Katharine; she trusted
her; she felt a respect for her. The first step of confidence was comparatively simple; but a further confidence had revealed itself, as
Katharine spoke, which was not so simple, and yet it impressed itself
upon her as a necessity; she must tell Katharine what it was clear that
she had no conception of – she must tell Katharine that Ralph was in
love with her.

'I don't know what he means to do,' she said hurriedly, seeking time
against the pressure of her own conviction. 'I've not seen him since
Christmas.'

Katharine reflected that this was odd; perhaps, after all, she had
misunderstood the position. She was in the habit of assuming, however,
that she was rather unobservant of the finer shades of feeling, and she
noted her present failure as another proof that she was a practical,
abstract-minded person, better fitted to deal with figures than with the
feelings of men and women. Anyhow, William Rodney would say so.

'And now – ' she said.

'Oh, please stay!' Mary exclaimed, putting out her hand to stop her. Directly Katharine moved she felt, inarticulately and violently, that she could not bear to let her go. If Katharine went, her only chance of speaking was lost; her only chance of saying something tremendously important was lost. Half a dozen words were sufficient to wake Katharine's attention, and put flight and further silence beyond her power. But although the words came to her lips, her throat closed upon them and drove them back. After all, she considered, why should she speak? Because it is right, her instinct told her; right to expose oneself without reservations to other human beings. She flinched from the thought. It asked too much of one already stripped bare. Something she must keep of her own. But if she did keep something of her own? Immediately she figured an immured life, continuing for an immense period, the same feelings living for ever, neither dwindling nor changing within the ring of a thick stone wall. The imagination of this loneliness frightened her, and yet to speak – to lose her loneliness, for it had already become dear to her, was beyond her power.

Her hand went down to the hem of Katharine's skirt, and, fingering a line of fur, she bent her head as if to examine it.

'I like this fur,' she said, 'I like your clothes. And you mustn't think that I'm going to marry Ralph,' she continued, in the same tone, 'because he doesn't care for me at all. He cares for someone else.' Her head remained bent, and her hand still rested upon the skirt.

'It's a shabby old dress,' said Katharine, and the only sign that Mary's words had reached her was that she spoke with a little jerk.

'You don't mind my telling you that?' said Mary, raising herself.

'No, no,' said Katharine; 'but you're mistaken, aren't you?' She was, in truth, horribly uncomfortable, dismayed, indeed, disillusioned. She disliked the turn things had taken quite intensely. The indecency of it afflicted her. The suffering implied by the tone appalled her. She looked at Mary furtively, with eyes that were full of apprehension. But if she had hoped to find that these words had been spoken without understanding of their meaning, she was at once disappointed. Mary lay back in her chair, frowning slightly, and looking, Katharine thought, as if she had lived fifteen years or so in the space of a few minutes.

'There are some things, don't you think, that one can't be mistaken about?' Mary said, quietly and almost coldly. 'That is what puzzles me about this question of being in love. I've always prided myself upon being reasonable,' she added. 'I didn't think I could have felt this – I mean if the other person didn't. I was foolish. I let myself pretend.'

Here she paused. 'For, you see, Katharine,' she proceeded, rousing herself and speaking with greater energy, 'I *am* in love. There's no doubt about that . . . I'm tremendously in love . . . with Ralph.' The little forward shake of her head, which shook a lock of hair, together with her brighter colour, gave her an appearance at once proud and defiant.

Katharine thought to herself, 'That's how it feels then.' She hesitated, with a feeling that it was not for her to speak; and then said, in a low tone, 'You've got that.'

'Yes,' said Mary; 'I've got that. One wouldn't *not* be in love . . . But I didn't mean to talk about that; I only wanted you to know. There's another thing I want to tell you . . . ' She paused. 'I haven't any authority from Ralph to say it; but I'm sure of this – he's in love with you.'

Katharine looked at her again, as if her first glance must have been deluded, for, surely, there must be some outward sign that Mary was talking in an excited, or bewildered, or fantastic manner. No; she still frowned, as if she sought her way through the clauses of a difficult argument, but she still looked more like one who reasons than one who feels.

'That proves that you're mistaken – utterly mistaken,' said Katharine, speaking reasonably, too. She had no need to verify the mistake by a glance at her own recollections when the fact was so clearly stamped upon her mind that if Ralph had any feeling towards her it was one of critical hostility. She did not give the matter another thought, and Mary, now that she had stated the fact, did not seek to prove it, but tried to explain to herself, rather than to Katharine, her motives in making the statement.

She had nerved herself to do what some large and imperious instinct demanded her doing; she had been swept on the breast of a wave beyond her reckoning.

'I've told you,' she said, 'because I want you to help me. I don't want to be jealous of you. And I am – I'm fearfully jealous. The only way, I thought, was to tell you.'

She hesitated, and groped in her endeavour to make her feelings clear to herself.

'If I tell you, then we can talk; and when I'm jealous, I can tell you. And if I'm tempted to do something frightfully mean, I can tell you; you could make me tell you. I find talking so difficult; but loneliness frightens me. I should shut it up in my mind. Yes, that's what I'm afraid of. Going about with something in my mind all my life that never changes. I find it so difficult to change. When I think a thing's wrong I never stop thinking it wrong, and Ralph was quite right, I see, when he said that there's no such thing as right and wrong; no such thing, I mean, as judging people – '

'Ralph Denham said that?' said Katharine, with considerable indignation. In order to have produced such suffering in Mary, it seemed to her that he must have behaved with extreme callousness. It seemed to her that he had discarded the friendship, when it suited his convenience to do so, with some falsely philosophical theory which made his conduct all the worse. She was going on to express herself thus, had not Mary at once interrupted her.

'No, no,' she said; 'you don't understand. If there's any fault it's mine entirely; after all, if one chooses to run risks – '

Her voice faltered into silence. It was borne in upon her how completely in running her risk she had lost her prize, lost it so entirely that she had no longer the right, in talking of Ralph, to presume that her knowledge of him supplanted all other knowledge. She no longer completely possessed her love, since his share in it was doubtful; and now, to make things yet more bitter, her clear vision of the way to face life was rendered tremulous and uncertain, because another was witness of it. Feeling her desire for the old unshared intimacy too great to be borne without tears, she rose, walked to the farther end of the room, held the curtains apart, and stood there mastered for a moment. The grief itself was not ignoble; the sting of it lay in the fact that she had been led to this act of treachery against herself. Trapped, cheated, robbed, first by Ralph and then by Katharine, she seemed all dissolved in humiliation, and bereft of anything she could call her own. Tears of weakness welled up and rolled down her cheeks. But tears, at least, she could control, and would this instant, and then, turning, she would face Katharine, and retrieve what could be retrieved of the collapse of her courage.

She turned. Katharine had not moved; she was leaning a little forward in her chair and looking into the fire. Something in the attitude reminded Mary of Ralph. So he would sit, leaning forward, looking rather fixedly in front of him, while his mind went far away, exploring, speculating, until he broke off with his, 'Well, Mary?' – and the silence, that had been so full of romance to her, gave way to the most delightful talk that she had ever known.

Something unfamiliar in the pose of the silent figure, something still, solemn, significant about it, made her hold her breath. She paused. Her thoughts were without bitterness. She was surprised by her own quiet and confidence. She came back silently, and sat once more by Katharine's side. Mary had no wish to speak. In the silence she seemed to have lost her isolation; she was at once the sufferer and the pitiful spectator of suffering; she was happier than she had ever been; she was more bereft; she was rejected, and she was immensely beloved. Attempt to express these sensations was vain, and, moreover, she could not help believing that, without any words on her side, they were shared. Thus for some time longer they sat silent, side by side, while Mary fingered the fur on the skirt of the old dress.

Chapter 22

The fact that she would be late in keeping her engagement with William was not the only reason which sent Katharine almost at racing speed along the Strand in the direction of his rooms. Punctuality might have been achieved by taking a cab, had she not wished the open air to fan into flame the glow kindled by Mary's words. For among all the impressions of the evening's talk one was of the nature of a revelation and subdued the rest to insignificance. Thus one looked; thus one spoke; such was love.

'She sat up straight and looked at me, and then she said, "I'm in love," ' Katharine mused, trying to set the whole scene in motion. It was a scene to dwell on with so much wonder that not a grain of pity occurred to her; it was a flame blazing suddenly in the dark; by its light Katharine perceived far too vividly for her comfort the mediocrity, indeed the entirely fictitious character of her own feelings so far as they pretended to correspond with Mary's feelings. She made up her mind to act instantly upon the knowledge thus gained, and cast her mind in amazement back to the scene upon the heath, when she had yielded, heaven knows why, for reasons which seemed now imperceptible. So in broad daylight one might revisit the place where one has groped and turned and succumbed to utter bewilderment in a fog.

'It's all so simple,' she said to herself. 'There can't be any doubt. I've only got to speak now. I've only got to speak,' she went on saying, in time to her own footsteps, and completely forgot Mary Datchet.

William Rodney, having come back earlier from the office than he expected, sat down to pick out the melodies in *The Magic Flute* upon the piano. Katharine was late, but that was nothing new, and, as she had no particular liking for music, and he felt in the mood for it, perhaps it was as well. This defect in Katharine was the more strange, William reflected, because, as a rule, the women of her family were unusually musical. Her cousin, Cassandra Otway, for example, had a very fine taste in music, and he had charming recollections of her in a light fantastic attitude, playing the flute in the morning-room at Stogdon House. He recalled with pleasure the amusing way in which her nose, long like all the Otway noses, seemed to extend itself into the flute, as if she were some inimitably graceful species of musical mole. The little picture suggested very happily her melodious and whimsical temperament. The enthusiasms of a young girl of distinguished upbringing appealed to William, and suggested a thousand ways in which, with his training and accomplishments, he could be of service to her. She ought to be given the chance of hearing good music, as it is played by those who have inherited the great tradition. Moreover, from one or two remarks let fall in the course of conversation, he thought it possible that she had what Katharine professed to lack, a passionate, if untaught, appreciation of literature. He had lent her his play. Meanwhile, as Katharine was certain to be late, and *The Magic Flute* is nothing without a voice, he felt inclined to spend the time of waiting in writing a letter to Cassandra, exhorting her to read Pope in preference to Dostoevsky,[69] until her feeling for form was more highly developed. He set himself down to compose this piece of advice in a shape which was light and playful, and yet did no injury to a cause which he had near at heart, when he heard Katharine upon the stairs. A moment later it was plain that he had been mistaken, it was not Katharine; but he could not settle himself to his letter. His temper had changed from one of urbane contentment – indeed of delicious expansion – to one of uneasiness and expectation. The dinner was brought in, and had to be set by the fire to keep hot. It was now a quarter of an hour beyond the specified time. He bethought him of a piece of news which had depressed him in the earlier part of the day. Owing to the illness of one of his fellow-clerks, it was likely that he would get no holiday until later in the year, which would mean the postponement of their marriage. But this possibility, after all, was not so disagreeable as the probability which forced itself upon him with every tick of the clock that Katharine had completely forgotten her engagement. Such things had happened less frequently since Christmas, but what if they were going to begin to happen again? What if their marriage should turn out, as she had said, a farce? He acquitted her of any wish to hurt him wantonly, but there was something in her character which made it impossible for her to help hurting people. Was she cold? Was she self-absorbed? He tried to fit her with each of these descriptions, but he had to own that she puzzled him.

'There are so many things that she doesn't understand,' he reflected, glancing at the letter to Cassandra which he had begun and laid aside. What prevented him from finishing the letter which he had so much enjoyed beginning? The reason was that Katharine might, at any moment, enter the room. The thought, implying his bondage to her, irritated him acutely. It occurred to him that he would leave the letter lying open for her to see, and he would take the opportunity of telling her that he had sent his play to Cassandra for her to criticise. Possibly, but not by any means certainly, this would annoy her – and as he reached the doubtful comfort of this conclusion, there was a knock on the door and Katharine came in. They kissed each other coldly and she made no apology for being late. Nevertheless, her mere presence moved him strangely; but he was determined that this should not weaken his resolution to make some kind of stand against her; to get at the truth about her. He let her make her own disposition of clothes and busied himself with the plates.

'I've got a piece of news for you, Katharine,' he said directly they sat down to table; 'I shan't get my holiday in April. We shall have to put off our marriage.'

He rapped the words out with a certain degree of briskness. Katharine started a little, as if the announcement disturbed her thoughts.

'That won't make any difference, will it? I mean the lease isn't signed,' she replied. 'But why? What has happened?'

He told her, in an off-hand way, how one of his fellow-clerks had broken down, and might have to be away for months, six months even, in which case they would have to think over their position. He said it in a way which struck her, at last, as oddly casual. She looked at him. There was no outward sign that he was annoyed with her. Was she well dressed? She thought sufficiently so. Perhaps she was late? She looked for a clock.

'It's a good thing we didn't take the house then,' she repeated thoughtfully.

'It'll mean, too, I'm afraid, that I shan't be as free for a considerable time as I have been,' he continued. She had time to reflect that she gained something by all this, though it was too soon to determine what. But the light which had been burning with such intensity as she came along was suddenly overclouded, as much by his manner as by his news. She had been prepared to meet opposition, which is simple to encounter compared with – she did not know what it was that she had to encounter. The meal passed in quiet, well-controlled talk about indifferent things. Music was not a subject about which she knew anything, but she liked him to tell her things; and could, she mused, as he talked, fancy the evenings of married life spent thus, over the fire; spent thus, or with a book, perhaps, for then she would have time to read her books, and to grasp firmly with every muscle of her unused mind what she longed to know. The atmosphere was very free. Suddenly William broke off. She looked up apprehensively, brushing aside these thoughts with annoyance.

'Where should I address a letter to Cassandra?' he asked her. It was obvious again that William had some meaning or other tonight, or was in some mood. 'We've struck up a friendship,' he added.

'She's at home, I think,' Katharine replied.

'They keep her too much at home,' said William. 'Why don't you ask her to stay with you, and let her hear a little good music? I'll just finish what I was saying, if you don't mind, because I'm particularly anxious that she should hear tomorrow.'

Katharine sank back in her chair, and Rodney took the paper on his knees, and went on with his sentence. 'Style, you know, is what we tend to neglect – '; but he was far more conscious of Katharine's eye upon him than of what he was saying about style. He knew that she was looking at him, but whether with irritation or indifference he could not guess.

In truth, she had fallen sufficiently into his trap to feel uncomfortably roused and disturbed and unable to proceed on the lines laid down for herself. This indifferent, if not hostile, attitude on William's part made it impossible to break off without animosity, largely and completely. Infinitely preferable was Mary's state, she thought, where there was a simple thing to do and one did it. In fact, she could not help supposing that some littleness of nature had a part in all the refinements, reserves and subtleties of feeling for which her friends and family were so distinguished. For example, although she liked Cassandra well enough, her fantastic method of life struck her as purely frivolous; now it was socialism, now it was silkworms, now it was music – which last she supposed was the cause of William's sudden interest in her. Never before had William wasted the minutes of her presence in writing his letters. With a curious sense of light opening where all, hitherto, had been opaque, it dawned upon her that, after all, possibly, yes, probably, nay, certainly, the devotion which she had almost wearily taken for granted existed in a much slighter degree than she had suspected, or existed no longer. She looked at him attentively as if this discovery of hers must show traces in his face. Never had she seen so much to respect in his appearance, so much that attracted her by its sensitiveness and intelligence, although she saw these qualities as if they were those one responds to, dumbly, in the face of a stranger. The head bent over the paper, thoughtful as usual, had now a composure which seemed somehow to place it at a distance, like a face seen talking to someone else behind glass.

He wrote on, without raising his eyes. She would have spoken, but could not bring herself to ask him for signs of affection which she had no right to claim. The conviction that he was thus strange to her filled her with despondency, and illustrated quite beyond doubt the infinite loneliness of human beings. She had never felt the truth of this so strongly before. She looked away into the fire; it seemed to her that even physically they were now scarcely within speaking distance; and spiritually there was certainly no human being with whom she could claim comradeship; no dream that satisfied her as she was used to be satisfied; nothing remained in whose reality she could believe, save those abstract ideas – figures, laws, stars, facts, which she could hardly hold to for lack of knowledge and a kind of shame.

When Rodney owned to himself the folly of this prolonged silence, and the meanness of such devices, and looked up ready to seek some excuse for a good laugh, or opening for a confession, he was disconcerted by what he saw. Katharine seemed equally oblivious of what was bad or of what was good in him. Her expression suggested concentration upon something entirely remote from her surroundings. The carelessness of her attitude seemed to him rather masculine than feminine. His impulse to break up the constraint was chilled, and once more the exasperating sense of his own impotency returned to him. He could not help contrasting Katharine with his vision of the engaging, whimsical Cassandra; Katharine undemonstrative, inconsiderate, silent, and yet so notable that he could never do without her good opinion.

She veered round upon him a moment later, as if, when her train of thought was ended, she became aware of his presence.

'Have you finished your letter?' she asked. He thought he heard faint amusement in her tone, but not a trace of jealousy.

'No, I'm not going to write any more tonight,' he said. 'I'm not in the mood for it for some reason. I can't say what I want to say.'

'Cassandra won't know if it's well written or badly written,' Katharine remarked.

'I'm not so sure about that. I should say she has a good deal of literary feeling.'

'Perhaps,' said Katharine indifferently. 'You've been neglecting my education lately, by the way. I wish you'd read something. Let me choose a book.' So speaking, she went across to his bookshelves and began looking in a desultory way among his books. Anything, she thought, was better than bickering or the strange silence which drove home to her the distance between them. As she pulled one book forward and then another she thought ironically of her own certainty not an hour ago; how it had vanished in a moment, how she was merely marking time as best she could, not knowing in the least where they stood, what they felt, or whether William loved her or not. More and more the condition of Mary's mind seemed to her wonderful and enviable – if, indeed, it could be quite as she figured it – if, indeed, simplicity existed for any one of the daughters of women.

'Swift,' she said, at last, taking out a volume at haphazard to settle this question at least. 'Let us have some Swift.'

Rodney took the book, held it in front of him, inserted one finger between the pages, but said nothing. His face wore a queer expression of deliberation, as if he were weighing one thing with another, and would not say anything until his mind were made up.

Katharine, taking her chair beside him, noted his silence and looked at him with sudden apprehension. What she hoped or feared, she could not have said; a most irrational and indefensible desire for some assurance of his affection was, perhaps, uppermost in her mind. Peevishness, complaints, exacting cross-examination she was used to, but this attitude of composed quiet, which seemed to come from the consciousness of power within, puzzled her. She did not know what was going to happen next.

At last William spoke.

'I think it's a little odd, don't you?' he said, in a voice of detached reflection. 'Most people, I mean, would be seriously upset if their marriage was put off for six months or so. But we aren't; now how do you account for that?'

She looked at him and observed his judicial attitude as of one holding far aloof from emotion.

'I attribute it,' he went on, without waiting for her to answer, 'to the fact that neither of us is in the least romantic about the other. That may be partly, no doubt, because we've known each other so long; but I'm inclined to think there's more in it than that. There's something temperamental. I think you're a trifle cold, and I suspect I'm a trifle self-absorbed. If that were so it goes a long way to explaining our odd lack of illusion about each other. I'm not saying that the most satisfactory marriages aren't founded upon this sort of understanding. But certainly it struck me as odd this morning, when Wilson told me, how little upset I felt. By the way, you're sure we haven't committed ourselves to that house?'

'I've kept the letters, and I'll go through them tomorrow; but I'm certain we're on the safe side.'

'Thanks. As to the psychological problem,' he continued, as if the question interested him in a detached way, 'there's no doubt, I think, that either of us is capable of feeling what, for reasons of simplicity, I call romance for a third person – at least, I've little doubt in my own case.'

It was, perhaps, the first time in all her knowledge of him that Katharine had known William enter thus deliberately and without sign of emotion upon a statement of his own feelings. He was wont to discourage such intimate discussions by a little laugh or turn of the conversation, as much as to say that men, or men of the world, find such topics a little silly, or in doubtful taste. His obvious wish to explain something puzzled her, interested her, and neutralised the wound to her vanity. For some reason, too, she felt more at ease with him than usual; or her ease was more the ease of equality – she could not stop to think of that at the moment though. His remarks interested her too much for the light that they threw upon certain problems of her own.

'What is this romance?' she mused.

'Ah, that's the question. I've never come across a definition that satisfied me, though there are some very good ones' – he glanced in the direction of his books.

'It's not altogether knowing the other person, perhaps – it's ignorance,' she hazarded.

'Some authorities say it's a question of distance – romance in literature, that is – '

'Possibly, in the case of art. But in the case of people it may be – ' she hesitated.

'Have you no personal experience of it?' he asked, letting his eyes rest upon her swiftly for a moment.

'I believe it's influenced me enormously,' she said, in the tone of one absorbed by the possibilities of some view just presented to them; 'but in my life there's so little scope for it,' she added. She reviewed her daily task, the perpetual demands upon her for good sense, self-control and accuracy in a house containing a romantic mother. Ah, but her romance wasn't *that* romance. It was a desire, an echo, a sound; she could drape it in colour, see it in form, hear it in music, but not in words; no, never in words. She sighed, teased by desires so incoherent, so incommunicable.

'But isn't it curious,' William resumed, 'that you should neither feel it for me, nor I for you?'

Katharine agreed that it was curious – very; but even more curious to her was the fact that she was discussing the question with William. It revealed possibilities which opened a prospect of a new relationship altogether. Somehow it seemed to her that he was helping her to understand what she had never understood; and in her gratitude she was conscious of a most sisterly desire to help him, too – sisterly, save for one pang, not quite to be subdued, that for him she was without romance.

'I think you might be very happy with someone you loved in that way,' she said.

'You assume that romance survives a closer knowledge of the person one loves?'

He asked the question formally, to protect himself from the sort of personality which he dreaded. The whole situation needed the most careful management lest it should degenerate into some degrading and disturbing exhibition such as the scene, which he could never think of without shame, upon the heath among the dead leaves. And yet each sentence brought him relief. He was coming to understand something or other about his own desires hitherto undefined by him, the source of his difficulty with Katharine. The wish to hurt her, which had urged him to begin, had completely left him, and he felt that it was only Katharine now who could help him to be sure. He must take his time. There were so many things that he could not say without the greatest difficulty – that name, for example, Cassandra. Nor could he move his eyes from a certain spot, a fiery glen surrounded by high mountains, in the heart of the coals. He waited in suspense for Katharine to continue. She had said that he might be very happy with someone he loved in that way.

'I don't see why it shouldn't last with you,' she resumed. 'I can imagine a certain sort of person – ' she paused; she was aware that he was listening with the greatest intentness, and that his formality was merely the cover for an extreme anxiety of some sort. There was some person then – some woman – who could it be? Cassandra? Ah, possibly –

'A person,' she added, speaking in the most matter-of-fact tone she could command, 'like Cassandra Otway, for instance. Cassandra is the most interesting of the Otways – with the exception of Henry. Even so, I like Cassandra better. She has more than mere cleverness. She is a character – a person by herself.'

'Those dreadful insects!' burst from William, with a nervous laugh, and a little spasm went through him as Katharine noticed. It *was* Cassandra then. Automatically and dully she replied, 'You could insist that she confined herself to – to – something else . . . But she cares for music; I believe she writes poetry; and there can be no doubt that she has a peculiar charm – '

She ceased, as if defining to herself this peculiar charm. After a moment's silence William jerked out: 'I thought her affectionate?'

'Extremely affectionate. She worships Henry. When you think what a house that is – Uncle Francis always in one mood or another – '

'Dear, dear, dear,' William muttered.

'And you have so much in common.'

'My dear Katharine!' William exclaimed, flinging himself back in his chair, and uprooting his eyes from the spot in the fire. 'I really don't know what we're talking about . . . I assure you . . .'

He was covered with an extreme confusion.

He withdrew the finger that was still thrust between the pages of *Gulliver*, opened the book, and ran his eye down the list of chapters, as though he were about to select the one most suitable for reading aloud. As Katharine watched him, she was seized with preliminary symptoms of his own panic. At the same time she was convinced that, should he find the right page, take out his spectacles, clear his throat, and open his lips, a chance that would never come again in all their lives would be lost to them both.

'We're talking about things that interest us both very much,' she said. 'Shan't we go on talking, and leave Swift for another time? I don't feel in the mood for Swift, and it's a pity to read anyone when that's the case – particularly Swift.'

The presence of wise literary speculation, as she calculated, restored William's confidence in his security, and he replaced the book in the bookcase, keeping his back turned to her as he did so, and taking advantage of this circumstance to summon his thoughts together.

But a second of introspection had the alarming result of showing him that his mind, when looked at from within, was no longer familiar ground. He felt, that is to say, what he had never consciously felt before; he was revealed to himself as other than he was wont to think him; he was afloat upon a sea of unknown and tumultuous possibilities. He paced once up and down the room, and then flung himself impetuously into the chair by Katharine's side. He had never felt anything like this before; he put himself entirely into her hands; he cast off all responsibility. He very nearly exclaimed aloud: 'You've stirred up all these odious and violent emotions, and now you must do the best you can with them.'

Her near presence, however, had a calming and reassuring effect upon his agitation, and he was conscious only of an implicit trust that, somehow, he was safe with her, that she would see him through, find out what it was that he wanted, and procure it for him.

'I wish to do whatever you tell me to do,' he said. 'I put myself entirely in your hands, Katharine.'

'You must try to tell me what you feel,' she said.

'My dear, I feel a thousand things every second. I don't know, I'm sure, what I feel. That afternoon on the heath – it was then – then – ' He broke off; he did not tell her what had happened then. 'Your ghastly good sense, as usual, has convinced me – for the moment – but what the truth is, heaven only knows!' he exclaimed.

'Isn't it the truth that you are, or might be, in love with Cassandra?' she said gently.

William bowed his head. After a moment's silence he murmured: 'I believe you're right, Katharine.'

She sighed, involuntarily. She had been hoping all this time, with an intensity that increased second by second against the current of her words, that it would not in the end come to this. After a moment of surprising anguish, she summoned her courage to tell him how she wished only that she might help him, and had framed the first words of her speech when a knock, terrific and startling to people in their over-wrought condition, sounded upon the door.

'Katharine, I worship you,' he urged, half in a whisper.

'Yes,' she replied, withdrawing with a little shiver, 'but you must open the door.'

Chapter 23

When Ralph Denham entered the room and saw Katharine seated with her back to him, he was conscious of a change in the grade of the atmosphere such as a traveller meets with sometimes upon the roads, particularly after sunset, when, without warning, he runs from clammy chill to a hoard of unspent warmth in which the sweetness of hay and beanfield is cherished, as if the sun still shone although the moon is up. He hesitated; he shuddered; he walked elaborately to the window and laid aside his coat. He balanced his stick most carefully against the folds of the curtain. Thus occupied with his own sensations and preparations, he had little time to observe what either of the other two was feeling. Such symptoms of agitation as he might perceive (and they had left their tokens in brightness of eye and pallor of cheeks) seemed to him well befitting the actors in so great a drama as that of Katharine Hilbery's daily life. Beauty and passion were the breath of her being, he thought.

She scarcely noticed his presence, or only as it forced her to adopt a manner of composure, which she was certainly far from feeling. William, however, was even more agitated than she was, and her first instalment of promised help took the form of some commonplace upon the age of the building or the architect's name, which gave him an excuse to fumble in a drawer for certain designs, which he laid upon the table between the three of them.

Which of the three followed the designs most carefully it would be difficult to tell, but it is certain that not one of the three found for the moment anything to say. Years of training in a drawing-room came at length to Katharine's help, and she said something suitable, at the same moment withdrawing her hand from the table because she perceived that it trembled. William agreed effusively; Denham corroborated him, speaking in rather high-pitched tones; they thrust aside the plans, and drew nearer to the fireplace.

'I'd rather live here than anywhere in the whole of London,' said Denham.

('And I've got nowhere to live,') Katharine thought, as she agreed aloud.

'You could get rooms here, no doubt, if you wanted to,' Rodney replied.

'But I'm just leaving London for good – I've taken that cottage I was telling you about.' The announcement seemed to convey very little to either of his hearers.

'Indeed? – that's sad . . . You must give me your address. But you won't cut yourself off altogether, surely – '

'You'll be moving, too, I suppose,' Denham remarked.

William showed such visible signs of floundering that Katharine collected herself and asked: 'Where is the cottage you've taken?'

In answering her, Denham turned and looked at her. As their eyes met, she realised for the first time that she was talking to Ralph Denham, and she remembered, without recalling any details, that she had been speaking of him quite lately, and that she had reason to think ill of him. What Mary had said she could not remember, but she felt that there was a mass of knowledge in her mind which she had not had time to examine – knowledge now lying on the far side of a gulf. But her agitation flashed the queerest lights upon her past. She must get through the matter in hand, and then think it out in quiet. She bent her mind to follow what Ralph was saying. He was telling her that he had taken a cottage in Norfolk, and she was saying that she knew, or did not know, that particular neighbourhood. But after a moment's attention her mind flew to Rodney, and she had an unusual, indeed unprecedented, sense that they were in touch and shared each other's thoughts. If only Ralph were not there, she would at once give way to her desire to take William's hand, then to bend his head upon her shoulder, for this was what she wanted to do more than anything at the moment, unless, indeed, she wished more than anything to be alone – yes, that was what she wanted. She was sick to death of these discussions; she shivered at the effort to reveal her feelings. She had forgotten to answer. William was speaking now.

'But what will you find to do in the country?' she asked at random, striking into a conversation which she had only half heard in such a way as to make both Rodney and Denham look at her with a little surprise. But directly she took up the conversation, it was William's turn to fall silent. He at once forgot to listen to what they were saying, although he interposed nervously at intervals, 'Yes, yes, yes.' As the minutes passed, Ralph's presence became more and more intolerable to him, since there was so much that he must say to Katharine; the moment he could not talk to her, terrible doubts, unanswerable questions accumulated, which he must lay before Katharine, for she alone could help him now. Unless he could see her alone, it would be impossible for him ever to sleep, or to know what he had said in a moment of madness, which was not altogether mad, or was it mad? He nodded his head, and said, nervously, 'Yes, yes,' and looked at Katharine, and thought how beautiful she looked; there was no one in the world that he admired more. There was an emotion in her face which lent it an expression he had never seen there. Then, as he was turning over means by which he could speak to her alone, she rose, and he was taken by surprise, for he had counted on the fact that she would outstay Denham. His only chance, then, of saying something to her in private, was to take her downstairs and walk with her to the street. While he hesitated, however, overcome with the difficulty of putting one simple thought into words when all his thoughts were scattered about, and all were too strong for utterance, he was struck silent by something that was still more unexpected. Denham got up from his chair, looked at Katharine, and said: 'I'm going, too. Shall we go together?'

And before William could see any way of detaining him – or would it be better to detain Katharine? – he had taken his hat, stick, and was holding the door open for Katharine to pass out. The most that William could do was to stand at the head of the stairs and say good-night. He could not offer to go with them. He could not insist that she should stay. He watched her descend, rather slowly, owing to the dusk of the staircase, and he had a last sight of Denham's head and of Katharine's head near together, against the panels, when suddenly a pang of acute jealousy overcame him, and had he not remained conscious of the slippers upon his feet, he would have run after them or cried out. As it was he could not move from the spot. At the turn of the staircase Katharine turned to look back, trusting to this last glance to seal their compact of good friendship. Instead of returning her silent greeting, William grinned back at her a cold stare of sarcasm or of rage.

She stopped dead for a moment, and then descended slowly into the court. She looked to the right and to the left, and once up into the sky. She was only conscious of Denham as a block upon her thoughts. She measured the distance that must be traversed before she would be alone. But when they came to the Strand no cabs were to be seen, and Denham broke the silence by saying: 'There seem to be no cabs. Shall we walk on a little?'

'Very well,' she agreed, paying no attention to him.

Aware of her preoccupation, or absorbed in his own thoughts, Ralph said nothing further; and in silence they walked some distance along the Strand. Ralph was doing his best to put his thoughts into such order that one came before the rest, and the determination that when he spoke he should speak worthily, made him put off the moment of speaking till he had found the exact words and even the place that best suited him. The Strand was too busy. There was too much risk, also, of finding an empty cab. Without a word of explanation he turned to the left, down one of the side streets leading to the river. On no account must they part until something of the very greatest importance had happened. He knew perfectly well what he wished to say, and had arranged not only the substance, but the order in which he was to say it. Now, however, that he was alone with her, not only did he find the difficulty of speaking almost insurmountable, but he was aware that he was angry with her for thus disturbing him, and casting, as it was so easy for a person of her advantages to do, these phantoms and pitfalls across his path. He was determined that he would question her as severely as he would question himself; and make them both, once and for all, either justify her dominance or renounce it. But the longer they walked thus alone, the more he was disturbed by the sense of her actual presence.

Her skirt blew; the feathers in her hat waved; sometimes he saw her a step or two ahead of him, or had to wait for her to catch him up.

The silence was prolonged, and at length drew her attention to him. First she was annoyed that there was no cab to free her from his company; then she recalled vaguely something that Mary had said to make her think ill of him; she could not remember what, but the recollection, combined with his masterful ways – why did he walk so fast down this side street? – made her more and more conscious of a person of marked, though disagreeable, force by her side. She stopped and, looking round her for a cab, sighted one in the distance. He was thus precipitated into speech.

'Should you mind if we walked a little farther?' he asked. 'There's something I want to say to you.'

'Very well,' she replied, guessing that his request had something to do with Mary Datchet.

'It's quieter by the river,' he said, and instantly he crossed over. 'I want to ask you merely this,' he began. But he paused so long that she could see his head against the sky; the slope of his thin cheek and his large, strong nose were clearly marked against it. While he paused, words that were quite different from those he intended to use presented themselves.

'I've made you my standard ever since I saw you. I've dreamt about you; I've thought of nothing but you; you represent to me the only reality in the world.'

His words, and the queer strained voice in which he spoke them, made it appear as if he addressed some person who was not the woman beside him, but someone far away.

'And now things have come to such a pass that, unless I can speak to you openly, I believe I shall go mad. I think of you as the most beautiful, the truest thing in the world,' he continued, filled with a sense of exaltation, and feeling that he had no need now to choose his words with pedantic accuracy, for what he wanted to say was suddenly become plain to him.

'I see you everywhere, in the stars, in the river; to me you're everything that exists; the reality of everything. Life, I tell you, would be impossible without you. And now I want – '

She had heard him so far with a feeling that she had dropped some material word which made sense of the rest. She could hear no more of this unintelligible rambling without checking him. She felt that she was overhearing what was meant for another.

'I don't understand,' she said. 'You're saying things that you don't mean.'

'I mean every word I say,' he replied, emphatically. He turned his head towards her. She recovered the words she was searching for while he spoke. 'Ralph Denham is in love with you.' They came back to her in Mary Datchet's voice. Her anger blazed up in her.

'I saw Mary Datchet this afternoon,' she exclaimed.

He made a movement as if he were surprised or taken aback, but answered in a moment: 'She told you that I had asked her to marry me, I suppose?'

'No!' Katharine exclaimed, in surprise.

'I did though. It was the day I saw you at Lincoln,' he continued. 'I had meant to ask her to marry me, and then I looked out of the window and saw you. After that I didn't want to ask anyone to marry me. But I did it; and she knew I was lying, and refused me. I thought then, and still think, that she cares for me. I behaved very badly. I don't defend myself.'

'No,' said Katharine, 'I should hope not. There's no defence that I can think of. If any conduct is wrong, that is.' She spoke with an energy that was directed even more against herself than against him. 'It seems to me,' she continued, with the same energy, 'that people are bound to be honest. There's no excuse for such behaviour.' She could now see plainly before her eyes the expression on Mary Datchet's face.

After a short pause, he said: 'I am not telling you that I am in love with you. I am not in love with you.'

'I didn't think that,' she replied, conscious of some bewilderment.

'I have not spoken a word to you that I do not mean,' he added.

'Tell me then what it is that you mean,' she said at length.

As if obeying a common instinct, they both stopped and, bending slightly over the balustrade of the river, looked into the flowing water.

'You say that we've got to be honest,' Ralph began. 'Very well. I will try to tell you the facts; but I warn you, you'll think me mad. It's a fact, though, that since I first saw you four or five months ago I have made you, in an utterly absurd way, I expect, my ideal. I'm almost ashamed to tell you what lengths I've gone to. It's become the thing that matters most in my life.' He checked himself. 'Without knowing you, except that you're beautiful, and all that, I've come to believe that we're in some sort of agreement; that we're after something together; that we see something . . . I've got into the habit of imagining you; I'm always thinking what you'd say or do; I walk along the street talking to you; I dream of you. It's merely a bad habit, a schoolboy habit, daydreaming; it's a common experience; half one's friends do the same; well, those are the facts.'

Simultaneously, they both walked on very slowly.

'If you were to know me you would feel none of this,' she said. 'We don't know each other – we've always been – interrupted . . . Were you going to tell me this that day my aunts came?' she asked, recollecting the whole scene.

He bowed his head.

'The day you told me of your engagement,' he said.

She thought, with a start, that she was no longer engaged.

'I deny that I should cease to feel this if I knew you,' he went on. 'I should feel it more reasonably – that's all. I shouldn't talk the kind of nonsense I've talked tonight . . . But it wasn't nonsense. It was the truth,' he said doggedly. 'It's the important thing. You can force me to talk as if this feeling for you were an hallucination, but all our feelings are that. The best of them are half illusions. Still,' he added, as if arguing to himself, 'if it weren't as real a feeling as I'm capable of, I shouldn't be changing my life on your account.'

'What do you mean?' she enquired.

'I told you. I'm taking a cottage. I'm giving up my profession.'

'On my account?' she asked, in amazement.

'Yes, on your account,' he replied. He explained his meaning no further.

'But I don't know you or your circumstances,' she said at last, as he remained silent.

'You have no opinion about me one way or the other?'

'Yes, I suppose I have an opinion – ' she hesitated.

He controlled his wish to ask her to explain herself, and much to his pleasure she went on, appearing to search her mind.

'I thought that you criticised me – perhaps disliked me. I thought of you as a person who judges – '

'No; I'm a person who feels,' he said, in a low voice.

'Tell me, then, what has made you do this?' she asked, after a break.

He told her in an orderly way, betokening careful preparation, all that he had meant to say at first; how he stood with regard to his brothers and sisters; what his mother had said, and his sister Joan had refrained from saying; exactly how many pounds stood in his name at the bank; what prospect his brother had of earning a livelihood in America; how much of their income went on rent, and other details known to him by heart. She listened to all this, so that she could have passed an examination in it by the time Waterloo Bridge was in sight; and yet she was no more listening to it than she was counting the paving-stones at her feet. She was feeling happier than she had felt in her life. If Denham could have seen how visibly books of algebraic symbols, pages all speckled with dots and dashes and twisted bars, came before her eyes as they trod the Embankment, his secret joy in her attention might have been dispersed. She went on, saying, 'Yes, I see . . . But how would that help you? . . . Your brother has passed his examination?' so sensibly, that he had constantly to keep his brain in check; and all the time she was in fancy looking up through a telescope at white shadow-cleft disks which were other worlds, until she felt herself possessed of two bodies, one walking by the river with Denham, the other concentrated to a silver globe aloft in the fine blue space above the scum of vapours that was covering the visible world. She looked at the sky once, and saw that no star was keen enough to pierce the flight of watery clouds now coursing rapidly before the west wind. She looked down hurriedly again. There was no reason, she assured herself, for this feeling of happiness; she was not free; she was not alone; she was still bound to earth by a million fibres; every step took her nearer home. Nevertheless, she exulted as she had never exulted before. The air was fresher, the lights more distinct, the cold stone of the balustrade colder and harder when by chance or purpose she struck her hand against it. No feeling of annoyance with Denham remained; he certainly did not hinder any flight she might choose to make, whether in the direction of the sky or of her home; but that her condition was due to him, or to anything that he had said, she had no consciousness of at all.

They were now within sight of the stream of cabs and omnibuses crossing to and from the Surrey side of the river; the sound of the traffic, the hooting of motor-horns and the light chime of tram-bells sounded more and more distinctly, and, with the increase of noise, they both became silent. With a common instinct they slackened their pace, as if to lengthen the time of semi-privacy allowed them. To Ralph, the pleasure of these last yards of the walk with Katharine was so great that he could not look beyond the present moment to the time when she should have left him. He had no wish to use the last moments of their companionship in adding fresh words to what he had already said. Since they had stopped talking, she had become to him not so much a real person, as the very woman he dreamt of; but his solitary dreams had never produced any such keenness of sensation as that which he felt in her presence. He himself was also strangely transfigured. He had complete mastery of all his faculties. For the first time he was in possession of his full powers. The vistas which opened before him seemed to have no perceptible end. But the mood had none of the restlessness or feverish desire to add one delight to another

which had hitherto marked, and somewhat spoilt, the most rapturous of
his imaginings. It was a mood that took such clear-eyed account of the
conditions of human life that he was not disturbed in the least by the
gliding presence of a taxicab, and without agitation he perceived that
Katharine was conscious of it also, and turned her head in that direction.
Their halting steps acknowledged the desirability of engaging the cab;
and they stopped simultaneously, and signed to it.

'Then you will let me know your decision as soon as you can?' he
asked, with his hand on the door.

She hesitated for a moment. She could not immediately recall what
the question was that she had to decide.

'I will write,' she said vaguely. 'No,' she added, in a second, bethinking
her of the difficulties of writing anything decided upon a question to
which she had paid no attention, 'I don't see how to manage it.'

She stood looking at Denham, considering and hesitating, with her
foot upon the step. He guessed her difficulties; he knew in a second that
she had heard nothing; he knew everything that she felt.

'There's only one place to discuss things satisfactorily that I know of,'
he said quickly; 'that's Kew.'[70]

'Kew?'

'Kew,' he repeated, with immense decision. He shut the door and
gave her address to the driver. She instantly was conveyed away from
him, and her cab joined the knotted stream of vehicles, each marked by
a light, and indistinguishable one from the other. He stood watching
for a moment, and then, as if swept by some fierce impulse, from the
spot where they had stood, he turned, crossed the road at a rapid pace,
and disappeared.

He walked on upon the impetus of this last mood of almost super-
natural exaltation until he reached a narrow street, at this hour empty of
traffic and passengers. Here, whether it was the shops with their shuttered
windows, the smooth and silvered curve of the wood pavement or a
natural ebb of feeling, his exaltation slowly oozed and deserted him. He
was now conscious of the loss that follows any revelation; he had lost
something in speaking to Katharine, for, after all, was the Katharine
whom he loved the same as the real Katharine? She had transcended
her entirely at moments; her skirt had blown, her feather waved, her
voice spoken; yes, but how terrible sometimes the pause between the
voice of one's dreams and the voice that comes from the object of
one's dreams! He felt a mixture of disgust and pity at the figure cut by
human beings when they try to carry out, in practice, what they have
the power to conceive. How small both he and Katharine had appeared

when they issued from the cloud of thought that enveloped them! He recalled the small, inexpressive, commonplace words in which they had tried to communicate with each other; he repeated them over to himself. By repeating Katharine's words, he came in a few moments to such a sense of her presence that he worshipped her more than ever. But she was engaged to be married, he remembered with a start. The strength of his feeling was revealed to him instantly, and he gave himself up to an irresistible rage and sense of frustration. The image of Rodney came before him with every circumstance of folly and indignity. That little pink-cheeked dancing-master to marry Katharine? that gibbering ass with the face of a monkey on an organ? that posing, vain, fantastical fop? with his tragedies and his comedies, his innumerable spites and prides and pettinesses? Lord! marry Rodney! She must be as great a fool as he was. His bitterness took possession of him, and as he sat in the corner of the Underground carriage, he looked as stark an image of unapproachable severity as could be imagined. Directly he reached home he sat down at his table and began to write Katharine a long, wild, mad letter, begging her for both their sakes to break with Rodney, imploring her not to do what would destroy for ever the one beauty, the one truth, the one hope; not to be a traitor, not to be a deserter, for if she were – and he wound up with a quiet and brief assertion that, whatever she did or left undone, he would believe to be the best, and accept from her with gratitude. He covered sheet after sheet, and heard the early carts starting for London before he went to bed.

Chapter 24

The first signs of spring, even such as make themselves felt towards the middle of February, not only produce little white and violet flowers in the more sheltered corners of woods and gardens, but bring to birth thoughts and desires comparable to those faintly coloured and sweetly scented petals in the minds of men and women. Lives frozen by age, so far as the present is concerned, to a hard surface, which neither reflects nor yields, at this season become soft and fluid, reflecting the shapes and colours of the present, as well as the shapes and colours of the past. In the case of Mrs Hilbery, these early spring days were chiefly upsetting inasmuch as they caused a general quickening of her emotional powers, which, as far as the past was concerned, had never suffered much diminution. But in the spring her desire for expression invariably increased. She was haunted by the ghosts of phrases. She gave herself up to a sensual delight in the combinations of words. She sought them in the pages of her favourite authors. She made them for herself on scraps of paper, and rolled them on her tongue when there seemed no occasion for such eloquence. She was upheld in these excursions by the certainty that no language could outdo the splendour of her father's memory, and although her efforts did not notably further the end of his biography, she was under the impression of living more in his shade at such times than at others. No one can escape the power of language, let alone those of English birth brought up from childhood, as Mrs Hilbery had been, to disport themselves now in the Saxon plainness, now in the Latin splendour of the tongue, and stored with memories, as she was, of old poets exuberating in an infinity of vocables. Even Katharine was slightly affected against her better judgement by her mother's enthusiasm. Not that her judgement could altogether acquiesce in the necessity for a study of Shakespeare's sonnets[71] as a preliminary to the fifth chapter of her grandfather's biography. Beginning with a perfectly frivolous jest, Mrs Hilbery had evolved a theory that Anne Hathaway had a way, among other things, of writing Shakespeare's sonnets; the idea, struck out to enliven a party of professors, who forwarded a number of privately printed manuals within the next few days for her instruction, had submerged her in a flood of Elizabethan literature; she had come half to believe in her joke, which was, she said, at least as good as other people's facts, and all her fancy for the time being centred upon Stratford-upon-Avon. She had a plan, she told Katharine, when, rather later than usual, Katharine came into the room the morning after her walk by the river, for visiting Shakespeare's tomb. Any fact about the poet had become, for the moment, of far greater interest to her than the immediate present, and the certainty that there was existing in England a spot of ground where Shakespeare had undoubtedly stood, where his very bones lay directly beneath one's feet, was so absorbing to her on this particular occasion that she greeted her daughter with the exclamation: 'D'you think he ever passed this house?'

The question, for the moment, seemed to Katharine to have reference to Ralph Denham.

'On his way to Blackfriars, I mean,' Mrs Hilbery continued, 'for you know the latest discovery is that he owned a house there.'

Katharine still looked about her in perplexity, and Mrs Hilbery added: 'Which is a proof that he wasn't as poor as they've sometimes said. I should like to think that he had enough, though I don't in the least want him to be rich.'

Then, perceiving her daughter's expression of perplexity, Mrs Hilbery burst out laughing.

'My dear, I'm not talking about *your* William, though that's another reason for liking him. I'm talking, I'm thinking, I'm dreaming of *my* William – William Shakespeare, of course. Isn't it odd,' she mused, standing at the window and tapping gently upon the pane, 'that for all one can see, that dear old thing in the blue bonnet, crossing the road with her basket on her arm, has never heard that there was such a person? Yet it all goes on: lawyers hurrying to their work, cabmen squabbling for their fares, little boys rolling their hoops, little girls throwing bread to the gulls, as if there weren't a Shakespeare in the world. I should like to stand at that crossing all day long and say: "People, read Shakespeare!" '

Katharine sat down at her table and opened a long dusty envelope. As Shelley was mentioned in the course of the letter as if he were alive, it had, of course, considerable value. Her immediate task was to decide whether the whole letter should be printed, or only the paragraph which mentioned Shelley's name, and she reached out for a pen and held it in readiness to do justice upon the sheet. Her pen, however, remained in the air. Almost surreptitiously she slipped a clean sheet in front of her, and her hand, descending, began drawing square boxes halved and quartered by straight lines, and then circles which underwent the same process of dissection.

'Katharine! I've hit upon a brilliant idea!' Mrs Hilbery exclaimed – 'to lay out, say, a hundred pounds or so on copies of Shakespeare, and give them to working men. Some of your clever friends who get up meetings might help us, Katharine. And that might lead to a playhouse, where we could all take parts. You'd be Rosalind – but you've a dash of the old nurse in you.[72] Your father's Hamlet, come to years of discretion; and I'm – well, I'm a bit of them all; I'm quite a large bit of the fool, but the fools in Shakespeare say all the clever things. Now who shall William be? A hero? Hotspur?[73] Henry the Fifth? No, William's got a touch of Hamlet in him, too. I can fancy that William talks to himself when he's alone. Ah, Katharine, you must say very beautiful things when you're together!' she added wistfully, with a glance at her daughter, who had told her nothing about the dinner the night before.

'Oh, we talk a lot of nonsense,' said Katharine, hiding her slip of paper as her mother stood by her, and spreading the old letter about Shelley in front of her.

'It won't seem to you nonsense in ten years' time,' said Mrs Hilbery. 'Believe me, Katharine, you'll look back on these days afterwards; you'll remember all the silly things you've said; and you'll find that your life has been built on them. The best of life is built on what we say when we're in love. It isn't nonsense, Katharine,' she urged, 'it's the truth, it's the only truth.'

Katharine was on the point of interrupting her mother, and then she was on the point of confiding in her. They came strangely close together sometimes. But, while she hesitated and sought for words not too direct, her mother had recourse to Shakespeare, and turned page after page, set upon finding some quotation which said all this about love far, far better than she could. Accordingly, Katharine did nothing but scrub one of her circles an intense black with her pencil, in the midst of which process the telephone-bell rang, and she left the room to answer it.

When she returned, Mrs Hilbery had found not the passage she wanted, but another of exquisite beauty as she justly observed, looking up for a second to ask Katharine who that was?

'Mary Datchet,' Katharine replied briefly.

'Ah – I half wish I'd called you Mary, but it wouldn't have gone with Hilbery, and it wouldn't have gone with Rodney. Now this isn't the passage I wanted. (I never can find what I want.) But it's spring; it's the daffodils; it's the green fields; it's the birds.'

She was cut short in her quotation by another imperative telephone-bell. Once more Katharine left the room.

'My dear child, how odious the triumphs of science are!' Mrs Hilbery exclaimed on her return. 'They'll be linking us with the moon next – but who was that?'

'William,' Katharine replied yet more briefly.

'I'll forgive William anything, for I'm certain that there aren't any Williams in the moon. I hope he's coming to luncheon?'

'He's coming to tea.'

'Well, that's better than nothing, and I promise to leave you alone.'

'There's no need for you to do that,' said Katharine.

She swept her hand over the faded sheet, and drew herself up squarely to the table as if she refused to waste time any longer. The gesture was not lost upon her mother. It hinted at the existence of something stern and unapproachable in her daughter's character, which struck chill upon her, as the sight of poverty, or drunkenness, or the logic with which Mr Hilbery sometimes thought good to demolish her certainty of an approaching millennium struck chill upon her. She went back to her own table, and putting on her spectacles with a curious expression of quiet humility, addressed herself for the first time that morning to the task before her. The shock with an unsympathetic world had a sobering effect on her. For once, her industry surpassed her daughter's. Katharine could not reduce the world to that particular perspective in which Harriet Martineau,[74] for instance, was a figure of solid importance, and possessed of a genuine relationship to this figure or to that date. Singularly enough, the sharp call of the telephone-bell still echoed in her ear, and her body and mind were in a state of tension, as if, at any moment, she might hear another summons of greater interest to her than the whole of the nineteenth century. She did not clearly realise what this call was to be; but when the ears have got into the habit of listening, they go on listening involuntarily, and thus Katharine spent the greater part of the morning in listening to a variety of sounds in the back streets of Chelsea. For the first time in her life, probably, she wished that Mrs Hilbery would not keep so closely to her work. A quotation from Shakespeare would not have come amiss. Now and again she heard a sigh from her mother's table, but that was the only proof she gave of her existence, and Katharine did not think of connecting it with the square aspect of her own position at the table, or, perhaps, she would have thrown her pen down and told her mother the reason for her restlessness. The only writing she managed to accomplish in the course of the morning was one letter, addressed to her cousin Cassandra Otway – a rambling letter, long, affectionate, playful and commanding all at once. She bade Cassandra put her creatures in the charge of a groom, and come to them for a week or so. They would go and hear some music together. Cassandra's dislike of rational society, she said, was an affectation fast hardening into a prejudice, which would, in the long run, isolate her from all interesting people and pursuits. She was finishing the sheet when the sound she was anticipating all the time actually struck upon her ears. She jumped up hastily, and slammed the door with a sharpness which made Mrs Hilbery start. Where was Katharine off to? In her preoccupied state she had not heard the bell.

The alcove on the stairs, in which the telephone was placed, was screened for privacy by a curtain of purple velvet. It was a pocket for superfluous possessions, such as exist in most houses which harbour the wreckage of three generations. Prints of great-uncles, famed for their prowess in the East, hung above Chinese teapots, whose sides were riveted by little gold stitches, and the precious teapots, again, stood upon bookcases containing the complete works of William Cowper[75] and Sir Walter Scott.[76] The thread of sound, issuing from the telephone, was always coloured by the surroundings which received it, so it seemed to Katharine. Whose voice was now going to combine with them, or to strike a discord?

'Whose voice?' she asked herself, hearing a man enquire, with great determination, for her number. The unfamiliar voice now asked for Miss Hilbery. Out of all the welter of voices which crowd round the far end of the telephone, out of the enormous range of possibilities, whose voice, what possibility, was this? A pause gave her time to ask herself this question. It was solved next moment.

'I've looked out the train . . . Early on Saturday afternoon would suit me best . . . I'm Ralph Denham . . . But I'll write it down . . . '

With more than the usual sense of being impinged upon the point of a bayonet, Katharine replied: 'I think I could come. I'll look at my engagements . . . Hold on.'

She dropped the machine, and looked fixedly at the print of the great-uncle who had not ceased to gaze, with an air of amiable authority, into a world which, as yet, beheld no symptoms of the Indian Mutiny.[77] And yet, gently swinging against the wall, within the black tube, was a voice which recked nothing of Uncle James, of china teapots or of red velvet curtains. She watched the oscillation of the tube, and at the same moment became conscious of the individuality of the house in which she stood; she heard the soft domestic sounds of regular existence upon staircases and floors above her head, and movements through the wall in the house next door. She had no very clear vision of Denham himself when she lifted the telephone to her lips and replied that she thought Saturday would suit her. She hoped that he would not say goodbye at once, although she felt no particular anxiety to attend to what he was saying, and began, even while he spoke, to think of her own upper room, with its books, its papers pressed between the leaves of dictionaries, and the table that could be cleared for work. She replaced the instrument, thoughtfully; her restlessness was assuaged; she finished her letter to Cassandra without difficulty, addressed the envelope, and fixed the stamp with her usual quick decision.

A bunch of anemones caught Mrs Hilbery's eye when they had finished luncheon. The blue and purple and white of the bowl, standing in a pool of variegated light on a polished Chippendale table in the drawing-room window, made her stop dead with an exclamation of pleasure.

'Who is lying ill in bed, Katharine?' she demanded. 'Which of our friends wants cheering up? Who feels that they've been forgotten and passed over, and that nobody wants them? Whose water rates are overdue, and the cook leaving in a temper without waiting for her wages? There was somebody I know – ' she concluded, but for the moment the name of this desirable acquaintance escaped her. The best representative of the forlorn company whose day would be brightened by a bunch of anemones was, in Katharine's opinion, the widow of a general living in the Cromwell Road.[78] In default of the actually destitute and starving, whom she would much have preferred, Mrs Hilbery was forced to acknowledge her claims, for though in comfortable circumstances, she was extremely dull, unattractive, connected in some oblique fashion with literature, and had been touched to the verge of tears, on one occasion, by an afternoon call.

It happened that Mrs Hilbery had an engagement elsewhere, so that the task of taking the flowers to the Cromwell Road fell upon Katharine. She took her letter to Cassandra with her, meaning to post it in the first pillar-box she came to. When, however, she was fairly out of doors, and constantly invited by pillar-boxes and post-offices to slip her envelope down their scarlet throats, she forbore. She made absurd excuses, as that she did not wish to cross the road, or that she was certain to pass another post-office in a more central position a little farther on. The longer she held the letter in her hand, however, the more persistently certain questions pressed upon her, as if from a collection of voices in the air. These invisible people wished to be informed whether she was engaged to William Rodney, or was the engagement broken off? Was it right, they asked, to invite Cassandra for a visit, and was William Rodney in love with her, or likely to fall in love? Then the questioners paused for a moment, and resumed as if another side of the problem had just come to their notice. What did Ralph Denham mean by what he said to you last night? Do you consider that he is in love with you? Is it right to consent to a solitary walk with him, and what advice are you going to give him about his future? Has William Rodney cause to be jealous of your conduct, and what do you propose to do about Mary Datchet? What are you going to do? What does honour require you to do? they repeated.

'Good heavens!' Katharine exclaimed, after listening to all these remarks, 'I suppose I ought to make up my mind.'

But the debate was a formal skirmishing, a pastime to gain breathing-space. Like all people brought up in a tradition, Katharine was able, within ten minutes or so, to reduce any moral difficulty to its traditional shape and solve it by the traditional answers. The book of wisdom lay open, if not upon her mother's knee, upon the knees of many uncles and aunts. She had only to consult them, and they would at once turn to the right page and read out an answer exactly suited to one in her position. The rules which should govern the behaviour of an unmarried woman are written in red ink, graved upon marble, if, by some freak of nature, it should fall out that the unmarried woman has not the same writing scored upon her heart. She was ready to believe that some people are fortunate enough to reject, accept, resign or lay down their lives at the bidding of traditional authority; she could envy them; but in her case the questions became phantoms directly she tried seriously to find an answer, which proved that the traditional answer would be of no use to her individually. Yet it had served so many people, she thought, glancing at the rows of houses on either side of her, where families, whose incomes must be between a thousand and fifteen-hundred a year lived, and kept, perhaps, three servants, and draped their windows with curtains which were always thick and generally dirty, and must, she thought, since you could only see a looking-glass gleaming above a sideboard on which a dish of apples was set, keep the room inside very dark. But she turned her head away, observing that this was not a method of thinking the matter out.

The only truth which she could discover was the truth of what she herself felt – a frail beam when compared with the broad illumination shed by the eyes of all the people who are in agreement to see together; but having rejected the visionary voices, she had no choice but to make this her guide through the dark masses which confronted her. She tried to follow her beam, with an expression upon her face which would have made any passer-by think her reprehensibly and almost ridiculously detached from the surrounding scene. One would have felt alarmed lest this young and striking woman were about to do something eccentric. But her beauty saved her from the worst fate that can befall a pedestrian; people looked at her, but they did not laugh. To seek a true feeling among the chaos of the unfeelings or half-feelings of life, to recognise it when found, and to accept the consequences of the discovery, draws lines upon the smoothest brow, while it quickens the light of the eyes; it is a pursuit which is alternately bewildering, debasing and exalting, and, as Katharine speedily found, her discoveries gave her equal cause for surprise, shame and intense anxiety. Much depended, as usual, upon the interpretation of the word love; which word came up again and again, whether she considered Rodney, Denham, Mary Datchet or herself; and in each case it seemed to stand for something different, and yet for something unmistakable and something not to be passed by. For the more she looked into the confusion of lives which, instead of running parallel, had suddenly intersected each other, the more distinctly she seemed to convince herself that there was no other light on them than was shed by this strange illumination, and no other path save the one upon which it threw its beams. Her blindness in the case of Rodney, her attempt to match his true feeling with her false feeling, was a failure never to be sufficiently condemned; indeed, she could only pay it the tribute of leaving it a black and naked landmark unburied by attempt at oblivion or excuse.

With this to humiliate there was much to exalt. She thought of three different scenes; she thought of Mary sitting upright and saying, 'I'm in love – I'm in love'; she thought of Rodney losing his self-consciousness among the dead leaves, and speaking with the abandonment of a child; she thought of Denham leaning upon the stone parapet and talking to the distant sky, so that she thought him mad. Her mind, passing from Mary to Denham, from William to Cassandra, and from Denham to herself – if, as she rather doubted, Denham's state of mind was connected with herself – seemed to be tracing out the lines of some symmetrical pattern, some arrangement of life, which invested, if not herself, at least the others, not only with interest, but with a kind of tragic beauty. She had a fantastic picture of them upholding splendid palaces upon their bent backs. They were the lantern-bearers, whose lights, scattered among the crowd, wove a pattern, dissolving, joining, meeting again in combination. Half forming such conceptions as these in her rapid walk along the dreary streets of South Kensington, she determined that, whatever else might be obscure, she must further the objects of Mary, Denham, William and Cassandra. The way was not apparent. No course of action seemed to her indubitably right. All she achieved by her thinking was the conviction that, in such a cause, no risk was too great; and that, far from making any rules for herself or others, she would let difficulties accumulate unsolved, situations widen their jaws unsatiated, while she maintained a position of absolute and fearless independence. So she could best serve the people who loved.

Read in the light of this exaltation, there was a new meaning in the words which her mother had pencilled upon the card attached to the bunch of anemones. The door of the house in the Cromwell Road opened; gloomy vistas of passage and staircase were revealed; such light as there was seemed to be concentrated upon a silver salver of visiting-cards, whose black borders suggested that the widow's friends had all suffered the same bereavement. The parlour-maid could hardly be expected to fathom the meaning of the grave tone in which the young lady proffered the flowers, with Mrs Hilbery's love; and the door shut upon the offering.

The sight of a face, the slam of a door, are both rather destructive of exaltation in the abstract; and, as she walked back to Chelsea, Katharine had her doubts whether anything would come of her resolves. If you cannot make sure of people, however, you can hold fairly fast to figures, and in some way or other her thought about such problems as she was wont to consider worked in happily with her mood as to her friends' lives. She reached home rather late for tea.

On the ancient Dutch chest in the hall she perceived one or two hats, coats and walking-sticks, and the sound of voices reached her as she stood outside the drawing-room door. Her mother gave a little cry as she came in; a cry which conveyed to Katharine the fact that she was late, that the teacups and milk-jugs were in a conspiracy of disobedience, and that she must immediately take her place at the head of the table and pour out tea for the guests. Augustus Pelham, the diarist, liked a calm atmosphere in which to tell his stories; he liked attention; he liked to elicit little facts, little stories, about the past and the great dead, from such distinguished characters as Mrs Hilbery for the nourishment of his diary, for whose sake he frequented tea-tables and ate yearly an enormous quantity of buttered toast. He, therefore, welcomed Katharine with relief, and she had merely to shake hands with Rodney and to greet the American lady who had come to be shown the relics, before the talk started again on the broad lines of reminiscence and discussion which were familiar to her.

Yet, even with this thick veil between them, she could not help looking at Rodney, as if she could detect what had happened to him since they met. It was in vain. His clothes, even the white slip,[79] the pearl in his tie, seemed to intercept her quick glance, and to proclaim the futility of such enquiries of a discreet, urbane gentleman, who balanced his cup of tea and poised a slice of bread and butter on the edge of the saucer. He would not meet her eye, but that could be accounted for by his activity in serving and helping, and the polite alacrity with which he was answering the questions of the American visitor.

It was certainly a sight to daunt anyone coming in with a head full of theories about love. The voices of the invisible questioners were re-inforced by the scene round the table, and sounded with a tremendous self-confidence, as if they had behind them the common sense of twenty generations, together with the immediate approval of Mr Augustus Pelham, Mrs Vermont Bankes, William Rodney and, possibly, Mrs Hilbery herself. Katharine set her teeth, not entirely in the meta-phorical sense, for her hand, obeying the impulse towards definite action, laid firmly upon the table beside her an envelope which she had been grasping all this time in complete forgetfulness. The address was uppermost, and a moment later she saw William's eye rest upon it as he rose to fulfil some duty with a plate. His expression instantly changed. He did what he was on the point of doing, and then looked at Katharine with a look which revealed enough of his confusion to show her that he was not entirely represented by his appearance. In a minute or two he proved himself at a loss with Mrs Vermont Bankes, and Mrs Hilbery, aware of the silence with her usual quickness, suggested that, perhaps, it was now time that Mrs Bankes should be shown 'our things'.

Katharine accordingly rose, and led the way to the little inner room with the pictures and the books. Mrs Bankes and Rodney followed her.

She turned on the lights, and began directly in her low, pleasant voice: 'This table is my grandfather's writing-table. Most of the later poems were written at it. And this is his pen – the last pen he ever used.' She took it in her hand and paused for the right number of seconds. 'Here,' she continued, 'is the original manuscript of the "Ode to Winter". The early manuscripts are far less corrected than the later ones, as you will see directly . . . Oh, do take it yourself,' she added, as Mrs Bankes asked, in an awestruck tone of voice, for that privilege, and began a preliminary unbuttoning of her white kid gloves.

'You are wonderfully like your grandfather, Miss Hilbery,' the American lady observed, gazing from Katharine to the portrait, 'especially about the eyes. Come, now, I expect she writes poetry herself, doesn't she?' she asked in a jocular tone, turning to William. 'Quite one's ideal of a poet, is it not, Mr Rodney? I cannot tell you what a privilege I feel it to be standing just here with the poet's granddaughter. You must know we think a great deal of your grandfather in America, Miss Hilbery. We have societies for reading him aloud. What! His very own slippers!' Laying aside the manuscript, she hastily grasped the old shoes, and remained for a moment dumb in contemplation of them.

While Katharine went on steadily with her duties as show-woman, Rodney examined intently a row of little drawings which he knew by heart already. His disordered state of mind made it necessary for him to take advantage of these little respites, as if he had been out in a high wind and must straighten his dress in the first shelter he reached. His calm was only superficial, as he knew too well; it did not exist much below the surface of tie, waistcoat and white slip.

On getting out of bed that morning he had fully made up his mind to ignore what had been said the night before; he had been convinced, by the sight of Denham, that his love for Katharine was passionate, and when he addressed her early that morning on the telephone, he had meant his cheerful but authoritative tones to convey to her the fact that,

after a night of madness, they were as indissolubly engaged as ever. But
when he reached his office his torments began. He found a letter from
Cassandra waiting for him. She had read his play, and had taken the
very first opportunity to write and tell him what she thought of it. She
knew, she wrote, that her praise meant absolutely nothing; but still, she
had sat up all night; she thought this, that and the other; she was full of
enthusiasm most elaborately scratched out in places, but enough was
written plain to gratify William's vanity exceedingly. She was quite
intelligent enough to say the right things, or, even more charmingly, to
hint at them. In other ways, too, it was a very charming letter. She told
him about her music, and about a Suffrage meeting to which Henry had
taken her, and she asserted, half seriously, that she had learnt the Greek
alphabet, and found it 'fascinating'. The word was underlined. Had she
laughed when she drew that line? Was she ever serious? Didn't the
letter show the most engaging compound of enthusiasm and spirit and
whimsicality, all tapering into a flame of girlish freakishness, which
flitted, for the rest of the morning, as a will-o'-the-wisp, across Rodney's
landscape. He could not resist beginning an answer to her there and
then. He found it particularly delightful to shape a style which should
express the bowing and curtsying, advancing and retreating, which are
characteristic of one of the many million partnerships of men and
women. Katharine never trod that particular measure, he could not
help reflecting; Katharine – Cassandra; Cassandra – Katharine; they
alternated in his consciousness all day long. It was all very well to dress
oneself carefully, compose one's face, and start off punctually at half-
past four to a tea-party in Cheyne Walk, but heaven only knew what
would come of it all, and when Katharine, after sitting silent with her
usual immobility, wantonly drew from her pocket and slapped down on
the table beneath his eyes a letter addressed to Cassandra herself, his
composure deserted him. What did she mean by her behaviour?

He looked up sharply from his row of little pictures. Katharine was
disposing of the American lady in far too arbitrary a fashion. Surely the
victim herself must see how foolish her enthusiasms appeared in the
eyes of the poet's granddaughter. Katharine never made any attempt to
spare people's feelings, he reflected; and, being himself very sensitive to
all shades of comfort and discomfort, he cut short the auctioneer's
catalogue, which Katharine was reeling off more and more absent-
mindedly, and took Mrs Vermont Bankes, with a queer sense of fellow-
ship in suffering, under his own protection.

But within a few minutes the American lady had completed her
inspection, and inclining her head in a little nod of reverential farewell

to the poet and his shoes, she was escorted downstairs by Rodney. Katharine stayed by herself in the little room. The ceremony of ancestor-worship had been more than usually oppressive to her. Moreover, the room was becoming crowded beyond the bounds of order. Only that morning a heavily insured proof-sheet had reached them from a collector in Australia, which recorded a change of the poet's mind about a very famous phrase, and, therefore, had claims to the honour of glazing and framing. But was there room for it? Must it be hung on the staircase, or should some other relic give place to do it honour? Feeling unable to decide the question, Katharine glanced at the portrait of her grandfather, as if to ask his opinion. The artist who had painted it was now out of fashion, and by dint of showing it to visitors, Katharine had almost ceased to see anything but a glow of faintly pleasing pink and brown tints, enclosed within a circular scroll of gilt laurel-leaves. The young man who was her grandfather looked vaguely over her head. The sensual lips were slightly parted, and gave the face an expression of beholding something lovely or miraculous vanishing or just rising upon the rim of the distance. The expression repeated itself curiously upon Katharine's face as she gazed up into his. They were the same age, or very nearly so. She wondered what he was looking for; were there waves beating upon a shore for him, too, she wondered, and heroes riding through the leaf-hung forests? For perhaps the first time in her life she thought of him as a man, young, unhappy, tempestuous, full of desires and faults; for the first time she realised him for herself, and not from her mother's memory. He might have been her brother, she thought. It seemed to her that they were akin, with the mysterious kinship of blood which makes it seem possible to interpret the sights which the eyes of the dead behold so intently, or even to believe that they look with us upon our present joys and sorrows. He would have understood, she thought, suddenly; and instead of laying her withered flowers upon his shrine, she brought him her own perplexities – perhaps a gift of greater value, should the dead be conscious of gifts, than flowers and incense and adoration. Doubts, questionings and despondencies she felt, as she looked up, would be more welcome to him than homage, and he would hold them but a very small burden if she gave him, also, some share in what she suffered and achieved. The depth of her own pride and love were not more apparent to her than the sense that the dead asked neither flowers nor regrets, but a share in the life which they had given her, the life which they had lived.

Rodney found her a moment later sitting beneath her grandfather's

portrait. She laid her hand on the seat next her in a friendly way, and
said: 'Come and sit down, William. How glad I was you were here! I
felt myself getting ruder and ruder.'

'You are not good at hiding your feelings,' he returned dryly.

'Oh, don't scold me – I've had a horrid afternoon.' She told him
how she had taken the flowers to Mrs McCormick, and how South
Kensington impressed her as the preserve of officers' widows. She
described how the door had opened, and what gloomy avenues of busts
and palm trees and umbrellas had been revealed to her. She spoke
lightly, and succeeded in putting him at his ease. Indeed, he rapidly
became too much at his ease to persist in a condition of cheerful
neutrality. He felt his composure slipping from him. Katharine made it
seem so natural to ask her to help him, or advise him, to say straight out
what he had in his mind. The letter from Cassandra was heavy in his
pocket. There was also the letter to Cassandra lying on the table in the
next room. The atmosphere seemed charged with Cassandra. But,
unless Katharine began the subject of her own accord, he could not
even hint – he must ignore the whole affair; it was the part of a
gentleman to preserve a bearing that was, as far as he could make it, the
bearing of an undoubting lover. At intervals he sighed deeply. He talked
rather more quickly than usual about the possibility that some of the
operas of Mozart would be played in the summer. He had received a
notice, he said, and at once produced a pocket-book stuffed with papers,
and began shuffling them in search. He held a thick envelope between
his finger and thumb, as if the notice from the opera company had
become in some way inseparably attached to it.

'A letter from Cassandra?' said Katharine, in the easiest voice in the
world, looking over his shoulder. 'I've just written to ask her to come
here, only I forgot to post it.'

He handed her the envelope in silence. She took it, extracted the
sheets, and read the letter through.

The reading seemed to Rodney to take an intolerably long time.

'Yes,' she observed at length, 'a very charming letter.'

Rodney's face was half turned away, as if in bashfulness. Her view of
his profile almost moved her to laughter. She glanced through the
pages once more.

'I see no harm,' William blurted out, 'in helping her – with Greek,
for example – if she really cares for that sort of thing.'

'There's no reason why she shouldn't care,' said Katharine, consulting
the pages once more. 'In fact – ah, here it is – "The Greek alphabet is
absolutely *fascinating*." Obviously she does care.'

'Well, Greek may be rather a large order. I was thinking chiefly of English. Her criticisms of my play, though they're too generous, evidently immature – she can't be more than twenty-two, I suppose? – they certainly show the sort of thing one wants: real feeling for poetry, understanding, not formed, of course, but it's at the root of everything after all. There'd be no harm in lending her books?'

'No. Certainly not.'

'But if it – hum – led to a correspondence? I mean, Katharine, I take it, without going into matters which seem to me a little morbid, I mean,' he floundered, 'you, from your point of view, feel that there's nothing disagreeable to you in the notion? If so, you've only to speak, and I will never think of it again.'

She was surprised by the violence of her desire that he never should think of it again. For an instant it seemed to her impossible to surrender an intimacy, which might not be the intimacy of love, but was certainly the intimacy of true friendship, to any woman in the world. Cassandra would never understand him – she was not good enough for him. The letter seemed to her a letter of flattery – a letter addressed to his weakness, which it made her angry to think was known to another. For he was not weak; he had the rare strength of doing what he promised – she had only to speak, and he would never think of Cassandra again.

She paused. Rodney guessed the reason. He was amazed.

'She loves me,' he thought. The woman he admired more than anyone in the world, loved him, as he had given up hope that she would ever love him. And now that for the first time he was sure of her love, he resented it. He felt it as a fetter, an encumbrance, something which made them both, but him in particular, ridiculous. He was in her power completely, but his eyes were open and he was no longer her slave or her dupe. He would be her master in future. The instant prolonged itself as Katharine realised the strength of her desire to speak the words that should keep William for ever, and the baseness of the temptation which assailed her to make the movement, or speak the word, which he had often begged her for, which she was now near enough to feeling. She held the letter in her hand. She sat silent.

At this moment there was a stir in the other room; the voice of Mrs Hilbery was heard talking of proof-sheets rescued by miraculous providence from butcher's ledgers in Australia; the curtain separating one room from the other was drawn apart, and Mrs Hilbery and Augustus Pelham stood in the doorway. Mrs Hilbery stopped short. She looked at her daughter, and at the man her daughter was to marry, with her peculiar smile that always seemed to tremble on the brink of satire.

'The best of all my treasures, Mr Pelham!' she exclaimed. 'Don't move, Katharine. Sit still, William. Mr Pelham will come another day.'

Mr Pelham looked, smiled, bowed, and, as his hostess had moved on, followed her without a word. The curtain was drawn again either by him or by Mrs Hilbery.

But her mother had settled the question somehow. Katharine doubted no longer.

'As I told you last night,' she said, 'I think it's your duty, if there's a chance that you care for Cassandra, to discover what your feeling is for her now. It's your duty to her, as well as to me. But we must tell my mother. We can't go on pretending.'

'That is entirely in your hands, of course,' said Rodney, with an immediate return to the manner of a formal man of honour.

'Very well,' said Katharine.

Directly he left her she would go to her mother, and explain that the engagement was at an end – or it might be better that they should go together?

'But, Katharine,' Rodney began, nervously attempting to stuff Cassandra's sheets back into their envelope; 'if Cassandra – should Cassandra – you've asked Cassandra to stay with you.'

'Yes; but I've not posted the letter.'

He crossed his knees in a discomfited silence. By all his codes it was impossible to ask a woman with whom he had just broken off his engagement to help him to become acquainted with another woman with a view to his falling in love with her. If it was announced that their engagement was over, a long and complete separation would inevitably follow; in those circumstances, letters and gifts were returned; after years of distance the severed couple met, perhaps at an evening party, and touched hands uncomfortably with an indifferent word or two. He would be cast off completely; he would have to trust to his own resources. He could never mention Cassandra to Katharine again; for months, and doubtless years, he would never see Katharine again; anything might happen to her in his absence.

Katharine was almost as well aware of his perplexities as he was. She knew in what direction complete generosity pointed the way; but pride – for to remain engaged to Rodney and to cover his experiments hurt what was nobler in her than mere vanity – fought for its life.

'I'm to give up my freedom for an indefinite time,' she thought, 'in order that William may see Cassandra here at his ease. He's not the courage to manage it without my help – he's too much of a coward to tell me openly what he wants. He hates the notion of a public breach. He wants to keep us both.'

When she reached this point, Rodney pocketed the letter and elaborately looked at his watch. Although the action meant that he resigned Cassandra, for he knew his own incompetence and distrusted himself entirely, and lost Katharine, for whom his feeling was profound though unsatisfactory, still it appeared to him that there was nothing else left for him to do. He was forced to go, leaving Katharine free, as he had said, to tell her mother that the engagement was at an end. But to do what plain duty required of an honourable man cost an effort which only a day or two ago would have been inconceivable to him. That a relationship such as he had glanced at with desire could be possible between him and Katharine, he would have been the first, two days ago, to deny with indignation. But now his life had changed; his attitude had changed; his feelings were different; new aims and possibilities had been shown him, and they had an almost irresistible fascination and force. The training of a life of thirty-five years had not left him defenceless; he was still master of his dignity; he rose, with a mind made up to an irrevocable farewell.

'I leave you, then,' he said, standing up and holding out his hand with an effort that left him pale, but lent him dignity, 'to tell your mother that our engagement is ended by your desire.'

She took his hand and held it.

'You don't trust me?' she said.

'I do, absolutely,' he replied.

'No. You don't trust me to help you . . . I could help you?'

'I'm hopeless without your help!' he exclaimed passionately, but withdrew his hand and turned his back. When he faced her, she thought that she saw him for the first time without disguise.

'It's useless to pretend that I don't understand what you're offering, Katharine. I admit what you say. Speaking to you perfectly frankly, I believe at this moment that I do love your cousin; there is a chance that, with your help, I might – but no,' he broke off, 'it's impossible, it's wrong – I'm infinitely to blame for having allowed this situation to arise.'

'Sit beside me. Let's consider sensibly – '

'Your sense has been our undoing – ' he groaned.

'I accept the responsibility.'

'Ah, but can I allow that?' he exclaimed. 'It would mean – for we must face it, Katharine – that we let our engagement stand for the time nominally; in fact, of course, your freedom would be absolute.'

'And yours too.'

'Yes, we should both be free. Let us say that I saw Cassandra once, twice, perhaps, under these conditions; and then if, as I think certain, the whole thing proves a dream, we tell your mother instantly. Why not tell her now, indeed, under pledge of secrecy?'

'Why not? It would be over London in ten minutes, besides, she would never even remotely understand.'

'Your father, then? This secrecy is detestable – it's dishonourable.'

'My father would understand even less than my mother.'

'Ah, who could be expected to understand?' Rodney groaned; 'but it's from your point of view that we must look at it. It's not only asking too much, it's putting you into a position – a position in which I could not endure to see my own sister.'

'We're not brothers and sisters,' she said impatiently, 'and if we can't decide, who can? I'm not talking nonsense,' she proceeded. 'I've done my best to think this out from every point of view, and I've come to the conclusion that there are risks which have to be taken – though I don't deny that they hurt horribly.'

'Katharine, you mind? You'll mind too much.'

'No I shan't,' she said stoutly. 'I shall mind a good deal, but I'm prepared for that; I shall get through it, because you will help me. You'll both help me. In fact, we'll help each other. That's a Christian doctrine, isn't it?'

'It sounds more like paganism to me,' Rodney groaned, as he reviewed the situation into which her Christian doctrine was plunging them.

And yet he could not deny that a divine relief possessed him, and that the future, instead of wearing a lead-coloured mask, now blossomed with a thousand varied gaieties and excitements. He was actually to see Cassandra within a week or perhaps less, and he was more anxious to know the date of her arrival than he could own even to himself. It seemed base to be so anxious to pluck this fruit of Katharine's unexampled generosity and of his own contemptible baseness. And yet, though he used these words automatically, they had now no meaning. He was not debased in his own eyes by what he had done, and as for praising Katharine, were they not partners, conspirators, people bent upon the same quest together, so that to praise the pursuit of a common end as an act of generosity was meaningless. He took her hand and pressed it, not in thanks so much as in an ecstasy of comradeship.

'We will help each other,' he said, repeating her words, seeking her eyes in an enthusiasm of friendship.

Her eyes were grave but dark with sadness as they rested on him.

'He's already gone,' she thought, 'far away – he thinks of me no more.'
And the fancy came to her that, as they sat side by side, hand in hand,
she could hear the earth pouring from above to make a barrier between
them, so that, as they sat, they were separated second by second by an
impenetrable wall. The process, which affected her as that of being
sealed away and for ever from all companionship with the person she
cared for most, came to an end at last, and by common consent they
unclasped their fingers, Rodney touching hers with his lips, as the
curtain parted, and Mrs Hilbery peered through the opening with
her benevolent and sarcastic expression to ask whether Katharine
could remember was it Tuesday or Wednesday, and did she dine in
Westminster?

'Dearest William,' she said, pausing, as if she could not resist the
pleasure of encroaching for a second upon this wonderful world of
love and confidence and romance. 'Dearest children,' she added, disappearing with an impulsive gesture, as if she forced herself to draw
the curtain upon a scene which she refused all temptation to interrupt.

Chapter 25

At a quarter-past three in the afternoon of the following Saturday
Ralph Denham sat on the bank of the lake in Kew Gardens, dividing
the dial-plate of his watch into sections with his forefinger. The just
and inexorable nature of time itself was reflected in his face. He might
have been composing a hymn to the unhasting and unresting march of
that divinity. He seemed to greet the lapse of minute after minute with
stern acquiescence in the inevitable order. His expression was so severe,
so serene, so immobile, that it seemed obvious that for him at least
there was a grandeur in the departing hour which no petty irritation on
his part was to mar, although the wasting time wasted also high private
hopes of his own.

His face was no bad index to what went on within him. He was in a
condition of mind rather too exalted for the trivialities of daily life. He
could not accept the fact that a lady was fifteen minutes late in keeping
her appointment without seeing in that accident the frustration of his
entire life. Looking at his watch, he seemed to look deep into the
springs of human existence, and by the light of what he saw there
altered his course towards the north and the midnight . . . Yes, one's
voyage must be made absolutely without companions through ice and

black water – towards what goal? Here he laid his finger upon the half-hour, and decided that when the minute-hand reached that point he would go, at the same time answering the question put by another of the many voices of consciousness with the reply that there was undoubtedly a goal, but that it would need the most relentless energy to keep anywhere in its direction. Still, still, one goes on, the ticking seconds seemed to assure him, with dignity, with open eyes, with determination not to accept the second-rate, not to be tempted by the unworthy, not to yield, not to compromise. Twenty-five minutes past three were now marked upon the face of the watch. The world, he assured himself, since Katharine Hilbery was now half an hour behind her time, offers no happiness, no rest from struggle, no certainty. In a scheme of things utterly bad from the start the only unpardonable folly is that of hope. Raising his eyes for a moment from the face of his watch, he rested them upon the opposite bank, reflectively and not without a certain wistfulness, as if the sternness of their gaze were still capable of mitigation. Soon a look of the deepest satisfaction filled them, though, for a moment, he did not move. He watched a lady who came rapidly, and yet with a trace of hesitation, down the broad grass-walk towards him. She did not see him. Distance lent her figure an indescribable height, and romance seemed to surround her from the floating of a purple veil which the light air filled and curved from her shoulders.

'Here she comes, like a ship in full sail,'[80] he said to himself, half remembering some line from a play or poem where the heroine bore down thus with feathers flying and airs saluting her. The greenery and the high presences of the trees surrounded her as if they stood forth at her coming. He rose, and she saw him; her little exclamation proved that she was glad to find him, and then that she blamed herself for being late.

'Why did you never tell me? I didn't know there was this,' she remarked, alluding to the lake, the broad green space, the vista of trees, with the ruffled gold of the Thames in the distance and the ducal castle[81] standing in its meadows. She paid the rigid tail of the ducal lion the tribute of incredulous laughter.

'You've never been to Kew?' Denham remarked.

But it appeared that she had come once as a small child, when the geography of the place was entirely different, and the fauna included certainly flamingos and, possibly, camels. They strolled on, refashioning these legendary gardens. She was, as he felt, glad merely to stroll and loiter and let her fancy touch upon anything her eyes encountered – a bush, a park-keeper, a decorated goose – as if the relaxation soothed her.

The warmth of the afternoon, the first of spring, tempted them to sit upon a seat in a glade of beech trees, with forest drives striking green paths this way and that around them. She sighed deeply.

'It's so peaceful,' she said, as if in explanation of her sigh. Not a single person was in sight, and the stir of the wind in the branches, that sound so seldom heard by Londoners, seemed to her as if wafted from fathomless oceans of sweet air in the distance.

While she breathed and looked, Denham was engaged in uncovering with the point of his stick a group of green spikes half smothered by the dead leaves. He did this with the peculiar touch of the botanist. In naming the little green plant to her he used the Latin name, thus disguising some flower familiar even to Chelsea, and making her exclaim, half in amusement, at his knowledge. Her own ignorance was vast, she confessed. What did one call that tree opposite, for instance, supposing one condescended to call it by its English name? Beech or elm or sycamore? It chanced, by the testimony of a dead leaf, to be oak; and a little attention to a diagram which Denham proceeded to draw upon an envelope soon put Katharine in possession of some of the fundamental distinctions between our British trees. She then asked him to inform her about flowers. To her they were variously shaped and coloured petals, poised, at different seasons of the year, upon very similar green stalks; but to him they were, in the first instance, bulbs or seeds, and later, living things endowed with sex, and pores, and susceptibilities which adapted themselves by all manner of ingenious devices to live and beget life, and could be fashioned squat or tapering, flame-coloured or pale, pure or spotted, by processes which might reveal the secrets of human existence. Denham spoke with increasing ardour of a hobby which had long been his in secret. No discourse could have worn a more welcome sound in Katharine's ears. For weeks she had heard nothing that made such pleasant music in her mind. It wakened echoes in all those remote fastnesses of her being where loneliness had brooded so long undisturbed.

She wished he would go on for ever talking of plants, and showing her how science felt not quite blindly for the law that ruled their endless variations. A law that might be inscrutable but was certainly omnipotent appealed to her at the moment, because she could find nothing like it in possession of human lives. Circumstances had long forced her, as they force most women in the flower of youth, to consider, painfully and minutely, all that part of life which is conspicuously without order; she had had to consider moods and wishes, degrees of liking or disliking, and their effect upon the destiny of people dear to her; she had been forced to deny herself any contemplation of that other part of life where thought constructs a destiny which is independent of human beings. As Denham spoke, she followed his words and considered their bearing with an easy vigour which spoke of a capacity long hoarded and unspent. The very trees and the green merging into the blue distance became symbols of the vast external world which recks so little of the happiness, of the marriages or deaths of individuals. In order to give her examples of what he was saying, Denham led the way, first to the Rock Garden, and then to the Orchid House.

For him there was safety in the direction which the talk had taken. His emphasis might come from feelings more personal than those science roused in him, but it was disguised, and naturally he found it easy to expound and explain. Nevertheless, when he saw Katharine among the orchids, her beauty strangely emphasised by the fantastic plants, which seemed to peer and gape at her from striped hoods and fleshy throats, his ardour for botany waned, and a more complex feeling replaced it. She fell silent. The orchids seemed to suggest absorbing reflections. In defiance of the rules she stretched her ungloved hand and touched one. The sight of the rubies upon her finger affected him so disagreeably that he started and turned away. But next moment he controlled himself; he looked at her taking in one strange shape after another with the contemplative, considering gaze of a person who sees not exactly what is before him, but gropes in regions that lie beyond it. The far-away look entirely lacked self-consciousness. Denham doubted whether she remembered his presence. He could recall himself, of course, by a word or a movement – but why? She was happier thus. She needed nothing that he could give her. And for him, too, perhaps, it was best to keep aloof, only to know that she existed, to preserve what he already had – perfect, remote and unbroken. Further, her still look, standing among the orchids in that hot atmosphere, strangely illustrated some scene that he had imagined in his room at home. The sight, mingling with his recollection, kept him silent when the door was shut and they were walking on again.

But though she did not speak, Katharine had an uneasy sense that silence on her part was selfishness. It was selfish of her to continue, as she wished to do, a discussion of subjects not remotely connected with any human beings. She roused herself to consider their exact position upon the turbulent map of the emotions. Oh yes – it was a question whether Ralph Denham should live in the country and write a book; it was getting late; they must waste no more time; Cassandra arrived tonight for dinner; she flinched and roused herself, and discovered that she ought to be holding something in her hands. But they were empty. She held them out with an exclamation.

'I've left my bag somewhere – where?' The gardens had no points of the compass, so far as she was concerned. She had been walking for the most part on grass – that was all she knew. Even the road to the Orchid House had now split itself into three. But there was no bag in the Orchid House. It must, therefore, have been left upon the seat. They retraced their steps in the preoccupied manner of people who have to think about something that is lost. What did this bag look like? What did it contain?

'A purse – a ticket – some letters, papers,' Katharine counted, becoming more agitated as she recalled the list. Denham went on quickly in advance of her, and she heard him shout that he had found it before she reached the seat. In order to make sure that all was safe she spread the contents on her knee. It was a queer collection, Denham thought, gazing with the deepest interest. Loose gold coins were tangled in a narrow strip of lace; there were letters which somehow suggested the extreme of intimacy; there were two or three keys, and lists of commissions against which crosses were set at intervals. But she did not seem satisfied until she had made sure of a certain paper so folded that Denham could not judge what it contained. In her relief and gratitude she began at once to say that she had been thinking over what Denham had told her of his plans.

He cut her short. 'Don't let's discuss that dreary business.'

'But I thought – '

'It's a dreary business. I ought never to have bothered you – '

'Have you decided, then?'

He made an impatient sound. 'It's not a thing that matters.'

She could only say rather flatly, 'Oh!'

'I mean it matters to me, but it matters to no one else. Anyhow,' he continued, more amiably, 'I see no reason why you should be bothered with other people's nuisances.'

She supposed that she had let him see too clearly her weariness of this side of life.

'I'm afraid I've been absent-minded,' she began, remembering how often William had brought this charge against her.

'You have a good deal to make you absent-minded,' he replied.

'Yes,' she replied, flushing. 'No,' she contradicted herself. 'Nothing particular, I mean. But I was thinking about plants. I was enjoying myself. In fact, I've seldom enjoyed an afternoon more. But I want to hear what you've settled, if you don't mind telling me.'

'Oh, it's all settled,' he replied. 'I'm going to this infernal cottage to write a worthless book.'

'How I envy you,' she replied, with the utmost sincerity.

'Well, cottages are to be had for fifteen shillings a week.'

'Cottages are to be had – yes,' she replied. 'The question is – ' She checked herself. 'Two rooms are all I should want,' she continued, with a curious sigh; 'one for eating, one for sleeping. Oh, but I should like another, a large one at the top, and a little garden where one could grow flowers. A path – so – down to a river, or up to a wood, and the sea not very far off, so that one could hear the waves at night. Ships just vanishing on the horizon – ' She broke off. 'Shall you be near the sea?'

'My notion of perfect happiness,' he began, not replying to her question, 'is to live as you've said.'

'Well, now you can. You will work, I suppose,' she continued; 'you'll work all the morning and again after tea and perhaps at night. You won't have people always coming about you to interrupt.'

'How far can one live alone?' he asked. 'Have you tried ever?'

'Once for three weeks,' she replied. 'My father and mother were in Italy, and something happened so that I couldn't join them. For three weeks I lived entirely by myself, and the only person I spoke to was a stranger in a shop where I lunched – a man with a beard. Then I went back to my room by myself and – well, I did what I liked. It doesn't make me out an amiable character, I'm afraid,' she added, 'but I can't endure living with other people. An occasional man with a beard is interesting; he's detached; he lets me go my way, and we know we shall never meet again. Therefore, we are perfectly sincere – a thing not possible with one's friends.'

'Nonsense,' Denham replied abruptly.

'Why "nonsense"?' she enquired.

'Because you don't mean what you say,' he expostulated.

'You're very positive,' she said, laughing and looking at him. How arbitrary, hot-tempered and imperious he was! He had asked her to come to Kew to advise him; he then told her that he had settled the question already; he then proceeded to find fault with her. He was the very opposite of William Rodney, she thought; he was shabby, his clothes were badly made, he was ill versed in the amenities of life; he was tongue-tied and awkward to the verge of obliterating his real character. He was awkwardly silent; he was awkwardly emphatic. And yet she liked him.

'I don't mean what I say,' she repeated good-humouredly. 'Well – ?'

'I doubt whether you make absolute sincerity your standard in life,' he answered significantly.

She flushed. He had penetrated at once to the weak spot – her engagement, and had reason for what he said. He was not altogether justified now, at any rate, she was glad to remember; but she could not enlighten him and must bear his insinuations, though from the lips of a man who had behaved as he had behaved their force should not have been sharp. Nevertheless, what he said had its force, she mused; partly because he seemed unconscious of his own lapse in the case of Mary Datchet, and thus baffled her insight; partly because he always spoke with force, for what reason she did not yet feel certain.

'Absolute sincerity is rather difficult, don't you think?' she enquired, with a touch of irony.

'There are people one credits even with that,' he replied a little vaguely. He was ashamed of his savage wish to hurt her, and yet it was not for the sake of hurting her, who was beyond his shafts, but in order to mortify his own incredibly reckless impulse of abandonment to the spirit which seemed, at moments, about to rush him to the uttermost ends of the earth. She affected him beyond the scope of his wildest dreams. He seemed to see that beneath the quiet surface of her manner, which was almost pathetically at hand and within reach for all the trivial demands of daily life, there was a spirit which she reserved or repressed for some reason either of loneliness or – could it be possible – of love. Was it given to Rodney to see her unmasked, unrestrained, unconscious of her duties? a creature of uncalculating passion and instinctive freedom? No; he refused to believe it. It was in her loneliness that Katharine was unreserved. 'I went back to my room by myself and I did – what I liked.' She had said that to him, and in saying it had given him a glimpse of possibilities, even of confidences, as if he might be the one to share her loneliness, the mere hint of which made his heart beat faster and his brain spin. He checked himself as brutally as he could. He saw her redden, and in the irony of her reply he heard her resentment.

He began slipping his smooth, silver watch in his pocket, in the hope that somehow he might help himself back to that calm and fatalistic mood which had been his when he looked at its face upon the bank of the lake, for that mood must, at whatever cost, be the mood of his intercourse with Katharine. He had spoken of gratitude and acquiescence in the letter which he had never sent, and now all the force of his character must make good those vows in her presence.

She, thus challenged, tried meanwhile to define her points. She wished to make Denham understand.

'Don't you see that if you have no relations with people it's easier to be honest with them?' she enquired. 'That is what I meant. One needn't cajole them; one's under no obligation to them. Surely you must have found with your own family that it's impossible to discuss what matters to you most because you're all herded together, because you're in a conspiracy, because the position is false – ' Her reasoning suspended itself a little inconclusively, for the subject was complex, and she found herself in ignorance whether Denham had a family or not. Denham was agreed with her as to the destructiveness of the family system, but he did not wish to discuss the problem at that moment.

He turned to a problem which was of greater interest to him.

'I'm convinced,' he said, 'that there are cases in which perfect sincerity is possible – cases where there's no relationship, though the people live together, if you like, where each is free, where there's no obligation upon either side.'

'For a time perhaps,' she agreed, a little despondently. 'But obligations always grow up. There are feelings to be considered. People aren't simple, and though they may mean to be reasonable, they end' – in the condition in which she found herself, she meant, but added lamely – 'in a muddle.'

'Because,' Denham instantly intervened, 'they don't make themselves understood at the beginning. I could undertake, at this instant,' he continued, with a reasonable intonation which did much credit to his self-control, 'to lay down terms for a friendship which should be perfectly sincere and perfectly straightforward.'

She was curious to hear them, but, besides feeling that the topic concealed dangers better known to her than to him, she was reminded by his tone of his curious abstract declaration upon the Embankment. Anything that hinted at love for the moment alarmed her; it was as much an infliction to her as the rubbing of a skinless wound.

But he went on, without waiting for her invitation.

'In the first place, such a friendship must be unemotional,' he laid it down emphatically. 'At least, on both sides it must be understood that if either chooses to fall in love, he or she does so entirely at his own risk. Neither is under any obligation to the other. They must be at liberty to break or to alter at any moment. They must be able to say whatever they wish to say. All this must be understood.'

'And they gain something worth having?' she asked.

'It's a risk – of course it's a risk,' he replied. The word was one that she had been using frequently in her arguments with herself of late. 'But it's the only way – if you think friendship worth having,' he concluded.

'Perhaps under those conditions it might be,' she said reflectively.

'Well,' he said, 'those are the terms of the friendship I wish to offer you.' She had known that this was coming, but, none the less, felt a little shock, half of pleasure, half of reluctance, when she heard the formal statement.

'I should like it,' she began, 'but – '

'Would Rodney mind?'

'Oh no,' she replied quickly. 'No, no, it isn't that,' she went on, and again came to an end.

She had been touched by the unreserved and yet ceremonious way in which he had made what he called his offer of terms, but if he was generous it was the more necessary for her to be cautious. They would find themselves in difficulties, she speculated; but, at this point, which was not very far, after all, upon the road of caution, her foresight deserted her. She sought for some definite catastrophe into which they must inevitably plunge. But she could think of none. It seemed to her that these catastrophes were fictitious; life went on and on – life was different altogether from what people said. And not only was she at an end of her stock of caution, but it seemed suddenly altogether super-fluous. Surely if anyone could take care of himself, Ralph Denham could; he had told her that he did not love her. And, further, she meditated, walking on beneath the beech trees and swinging her umbrella, as in her thought she was accustomed to complete freedom, why should she perpetually apply so different a standard to her behaviour in practice? Why, she reflected, should there be this perpetual disparity between the thought and the action, between the life of solitude and the life of society, this astonishing precipice on one side of which the soul was active and in broad daylight, on the other side of which it was contemplative and dark as night? Was it not possible to step from one to the other, erect, and without essential change? Was this not the chance he offered her – the rare and wonderful chance of friendship? At any rate, she told Denham, with a sigh in which he heard both impatience and relief, that she agreed; she thought him right; she would accept his terms of friendship.

'Now,' she said, 'let's go and have tea.'

In fact, these principles having been laid down, a great lightness of spirit showed itself in both of them. They were both convinced that something of profound importance had been settled, and could now give their attention to their tea and the Gardens. They wandered in and out of glasshouses, saw lilies swimming in tanks, breathed in the scent of thousands of carnations, and compared their respective tastes in the matter of trees and lakes. While talking exclusively of what they saw, so that anyone might have overheard them, they felt that the compact between them was made firmer and deeper by the number of people who passed them and suspected nothing of the kind. The question of Ralph's cottage and future was not mentioned again.

Chapter 26

Although the old coaches, with their gay panels and the guard's horn, and the humours of the box and the vicissitudes of the road, have long moldered into dust so far as they were matter, and are preserved in the printed pages of our novelists so far as they partook of the spirit, a journey to London by express train can still be a very pleasant and romantic adventure. Cassandra Otway, at the age of twenty-two, could imagine few things more pleasant. Satiated with months of green fields as she was, the first row of artisans' villas on the outskirts of London seemed to have something serious about it, which positively increased the importance of every person in the railway carriage, and even, to her impressionable mind, quickened the speed of the train and gave a note of stern authority to the shriek of the engine-whistle. They were bound for London; they must have precedence of all traffic not similarly destined. A different demeanour was necessary directly one stepped out upon Liverpool Street platform, and became one of those preoccupied and hasty citizens for whose needs innumerable taxi-cabs, motor-omnibuses and underground railways were in waiting. She did her best to look dignified and preoccupied too, but as the cab carried her away, with a determination which alarmed her a little, she became more and more forgetful of her station as a citizen of London, and turned her head from one window to another, picking up eagerly a building on this side or a street scene on that to feed her intense curiosity. And yet, while the drive lasted no one was real, nothing was ordinary; the crowds, the government buildings, the tide of men and women washing the base of the great glass windows, were all generalised, and affected her as if she saw them on the stage.

All these feelings were sustained and partly inspired by the fact that her journey took her straight to the centre of her most romantic world. A thousand times in the midst of her pastoral landscape her thoughts took this precise road, were admitted to the house in Chelsea, and went directly upstairs to Katharine's room, where, invisible themselves, they had the better chance of feasting upon the privacy of the room's adorable and mysterious mistress. Cassandra adored her cousin; the adoration might have been foolish, but was saved from that excess and lent an engaging charm by the volatile nature of Cassandra's temperament. She had adored a great many things and people in the course of twenty-two years; she had been alternately the pride and the desperation of her teachers. She had worshipped architecture and music, natural history and humanity, literature and art, but always at the height of her enthusiasm, which was accompanied by a brilliant degree of accomplishment, she changed her mind and bought, surreptitiously, another grammar. The terrible results which governesses had predicted from such mental dissipation were certainly apparent now that Cassandra was twenty-two, and had never passed an examination, and daily showed herself less and less capable of passing one. The more serious prediction that she could never possibly earn her living was also verified. But from all these short strands of different accomplishments Cassandra wove for herself an attitude, a cast of mind, which, if useless, was found by some people to have the not despicable virtues of vivacity and freshness. Katharine, for example, thought her a most charming companion. The cousins seemed to assemble between them a great range of qualities which are never found united in one person and seldom in half a dozen people. Where Katharine was simple, Cassandra was complex; where Katharine was solid and direct, Cassandra was vague and evasive. In short, they represented very well the manly and the womanly sides of the feminine nature, and, for foundation, there was the profound unity of common blood between them. If Cassandra adored Katharine she was incapable of adoring anyone without refreshing her spirit with frequent draughts of raillery and criticism, and Katharine enjoyed her laughter at least as much as her respect.

Respect was certainly uppermost in Cassandra's mind at the present moment. Katharine's engagement had appealed to her imagination as the first engagement in a circle of contemporaries is apt to appeal to the imaginations of the others; it was solemn, beautiful, and mysterious; it gave both parties the important air of those who have been initiated into some rite which is still concealed from the rest of the group. For Katharine's sake Cassandra thought William a most distinguished and interesting character, and welcomed first his conversation and then his manuscript as the marks of a friendship which it flattered and delighted her to inspire.

Katharine was still out when she arrived at Cheyne Walk. After greeting her uncle and aunt and receiving, as usual, a present of two

sovereigns for 'cab fares and dissipation' from Uncle Trevor, whose
favourite niece she was, she changed her dress and wandered into
Katharine's room to await her. What a great looking-glass Katharine
had, she thought, and how mature all the arrangements upon the
dressing-table were compared to what she was used to at home.
Glancing round, she thought that the bills stuck upon a skewer and
stood for ornament upon the mantelpiece were astonishingly like
Katharine, There wasn't a photograph of William anywhere to be
seen. The room, with its combination of luxury and bareness, its silk
dressing-gowns and crimson slippers, its shabby carpet and bare walls,
had a powerful air of Katharine herself; she stood in the middle of the
room and enjoyed the sensation; and then, with a desire to finger what
her cousin was in the habit of fingering, Cassandra began to take down
the books which stood in a row upon the shelf above the bed. In most
houses this shelf is the ledge upon which the last relics of religious belief
lodge themselves as if, late at night, in the heart of privacy, people,
sceptical by day, find solace in sipping one draught of the old charm for
such sorrows or perplexities as may steal from their hiding-places in the
dark. But there was no hymn-book here. By their battered covers and
enigmatical contents, Cassandra judged them to be old schoolbooks
belonging to Uncle Trevor, and piously, though eccentrically, preserved
by his daughter. There was no end, she thought, to the unexpectedness
of Katharine. She had once had a passion for geometry herself,
and, curled upon Katharine's quilt, she became absorbed in trying to
remember how far she had forgotten what she once knew. Katharine,
coming in a little later, found her deep in this characteristic pursuit.

'My dear,' Cassandra exclaimed, shaking the book at her cousin, 'my
whole life's changed from this moment! I must write the man's name
down at once, or I shall forget – '

Whose name, what book, which life was changed Katharine proceeded to ascertain. She began to lay aside her clothes hurriedly, for she
was very late.

'May I sit and watch you?' Cassandra asked, shutting up her book. 'I
got ready on purpose.'

'Oh, you're ready, are you?' said Katharine, half turning in the midst
of her operations, and looking at Cassandra, who sat, clasping her
knees, on the edge of the bed.

'There are people dining here,' she said, taking in the effect of
Cassandra from a new point of view. After an interval, the distinction,
the irregular charm, of the small face with its long tapering nose and its
bright oval eyes were very notable. The hair rose up off the forehead

rather stiffly, and, given a more careful treatment by hairdressers and dressmakers, the light angular figure might possess a likeness to a French lady of distinction in the eighteenth century.

'Who's coming to dinner?' Cassandra asked, anticipating further possibilities of rapture.

'There's William, and, I believe, Aunt Eleanor and Uncle Aubrey.'

'I'm so glad William is coming. Did he tell you that he sent me his manuscript? I think it's wonderful – I think he's almost good enough for you, Katharine.'

'You shall sit next to him and tell him what you think of him.'

'I shan't dare do that,' Cassandra asserted.

'Why? You're not afraid of him, are you?'

'A little – because he's connected with you.'

Katharine smiled.

'But then, with your well-known fidelity, considering that you're staying here at least a fortnight, you won't have any illusions left about me by the time you go. I give you a week, Cassandra. I shall see my power fading day by day. Now it's at the climax; but tomorrow it'll have begun to fade. What am I to wear, I wonder? Find me a blue dress, Cassandra, over there in the long wardrobe.'

She spoke disconnectedly, handling brush and comb, and pulling out the little drawers in her dressing-table and leaving them open. Cassandra, sitting on the bed behind her, saw the reflection of her cousin's face in the looking-glass. The face in the looking-glass was serious and intent, apparently occupied with other things besides the straightness of the parting which, however, was being driven as straight as a Roman road through the dark hair. Cassandra was impressed again by Katharine's maturity; and, as she enveloped herself in the blue dress which filled almost the whole of the long looking-glass with blue light and made it the frame of a picture, holding not only the slightly moving effigy of the beautiful woman, but shapes and colours of objects reflected from the background, Cassandra thought that no sight had ever been quite so romantic. It was all in keeping with the room and the house and the city round them; for her ears had not yet ceased to notice the hum of distant wheels.

They went downstairs rather late, in spite of Katharine's extreme speed in getting ready. To Cassandra's ears the buzz of voices inside the drawing-room was like the tuning up of the instruments of the orchestra. It seemed to her that there were numbers of people in the room, and that they were strangers, and that they were beautiful and dressed with the greatest distinction, although they proved to be mostly her relations, and the distinction of their clothing was confined, in the eyes of an impartial observer, to the white waistcoat which Rodney wore. But they all rose simultaneously, which was by itself impressive, and they all exclaimed, and shook hands, and she was introduced to Mr Peyton, and the door sprang open, and dinner was announced, and they filed off, William Rodney offering her his slightly bent black arm, as she had secretly hoped he would. In short, had the scene been looked at only through her eyes, it must have been described as one of magical brilliancy. The pattern of the soup-plates, the stiff folds of the napkins, which rose by the side of each plate in the shape of arum lilies, the long sticks of bread tied with pink ribbon, the silver dishes and the sea-coloured champagne glasses, with the flakes of gold congealed in their stems – all these details, together with a curiously pervasive smell of kid gloves, contributed to her exhilaration, which must be repressed, however, because she was grown up, and the world held no more for her to marvel at.

The world held no more for her to marvel at, it is true; but it held other people; and each other person possessed in Cassandra's mind some fragment of what privately she called 'reality'. It was a gift that they would impart if you asked them for it, and thus no dinner-party could possibly be dull, and little Mr Peyton on her right and William Rodney on her left were in equal measure endowed with the quality which seemed to her so unmistakable and so precious that the way people neglected to demand it was a constant source of surprise to her. She scarcely knew, indeed, whether she was talking to Mr Peyton or to William Rodney. But to one who, by degrees, assumed the shape of an elderly man with a moustache, she described how she had arrived in London that very afternoon, and how she had taken a cab and driven through the streets. Mr Peyton, an editor of fifty years, bowed his bald head repeatedly, with apparent understanding. At least, he understood that she was very young and pretty, and saw that she was excited, though he could not gather at once from her words or remember from his own experience what there was to be excited about. 'Were there any buds on the trees?' he asked. 'Which line did she travel by?'

He was cut short in these amiable enquiries by her desire to know whether he was one of those who read, or one of those who look out of the window? Mr Peyton was by no means sure which he did. He rather thought he did both. He was told that he had made a most dangerous confession. She could deduce his entire history from that one fact. He challenged her to proceed; and she proclaimed him a Liberal Member of Parliament.

William, nominally engaged in a desultory conversation with Aunt Eleanor, heard every word, and taking advantage of the fact that elderly ladies have little continuity of conversation, at least with those whom they esteem for their youth and their sex, he asserted his presence by a very nervous laugh.

Cassandra turned to him directly. She was enchanted to find that, instantly and with such ease, another of these fascinating beings was offering untold wealth for her extraction.

'There's no doubt what *you* do in a railway carriage, William,' she said, making use in her pleasure of his first name. 'You never *once* look out of the window; you read *all* the time.'

'And what facts do you deduce from that?' Mr Peyton asked.

'Oh, that he's a poet, of course,' said Cassandra. 'But I must confess that I knew that before, so it isn't fair. I've got your manuscript with me,' she went on, disregarding Mr Peyton in a shameless way. 'I've got all sorts of things I want to ask you about it.'

William inclined his head and tried to conceal the pleasure that her remark gave him. But the pleasure was not unalloyed. However susceptible to flattery William might be, he would never tolerate it from people who showed a gross or emotional taste in literature, and if Cassandra erred even slightly from what he considered essential in this respect he would express his discomfort by flinging out his hands and wrinkling his forehead; he would find no pleasure in her flattery after that.

'First of all,' she proceeded, 'I want to know why you chose to write a play?'

'Ah! You mean it's not dramatic?'

'I mean that I don't see what it would gain by being acted. But then does Shakespeare gain? Henry and I are always arguing about Shakespeare. I'm certain he's wrong, but I can't prove it because I've only seen Shakespeare acted once in Lincoln. But I'm quite positive,' she insisted, 'that Shakespeare wrote for the stage.'

'You're perfectly right,' Rodney exclaimed. 'I was hoping you were on that side. Henry's wrong – entirely wrong. Of course, I've failed, as all the moderns fail. Dear, dear, I wish I'd consulted you before.'

From this point they proceeded to go over, as far as memory served them, the different aspects of Rodney's drama. She said nothing that jarred upon him, and untrained daring had the power to stimulate experience to such an extent that Rodney was frequently seen to hold his fork suspended before him, while he debated the first principles of the art. Mrs Hilbery thought to herself that she had never seen him to such advantage; yes, he was somehow different; he reminded her of someone who was dead, someone who was distinguished – she had forgotten his name.

Cassandra's voice rose high in its excitement.

'You've not read *The Idiot*!' she exclaimed.

'I've read *War and Peace*,'[82] William replied, a little testily.

'*War and Peace*!' she echoed, in a tone of derision.

'I confess I don't understand the Russians.'

'Shake hands! Shake hands!' boomed Uncle Aubrey from across the table. 'Neither do I. And I hazard the opinion that they don't themselves.'

The old gentleman had ruled a large part of the Indian Empire, but he was in the habit of saying that he had rather have written the works of Dickens. The table now took possession of a subject much to its liking. Aunt Eleanor showed premonitory signs of pronouncing an opinion. Although she had blunted her taste upon some form of philanthropy for twenty-five years, she had a fine natural instinct for an upstart or a pretender, and knew to a hair's breadth what literature should be and what it should not be. She was born to the knowledge, and scarcely thought it a matter to be proud of.

'Insanity is not a fit subject for fiction,' she announced positively.

'There's the well-known case of Hamlet,' Mr Hilbery interposed, in his leisurely, half-humorous tones.

'Ah, but poetry's different, Trevor,' said Aunt Eleanor, as if she had special authority from Shakespeare to say so. 'Different altogether. And I've never thought, for my part, that Hamlet was as mad as they make out. What is your opinion, Mr Peyton?' For, as there was a minister of literature present in the person of the editor of an esteemed review, she deferred to him.

Mr Peyton leant a little back in his chair, and, putting his head rather on one side, observed that that was a question that he had never been able to answer entirely to his satisfaction. There was much to be said on both sides, but as he considered upon which side he should say it, Mrs Hilbery broke in upon his judicious meditations.

'Lovely, lovely Ophelia!' she exclaimed. 'What a wonderful power it is – poetry! I wake up in the morning all bedraggled; there's a yellow fog outside; little Emily turns on the electric light when she brings me my tea, and says, "Oh, ma'am, the water's frozen in the cistern, and cook's cut her finger to the bone." And then I open a little green book, and the birds are singing, the stars shining, the flowers twinkling – ' She looked about her as if these presences had suddenly manifested themselves round her dining-room table.

'Has the cook cut her finger badly?' Aunt Eleanor demanded, addressing herself naturally to Katharine.

'Oh, the cook's finger is only my way of putting it,' said Mrs Hilbery. 'But if she had cut her arm off, Katharine would have sewn it on again,' she remarked, with an affectionate glance at her daughter, who looked, she thought, a little sad. 'But what horrid, horrid thoughts,' she wound up, laying down her napkin and pushing her chair back. 'Come, let us find something more cheerful to talk about upstairs.'

Upstairs in the drawing-room Cassandra found fresh sources of pleasure, first in the distinguished and expectant look of the room, and then in the chance of exercising her divining-rod upon a new assortment of human beings. But the low tones of the women, their meditative silences, the beauty which, to her at least, shone even from black satin and the knobs of amber which encircled elderly necks, changed her wish to chatter to a more subdued desire merely to watch and to whisper. She entered with delight into an atmosphere in which private matters were being interchanged freely, almost in monosyllables, by the older women who now accepted her as one of themselves. Her expression became very gentle and sympathetic, as if she, too, were full of solicitude for the world which was somehow being cared for, managed and deprecated by Aunt Maggie and Aunt Eleanor. After a time she perceived that Katharine was outside the community in some way, and, suddenly, she threw aside her wisdom and gentleness and concern and began to laugh.

'What are you laughing at?' Katharine asked.

A joke so foolish and unfilial wasn't worth explaining.

'It was nothing – ridiculous – in the worst of taste, but still, if you half shut your eyes and looked – ' Katharine half shut her eyes and looked, but she looked in the wrong direction, and Cassandra laughed more than ever, and was still laughing and doing her best to explain in a whisper that Aunt Eleanor, through half-shut eyes, was like the parrot in the cage at Stogdon House, when the gentlemen came in and Rodney walked straight up to them and wanted to know what they were laughing at.

'I utterly refuse to tell you!' Cassandra replied, standing up straight, clasping her hands in front of her, and facing him. Her mockery was delicious to him. He had not even for a second the fear that she had been laughing at him. She was laughing because life was so adorable, so enchanting.

'Ah, but you're cruel to make me feel the barbarity of my sex,' he replied, drawing his feet together and pressing his fingertips upon an imaginary opera-hat or malacca cane. 'We've been discussing all sorts of dull things, and now I shall never know what I want to know more than anything in the world.'

'You don't deceive us for a minute!' she cried. 'Not for a second. We both know that you've been enjoying yourself immensely. Hasn't he, Katharine?'

'No,' she replied, 'I think he's speaking the truth. He doesn't care much for politics.'

Her words, though spoken simply, produced a curious change in the light, sparkling atmosphere. William at once lost his look of animation and said seriously: 'I detest politics.'

'I don't think any man has the right to say that,' said Cassandra, almost severely.

'I agree. I mean that I detest politicians,' he corrected himself quickly.

'You see, I believe Cassandra is what they call a Feminist,' Katharine went on. 'Or rather, she was a Feminist six months ago, but it's no good supposing that she is now what she was then. That is one of her greatest charms in my eyes. One never can tell.' She smiled at her as an elder sister might smile.

'Katharine, you make one feel so horribly small!' Cassandra exclaimed.

'No, no, that's not what she means,' Rodney interposed. 'I quite agree that women have an immense advantage over us there. One misses a lot by attempting to know things thoroughly.'

'He knows Greek thoroughly,' said Katharine. 'But then he also knows a good deal about painting, and a certain amount about music. He's very cultivated – perhaps the most cultivated person I know.'

'And poetry,' Cassandra added.

'Yes, I was forgetting his play,' Katharine remarked, and turning her head as though she saw something that needed her attention in a far corner of the room, she left them.

For a moment they stood silent, after what seemed a deliberate introduction to each other, and Cassandra watched her crossing the room.

'Henry,' she said next moment, 'would say that a stage ought to be no bigger than this drawing-room. He wants there to be singing and dancing as well as acting – only all the opposite of Wagner – you understand?'

They sat down, and Katharine, turning when she reached the window, saw William with his hand raised in gesticulation and his mouth open, as if ready to speak the moment Cassandra ceased.

Katharine's duty, whether it was to pull a curtain or move a chair, was either forgotten or discharged, but she continued to stand by the window without doing anything. The elderly people were all grouped together round the fire. They seemed an independent, middle-aged community busy with its own concerns. They were telling stories very well and listening to them very graciously. But for her there was no obvious employment.

'If anybody says anything, I shall say that I'm looking at the river,' she thought, for in her slavery to her family traditions, she was ready to pay for her transgression with some plausible falsehood. She pushed aside the blind and looked at the river. But it was a dark night and the water was barely visible. Cabs were passing, and couples were loitering slowly along the road, keeping as close to the railings as possible, though the trees had as yet no leaves to cast shadow upon their embraces. Katharine, thus withdrawn, felt her loneliness. The evening had been one of pain, offering her, minute after minute, plainer proof that things would fall out as she had foreseen. She had faced tones, gestures, glances; she knew, with her back to them, that William, even now, was plunging deeper and deeper into the delight of unexpected understanding with Cassandra. He had almost told her that he was finding it infinitely better than he could have believed. She looked out of the window, sternly determined to forget private misfortunes, to forget herself, to forget individual lives. With her eyes upon the dark sky, voices reached her from the room in which she was standing. She heard them as if they came from people in another world, a world antecedent to her world, a world that was the prelude, the antechamber to reality; it was as if, lately dead, she heard the living talking. The dream nature of our life had never been more apparent to her, never had life been more certainly an affair of four walls, whose objects existed only within the range of lights and fires, beyond which lay nothing, or nothing more than darkness. She seemed physically to have stepped beyond the region where the light of illusion still makes it desirable to possess, to love, to struggle. And yet her melancholy brought her no serenity. She still heard the voices within the room. She was still tormented by desires. She wished to be beyond their range. She wished inconsistently enough that she could find herself driving rapidly through the streets; she was even anxious to be with someone who, after a moment's groping, took a definite shape and solidified into the person of Mary Datchet. She drew the curtains so that the draperies met in deep folds in the middle of the window.

'Ah, there she is,' said Mr Hilbery, who was standing swaying affably from side to side, with his back to the fire. 'Come here, Katharine. I

couldn't see where you'd got to – our children,' he observed parenthetically, 'have their uses – I want you to go to my study, Katharine;
go to the third shelf on the right-hand side of the door; take down
Trelawny's *Recollections of Shelley*;[83] bring it to me. Then, Peyton, you
will have to admit to the assembled company that you have been
mistaken.'

'Trelawny's *Recollections of Shelley*. The third shelf on the right of the
door,' Katharine repeated. After all, one does not check children in
their play, or rouse sleepers from their dreams. She passed William and
Cassandra on her way to the door.

'Stop, Katharine,' said William, speaking almost as if he were conscious of her against his will. 'Let me go.' He rose, after a second's
hesitation, and she understood that it cost him an effort. She knelt one
knee upon the sofa where Cassandra sat, looking down at her cousin's
face, which still moved with the speed of what she had been saying.

'Are you – happy?' she asked.

'Oh, my dear!' Cassandra exclaimed, as if no further words were
needed. 'Of course, we disagree about every subject under the sun,' she
exclaimed, 'but I think he's the cleverest man I've ever met – and you're
the most beautiful woman,' she added, looking at Katharine, and as she
looked her face lost its animation and became almost melancholy in
sympathy with Katharine's melancholy, which seemed to Cassandra the
last refinement of her distinction.

'Ah, but it's only ten o'clock,' said Katharine darkly.

'As late as that! Well – ?' She did not understand.

'At twelve my horses turn into rats and off I go. The illusion fades.
But I accept my fate. I make hay while the sun shines.' Cassandra
looked at her with a puzzled expression.

'Here's Katharine talking about rats, and hay, and all sorts of odd
things,' she said, as William returned to them. He had been quick. 'Can
you make her out?'

Katharine perceived from his little frown and hesitation that he did
not find that particular problem to his taste at present. She stood upright
at once and said in a different tone: 'I really am off, though. I wish you'd
explain if they say anything, William. I shan't be late, but I've got to see
someone.'

'At this time of night?' Cassandra exclaimed.

'Whom have you got to see?' William demanded.

'A friend,' she remarked, half turning her head towards him. She
knew that he wished her to stay, not, indeed, with them, but in their
neighbourhood, in case of need.

'Katharine has a great many friends,' said William rather lamely, sitting down once more, as Katharine left the room.

She was soon driving quickly, as she had wished to drive, through the lamp-lit streets. She liked both light and speed, and the sense of being out of doors alone, and the knowledge that she would reach Mary in her high, lonely room at the end of the drive. She climbed the stone steps quickly, remarking the queer look of her blue silk skirt and blue shoes upon the stone, dusty with the boots of the day, under the light of an occasional jet of flickering gas.

The door was opened in a second by Mary herself, whose face showed not only surprise at the sight of her visitor, but some degree of embarrassment. She greeted her cordially, and, as there was no time for explanations, Katharine walked straight into the sitting-room, and found herself in the presence of a young man who was lying back in a chair and holding a sheet of paper in his hand, at which he was looking as if he expected to go on immediately with what he was in the middle of saying to Mary Datchet. The apparition of an unknown lady in full evening dress seemed to disturb him. He took his pipe from his mouth, rose stiffly, and sat down again with a jerk.

'Have you been dining out?' Mary asked.

'Are you working?' Katharine enquired simultaneously.

The young man shook his head, as if he disowned his share in the question with some irritation.

'Well, not exactly,' Mary replied. 'Mr Basnett had brought some papers to show me. We were going through them, but we'd almost done . . . Tell us about your party.'

Mary had a ruffled appearance, as if she had been running her fingers through her hair in the course of her conversation; she was dressed more or less like a Russian peasant girl. She sat down again in a chair which looked as if it had been her seat for some hours; the saucer which stood upon the arm contained the ashes of many cigarettes. Mr Basnett, a very young man with a fresh complexion and a high forehead from which the hair was combed straight back, was one of that group of 'very able young men' suspected by Mr Clacton, justly as it turned out, of an influence upon Mary Datchet. He had come down from one of the universities not long ago, and was now charged with the reformation of society. In connection with the rest of the group of very able young men he had drawn up a scheme for the education of labour, for the amalgamation of the middle class and the working class, and for a joint assault of the two bodies, combined in the Society for the Education of Democracy,[84] upon capital. The scheme had already reached the stage in which it was permissible to hire an office and engage a secretary, and he had been deputed to expound the scheme to Mary, and make her an offer of the secretaryship, to which, as a matter of principle, a small salary was attached. Since seven o'clock that evening he had been reading out loud the document in which the faith of the new reformers was expounded, but the reading was so frequently interrupted by discussion, and it was so often necessary to inform Mary 'in strictest confidence' of the private characters and evil designs of certain individuals and societies that they were still only halfway through the manuscript. Neither of them realised that the talk had already lasted three hours. In their absorption they had forgotten even to feed the fire, and yet both Mr Basnett in his exposition, and Mary in her interrogation, carefully preserved a kind of formality calculated to check the desire of the human mind for irrelevant discussion. Her questions frequently began, 'Am I to understand – ' and his replies invariably represented the views of someone called 'we'.

By this time Mary was almost persuaded that she, too, was included in the 'we', and agreed with Mr Basnett in believing that 'our' views, 'our' society, 'our' policy, stood for something quite definitely segregated from the main body of society in a circle of superior illumination.

The appearance of Katharine in this atmosphere was extremely incongruous, and had the effect of making Mary remember all sorts of things that she had been glad to forget.

'You've been dining out?' she asked again, looking, with a little smile, at the blue silk and the pearl-sewn shoes.

'No, at home. Are you starting something new?' Katharine hazarded, rather hesitatingly, looking at the papers.

'We are,' Mr Basnett replied. He said no more.

'I'm thinking of leaving our friends in Russell Square,' Mary explained.

'I see. And then you will do something else.'

'Well, I'm afraid I like working,' said Mary.

'Afraid,' said Mr Basnett, conveying the impression that, in his opinion, no sensible person could be afraid of liking to work.

'Yes,' said Katharine, as if he had stated this opinion aloud. 'I should like to start something – something off one's own bat – that's what I should like.'

'Yes, that's the fun,' said Mr Basnett, looking at her for the first time rather keenly, and refilling his pipe.

'But you can't limit work – that's what I mean,' said Mary. 'I mean there are other sorts of work. No one works harder than a woman with little children.'

'Quite so,' said Mr Basnett. 'It's precisely the women with babies we want to get hold of.' He glanced at his document, rolled it into a cylinder between his fingers, and gazed into the fire. Katharine felt that in this company anything that one said would be judged upon its merits; one had only to say what one thought, rather barely and tersely, with a curious assumption that the number of things that could properly be thought about was strictly limited. And Mr Basnett was only stiff upon the surface; there was an intelligence in his face which attracted her intelligence.

'When will the public know?' she asked.

'What d'you mean – about us?' Mr Basnett asked, with a little smile.

'That depends upon many things,' said Mary. The conspirators looked pleased, as if Katharine's question, with the belief in their existence which it implied, had a warming effect upon them.

'In starting a society such as we wish to start (we can't say any more at present),' Mr Basnett began, with a little jerk of his head, 'there are two things to remember – the press and the public. Other societies, which shall be nameless, have gone under because they've appealed only to cranks. If you don't want a mutual admiration society, which dies as soon as you've all discovered each other's faults, you must nobble the press. You must appeal to the public.'

'That's the difficulty,' said Mary thoughtfully.

'That's where she comes in,' said Mr Basnett, jerking his head in Mary's direction. 'She's the only one of us who's a capitalist. She can make a whole-time job of it. I'm tied to an office; I can only give my spare time. Are you, by any chance, on the look-out for a job?' he asked Katharine, with a queer mixture of distrust and deference.

'Marriage is her job at present,' Mary replied for her.

'Oh, I see,' said Mr Basnett. He made allowances for that; he and his friends had faced the question of sex, along with all others, and assigned it an honourable place in their scheme of life. Katharine felt this beneath the roughness of his manner; and a world entrusted to the guardianship of Mary Datchet and Mr Basnett seemed to her a good world, although not a romantic or beautiful place or, to put it figuratively, a place where any line of blue mist softly linked tree to tree upon the horizon. For a moment she thought she saw in his face, bent now over the fire, the features of that original man whom we still recall every now and then, although we know only the clerk, barrister, governmental official, or working-man variety of him. Not that Mr Basnett, giving his days to commerce and his spare time to social reform, would long carry about him any trace of his possibilities of completeness; but, for the moment, in his youth and ardour, still speculative, still uncramped, one might imagine him the citizen of a nobler state than ours. Katharine turned over her small stock of information, and wondered what their society might be going to attempt. Then she remembered that she was hindering their business, and rose, still thinking of this society, and thus thinking, she said to Mr Basnett: 'Well, you'll ask me to join when the time comes, I hope.'

He nodded, and took his pipe from his mouth, but, being unable to think of anything to say, he put it back again, although he would have been glad if she had stayed.

Against her wish, Mary insisted upon taking her downstairs, and then, as there was no cab to be seen, they stood in the street together, looking about them.

'Go back,' Katharine urged her, thinking of Mr Basnett with his papers in his hand.

'You can't wander about the streets alone in those clothes,' said Mary, but the desire to find a cab was not her true reason for standing beside Katharine for a minute or two. Unfortunately for her composure, Mr Basnett and his papers seemed to her an incidental diversion of life's serious purpose compared with some tremendous fact which manifested itself as she stood alone with Katharine. It may have been their common womanhood.

'Have you seen Ralph?' she asked suddenly, without preface.

'Yes,' said Katharine directly, but she did not remember when or where she had seen him. It took her a moment or two to remember why Mary should ask her if she had seen Ralph.

'I believe I'm jealous,' said Mary.

'Nonsense, Mary,' said Katharine, rather distractedly, taking her arm and beginning to walk up the street in the direction of the main road. 'Let me see; we went to Kew, and we agreed to be friends. Yes, that's what happened.' Mary was silent, in the hope that Katharine would tell her more. But Katharine said nothing.

'It's not a question of friendship,' Mary exclaimed, her anger rising, to her own surprise. 'You know it's not. How can it be? I've no right to interfere – ' She stopped. 'Only I'd rather Ralph wasn't hurt,' she concluded.

'I think he seems able to take care of himself,' Katharine observed. Without either of them wishing it, a feeling of hostility had risen between them.

'Do you really think it's worth it?' said Mary, after a pause.

'How can one tell?' Katharine asked.

'Have you ever cared for anyone?' Mary demanded rashly and foolishly.

'I can't wander about London discussing my feelings – Here's a cab – no, there's someone in it.'

'We don't want to quarrel,' said Mary.

'Ought I to have told him that I wouldn't be his friend?' Katharine asked. 'Shall I tell him that? If so, what reason shall I give him?'

'Of course you can't tell him that,' said Mary, controlling herself.

'I believe I shall, though,' said Katharine suddenly.

'I lost my temper, Katharine; I shouldn't have said what I did.'

'The whole thing's foolish,' said Katharine, peremptorily. 'That's what I say. It's not worth it.' She spoke with unnecessary vehemence, but it was not directed against Mary Datchet. Their animosity had completely disappeared, and upon both of them a cloud of difficulty and darkness rested, obscuring the future, in which they had both to find a way.

'No, no, it's not worth it,' Katharine repeated. 'Suppose, as you say, it's out of the question – this friendship; he falls in love with me. I don't want that. Still,' she added, 'I believe you exaggerate; love's not everything; marriage itself is only one of the things – ' They had reached the main thoroughfare, and stood looking at the omnibuses and passers-by, who seemed, for the moment, to illustrate what Katharine had said of the diversity of human interests. For both of them it had become one of those moments of extreme detachment, when it seems unnecessary ever again to shoulder the burden of happiness and self-assertive existence. Their neighbours were welcome to their possessions.

'I don't lay down any rules,'' said Mary, recovering herself first, as they turned after a long pause of this description. 'All I say is that you should know what you're about – for certain; but,' she added, 'I expect you do.'

At the same time she was profoundly perplexed, not only by what she knew of the arrangements for Katharine's marriage, but by the impression which she had of her, there on her arm, dark and inscrutable.

They walked back again and reached the steps which led up to Mary's flat. Here they stopped and paused for a moment, saying nothing.

'You must go in,' said Katharine, rousing herself. 'He's waiting all this time to go on with his reading.' She glanced up at the lighted window near the top of the house, and they both looked at it and waited for a moment. A flight of semicircular steps ran up to the hall, and Mary slowly mounted the first two or three, and paused, looking down upon Katharine.

'I think you underrate the value of that emotion,' she said slowly, and a little awkwardly. She climbed another step and looked down once more upon the figure that was only partly lit up, standing in the street with a colourless face turned upwards. As Mary hesitated, a cab came by and Katharine turned and stopped it, saying as she opened the door: 'Remember, I want to belong to your society – remember,' she added, having to raise her voice a little, and shutting the door upon the rest of her words.

Mary mounted the stairs step by step, as if she had to lift her body up an extremely steep ascent. She had had to wrench herself forcibly away from Katharine, and every step vanquished her desire. She held on grimly, encouraging herself as though she were actually making some great physical effort in climbing a height. She was conscious that Mr Basnett, sitting at the top of the stairs with his documents, offered her solid footing if she were capable of reaching it. The knowledge gave her a faint sense of exaltation.

Mr Basnett raised his eyes as she opened the door.

'I'll go on where I left off,' he said. 'Stop me if you want anything explained.'

He had been rereading the document, and making pencil notes in the margin while he waited, and he went on again as if there had been no interruption. Mary sat down among the flat cushions, lit another cigarette, and listened with a frown upon her face.

Katharine leant back in the corner of the cab that carried her to Chelsea, conscious of fatigue, and conscious, too, of the sober and satisfactory nature of such industry as she had just witnessed. The thought of it composed and calmed her. When she reached home she let herself in as quietly as she could, in the hope that the household was already gone to bed. But her excursion had occupied less time than she thought, and she heard sounds of unmistakable liveliness upstairs. A door opened, and she drew herself into a ground-floor room in case the sound meant that Mr Peyton were taking his leave. From where she stood she could see the stairs, though she was herself invisible. Someone was coming down the stairs, and now she saw that it was William Rodney. He looked a little strange, as if he were walking in his sleep; his lips moved as if he were acting some part to himself. He came down very slowly, step by step, with one hand upon the banisters to guide himself. She thought he looked as if he were in some mood of high exaltation, which it made her uncomfortable to witness any longer unseen. She stepped into the hall. He gave a great start upon seeing her and stopped.

'Katharine!' he exclaimed. 'You've been out?' he asked.

'Yes . . . Are they still up?'

He did not answer, and walked into the ground-floor room through the door which stood open.

'It's been more wonderful than I can tell you,' he said, 'I'm incredibly happy – '

He was scarcely addressing her, and she said nothing. For a moment they stood at opposite sides of a table saying nothing. Then he asked her quickly, 'But tell me, how did it seem to you? What did you think, Katharine? Is there a chance that she likes me? Tell me, Katharine!'

Before she could answer a door opened on the landing above and disturbed them. It disturbed William excessively. He started back, walked rapidly into the hall, and said in a loud and ostentatiously ordinary tone: 'Good-night, Katharine. Go to bed now. I shall see you soon. I hope I shall be able to come tomorrow.'

Next moment he was gone. She went upstairs and found Cassandra on the landing. She held two or three books in her hand, and she was stooping to look at others in a little bookcase. She said that she could never tell which book she wanted to read in bed, poetry, biography or metaphysics.

'What do you read in bed, Katharine?' she asked, as they walked upstairs side by side.

'Sometimes one thing – sometimes another,' said Katharine vaguely. Cassandra looked at her.

'D'you know, you're extraordinarily queer,' she said. 'Everyone seems to me a little queer. Perhaps it's the effect of London.'

'Is William queer, too?' Katharine asked.

'Well, I think he is a little,' Cassandra replied. 'Queer, but very fascinating. I shall read Milton tonight. It's been one of the happiest nights of my life, Katharine,' she added, looking with shy devotion at her cousin's beautiful face.

Chapter 27

London, in the first days of spring, has buds that open and flowers that suddenly shake their petals – white, purple or crimson – in competition with the display in the garden beds, although these city flowers are merely so many doors flung wide in Bond Street and the neighbourhood, inviting you to look at a picture, or hear a symphony, or merely crowd and crush yourself among all sorts of vocal, excitable, brightly coloured human beings. But, all the same, it is no mean rival to the quieter process of vegetable florescence. Whether or not there is a generous motive at the root, a desire to share and impart, or whether the animation is purely that of insensate fervour and friction, the effect, while it lasts, certainly encourages those who are young, and those who are ignorant, to think the world one great bazaar, with banners fluttering and divans heaped with spoils from every quarter of the globe for their delight.

As Cassandra Otway went about London provided with shillings that opened turnstiles, or more often with large white cards that disregarded turnstiles, the city seemed to her the most lavish and hospitable of hosts. After visiting the National Gallery, or Hertford House,[85] or hearing Brahms or Beethoven at the Bechstein Hall,[86] she would come back to find a new person awaiting her, in whose soul were imbedded some grains of the invaluable substance which she still called reality, and still believed that she could find. The Hilberys, as the saying is, 'knew everyone', and that arrogant claim was certainly upheld by the number of houses which, within a certain area, lit their lamps at night, opened their doors after 3 o'clock, and admitted the Hilberys to their dining-rooms, say, once a month. An indefinable freedom and authority of manner, shared by most of the people who lived in these houses, seemed to indicate that whether it was a question of art, music or government they were well within the gates, and could smile indulgently at the vast mass of humanity which is forced to wait and struggle, and pay for entrance with common coin at the door. The gates opened instantly to admit Cassandra. She was naturally critical of what went on inside, and inclined to quote what Henry would have said; but she often succeeded in contradicting Henry, in his absence, and invariably paid her partner at dinner, or the kind old lady who remembered her grandmother, the compliment of believing that there was meaning in what they said. For the sake of the light in her eager eyes, much crudity of expression and some untidiness of person were forgiven her. It was generally felt that, given a year or two of experience, introduced to good dressmakers and preserved from bad influences, she would be an acquisition. Those elderly ladies, who sit on the edge of ballrooms sampling the stuff of humanity between finger and thumb and breathing so evenly that the necklaces, which rise and fall upon their breasts, seem to represent some elemental force, such as the waves upon the ocean of humanity, concluded, a little smilingly, that she would do. They meant that she would in all probability marry some young man whose mother they respected.

William Rodney was fertile in suggestions. He knew of little galleries, and select concerts, and private performances, and somehow made time to meet Katharine and Cassandra, and to give them tea or dinner or supper in his rooms afterwards. Each one of her fourteen days thus promised to bear some bright illumination in its sober text. But Sunday approached. The day is usually dedicated to nature. The weather was almost kindly enough for an expedition. But Cassandra rejected Hampton Court, Greenwich, Richmond and Kew in favour of the Zoological Gardens. She had once trifled with the psychology of animals, and still knew something about inherited characteristics. On Sunday afternoon, therefore, Katharine, Cassandra and William Rodney drove off to the Zoo. As their cab approached the entrance, Katharine bent forward and waved her hand to a young man who was walking rapidly in the same direction.

'There's Ralph Denham!' she exclaimed. 'I told him to meet us here,' she added. She had even come provided with a ticket for him. William's objection that he would not be admitted was, therefore, silenced directly. But the way in which the two men greeted each other was significant of what was going to happen. As soon as they had admired the little birds in the large cage, William and Cassandra lagged behind and Ralph and Katharine pressed on rather in advance. It was an arrangement in which William took his part, and one that suited his convenience, but he was annoyed all the same. He thought that Katharine should have told him that she had invited Denham to meet them.

'One of Katharine's friends,' he said rather sharply. It was clear that he was irritated, and Cassandra felt for his annoyance. They were standing by the pen of some Oriental hog, and she was prodding the brute gently with the point of her umbrella, when a thousand little observations seemed, in some way, to collect in one centre. The centre was one of intense and curious emotion. Were they happy? She dismissed the question as she asked it, scorning herself for applying such simple measures to the rare and splendid emotions of so unique a couple. Nevertheless, her manner became immediately different, as if, for the first time, she felt consciously womanly, and as if William might conceivably wish later on to confide in her. She forgot all about the psychology of animals, and the recurrence of blue eyes and brown, and became instantly engrossed in her feelings as a woman who could administer consolation, and she hoped that Katharine would keep ahead with Mr Denham, as a child who plays at being grown-up hopes that her mother won't come in just yet, and spoil the game. Or was it not rather that she had ceased to play at being grown-up, and was conscious, suddenly, that she was alarmingly mature and in earnest?

There was still unbroken silence between Katharine and Ralph Denham, but the occupants of the different cages served instead of speech.

'What have you been doing since we met?' Ralph asked at length.

'Doing?' she pondered. 'Walking in and out of other people's houses. I wonder if these animals are happy?' she speculated, stopping before a grey bear, who was philosophically playing with a tassel which once, perhaps, formed part of a lady's parasol.

'I'm afraid Rodney didn't like my coming,' Ralph remarked.

'No. But he'll soon get over that,' she replied. The detachment expressed by her voice puzzled Ralph, and he would have been glad if she had explained her meaning further. But he was not going to press her for explanations. Each moment was to be, as far as he could make it, complete in itself, owing nothing of its happiness to explanations, borrowing neither bright nor dark tints from the future.

'The bears seem happy,' he remarked. 'But we must buy them a bag of something. There's the place to buy buns. Let's go and get them.' They walked to the counter piled with little paper bags, and each simultaneously produced a shilling and pressed it upon the young lady, who did not know whether to oblige the lady or the gentleman, but decided, from conventional reasons, that it was the part of the gentleman to pay.

'I wish to pay,' said Ralph peremptorily, refusing the coin which Katharine tendered. 'I have a reason for what I do,' he added, seeing her smile at his tone of decision.

'I believe you have a reason for everything,' she agreed, breaking a bun into parts and tossing them down the bears' throats, 'but I can't believe it's a good one this time. What is your reason?'

He refused to tell her. He could not explain to her that he was offering up consciously all his happiness to her, and wished, absurdly enough, to pour every possession he had upon the blazing pyre, even his silver and gold. He wished to keep this distance between them – the distance which separates the devotee from the image in the shrine.

Circumstances conspired to make this easier than it would have been had they been seated in a drawing-room, for example, with a tea-tray between them. He saw her against a background of pale grottos and sleek hides; camels slanted their heavy-lidded eyes at her, giraffes fastidiously observed her from their melancholy eminence, and the pink-lined trunks of elephants cautiously abstracted buns from her outstretched hands. Then there were the hothouses. He saw her bending over pythons coiled upon the sand, or considering the brown rock breaking the stagnant water of the alligators' pool, or searching some minute section of tropical forest for the golden eye of a lizard or the indrawn movement of the green frogs' flanks. In particular, he saw her outlined against the deep green waters, in which squadrons of silvery fish wheeled incessantly or ogled her for a moment, pressing their distorted mouths against the glass, quivering their tails straight out behind them. Again, there was the insect house, where she lifted the blinds of the little cages, and marvelled at the purple circles marked upon the rich tussore wings of some lately emerged and semi-conscious butterfly, or at caterpillars immobile like the knobbed twigs of a pale-skinned tree, or at slim green snakes stabbing the glass wall again and again with their flickering cleft tongues. The heat of the air, and the bloom of heavy flowers, which swam in water or rose stiffly from great red jars, together with the display of curious patterns and fantastic shapes, produced an atmosphere in which human beings tended to look pale and to fall silent.

Opening the door of a house which rang with the mocking and profoundly unhappy laughter of monkeys, they discovered William and Cassandra. William appeared to be tempting some small reluctant animal to descend from an upper perch to partake of half an apple. Cassandra was reading out, in her high-pitched tones, an account of this creature's secluded disposition and nocturnal habits. She saw Katharine and exclaimed: 'Here you are! Do prevent William from torturing this unfortunate aye-aye.'

'We thought we'd lost you,' said William. He looked from one to the other, and seemed to take stock of Denham's unfashionable appearance. He seemed to wish to find some outlet for malevolence, but, failing one, he remained silent. The glance, the slight quiver of the upper lip, were not lost upon Katharine.

'William isn't kind to animals,' she remarked. 'He doesn't know what they like and what they don't like.'

'I take it you're well versed in these matters, Denham,' said Rodney, withdrawing his hand with the apple.

'It's mainly a question of knowing how to stroke them,' Denham replied.

'Which is the way to the Reptile House?' Cassandra asked him, not from a genuine desire to visit the reptiles, but in obedience to her new-born feminine susceptibility, which urged her to charm and conciliate the other sex. Denham began to give her directions, and Katharine and William moved on together.

'I hope you've had a pleasant afternoon,' William remarked.

'I like Ralph Denham,' she replied.

'Ça se voit,' William returned, with superficial urbanity.

Many retorts were obvious, but wishing, on the whole, for peace, Katharine merely enquired: 'Are you coming back to tea?'

'Cassandra and I thought of having tea at a little shop in Portland Place,' he replied. 'I don't know whether you and Denham would care to join us.'

'I'll ask him,' she replied, turning her head to look for him. But he and Cassandra were absorbed in the aye-aye once more.

William and Katharine watched them for a moment, and each looked curiously at the object of the other's preference. But resting his eye upon Cassandra, to whose elegance the dressmakers had now done justice, William said sharply: 'If you come, I hope you won't do your best to make me ridiculous.'

'If that's what you're afraid of I certainly shan't come,' Katharine replied.

They were professedly looking into the enormous central cage of monkeys, and being thoroughly annoyed by William, she compared him to a wretched misanthropical ape, huddled in a scrap of old shawl at the end of a pole, darting peevish glances of suspicion and distrust at his companions. Her tolerance was deserting her. The events of the past week had worn it thin. She was in one of those moods, perhaps not uncommon with either sex, when the other becomes very clearly distinguished, and of contemptible baseness, so that the necessity of association is degrading, and the tie, which at such moments is always extremely close, drags like a halter round the neck. William's exacting demands and his jealousy had pulled her down into some horrible swamp of her nature where the primeval struggle between man and woman still rages.

'You seem to delight in hurting me,' William persisted. 'Why did you say that just now about my behaviour to animals?' As he spoke he rattled his stick against the bars of the cage, which gave his words an accompaniment peculiarly exasperating to Katharine's nerves.

'Because it's true. You never see what anyone feels,' she said. 'You think of no one but yourself.'

'That is not true,' said William. By his determined rattling he had now collected the animated attention of some half-dozen apes. Either to propitiate them, or to show his consideration for their feelings, he proceeded to offer them the apple which he held.

The sight, unfortunately, was so comically apt in its illustration of the picture in her mind, the ruse was so transparent, that Katharine was seized with laughter. She laughed uncontrollably. William flushed red. No display of anger could have hurt his feelings more profoundly. It was not only that she was laughing at him; the detachment of the sound was horrible.

'I don't know what you're laughing at,' he muttered, and, turning, found that the other couple had rejoined them. As if the matter had been privately agreed upon, the couples separated once more, Katharine and Denham passing out of the house without more than a perfunctory glance round them. Denham obeyed what seemed to be Katharine's wish in thus making haste. Some change had come over her. He connected it with her laughter, and her few words in private with Rodney; he felt that she had become unfriendly to him. She talked, but her remarks were indifferent, and when he spoke her attention seemed to wander. This change of mood was at first extremely disagreeable to him; but soon he found it salutary. The pale drizzling atmosphere of the day affected him, also. The charm, the insidious magic in which he had luxuriated, were suddenly gone; his feeling had become one of friendly respect, and to his great pleasure he found himself thinking spontaneously of the relief of finding himself alone in his room that night. In his surprise at the suddenness of the change, and at the extent of his freedom, he bethought him of a daring plan, by which the ghost of Katharine could be more effectually exorcised than by mere abstinence. He would ask her to come home with him to tea. He would force her through the mill of family life; he would place her in a light unsparing and revealing. His family would find nothing to admire in her, and she, he felt certain, would despise them all, and this, too, would help him. He felt himself becoming more and more merciless towards her. By such courageous measures anyone, he thought, could end the absurd passions which were the cause of so much pain and waste. He could foresee a time when his experiences, his discovery and his triumph were made available for younger brothers who found themselves in the same predicament. He looked at his watch, and remarked that the gardens would soon be closed.

'Anyhow,' he added, 'I think we've seen enough for one afternoon. Where have the others got to?' He looked over his shoulder, and, seeing no trace of them, remarked at once: 'We'd better be independent of them. The best plan will be for you to come back to tea with me.'

'Why shouldn't you come with me?' she asked.

'Because we're next door to Highgate here,' he replied promptly.

She assented, having very little notion whether Highgate was next door to Regent's Park or not. She was only glad to put off her return to the family tea-table in Chelsea for an hour or two. They proceeded with dogged determination through the winding roads of Regent's Park, and the Sunday-stricken streets of the neighbourhood, in the direction of the Tube station. Ignorant of the way, she resigned herself entirely to him, and found his silence a convenient cover beneath which to continue her anger with Rodney.

When they stepped out of the train into the still greyer gloom of Highgate, she wondered, for the first time, where he was taking her. Had he a family, or did he live alone in rooms? On the whole she was inclined to believe that he was the only son of an aged, and possibly invalid, mother. She sketched lightly, upon the blank vista down which they walked, the little white house and the tremulous old lady rising from behind her tea-table to greet her with faltering words about 'my son's friends', and was on the point of asking Ralph to tell her what she might expect, when he jerked open one of the infinite number of identical wooden doors, and led her up a tiled path to a porch in the Alpine style of architecture. As they listened to the shaking of the bell in the basement, she could summon no vision to replace the one so rudely destroyed.

'I must warn you to expect a family party,' said Ralph. 'They're mostly in on Sundays. We can go to my room afterwards.'

'Have you many brothers and sisters?' she asked, without concealing her dismay.

'Six or seven,' he replied grimly, as the door opened.

While Ralph took off his coat, she had time to notice the ferns and photographs and draperies, and to hear a hum, or rather a babble, of voices talking each other down, from the sound of them. The rigidity of extreme shyness came over her. She kept as far behind Denham as she could, and walked stiffly after him into a room blazing with unshaded lights, which fell upon a number of people, of different ages, sitting round a large dining-room table untidily strewn with food, and unflinchingly lit up by incandescent gas. Ralph walked straight to the far end of the table.

'Mother, this is Miss Hilbery,' he said.

A large elderly lady, bent over an unsatisfactory spirit-lamp, looked up with a little frown, and observed: 'I beg your pardon. I thought you were one of my own girls. Dorothy,' she continued in the same breath, to catch the servant before she left the room, 'we shall want some more methylated spirits – unless the lamp itself is out of order. If one of you could invent a good spirit-lamp – ' she sighed, looking generally down the table, and then began seeking among the china before her for two clean cups for the newcomers.

The unsparing light revealed more ugliness than Katharine had seen in one room for a very long time. It was the ugliness of enormous folds of brown material, looped and festooned, of plush curtains, from which depended balls and fringes, partially concealing bookshelves swollen with black school-texts. Her eye was arrested by crossed scabbards of fretted wood upon the dull green wall, and wherever there was a high flat eminence, some fern waved from a pot of crinkled china, or a bronze horse reared so high that the stump of a tree had to sustain his forequarters. The waters of family life seemed to rise and close over her head, and she munched in silence.

At length Mrs Denham looked up from her teacups and remarked: 'You see, Miss Hilbery, my children all come in at different hours and want different things. (The tray should go up if you've done, Johnnie.) My boy Charles is in bed with a cold. What else can you expect? – standing in the wet playing football. We did try drawing-room tea, but it didn't do.'

A boy of sixteen, who appeared to be Johnnie, grumbled derisively both at the notion of drawing-room tea and at the necessity of carrying a tray up to his brother. But he took himself off, being enjoined by his mother to mind what he was doing, and shut the door after him.

'It's much nicer like this,' said Katharine, applying herself with determination to the dissection of her cake; they had given her too large a slice. She knew that Mrs Denham suspected her of critical comparisons. She knew that she was making poor progress with her cake. Mrs Denham had looked at her sufficiently often to make it clear to Katharine that she was asking who this young woman was, and why Ralph had brought her to tea with them. There was an obvious reason, which Mrs Denham had probably reached by this time. Outwardly, she was behaving with rather rusty and laborious civility. She was making conversation about the amenities of Highgate, its development and situation.

'When I first married,' she said, 'Highgate was quite separate from London, Miss Hilbery, and this house, though you wouldn't believe it, had a view of apple orchards. That was before the Middletons built their house in front of us.'

'It must be a great advantage to live at the top of a hill,' said Katharine. Mrs Denham agreed effusively, as if her opinion of Katharine's sense had risen.

'Yes, indeed, we find it very healthy,' she said, and she went on, as people who live in the suburbs so often do, to prove that it was healthier, more convenient, and less spoilt than any suburb round London. She spoke with such emphasis that it was quite obvious that she expressed unpopular views, and that her children disagreed with her.

'The ceiling's fallen down in the pantry again,' said Hester, a girl of eighteen, abruptly.

'The whole house will be down one of these days,' James muttered.

'Nonsense,' said Mrs Denham. 'It's only a little bit of plaster – I don't see how any house could be expected to stand the wear and tear you give it.' Here some family joke exploded, which Katharine could not follow. Even Mrs Denham laughed against her will.

'Miss Hilbery's thinking us all so rude,' she added reprovingly. Miss Hilbery smiled and shook her head, and was conscious that a great many eyes rested upon her, for a moment, as if they would find pleasure in discussing her when she was gone. Owing, perhaps, to this critical glance, Katharine decided that Ralph Denham's family was commonplace, unshapely, lacking in charm, and fitly expressed by the hideous nature of their furniture and decorations. She glanced along a mantelpiece ranged with bronze chariots, silver vases and china ornaments that were either facetious or eccentric.

She did not apply her judgement consciously to Ralph, but when she looked at him, a moment later, she rated him lower than at any other time of their acquaintanceship.

He had made no effort to tide over the discomforts of her introduction, and now, engaged in argument with his brother, apparently forgot her presence. She must have counted upon his support more than she realised, for this indifference, emphasised, as it was, by the insignificant commonplace of his surroundings, awoke her, not only to that ugliness, but to her own folly. She thought of one scene after another in a few seconds, with that shudder which is almost a blush. She had believed him when he spoke of friendship. She had believed in a spiritual light burning steadily and steadfastly behind the erratic disorder and incoherence of life. The light was now gone out, suddenly, as if a sponge had blotted it. The litter of the table and the tedious but exacting conversation of Mrs Denham remained: they struck, indeed, upon a mind bereft of all defences, and, keenly conscious of the degradation which is the result of strife whether victorious or not, she thought gloomily of her loneliness, of life's futility, of the barren prose of reality, of William Rodney, of her mother and the unfinished book.

Her answers to Mrs Denham were perfunctory to the verge of rudeness, and to Ralph, who watched her narrowly, she seemed further away than was compatible with her physical closeness. He glanced at her, and ground out further steps in his argument, determined that no folly should remain when this experience was over. Next moment, a silence, sudden and complete, descended upon them all. The silence of all these people round the untidy table was enormous and hideous; something horrible seemed about to burst from it, but they endured it obstinately. A second later the door opened and there was a stir of relief; cries of, 'Hello, Joan! There's nothing left for you to eat,' broke up the oppressive concentration of so many eyes upon the tablecloth, and set the waters of family life dashing in brisk little waves again. It was obvious that Joan had some mysterious and beneficent power upon her family. She went up to Katharine as if she had heard of her, and was very glad to see her at last. She explained that she had been visiting an uncle who was ill, and that had kept her. No, she hadn't had any tea, but a slice of bread would do. Someone handed up a hot cake, which had been keeping warm in the fender; she sat down by her mother's side, Mrs Denham's anxieties seemed to relax, and everyone began eating and drinking, as if tea had begun over again. Hester voluntarily explained to Katharine that she was reading to pass some examination, because she wanted more than anything in the whole world to go to Newnham.[87]

'Now, just let me hear you decline "amo" – I love,' Johnnie demanded.

'No, Johnnie, no Greek at mealtimes,'[88] said Joan, overhearing him instantly. 'She's up at all hours of the night over her books, Miss Hilbery, and I'm sure that's not the way to pass examinations,' she went on, smiling at Katharine, with the worried humorous smile of the elder sister whose younger brothers and sisters have become almost like children of her own.

'Joan, you don't really think that "amo" is Greek?' Ralph asked.

'Did I say Greek? Well, never mind. No dead languages at teatime. My dear boy, don't trouble to make me any toast – '

'Or if you do, surely there's the toasting-fork somewhere?' said Mrs Denham, still cherishing the belief that the breadknife could be spoilt. 'Do one of you ring and ask for one,' she said, without any conviction that she would be obeyed. 'But is Ann coming to be with Uncle Joseph?' she continued. 'If so, surely they had better send Amy to us – ' and in the mysterious delight of learning further details of these arrangements, and suggesting more sensible plans of her own, which, from the aggrieved way in which she spoke, she did not seem to expect anyone to adopt, Mrs Denham completely forgot the presence of a well-dressed visitor, who had to be informed about the amenities of Highgate. As soon as Joan had taken her seat, an argument had sprung up on either side of Katharine as to whether the Salvation Army[89] has any right to play hymns at street corners on Sunday mornings, thereby making it impossible for James to have his sleep out, and tampering with the rights of individual liberty.

'You see, James likes to lie in bed and sleep like a hog,' said Johnnie, explaining himself to Katharine, whereupon James fired up and, making her his goal, also exclaimed: 'Because Sundays are my one chance in the week of having my sleep out. Johnnie messes with stinking chemicals in the pantry – '

They appealed to her, and she forgot her cake and began to laugh and talk and argue with sudden animation. The large family seemed to her so warm and various that she forgot to censure them for their taste in pottery. But the personal question between James and Johnnie merged into some argument already, apparently, debated, so that the parts had been distributed among the family, in which Ralph took the lead; and Katharine found herself opposed to him and the champion of Johnnie's cause, who, it appeared, always lost his head and got excited in argument with Ralph.

'Yes, yes, that's what I mean. She's got it right,' he exclaimed, after Katharine had restated his case, and made it more precise. The debate was left almost solely to Katharine and Ralph. They looked into each other's eyes fixedly, like wrestlers trying to see what movement is coming next, and while Ralph spoke, Katharine bit her lower lip, and was always ready with her next point as soon as he had done. They were very well matched, and held the opposite views.

But at the most exciting stage of the argument, for no reason that Katharine could see, all chairs were pushed back, and one after another the Denham family got up and went out of the door, as if a bell had summoned them. She was not used to the clockwork regulations of a large family. She hesitated in what she was saying, and rose. Mrs Denham and Joan had drawn together and stood by the fireplace, slightly raising their skirts above their ankles, and discussing something which had an air of being very serious and very private. They appeared to have forgotten her presence among them. Ralph stood holding the door open for her.

'Won't you come up to my room?' he said. And Katharine, glancing back at Joan, who smiled at her in a preoccupied way, followed Ralph upstairs. She was thinking of their argument, and when, after the long climb, he opened his door, she began at once.

'The question is, then, at what point is it right for the individual to assert his will against the will of the state.'

For some time they continued the argument, and then the intervals between one statement and the next became longer and longer, and they spoke more speculatively and less pugnaciously, and at last fell silent. Katharine went over the argument in her mind, remembering how, now and then, it had been set conspicuously on the right course by some remark offered either by James or by Johnnie.

'Your brothers are very clever,' she said. 'I suppose you're in the habit of arguing?'

'James and Johnnie will go on like that for hours,' Ralph replied. 'So will Hester, if you start her upon Elizabethan dramatists.'

'And the little girl with the pigtail?'

'Molly? She's only ten. But they're always arguing among themselves.'

He was immensely pleased by Katharine's praise of his brothers and sisters. He would have liked to go on telling her about them, but he checked himself.

'I see that it must be difficult to leave them,' Katharine continued. His deep pride in his family was more evident to him, at that moment, than ever before, and the idea of living alone in a cottage was ridiculous. All that brotherhood and sisterhood and a common childhood in a common past mean, all the stability, the unambitious comradeship and tacit understanding of family life at its best, came to his mind, and he thought of them as a company, of which he was the leader, bound on a difficult, dreary, but glorious voyage. And it was Katharine who had opened his eyes to this, he thought.

A little dry chirp from the corner of the room now roused her attention.

'My tame rook,' he explained briefly. 'A cat had bitten one of its legs.' She looked at the rook, and her eyes went from one object to another.

'You sit here and read?' she said, her eyes resting upon his books. He said that he was in the habit of working there at night.

'The great advantage of Highgate is the view over London. At night the view from my window is splendid.' He was extremely anxious that she should appreciate his view, and she rose to see what was to be seen. It was already dark enough for the turbulent haze to be yellow with the light of street lamps, and she tried to determine the quarters of the city beneath her. The sight of her gazing from his window gave him a peculiar satisfaction. When she turned, at length, he was still sitting motionless in his chair.

'It must be late,' she said. 'I must be going.' She settled upon the arm of the chair irresolutely, thinking that she had no wish to go home. William would be there, and he would find some way of making things unpleasant for her, and the memory of their quarrel came back to her.

She had noticed Ralph's coldness, too. She looked at him, and from his fixed stare she thought that he must be working out some theory, some argument. He had thought, perhaps, of some fresh point in his position, as to the bounds of personal liberty. She waited, silently, thinking about liberty.

'You've won again,' he said at last, without moving.

'I've won?' she repeated, thinking of the argument.

'I wish to God I hadn't asked you here,' he burst out.

'What do you mean?'

'When you're here, it's different – I'm happy. You've only to walk to the window – you've only to talk about liberty. When I saw you down there among them all – ' He stopped short.

'You thought how ordinary I was.'

'I tried to think so. But I thought you more wonderful than ever.'

An immense relief, and a reluctance to enjoy that relief, conflicted in her heart.

She slid down into the chair.

'I thought you disliked me,' she said.

'God knows I tried,' he replied. 'I've done my best to see you as you are, without any of this damned romantic nonsense. That was why I asked you here, and it's increased my folly. When you're gone I shall look out of that window and think of you. I shall waste the whole evening thinking of you. I shall waste my whole life, I believe.'

He spoke with such vehemence that her relief disappeared; she frowned; and her tone changed to one almost of severity.

'This is what I foretold. We shall gain nothing but unhappiness. Look at me, Ralph.' He looked at her. 'I assure you that I'm far more ordinary than I appear. Beauty means nothing whatever. In fact, the most beautiful women are generally the most stupid. I'm not that, but I'm a matter-of-fact, prosaic, rather ordinary character; I order the dinner, I pay the bills, I do the accounts, I wind up the clock, and I never look at a book.'

'You forget – ' he began, but she would not let him speak.

'You come and see me among flowers and pictures, and think me mysterious, romantic, and all the rest of it. Being yourself very inexperienced and very emotional, you go home and invent a story about me, and now you can't separate me from the person you've imagined me to be. You call that, I suppose, being in love; as a matter of fact it's being in delusion. All romantic people are the same,' she added. 'My mother spends her life in making stories about the people she's fond of. But I won't have you do it about me, if I can help it.'

'You can't help it,' he said.

'I warn you it's the source of all evil.'

'And of all good,' he added.

'You'll find out that I'm not what you think me.'

'Perhaps. But I shall gain more than I lose.'

'If such gain's worth having.'

They were silent for a space.

'That may be what we have to face,' he said. 'There may be nothing else. Nothing but what we imagine.'

'The reason of our loneliness,' she mused, and they were silent for a time.

'When are you to be married?' he asked abruptly, with a change of tone.

'Not till September, I think. It's been put off.'

'You won't be lonely then,' he said. 'According to what people say, marriage is a very queer business. They say it's different from anything else. It may be true. I've known one or two cases where it seems to be true.' He hoped that she would go on with the subject. But she made no reply. He had done his best to master himself, and his voice was sufficiently indifferent, but her silence tormented him. She would never speak to him of Rodney of her own accord, and her reserve left a whole continent of her soul in darkness.

'It may be put off even longer than that,' she said, as if by an afterthought. 'Someone in the office is ill, and William has to take his place. We may put it off for some time in fact.'

'That's rather hard on him, isn't it?' Ralph asked.

'He has his work,' she replied. 'He has lots of things that interest him . . . I know I've been to that place,' she broke off, pointing to a photograph. 'But I can't remember where it is – oh, of course, it's Oxford. Now, what about your cottage?'

'I'm not going to take it.'

'How you change your mind!' she smiled.

'It's not that,' he said impatiently. 'It's that I want to be where I can see you.'

'Our compact is going to hold in spite of all I've said?' she asked.

'For ever, so far as I'm concerned,' he replied.

'You're going to go on dreaming and imagining and making up stories about me as you walk along the street, and pretending that we're riding in a forest, or landing on an island – '

'No. I shall think of you ordering dinner, paying bills, doing the accounts, showing old ladies the relics – '

'That's better,' she said. 'You can think of me tomorrow morning looking up dates in the *Dictionary of National Biography*.'[90]

'And forgetting your purse,' Ralph added.

At this she smiled, but in another moment her smile faded, either because of his words or of the way in which he spoke them. She was capable of forgetting things. He saw that. But what more did he see? Was he not looking at something she had never shown to anybody? Was it not something so profound that the notion of his seeing it almost shocked her? Her smile faded, and for a moment she seemed upon the point of speaking, but looking at him in silence, with a look that seemed to ask what she could not put into words, she turned and bade him good-night.

Chapter 28

Like a strain of music, the effect of Katharine's presence slowly died from the room in which Ralph sat alone. The music had ceased in the rapture of its melody. He strained to catch the faintest lingering echoes; for a moment the memory lulled him into peace; but soon it failed, and he paced the room so hungry for the sound to come again that he was conscious of no other desire left in life. She had gone without speaking; abruptly a chasm had been cut in his course, down which the tide of his being plunged in disorder; fell upon rocks; flung itself to destruction. The distress had an effect of physical ruin and disaster. He trembled; he was white; he felt exhausted, as if by a great physical effort. He sank at last into a chair standing opposite her empty one, and marked, mechanically, with his eye upon the clock, how she went farther and farther from him, was home now, and now, doubtless, again with Rodney. But it was long before he could realise these facts; the immense desire for her presence churned his senses into foam, into froth, into a haze of emotion that removed all facts from his grasp, and gave him a strange sense of distance, even from the material shapes of wall and window by which he was surrounded. The prospect of the future, now that the strength of his passion was revealed to him, appalled him.

The marriage would take place in September, she had said; that allowed him, then, six full months in which to undergo these terrible extremes of emotion. Six months of torture, and after that the silence of the grave, the isolation of the insane, the exile of the damned; at best, a life from which the chief good was knowingly and for ever excluded. An impartial judge might have assured him that his chief hope of recovery lay in this mystic temper, which identified a living woman with much that no human beings long possess in the eyes of each other; she would pass, and the desire for her vanish, but his belief in what she stood for, detached from her, would remain. This line of thought offered, perhaps, some respite, and possessed of a brain that had its station considerably above the tumult of the senses, he tried to reduce the vague and wandering incoherency of his emotions to order. The sense of self-preservation was strong in him, and Katharine herself had strangely revived it by convincing him that his family deserved and needed all his strength. She was right, and for their sake, if not for his own, this passion, which could bear no fruit, must be cut off, uprooted, shown to be as visionary and baseless as she had maintained. The best way of achieving this was not to run away from her, but to face her, and having steeped himself in her qualities, to convince his reason that they were, as she assured him, not those that he imagined. She was a practical woman, a domestic wife for an inferior poet, endowed with romantic beauty by some freak of unintelligent nature. No doubt her beauty itself would not stand examination. He had the means of settling this point at least. He possessed a book of photographs from the Greek statues; the head of a goddess, if the lower part were concealed, had often given him the ecstasy of being in Katharine's presence. He took it down from the shelf and found the picture. To this he added a note from her, bidding him meet her at the Zoo. He had a flower which he had picked at Kew to teach her botany. Such were his relics. He placed them before him, and set himself to visualise her so clearly that no deception or delusion was possible. In a second he could see her, with the sun slanting across her dress, coming towards him down the green walk at Kew. He made her sit upon the seat beside him. He heard her voice, so low and yet so decided in its tone; she spoke reasonably of indifferent matters. He could see her faults, and analyse her virtues. His pulse became quieter, and his brain increased in clarity. This time she could not escape him. The illusion of her presence became more and more complete. They seemed to pass in and out of each other's minds, questioning and answering. The utmost fullness of communion seemed to be theirs. Thus united, he felt himself raised to an eminence, exalted, and filled with a power of achievement such as he had never known in singleness. Once more he told over conscientiously her faults, both of face and character; they were clearly known to him; but they merged themselves in the flawless union that was born of their association. They surveyed life to its uttermost limits. How deep it was when looked at from this height! How sublime! How the commonest things moved him almost to tears! Thus, he forgot the inevitable limitations; he forgot her absence, he thought it of no account whether she married him or another; nothing mattered, save that she should exist, and that he should love her. Some words of these reflections were uttered aloud, and it happened that among them were the words, 'I love her.' It was the first time that he had used the word 'love' to describe his feeling; madness, romance, hallucination – he had called it by these names before; but having, apparently by accident, stumbled upon the word 'love', he repeated it again and again with a sense of revelation.

'But I'm in love with you!' he exclaimed, with something like dismay. He leant against the window-sill, looking over the city as she had looked. Everything had become miraculously different and completely distinct. His feelings were justified and needed no further explanation. But he must impart them to someone, because his discovery was so important that it concerned other people too. Shutting the book of Greek photographs, and hiding his relics, he ran downstairs, snatched his coat, and passed out of doors.

The lamps were being lit, but the streets were dark enough and empty enough to let him walk his fastest, and to talk aloud as he walked. He had no doubt where he was going. He was going to find Mary Datchet. The desire to share what he felt, with someone who understood it, was so imperious that he did not question it. He was soon in her street. He ran up the stairs leading to her flat two steps at a time, and it never crossed his mind that she might not be at home. As he rang her bell, he seemed to himself to be announcing the presence of something wonderful that was separate from himself, and gave him power and authority over all other people. Mary came to the door after a moment's pause. He was perfectly silent, and in the dusk his face looked completely white. He followed her into her room.

'Do you know each other?' she said, to his extreme surprise, for he had counted on finding her alone. A young man rose, and said that he knew Ralph by sight.

'We were just going through some papers,' said Mary. 'Mr Basnett has to help me, because I don't know much about my work yet. It's the new society,' she explained. 'I'm the secretary. I'm no longer at Russell Square.'

The voice in which she gave this information was so constrained as to sound almost harsh.

'What are your aims?' said Ralph. He looked neither at Mary nor at

Mr Basnett. Mr Basnett thought he had seldom seen a more disagreeable or formidable man than this friend of Mary's, this sarcastic-
looking, white-faced Mr Denham, who seemed to demand, as if by
right, an account of their proposals, and to criticise them before he had
heard them. Nevertheless, he explained his projects as clearly as he
could, and knew that he wished Mr Denham to think well of them.

'I see,' said Ralph, when he had done. 'D'you know, Mary,' he
suddenly remarked, 'I believe I'm in for a cold. Have you any quinine?'[91]
The look which he cast at her frightened her; it expressed mutely,
perhaps without his own consciousness, something deep, wild
and passionate. She left the room at once. Her heart beat fast at the
knowledge of Ralph's presence; but it beat with pain, and with an
extraordinary fear. She stood listening for a moment to the voices in the
next room.

'Of course, I agree with you,' she heard Ralph say, in this strange
voice, to Mr Basnett. 'But there's more that might be done. Have you
seen Judson, for instance? You should make a point of getting him.'

Mary returned with the quinine.

'Judson's address?' Mr Basnett enquired, pulling out his notebook
and preparing to write. For twenty minutes, perhaps, he wrote down
names, addresses, and other suggestions that Ralph dictated to him.
Then, when Ralph fell silent, Mr Basnett felt that his presence was not
desired, and thanking Ralph for his help, with a sense that he was very
young and ignorant compared with him, he said goodbye.

'Mary,' said Ralph, directly Mr Basnett had shut the door and they
were alone together. 'Mary,' he repeated. But the old difficulty of
speaking to Mary without reserve prevented him from continuing. His
desire to proclaim his love for Katharine was still strong in him, but he
had felt, directly he saw Mary, that he could not share it with her. The
feeling increased as he sat talking to Mr Basnett. And yet all the time he
was thinking of Katharine, and marvelling at his love. The tone in
which he spoke Mary's name was harsh.

'What is it, Ralph?' she asked, startled by his tone. She looked at him
anxiously, and her little frown showed that she was trying painfully to
understand him, and was puzzled. He could feel her groping for his
meaning, and he was annoyed with her, and thought how he had always
found her slow, painstaking and clumsy. He had behaved badly to her,
too, which made his irritation the more acute. Without waiting for him
to answer, she rose as if his answer were indifferent to her, and began to
put in order some papers that Mr Basnett had left on the table. She
hummed a scrap of a tune under her breath, and moved about the room

as if she were occupied in making things tidy, and had no other concern.

'You'll stay and dine?' she said casually, returning to her seat.

'No,' Ralph replied. She did not press him further. They sat side by side without speaking, and Mary reached her hand for her work-basket, and took out her sewing and threaded a needle.

'That's a clever young man,' Ralph observed, referring to Mr Basnett.

'I'm glad you thought so. It's tremendously interesting work, and considering everything, I think we've done very well. But I'm inclined to agree with you; we ought to try to be more conciliatory. We're absurdly strict. It's difficult to see that there may be sense in what one's opponents say, though they are one's opponents. Horace Basnett is certainly too uncompromising. I mustn't forget to see that he writes that letter to Judson. You're too busy, I suppose, to come on to our committee?' She spoke in the most impersonal manner.

'I may be out of town,' Ralph replied, with equal distance of manner.

'Our executive meets every week, of course,' she observed. 'But some of our members don't come more than once a month. Members of Parliament are the worst; it was a mistake, I think, to ask them.'

She went on sewing in silence.

'You've not taken your quinine,' she said, looking up and seeing the tabloids upon the mantelpiece.

'I don't want it,' said Ralph shortly.

'Well, you know best,' she replied tranquilly.

'Mary, I'm a brute!' he exclaimed. 'Here I come and waste your time, and do nothing but make myself disagreeable.'

'A cold coming on does make one feel wretched,' she replied.

'I've not got a cold. That was a lie. There's nothing the matter with me. I'm mad, I suppose. I ought to have had the decency to keep away. But I wanted to see you – I wanted to tell you – I'm in love, Mary.' He spoke the word, but, as he spoke it, it seemed robbed of substance.

'In love, are you?' she said quietly. 'I'm glad, Ralph.'

'I suppose I'm in love. Anyhow, I'm out of my mind. I can't think, I can't work, I don't care a hang for anything in the world. Good heavens, Mary! I'm in torment! One moment I'm happy; next I'm miserable. I hate her for half an hour; then I'd give my whole life to be with her for ten minutes; all the time I don't know what I feel, or why I feel it; it's insanity, and yet it's perfectly reasonable. Can you make any sense of it? Can you see what's happened? I'm raving, I know; don't listen, Mary; go on with your work.'

He rose and began, as usual, to pace up and down the room. He knew that what he had just said bore very little resemblance to what he felt, for Mary's presence acted upon him like a very strong magnet, drawing from him certain expressions which were not those he made use of when he spoke to himself, nor did they represent his deepest feelings. He felt a little contempt for himself at having spoken thus; but somehow he had been forced into speech.

'Do sit down,' said Mary suddenly. 'You make me so – ' She spoke with unusual irritability, and Ralph, noticing it with surprise, sat down at once.

'You haven't told me her name – you'd rather not, I suppose?'

'Her name? Katharine Hilbery.'

'But she's engaged – '

'To Rodney. They're to be married in September.'

'I see,' said Mary. But in truth the calm of his manner, now that he was sitting down once more, wrapped her in the presence of something which she felt to be so strong, so mysterious, so incalculable, that she scarcely dared to attempt to intercept it by any word or question that she was able to frame. She looked at Ralph blankly, with a kind of awe in her face, her lips slightly parted, and her brows raised. He was apparently quite unconscious of her gaze. Then, as if she could look no longer, she leant back in her chair, and half closed her eyes. The distance between them hurt her terribly; one thing after another came into her mind, tempting her to assail Ralph with questions, to force him to confide in her, and to enjoy once more his intimacy. But she rejected every impulse, for she could not speak without doing violence to some reserve which had grown between them, putting them a little far from each other, so that he seemed to her dignified and remote, like a person she no longer knew well.

'Is there anything that I could do for you?' she asked gently, and even with courtesy, at length.

'You could see her – no, that's not what I want; you mustn't bother about me, Mary.' He, too, spoke very gently.

'I'm afraid no third person can do anything to help,' she added.

'No,' he shook his head. 'Katharine was saying today how lonely we are.' She saw the effort with which he spoke Katharine's name, and believed that he forced himself to make amends now for his concealment in the past. At any rate, she was conscious of no anger against him; but rather of a deep pity for one condemned to suffer as she had suffered. But in the case of Katharine it was different; she was indignant with Katharine.

'There's always work,' she said, a little aggressively.

Ralph moved directly.

'Do you want to be working now?' he asked.

'No, no. It's Sunday,' she replied. 'I was thinking of Katharine. She doesn't understand about work. She's never had to. She doesn't know what work is. I've only found out myself quite lately. But it's the thing that saves one – I'm sure of that.'

'There are other things, aren't there?' he hesitated.

'Nothing that one can count upon,' she returned. 'After all, other people – ' she stopped, but forced herself to go on. 'Where should I be now if I hadn't got to go to my office every day? Thousands of people would tell you the same thing – thousands of women. I tell you, work is the only thing that saved me, Ralph.' He set his mouth, as if her words rained blows on him; he looked as if he had made up his mind to bear anything she might say, in silence. He had deserved it, and there would be relief in having to bear it. But she broke off, and rose as if to fetch something from the next room. Before she reached the door she turned back, and stood facing him, self-possessed, and yet defiant and formidable in her composure.

'It's all turned out splendidly for me,' she said. 'It will for you, too. I'm sure of that. Because, after all, Katharine is worth it.'

'Mary – !' he exclaimed. But her head was turned away, and he could not say what he wished to say. 'Mary, you're splendid,' he concluded. She faced him as he spoke, and gave him her hand. She had suffered and relinquished, she had seen her future turned from one of infinite promise to one of barrenness, and yet, somehow, over what she scarcely knew, and with what results she could hardly foretell, she had conquered. With Ralph's eyes upon her, smiling straight back at him serenely and proudly, she knew, for the first time, that she had conquered. She let him kiss her hand.

The streets were empty enough on Sunday night, and if the Sabbath, and the domestic amusements proper to the Sabbath, had not kept people indoors, a high strong wind might very probably have done so. Ralph Denham was aware of a tumult in the street much in accordance with his own sensations. The gusts, sweeping along the Strand, seemed at the same time to blow a clear space across the sky in which stars appeared, and for a short time the quick-speeding silver moon riding through clouds, as if they were waves of water surging round her and over her. They swamped her, but she emerged; they broke over her and covered her again; she issued forth indomitable. In the country fields all the wreckage of winter was being dispersed; the dead leaves, the withered bracken, the dry and discoloured grass, but no bud would be broken, nor would the new stalks that showed above the earth take any harm, and perhaps tomorrow a line of blue or yellow would show through a slit in their green. But the whirl of the atmosphere alone was in Denham's mood, and what of star or blossom appeared was only as a light gleaming for a second upon heaped waves fast following each other. He had not been able to speak to Mary, though for a moment he had come near enough to be tantalised by a wonderful possibility of understanding. But the desire to communicate something of the very greatest importance possessed him completely; he still wished to bestow this gift upon some other human being; he sought their company. More by instinct than by conscious choice, he took the direction which led to Rodney's rooms. He knocked loudly upon his door; but no one answered. He rang the bell. It took him some time to accept the fact that Rodney was out. When he could no longer pretend that the sound of the wind in the old building was the sound of someone rising from his chair, he ran downstairs again, as if his goal had been altered and only just revealed to him. He walked in the direction of Chelsea.

But physical fatigue, for he had not dined and had tramped both far and fast, made him sit for a moment upon a seat on the Embankment. One of the regular occupants of those seats, an elderly man who had drunk himself, probably, out of work and lodging, drifted up, begged a match and sat down beside him. It was a windy night, he said; times were hard; some long story of bad luck and injustice followed, told so often that the man seemed to be talking to himself, or, perhaps, the neglect of his audience had long made any attempt to catch their attention seem scarcely worth while. When he began to speak Ralph had a wild desire to talk to him; to question him; to make him understand. He did, in fact, interrupt him at one point; but it was useless. The ancient story of failure, ill-luck, undeserved disaster, went down the wind, disconnected syllables flying past Ralph's ears with a queer alternation of loudness and faintness as if, at certain moments, the man's memory of his wrongs revived and then flagged, dying down at last into a grumble of resignation, which seemed to represent a final lapse into the accustomed despair. The unhappy voice afflicted Ralph, but it also angered him. And when the elderly man refused to listen and mumbled on, an odd image came to his mind of a lighthouse[92] besieged by the flying bodies of lost birds, who were dashed senseless, by the gale, against the glass. He had a strange sensation that he was both lighthouse and bird; he was steadfast and brilliant; and at the same time he was whirled, with all other things, senseless against the glass. He got up, left his tribute of silver, and pressed on, with the wind against him. The image of the lighthouse and the storm full of birds persisted, taking the place of more definite thoughts, as he walked past the Houses of Parliament and down Grosvenor Road, by the side of the river. In his state of physical fatigue, details merged themselves in the vaster prospect, of which the flying gloom and the intermittent lights of lamp-posts and private houses were the outward token, but he never lost his sense of walking in the direction of Katharine's house. He took it for granted that something would then happen, and, as he walked on, his mind became more and more full of pleasure and expectancy. Within a certain radius of her house the streets came under the influence of her presence. Each house had an individuality known to Ralph, because of the tremendous individuality of the house in which she lived. For some yards before reaching the Hilberys' door he walked in a trance of pleasure, but when he reached it, and pushed the gate of the little garden open, he hesitated. He did not know what to do next. There was no hurry, however, for the outside of the house held pleasure enough to last him some time longer. He crossed the road, and leant against the balustrade of the Embankment, fixing his eyes upon the house.

Lights burnt in the three long windows of the drawing-room. The space of the room behind became, in Ralph's vision, the centre of the dark, flying wilderness of the world; the justification for the welter of confusion surrounding it; the steady light which cast its beams, like those of a lighthouse, with searching composure over the trackless waste. In this little sanctuary were gathered together several different people, but their identity was dissolved in a general glory of something that might, perhaps, be called civilisation; at any rate, all dryness, all safety, all that stood up above the surge and preserved a consciousness of its own, was centred in the drawing-room of the Hilberys. Its purpose was beneficent; and yet so far above his level as to have something austere about it, a light that cast itself out and yet kept itself aloof. Then he began, in his mind, to distinguish different individuals within, consciously refusing as yet to attack the figure of Katharine. His thoughts lingered over Mrs Hilbery and Cassandra; and then he turned to Rodney and Mr Hilbery. Physically, he saw them bathed in that steady flow of yellow light which filled the long oblongs of the windows; in their movements they were beautiful; and in their speech he figured a reserve of meaning, unspoken, but understood. At length, after all this half-conscious selection and arrangement, he allowed himself to approach the figure of Katharine herself; and instantly the scene was flooded with excitement. He did not see her in the body; he seemed curiously to see her as a shape of light, the light itself; he seemed, simplified and exhausted as he was, to be like one of those lost birds fascinated by the lighthouse and held to the glass by the splendour of the blaze.

These thoughts drove him to tramp a beat up and down the pavement before the Hilberys' gate. He did not trouble himself to make any plans for the future. Something of an unknown kind would decide both the coming year and the coming hour. Now and again, in his vigil, he sought the light in the long windows, or glanced at the ray which gilded a few leaves and a few blades of grass in the little garden. For a long time the light burnt without changing. He had just reached the limit of his beat and was turning, when the front door opened, and the aspect of the house was entirely changed. A black figure came down the little pathway and paused at the gate. Denham understood instantly that it was Rodney. Without hesitation, and conscious only of a great friendliness for anyone coming from that lighted room, he walked straight up to him and stopped him. In the flurry of the wind Rodney was taken aback, and for the moment tried to press on, muttering something, as if he suspected a demand upon his charity.

'Goodness, Denham, what are you doing here?' he exclaimed, recognising him.

Ralph mumbled something about being on his way home. They walked on together, though Rodney walked quick enough to make it plain that he had no wish for company.

He was very unhappy. That afternoon Cassandra had repulsed him; he had tried to explain to her the difficulties of the situation, and to suggest the nature of his feelings for her without saying anything definite or anything offensive to her. But he had lost his head; under the goad of Katharine's ridicule he had said too much, and Cassandra, superb in her dignity and severity, had refused to hear another word, and threatened an immediate return to her home. His agitation, after an evening spent between the two women, was extreme. Moreover, he could not help suspecting that Ralph was wandering near the Hilberys' house, at this hour, for reasons connected with Katharine. There was probably some understanding between them – not that anything of the kind mattered to him now. He was convinced that he had never cared for anyone save Cassandra, and Katharine's future was no concern of his. Aloud, he said, shortly, that he was very tired and wished to find a cab. But on Sunday night, on the Embankment, cabs were hard to come by, and Rodney found himself constrained to walk some distance, at any rate, in Denham's company. Denham maintained his silence. Rodney's irritation lapsed. He found the silence oddly suggestive of the good masculine qualities which he much respected, and had at this moment great reason to need. After the mystery, difficulty and uncertainty of dealing with the other sex, intercourse with one's own is apt to have a composing and even ennobling influence, since plain speaking is possible and subterfuges of no avail. Rodney, too, was much in need of a confidant; Katharine, despite her promises of help, had failed him at the critical moment; she had gone off with Denham; she was, perhaps, tormenting Denham as she had tormented him. How grave and stable he seemed, speaking little, and walking firmly, compared with what Rodney knew of his own torments and indecisions! He began to cast about for some way of telling the story of his relations with Katharine and Cassandra that would not lower him in Denham's eyes. It then occurred to him that, perhaps, Katharine herself had confided in Denham; they had something in common; it was likely that they had discussed him that very afternoon. The desire to discover what they had said of him now came uppermost in his mind. He recalled Katharine's laugh; he remembered that she had gone, laughing, to walk with Denham.

'Did you stay long after we'd left?' he asked abruptly.

'No. We went back to my house.'

This seemed to confirm Rodney's belief that he had been discussed. He turned over the unpalatable idea for a while, in silence.

'Women are incomprehensible creatures, Denham!' he then exclaimed.

'Um,' said Denham, who seemed to himself possessed of complete understanding, not merely of women, but of the entire universe. He could read Rodney, too, like a book. He knew that he was unhappy, and he pitied him, and wished to help him.

'You say something and they – fly into a passion. Or for no reason at all, they laugh. I take it that no amount of education will – ' The remainder of the sentence was lost in the high wind, against which they had to struggle; but Denham understood that he referred to Katharine's laughter, and that the memory of it was still hurting him. In comparison with Rodney, Denham felt himself very secure; he saw Rodney as one of the lost birds dashed senseless against the glass; one of the flying bodies of which the air was full. But he and Katharine were alone together, aloft, splendid, and luminous with a twofold radiance. He pitied the unstable creature beside him; he felt a desire to protect him, exposed without the knowledge which made his own way so direct. They were united as the adventurous are united, though one reaches the goal and the other perishes by the way.

'You couldn't laugh at someone you cared for.'

This sentence, apparently addressed to no other human being, reached Denham's ears. The wind seemed to muffle it and fly away with it directly. Had Rodney spoken those words?

'You love her.' Was that his own voice, which seemed to sound in the air several yards in front of him?

'I've suffered tortures, Denham, tortures!'

'Yes, yes, I know that.'

'She's laughed at me.'

'Never – to me.'

The wind blew a space between the words – blew them so far away that they seemed unspoken.

'How I've loved her!'

This was certainly spoken by the man at Denham's side. The voice had all the marks of Rodney's character, and recalled, with strange vividness, his personal appearance. Denham could see him against the blank buildings and towers of the horizon. He saw him dignified, exalted and tragic, as he might have appeared thinking of Katharine alone in his rooms at night.

'I am in love with Katharine myself. That is why I am here tonight.'

Ralph spoke distinctly and deliberately, as if Rodney's confession had made this statement necessary.

Rodney exclaimed something inarticulate.

'Ah, I've always known it,' he cried, 'I've known it from the first. You'll marry her!'

The cry had a note of despair in it. Again the wind intercepted their words. They said no more. At length they drew up beneath a lamp-post, simultaneously.

'My God, Denham, what fools we both are!' Rodney exclaimed. They looked at each other, queerly, in the light of the lamp. Fools! They seemed to confess to each other the extreme depths of their folly. For the moment, under the lamp-post, they seemed to be aware of some common knowledge which did away with the possibility of rivalry, and made them feel more sympathy for each other than for anyone else in the world. Giving simultaneously a little nod, as if in confirmation of this understanding, they parted without speaking again.

Chapter 29

Between twelve and one that Sunday night Katharine lay in bed, not asleep, but in that twilight region where a detached and humorous view of our own lot is possible; or if we must be serious, our seriousness is tempered by the swift oncome of slumber and oblivion. She saw the forms of Ralph, William, Cassandra and herself as if they were all equally unsubstantial, and, in putting off reality, had gained a kind of dignity which rested upon each impartially. Thus rid of any uncomfortable warmth of partisanship or load of obligation, she was dropping off to sleep when a light tap sounded upon her door. A moment later Cassandra stood beside her, holding a candle and speaking in the low tones proper to the time of night.

'Are you awake, Katharine?'

'Yes, I'm awake. What is it?'

She roused herself, sat up, and asked what in heaven's name Cassandra was doing?

'I couldn't sleep, and I thought I'd come and speak to you – only for a moment, though. I'm going home tomorrow.'

'Home? Why, what has happened?'

'Something happened today which makes it impossible for me to stay here.'

Cassandra spoke formally, almost solemnly; the announcement was clearly prepared and marked a crisis of the utmost gravity. She continued what seemed to be part of a set speech.

'I have decided to tell you the whole truth, Katharine. William allowed himself to behave in a way which made me extremely uncomfortable today.'

Katharine seemed to waken completely, and at once to be in control of herself.

'At the Zoo?' she asked.

'No, on the way home. When we had tea.'

As if foreseeing that the interview might be long, and the night chilly, Katharine advised Cassandra to wrap herself in a quilt. Cassandra did so with unbroken solemnity.

'There's a train at eleven,' she said. 'I shall tell Aunt Maggie that I have to go suddenly . . . I shall make Violet's visit an excuse. But, after thinking it over, I don't see how I can go without telling you the truth.'

She was careful to abstain from looking in Katharine's direction. There was a slight pause.

'But I don't see the least reason why you should go,' said Katharine eventually. Her voice sounded so astonishingly equable that Cassandra glanced at her. It was impossible to suppose that she was either indignant or surprised; she seemed, on the contrary, sitting up in bed, with her arms clasped round her knees and a little frown on her brow, to be thinking closely upon a matter of indifference to her.

'Because I can't allow any man to behave to me in that way,' Cassandra replied, and she added, 'particularly when I know that he is engaged to someone else.'

'But you like him, don't you?' Katharine enquired.

'That's got nothing to do with it,' Cassandra exclaimed indignantly. 'I consider his conduct, under the circumstances, most disgraceful.'

This was the last of the sentences of her premeditated speech; and having spoken it she was left unprovided with any more to say in that particular style. When Katharine remarked: 'I should say it had everything to do with it,' Cassandra's self-possession deserted her.

'I don't understand you in the least, Katharine. How can you behave as you behave? Ever since I came here I've been amazed by you!'

'You've enjoyed yourself, haven't you?' Katharine asked.

'Yes, I have,' Cassandra admitted.

'Anyhow, my behaviour hasn't spoiled your visit.'

'No,' Cassandra allowed once more. She was completely at a loss. In her forecast of the interview she had taken it for granted that Katharine, after an outburst of incredulity, would agree that Cassandra must return home as soon as possible. But Katharine, on the contrary, accepted her statement at once, seemed neither shocked nor surprised, and merely looked rather more thoughtful than usual. From being a mature woman charged with an important mission, Cassandra shrank to the stature of an inexperienced child.

'Do you think I've been very foolish about it?' she asked.

Katharine made no answer, but still sat deliberating silently, and a certain feeling of alarm took possession of Cassandra. Perhaps her words had struck far deeper than she had thought, into depths beyond her reach, as so much of Katharine was beyond her reach. She thought suddenly that she had been playing with very dangerous tools.

Looking at her at length, Katharine asked slowly, as if she found the question very difficult to ask, 'But do you care for William?'

She marked the agitation and bewilderment of the girl's expression, and how she looked away from her.

'Do you mean, am I in love with him?' Cassandra asked, breathing quickly, and nervously moving her hands.

'Yes, in love with him,' Katharine repeated.

'How can I love the man you're engaged to marry?' Cassandra burst out.

'He may be in love with you.'

'I don't think you've any right to say such things, Katharine,' Cassandra exclaimed. 'Why do you say them? Don't you mind in the least how William behaves to other women? If I were engaged, I couldn't bear it!'

'We're not engaged,' said Katharine, after a pause.

'Katharine!' Cassandra cried.

'No, we're not engaged,' Katharine repeated. 'But no one knows it but ourselves.'

'But why – I don't understand – you're not engaged!' Cassandra said again. 'Oh, that explains it! You're not in love with him! You don't want to marry him!'

'We aren't in love with each other any longer,' said Katharine, as if disposing of something for ever and ever.

'How queer, how strange, how unlike other people you are, Katharine,' Cassandra said, her whole body and voice seeming to fall and collapse together, and no trace of anger or excitement remaining, but only a dreamy quietude.

'You're not in love with him?'

'But I love him,' said Katharine.

Cassandra remained bowed, as if by the weight of the revelation, for some little while longer. Nor did Katharine speak. Her attitude was that of someone who wishes to be concealed as much as possible from observation. She sighed profoundly; she was absolutely silent, and apparently overcome by her thoughts.

'D'you know what time it is?' she said at length, and shook her pillow, as if making ready for sleep.

Cassandra rose obediently, and once more took up her candle. Perhaps the white dressing-gown, and the loosened hair and something unseeing in the expression of the eyes gave her a likeness to a woman walking in her sleep. Katharine, at least, thought so.

'There's no reason why I should go home, then?' Cassandra said, pausing. 'Unless you want me to go, Katharine? What *do* you want me to do?'

For the first time their eyes met.

'You wanted us to fall in love,' Cassandra exclaimed, as if she read the certainty there. But as she looked she saw a sight that surprised her. The tears rose slowly in Katharine's eyes and stood there, brimming but contained – the tears of some profound emotion, happiness, grief, renunciation; an emotion so complex in its nature that to express it was impossible, and Cassandra, bending her head and receiving the tears upon her cheek, accepted them in silence as the consecration of her love.

'Please, miss,' said the maid, about eleven o'clock on the following morning, 'Mrs Milvain is in the kitchen.'

A long wicker basket of flowers and branches had arrived from the country, and Katharine, kneeling upon the floor of the drawing-room, was sorting them while Cassandra watched her from an armchair, and absent-mindedly made spasmodic offers of help which were not accepted. The maid's message had a curious effect upon Katharine.

She rose, walked to the window, and, the maid being gone, said emphatically and even tragically: 'You know what that means.'

Cassandra had understood nothing.

'Aunt Celia is in the kitchen,' Katharine repeated.

'Why in the kitchen?' Cassandra asked, not unnaturally.

'Probably because she's discovered something,' Katharine replied. Cassandra's thoughts flew to the subject of her preoccupation.

'About us?' she enquired.

'Heaven knows,' Katharine replied. 'I shan't let her stay in the kitchen, though. I shall bring her up here.'

The sternness with which this was said suggested that to bring Aunt Celia upstairs was, for some reason, a disciplinary measure.

'For goodness' sake, Katharine,' Cassandra exclaimed, jumping from her chair and showing signs of agitation, 'don't be rash. Don't let her suspect. Remember, nothing's certain – '

Katharine assured her by nodding her head several times, but the manner in which she left the room was not calculated to inspire complete confidence in her diplomacy.

Mrs Milvain was sitting, or rather perching, upon the edge of a chair in the servants' room. Whether there was any sound reason for her choice of a subterranean chamber, or whether it corresponded with the spirit of her quest, Mrs Milvain invariably came in by the back door and sat in the servants' room when she was engaged in confidential family transactions. The ostensible reason she gave was that neither Mr nor Mrs Hilbery should be disturbed. But, in truth, Mrs Milvain depended even more than most elderly women of her generation upon the delicious emotions of intimacy, agony and secrecy, and the additional thrill provided by the basement was one not lightly to be forfeited. She protested almost plaintively when Katharine proposed to go upstairs.

'I've something that I want to say to you in *private*,' she said, hesitating reluctantly upon the threshold of her ambush.

'The drawing-room is empty –'

'But we might meet your mother upon the stairs. We might disturb your father,' Mrs Milvain objected, taking the precaution to speak in a whisper already.

But as Katharine's presence was absolutely necessary to the success of the interview, and as Katharine obstinately receded up the kitchen stairs, Mrs Milvain had no course but to follow her. She glanced furtively about her as she proceeded upstairs, drew her skirts together, and stepped with circumspection past all doors, whether they were open or shut.

'Nobody will overhear us?' she murmured, when the comparative sanctuary of the drawing-room had been reached. 'I see that I have interrupted you,' she added, glancing at the flowers strewn upon the floor. A moment later she enquired, 'Was someone sitting with you?' noticing a handkerchief that Cassandra had dropped in her flight.

'Cassandra was helping me to put the flowers in water,' said Katharine, and she spoke so firmly and clearly that Mrs Milvain glanced nervously at the main door and then at the curtain which divided the little room with the relics from the drawing-room.

'Ah, Cassandra is still with you,' she remarked. 'And did William send you those lovely flowers?'

Katharine sat down opposite her aunt and said neither yes nor no. She looked past her, and it might have been thought that she was considering very critically the pattern of the curtains. Another advantage of the basement, from Mrs Milvain's point of view, was that it made it necessary to sit very close together, and the light was dim compared with that which now poured through three windows upon Katharine and the basket of flowers, and gave even the slight angular figure of Mrs Milvain herself a halo of gold.

'They're from Stogdon House,' said Katharine abruptly, with a little jerk of her head.

Mrs Milvain felt that it would be easier to tell her niece what she wished to say if they were actually in physical contact, for the spiritual distance between them was formidable. Katharine, however, made no overtures, and Mrs Milvain, who was possessed of rash but heroic courage, plunged without preface: 'People are talking about you, Katharine. That is why I have come this morning. You forgive me for saying what I'd much rather not say? What I say is only for your own sake, my child.'

'There's nothing to forgive yet, Aunt Celia,' said Katharine, with apparent good humor.

'People are saying that William goes everywhere with you and Cassandra, and that he is always paying her attentions. At the Markhams' dance he sat out five dances with her. At the Zoo they were seen alone together. They left together. They never came back here till seven in the evening. But that is not all. They say his manner is very marked – he is quite different when she is there.'

Mrs Milvain, whose words had run themselves together, and whose voice had raised its tone almost to one of protest, here ceased, and looked intently at Katharine, as if to judge the effect of her communication. A slight rigidity had passed over Katharine's face. Her lips were pressed together; her eyes were contracted, and they were still fixed upon the curtain. These superficial changes covered an extreme inner loathing such as might follow the display of some hideous or indecent spectacle. The indecent spectacle was her own action beheld for the first time from the outside; her aunt's words made her realise how infinitely repulsive the body of life is without its soul.

'Well?' she said at length.

Mrs Milvain made a gesture as if to bring her closer, but it was not returned.

'We all know how good you are – how unselfish – how you sacrifice yourself to others. But you've been too unselfish, Katharine. You have made Cassandra happy, and she has taken advantage of your goodness.'

'I don't understand, Aunt Celia,' said Katharine. 'What has Cassandra done?'

'Cassandra has behaved in a way that I could not have thought possible,' said Mrs Milvain warmly. 'She has been utterly selfish – utterly heartless. I must speak to her before I go.'

'I don't understand,' Katharine persisted.

Mrs Milvain looked at her. Was it possible that Katharine really doubted? That there was something that Mrs Milvain herself did not understand? She braced herself, and pronounced the tremendous words: 'Cassandra has stolen William's love.'

Still the words seemed to have curiously little effect.

'Do you mean,' said Katharine, 'that he has fallen in love with her?'

'There are ways of *making* men fall in love with one, Katharine.'

Katharine remained silent. The silence alarmed Mrs Milvain, and she began hurriedly: 'Nothing would have made me say these things but your own good. I have not wished to interfere; I have not wished to give you pain. I am a useless old woman. I have no children of my own. I only want to see you happy, Katharine.'

Again she stretched forth her arms, but they remained empty.

'You are not going to say these things to Cassandra,' said Katharine suddenly. 'You've said them to me; that's enough.'

Katharine spoke so low and with such restraint that Mrs Milvain had to strain to catch her words, and when she heard them she was dazed by them.

'I've made you angry! I knew I should!' she exclaimed. She quivered, and a kind of sob shook her; but even to have made Katharine angry was some relief, and allowed her to feel some of the agreeable sensations of martyrdom.

'Yes,' said Katharine, standing up, 'I'm so angry that I don't want to say anything more. I think you'd better go, Aunt Celia. We don't understand each other.'

At these words Mrs Milvain looked for a moment terribly apprehensive; she glanced at her niece's face, but read no pity there, whereupon she folded her hands upon a black velvet bag which she carried in an attitude that was almost one of prayer. Whatever divinity she prayed to, if pray she did, at any rate she recovered her dignity in a singular way and faced her niece.

'Married love,' she said slowly and with emphasis upon every word, 'is the most sacred of all loves. The love of husband and wife is the most holy we know. That is the lesson mama's children learnt from her; that is what they can never forget. I have tried to speak as she would have wished her daughter to speak. You are her grandchild.'

Katharine seemed to judge this defence upon its merits, and then to convict it of falsity.

'I don't see that there is any excuse for your behaviour,' she said.

At these words Mrs Milvain rose and stood for a moment beside her niece. She had never met with such treatment before, and she did not know with what weapons to break down the terrible wall of resistance offered her by one who, by virtue of youth and beauty and sex, should have been all tears and supplications. But Mrs Milvain herself was obstinate; upon a matter of this kind she could not admit that she was either beaten or mistaken. She beheld herself the champion of married love in its purity and supremacy; what her niece stood for she was quite unable to say, but she was filled with the gravest suspicions. The old woman and the young woman stood side by side in unbroken silence. Mrs Milvain could not make up her mind to withdraw while her principles trembled in the balance and her curiosity remained un-appeased. She ransacked her mind for some question that should force Katharine to enlighten her, but the supply was limited, the choice difficult, and while she hesitated the door opened and William Rodney came in. He carried in his hand an enormous and splendid bunch of white and purple flowers, and, either not seeing Mrs Milvain, or disregarding her, he advanced straight to Katharine and presented the flowers with the words: 'These are for you, Katharine.'

Katharine took them with a glance that Mrs Milvain did not fail to intercept. But with all her experience, she did not know what to make of it. She watched anxiously for further illumination. William greeted her without obvious sign of guilt, and, explaining that he had a holiday, both he and Katharine seemed to take it for granted that his holiday should be celebrated with flowers and spent in Cheyne Walk. A pause followed; that, too, was natural; and Mrs Milvain began to feel that she laid herself open to a charge of selfishness if she stayed. The mere presence of a young man had altered her disposition curiously, and filled her with a desire for a scene which should end in an emotional forgiveness. She would have given much to clasp both nephew and niece in her arms. But she could not flatter herself that any hope of the customary exaltation remained.

'I must go,' she said, and she was conscious of an extreme flatness of spirit.

Neither of them said anything to stop her. William politely escorted her downstairs, and somehow, among her protests and embarrass-ments, Mrs Milvain forgot to say goodbye to Katharine. She departed, murmuring words about masses of flowers and a drawing-room always beautiful even in the depths of winter.

William came back to Katharine; he found her standing where he had left her.

'I've come to be forgiven,' he said. 'Our quarrel was perfectly hateful to me. I've not slept all night. You're not angry with me, are you, Katharine?'

She could not bring herself to answer him until she had rid her mind of the impression that her aunt had made on her. It seemed to her that the very flowers were contaminated, and Cassandra's pocket-handkerchief, for Mrs Milvain had used them for evidence in her investigations.

'She's been spying upon us,' she said, 'following us about London, overhearing what people are saying – '

'Mrs Milvain?' Rodney exclaimed. 'What has she told you?'

His air of open confidence entirely vanished.

'Oh, people are saying that you're in love with Cassandra, and that you don't care for me.'

'They have seen us?' he asked.

'Everything we've done for a fortnight has been seen.'

'I told you that would happen!' he exclaimed.

He walked to the window in evident perturbation. Katharine was too indignant to attend to him. She was swept away by the force of her own anger. Clasping Rodney's flowers, she stood upright and motionless.

Rodney turned away from the window.

'It's all been a mistake,' he said. 'I blame myself for it. I should have known better. I let you persuade me in a moment of madness. I beg you to forget my insanity, Katharine.'

'She wished even to persecute Cassandra!' Katharine burst out, not listening to him. 'She threatened to speak to her. She's capable of it – she's capable of anything!'

'Mrs Milvain is not tactful, I know, but you exaggerate, Katharine. People are talking about us. She was right to tell us. It only confirms my own feeling – the position is monstrous.'

At length Katharine realised some part of what he meant.

'You don't mean that this influences you, William?' she asked in amazement.

'It does,' he said, flushing. 'It's intensely disagreeable to me. I can't endure that people should gossip about us. And then there's your cousin – Cassandra – ' He paused in embarrassment.

'I came here this morning, Katharine,' he resumed, with a change of voice, 'to ask you to forget my folly, my bad temper, my inconceivable behaviour. I came, Katharine, to ask whether we can't return to the position we were in before this – this season of lunacy. Will you take me back, Katharine, once more and for ever?'

No doubt her beauty, intensified by emotion and enhanced by the flowers of bright colour and strange shape which she carried, wrought upon Rodney, and had its share in bestowing upon her the old romance. But a less noble passion worked in him, too; he was inflamed by jealousy. His tentative offer of affection had been rudely and, as he thought, completely repulsed by Cassandra on the preceding day. Denham's confession was in his mind. And ultimately, Katharine's dominion over him was of the sort that the fevers of the night cannot exorcise.

'I was as much to blame as you were yesterday,' she said gently, disregarding his question. 'I confess, William, the sight of you and

Cassandra together made me jealous, and I couldn't control myself. I laughed at you, I know.'

'You jealous!' William exclaimed. 'I assure you, Katharine, you've not the slightest reason to be jealous. Cassandra dislikes me, so far as she feels about me at all. I was foolish enough to try to explain the nature of our relationship. I couldn't resist telling her what I supposed myself to feel for her. She refused to listen, very rightly. But she left me in no doubt of her scorn.'

Katharine hesitated. She was confused, agitated, physically tired, and had already to reckon with the violent feeling of dislike aroused by her aunt which still vibrated through all the rest of her feelings. She sank into a chair and dropped her flowers upon her lap.

'She charmed me,' Rodney continued. 'I thought I loved her. But that's a thing of the past. It's all over, Katharine. It was a dream – an hallucination. We were both equally to blame, but no harm's done if you believe how truly I care for you. Say you believe me!'

He stood over her, as if in readiness to seize the first sign of her assent. Precisely at that moment, owing, perhaps, to her vicissitudes of feeling, all sense of love left her, as in a moment a mist lifts from the earth. And when the mist departed a skeleton world and blankness alone remained – a terrible prospect for the eyes of the living to behold. He saw the look of terror in her face, and without understanding its origin, took her hand in his. With the sense of companionship returned a desire, like that of a child for shelter, to accept what he had to offer her – and at that moment it seemed that he offered her the only thing that could make it tolerable to live. She let him press his lips to her cheek, and leant her head upon his arm. It was the moment of his triumph. It was the only moment in which she belonged to him and was dependent upon his protection.

'Yes, yes, yes,' he murmured, 'you accept me, Katharine. You love me.'

For a moment she remained silent. He then heard her murmur: 'Cassandra loves you more than I do.'

'Cassandra?' he whispered.

'She loves you,' Katharine repeated. She raised herself and repeated the sentence yet a third time. 'She loves you.'

William slowly raised himself. He believed instinctively what Katharine said, but what it meant to him he was unable to understand. Could Cassandra love him? Could she have told Katharine that she loved him? The desire to know the truth of this was urgent, unknown though the consequences might be. The thrill of excitement associated with the thought of Cassandra once more took possession of him. No longer was it the excitement of anticipation and ignorance; it was the excitement of something greater than a possibility, for now he knew her and had measure of the sympathy between them. But who could give him certainty? Could Katharine, Katharine who had lately lain in his arms, Katharine herself the most admired of women? He looked at her, with doubt, and with anxiety, but said nothing.

'Yes, yes,' she said, interpreting his wish for assurance, 'it's true. I know what she feels for you.'

'She loves me?'

Katharine nodded.

'Ah, but who knows what I feel? How can I be sure of my feeling myself? Ten minutes ago I asked you to marry me. I still wish it – I don't know what I wish – '

He clenched his hands and turned away. He suddenly faced her and demanded: 'Tell me what you feel for Denham.'

'For Ralph Denham?' she asked. 'Yes!' she exclaimed, as if she had found the answer to some momentarily perplexing question. 'You're jealous of me, William; but you're not in love with me. I'm jealous of you. Therefore, for both our sakes, I say, speak to Cassandra at once.'

He tried to compose himself. He walked up and down the room; he paused at the window and surveyed the flowers strewn upon the floor. Meanwhile his desire to have Katharine's assurance confirmed became so insistent that he could no longer deny the over-mastering strength of his feeling for Cassandra.

'You're right,' he exclaimed, coming to a standstill and rapping his knuckles sharply upon a small table carrying one slender vase. 'I love Cassandra.'

As he said this, the curtains hanging at the door of the little room parted, and Cassandra herself stepped forth.

'I have overheard every word!' she exclaimed.

A pause succeeded this announcement. Rodney made a step forward and said: 'Then you know what I wish to ask you. Give me your answer – '

She put her hands before her face; she turned away and seemed to shrink from both of them.

'What Katharine said,' she murmured. 'But,' she added, raising her head with a look of fear from the kiss with which he greeted her admission, 'how frightfully difficult it all is! Our feelings, I mean – yours and mine and Katharine's. Katharine, tell me, are we doing right?'

'Right – of course we're doing right,' William answered her, 'if, after what you've heard, you can marry a man of such incomprehensible confusion, such deplorable – '

'Don't, William,' Katharine interposed; 'Cassandra has heard us; she can judge what we are; she knows better than we could tell her.'

But, still holding William's hand, questions and desires welled up in Cassandra's heart. Had she done wrong in listening? Why did Aunt Celia blame her? Did Katharine think her right? Above all, did William really love her, for ever and ever, better than anyone?

'I must be first with him, Katharine!' she exclaimed. 'I can't share him even with you.'

'I shall never ask that,' said Katharine. She moved a little away from where they sat and began half-consciously sorting her flowers.

'But you've shared with me,' Cassandra said. 'Why can't I share with you? Why am I so mean? I know why it is,' she added. 'We understand each other, William and I. You've never understood each other. You're too different.'

'I've never admired anybody more,' William interposed.

'It's not that' – Cassandra tried to enlighten him – 'it's understanding.'

'Have I never understood you, Katharine? Have I been very selfish?'

'Yes,' Cassandra interposed. 'You've asked her for sympathy, and she's not sympathetic; you've wanted her to be practical, and she's not practical. You've been selfish; you've been exacting – and so has Katharine – but it wasn't anybody's fault.'

Katharine had listened to this attempt at analysis with keen attention. Cassandra's words seemed to rub the old blurred image of life and freshen it so marvellously that it looked new again. She turned to William.

'It's quite true,' she said. 'It was nobody's fault.'

'There are many things that he'll always come to you for,' Cassandra continued, still reading from her invisible book. 'I accept that, Katharine. I shall never dispute it. I want to be generous as you've been generous. But being in love makes it more difficult for me.'

They were silent. At length William broke the silence.

'One thing I beg of you both,' he said, and the old nervousness of manner returned as he glanced at Katharine. 'We will never discuss these matters again. It's not that I'm timid and conventional, as you think, Katharine. It's that it spoils things to discuss them; it unsettles people's minds; and now we're all so happy – '

Cassandra ratified this conclusion so far as she was concerned, and William, after receiving the exquisite pleasure of her glance, with its absolute affection and trust, looked anxiously at Katharine.

'Yes, I'm happy,' she assured him. 'And I agree. We will never talk about it again.'

'Oh, Katharine, Katharine!' Cassandra cried, holding out her arms while the tears ran down her cheeks.

Chapter 30

The day was so different from other days to three people in the house that the common routine of household life – the maid waiting at table, Mrs Hilbery writing a letter, the clock striking, and the door opening, and all the other signs of long-established civilisation appeared suddenly to have no meaning save as they lulled Mr and Mrs Hilbery into the belief that nothing unusual had taken place. It chanced that Mrs Hilbery was depressed without visible cause, unless a certain crudeness verging upon coarseness in the temper of her favourite Elizabethans could be held responsible for the mood. At any rate, she had shut up *The Duchess of Malfi* with a sigh, and wished to know, so she told Rodney at dinner, whether there wasn't some young writer with a touch of the great spirit – somebody who made you believe that life was *beautiful*? She got little help from Rodney, and after singing her plaintive requiem for the death of poetry by herself, she charmed herself into good spirits again by remembering the existence of Mozart. She begged Cassandra to play to her, and when they went upstairs Cassandra opened the piano directly, and did her best to create an atmosphere of unmixed beauty. At the sound of the first notes Katharine and Rodney both felt an enormous sense of relief at the licence which the music gave them to loosen their hold upon the mechanism of behaviour. They lapsed into the depths of thought. Mrs Hilbery was soon spirited away into a perfectly congenial mood, that was half reverie and half slumber, half delicious melancholy and half pure bliss. Mr Hilbery alone attended. He was extremely musical, and made Cassandra aware that he listened to every note. She played her best, and won his approval. Leaning slightly forward in his chair, and turning his little green stone, he weighed the intention of her phrases approvingly, but stopped her suddenly to complain of a noise behind him. The window was unhasped. He signed to Rodney, who crossed the room immediately to put the matter right. He stayed a moment longer by the window than was, perhaps, necessary, and having done what was needed, drew his chair a little closer than before to Katharine's side. The music went on. Under cover of some exquisite run of melody, he leant towards her and whispered something. She glanced at her father and mother, and a moment later left the room, almost unobserved, with Rodney.

'What is it?' she asked, as soon as the door was shut.

Rodney made no answer, but led her downstairs into the dining-room on the ground floor. Even when he had shut the door he said nothing, but went straight to the window and parted the curtains. He beckoned to Katharine.

'There he is again,' he said. 'Look, there – under the lamp-post.'

Katharine looked. She had no idea what Rodney was talking about. A vague feeling of alarm and mystery possessed her. She saw a man standing on the opposite side of the road facing the house beneath a lamp-post. As they looked the figure turned, walked a few steps, and came back again to his old position. It seemed to her that he was looking fixedly at her, and was conscious of her gaze on him. She knew, in a flash, who the man was who was watching them. She drew the curtain abruptly.

'Denham,' said Rodney. 'He was there last night too.' He spoke sternly. His whole manner had become full of authority. Katharine felt almost as if he accused her of some crime. She was pale and uncomfortably agitated, as much by the strangeness of Rodney's behaviour as by the sight of Ralph Denham.

'If he chooses to come – ' she said defiantly.

'You can't let him wait out there. I shall tell him to come in.' Rodney spoke with such decision that when he raised his arm Katharine expected him to draw the curtain instantly. She caught his hand with a little exclamation.

'Wait!' she cried. 'I don't allow you.'

'You can't wait,' he replied. 'You've gone too far.' His hand remained upon the curtain. 'Why don't you admit, Katharine,' he broke out, looking at her with an expression of contempt as well as of anger, 'that you love him? Are you going to treat him as you treated me?'

She looked at him, wondering, in spite of all her perplexity, at the spirit that possessed him.

'I forbid you to draw the curtain,' she said.

He reflected, and then took his hand away.

'I've no right to interfere,' he concluded. 'I'll leave you. Or, if you like, we'll go back to the drawing-room.'

'No. I can't go back,' she said, shaking her head. She bent her head in thought.

'You love him, Katharine,' Rodney said suddenly. His tone had lost something of its sternness, and might have been used to urge a child to confess its fault. She raised her eyes and fixed them upon him.

'I love him?' she repeated. He nodded. She searched his face, as if for further confirmation of his words, and, as he remained silent and expectant, turned away once more and continued her thoughts. He observed her closely, but without stirring, as if he gave her time to make up her mind to fulfil her obvious duty. The strains of Mozart reached them from the room above.

'Now,' she said suddenly, with a sort of desperation, rising from her chair and seeming to command Rodney to fulfil his part. He drew the curtain instantly, and she made no attempt to stop him. Their eyes at once sought the same spot beneath the lamp-post.

'He's not there!' she exclaimed.

No one was there. William threw the window up and looked out. The wind rushed into the room, together with the sound of distant wheels, footsteps hurrying along the pavement and the cries of sirens hooting down the river.

'Denham!' William cried.

'Ralph!' said Katharine, but she spoke scarcely louder than she might have spoken to someone in the same room. With their eyes fixed upon the opposite side of the road, they did not notice a figure close to the railing which divided the garden from the street. But Denham had crossed the road and was standing there. They were startled by his voice close at hand.

'Rodney!'

'There you are! Come in, Denham.' Rodney went to the front door and opened it. 'Here he is,' he said, bringing Ralph with him into the dining-room where Katharine stood, with her back to the open window. Their eyes met for a second. Denham looked half dazed by the strong light, and, buttoned in his overcoat, with his hair ruffled across his forehead by the wind, he seemed like somebody rescued from an open boat out at sea. William promptly shut the window and drew the curtains. He acted with a cheerful decision as if he were master of the situation, and knew exactly what he meant to do.

'You're the first to hear the news, Denham,' he said. 'Katharine isn't going to marry me, after all.'

'Where shall I put – ' Ralph began vaguely, holding out his hat and glancing about him; he balanced it carefully against a silver bowl that stood upon the sideboard. He then sat himself down rather heavily at the head of the oval dinner-table. Rodney stood on one side of him and

Katharine on the other. He appeared to be presiding over some meeting from which most of the members were absent. Meanwhile, he waited, and his eyes rested upon the glow of the beautifully polished mahogany table.

'William is engaged to Cassandra,' said Katharine briefly.

At that Denham looked up quickly at Rodney. Rodney's expression changed. He lost his self-possession. He smiled a little nervously, and then his attention seemed to be caught by a fragment of melody from the floor above. He seemed for a moment to forget the presence of the others. He glanced towards the door.

'I congratulate you,' said Denham.

'Yes, yes. We're all mad – quite out of our minds, Denham,' he said. 'It's partly Katharine's doing – partly mine.' He looked oddly round the room as if he wished to make sure that the scene in which he played a part had some real existence. 'Quite mad,' he repeated. 'Even Katharine – ' His gaze rested upon her finally, as if she, too, had changed from his old view of her. He smiled at her as if to encourage her. 'Katharine shall explain,' he said, and giving a little nod to Denham, he left the room.

Katharine sat down at once, and leant her chin upon her hands. So long as Rodney was in the room the proceedings of the evening had seemed to be in his charge, and had been marked by a certain unreality. Now that she was alone with Ralph she felt at once that a constraint had been taken from them both. She felt that they were alone at the bottom of the house, which rose, storey upon storey, upon the top of them.

'Why were you waiting out there?' she asked.

'For the chance of seeing you,' he replied.

'You would have waited all night if it hadn't been for William. It's windy too. You must have been cold. What could you see? Nothing but our windows.'

'It was worth it. I heard you call me.'

'I called you?' She had called unconsciously.

'They were engaged this morning,' she told him, after a pause.

'You're glad?' he asked.

She bent her head. 'Yes, yes,' she sighed. 'But you don't know how good he is – what he's done for me – ' Ralph made a sound of understanding. 'You waited there last night too?' she asked.

'Yes. I can wait,' Denham replied.

The words seemed to fill the room with an emotion which Katharine connected with the sound of distant wheels, the footsteps hurrying along the pavement, the cries of sirens hooting down the river, the darkness and the wind. She saw the upright figure standing beneath the lamp-post.

'Waiting in the dark,' she said, glancing at the window, as if he saw what she was seeing. 'Ah, but it's different – ' She broke off. 'I'm not the person you think me. Until you realise that it's impossible – '

Placing her elbows on the table, she slid her ruby ring up and down her finger abstractedly. She frowned at the rows of leather-bound books opposite her. Ralph looked keenly at her. Very pale, but sternly concentrated upon her meaning, beautiful but so little aware of herself as to seem remote from him also, there was something distant and abstract about her which exalted him and chilled him at the same time.

'No, you're right,' he said. 'I don't know you. I've never known you.'

'Yet perhaps you know me better than anyone else,' she mused.

Some detached instinct made her aware that she was gazing at a book which belonged by rights to some other part of the house. She walked over to the shelf, took it down, and returned to her seat, placing the book on the table between them. Ralph opened it and looked at the portrait of a man with a voluminous white shirt-collar, which formed the frontispiece.

'I say I do know you, Katharine,' he affirmed, shutting the book. 'It's only for moments that I go mad.'

'Do you call two whole nights a moment?'

'I swear to you that now, at this instant, I see you precisely as you are. No one has ever known you as I know you . . . Could you have taken down that book just now if I hadn't known you?'

'That's true,' she replied, 'but you can't think how I'm divided – how I'm at my ease with you, and how I'm bewildered. The unreality – the dark – the waiting outside in the wind – yes, when you look at me, not seeing me, and I don't see you either . . . But I do see,' she went on quickly, changing her position and frowning again, 'heaps of things, only not you.'

'Tell me what you see,' he urged.

But she could not reduce her vision to words, since it was no single shape coloured upon the dark, but rather a general excitement, an atmosphere, which, when she tried to visualise it, took form as a wind scouring the flanks of northern hills and flashing light upon cornfields and pools.

'Impossible,' she sighed, laughing at the ridiculous notion of putting any part of this into words.

'Try, Katharine,' Ralph urged her.

'But I can't – I'm talking a sort of nonsense – the sort of nonsense one talks to oneself.' She was dismayed by the expression of longing and despair upon his face. 'I was thinking about a mountain in the North of England,' she attempted. 'It's too silly – I won't go on.'

'We were there together?' he pressed her.

'No. I was alone.' She seemed to be disappointing the desire of a child. His face fell.

'You're always alone there?'

'I can't explain.' She could not explain that she was essentially alone there. 'It's not a mountain in the North of England. It's an imagination – a story one tells oneself. You have yours too?'

'You're with me in mine. You're the thing I make up, you see.'

'Oh, I see,' she sighed. 'That's why it's so impossible.' She turned upon him almost fiercely. 'You must try to stop it,' she said.

'I won't,' he replied roughly, 'because I – ' He stopped. He realised that the moment had come to impart that news of the utmost importance which he had tried to impart to Mary Datchet, to Rodney upon the Embankment, to the drunken tramp upon the seat. How should he offer it to Katharine? He looked quickly at her. He saw that she was only half attentive to him; only a section of her was exposed to him. The sight roused in him such desperation that he had much ado to control his impulse to rise and leave the house. Her hand lay loosely curled upon the table. He seized it and grasped it firmly as if to make sure of her existence and of his own. 'Because I love you, Katharine,' he said.

Some roundness or warmth essential to that statement was absent from his voice, and she had merely to shake her head very slightly for him to drop her hand and turn away in shame at his own impotence. He thought that she had detected his wish to leave her. She had discerned the break in his resolution, the blankness in the heart of his vision. It was true that he had been happier out in the street, thinking of her, than now that he was in the same room with her. He looked at her with a guilty expression on his face. But her look expressed neither disappointment nor reproach. Her pose was easy, and she seemed to give effect to a mood of quiet speculation by the spinning of her ruby ring upon the polished table. Denham forgot his despair in wondering what thoughts now occupied her.

'You don't believe me?' he said. His tone was humble, and made her smile at him.

'As far as I understand you – but what should you advise me to do with this ring?' she asked, holding it out.

'I should advise you to let me keep it for you,' he replied, in the same tone of half-humorous gravity.

'After what you've said, I can hardly trust you – unless you'll unsay what you've said?'

'Very well. I'm not in love with you.'

'But I think you *are* in love with me . . . As I am with you,' she added casually enough. 'At least,' she said slipping her ring back to its old position, 'what other word describes the state we're in?'

She looked at him gravely and enquiringly, as if in search of help.

'It's when I'm with you that I doubt it, not when I'm alone,' he stated.

'So I thought,' she replied.

In order to explain to her his state of mind, Ralph recounted his experience with the photograph, the letter and the flower picked at Kew. She listened very seriously.

'And then you went raving about the streets,' she mused. 'Well, it's bad enough. But my state is worse than yours, because it hasn't anything to do with facts. It's an hallucination, pure and simple – an intoxication . . . One can be in love with pure reason?' she hazarded. 'Because if you're in love with a vision, I believe that that's what I'm in love with.'

This conclusion seemed fantastic and profoundly unsatisfactory to Ralph, but after the astonishing variations of his own sentiments during the past half-hour he could not accuse her of fanciful exaggeration.

'Rodney seems to know his own mind well enough,' he said almost bitterly. The music, which had ceased, had now begun again, and the melody of Mozart seemed to express the easy and exquisite love of the two upstairs.

'Cassandra never doubted for a moment. But we – ' she glanced at him as if to ascertain his position, 'we see each other only now and then – '

'Like lights in a storm – '

'In the midst of a hurricane,' she concluded, as the window shook beneath the pressure of the wind. They listened to the sound in silence.

Here the door opened with considerable hesitation, and Mrs Hilbery's head appeared, at first with an air of caution, but having made sure that she had admitted herself to the dining-room and not to some more unusual region, she came completely inside and seemed in no way taken aback by the sight she saw. She seemed, as usual, bound on some quest of her own which was interrupted pleasantly but strangely by running into one of those queer, unnecessary ceremonies that other people thought fit to indulge in.

'Please don't let me interrupt you, Mr – ' she was at a loss, as usual, for the name, and Katharine thought that she did not recognise him. 'I hope you've found something nice to read,' she added, pointing to the book upon the table. 'Byron – ah, Byron. I've known people who knew Lord Byron,' she said.

Katharine, who had risen in some confusion, could not help smiling at the thought that her mother found it perfectly natural and desirable that her daughter should be reading Byron in the dining-room late at night alone with a strange young man. She blessed a disposition that was so convenient, and felt tenderly towards her mother and her mother's eccentricities. But Ralph observed that although Mrs Hilbery held the book so close to her eyes she was not reading a word.

'My dear mother, why aren't you in bed?' Katharine exclaimed, changing astonishingly in the space of a minute to her usual condition of authoritative good sense. 'Why are you wandering about?'

'I'm sure I should like your poetry better than I like Lord Byron's,' said Mrs Hilbery, addressing Ralph Denham.

'Mr Denham doesn't write poetry; he has written articles for father, for the *Review*,' Katharine said, as if prompting her memory.

'Oh dear! How dull!' Mrs Hilbery exclaimed, with a sudden laugh that rather puzzled her daughter.

Ralph found that she had turned upon him a gaze that was at once very vague and very penetrating.

'But I'm sure you read poetry at night. I always judge by the expression of the eyes,' Mrs Hilbery continued. (' "The windows of the soul",' she added parenthetically.) 'I don't know much about the law,' she went on, 'though many of my relations were lawyers. Some of them looked very handsome, too, in their wigs. But I think I do know a little about poetry,' she added. 'And all the things that aren't written down, but – but – ' She waved her hand, as if to indicate the wealth of unwritten poetry all about them. 'The night and the stars, the dawn coming up, the barges swimming past, the sun setting . . . Ah dear,' she sighed, 'well, the sunset is very lovely too. I sometimes think that poetry isn't so much what we write as what we feel, Mr Denham.'

During this speech of her mother's Katharine had turned away, and Ralph felt that Mrs Hilbery was talking to him apart, with a desire to ascertain something about him which she veiled purposely by the vagueness of her words. He felt curiously encouraged and heartened by the beam in her eye rather than by her actual words. From the distance of her age and sex she seemed to be waving to him, hailing him as a ship sinking beneath the horizon might wave its flag of greeting to another setting out upon the same voyage. He bent his head, saying nothing, but with a curious certainty that she had read an answer to her enquiry that satisfied her. At any rate, she rambled off into a description of the

Law Courts which turned to a denunciation of English justice, which, according to her, imprisoned poor men who couldn't pay their debts. 'Tell me, shall we ever do without it all?' she asked, but at this point Katharine gently insisted that her mother should go to bed. Looking back from halfway up the staircase, Katharine seemed to see Denham's eyes watching her steadily and intently with an expression that she had guessed in them when he stood looking at the windows across the road.

Chapter 31

The tray which brought Katharine's cup of tea the next morning brought, also, a note from her mother, announcing that it was her intention to catch an early train to Stratford-upon-Avon that very day.

'Please find out the best way of getting there,' the note ran, 'and wire to dear Sir John Burdett to expect me, with my love. I've been dreaming all night of you and Shakespeare, dearest Katharine.'

This was no momentary impulse. Mrs Hilbery had been dreaming of Shakespeare any time these six months, toying with the idea of an excursion to what she considered the heart of the civilised world. To stand six feet above Shakespeare's bones, to see the very stones worn by his feet, to reflect that the oldest man's oldest mother had very likely seen Shakespeare's daughter – such thoughts roused an emotion in her, which she expressed at unsuitable moments, and with a passion that would not have been unseemly in a pilgrim to a sacred shrine. The only strange thing was that she wished to go by herself. But, naturally enough, she was well provided with friends who lived in the neighbourhood of Shakespeare's tomb and were delighted to welcome her; and she left later to catch her train in the best of spirits. There was a man selling violets in the street. It was a fine day. She would remember to send Mr Hilbery the first daffodil she saw. And, as she ran back into the hall to tell Katharine, she felt, she had always felt, that Shakespeare's command to leave his bones undisturbed applied only to odious curiosity-mongers – not to dear Sir John and herself. Leaving her daughter to cogitate the theory of Anne Hathaway's sonnets, and the buried manuscripts here referred to, with the implied menace to the safety of the heart of civilisation itself, she briskly shut the door of her taxi-cab, and was whirled off upon the first stage of her pilgrimage.

The house was oddly different without her. Katharine found the maids already in possession of her room, which they meant to clean thoroughly during her absence. To Katharine it seemed as if they had brushed away sixty years or so with the first flick of their damp dusters. It seemed to her that the work she had tried to do in that room was being swept into a very insignificant heap of dust. The china shepherdesses were already shining from a bath of hot water. The writing-table might have belonged to a professional man of methodical habits.

Gathering together a few papers upon which she was at work, Katharine proceeded to her own room with the intention of looking through them, perhaps, in the course of the morning. But she was met on the stairs by Cassandra, who followed her up, but with such intervals between each step that Katharine began to feel her purpose dwindling before they had reached the door. Cassandra leant over the banisters, and looked down upon the Persian rug that lay on the floor of the hall.

'Doesn't everything look odd this morning?' she enquired. 'Are you really going to spend the morning with those dull old letters, because if so – '

The dull old letters, which would have turned the heads of the most sober of collectors, were laid upon a table, and, after a moment's pause, Cassandra, looking grave all of a sudden, asked Katharine where she should find the *History of England* by Lord Macaulay.[93] It was downstairs in Mr Hilbery's study. The cousins descended together in search of it. They diverged into the drawing-room for the good reason that the door was open. The portrait of Richard Alardyce attracted their attention.

'I wonder what he was like?' It was a question that Katharine had often asked herself lately.

'Oh, a fraud like the rest of them – at least Henry says so,' Cassandra replied. 'Though I don't believe everything Henry says,' she added a little defensively.

Down they went into Mr Hilbery's study, where they began to look among his books. So desultory was this examination that some fifteen minutes failed to discover the work they were in search of.

'Must you read Macaulay's *History*, Cassandra?' Katharine asked, with a stretch of her arms.

'I must,' Cassandra replied briefly.

'Well, I'm going to leave you to look for it by yourself.'

'Oh, no, Katharine. Please stay and help me. You see – you see – I told William I'd read a little every day. And I want to tell him that I've begun when he comes.'

'When does William come?' Katharine asked, turning to the shelves again.

'To tea, if that suits you?'

'If it suits me to be out, I suppose you mean.'

'Oh, you're horrid . . . Why shouldn't you – ?'

'Yes ?'

'Why shouldn't you be happy too?'

'I am quite happy,' Katharine replied.

'I mean as I am. Katharine,' she said impulsively, 'do let's be married on the same day.'

'To the same man?'

'Oh, no, no. But why shouldn't you marry – someone else?'

'Here's your Macaulay,' said Katharine, turning round with the book in her hand. 'I should say you'd better begin to read at once if you mean to be educated by teatime.'

'Damn Lord Macaulay!' cried Cassandra, slapping the book upon the table. 'Would you rather not talk?'

'We've talked enough already,' Katharine replied evasively.

'I know I shan't be able to settle to Macaulay,' said Cassandra, looking ruefully at the dull red cover of the prescribed volume, which, however, possessed a talismanic property, since William admired it. He had advised a little serious reading for the morning hours.

'Have *you* read Macaulay?' she asked.

'No. William never tried to educate me.' As she spoke she saw the light fade from Cassandra's face, as if she had implied some other, more mysterious, relationship. She was stung with compunction. She marvelled at her own rashness in having influenced the life of another, as she had influenced Cassandra's life.

'We weren't serious,' she said quickly.

'But I'm fearfully serious,' said Cassandra, with a little shudder, and her look showed that she spoke the truth. She turned and glanced at Katharine as she had never glanced at her before. There was fear in her glance, which darted on her and then dropped guiltily. Oh, Katharine had everything – beauty, mind, character. She could never compete with Katharine; she could never be safe so long as Katharine brooded over her, dominating her, disposing of her. She called her cold, unseeing, unscrupulous, but the only sign she gave outwardly was a curious one – she reached out her hand and grasped the volume of history. At that moment the bell of the telephone rang and Katharine went to answer it. Cassandra, released from observation, dropped her book and clenched her hands. She suffered more fiery torture in those few minutes than she had suffered in the whole of her life; she learnt more of her capacities for feeling. But when Katharine reappeared she was calm, and had gained a look of dignity that was new to her.

'Was that him?' she asked.

'It was Ralph Denham,' Katharine replied.

'I meant Ralph Denham.'

'Why did you mean Ralph Denham? What has William told you about Ralph Denham?' The accusation that Katharine was calm, callous and indifferent was not possible in face of her present air of animation. She gave Cassandra no time to frame an answer. 'Now, when are you and William going to be married?' she asked.

Cassandra made no reply for some moments. It was, indeed, a very difficult question to answer. In conversation the night before, William had indicated to Cassandra that, in his belief, Katharine was becoming engaged to Ralph Denham in the dining-room. Cassandra, in the rosy light of her own circumstances, had been disposed to think that the matter must be settled already. But a letter which she had received that morning from William, while ardent in its expression of affection, had conveyed to her obliquely that he would prefer the announcement of their engagement to coincide with that of Katharine's. This document Cassandra now produced, and read aloud, with considerable excisions and much hesitation.

' . . . a thousand pities – ahem – I fear we shall cause a great deal of natural annoyance. If, on the other hand, what I have reason to think will happen, should happen – within reasonable time, and the present position is not in any way offensive to you, delay would, in my opinion, serve all our interests better than a premature explanation, which is bound to cause more surprise than is desirable – '

'Very like William,' Katharine exclaimed, having gathered the drift of these remarks with a speed that, by itself, disconcerted Cassandra.

'I quite understand his feelings,' Cassandra replied. 'I quite agree with them. I think it would be much better, if you intend to marry Mr Denham, that we should wait as William says.'

'But, then, if I don't marry him for months – or, perhaps, not at all?'

Cassandra was silent. The prospect appalled her. Katharine had been telephoning to Ralph Denham; she looked queer, too; she must be, or about to become, engaged to him. But if Cassandra could have overheard the conversation upon the telephone, she would not have felt so certain that it tended in that direction. It was to this effect: 'I'm Ralph Denham speaking. I'm in my right senses now.'

'How long did you wait outside the house?'

'I went home and wrote you a letter. I tore it up.'

'I shall tear up everything too.'

'I shall come.'

'Yes. Come today.'

'I must explain to you – '

'Yes. We must explain – '

A long pause followed. Ralph began a sentence, which he cancelled with the word, 'Nothing.' Suddenly, together, at the same moment, they said goodbye. And yet, if the telephone had been miraculously connected with some higher atmosphere pungent with the scent of thyme and the savour of salt, Katharine could hardly have breathed in a keener sense of exhilaration. She ran downstairs on the crest of it. She was amazed to find herself already committed by William and Cassandra to marry the owner of the halting voice she had just heard on the telephone. The tendency of her spirit seemed to be in an altogether different direction; and of a different nature. She had only to look at Cassandra to see what the love that results in an engagement and marriage means. She considered for a moment, and then said: 'If you don't want to tell people yourselves, I'll do it for you. I know William has feelings about these matters that make it very difficult for him to do anything.'

'Because he's fearfully sensitive about other people's feelings,' said Cassandra. 'The idea that he could upset Aunt Maggie or Uncle Trevor would make him ill for weeks.'

This interpretation of what she was used to call William's conventionality was new to Katharine. And yet she felt it now to be the true one.

'Yes, you're right,' she said.

'And then he worships beauty. He wants life to be beautiful in every part of it. Have you ever noticed how exquisitely he finishes everything? Look at the address on that envelope. Every letter is perfect.'

Whether this applied also to the sentiments expressed in the letter, Katharine was not so sure; but when William's solicitude was spent upon Cassandra it not only failed to irritate her, as it had done when she was the object of it, but appeared, as Cassandra said, the fruit of his love of beauty.

'Yes,' she said, 'he loves beauty.'

'I hope we shall have a great many children,' said Cassandra. 'He loves children.'

This remark made Katharine realise the depths of their intimacy better than any other words could have done; she was jealous for one moment; but the next she was humiliated. She had known William for years, and she had never once guessed that he loved children. She looked at the queer glow of exaltation in Cassandra's eyes, through which she was beholding the true spirit of a human being, and wished that she would go on talking about William for ever. Cassandra was not unwilling to gratify her. She talked on. The morning slipped away. Katharine scarcely changed her position on the edge of her father's writing-table, and Cassandra never opened the *History of England*.

And yet it must be confessed that there were vast lapses in the attention which Katharine bestowed upon her cousin. The atmosphere was wonderfully congenial for thoughts of her own. She lost herself sometimes in such deep reverie that Cassandra, pausing, could look at her for moments unperceived. What could Katharine be thinking about, unless it were Ralph Denham? She was satisfied, by certain random replies, that Katharine had wandered a little from the subject of William's perfections. But Katharine made no sign. She always ended these pauses by saying something so natural that Cassandra was deluded into giving fresh examples of her absorbing theme. Then they lunched, and the only sign that Katharine gave of abstraction was to forget to help the pudding. She looked so like her mother, as she sat there oblivious of the tapioca, that Cassandra was startled into exclaiming: 'How like Aunt Maggie you look!'

'Nonsense,' said Katharine, with more irritation than the remark seemed to call for.

In truth, now that her mother was away, Katharine did feel less sensible than usual, but as she argued it to herself, there was much less need for sense. Secretly, she was a little shaken by the evidence which the morning had supplied of her immense capacity for – what could one call it? – rambling over an infinite variety of thoughts that were too foolish to be named. She was, for example, walking down a road in Northumberland in the August sunset; at the inn she left her companion, who was Ralph Denham, and was transported, not so much by her own feet as by some invisible means, to the top of a high hill. Here the scents, the sounds among the dry heather-roots, the grass-blades pressed upon the palm of her hand, were all so perceptible that she could experience each one separately. After this her mind made excursions into the dark of the air, or settled upon the surface of the sea, which could be discovered over there, or with equal unreason it returned to its couch of bracken beneath the stars of midnight, and visited the snow valleys of the moon. These fancies would have been in no way strange, since the walls of every mind are decorated with some such tracery, but she found herself suddenly pursuing such thoughts with an extreme ardour, which became a desire to change her actual condition for something matching the conditions of her dream. Then she started; then she awoke to the fact that Cassandra was looking at her in amazement.

Cassandra would have liked to feel certain that, when Katharine made no reply at all or one wide of the mark, she was making up her mind to get married at once, but it was difficult, if this were so, to account for some remarks that Katharine let fall about the future. She recurred several times to the summer, as if she meant to spend that season in solitary wandering. She seemed to have a plan in her mind which required *Bradshaw's* [94] and the names of inns.

Cassandra was driven finally, by her own unrest, to put on her clothes and wander out along the streets of Chelsea, on the pretence that she must buy something. But, in her ignorance of the way, she became panic-stricken at the thought of being late, and no sooner had she found the shop she wanted, than she fled back again in order to be at home when William came. He came, indeed, five minutes after she had sat down by the tea-table, and she had the happiness of receiving him alone. His greeting put her doubts of his affection at rest, but the first question he asked was: 'Has Katharine spoken to you?'

'Yes. But she says she's not engaged. She doesn't seem to think she's ever going to be engaged.'

William frowned, and looked annoyed.

'They telephoned this morning, and she behaves very oddly. She forgets to help the pudding,' Cassandra added by way of cheering him.

'My dear child, after what I saw and heard last night, it's not a question of guessing or suspecting. Either she's engaged to him – or – '

He left his sentence unfinished, for at this point Katharine herself appeared. With his recollections of the scene the night before, he was too self-conscious even to look at her, and it was not until she told him of her mother's visit to Stratford-upon-Avon that he raised his eyes. It was clear that he was greatly relieved. He looked round him now, as if he felt at his ease, and Cassandra exclaimed: 'Don't you think everything looks quite different?'

'You've moved the sofa?' he asked.

'No. Nothing's been touched,' said Katharine. 'Everything's exactly the same.' But as she said this, with a decision which seemed to make it imply that more than the sofa was unchanged, she held out a cup into which she had forgotten to pour any tea. Being told of her forgetfulness, she frowned with annoyance, and said that Cassandra was demoralising her. The glance she cast upon them, and the resolute way in which she plunged them into speech, made William and Cassandra feel like children who had been caught prying. They followed her obediently, making conversation. Anyone coming in might have judged them acquaintances met, perhaps, for the third time. If that were so, one must have concluded that the hostess suddenly bethought her of an engagement pressing for fulfilment. First Katharine looked at her watch, and then she asked William to tell her the right time. When told that it was ten minutes to five she rose at once, and said: 'Then I'm afraid I must go.'

She left the room, holding her unfinished bread and butter in her hand. William glanced at Cassandra.

'Well, she *is* queer!' Cassandra exclaimed.

William looked perturbed. He knew more of Katharine than Cassandra did, but even he could not tell – In a second Katharine was back again dressed in outdoor things, still holding her bread and butter in her bare hand.

'If I'm late, don't wait for me,' she said. 'I shall have dined,' and so saying, she left them.

'But she can't – ' William exclaimed, as the door shut, 'not without any gloves and bread and butter in her hand!' They ran to the window, and saw her walking rapidly along the street towards the City. Then she vanished.

'She must have gone to meet Mr Denham,' Cassandra exclaimed.

'Goodness knows!' William interjected.

The incident impressed them both as having something queer and ominous about it out of all proportion to its surface strangeness.

'It's the sort of way Aunt Maggie behaves,' said Cassandra, as if in explanation.

William shook his head, and paced up and down the room looking extremely perturbed.

'This is what I've been foretelling,' he burst out. 'Once set the ordinary conventions aside – Thank heaven Mrs Hilbery is away. But there's Mr Hilbery. How are we to explain it to him? I shall have to leave you.'

'But Uncle Trevor won't be back for hours, William!' Cassandra implored.

'You never can tell. He may be on his way already. Or suppose Mrs Milvain – your Aunt Celia – or Mrs Cosham, or any other of your aunts or uncles should be shown in and find us alone together. You know what they're saying about us already.'

Cassandra was equally stricken by the sight of William's agitation, and appalled by the prospect of his desertion.

'We might hide,' she exclaimed wildly, glancing at the curtain which separated the room with the relics.

'I refuse entirely to get under the table,' said William sarcastically.

She saw that he was losing his temper with the difficulties of the situation. Her instinct told her that an appeal to his affection, at this moment, would be extremely ill-judged. She controlled herself, sat down, poured out a fresh cup of tea, and sipped it quietly. This natural action, arguing complete self-mastery, and showing her in one of those feminine attitudes which William found adorable, did more than any argument to compose his agitation. It appealed to his chivalry. He accepted a cup. Next she asked for a slice of cake. By the time the cake was eaten and the tea drunk the personal question had lapsed, and they were discussing poetry. Insensibly they turned from the question of dramatic poetry in general, to the particular example which reposed in William's pocket, and when the maid came in to clear away the tea-things, William had asked permission to read a short passage aloud, 'unless it bored her?'

Cassandra bent her head in silence, but she showed a little of what she felt in her eyes, and thus fortified, William felt confident that it would take more than Mrs Milvain herself to rout him from his position. He read aloud.

Meanwhile Katharine walked rapidly along the street. If called upon to explain her impulsive action in leaving the tea-table, she could have traced it to no better cause than that William had glanced at Cassandra; Cassandra at William. Yet, because they had glanced, her position was impossible. If one forgot to pour out a cup of tea they rushed to the conclusion that she was engaged to Ralph Denham. She knew that in half an hour or so the door would open, and Ralph Denham would appear. She could not sit there and contemplate seeing him with William's and Cassandra's eyes upon them, judging their exact degree of intimacy, so that they might fix the wedding-day. She promptly decided that she would meet Ralph out of doors; she still had time to reach Lincoln's Inn Fields before he left his office. She hailed a cab, and bade it take her to a shop for selling maps which she remembered in Great Queen Street, since she hardly liked to be set down at his door. Arrived at the shop, she bought a large scale map of Norfolk, and thus provided, hurried into Lincoln's Inn Fields, and assured herself of the position of Messrs Hoper and Grateley's office. The great gas chandeliers were alight in the office windows. She conceived that he sat at an enormous table laden with papers beneath one of them in the front room with the three tall windows. Having settled his position there, she began walking to and fro upon the pavement. Nobody of his build appeared. She scrutinised each male figure as it approached and passed her. Each male figure had, nevertheless, a look of him, due, perhaps, to the professional dress, the quick step, the keen glance which they cast upon her as they hastened home after the day's work. The square itself, with its immense houses all so fully occupied and stern of aspect, its atmosphere of industry and power, as if even the sparrows and the children were earning their daily bread, as if the sky itself, with its grey and scarlet clouds, reflected the serious intention of the city beneath it, spoke of him. Here was the fit place for their meeting, she thought; here was the fit place for her to walk thinking of him. She could not help comparing it with the domestic streets of Chelsea. With this comparison in her mind, she extended her range a little, and turned into the main road. The great torrent of vans and carts was sweeping down Kingsway; pedestrians were streaming in two currents along the pavements. She stood fascinated at the corner. The deep roar filled her ears; the changing tumult had the inexpressible fascination of varied life pouring ceaselessly with a purpose which, as she looked, seemed to her, somehow, the normal purpose for which life was framed; its complete indifference to the individuals, whom it swallowed up and rolled onwards, filled her with at least a temporary exaltation. The blend of daylight and of lamplight made her an invisible spectator, just as it gave the people who passed her a semi-transparent quality, and left the faces pale ivory ovals in which the eyes alone were dark. They tended the enormous rush of the current – the great flow, the deep stream, the unquenchable tide. She stood unobserved and absorbed, glorying openly in the rapture that had run subterraneously all day. Suddenly she was clutched, unwilling, from the outside, by the recollection of her purpose in coming there. She had come to find Ralph Denham. She hastily turned back into Lincoln's Inn Fields, and looked for her land-mark – the light in the three tall windows. She sought in vain. The faces of the houses had now merged in the general darkness, and she had difficulty in determining which she sought. Ralph's three windows gave back on their ghostly glass panels only a reflection of the grey and greenish sky. She rang the bell, peremptorily, under the painted name of the firm. After some delay she was answered by a caretaker, whose pail and brush of themselves told her that the working day was over and the workers gone. Nobody, save perhaps Mr Grateley himself, was left, she assured Katharine; everyone else had been gone these ten minutes.

The news woke Katharine completely. Anxiety gained upon her. She hastened back into Kingsway, looking at people who had miraculously regained their solidity. She ran as far as the Tube station, overhauling clerk after clerk, solicitor after solicitor. Not one of them even faintly resembled Ralph Denham. More and more plainly did she see him; and more and more did he seem to her unlike anyone else. At the door of the station she paused, and tried to collect her thoughts. He had gone to her house. By taking a cab she could be there probably in advance of him. But she pictured herself opening the drawing-room door, and William and Cassandra looking up, and Ralph's entrance a moment later, and the glances – the insinuations. No; she could not face it. She would write him a letter and take it at once to his house. She bought paper and pencil at the bookstall, and entered an ABC shop,[95] where, by ordering a cup of coffee, she secured an empty table, and began at once to write: 'I came to meet you and I have missed you. I could not face William and Cassandra. They want us – ' here she paused. 'They insist that we are engaged,' she substituted, 'and we couldn't talk at all, or explain anything. I want – ' Her wants were so vast, now that she was in communication with Ralph, that the pencil was utterly inadequate to conduct them on to the paper; it seemed as if the whole torrent of Kingsway had to run down her pencil. She gazed intently at a notice hanging on the gold-encrusted wall opposite. ' . . . to say all kinds of things,' she added, writing each word with the painstaking of a child. But, when she raised her eyes again to meditate the next sentence, she was aware of a waitress, whose expression intimated that it was closing time, and, looking round, Katharine saw herself almost the last person left in the shop. She took up her letter, paid her bill, and found herself once more in the street. She would now take a cab to Highgate. But at that moment it flashed upon her that she could not remember the address. This check seemed to let fall a barrier across a very powerful current of desire. She ransacked her memory in desperation, hunting for the name, first by remembering the look of the house, and then by trying, in memory, to retrace the words she had written once, at least, upon an envelope. The more she pressed the farther the words receded. Was the house an Orchard Something, on the street a Hill? She gave it up. Never, since she was a child, had she felt anything like this blankness and desolation. There rushed in upon her, as if she were waking from some dream, all the consequences of her inexplicable indolence. She figured Ralph's face as he turned from her door without a word of explanation, receiving his dismissal as a blow from herself, a callous intimation that she did not wish to see him. She followed his departure from her door; but it was far more easy to see him marching far and fast in any direction for any length of time than to conceive that he would turn back to Highgate. Perhaps he would try once more to see her in Cheyne Walk? It was proof of the clearness with which she saw him, that she started forward as this possibility occurred to her, and almost raised her hand to beckon to a cab. No; he was too proud to come again; he rejected the desire and walked on and on, on and on – If only she could read the names of those visionary streets down which he passed! But her imagination betrayed her at this point, or mocked her with a sense of their strangeness, darkness and distance. Indeed, instead of helping herself to any decision, she only filled her mind with the vast extent of London and the impossibility of finding any single figure that wandered off this way and that way, turned to the right and to the left, chose that dingy little back street where the children were playing in the road, and so – She roused herself impatiently. She walked rapidly along Holborn. Soon she turned and walked as rapidly in the other direction. This indecision was not merely odious, but had something that alarmed her about it, as she had been alarmed slightly once or twice already that day; she felt unable to cope with the strength of her own desires. To a person controlled by habit, there was humiliation as well as alarm in this sudden release of what appeared to be a very powerful as well as an unreasonable force. An aching in the muscles of her right hand now showed her that she was crushing her gloves and the map of Norfolk in a grip sufficient to crack a more solid object. She relaxed her grasp; she looked anxiously at the faces of the passers-by to see whether their eyes rested on her for a moment longer than was natural, or with any curiosity. But having smoothed out her gloves, and done what she could to look as usual, she forgot spectators, and was once more given up to her desperate desire to find Ralph Denham. It was a desire now – wild, irrational, unexplained, resembling something felt in childhood. Once more she blamed herself bitterly for her carelessness. But finding herself opposite the Tube station, she pulled herself up and took counsel swiftly, as of old. It flashed upon her that she would go at once to Mary Datchet, and ask her to give her Ralph's address. The decision was a relief, not only in giving her a goal, but in providing her with a rational excuse for her own actions. It gave her a goal certainly, but the fact of having a goal led her to dwell exclusively upon her obsession; so that when she rang the bell of Mary's flat, she did not for a moment consider how this demand would strike Mary. To her extreme annoyance Mary was not at home; a charwoman opened the door. All Katharine could do was to accept the invitation to wait. She waited for, perhaps, fifteen minutes, and spent them in pacing from one end of the room to the other without intermission. When she heard Mary's key in the door she paused in front of the fireplace, and Mary found her standing upright, looking at once expectant and determined, like a person who has come on an errand of such importance that it must be broached without preface.

Mary exclaimed in surprise.

'Yes, yes,' Katharine said, brushing these remarks aside, as if they were in the way.

'Have you had tea?'

'Oh yes,' she said, thinking that she had had tea hundreds of years ago, somewhere or other.

Mary paused, took off her gloves, and, finding matches, proceeded to light the fire.

Katharine checked her with an impatient movement, and said: 'Don't light the fire for me . . . I want to know Ralph Denham's address.'

She was holding a pencil and preparing to write on the envelope. She waited with an imperious expression.

'The Apple Orchard, Mount Ararat Road, Highgate,' Mary said, speaking slowly and rather strangely.

'Oh, I remember now!' Katharine exclaimed, with irritation at her own stupidity. 'I suppose it wouldn't take twenty minutes to drive there?' She gathered up her purse and gloves and seemed about to go.

'But you won't find him,' said Mary, pausing with a match in her hand. Katharine, who had already turned towards the door, stopped and looked at her.

'Why? Where is he?' she asked.

'He won't have left his office.'

'But he has left the office,' she replied. 'The only question is will he have reached home yet? He went to see me at Chelsea; I tried to meet him and missed him. He will have found no message to explain. So I must find him – as soon as possible.'

Mary took in the situation at her leisure.

'But why not telephone?' she said.

Katharine immediately dropped all that she was holding; her strained expression relaxed, and exclaiming, 'Of course! Why didn't I think of that!' she seized the telephone receiver and gave her number. Mary looked at her steadily, and then left the room. At length Katharine heard, through all the superimposed weight of London, the mysterious sound of feet in her own house mounting to the little room, where she could almost see the pictures and the books; she listened with extreme intentness to the preparatory vibrations, and then established her identity.

'Has Mr Denham called?'

'Yes, miss.'

'Did he ask for me?'

'Yes. We said you were out, miss.'

'Did he leave any message?'

'No. He went away. About twenty minutes ago, miss.'

Katharine hung up the receiver. She walked the length of the room in such acute disappointment that she did not at first perceive Mary's absence. Then she called in a harsh and peremptory tone: 'Mary.'

Mary was taking off her outdoor things in the bedroom. She heard Katharine call her. 'Yes,' she said, 'I shan't be a moment.' But the moment prolonged itself, as if for some reason Mary found satisfaction in making herself not only tidy, but seemly and ornamented. A stage in her life had been accomplished in the last months which left its traces for ever upon her bearing. Youth, and the bloom of youth, had receded, leaving the purpose in her face to show itself in the hollower cheeks, the firmer lips, the eyes no longer spontaneously observing at random, but narrowed upon an end which was not near at hand. This woman was now a serviceable human being, mistress of her own destiny, and thus, by some combination of ideas, fit to be adorned with the dignity of silver chains and glowing brooches. She came in at her leisure and asked: 'Well, did you get an answer?'

'He has left Chelsea already,' Katharine replied.

'Still, he won't be home yet,' said Mary.

Katharine was once more irresistibly drawn to gaze upon an imaginary map of London, to follow the twists and turns of unnamed streets.

'I'll ring up his home and ask whether he's back.' Mary crossed to the telephone and, after a series of brief remarks, announced: 'No. His sister says he hasn't come back yet.'

'Ah!' She applied her ear to the telephone once more. 'They've had a message. He won't be back to dinner.'

'Then what is he going to do?'

Very pale, and with her large eyes fixed not so much upon Mary as upon vistas of unresponding blankness, Katharine addressed herself also not so much to Mary as to the unrelenting spirit which now appeared to mock her from every quarter of her survey.

After waiting a little time Mary remarked indifferently: 'I really don't know.' Slackly lying back in her armchair, she watched the little flames beginning to creep among the coals indifferently, as if they, too, were very distant and indifferent.

Katharine looked at her indignantly and rose.

'Possibly he may come here,' Mary continued, without altering the abstract tone of her voice. 'It would be worth your while to wait if you want to see him tonight.' She bent forward and touched the wood, so that the flames slipped in between the interstices of the coal.

Katharine reflected. 'I'll wait half an hour,' she said.

Mary rose, went to the table, spread out her papers under the green-shaded lamp and, with an action that was becoming a habit, twisted a lock of hair round and round in her fingers. Once she looked unperceived at her visitor, who never moved, who sat so still, with eyes so intent, that you could almost fancy that she was watching something, some face that never looked up at her. Mary found herself unable to go on writing. She turned her eyes away, but only to be aware of the presence of what Katharine looked at. There were ghosts in the room, and one, strangely and sadly, was the ghost of herself. The minutes went by.

'What would be the time now?' said Katharine at last. The half-hour was not quite spent.

'I'm going to get dinner ready,' said Mary, rising from her table.

'Then I'll go,' said Katharine.

'Why don't you stay? Where are you going?'

Katharine looked round the room, conveying her uncertainty in her glance.

'Perhaps I might find him,' she mused.

'But why should it matter? You'll see him another day.'

Mary spoke, and intended to speak, cruelly enough.

'I was wrong to come here,' Katharine replied.

Their eyes met with antagonism, and neither flinched.

'You had a perfect right to come here,' Mary answered.

A loud knocking at the door interrupted them. Mary went to open it, and returned with some note or parcel; Katharine looked away so that Mary might not read her disappointment.

'Of course you had a right to come,' Mary repeated, laying the note upon the table.

'No,' said Katharine. 'Except that when one's desperate one has a sort of right. I am desperate. How do I know what's happening to him now? He may do anything. He may wander about the streets all night. Anything may happen to him.'

She spoke with a self-abandonment that Mary had never seen in her.

'You know you exaggerate; you're talking nonsense,' she said roughly.

'Mary, I must talk – I must tell you – '

'You needn't tell me anything,' Mary interrupted her. 'Can't I see for myself?'

'No, no,' Katharine exclaimed. 'It's not that – '

Her look, passing beyond Mary, beyond the verge of the room and out beyond any words that came her way, wildly and passionately, convinced Mary that she, at any rate, could not follow such a glance to its end. She was baffled; she tried to think herself back again into the height of her love for Ralph. Pressing her fingers upon her eyelids, she murmured: 'You forget that I loved him too. I thought I knew him. I *did* know him.'

And yet, what had she known? She could not remember it any more. She pressed her eyeballs until they struck stars and suns into her darkness. She convinced herself that she was stirring among ashes. She desisted. She was astonished at her discovery. She did not love Ralph any more. She looked back dazed into the room, and her eyes rested upon the table with its lamp-lit papers. The steady radiance seemed for a second to have its counterpart within her; she shut her eyes; she opened them and looked at the lamp again; another love burnt in the place of the old one, or so, in a momentary glance of amazement, she guessed before the revelation was over and the old surroundings asserted themselves. She leant in silence against the mantelpiece.

'There are different ways of loving,' she murmured, half to herself, at length.

Katharine made no reply and seemed unaware of her words. She seemed absorbed in her own thoughts.

'Perhaps he's waiting in the street again tonight,' she exclaimed. 'I'll go now. I might find him.'

'It's far more likely that he'll come here,' said Mary, and Katharine, after considering for a moment, said: 'I'll wait another half-hour.'

She sank down into her chair again, and took up the same position which Mary had compared to the position of one watching an unseeing face. She watched, indeed, not a face, but a procession, not of people, but of life itself: the good and bad; the meaning; the past, the present and the future. All this seemed apparent to her, and she was not ashamed of her extravagance so much as exalted to one of the pinnacles of existence, where it behoved the world to do her homage. No one but she herself knew what it meant to miss Ralph Denham on that particular night; into this inadequate event crowded feelings that the great crises of life might have failed to call forth. She had missed him, and knew the bitterness of all failure; she desired him, and knew the torment of all passion. It did not matter what trivial accidents led to this culmination. Nor did she care how extravagant she appeared, nor how openly she showed her feelings.

When the dinner was ready Mary told her to come, and she came submissively, as if she let Mary direct her movements for her. They ate and drank together almost in silence, and when Mary told her to eat more, she ate more; when she was told to drink wine, she drank it. Nevertheless, beneath this superficial obedience, Mary knew that she was following her own thoughts unhindered. She was not inattentive so much as remote; she looked at once so unseeing and so intent upon some vision of her own that Mary gradually felt more than protective – she became actually alarmed at the prospect of some collision between Katharine and the forces of the outside world. Directly they had done, Katharine announced her intention of going.

'But where are you going to?' Mary asked, desiring vaguely to hinder her.

'Oh, I'm going home – no, to Highgate perhaps.'

Mary saw that it would be useless to try to stop her. All she could do was to insist upon coming too, but she met with no opposition; Katharine seemed indifferent to her presence. In a few minutes they were walking along the Strand. They walked so rapidly that Mary was deluded into the belief that Katharine knew where she was going. She herself was not attentive. She was glad of the movement along lamp-lit streets in the open air. She was fingering, painfully and with fear, yet with strange hope, too, the discovery which she had stumbled upon unexpectedly that night. She was free once more at the cost of a gift, the best, perhaps, that she could offer, but she was, thank heaven, in love no longer. She was tempted to spend the first instalment of her freedom in some dissipation; in the pit of the Coliseum,[96] for example, since they were now passing the door. Why not go in and celebrate her independence of the tyranny of love? Or, perhaps, the top of an omnibus bound for some remote place such as Camberwell, or Sidcup, or the Welsh Harp[97] would suit her better. She noticed these names painted on little boards for the first time for weeks. Or should she return to her room, and spend the night working out the details of a very enlightened and ingenious scheme? Of all possibilities this appealed to her most, and brought to mind the fire, the lamplight, the steady glow which had seemed lit in the place where a more passionate flame had once burnt.

Now Katharine stopped, and Mary woke to the fact that instead of having a goal she had evidently none. She paused at the edge of the crossing, and looked this way and that, and finally made as if in the direction of Haverstock Hill.

'Look here – where are you going?' Mary cried, catching her by the hand. 'We must take that cab and go home.' She hailed a cab and insisted that Katharine should get in, while she directed the driver to take them to Cheyne Walk.

Katharine submitted. 'Very well,' she said. 'We may as well go there as anywhere else.'

A gloom seemed to have fallen on her. She lay back in her corner, silent and apparently exhausted. Mary, in spite of her own preoccupation, was struck by her pallor and her attitude of dejection.

'I'm sure we shall find him,' she said more gently than she had yet spoken.

'It may be too late,' Katharine replied. Without understanding her, Mary began to pity her for what she was suffering.

'Nonsense,' she said, taking her hand and rubbing it. 'If we don't find him there we shall find him somewhere else.'

'But suppose he's walking about the streets – for hours and hours?' She leant forward and looked out of the window.

'He may refuse ever to speak to me again,' she said in a low voice, almost to herself.

The exaggeration was so immense that Mary did not attempt to cope with it, save by keeping hold of Katharine's wrist. She half expected that Katharine might open the door suddenly and jump out. Perhaps Katharine perceived the purpose with which her hand was held.

'Don't be frightened,' she said, with a little laugh. 'I'm not going to jump out of the cab. It wouldn't do much good after all.'

Upon this, Mary ostentatiously withdrew her hand.

'I ought to have apologised,' Katharine continued, with an effort, 'for bringing you into all this business; I haven't told you half, either. I'm no longer engaged to William Rodney. He is to marry Cassandra Otway. It's all arranged – all perfectly right . . . And after he'd waited in the streets for hours and hours, William made me bring him in. He was standing under the lamp-post watching our windows. He was perfectly white when he came into the room. William left us alone, and we sat and talked. It seems ages and ages ago, now. Was it last night? Have I been out long? What's the time?' She sprang forward to catch sight of a clock, as if the exact time had some important bearing on her case.

'Only half-past eight!' she exclaimed. 'Then he may be there still.' She leant out of the window and told the cabman to drive faster.

'But if he's not there, what shall I do? Where could I find him? The streets are so crowded.'

'We shall find him,' Mary repeated.

Mary had no doubt but that somehow or other they would find him. But suppose they did find him? She began to think of Ralph with a sort of strangeness, in her effort to understand how he could be capable of satisfying this extraordinary desire. Once more she thought herself back to her old view of him and could, with an effort, recall the haze which surrounded his figure, and the sense of confused, heightened exhilaration which lay all about his neighbourhood, so that for months at a time she had never exactly heard his voice or seen his face – or so it now seemed to her. The pain of her loss shot through her. Nothing would ever make up – not success, or happiness, or oblivion. But this pang was immediately followed by the assurance that now, at any rate, she knew the truth; and Katharine, she thought, stealing a look at her, did not know the truth; yes, Katharine was immensely to be pitied.

The cab, which had been caught in the traffic, was now liberated and sped on down Sloane Street. Mary was conscious of the tension with which Katharine marked its progress, as if her mind were fixed upon a point in front of them, and marked, second by second, their approach to it. She said nothing, and in silence Mary began to fix her mind, in sympathy at first, and later in forgetfulness of her companion, upon a point in front of them. She imagined a point distant as a low star upon the horizon of the dark. There for her too, for them both, was the goal for which they were striving, and the end for the ardours of their spirits was the same: but where it was, or what it was, or why she felt convinced that they were united in search of it, as they drove swiftly down the streets of London side by side, she could not have said.

'At last,' Katharine breathed, as the cab drew up at the door. She jumped out and scanned the pavement on either side. Mary, meanwhile, rang the bell. The door opened as Katharine assured herself that no one of the people within view had any likeness to Ralph. On seeing her, the maid said at once: 'Mr Denham called again, miss. He has been waiting for you for some time.'

Katharine vanished from Mary's sight. The door shut between them, and Mary walked slowly and thoughtfully up the street alone.

Katharine turned at once to the dining-room. But with her fingers upon the handle, she held back. Perhaps she realised that this was a moment which would never come again. Perhaps, for a second, it seemed to her that no reality could equal the imagination she had formed. Perhaps she was restrained by some vague fear or anticipation, which made her dread any exchange or interruption. But if these doubts and fears or this supreme bliss restrained her, it was only for a moment. In another second she had turned the handle and, biting her lip to control herself, she opened the door upon Ralph Denham. An extraordinary clearness of sight seemed to possess her on beholding him. So little, so single, so separate from all else he appeared, who had been the cause of these extreme agitations and aspirations. She could have laughed in his face. But, gaining upon this clearness of sight against her will, and to her dislike, was a flood of confusion, of relief, of certainty, of humility, of desire no longer to strive and to discriminate, yielding to which, she let herself sink within his arms and confessed her love.

Chapter 32

Nobody asked Katharine any questions next day. If cross-examined she might have said that nobody spoke to her. She worked a little, wrote a little, ordered the dinner, and sat, for longer than she knew, with her head on her hand piercing whatever lay before her, whether it was a letter or a dictionary, as if it were a film upon the deep prospects that revealed themselves to her kindling and brooding eyes. She rose once, and going to the bookcase, took out her father's Greek dictionary and spread the sacred pages of symbols and figures before her. She smoothed the sheets with a mixture of affectionate amusement and hope. Would other eyes look on them with her one day? The thought, long intolerable, was now just bearable.

She was quite unaware of the anxiety with which her movements were watched and her expression scanned. Cassandra was careful not to be caught looking at her, and their conversation was so prosaic that were it not for certain jolts and jerks between the sentences, as if the mind were kept with difficulty to the rails, Mrs Milvain herself could have detected nothing of a suspicious nature in what she overheard.

William, when he came in late that afternoon and found Cassandra alone, had a very serious piece of news to impart. He had just passed Katharine in the street and she had failed to recognise him.

'That doesn't matter with me, of course, but suppose it happened with somebody else? What would they think? They would suspect something merely from her expression. She looked – she looked' – he hesitated – 'like someone walking in her sleep.'

To Cassandra the significant thing was that Katharine had gone out without telling her, and she interpreted this to mean that she had gone out to meet Ralph Denham. But to her surprise William drew no comfort from this probability.

'Once throw conventions aside,' he began, 'once do the things that people don't do –' and the fact that you are going to meet a young man is no longer proof of anything, except, indeed, that people will talk.

Cassandra saw, not without a pang of jealousy, that he was extremely solicitous that people should not talk about Katharine, as if his interest in her were still proprietary rather than friendly. As they were both ignorant of Ralph's visit the night before they had not that reason to comfort themselves with the thought that matters were hastening to a crisis. These absences of Katharine's, moreover, left them exposed to interruptions which almost destroyed their pleasure in being alone together. The rainy evening made it impossible to go out; and, indeed, according to William's code, it was considerably more damning to be seen out of doors than surprised within. They were so much at the mercy of bells and doors that they could hardly talk of Macaulay with any conviction, and William preferred to defer the second act of his tragedy until another day.

Under these circumstances Cassandra showed herself at her best. She sympathised with William's anxieties and did her utmost to share them; but still, to be alone together, to be running risks together, to be partners in the wonderful conspiracy, was to her so enthralling that she was always forgetting discretion, breaking out into exclamations and admirations which finally made William believe that, although deplorable and upsetting, the situation was not without its sweetness.

When the door did open, he started, but braved the forthcoming revelation. It was not Mrs Milvain, however, but Katharine herself who entered, closely followed by Ralph Denham. With a set expression which showed what an effort she was making, Katharine encountered their eyes, and saying, 'We're not going to interrupt you,' she led Denham behind the curtain which hung in front of the room with the relics. This refuge was none of her willing, but confronted with wet pavements and only some belated museum or Tube station for shelter, she was forced, for Ralph's sake, to face the discomforts of her own house. Under the street lamps she had thought him looking both tired and strained.

Thus separated, the two couples remained occupied for some time with their own affairs. Only the lowest murmurs penetrated from one section of the room to the other. At length the maid came in to bring a message that Mr Hilbery would not be home for dinner. It was true that there was no need that Katharine should be informed, but William began to enquire Cassandra's opinion in such a way as to show that, with or without reason, he wished very much to speak to her.

From motives of her own Cassandra dissuaded him.

'But don't you think it's a little unsociable?' he hazarded. 'Why not do something amusing? – go to the play, for instance? Why not ask Katharine and Ralph, eh?' The coupling of their names in this manner caused Cassandra's heart to leap with pleasure.

'Don't you think they must be – ?' she began, but William hastily took her up.

'Oh, I know nothing about that. I only thought we might amuse ourselves, as your uncle's out.'

He proceeded on his embassy with a mixture of excitement and embarrassment which caused him to turn aside with his hand on the curtain, and to examine intently for several moments the portrait of a lady, optimistically said by Mrs Hilbery to be an early work of Sir Joshua Reynolds. Then, with some unnecessary fumbling, he drew aside the curtain, and with his eyes fixed upon the ground, repeated his message and suggested that they should all spend the evening at the play. Katharine accepted the suggestion with such cordiality that it was strange to find her of no clear mind as to the precise spectacle she wished to see. She left the choice entirely to Ralph and William, who, taking counsel fraternally over an evening paper, found themselves in agreement as to the merits of a music-hall. This being arranged, everything else followed easily and enthusiastically. Cassandra had never been to a music-hall. Katharine instructed her in the peculiar delights of an entertainment where Polar bears follow directly upon ladies in full evening dress, and the stage is alternately a garden of mystery, a milliner's band-box and a fried-fish shop in the Mile End Road. Whatever the exact nature of the programme that night, it fulfilled the highest purposes of dramatic art, so far, at least, as four of the audience were concerned.

No doubt the actors and the authors would have been surprised to learn in what shape their efforts reached those particular eyes and ears; but they could not have denied that the effect as a whole was tremendous. The hall resounded with brass and strings, alternately of enormous pomp and majesty, and then of sweetest lamentation. The reds and creams of the background, the lyres and harps and urns and skulls, the protuberances of plaster, the fringes of scarlet plush, the sinking and blazing of innumerable electric lights, could scarcely have been surpassed for decorative effect by any craftsman of the ancient or modern world.

Then there was the audience itself, bare-shouldered, tufted and garlanded in the stalls, decorous but festal in the balconies, and frankly fit for daylight and street life in the galleries. But, however they differed when looked at separately, they shared the same huge, lovable nature in the bulk, which murmured and swayed and quivered all the time the dancing and juggling and love-making went on in front of it, slowly laughed and reluctantly left off laughing, and applauded with a helter-skelter generosity which sometimes became unanimous and overwhelming. Once William saw Katharine leaning forward and clapping her hands with an abandonment that startled him. Her laugh rang out with the laughter of the audience.

For a second he was puzzled, as if this laughter disclosed something that he had never suspected in her. But then Cassandra's face caught his eye, gazing with astonishment at the buffoon, not laughing, too deeply intent and surprised to laugh at what she saw, and for some moments he watched her as if she were a child.

The performance came to an end, the illusion dying out first here and then there, as some rose to put on their coats, others stood upright to salute 'God Save the King', the musicians folded their music and encased their instruments, and the lights sank one by one until the house was empty, silent and full of great shadows. Looking back over her shoulder as she followed Ralph through the swing doors, Cassandra marvelled to see how the stage was already entirely without romance. But, she wondered, did they really cover all the seats in brown holland every night?

The success of this entertainment was such that before they separated another expedition had been planned for the next day. The next day was Saturday; therefore both William and Ralph were free to devote the whole afternoon to an expedition to Greenwich, which Cassandra had never seen, and Katharine confused with Dulwich. On this occasion Ralph was their guide. He brought them without accident to Greenwich.

What exigencies of state or fantasies of imagination first gave birth to the cluster of pleasant places by which London is surrounded is matter of indifference now that they have adapted themselves so admirably to the needs of people between the ages of twenty and thirty with Saturday afternoons to spend. Indeed, if ghosts have any interest in the affections of those who succeed them they must reap their richest harvests when the fine weather comes again and the lovers, the sightseers and the holiday-makers pour themselves out of trains and omnibuses into their old pleasure-grounds. It is true that they go, for the most part, unthanked by name, although upon this

occasion William was ready to give such discriminating praise as the
dead architects and painters received seldom in the course of the year.
They were walking by the riverbank, and Katharine and Ralph, lagging
a little behind, caught fragments of his lecture. Katharine smiled at
the sound of his voice; she listened as if she found it a little unfamiliar,
intimately though she knew it; she tested it. The note of assurance and
happiness was new. William was very happy. She learnt every hour
what sources of his happiness she had neglected. She had never asked
him to teach her anything; she had never consented to read Macaulay;
she had never expressed her belief that his play was second only to the
works of Shakespeare. She followed dreamily in their wake, smiling
and delighting in the sound which conveyed, she knew, the rapturous
and yet not servile assent of Cassandra.

Then she murmured, 'How can Cassandra – ' but changed her
sentence to the opposite of what she meant to say and ended, 'how
could she herself have been so blind?' But it was unnecessary to follow
out such riddles when the presence of Ralph supplied her with more
interesting problems, which somehow became involved with the little
boat crossing the river, the majestic and careworn City, and the steamers
homecoming with their treasury, or starting in search of it, so that
infinite leisure would be necessary for the proper disentanglement of
one from the other. He stopped, moreover, and began enquiring of an
old boatman as to the tides and the ships. In thus talking he seemed
different, and even looked different, she thought, against the river, with
the steeples and towers for background. His strangeness, his romance,
his power to leave her side and take part in the affairs of men, the
possibility that they should together hire a boat and cross the river, the
speed and wildness of this enterprise filled her mind and inspired her
with such rapture, half of love and half of adventure, that William and
Cassandra were startled from their talk, and Cassandra exclaimed, 'She
looks as if she were offering up a sacrifice! Very beautiful,' she added
quickly, though she repressed, in deference to William, her own wonder
that the sight of Ralph Denham talking to a boatman on the banks of
the Thames could move anyone to such an attitude of adoration.

That afternoon, what with tea and the curiosities of the Thames
tunnel[98] and the unfamiliarity of the streets, passed so quickly that the
only method of prolonging it was to plan another expedition for the
following day. Hampton Court was decided upon, in preference to
Hampstead, for though Cassandra had dreamt as a child of the brigands
of Hampstead, she had now transferred her affections completely and
for ever to William III.[99] Accordingly, they arrived at Hampton Court

about lunchtime on a fine Sunday morning. Such unity marked their expressions of admiration for the red-brick building that they might have come there for no other purpose than to assure each other that this palace was the stateliest palace in the world. They walked up and down the terrace, four abreast, and fancied themselves the owners of the place, and calculated the amount of good to the world produced indubitably by such a tenancy.

'The only hope for us,' said Katharine, 'is that William shall die, and Cassandra shall be given rooms as the widow of a distinguished poet.'

'Or – ' Cassandra began, but checked herself from the liberty of envisaging Katharine as the widow of a distinguished lawyer. Upon this, the third day of junketing, it was tiresome to have to restrain oneself even from such innocent excursions of fancy. She dared not question William; he was inscrutable; he never seemed even to follow the other couple with curiosity when they separated, as they frequently did, to name a plant, or examine a fresco. Cassandra was constantly studying their backs. She noticed how sometimes the impulse to move came from Katharine, and sometimes from Ralph; how, sometimes, they walked slow, as if in profound intercourse, and sometimes fast, as if in passionate. When they came together again nothing could be more unconcerned than their manner.

'We have been wondering whether they ever catch a fish . . . ' or, 'We must leave time to visit the Maze.' Then, to puzzle her further, William and Ralph filled in all interstices of mealtimes or railway journeys with perfectly good-tempered arguments; or they discussed politics, or they told stories, or they did sums together upon the backs of old envelopes to prove something. She suspected that Katharine was absent-minded, but it was impossible to tell. There were moments when she felt so young and inexperienced that she almost wished herself back with the silkworms at Stogdon House, and not embarked upon this bewildering intrigue.

These moments, however, were only the necessary shadow or chill which proved the substance of her bliss, and did not damage the radiance which seemed to rest equally upon the whole party. The fresh air of spring, the sky washed of clouds and already shedding warmth from its blue, seemed the reply vouchsafed by nature to the mood of her chosen spirits. These chosen spirits were to be found also among the deer, dumbly basking, and among the fish, set still in mid-stream, for they were mute sharers in a benignant state not needing any exposition by the tongue. No words that Cassandra could come by expressed the stillness, the brightness, the air of expectancy which lay upon the orderly beauty of the grass walks and gravel paths down which they went walking four abreast that Sunday afternoon. Silently the shadows of the trees lay across the broad sunshine; silence wrapped her heart in its folds. The quivering stillness of the butterfly on the half-opened flower, the silent grazing of the deer in the sun, were the sights her eye rested upon and received as the images of her own nature laid open to happiness and trembling in its ecstasy.

But the afternoon wore on, and it became time to leave the gardens. As they drove from Waterloo to Chelsea, Katharine began to have some compunction about her father, which, together with the opening of offices and the need of working in them on Monday, made it difficult to plan another festival for the following day. Mr Hilbery had taken their absence, so far, with paternal benevolence, but they could not trespass upon it indefinitely. Indeed, had they known it, he was already suffering from their absence, and longing for their return.

He had no dislike of solitude, and Sunday, in particular, was pleasantly adapted for letter-writing, paying calls, or a visit to his club. He was leaving the house on some such suitable expedition towards teatime when he found himself stopped on his own doorstep by his sister, Mrs Milvain. She should, on hearing that no one was at home, have withdrawn submissively, but instead she accepted his half-hearted invitation to come in, and he found himself in the melancholy position of being forced to order tea for her and sit in the drawing-room while she drank it. She speedily made it plain that she was only thus exacting because she had come on a matter of business. He was by no means exhilarated at the news.

'Katharine is out this afternoon,' he remarked. 'Why not come round later and discuss it with her – with us both, eh?'

'My dear Trevor, I have particular reasons for wishing to talk to you alone . . . Where is Katharine?'

'She's out with her young man, naturally. Cassandra plays the part of chaperone very usefully. A charming young woman that – a great favourite of mine.' He turned his stone between his fingers, and conceived different methods of leading Celia away from her obsession, which, he supposed, must have reference to the domestic affairs of Cyril as usual.

'With Cassandra,' Mrs Milvain repeated significantly. 'With Cassandra.'

'Yes, with Cassandra,' Mr Hilbery agreed urbanely, pleased at the diversion. 'I think they said they were going to Hampton Court, and I rather believe they were taking a protégé of mine, Ralph Denham, a very clever fellow, too, to amuse Cassandra. I thought the arrangement very suitable.' He was prepared to dwell at some length upon this safe topic, and trusted that Katharine would come in before he had done with it.

'Hampton Court always seems to me an ideal spot for engaged couples. There's the Maze, there's a nice place for having tea – I forget what they call it – and then, if the young man knows his business he contrives to take his lady upon the river. Full of possibilities – full. Cake, Celia?' Mr Hilbery continued. 'I respect my dinner too much, but that can't possibly apply to you. You've never observed that feast, so far as I can remember.'

Her brother's affability did not deceive Mrs Milvain; it slightly saddened her; she well knew the cause of it. Blind and infatuated as usual!

'Who is this Mr Denham?' she asked.

'Ralph Denham?' said Mr Hilbery, in relief that her mind had taken this turn. 'A very interesting young man. I've a great belief in him. He's an authority upon our mediaeval institutions, and if he weren't forced to earn his living he would write a book that very much wants writing – '

'He is not well off, then?' Mrs Milvain interposed.

'Hasn't a penny, I'm afraid, and a family more or less dependent on him.'

'A mother and sisters? – His father is dead?'

'Yes, his father died some years ago,' said Mr Hilbery, who was prepared to draw upon his imagination, if necessary, to keep Mrs Milvain supplied with facts about the private history of Ralph Denham since, for some inscrutable reason, the subject took her fancy.

'His father has been dead some time, and this young man had to take his place – '

'A legal family?' Mrs Milvain enquired. 'I fancy I've seen the name somewhere.'

Mr Hilbery shook his head. 'I should be inclined to doubt whether they were altogether in that walk of life,' he observed. 'I fancy that Denham once told me that his father was a corn merchant. Perhaps he said a stockbroker. He came to grief, anyhow, as stockbrokers have a way of doing. I've a great respect for Denham,' he added. The remark sounded to his ears unfortunately conclusive, and he was afraid that there was nothing more to be said about Denham. He examined the tips of his fingers carefully. 'Cassandra's grown into a very charming young woman,' he started afresh. 'Charming to look at, and charming to talk to, though her historical knowledge is not altogether profound. Another cup of tea?'

Mrs Milvain had given her cup a little push, which seemed to indicate some momentary displeasure. But she did not want any more tea.

'It is Cassandra that I have come about,' she began. 'I am very sorry to say that Cassandra is not at all what you think her, Trevor. She has imposed upon your and Maggie's goodness. She has behaved in a way that would have seemed incredible – in this house of all houses – were it not for other circumstances that are still more incredible.'

Mr Hilbery looked taken aback, and was silent for a second.

'It all sounds very black,' he remarked urbanely, continuing his examination of his fingernails. 'But I own I am completely in the dark.'

Mrs Milvain became rigid, and emitted her message in little short sentences of extreme intensity.

'Who has Cassandra gone out with? William Rodney. Who has Katharine gone out with? Ralph Denham. Why are they for ever meeting each other round street corners, and going to music-halls, and taking cabs late at night? Why will Katharine not tell me the truth when I question her? I understand the reason now. Katharine has entangled herself with this unknown lawyer; she has seen fit to condone Cassandra's conduct.'

There was another slight pause.

'Ah, well, Katharine will no doubt have some explanation to give me,' Mr Hilbery replied imperturbably. 'It's a little too complicated for me to take in all at once, I confess – and, if you won't think me rude, Celia, I think I'll be getting along towards Knightsbridge.'

Mrs Milvain rose at once.

'She has condoned Cassandra's conduct and entangled herself with Ralph Denham,' she repeated. She stood very erect with the dauntless air of one testifying to the truth regardless of consequences. She knew from past discussions that the only way to counter her brother's indolence and indifference was to shoot her statements at him in a compressed form once finally upon leaving the room. Having spoken thus, she restrained herself from adding another word, and left the house with the dignity of one inspired by a great ideal.

She had certainly framed her remarks in such a way as to prevent her brother from paying his call in the region of Knightsbridge. He had no fears for Katharine, but there was a suspicion at the back of his mind that Cassandra might have been, innocently and ignorantly, led into some foolish situation in one of their unshepherded dissipations. His wife was an erratic judge of the conventions; he himself was lazy;

and with Katharine absorbed, very naturally – Here he recalled, as
well as he could, the exact nature of the charge. 'She has condoned
Cassandra's conduct and entangled herself with Ralph Denham.' From
which it appeared that Katharine was *not* absorbed, or which of them
was it that had entangled herself with Ralph Denham? From this
maze of absurdity Mr Hilbery saw no way out until Katharine herself
came to his help, so that he applied himself, very philosophically on
the whole, to a book.

No sooner had he heard the young people come in and go upstairs
than he sent a maid to tell Miss Katharine that he wished to speak to
her in the study. She was slipping furs loosely on to the floor in the
drawing-room in front of the fire. They were all gathered round,
reluctant to part. The message from her father surprised Katharine,
and the others caught from her look, as she turned to go, a vague sense
of apprehension.

Mr Hilbery was reassured by the sight of her. He congratulated
himself, he prided himself, upon possessing a daughter who had a sense
of responsibility and an understanding of life profound beyond her
years. Moreover, she was looking today unusual; he had come to take
her beauty for granted; now he remembered it and was surprised by it.
He thought instinctively that he had interrupted some happy hour of
hers with Rodney, and apologised.

'I'm sorry to bother you, my dear. I heard you come in, and thought
I'd better make myself disagreeable at once – as it seems, unfortunately,
that fathers are expected to make themselves disagreeable. Now, your
Aunt Celia has been to see me; your Aunt Celia has taken it into her
head apparently that you and Cassandra have been – let us say a little
foolish. This going about together – these pleasant little parties – there's
been some kind of misunderstanding. I told her I saw no harm in it, but
I should just like to hear from yourself. Has Cassandra been left a little
too much in the company of Mr Denham?'

Katharine did not reply at once, and Mr Hilbery tapped the coal
encouragingly with the poker. Then she said, without embarrassment
or apology: 'I don't see why I should answer Aunt Celia's questions. I've
told her already that I won't.'

Mr Hilbery was relieved and secretly amused at the thought of the
interview, although he could not license such irreverence outwardly.

'Very good. Then you authorise me to tell her that she's been mistaken, and there was nothing but a little fun in it? You've no doubt,
Katharine, in your own mind? Cassandra is in our charge, and I don't
intend that people should gossip about her. I suggest that you should be

a little more careful in future. Invite me to your next entertainment.'

She did not respond, as he had hoped, with any affectionate or humorous reply. She meditated, pondering something or other, and he reflected that even his Katharine did not differ from other women in the capacity to let things be. Or had she something to say?

'Have you a guilty conscience?' he enquired lightly. 'Tell me, Katharine,' he said more seriously, struck by something in the expression of her eyes.

'I've been meaning to tell you for some time,' she said. 'I'm not going to marry William.'

'You're not going – !' he exclaimed, dropping the poker in his immense surprise. 'Why? When? Explain yourself, Katharine.'

'Oh, some time ago – a week, perhaps more.' Katharine spoke hurriedly and indifferently, as if the matter could no longer concern anyone.

'But may I ask – why have I not been told of this – what do you mean by it?'

'We don't wish to be married – that's all.'

'This is William's wish as well as yours?'

'Oh, yes. We agree perfectly.'

Mr Hilbery had seldom felt more completely at a loss. He thought that Katharine was treating the matter with curious unconcern; she scarcely seemed aware of the gravity of what she was saying; he did not understand the position at all. But his desire to smooth everything over comfortably came to his relief. No doubt there was some quarrel, some whimsey on the part of William, who, though a good fellow, was a little exacting sometimes – something that a woman could put right. But though he inclined to take the easiest view of his responsibilities, he cared too much for his daughter to let things be.

'I confess I find great difficulty in following you. I should like to hear William's side of the story,' he said irritably. 'I think he ought to have spoken to me in the first instance.'

'I wouldn't let him,' said Katharine. 'I know it must seem to you very strange,' she added. 'But I assure you, if you'd wait a little – until mother comes back.'

This appeal for delay was much to Mr Hilbery's liking. But his conscience would not suffer it. People were talking. He could not endure that his daughter's conduct should be in any way considered irregular. He wondered whether, in the circumstances, it would be better to wire to his wife, to send for one of his sisters, to forbid William the house, to pack Cassandra off home – for he was vaguely conscious of responsibilities in her direction, too. His forehead was becoming more and more wrinkled by the multiplicity of his anxieties, which he was sorely tempted to ask Katharine to solve for him, when the door opened and William Rodney appeared. This necessitated a complete change, not only of manner, but of position also.

'Here's William,' Katharine exclaimed, in a tone of relief. 'I've told father we're not engaged,' she said to him. 'I've explained that I prevented you from telling him.'

William's manner was marked by the utmost formality. He bowed very slightly in the direction of Mr Hilbery, and stood erect, holding one lapel of his coat, and gazing into the centre of the fire. He waited for Mr Hilbery to speak.

Mr Hilbery also assumed an appearance of formidable dignity. He had risen to his feet, and now bent the top part of his body slightly forward.

'I should like your account of this affair, Rodney – if Katharine no longer prevents you from speaking.'

William waited two seconds at least.

'Our engagement is at an end,' he said, with the utmost stiffness.

'Has this been arrived at by your joint desire?'

After a perceptible pause, William bent his head, and Katharine said, as if by an afterthought: 'Oh, yes.'

Mr Hilbery swayed to and fro, and moved his lips as if to utter remarks which remained unspoken.

'I can only suggest that you should postpone any decision until the effect of this misunderstanding has had time to wear off. You have now known each other – ' he began.

'There's been no misunderstanding,' Katharine interposed. 'Nothing at all.' She moved a few paces across the room, as if she intended to leave them. Her preoccupied naturalness was in strange contrast to her father's pomposity and to William's military rigidity. He had not once raised his eyes. Katharine's glance, on the other hand, ranged past the two gentlemen, along the books, over the tables, towards the door. She was paying the least possible attention, it seemed, to what was happening. Her father looked at her with a sudden clouding and troubling of his expression. Somehow his faith in her stability and sense was queerly shaken. He no longer felt that he could ultimately entrust her with the whole conduct of her own affairs after a superficial show of directing them. He felt, for the first time in many years, responsible for her.

'Look here, we must get to the bottom of this,' he said, dropping his formal manner and addressing Rodney as if Katharine were not present.

'You've had some difference of opinion, eh? Take my word for it, most people go through this sort of thing when they're engaged. I've seen more trouble come from long engagements than from any other form of human folly. Take my advice and put the whole matter out of your minds – both of you. I prescribe a complete abstinence from emotion. Visit some cheerful seaside resort, Rodney.'

He was struck by William's appearance, which seemed to him to indicate profound feeling resolutely held in check. No doubt, he reflected, Katharine had been very trying, unconsciously trying, and had driven him to take up a position which was none of his willing. Mr Hilbery certainly did not overrate William's sufferings. No minutes in his life had hitherto extorted from him such intensity of anguish. He was now facing the consequences of his insanity. He must confess himself entirely and fundamentally other than Mr Hilbery thought him. Everything was against him. Even the Sunday evening and the fire and the tranquil library scene were against him. Mr Hilbery's appeal to him as a man of the world was terribly against him. He was no longer a man of any world that Mr Hilbery cared to recognise. But some power compelled him, as it had compelled him to come downstairs, to make his stand here and now, alone and unhelped by anyone, without prospect of reward. He fumbled with various phrases; and then jerked out: 'I love Cassandra.'

Mr Hilbery's face turned a curious dull purple. He looked at his daughter. He nodded his head, as if to convey his silent command to her to leave the room; but either she did not notice it or preferred not to obey.

'You have the impudence – ' Mr Hilbery began, in a dull, low voice that he himself had never heard before, when there was a scuffling and exclaiming in the hall, and Cassandra, who appeared to be insisting against some dissuasion on the part of another, burst into the room.

'Uncle Trevor,' she exclaimed, 'I insist upon telling you the truth!' She flung herself between Rodney and her uncle, as if she sought to intercept their blows. As her uncle stood perfectly still, looking very large and imposing, and as nobody spoke, she shrank back a little, and looked first at Katharine and then at Rodney. 'You must know the truth,' she said, a little lamely.

'You have the impudence to tell me this in Katharine's presence?' Mr Hilbery continued, speaking with complete disregard of Cassandra's interruption.

'I am aware, quite aware – ' Rodney's words, which were broken in sense, spoken after a pause, and with his eyes upon the ground, nevertheless expressed an astonishing amount of resolution. 'I am quite aware what you must think of me,' he brought out, looking Mr Hilbery directly in the eyes for the first time.

'I could express my views on the subject more fully if we were alone,' Mr Hilbery returned.

'But you forget me,' said Katharine. She moved a little towards Rodney, and her movement seemed to testify mutely to her respect for him, and her alliance with him. 'I think William has behaved perfectly rightly, and, after all, it is I who am concerned – I and Cassandra.'

Cassandra, too, gave an indescribably slight movement which seemed to draw the three of them into alliance together. Katharine's tone and glance made Mr Hilbery once more feel completely at a loss, and in addition, painfully and angrily obsolete; but in spite of an awful inner hollowness he was outwardly composed.

'Cassandra and Rodney have a perfect right to settle their own affairs according to their own wishes; but I see no reason why they should do so either in my room or in my house . . . I wish to be quite clear on this point, however: you are no longer engaged to Rodney.'

He paused, and his pause seemed to signify that he was extremely thankful for his daughter's deliverance.

Cassandra turned to Katharine, who drew her breath as if to speak and checked herself; Rodney, too, seemed to await some movement on her part; her father glanced at her as if he half anticipated some further revelation. She remained perfectly silent. In the silence they heard distinctly steps descending the staircase, and Katharine went straight to the door.

'Wait,' Mr Hilbery commanded. 'I wish to speak to you – alone,' he added.

She paused, holding the door ajar.

'I'll come back,' she said, and as she spoke she opened the door and went out. They could hear her immediately speak to someone outside, though the words were inaudible.

Mr Hilbery was left confronting the guilty couple, who remained standing as if they did not accept their dismissal, and the disappearance of Katharine had brought some change into the situation. So, in his secret heart, Mr Hilbery felt that it had, for he could not explain his daughter's behaviour to his own satisfaction.

'Uncle Trevor,' Cassandra exclaimed impulsively, 'don't be angry, please. I couldn't help it; I do beg you to forgive me.'

Her uncle still refused to acknowledge her identity, and still talked over her head as if she did not exist.

'I suppose you have communicated with the Otways,' he said to Rodney grimly.

'Uncle Trevor, we wanted to tell you,' Cassandra replied for him. 'We waited – ' she looked appealingly at Rodney, who shook his head ever so slightly.

'Yes? What were you waiting for?' her uncle asked sharply, looking at her at last.

The words died on her lips. It was apparent that she was straining her ears as if to catch some sound outside the room that would come to her help. He received no answer. He listened, too.

'This is a most unpleasant business for all parties,' he concluded, sinking into his chair again, hunching his shoulders and regarding the flames. He seemed to speak to himself, and Rodney and Cassandra looked at him in silence.

'Why don't you sit down?' he said suddenly. He spoke gruffly, but the force of his anger was evidently spent, or some preoccupation had turned his mood to other regions. While Cassandra accepted his invitation, Rodney remained standing.

'I think Cassandra can explain matters better in my absence,' he said, and left the room, Mr Hilbery giving his assent by a slight nod of the head.

Meanwhile, in the dining-room next door, Denham and Katharine were once more seated at the mahogany table. They seemed to be continuing a conversation broken off in the middle, as if each remembered the precise point at which they had been interrupted, and was eager to go on as quickly as possible. Katharine, having interposed a short account of the interview with her father, Denham made no comment, but said: 'Anyhow, there's no reason why we shouldn't see each other.'

'Or stay together. It's only marriage that's out of the question,' Katharine replied.

'But if I find myself coming to want you more and more?'

'If our lapses come more and more often?'

He sighed impatiently, and said nothing for a moment.

'But at least,' he renewed, 'we've established the fact that my lapses are still in some odd way connected with you; yours have nothing to do with me. Katharine,' he added, his assumption of reason broken up by his agitation, 'I assure you that we are in love – what other people call love. Remember that night. We had no doubts whatever then. We were absolutely happy for half an hour. You had no lapse until the day after; I had no lapse until yesterday morning. We've been happy at intervals all day until I – went off my head, and you, quite naturally, were bored.'

'Ah,' she exclaimed, as if the subject chafed her, 'I can't make you understand. It's not boredom – I'm never bored. Reality – reality,' she ejaculated, tapping her finger upon the table as if to emphasise and perhaps explain her isolated utterance of this word. 'I cease to be real to you. It's the faces in a storm again – the vision in a hurricane. We come together for a moment and we part. It's my fault, too. I'm as bad as you are – worse, perhaps.'

They were trying to explain, not for the first time, as their weary gestures and frequent interruptions showed, what in their common language they had christened their 'lapses'; a constant source of distress to them, in the past few days, and the immediate reason why Ralph was on his way to leave the house when Katharine, listening anxiously, heard him and prevented him. What was the cause of these lapses? Either because Katharine looked more beautiful, or more strange, because she wore something different, or said something unexpected, Ralph's sense of her romance welled up and overcame him either into silence or into inarticulate expressions, which Katharine, with un-intentional but invariable perversity, interrupted or contradicted with some severity or assertion of prosaic fact. Then the vision disappeared, and Ralph expressed vehemently in his turn the conviction that he only loved her shadow and cared nothing for her reality. If the lapse was on her side it took the form of gradual detachment until she became completely absorbed in her own thoughts, which carried her away with such intensity that she sharply resented any recall to her companion's side. It was useless to assert that these trances were always originated by Ralph himself, however little in their later stages they had to do with him. The fact remained that she had no need of him and was very loath to be reminded of him. How, then, could they be in love? The fragmentary nature of their relationship was but too apparent.

Thus they sat depressed to silence at the dining-room table, oblivious of everything, while Rodney paced the drawing-room overhead in such agitation and exaltation of mind as he had never conceived possible, and Cassandra remained alone with her uncle. Ralph, at length, rose and walked gloomily to the window. He pressed close to the pane. Outside were truth and freedom and the immensity only to be apprehended by the mind in loneliness, and never communicated to another. What worse sacrilege was there than to attempt to violate what he perceived by seeking to impart it? Some movement behind him made him reflect that Katharine had the power, if she chose, to be in person what he dreamed of her spirit. He turned sharply to implore her help, when again he was struck cold by her look of distance, her expression of intentness upon some far object. As if conscious of his look upon her she rose and came to him, standing close by his side, and looking with him out into the dusky atmosphere. Their physical closeness was to him a bitter enough comment upon the distance between their minds. Yet distant as she was, her presence by his side transformed the world. He saw himself performing wonderful deeds of courage; saving the drowning, rescuing the forlorn. Impatient with this form of egotism, he could not shake off the conviction that somehow life was wonderful, romantic, a master worth serving so long as she stood there. He had no wish that she should speak; he did not look at her or touch her; she was apparently deep in her own thoughts and oblivious of his presence.

The door opened without their hearing the sound. Mr Hilbery looked round the room, and for a moment failed to discover the two figures in the window. He started with displeasure when he saw them, and observed them keenly before he appeared able to make up his mind to say anything. He made a movement finally that warned them of his presence; they turned instantly. Without speaking, he beckoned to Katharine to come to him, and, keeping his eyes from the region of the room where Denham stood, he shepherded her in front of him back to the study. When Katharine was inside the room he shut the study door carefully behind him as if to secure himself from something that he disliked.

'Now, Katharine,' he said, taking up his stand in front of the fire, 'you will, perhaps, have the kindness to explain – ' She remained silent. 'What inferences do you expect me to draw?' he said sharply . . . 'You tell me that you are not engaged to Rodney; I see you on what appear to be extremely intimate terms with another – with Ralph Denham. What am I to conclude? Are you,' he added, as she still said nothing, 'engaged to Ralph Denham?'

'No,' she replied.

His sense of relief was great; he had been certain that her answer would have confirmed his suspicions, but that anxiety being set at rest, he was the more conscious of annoyance with her for her behaviour.

'Then all I can say is that you've very strange ideas of the proper way to behave . . . People have drawn certain conclusions, nor am I surprised . . . The more I think of it the more inexplicable I find it,' he went on, his anger rising as he spoke. 'Why am I left in ignorance of what is going on in my own house? Why am I left to hear of these events for the first time from my sister? Most disagreeable – most upsetting. How I'm to explain to your Uncle Francis – but I wash my hands of it. Cassandra goes tomorrow. I forbid Rodney the house. As for the other young man, the sooner he makes himself scarce the better. After placing the most implicit trust in you, Katharine – ' He broke off, disquieted by the ominous silence with which his words were received, and looked at his daughter with the curious doubt as to her state of mind which he had felt before, for the first time, this evening. He perceived once more that she was not attending to what he said, but was listening, and for a moment he, too, listened, for sounds outside the room. His certainty that there was some understanding between Denham and Katharine returned, but with a most unpleasant suspicion that there was something illicit about it, as the whole position between the young people seemed to him gravely illicit.

'I'll speak to Denham,' he said, on the impulse of his suspicion, moving as if to go.

'I shall come with you,' Katharine said instantly, starting forward.

'You will stay here,' said her father.

'What are you going to say to him?' she asked.

'I suppose I may say what I like in my own house?' he returned.

'Then I go, too,' she replied.

At these words, which seemed to imply a determination to go – to go for ever, Mr Hilbery returned to his position in front of the fire, and began swaying slightly from side to side without for the moment making any remark.

'I understood you to say that you were not engaged to him,' he said at length, fixing his eyes upon his daughter.

'We are not engaged,' she said.

'It should be a matter of indifference to you, then, whether he comes here or not – I will not have you listening to other things when I am speaking to you!' he broke off angrily, perceiving a slight movement on her part to one side. 'Answer me frankly, what is your relationship with this young man?'

'Nothing that I can explain to a third person,' she said obstinately.

'I will have no more of these equivocations,' he replied.

'I refuse to explain,' she returned, and as she said it the front door banged to. 'There!' she exclaimed. 'He is gone!' She flashed such a look of fiery indignation at her father that he lost his self-control for a moment.

'For God's sake, Katharine, control yourself!' he cried.

She looked for a moment like a wild animal caged in a civilised dwelling-place. She glanced over the walls covered with books, as if for a second she had forgotten the position of the door. Then she made as if to go, but her father laid his hand upon her shoulder. He compelled her to sit down.

'These emotions have been very upsetting, naturally,' he said. His manner had regained all its suavity, and he spoke with a soothing assumption of paternal authority. 'You've been placed in a very difficult position, as I understand from Cassandra. Now let us come to terms; we will leave these agitating questions in peace for the present. Meanwhile, let us try to behave like civilised beings. Let us read Sir Walter Scott. What d'you say to *The Antiquary*, eh? or *The Bride of Lammermoor*?'

He made his own choice, and before his daughter could protest or make her escape, she found herself being turned by the agency of Sir Walter Scott into a civilised human being.

Yet Mr Hilbery had grave doubts, as he read, whether the process was more than skin-deep. Civilisation had been very profoundly and unpleasantly overthrown that evening; the extent of the ruin was still undetermined; he had lost his temper, a physical disaster not to be matched for the space of ten years or so; and his own condition urgently required soothing and renovating at the hands of the classics. His house was in a state of revolution; he had a vision of unpleasant encounters on the staircase; his meals would be poisoned for days to come; was literature itself a specific against such disagreeables? A note of hollowness was in his voice as he read.

Chapter 33

Considering that Mr Hilbery lived in a house which was accurately numbered in order with its fellows, and that he filled up forms, paid rent, and had seven more years of tenancy to run, he had an excuse for laying down laws for the conduct of those who lived in his house, and this excuse, though profoundly inadequate, he found useful during the interregnum of civilisation with which he now found himself faced. In obedience to those laws, Rodney disappeared; Cassandra was dispatched to catch the eleven-thirty on Monday morning; Denham was seen no more; so that only Katharine, the lawful occupant of the upper rooms, remained, and Mr Hilbery thought himself competent to see that she did nothing further to compromise herself. As he bade her good-morning next day he was aware that he knew nothing of what she was thinking, but, as he reflected with some bitterness, even this was an advance upon the ignorance of the previous mornings. He went to his study and wrote, tore up and wrote again a letter to his wife, asking her to come back on account of domestic difficulties which he specified at first, but in a later draft more discreetly left unspecified. Even if she started the very moment that she got it, he reflected, she would not be home till Tuesday night, and he counted lugubriously the number of hours that he would have to spend in a position of detestable authority alone with his daughter.

What was she doing now, he wondered, as he addressed the envelope to his wife. He could not control the telephone. He could not play the spy. She might be making any arrangements she chose. Yet the thought did not disturb him so much as the strange, unpleasant, illicit atmosphere of the whole scene with the young people the night before. His sense of discomfort was almost physical.

Had he known it, Katharine was far enough withdrawn, both physically and spiritually, from the telephone. She sat in her room with the dictionaries spreading their wide leaves on the table before her, and all the pages which they had concealed for so many years arranged in a pile. She worked with the steady concentration that is produced by the successful effort to think down some unwelcome thought by means of another thought. Having absorbed the unwelcome thought, her mind went on with additional vigour, derived from the victory; on a sheet of paper lines of figures and symbols frequently and firmly written down marked the different stages of its progress. And yet it was broad daylight; there were sounds of knocking and sweeping, which proved that living people were at work on the other side of the door, and the door, which could be thrown open in a second, was her only protection against the world. But she had somehow risen to be mistress in her own kingdom, assuming her sovereignty unconsciously.

Steps approached her unheard. It is true that they were steps that lingered, divagated and mounted with the deliberation natural to one past sixty whose arms, moreover, are full of leaves and blossoms; but they came on steadily, and soon a tap of laurel boughs against the door arrested Katharine's pencil as it touched the page. She did not move, however, and sat blank-eyed as if waiting for the interruption to cease. Instead, the door opened. At first, she attached no meaning to the moving mass of green which seemed to enter the room independently of any human agency. Then she recognised parts of her mother's face and person behind the yellow flowers and soft velvet of the palm-buds.

'From Shakespeare's tomb!'[100] exclaimed Mrs Hilbery, dropping the entire mass upon the floor, with a gesture that seemed to indicate an act of dedication. Then she flung her arms wide and embraced her daughter.

'Thank God, Katharine!' she exclaimed. 'Thank God!' she repeated.

'You've come back?' said Katharine, very vaguely, standing up to receive the embrace.

Although she recognised her mother's presence, she was very far from taking part in the scene, and yet felt it to be amazingly appropriate that her mother should be there, thanking God emphatically for unknown blessings, and strewing the floor with flowers and leaves from Shakespeare's tomb.

'Nothing else matters in the world!' Mrs Hilbery continued. 'Names aren't everything; it's what we feel that's everything. I didn't want silly, kind, interfering letters. I didn't want your father to tell me. I knew it from the first. I prayed that it might be so.'

'You knew it?' Katharine repeated her mother's words softly and vaguely, looking past her. 'How did you know it?' She began, like a child, to finger a tassel hanging from her mother's cloak.

'The first evening you told me, Katharine. Oh, and thousands of times – dinner-parties – talking about books – the way he came into the room – your voice when you spoke of him.'

Katharine seemed to consider each of these proofs separately. Then she said gravely: 'I'm not going to marry William. And then there's Cassandra – '

'Yes, there's Cassandra,' said Mrs Hilbery. 'I own I was a little grudging at first, but, after all, she plays the piano so beautifully. Do tell me, Katharine,' she asked impulsively, 'where did you go that evening she played Mozart, and you thought I was asleep?'

Katharine recollected with difficulty.

'To Mary Datchet's,' she remembered.

'Ah!' said Mrs Hilbery, with a slight note of disappointment in her voice. 'I had my little romance – my little speculation.' She looked at her daughter. Katharine faltered beneath that innocent and penetrating gaze; she flushed, turned away, and then looked up with very bright eyes.

'I'm not in love with Ralph Denham,' she said.

'Don't marry unless you're in love!' said Mrs Hilbery very quickly. 'But,' she added, glancing momentarily at her daughter, 'aren't there different ways, Katharine – different – ?'

'We want to meet as often as we like, but to be free,' Katharine continued.

'To meet here, to meet in his house, to meet in the street.' Mrs Hilbery ran over these phrases as if she were trying chords that did not quite satisfy her ear. It was plain that she had her sources of information, and, indeed, her bag was stuffed with what she called 'kind letters' from the pen of her sister-in-law.

'Yes. Or to stay away in the country,' Katharine concluded.

Mrs Hilbery paused, looked unhappy, and sought inspiration from the window.

'What a comfort he was in that shop – how he took me and found the ruins at once – how *safe* I felt with him – '

'Safe? Oh, no, he's fearfully rash – he's always taking risks. He wants to throw up his profession and live in a little cottage and write books, though he hasn't a penny of his own, and there are any number of sisters and brothers dependent on him.'

'Ah, he has a mother?' Mrs Hilbery enquired.

'Yes. Rather a fine-looking old lady, with white hair.' Katharine began to describe her visit, and soon Mrs Hilbery elicited the facts that not only was the house of excruciating ugliness, which Ralph bore without complaint, but that it was evident that everyone depended on him, and he had a room at the top of the house, with a wonderful view over London, and a rook.

'A wretched old bird in a corner, with half its feathers out,' she said, with a tenderness in her voice that seemed to commiserate the sufferings of humanity while resting assured in the capacity of Ralph Denham to alleviate them, so that Mrs Hilbery could not help exclaiming: 'But, Katharine, you *are* in love!' at which Katharine flushed, looked startled, as if she had said something that she ought not to have said, and shook her head.

Hastily Mrs Hilbery asked for further details of this extraordinary house, and interposed a few speculations about the meeting between Keats and Coleridge[101] in a lane, which tided over the discomfort of the moment, and drew Katharine on to further descriptions and in-discretions. In truth, she found an extraordinary pleasure in being thus free to talk to someone who was equally wise and equally benignant, the mother of her earliest childhood, whose silence seemed to answer questions that were never asked. Mrs Hilbery listened without making any remark for a considerable time. She seemed to draw her conclusions rather by looking at her daughter than by listening to her, and, if cross-examined, she would probably have given a highly inaccurate version of Ralph Denham's life-history except that he was penniless, fatherless, and lived at Highgate – all of which was much in his favour. But by means of these furtive glances she had assured herself that Katharine was in a state which gave her, alternately, the most exquisite pleasure and the most profound alarm.

She could not help ejaculating at last: 'It's all done in five minutes at a registry office nowadays, if you think the church service a little florid – which it is, though there are noble things in it.'

'But we don't want to be married,' Katharine replied emphatically, and added, 'Why, after all, isn't it perfectly possible to live together without being married?'

Again Mrs Hilbery looked discomposed, and, in her trouble, took up the sheets which were lying upon the table, and began turning them over this way and that, and muttering to herself as she glanced: 'A plus B minus C equals "x y z". It's so dreadfully ugly, Katharine. That's what I feel – so dreadfully ugly.'

Katharine took the sheets from her mother's hand and began shuffling them absent-mindedly together, for her fixed gaze seemed to show that her thoughts were intent upon some other matter.

'Well, I don't know about ugliness,' she said at length.

'But he doesn't ask it of you?' Mrs Hilbery exclaimed. 'Not that grave young man with the steady brown eyes?'

'He doesn't ask anything – we neither of us ask anything.'

'If I could help you, Katharine, by the memory of what I felt – '

'Yes, tell me what you felt.'

Mrs Hilbery, her eyes growing blank, peered down the enormously long corridor of days at the far end of which the little figures of herself and her husband appeared fantastically attired, clasping hands upon a moonlit beach, with roses swinging in the dusk.

'We were in a little boat going out to a ship at night,' she began. 'The sun had set and the moon was rising over our heads. There were lovely silver lights upon the waves and three green lights upon the steamer in the middle of the bay. Your father's head looked so grand against the mast. It was life, it was death. The great sea was round us. It was the voyage for ever and ever.'

The ancient fairytale fell roundly and harmoniously upon Katharine's ears. Yes, there was the enormous space of the sea; there were the three green lights upon the steamer; the cloaked figures climbed up on deck. And so, voyaging over the green and purple waters, past the cliffs and the sandy lagoons and through pools crowded with the masts of ships and the steeples of churches – here they were. The river seemed to have brought them and deposited them here at this precise point. She looked admiringly at her mother, that ancient voyager.

'Who knows,' exclaimed Mrs Hilbery, continuing her reveries, 'where we are bound for, or why, or who has sent us, or what we shall find – who knows anything, except that love is our faith – love – ' she crooned, and the soft sound beating through the dim words was heard by her daughter as the breaking of waves solemnly in order upon the vast shore that she gazed upon. She would have been content for her mother to repeat that word almost indefinitely – a soothing word when uttered by another, a riveting together of the shattered fragments of the world. But Mrs Hilbery, instead of repeating the word love, said pleadingly: 'And you won't think those ugly thoughts again, will you, Katharine?' at which words the ship which Katharine had been considering seemed to put into harbour and have done with its seafaring. Yet she was in great need, if not exactly of sympathy, of some form of advice, or, at least, of the opportunity of setting forth her problems before a third person so as to renew them in her own eyes.

'But then,' she said, ignoring the difficult problem of ugliness, 'you knew you were in love; but we're different. It seems,' she continued, frowning a little as she tried to fix the difficult feeling, 'as if something came to an end suddenly – gave out – faded – an illusion – as if when we think we're in love we make it up – we imagine what doesn't exist. That's why it's impossible that we should ever marry. Always to be finding the other an illusion, and going off and forgetting about them, never to be certain that you cared, or that he wasn't caring for someone not you at all, the horror of changing from one state to the other, being happy one moment and miserable the next – that's the reason why we can't possibly marry. At the same time,' she continued, 'we can't live without each other, because – ' Mrs Hilbery waited patiently for the sentence to be completed, but Katharine fell silent and fingered her sheet of figures.

'We have to have faith in our vision,' Mrs Hilbery resumed, glancing at the figures, which distressed her vaguely, and had some connection in her mind with the household accounts, 'otherwise, as you say – ' She cast a lightning glance into the depths of disillusionment which were, perhaps, not altogether unknown to her.

'Believe me, Katharine, it's the same for everyone – for me, too – for your father,' she said earnestly, and sighed. They looked together into the abyss and, as the elder of the two, she recovered herself first and asked: 'But where is Ralph? Why isn't he here to see me?'

Katharine's expression changed instantly.

'Because he's not allowed to come here,' she replied bitterly.

Mrs Hilbery brushed this aside.

'Would there be time to send for him before luncheon?' she asked.

Katharine looked at her as if, indeed, she were some magician. Once more she felt that instead of being a grown woman, used to advise and command, she was only a foot or two raised above the long grass and the little flowers and entirely dependent upon the figure of indefinite size whose head went up into the sky, whose hand was in hers, for guidance.

'I'm not happy without him,' she said simply.

Mrs Hilbery nodded her head in a manner which indicated complete understanding, and the immediate conception of certain plans for the future. She swept up her flowers, breathed in their sweetness, and, humming a little song about a miller's daughter,[102] left the room.

The case upon which Ralph Denham was engaged that afternoon was not apparently receiving his full attention, and yet the affairs of the late John Leake of Dublin were sufficiently confused to need all the care that a solicitor could bestow upon them, if the widow Leake and the five Leake children of tender age were to receive any pittance at all. But the appeal to Ralph's humanity had little chance of being heard today; he was no longer a model of concentration. The partition so carefully erected between the different sections of his life had been broken down, with the result that though his eyes were fixed upon the last Will and Testament, he saw through the page a certain drawing-room in Cheyne Walk.

He tried every device that had proved effective in the past for keeping up the partitions of the mind until he could decently go home; but a little to his alarm he found himself assailed so persistently, as if from outside, by Katharine, that he launched forth desperately into an imaginary interview with her. She obliterated a bookcase full of law reports, and the corners and lines of the room underwent a curious softening of outline like that which sometimes makes a room unfamiliar at the moment of waking from sleep. By degrees, a pulse or stress began to beat at regular intervals in his mind, heaping his thoughts into waves to which words fitted themselves, and without much consciousness of what he was doing, he began to write on a sheet of draft paper what had the appearance of a poem lacking several words in each line. Not many lines had been set down, however, before he threw away his pen as violently as if that were responsible for his misdeeds, and tore the paper into many separate pieces. This was a sign that Katharine had asserted herself and put to him a remark that could not be met poetically. Her remark was entirely destructive of poetry, since it was to the effect that poetry had nothing whatever to do with her; all her friends spent their lives in making up phrases, she said; all his feeling was an illusion, and next moment, as if to taunt him with his impotence, she had sunk into one of those dreamy states which took no account whatever of his existence. Ralph was roused by his passionate attempts to attract her attention to the fact that he was standing in the middle of his little private room in Lincoln's Inn Fields at a considerable distance from Chelsea. The physical distance increased his desperation. He began pacing in circles until the process sickened him, and then took a sheet of paper for the composition of a letter which, he vowed before he began it, should be sent that same evening.

It was a difficult matter to put into words; poetry would have done it better justice, but he must abstain from poetry. In an infinite number of half-obliterated scratches he tried to convey to her the possibility that although human beings are woefully ill-adapted for communication, still, such communion is the best we know; moreover, they make it possible for each to have access to another world independent of personal affairs, a world of law, of philosophy, or more strangely a world such as he had had a glimpse of the other evening when together they seemed to be sharing something, creating something, an ideal – a vision flung out in advance of our actual circumstances. If this golden rim were quenched, if life were no longer circled by an illusion (but was it an illusion after all?), then it would be too dismal an affair to carry to an end; so he wrote with a sudden spurt of conviction which made clear way for a space and left at least one sentence standing whole. Making every allowance for other desires, on the whole this conclusion appeared to him to justify their relationship. But the conclusion was mystical; it plunged him into thought. The difficulty with which even this amount was written, the inadequacy of the words, and the need of writing under them and over them others which, after all, did no better, led him to leave off before he was at ail satisfied with his production, and unable to resist the conviction that such rambling would never be fit for Katharine's eye. He felt himself more cut off from her than ever. In idleness, and because he could do nothing further with words, he began to draw little figures in the blank spaces, heads meant to resemble her head, blots fringed with flames meant to represent – perhaps the entire universe. From this occupation he was roused by the message that a lady wished to speak to him. He had scarcely time to run his hands through his hair in order to look as much like a solicitor as possible, and to cram his papers into his pocket, already overcome with shame that another eye should behold them, when he realised that his preparations were needless. The lady was Mrs Hilbery.

'I hope you're not disposing of somebody's fortune in a hurry,' she remarked, gazing at the documents on his table, 'or cutting off an entail at one blow, because I want to ask you to do me a favour. And Anderson won't keep his horse waiting. (Anderson is a perfect tyrant, but he drove my dear father to the Abbey the day they buried him.) I made bold to come to you, Mr Denham, not exactly in search of legal assistance (though I don't know who I'd rather come to, if I were in trouble), but in order to ask your help in settling some tiresome little domestic affairs that have arisen in my absence. I've been to Stratford-upon-Avon (I must tell you all about that one of these days), and there I got a letter from my sister-in-law, a dear kind goose who likes interfering with other people's children because she's got none of her own. (We're dreadfully afraid that she's going to lose the sight of one of her eyes, and I always feel that our physical ailments are so apt to turn into mental ailments. I think Matthew Arnold says something of the same kind about Lord Byron.)[103] But that's neither here nor there.'

The effect of these parentheses, whether they were introduced for that purpose or represented a natural instinct on Mrs Hilbery's part to embellish the bareness of her discourse, gave Ralph time to perceive that she possessed all the facts of their situation and was come, somehow, in the capacity of ambassador.

'I didn't come here to talk about Lord Byron,' Mrs Hilbery continued, with a little laugh, 'though I know that both you and Katharine, unlike other young people of your generation, still find him worth reading.' She paused. 'I'm so glad you've made Katharine read poetry, Mr Denham!' she exclaimed, 'and feel poetry, and look poetry! She can't talk it yet, but she will – oh, she will!'

Ralph, whose hand was grasped and whose tongue almost refused to articulate, somehow contrived to say that there were moments when he felt hopeless, utterly hopeless, though he gave no reason for this statement on his part.

'But you care for her?' Mrs Hilbery enquired.

'Good God!' he exclaimed, with a vehemence which admitted of no question.

'It's the Church of England service you both object to?' Mrs Hilbery enquired innocently.

'I don't care a damn what service it is,' Ralph replied.

'You would marry her in Westminster Abbey if the worst came to the worst?' Mrs Hilbery enquired.

'I would marry her in St Paul's Cathedral,' Ralph replied. His doubts upon this point, which were always roused by Katharine's presence, had vanished completely, and his strongest wish in the world was to be with her immediately, since every second he was away from her he imagined her slipping farther and farther from him into one of those states of mind in which he was unrepresented. He wished to dominate her, to possess her.

'Thank God!' exclaimed Mrs Hilbery. She thanked Him for a variety of blessings: for the conviction with which the young man spoke; and not least for the prospect that on her daughter's wedding-day the noble cadences, the stately periods, the ancient eloquence of the marriage service would resound over the heads of a distinguished congregation gathered together near the very spot where her father lay quiescent with the other poets of England. The tears filled her eyes; but she remembered simultaneously that her carriage was waiting, and with dim eyes she walked to the door. Denham followed her downstairs.

It was a strange drive. For Denham it was without exception the most unpleasant he had ever taken. His only wish was to go as straightly and quickly as possible to Cheyne Walk; but it soon appeared that Mrs Hilbery either ignored or thought fit to baffle this desire by interposing various errands of her own. She stopped the carriage at post-offices, and coffee-shops, and shops of inscrutable dignity where the aged attendants had to be greeted as old friends; and, catching sight of the dome of St Paul's above the irregular spires of Ludgate Hill, she pulled the cord impulsively, and gave directions that Anderson should drive them there. But Anderson had reasons of his own for discouraging afternoon worship, and kept his horse's nose obstinately towards the west. After some minutes, Mrs Hilbery realised the situation, and accepted it good-humouredly, apologising to Ralph for his disappointment.

'Never mind,' she said, 'we'll go to St Paul's another day, and it may turn out, though I can't promise that it *will*, that he'll take us past Westminster Abbey, which would be even better.'

Ralph was scarcely aware of what she went on to say. Her mind and body both seemed to have floated into another region of quick-sailing clouds rapidly passing across each other and enveloping everything in a vaporous indistinctness. Meanwhile he remained conscious of his own concentrated desire, his impotence to bring about anything he wished, and his increasing agony of impatience.

Suddenly Mrs Hilbery pulled the cord with such decision that even Anderson had to listen to the order which she leant out of the window to give him. The carriage pulled up abruptly in the middle of Whitehall before a large building dedicated to one of our government offices. In a second Mrs Hilbery was mounting the steps, and Ralph was left in too acute an irritation by this further delay even to speculate what errand took her now to the Board of Education. He was about to jump from the carriage and take a cab, when Mrs Hilbery reappeared talking genially to a figure who remained hidden behind her.

'There's plenty of room for us all,' she was saying. 'Plenty of room. We could find space for *four* of you, William,' she added, opening the door, and Ralph found that Rodney had now joined their company. The two men glanced at each other. If distress, shame, discomfort in its most acute form were ever visible upon a human face, Ralph could read them all expressed beyond the eloquence of words upon the face of his unfortunate companion. But Mrs Hilbery was either completely unseeing or determined to appear so. She went on talking; she talked, it seemed to both the young men, to someone outside, up in the air. She talked about Shakespeare, she apostrophised the human race, she proclaimed the virtues of divine poetry, she began to recite verses which broke down in the middle. The great advantage of her discourse was that it was self-supporting. It nourished itself until Cheyne Walk was reached upon half a dozen grunts and murmurs.

'Now,' she said, alighting briskly at her door, 'here we are!'

There was something airy and ironical in her voice and expression as she turned upon the doorstep and looked at them, which filled both Rodney and Denham with the same misgivings at having trusted their fortunes to such an ambassador; and Rodney actually hesitated upon the threshold and murmured to Denham: 'You go in, Denham. I . . . ' He was turning tail, but the door opening and the familiar look of the house asserting its charm, he bolted in on the wake of the others, and the door shut upon his escape. Mrs Hilbery led the way upstairs. She took them to the drawing-room. The fire burnt as usual, the little tables were laid with china and silver. There was nobody there.

'Ah,' she said, 'Katharine's not here. She must be upstairs in her room. You have something to say to her, I know, Mr Denham. You can find your way?' she vaguely indicated the ceiling with a gesture of her hand. She had become suddenly serious and composed, mistress in her own house. The gesture with which she dismissed him had a dignity that Ralph never forgot. She seemed to make him free with a wave of her hand to all that she possessed. He left the room.

The Hilberys' house was tall, possessing many storeys and passages with closed doors, all, once he had passed the drawing-room floor, unknown to Ralph. He mounted as high as he could and knocked at the first door he came to.

'May I come in?' he asked.

A voice from within answered, 'Yes.'

He was conscious of a large window, full of light, of a bare table, and of a long looking-glass. Katharine had risen, and was standing with some white papers in her hand, which slowly fluttered to the ground as she saw her visitor. The explanation was a short one. The sounds were inarticulate; no one could have understood the meaning save them—selves. As if the forces of the world were all at work to tear them asunder they sat, clasping hands, near enough to be taken even by the malicious eye of Time himself for a united couple, an indivisible unit.

'Don't move, don't go,' she begged of him, when he stooped to gather the papers she had let fall. But he took them in his hands and, giving her by a sudden impulse his own unfinished dissertation, with its mystical conclusion, they read each other's compositions in silence.

Katharine read his sheets to an end; Ralph followed her figures as far as his mathematics would let him. They came to the end of their tasks at about the same moment, and sat for a time in silence.

'Those were the papers you left on the seat at Kew,' said Ralph at length. 'You folded them so quickly that I couldn't see what they were.'

She blushed very deeply; but as she did not move or attempt to hide her face she had the appearance of someone disarmed of all defences, or Ralph likened her to a wild bird just settling with wings trembling to fold themselves within reach of his hand. The moment of exposure had been exquisitely painful – the light shed startlingly vivid. She had now to get used to the fact that someone shared her loneliness. The bewilderment was half shame and half the prelude to profound rejoicing. Nor was she unconscious that on the surface the whole thing must appear of the utmost absurdity. She looked to see whether Ralph smiled, but found his gaze fixed on her with such gravity that she turned to the belief that she had committed no sacrilege but enriched herself, perhaps immeasurably, perhaps eternally. She hardly dared steep herself in the infinite bliss. But his glance seemed to ask for some assurance upon another point of vital interest to him. It beseeched her mutely to tell him whether what she had read upon his confused sheet had any meaning or truth to her. She bent her head once more to the papers she held.

'I like your little dot with the flames round it,' she said meditatively.

Ralph nearly tore the page from her hand in shame and despair when he saw her actually contemplating the idiotic symbol of his most confused and emotional moments.

He was convinced that it could mean nothing to another, although somehow to him it conveyed not only Katharine herself but all those states of mind which had clustered round her since he first saw her pouring out tea on a Sunday afternoon. It represented by its circumference of smudges surrounding a central blot all that encircling glow which for him surrounded, inexplicably, so many of the objects of life, softening their sharp outline, so that he could see certain streets, books and situations wearing a halo [104] almost perceptible to the physical eye. Did she smile? Did she put the paper down wearily, condemning it not only for its inadequacy but for its falsity? Was she going to protest once more that he only loved the vision of her? But it did not occur to her that this diagram had anything to do with her. She said simply, and in the same tone of reflection: 'Yes, the world looks something like that to me too.'

He received her assurance with profound joy. Quietly and steadily there rose up behind the whole aspect of life that soft edge of fire which gave its red tint to the atmosphere and crowded the scene with shadows so deep and dark that one could fancy pushing farther into their density and still farther, exploring indefinitely. Whether there was any correspondence between the two prospects now opening before them they shared the same sense of the impending future, vast, mysterious, infinitely stored with undeveloped shapes which each would unwrap for the other to behold; but for the present the prospect of the future was enough to fill them with silent adoration. At any rate, their further attempts to communicate articulately were interrupted by a knock on the door, and the entrance of a maid who, with a due sense of mystery, announced that a lady wished to see Miss Hilbery, but refused to allow her name to be given.

When Katharine rose, with a profound sigh, to resume her duties, Ralph went with her, and neither of them formulated any guess, on their way downstairs, as to who this anonymous lady might prove to be. Perhaps the fantastic notion that she was a little black hunchback provided with a steel knife, which she would plunge into Katharine's heart, appeared to Ralph more probable than another, and he pushed first into the dining-room to avert the blow. Then he exclaimed, 'Cassandra!' with such heartiness at the sight of Cassandra Otway standing by the dining-room table that she put her finger to her lips and begged him to be quiet.

'Nobody must know I'm here,' she explained in a sepulchral whisper. 'I missed my train. I have been wandering about London all day. I can bear it no longer. Katharine, what am I to do?'

Katharine pushed forward a chair; Ralph hastily found wine and poured it out for her. If not actually fainting, she was very near it.

'William's upstairs,' said Ralph, as soon as she appeared to be recovered. 'I'll go and ask him to come down to you.' His own happiness had given him a confidence that everyone else was bound to be happy too. But Cassandra had her uncle's commands and anger too vividly in her mind to dare any such defiance. She became agitated and said that she must leave the house at once. She was not in a condition to go, had they known where to send her. Katharine's common sense, which had been in abeyance for the past week or two, still failed her, and she could only ask, 'But where's your luggage?' in the vague belief that to take lodgings depended entirely upon a sufficiency of luggage. Cassandra's reply, 'I've lost my luggage,' in no way helped her to a conclusion.

'You've lost your luggage,' she repeated. Her eyes rested upon Ralph, with an expression which seemed better fitted to accompany a profound thanksgiving for his existence or some vow of eternal devotion than a question about luggage. Cassandra perceived the look, and saw that it was returned; her eyes filled with tears. She faltered in what she was saying. She began bravely again to discuss the question of lodging when Katharine, who seemed to have communicated silently with Ralph, and obtained his permission, took her ruby ring from her finger and giving it to Cassandra, said: 'I believe it will fit you without any alteration.'

These words would not have been enough to convince Cassandra of what she very much wished to believe had not Ralph taken the bare hand in his and demanded: 'Why don't you tell us you're glad?' Cassandra was so glad that the tears ran down her cheeks. The certainty of Katharine's engagement not only relieved her of a thousand vague fears and self-reproaches, but entirely quenched that spirit of criticism which had lately impaired her belief in Katharine. Her old faith came back to her. She seemed to behold her with that curious intensity which she had lost; as a being who walks just beyond our sphere, so that life in their presence is a heightened process, illuminating not only ourselves but a considerable stretch of the surrounding world. Next moment she contrasted her own lot with theirs and gave back the ring.

'I won't take that unless William gives it me himself,' she said. 'Keep it for me, Katharine.'

'I assure you everything's perfectly all right,' said Ralph. 'Let me tell William – '

He was about, in spite of Cassandra's protest, to reach the door, when Mrs Hilbery, either warned by the parlour-maid or conscious with her usual prescience of the need for her intervention, opened the door and smilingly surveyed them.

'My dear Cassandra!' she exclaimed. 'How delightful to see you back again! What a coincidence!' she observed, in a general way. 'William is upstairs. The kettle boils over. Where's Katharine, I say?

I go to look, and I find Cassandra!' She seemed to have proved something to her own satisfaction, although nobody felt certain what thing precisely it was.

'I find Cassandra,' she repeated.

'She missed her train,' Katharine interposed, seeing that Cassandra was unable to speak.

'Life,' began Mrs Hilbery, drawing inspiration from the portraits on the wall apparently, 'consists in missing trains and in finding – ' But she pulled herself up and remarked that the kettle must have boiled completely over everything.

To Katharine's agitated mind it appeared that this kettle was an enormous kettle, capable of deluging the house in its incessant showers of steam, the enraged representative of all those household duties which she had neglected. She ran hastily up to the drawing-room, and the rest followed her, for Mrs Hilbery put her arm round Cassandra and drew her upstairs. They found Rodney observing the kettle with uneasiness but with such absence of mind that Katharine's catastrophe was in a fair way to be fulfilled. In putting the matter straight no greetings were exchanged, but Rodney and Cassandra chose seats as far apart as possible, and sat down with an air of people making a very temporary lodgment. Either Mrs Hilbery was impervious to their discomfort, or chose to ignore it, or thought it high time that the subject was changed, for she did nothing but talk about Shakespeare's tomb.

'So much earth and so much water and that sublime spirit brooding over it all,' she mused, and went on to sing her strange, half-earthly song of dawns and sunsets, of great poets, and the unchanged spirit of noble loving which they had taught, so that nothing changes, and one age is linked with another, and no one dies, and we all meet in spirit, until she appeared oblivious of anyone in the room. But suddenly her remarks seemed to contract the enormously wide circle in which they were soaring and to alight, airily and temporarily, upon matters of more immediate moment.

'Katharine and Ralph,' she said, as if to try the sound. 'William and Cassandra.'

'I feel myself in an entirely false position,' said William desperately, thrusting himself into this breach in her reflections. 'I've no right to be sitting here. Mr Hilbery told me yesterday to leave the house. I'd no intention of coming back again. I shall now – '

'I feel the same too,' Cassandra interrupted. 'After what Uncle Trevor said to me last night – '

'I have put you into a most odious position,' Rodney went on, rising from his seat, in which movement he was imitated simultaneously by Cassandra. 'Until I have your father's consent I have no right to speak to you – let alone in this house, where my conduct' – he looked at Katharine, stammered, and fell silent – 'where my conduct has been reprehensible and inexcusable in the extreme,' he forced himself to continue. 'I have explained everything to your mother. She is so generous as to try and make me believe that I have done no harm – you have convinced her that my behaviour, selfish and weak as it was – selfish and weak – ' he repeated, like a speaker who has lost his notes.

Two emotions seemed to be struggling in Katharine; one the desire to laugh at the ridiculous spectacle of William making her a formal speech across the tea-table, the other a desire to weep at the sight of something childlike and honest in him which touched her inexpressibly. To everyone's surprise she rose, stretched out her hand, and said: 'You've nothing to reproach yourself with – you've been always – ' but here her voice died away, and the tears forced themselves into her eyes, and ran down her cheeks, while William, equally moved, seized her hand and pressed it to his lips. No one perceived that the drawing-room door had opened itself sufficiently to admit at least half the person of Mr Hilbery, or saw him gaze at the scene round the tea-table with an expression of the utmost disgust and expostulation. He withdrew unseen. He paused outside on the landing trying to recover his self-control and to decide what course he might with most dignity pursue. It was obvious to him that his wife had entirely confused the meaning of his instructions. She had plunged them all into the most odious confusion. He waited a moment, and then, with much preliminary rattling of the handle, opened the door a second time. They had all regained their places; some incident of an absurd nature had now set them laughing and looking under the table, so that his entrance passed momentarily unperceived. Katharine, with flushed cheeks, raised her head and said: 'Well, that's my last attempt at the dramatic.'

'It's astonishing what a distance they roll,' said Ralph, stooping to turn up the corner of the hearth-rug.

'Don't trouble – don't bother. We shall find it – ' Mrs Hilbery began, and then saw her husband and exclaimed: 'Oh, Trevor, we're looking for Cassandra's engagement-ring!'

Mr Hilbery looked instinctively at the carpet. Remarkably enough, the ring had rolled to the very point where he stood. He saw the rubies touching the tip of his boot. Such is the force of habit that he could not refrain from stooping, with an absurd little thrill of pleasure at being the one to find what others were looking for, and, picking the

ring up, he presented it, with a bow that was courtly in the extreme, to
Cassandra. Whether the making of a bow released automatically feelings
of complaisance and urbanity, Mr Hilbery found his resentment
completely washed away during the second in which he bent and
straightened himself. Cassandra dared to offer her cheek and received
his embrace. He nodded with some degree of stiffness to Rodney and
Denham, who had both risen upon seeing him, and now altogether sat
down. Mrs Hilbery seemed to have been waiting for the entrance of her
husband, and for this precise moment in order to put to him a question
which, from the ardour with which she announced it, had evidently
been pressing for utterance for some time past.

'Oh, Trevor, please tell me, what was the date of the first performance
of *Hamlet*?'[105]

In order to answer her Mr Hilbery had to have recourse to the exact
scholarship of William Rodney, and before he had given his excellent
authorities for believing as he believed, Rodney felt himself admitted
once more to the society of the civilised and sanctioned by the authority
of no less a person than Shakespeare himself. The power of literature,
which had temporarily deserted Mr Hilbery, now came back to him,
pouring over the raw ugliness of human affairs its soothing balm, and
providing a form into which such passions as he had felt so painfully the
night before could be molded so that they fell roundly from the tongue
in shapely phrases, hurting nobody. He was sufficiently sure of his
command of language at length to look at Katharine and again at
Denham. All this talk about Shakespeare had acted as a soporific, or
rather as an incantation upon Katharine. She leaned back in her chair at
the head of the tea-table, perfectly silent, looking vaguely past them all,
receiving the most generalised ideas of human heads against pictures,
against yellow-tinted walls, against curtains of deep crimson velvet.
Denham, to whom he turned next, shared her immobility under his
gaze. But beneath his restraint and calm it was possible to detect a
resolution, a will, set now with unalterable tenacity, which made such
turns of speech as Mr Hilbery had at command appear oddly irrelevant.
At any rate, he said nothing. He respected the young man; he was a very
able young man; he was likely to get his own way. He could, he thought,
looking at his still and very dignified head, understand Katharine's
preference, and, as he thought this, he was surprised by a pang of acute
jealousy. She might have married Rodney without causing him a twinge.
This man she loved. Or what was the state of affairs between them? An
extraordinary confusion of emotion was beginning to get the better of
him, when Mrs Hilbery, who had been conscious of a sudden pause in

the conversation, and had looked wistfully at her daughter once or twice, remarked: 'Don't stay if you want to go, Katharine. There's the little room over there. Perhaps you and Ralph – '

'We're engaged,' said Katharine, waking with a start, and looking straight at her father. He was taken aback by the directness of the statement; he exclaimed as if an unexpected blow had struck him. Had he loved her to see her swept away by this torrent, to have her taken from him by this uncontrollable force, to stand by helpless, ignored? Oh, how he loved her! How he loved her! He nodded very curtly to Denham.

'I gathered something of the kind last night,' he said. 'I hope you'll deserve her.' But he never looked at his daughter, and strode out of the room, leaving in the minds of the women a sense, half of awe, half of amusement, at the extravagant, inconsiderate, uncivilised male, outraged somehow and gone bellowing to his lair with a roar which still sometimes reverberates in the most polished of drawing-rooms. Then Katharine, looking at the shut door, looked down again, to hide her tears.

Chapter 34

The lamps were lit; their lustre reflected itself in the polished wood; good wine was passed round the dinner-table; before the meal was far advanced civilisation had triumphed, and Mr Hilbery presided over a feast which came to wear more and more surely an aspect, cheerful, dignified, promising well for the future. To judge from the expression in Katharine's eyes it promised something – but he checked the approach to sentimentality. He poured out wine; he bade Denham help himself.

They went upstairs and he saw Katharine and Denham abstract themselves directly Cassandra had asked whether she might not play him something – some Mozart? some Beethoven? She sat down to the piano; the door closed softly behind them. His eyes rested on the closed door for some seconds unwaveringly, but, by degrees, the look of expectation died out of them, and, with a sigh, he listened to the music.

Katharine and Ralph were agreed with scarcely a word of discussion as to what they wished to do, and in a moment she joined him in the hall dressed for walking. The night was still and moonlit, fit for walking, though any night would have seemed so to them, desiring more than anything movement, freedom from scrutiny, silence, and the open air.

'At last!' she breathed, as the front door shut. She told him how she had waited, fidgeted, thought he was never coming, listened for the sound of doors, half expected to see him again under the lamp-post, looking at the house. They turned and looked at the serene front with its gold-rimmed windows, to him the shrine of so much adoration. In spite of her laugh and the little pressure of mockery on his arm, he would not resign his belief, but with her hand resting there, her voice quickened and mysteriously moving in his ears, he had not time – they had not the same inclination – other objects drew his attention.

How they came to find themselves walking down a street with many lamps, corners radiant with light, and a steady succession of motor-omnibuses plying both ways along it, they could neither of them tell; nor account for the impulse which led them suddenly to select one of these wayfarers and mount to the very front seat. After curving through streets of comparative darkness, so narrow that shadows on the blinds were pressed within a few feet of their faces, they came to one of those great knots of activity where the lights, having drawn close together, thin out again and take their separate ways. They were borne on until they saw the spires of the City churches pale and flat against the sky.

'Are you cold?' he asked, as they stopped by Temple Bar.

'Yes, I am rather,' she replied, becoming conscious that the splendid race of lights drawn past her eyes by the superb curving and swerving of the monster on which she sat was at an end. They had followed some such course in their thoughts too; they had been borne on, victors in the forefront of some triumphal car, spectators of a pageant enacted for them, masters of life. But standing on the pavement alone, this exaltation left them; they were glad to be alone together. Ralph stood still for a moment to light his pipe beneath a lamp.

She looked at his face isolated in the little circle of light.

'Oh, that cottage,' she said. 'We must take it and go there.'

'And leave all this?' he enquired.

'As you like,' she replied. She thought, looking at the sky above Chancery Lane, how the roof was the same everywhere; how she was now secure of all that this lofty blue and its steadfast lights meant to her: reality, was it, figures, love, truth?

'I've something on my mind,' said Ralph abruptly. 'I mean I've been thinking of Mary Datchet. We're very near her rooms now. Would you mind if we went there?'

She had turned before she answered him. She had no wish to see anyone tonight; it seemed to her that the immense riddle was answered; the problem had been solved; she held in her hands for one brief moment the globe which we spend our lives in trying to shape, round, whole and entire from the confusion of chaos. To see Mary was to risk the destruction of this globe.

'Did you treat her badly?' she asked rather mechanically, walking on.

'I could defend myself,' he said, almost defiantly. 'But what's the use, if one feels a thing? I won't be with her a minute,' he said. 'I'll just tell her – '

'Of course, you must tell her,' said Katharine, and now felt anxious for him to do what appeared to be necessary if he, too, were to hold his globe for a moment round, whole and entire.

'I wish – I wish – ' she sighed, for melancholy came over her and obscured at least a section of her clear vision. The globe swam before her as if obscured by tears.

'I regret nothing,' said Ralph firmly. She leant towards him almost as if she could thus see what he saw. She thought how obscure he still was to her, save only that more and more constantly he appeared to her a fire burning through its smoke, a source of life.

'Go on,' she said. 'You regret nothing – '

'Nothing – nothing,' he repeated.

'What a fire!' she thought to herself. She thought of him blazing splendidly in the night, yet so obscure that to hold his arm, as she held it, was only to touch the opaque substance surrounding the flame that roared upwards.

'Why nothing?' she asked hurriedly, in order that he might say more and so make more splendid, more red, more darkly intertwined with smoke this flame rushing upwards.

'What are you thinking of, Katharine?' he asked suspiciously, noticing her tone of dreaminess and the inapt words.

'I was thinking of you – yes, I swear it. Always of you, but you take such strange shapes in my mind. You've destroyed my loneliness. Am I to tell you how I see you? No, tell me – tell me from the beginning.'

Beginning with spasmodic words, he went on to speak more and more fluently, more and more passionately, feeling her leaning towards him, listening with wonder like a child, with gratitude like a woman. She interrupted him gravely now and then.

'But it was foolish to stand outside and look at the windows. Suppose William hadn't seen you. Would you have gone to bed?'

He capped her reproof with wonderment that a woman of her age could have stood in Kingsway looking at the traffic until she forgot.

'But it was then I first knew I loved you!' she exclaimed.

'Tell me from the beginning,' he begged her.

'No, I'm a person who can't tell things,' she pleaded. 'I shall say something ridiculous – something about flames – fires. No, I can't tell you.'

But he persuaded her into a broken statement, beautiful to him, charged with extreme excitement as she spoke of the dark red fire, and the smoke twined round it, making him feel that he had stepped over the threshold into the faintly lit vastness of another mind, stirring with shapes, so large, so dim, unveiling themselves only in flashes, and moving away again into the darkness, engulfed by it. They had walked by this time to the street in which Mary lived, and being engrossed by what they said and partly saw, passed her staircase without looking up. At this time of night there was no traffic and scarcely any foot-passengers, so that they could pace slowly without interruption, arm in arm, raising their hands now and then to draw something upon the vast blue curtain of the sky.

They brought themselves by these means, acting on a mood of profound happiness, to a state of clear-sightedness where the lifting of a finger had effect, and one word spoke more than a sentence. They lapsed gently into silence, travelling the dark paths of thought side by side towards something discerned in the distance which gradually possessed them both. They were victors, masters of life, but at the same time absorbed in the flame, giving their life to increase its brightness, to testify to their faith. Thus they had walked, perhaps, twice or three times up and down Mary Datchet's street before the recurrence of a light burning behind a thin, yellow blind caused them to stop without exactly knowing why they did so. It burned itself into their minds.

'That is the light in Mary's room,' said Ralph. 'She must be at home.' He pointed across the street. Katharine's eyes rested there too.

'Is she alone, working at this time of night? What is she working at?' she wondered. 'Why should we interrupt her?' she asked passionately. 'What have we got to give her? She's happy too,' she added. 'She has her work.' Her voice shook slightly, and the light swam like an ocean of gold behind her tears.

'You don't want me to go to her?' Ralph asked.

'Go, if you like; tell her what you like,' she replied.

He crossed the road immediately, and went up the steps into Mary's house. Katharine stood where he left her, looking at the window and expecting soon to see a shadow move across it; but she saw nothing; the blinds conveyed nothing; the light was not moved. It signalled to her across the dark street; it was a sign of triumph shining there for ever, not to be extinguished this side of the grave. She brandished her happiness as if in salute; she dipped it as if in reverence. 'How they burn!' she thought, and all the darkness of London seemed set with fires, roaring upwards; but her eyes came back to Mary's window and rested there satisfied. She had waited some time before a figure detached itself from the doorway and came across the road, slowly and reluctantly, to where she stood.

'I didn't go in – I couldn't bring myself,' he broke off. He had stood outside Mary's door unable to bring himself to knock; if she had come out she would have found him there, the tears running down his cheeks, unable to speak.

They stood for some moments, looking at the illuminated blind, an expression to them both of something impersonal and serene in the spirit of the woman within, working out her plans far into the night – her plans for the good of a world that none of them were ever to know. Then their minds jumped on and other little figures came by in procession, headed, in Ralph's view, by the figure of Sally Seal.

'Do you remember Sally Seal?' he asked. Katharine bent her head.

'Your mother and Mary?' he went on. 'Rodney and Cassandra? Old Joan up at Highgate?' He stopped in his enumeration, not finding it possible to link them together in any way that should explain the queer combination which he could perceive in them, as he thought of them. They appeared to him to be more than individuals; to be made up of many different things in cohesion; he had a vision of an orderly world.

'It's all so easy – it's all so simple,' Katherine quoted, remembering some words of Sally Seal's, and wishing Ralph to understand that she followed the track of his thought. She felt him trying to piece together in a laborious and elementary fashion fragments of belief, unsoldered and separate, lacking the unity of phrases fashioned by the old believers. Together they groped in this difficult region, where the unfinished, the unfulfilled, the unwritten, the unreturned, came together in their ghostly way and wore the semblance of the complete and the satisfactory. The future emerged more splendid than ever from this construction of the present. Books were to be written, and since books must be written in rooms, and rooms must have hangings, and outside the windows there must be land, and an horizon to that land, and trees perhaps, and a hill, they sketched a habitation for themselves upon the outline of great offices in the Strand and continued to make an account of the future upon the omnibus which took them towards Chelsea; and still, for both of them, it swam miraculously in the golden light of a large steady lamp.

As the night was far advanced they had the whole of the seats on the top of the omnibus to choose from, and the roads, save for an occasional couple, wearing even at midnight an air of sheltering their words from the public, were deserted. No longer did the shadow of a man sing to the shadow of a piano. A few lights in bedroom windows burnt but were extinguished one by one as the omnibus passed them.

They dismounted and walked down to the river. She felt his arm stiffen beneath her hand, and knew by this token that they had entered the enchanted region. She might speak to him, but with that strange tremor in his voice, those eyes blindly adoring, whom did he answer? What woman did he see? And where was she walking, and who was her companion? Moments, fragments, a second of vision, and then the flying waters, the winds dissipating and dissolving; then, too, the recollection from chaos, the return of security, the earth firm, superb and brilliant in the sun. From the heart of his darkness he spoke his thanksgiving; from a region as far, as hidden, she answered him. On a June night the nightingales sing, they answer each other across the plain; they are heard under the window among the trees in the garden. Pausing, they looked down into the river which bore its dark tide of waters, endlessly moving, beneath them. They turned and found themselves opposite the house. Quietly they surveyed the friendly place, burning its lamps either in expectation of them or because Rodney was still there talking to Cassandra. Katharine pushed the door half open and stood upon the threshold. The light lay in soft golden grains upon the deep obscurity of the hushed and sleeping household. For a moment they waited, and then loosed their hands. 'Good-night,' he breathed. 'Good-night,' she murmured back to him.

NOTES

Chapter 1

1 (p. 22) *Mr Fortescue, the eminent novelist*   Woolf had known Henry
James as a child; James is suggested here through Fortescue's
lengthy sentences and celebrity stature.

2 (p. 23) *He was an elderly man ... any result*   The description of Mr
Hilbery, while suggesting Sir Richmond Ritchie, Anne Thackeray's
husband, is closer in terms of profession to Sir Leslie Stephen,
Woolf's father, a distinguished biographer and man of letters.

3 (p. 25) *dear Mr Ruskin*   John Ruskin (1819–1900), poet, artist,
critic, social revolutionary and conservationist, was one of the
influential figures of the Victorian age.

4 (p. 25) *the great poet, Richard Alardyce*   Katharine's grandfather,
an imaginary figure, would have been a contemporary of Tennyson
or Browning, although his subject matter and poems are reminiscent
of the Romantic poets such as Keats or Shelley.

5 (p. 26) *Millington ... Havelock ... the Relief of Lucknow*   Millington
is an imaginary painter, ostensibly from a distinguished family, as
is Katharine's uncle who rode with Sir Henry Havelock to the
relief of Lucknow. General Sir Henry Havelock (1795–1857) led
the army which liberated Lucknow in India from occupation by
mutinous sepoys in September 1857.

Chapter 2

6 (p. 33) *college arms ... photographs of ... young men*   Ralph took a
degree at Oxford

7 (p. 38) *What is happiness?*   Part of a wider debate about the nature
of happiness within the novel and a question Woolf herself debated
in her diary (7 May 1919, *Diary*, I, p. 269).

Chapter 3

8 (p. 40) *Galton's 'Heriditary Genius'*   Sir Francis Galton (1822–1911),
founder of the science of eugenics, which he expounded in this
study. Galton was a friend of Woolf's father, Leslie Stephen, and
she read *Hereditary Genius* in 1905. Here Woolf satirises the
hereditarian mindset (see *A Concise Companion to Modernism*, David
Bradshaw [ed.], Blackwell, Oxford, 2002, p. 50).

9 (p. 42) *Poets' Corner*　the name given to a section of the south transept of Westminster Abbey. The first burial of a poet there was of Geoffrey Chaucer in 1400.

Chapter 4

10 (p. 49) *the army of workers*　In *On Being Ill* Woolf refers to the army of workers marching upright into battle. For Woolf it is those recumbent in illness that can momentarily halt time; having dropped out of the army of workers they can ponder on the sky, look at flowers.

11 (p. 49) *a Sussex down*　Woolf herself regularly stayed at Asheham on the Sussex downs but, although Mary imagines herself in a moonlit landscape of rolling hills, she is given no further connection to it.

12 (p. 50) *the great clock at Westminster*　Big Ben, whose quarterly chimes could be heard in the West End (as they are in *Mrs Dalloway*, 1925)

13 (p. 51) *I must reflect with Emerson that it's being and not doing that matters*　While Mary attributes this sentiment to Ralph Waldo Emerson (1803–82), the American philosopher, it is not a direct quotation. Meditative thought, for Emerson, because it puts us in tune with universal forces and laws, leads us to ways of being and doing that he believed are inherently right and successful.

14 (p. 56) *the death of the Duchess*　Rodney refers to John Webster's *The Duchess of Malfi* (1613). Mrs Hilbery reads the play in Chapter 30.

15 (p. 56) *'Insurance Bill'*　The 'Insurance Bill', part of the Liberals' welfare programme, proposed schemes for health and unemployment insurance financed from contributions. The bill was passed in 1911.

16 (p. 56) *if we had votes*　Women over thirty were given the vote in England in 1918 after years of pressure from, among others, Christabel and Emmeline Pankhurst. They and their followers were known as 'suffragettes'. The National Union of Women's Suffrage Societies, led by Millicent Fawcett, and known as the 'suffragists', favoured a more peaceful means of protest and it is to this sort of society that Mary belongs.

17 (p. 59) *ablative of mensa*　one of the first declensions to be learnt by a Latin student. Though Mary is inexperienced in the conduct of social relationships, by implication she is more experienced than Ralph.

Chapter 5

18 (p. 63) *With how sad steps . . . wan a face* Rodney misquotes the opening of Sonnet 31 from Philip Sidney's *Astrophil and Stella* (*c.* 1582):

> With how sad steps, O moon, thou climb'st the skies,
> How silently, and with how wan a face;

19 (p. 67) *Dr Johnson* Samuel Johnson (1709–84), a man of letters. His ghost is evoked to emphasise the eighteenth-century atmosphere of Rodney's chambers.

20 (p. 68) *The Baskerville Congreve* A rare edition of the work of the dramatist William Congreve (1670–1729) published in 1761. Woolf had planned to buy one (see *Diary*, I, pp. 126, 128).

21 (p. 69) *Sir Thomas Browne* (1605–82) admired greatly by Woolf and discussed in her essays 'Reading' and 'Sir Thomas Browne' (*Essays*, III, pp. 153–9, 368–71)

Chapter 6

22 (p. 74) *British Museum . . . Elgin Marbles . . . Ulysses* The British Museum houses the collection of classical Greek sculptures Lord Elgin brought back from Athens (1817). Among these was a head wearing a sailor's cap, thought to represent Ulysses. In *Jacob's Room* Fanny, who is in love with Jacob, associates this head with him.

23 (p. 75) *the housing of the poor, or the taxation of land values* In London, land values were increasing rapidly, and proposals to improve the conditions of the poor were closely linked to taxation of land.

24 (p. 76) *SRFR . . . SGS* abbreviations for the (fictional) societies with offices within the building

25 (p. 77) *Salford's affiliated* i.e. the society for suffrage reform at Salford (an industrial town in Lancashire) has joined the SGS. The societies designed to gain votes for women were not always united in their methods and were at times in rivalry with one another.

26 (p. 77) *Partridge . . . this Session* Partridge is an imaginary Member of Parliament who supports women's suffrage.

27 (p. 77) *COS* the Charity Organisation Society

28 (p. 79) *Punch* the humorous magazine which often had fun at the expense of the suffragettes

29 (p. 80) *Chénier and Hugo and Alfred de Musset* three French Romantic poets, André Chénier (1762–94), Victor Hugo (1802–85) and Alfred de Musset (1810–57)

30 (p. 81) *verse from the Psalms . . . the sowers and the seed*   The parable of the sower and the seed is not in the Psalms but in the Gospel of Luke 8:5–15.

31 (p. 83) *the Temple*   the Middle and Inner Temple, the Inns of Court

Chapter 7

32 (p. 87) *the name of the lady Hamlet was in love with*   Ophelia in Shakespeare's *Hamlet* of 1600. It is ironic that Mrs Hilbery turns to her daughter for assistance since Katharine claims she has not read Shakespeare.

33 (p. 90) *the periods of Henry Fielding*   the sentences of the English novelist Henry Fielding (1707–54); someone much admired by Leslie Stephen

Chapter 8

34 (p. 91) *teaching the young ladies of Bungay*   Bungay is a small town in Suffolk.

35 (p. 93) *the fruitful question as to whether Coleridge had wished to marry Dorothy Wordsworth*   The poet Samuel Taylor Coleridge (1772–1834) was a close friend of William Wordsworth and his sister Dorothy. There is no documentary evidence to suggest Coleridge ever wished to marry her.

36 (p. 94) *Isabella and the Pot of Basil*   Keats's poem *Isabella or The Pot of Basil* (1818)

37 (p. 94) *Ibsen and Butler*   Henrik Ibsen (1828–1906), dramatist, and Samuel Butler (1835–1902), novelist, had attacked the hypocrisy of bourgeois nineteenth-century society; see for example Butler's *The Way of All Flesh* (1903).

Chapter 9

38 (p. 97) *the Abbey*   Westminster Abbey

39 (p. 100) *the Empress*   Empress Eugénie, a frequent visitor to London, was the wife of Napoleon III.

40 (p. 102) *poor men's college . . . Kennington Road*   Kennington Road runs through a poor district of South London, not far from Waterloo Road, where Morley College was.

Chapter 10

41 (p. 108) *Tory to Radical*   a Tory, a Conservative Party supporter as opposed to a Radical, a left-wing Liberal Party supporter (the Labour Party was only just beginning to emerge in party politics)

42 (p. 109) *It's life that matters . . . all* Katharine quotes from Constance Garnett's translation of Fyodor Dostoevsky's *The Idiot* (1868), Part III, Chapter 5, final paragraph.

43 (p. 110) *Asquith . . . Suffrage Bill* Herbert Henry Asquith, Liberal Prime Minister (1908–16), was vehemently opposed to women's suffrage. However, male politicians were not all opposed to some form of female suffrage. A substantial section of the Liberal Party supported it, as did many leading Liberals, including Churchill, Lloyd George and Sir Edward Grey.

Chapter 12

44 (p. 122) *Romney* George Romney (1734–1802) was a famous English portrait painter. He wished to expand from portraiture into historical painting, a desire never fully achieved.

45 (p. 123) *Woking* Woking is located south-west of London in Surrey.

46 (p. 123) *De Quincey* Thomas de Quincey (1785–1859) was a journalist and autobiographer. His *Confessions of an Opium Eater* was a favourite of Woolf's mother (*Moments of Being*, p. 100). Edward, Baron Sackville West wrote a biography of him.

47 (p. 123) *your Belloc, your Chesterton, your Bernard Shaw* Hillaire Belloc (1870–1953), Catholic essayist, novelist and poet; G. K. Chesterton (1874–1936), Catholic essayist and polemicist. Bernard Shaw (1856–1950) berated Belloc and Chesterton for their socialist views and dubbed them the 'Chesterbelloc'.

48 (p. 125) *The Princess* A long narrative poem by poet laureate Alfred Tennyson (1809–92) published in 1847. It is the story of Ida, who founds a university for women, which is infiltrated by men in disguise and finally undermined and disbanded. Princess Ida, the head, despite her previous refusal of a marriage proposal, finally capitulates and marries the hero.

49 (p. 125) *Laura and Beatrice, Antigone and Cordelia* Laura was the muse and ideal of womanhood for Francesco Petrarch (1307–74), Italian poet and humanist. He first saw her in Avignon in 1327. Beatrice was the name Dante gave to a woman he fell in love with on first sighting her in the street and subsequently portrayed in his *Divine Comedy*. Antigone is the heroine of Sophocles' tragedy of that name. Cordelia, the youngest daughter of Lear in Shakespeare's *King Lear*, is the moral heroine of the play, sacrificing all and transcending the traditional female role for the sake of loyalty, love, and truth.

50 (p. 125) *Pendennis . . . Laura*   Ralph reminds her of George Warrington, friend of Arthur Pendennis in W. M. Thackeray's *The History of Pendennis*, published in monthly instalments from 1848–50. The heroine, Laura Bell, eventually marries Arthur rather than George. George Warrington, a cynical barrister, Pendennis's friend, warns him against marrying Fanny Bolton by telling him of his own unfortunate early marriage.

51 (p. 125) *George Eliot . . . and Lewes*   Mary Ann Evans (George Eliot, 1819–80), translator and novelist, lived with the writer George Henry Lewes (1817–78) from 1854. Lewes was estranged from his wife Agnes but could not obtain a divorce. By implication Laura, if she had so desired, could have established a relationship with Warrington despite his marriage.

52 (p. 126) *Swift*   Jonathan Swift (1667–1745), Irish cleric, satirist, novelist (author of *Gulliver's Travels*, 1726) and political pamphleteer. His satiric portraits of women could be unsparing.

53 (p. 126) *Millais . . . Ophelia*   Sir John Everett Millais (1829–96), painter. His painting of Ophelia floating down the stream is probably his best-known work. He was a founder, with Hunt and Rossetti, of the Pre-Raphaelite Brotherhood.

54 (p. 127) *To be imprisoned . . . The pendant world*   Shakespeare's *Measure for Measure*, Act III, Scene 2, ll. 126–8, the scene in which Claudio describes his fear of death to his sister Isabella

Chapter 14

55 (p. 138) *the Queen's Hall*   The Queen's Hall in Langham Place at the top of Regent Street opened in 1893 and became the principal concert hall in London with the closure of St James's Hall in 1905.

56 (p. 140) *Grafton Gallery . . . Titian*   a fashionable art gallery off Bond Street. Titian (1488/90–1576) was the greatest painter of the Venetian school, and famous for his deep colours, red especially.

57 (p. 142) *Flemish school*   The Flemish school of painting was a major movement in realist painting, running from the international Gothic period at the end of fourteenth century till the Baroque era in the seventeenth century. It mainly dealt with religious subjects and its exponents included Van Eyck and Van der Weyden.

58 (p. 142) *Rosalind, you know*   Rosalind, in Shakespeare's *As You Like It* (1599), spends much of the play dressed as a boy. She initiates a mock courtship with Orlando.

Chapter 15

59 (p. 143) *Disham* An imaginary village, possibly inspired by Wissett in Suffolk where Woolf stayed with her sister Vanessa in the summer of 1916.

60 (p. 147) *Edward's passion for Jorrocks* Edward's favourite reading is Robert Smith Surtees's (1803–64) *Jorrocks's Jaunts and Jollities, or the Exploits of that Renowned Sporting Citizen* (1838), a series of sketches about John Jorrocks, an eccentric London grocer turned Master of Foxhounds.

Chapter 16

61 (p. 157) *a barbarous clod of mud* Katharine refers to the star that led the Three Kings from the East to witness the birth of Jesus, but her thoughts of divinity quickly dissolve into evolutionary ones about man's animalistic origins.

Chapter 17

62 (p. 168) *palanquins* A palanquin (*palki*) is a covered sedan chair (or litter) for one, with a pole projecting before and behind, carried by two to six men in India and the Middle East.

63 (p. 171) *Simla* a town in the Indian state of Himachal Pradesh

Chapter 18

64 (p. 183) *I'm wandering about Lincoln looking for the ruins* Mrs Hilbery is searching for, and subsequently finds, Newport Arch, the best preserved of the many Roman remains in Lincoln. Newport Arch is a gateway across Bailgate, at the northern extremity of the old Roman city, where the Roman Ermine Street led north towards York.

65 (p. 191) *children in the fairy tale* the tale of the *Babes in the Wood*, abandoned by their parents and covered with leaves by the birds and animals. The expression has passed into popular usage, referring to inexperienced innocents encountering unawares any potentially dangerous or hostile situation.

Chapter 20

66 (p. 203) *the statue of one of London's heroes upon the Embankment* London's Victoria Embankment, near Mary's home, has a number of statues, including Sir Thomas Moore and Shakespeare.

67 (p. 204) *the statue of Francis, Duke of Bedford* a bronze monument by Sir Richard Westmacott (1775–1856), erected in 1809, celebrating the fifth duke stands in Russell Square, near Mary's offices

Chapter 21

68 (p. 208) *Westminster Gazette* The newspaper was established in
1893 and incorporated with the *Daily News* in 1928, which was
subsequently taken over by the *Daily Mail* in 1960. The *Westminster
Gazette* was known for publishing short stories and sketches.

Chapter 22

69 (p. 218) *Pope in preference to Dostoevsky* Alexander Pope (1688–
1744), Augustan poet, famous for his metrical skill, in contrast to
Dostoevsky, whose works are long and loosely structured

Chapter 23

70 (p. 234) *Kew*   the Royal Botanical Gardens in south-west London,
close to Richmond. The Gardens inspired her experimental short
story 'Kew Gardens' (written concurrently with *Night and Day*).

Chapter 24

71 (p. 236) *Anne Hathaway . . . Shakespeare's sonnets* Mrs Hilbery's
theory was originally put forward by Anne Thackeray Ritchie to
Samuel Butler in jest; one he failed to recognise. Woolf displaced
Shakespeare, not with Anne Hathaway, but with Shakespeare's
imaginary sister Judith, in *A Room of One's Own*.

72 (p. 237) *You'd be Rosalind – but you've a dash of the old nurse in you*
The 'old nurse' is Juliet's nurse in *Romeo and Juliet*.

73 (p. 237) *Hotspur*   The nickname of Henry Percy (1364–1403), son
of the Earl of Northumberland. He appears in Shakespeare's
Richard II and *Henry IV*. Both Katharine's resemblance to Rosalind
and William's to Hotspur in *Henry IV*, Part One, or *Henry V*, seem
flights of fancy.

74 (p. 239) *Harriet Martineau* Of French Huguenot extraction,
Harriet Martineau (1802–76) was more rigorously and formally
educated than most women of her time. She was a prolific writer
and strongly committed to various social causes; her major works
include *Illustrations of Political Economy*, 1832–4.

75 (p. 239) *William Cowper*   (1731–1800) poet and letter writer, author
of many works, including *The Task: A Poem in Six Books* (1785)

76 (p. 239) *Sir Walter Scott*   (1771–1832) Scott's novel *The Antiquary*
(1816) was a particular favourite of Woolf's family (see *Moments of
Being*, p. 86).

77 (p. 240) *the Indian Mutiny* The sepoy mutiny against British rule
broke out in Meerut in 1857, and after initial success was contained
by the British army in 1858.

78 (p. 241) *living in the Cromwell Road*   a street in South Kensington, largely occupied by gentlefolk reduced to poor circumstances

79 (p. 244) *the white slip*   a white waistcoat worn under a dinner suit

Chapter 25

80 (p. 254) *like a ship in full sail*   reminiscent of Mirabell's words announcing the arrival of Mrs Millamant in William Congreve's *The Way of the World* (1700): 'Here she comes i'faith full sail, with her fan spread and streamers out, and a shoal of fools for tenders' (Act II, Scene 5).

81 (p. 254) *the ducal castle*   Syon House, home of the Duke of Northumberland. The lion is the ducal badge.

Chapter 26

82 (p. 268) *The Idiot . . . War and Peace*   Here the allusion to Dostoevsky's novel is countered with one to Tolstoy's great realist Russian masterpiece (1864–9).

83 (p. 272) *Trelawney's Recollections of Shelley*   Edward John Trelawney (1792–1881) recovered Shelley's drowned body and wrote a memoir of the poet's last days, *Records of Shelley, Byron and the Author* (1858).

84 (p. 273) *Society for the Education of Democracy*   Mr Basnett's society is possibly a derivation from the Social Democratic Federation, a socialist society founded as the Democratic Federation in 1881 and renamed in 1884. It was led by H. M. Hyndman (1842–1921), a former conservative journalist and stockbroker who claimed Marx as his inspiration without obtaining recognition from his mentor. In 1911 it became the British Socialist Party.

Chapter 27

85 (p. 280) *Hertford House*   Hertford House in Manchester Square is home to the Wallace Collection, works of art collected in the eighteenth and nineteenth centuries by the first four marquesses of Hertford and Sir Richard Wallace, the son of the 4th Marquess. It was bequeathed to the public by Sir Richard's widow, Lady Wallace, in 1897.

86 (p. 280) *Bechstein Hall*   A concert hall in Wigmore Street, built by the German piano firm Bechstein in 1901; it was sold in 1917 and reopened the same year as Wigmore Hall.

87 (p. 289) *Newnham*   women's college at Cambridge University

88 (p. 289) *no Greek at mealtimes*   Hester is learning Latin; Joan shows her ignorance by supposing *amo* to be Greek.

89 (p. 289) *Salvation Army*   an evangelising body with a military-style
    organisation, founded in East London in 1865 by William and
    Catharine Booth. The name Salvation Army was adopted in 1878.

90 (p. 294) *Dictionary of National Biography*   Woolf's father Sir Leslie
    Stephen was editor of this vast publication from 1882 to 1891,
    when the editorship was taken over by Sidney Lee. Katharine's
    father spends much of his time working out trivial details of the
    biographies of Byron and Shelley, and he is perhaps a comic
    caricature of Woolf's father.

Chapter 28

91 (p. 297) *quinine*   a white powder with medicinal properties obtained
    from the bark of the cinchona tree, found in the Andes mountain
    range of Ecuador and Peru. Quinine was introduced into Europe
    around 1640.

92 (p. 301) *an odd image . . . of a lighthouse*   The 'beam' of steadfastness
    set against the storm of emotion figured as birds dashed against the
    windows recurs throughout the remaining chapters and later in *To
    the Lighthouse* (1927).

Chapter 31

93 (p. 327) *the History of England by Lord Macaulay*   Thomas Babington
    Macaulay (1800–59), politician and historian, author of the *History
    of England* in 5 volumes (1849–61). This work by her 'beloved
    Macaulay' was read and enjoyed by Woolf (see *Passionate Apprentice*,
    p. 87).

94 (p. 332) *Bradshaw's*   George Bradshaw's (1801–53) Railway Guides
    were timetables published monthly, the first issue having appeared
    in December 1841. By the time of his death the railway guides had
    become a national institution.

95 (p. 336) *an ABC shop*   The initials stood for the Aerated Bread
    Company, founded in 1862 by Dr John Dauglish, whose tearooms
    around London provided single women with somewhere to sit
    alone.

96 (p. 342) *the Coliseum*   The London Coliseum in St Martin's Lane
    is now home to the English National Opera Company. It was
    originally built as a variety theatre.

97 (p. 342) *the Welsh Harp*   The Welsh Harp Reservoir (opened in
    1838), named after the Old Welsh Harp Inn (demolished in 1971),
    is in Neasden in the north-west of London.

Chapter 32

98   (p. 349) *The Thames tunnel*   The first tunnel ever to be built
     beneath a large body of water runs between Rotherhithe and
     Wapping. Opened to the public in March 1843, it was built by
     Marc Isambard Brunel and his son Isambard Kingdom Brunel for
     pedestrian use. Converted to rail in the 1860s, it is still used by
     London Underground trains.

99   (p. 349) *Hampton Court . . . Hampstead . . . William III*   Hampton
     Court is a palace on the Thames, south-west of London. Built in
     the sixteenth century it was later renovated by William III who
     resided there and commissioned Sir Christopher Wren to remodel
     it. Woolf visited there on 5 July 1903 (see *Passionate Apprentice*, pp.
     172–5).

Chapter 33

100 (p. 364) *From Shakespeare's tomb*   Shakespeare's tomb is inside
     Holy Trinity Church but Woolf takes liberties here to visualise it
     as out of doors so that Mrs Hilbery can bring back flowers and
     branches from it.

101 (p. 366) *The meeting between Keats and Coleridge*   The only meeting
     between Keats and Coleridge took place in a Highgate Lane on 11
     April 1819.

102 (p. 369) *a little song about a miller's daughter*   possibly a popular
     song of the day or perhaps Mrs Hilbery is humming the words to
     Tennyson's (1809–92) poem 'The Miller's Daughter'

103 (p. 371) *Matthew Arnold says something . . . about Lord Byron*
     Matthew Arnold (1822–88), critic, educationist and poet, in his
     preface to his own selection of *Poetry of Byron* (1881), refers to
     Byron's shortcomings as a poet, and mentions his physical deformity
     and melancholy temperament, but without making any explicit link
     between them.

104 (p. 375) *that encircling glow . . . a halo*   In Woolf's essay 'Modern
     Novels', composed shortly after the completion of *Night and Day*,
     life is figured as ' the semi-transparent envelope, or luminous halo,
     surrounding us from the beginning of consciousness to the end'
     (*Essays*, III, p. 33).

105 (p. 379) *the date of the first performance of Hamlet*   It is believed that
     Hamlet was first performed between 1600 and 1601.

JACOB'S ROOM

Jacob's Room

—————◆—————

VIRGINIA WOOLF

A novel by
VIRGINIA WOOLF
first published in 1922

INTRODUCTION

> Sounding at the same moment as the bell, her son's voice
> mixed life and death inextricably, exhilaratingly.   [p. 428]

Jacob's Room shows an acute sense of the contemporary in contrast with
the heavily retrospective concerns of Woolf's *Night and Day*. *Jacob's
Room* is not about the protagonist Jacob in the way Woolf's subsequent
novel, *Mrs Dalloway*, is about Clarissa Dalloway. Rather, it is a book
about the mental and physical space occupied by Jacob Flanders, the
metaphorical and metaphysical 'room' that is his, whether his literal
room at Cambridge or in Lamb's Conduit Street, or, at another level,
Cambridge, London, Paris or Greece, or, on yet another level, the
metaphysical rooms nourished by Shakespeare, Homer and Byron. The
rooms remain when he does not, in the sense that the novel is about life
and the absence of life.

Woolf's representation of Jacob Flanders in *Jacob's Room* is of a young
man who dies an untimely death in war, his surname announcing his
ultimate destiny. The voice of the narrator lures us to the grave; the
sadness and pessimism pervading the novel are rooted in the recognition
of death as central to the whole edifice of Imperial culture; a society
that socially and culturally seemed drawn to war. The novel is concerned
with pre-First World War England viewed from a post-war perspective.
Jacob's surname recalls John McCrae's poem 'In Flanders Fields' which
first appeared in *Punch* in 1915 and, according to Paul Fussell, 'became
the most popular poem of the war':[1]

> In Flanders fields, the poppies blow,
> Between the crosses row on row
> [...]
> We are the Dead. Short days ago

---

[1]   *The Great War and Modern Memory*, p. 248. See Bibliography for full details.
Hereafter the name of the critic and/or the page number will appear in
brackets after the quotation.

We lived, felt dawn, saw sunset glow,
Loved and were loved, and now we lie,
In Flanders fields.

Jacob's Room can be seen as a rejoinder to McCrae's poem. Woolf depicts Jacob as both representative and victim of the social values which led Edwardian society into war. Critical of the inability of the press to communicate the war's brutality, she concluded her 1917 story 'The Mark on the Wall' with an anonymous figure announcing, ' "I'm going out to buy a newspaper [...] Though it's no good buying newspapers . . . Nothing ever happens. Curse this war; God damn this war!" ' (*Complete Shorter Fiction*, p. 83).[2] The story of the war, as Woolf well knew, was reflected in the faces of the wounded soldiers who had returned from the Somme, Passchendaele and Gallipoli. It is only fitting then that Jacob's life comes to an end in a manner altogether unheroic, in a death indistinguishable from thousands of others.

Katherine Mansfield, when reviewing Woolf's previous novel, *Night and Day*, for the *Athenaeum*, had criticised it for its refusal to engage with the war:

We had thought that this [pre-war] world was vanished for ever, that it was impossible to find on the great ocean of literature a ship that was unaware of what has been happening. Yet here is *Night and Day* fresh, new and exquisite, a novel in the tradition of the English novel. In the midst of our admiration it makes us feel old and chill: we had never thought to look upon its like again![3]

As Julia Briggs asserts: 'Mansfield did not know, and Woolf could not admit to herself, that in order to write *Night and Day* at all, she had withdrawn into the apparently stable, pre-war world where it seemed as if individuals could still decide for themselves what shape their lives might take – the war had interrupted all such expectations' (p. 86). With the coming of conscription in 1916 no one could call their lives their own, and the shadows of war were everywhere as 'The Mark on the Wall' and 'Kew Gardens' had registered. As she anticipates, *Jacob's Room* is the culmination of 'mark on the wall, K[ew]. G[ardens]. & unwritten novel taking hands & dancing in unity' (26 January 1920, *Diary*, II, p. 14). The discoveries made through writing these short pieces provided Woolf, alongside Mansfield's critical review, with the impetus to employ

---

2   hereafter *CSF*

3   Clare Hanson (ed.), *The Critical Writings of Katherine Mansfield*, p. 59

the experimental new techniques on a full-length work of fiction. *Jacob's Room*, published in 1922, 'marks', to use the words of Quentin Bell, 'the beginning of [Woolf's] maturity and her fame'.[4] This novel traces Woolf's discovery of how 'to say something in [her] own voice' (26 July 1922, *Diary*, II, p. 186). E. M. Forster put it this way:

> *Jacob's Room* [...] comes as a tremendous surprise. The impossible has occurred. The style closely resembles that of 'Kew Gardens' [...] The break with *Night and Day* and even with *The Voyage Out* is complete. A new type of fiction has swum into view.[5]

There is a consciousness of an immitigable sadness at the back of life reaching out from this novel. 'The human soul', Woolf suggests, 'orientates itself afresh every now & then. It is doing so now. No one can see it whole therefore [...] life has to be faced: to be rejected; then accepted on new terms with rapture' (*Letters*, II, 25 December 1922, pp. 598–9). *Jacob's Room* is often regarded as an elegy for Woolf's brother Thoby, but it can also be seen as an elegy for a lost generation of young men, for an age and for a world view that had altered for ever.[6] While late Victorian social conventions made grief an increasingly private matter, the post-war modernist aesthetics had foregrounded public experience, anger and outrage. Woolf's novel is more than a cultural critique, however, because its subtle discursive formations represent not simply Jacob's history, nor simply the histories of his generation, but the incongruous threads of life, random episodes that weave and interconnect, providing a sense of a fragmentary world.

It is the juxtaposition of seemingly irrelevant details in the difficult task of distinguishing the post-war world, narrating it in all of its indistinction, in its trivial or unheroic details, that marks Woolf's achievement in *Jacob's Room*. Presented in a series of episodes loosely strung together, the narrative calls for him as does his brother Archer in the opening pages: ' "Ja–cob! Ja–cob!" ' (p. 421), and his friend

---

4   Quentin Bell, *Virginia Woolf*, II, p. 88; 1922 also saw the publication of Joyce's *Ulysses* and Eliot's *The Waste Land*.

5   Robin Majumdar and Allen McLaurin (eds), *Virginia Woolf: The Critical Heritage*, p. 174

6   Thoby died in 1906, having contracted typhoid on a trip to Greece. Lytton Strachey wrote to Woolf (9 October 1922): 'Jacob I think is very successful – in a most remarkable and original way. Of course I see something of Thoby in him, as I suppose was intended' (Leonard Woolf and James Strachey [eds], *Virginia Woolf & Lytton Strachey Letters*, pp. 103–4).

Bonamy on the last: ' "Jacob! Jacob!" cried Bonamy, standing by the window' (p. 548). Jacob remains mysterious, opaque, an unknowing victim of the darkness at the heart of the cultural edifice while sharing in its illusions and enjoying its privileges. The identity of Jacob is always kept tantalisingly out of reach: 'what remains is mostly a matter of guesswork. Yet over him we hang, vibrating' (p. 471). In the words of David Bradshaw:[7]

> just as Betty Flanders looks down Dods Hill to see 'the whole of Scarborough from one end to the other laid out flat like a puzzle' (p. 428), so the vigilant reader finds herself, happily, in a similar position. There is plenty to observe, much to admire, bits to baffle over, missing pieces to infuriate, and no chance of ever being satisfied, for long, by any single solution.

From the vantage point of the essayist-narrator, an important characteristic of the narration and of Woolf's experimentation with form and voice, we are provided in *Jacob's Room* with a kaleidoscope of private and public scenes. The narrator can be seen, as Bishop observes,[8] as the novel's 'voice', its breath and spirit, its sensibility and intelligence, its soul and psyche, seeing into 'the cavern of mystery' that is Jacob. However, if this is a novel concerned with the social forces that shape characters' internal reality it would follow that the form of the narrative as well as the content would reflect and criticise those forces. In such a highly parodic novel, narration is not the monologue of a unitary voice, but the interplay of the many voices whose dialogue constructs the cultural edifice within which Jacob moves.

Both a paean to pre-war England and an elegy on its demise, *Jacob's Room* avoids 'strict representation' (*Letters*, II, 23 November 1922, p. 588). The war and Jacob's death are largely elided, assumed rather than accommodated, read into that which he leaves behind. As Ruth Gruber noted, 'The whole war is suggested in one line, almost obscured by its very simplicity. " 'The Kaiser', the far-away voice remarked in Whitehall, 'received me in audience' " ' (p. 546). Big Ben has struck five on the afternoon of 4 August 1914, and the far-away voice alluded to here is the voice of Prime Minister Asquith, announcing war to the other gentlemen in the cabinet. Later, the war breaks out, but as a distant echo; Jacob's death, sudden, unmotivated, is only suggested by the

---

7 David Bradshaw, 'Winking, Buzzing, Carpet-Beating: Reading *Jacob's Room*', p. 28
8 Edward, L. Bishop, 'The Subject in *Jacob's Room*', p. 166

desolation of his room. The room, once teeming with Jacob's presence, is suddenly replete with his absence.

Jacob is, indeed, first drawn to our attention by his absence: 'Well, if Jacob doesn't want to play [...] Where *is* that tiresome little boy?' (p. 421) Jacob is at once an elusive being that no net of words can capture and a puppet of fate, one of the war dead, a ghost. As Christine Froula suggests, 'Jacob dies in the gap between a founding ideal of European civilization – summed up as "Greek myth" or "illusion" – and modern barbarity' (p. 64). Presented in glimpses, and filtered through a third-person narrator, Jacob's story is of an unknowable self. Like a cubist portrait he is a disembodied assortment of shapes suggesting a complete image, yet remaining disjointed none the less. Jacob's absence over-shadows his presence and, as the narrator advises: 'It is no use trying to sum people up. One must follow hints, not exactly what is said, nor yet entirely what is done' (p. 439).

The play between absence and presence, between erasure and dis-course, is also established in *Jacob's Room* from the beginning with the opening blot on Betty Flanders' page: 'but the blot had spread [...] "if Jacob doesn't want to play" – what a horrid blot!' (p. 421) Betty's letter, like Jacob, is blotted out, evoking the poignancy, the mixture of sorrow, irony and regret that surrounds the defeat of young promise. As Clare Hanson points out, Betty Flanders' letter is 'linked with bodily fluids', bearing, as a mark of weakness or of woe, the 'horrid blot' made by her tears, which spreads and contaminates the page (p. 47). Humans are insubstantial and fragile; even Archer's heart-rending cry for his brother seems disembodied as he calls out the name ' "Ja–cob" ' three times in a voice of 'extraordinary sadness' (p. 422). At the end of the novel Jacob is absent once more, his tenuous presence in his empty room barely suggested through the wind rustling the leaves outside the window, a creaking chair, and finally and most poignantly Jacob's empty shoes held aloft by his mother as she exclaims: ' "What am I to do with these [...]?" ' (p. 548)

Why Shoes?

Shoes may seem an unlikely topic to dwell on, but they feature prominently in Woolf's fictional worlds. In her short story 'Kew Gardens', for example, Simon reminisces on the occasion when, fifteen years ago, he visited the gardens with Lily: 'All the time I spoke I saw her shoe and when it moved impatiently I knew without looking up what she was going to say: the whole of her seemed to be in her shoe'

(*CSF*, pp. 84–5). Feet, for the dwarf in 'Street Haunting', are 'the most important part of the whole person', as she tries on shoe after shoe:

> She sent for shoe after shoe; she tried on pair after pair [...] She was thinking that, after all, feet are the most important part of the whole person; women, she said to herself, have been loved for their feet alone. Seeing nothing but her feet, she imagined perhaps that the rest of her body was of a piece with those beautiful feet.
>
> [*The Death of the Moth and Other Essays*, p. 24]

Shoes take on an even greater significance in *Jacob's Room* where, apart from Jacob's empty shoes at the end of the novel, there are 'shoes with red tassels' (p. 508), 'silver-buckled shoes' (p. 501), 'pale men in muddy boots' (p. 442), and 'great boots march[ing] under the gowns' (p. 439). Just as in 'The Lady in the Looking Glass: A Reflection', where '[o]ne must put oneself in her shoes' (*CSF*, p. 218), we are asked to step inside Jacob's shoes, and use them as the key to the whole novel. They serve as material reminders of Jacob's body, a body that will not return and be buried at home, unlike his father whose tombstone read: ' "Merchant of this city" [...] though why Betty Flanders had chosen so to call him when, as many still remembered, he had only sat behind an office window for three months [...] Had he, then, been nothing?' (p. 427–8) The tombstone is one of a 'thousand white stones', a memorial for a husband and father 'who had gone out duck-shooting and refused to change his boots' (p. 427), foreshadowing the muddy fields of Flanders. Jacob's shoes contain his bodily imprint, casting them as a temporary private memorial in the absence of a lasting tombstone. The poignant portrayal of Jacob's shoes is emblematic of discarded body parts and of the suffering of the soldiers in the trenches, 'many' of whom, as in Wilfred Owen's 'Dulce et Decorum Est', 'had lost their boots/But limped on, blood-shod'.[9] I also dwell on Jacob's shoes because the image 'chillingly presages the horrors to come in the next war', atrocities still inconceivable in Woolf's time.[10] The words of the Yiddish poet Moses Schulstein, referring to mass genocide, could equally apply:

> We are the shoes,
> We are the last witnesses,
> We are shoes from grandchildren and grandfathers.
> From Prague, Paris and Amsterdam.

9 Wilfred Owen, 'Dulce et Decorum Est', *The Poems of Wilfred Owen*, p. 14, ll. 5–6
10 Ravit Reichman, *Novel: A Forum on Fiction*, Vol. 36/3, p. 417

And because we are only made of fabric and leather
And not of blood and flesh,
Each one of us avoided the Hellfire [11]

Here the shoes bear witness to the decomposition of a people under the Nazis.[12] The shoes' very presence signals the absence of those humans who once wore them, their materiality a metonymy[13] for a corporeality obliterated. The shoes as 'remains' stand in for, or take the place of, bodies now lost. The piles of empty shoes signal for the reader or viewer the enormity of the loss by metonymically materialising what has been rendered immaterial. The shoes of the war dead do indeed cry out.

Jacob's shoes are a signifier of both presence and absence; while the reader is given to understand that Jacob has died in France, his shoes remain as the trace of the feet which moulded them, a grotesque sloughed-off skin, a death cast. The shoes as remainder serve as revenant; as spectral reminder of absence. They become, in Jacques Derrida's words, 'the anonymous, lightened, voided support [...] of an absent subject whose name returns to haunt the open form'.[14] Jacob's shoes create a ghostly effect, as one seeks to restitute them, to render them to their rightful owner, as we wonder what it all amounts to, shoes and young men, objects and subjects, as the ghost of a shape answers the tapping of leaves outside and Bonamy's silent cry of anguish, " 'Jacob! Jacob!' " (p. 548); his death stands for that of a generation.

The empty shoes (or boots) appear especially grotesque and poignant, since Jacob is often seen walking in the novel, hiking up Olympian Hills, or climbing the path leading to the Acropolis, never doubting for a moment that he will get somewhere: ' "What for? What for?" Jacob never asked himself any such questions, to judge by the way he laced his boots' (p. 537). One of the few moments in *Jacob's Room* when Jacob

---

11 from 'I Saw a Mountain', translated by Mindelle Majsman and Bea Stadtler, quoted in Michael Berenbaum, *The World Must Know: The History of the Holocaust as Told in the United States Holocaust Memorial Museum*, pp. 145–7. This poem is printed above the huge pile of shoes in the Holocaust Museum in Washington DC.

12 See Ellen Carol Jones's chapter 'Empty Shoes', in *Footnotes: On Shoes*, Shari Benstock and Suzanne Ferriss (eds), pp. 197–232. She considers shoes – in photographs, paintings, poems and survivor testimonies from the Holocaust.

13 Metonymy is a figure of speech that works by association and in which an attribute of the thing itself is used to represent the whole.

14 Jacques Derrida, *The Truth in Painting*, p. 265

becomes intensely alive is in a passage where the prose mimetically
echoes the sound of footsteps, just as the narration itself keeps taking us
back to the young man's room – though in the end we find nothing
there; the feet have vanished:

> He went back to his rooms, and being the only man who walked at
> that moment back to his rooms, his footsteps rang out, his figure
> loomed large. Back from the Chapel, back from the Hall, back from
> the Library, came the sound of his footsteps, as if the old stone
> echoed with magisterial authority: 'The young man – the young
> man – the young man – back to his rooms.'   [p. 451]

Shoes (or boots) tell us where a person has been and where he or she
wants to go; they tell us the story of who people are and who they
would be. Worn and tattered shoes, like faces, are drawn into signatures,
inscribed through time and experience with identity. New shoes tell the
story of desires, of aspirations written, not only on the heart and soul
but, just as intimately, on the body.

Woolf's novel reminds us that the empty shoes of Jacob are there for
repeated lacing and re-lacing, for multiple repetitions which alter and
produce new effects. We are forced, by Woolf's verbal painting of the
empty shoes in *Jacob's Room*, to retrace our steps and re-evaluate the
entire novel, in the process stepping into Jacob's shoes in his absence.
Woolf delights in contradictory pairs, as Jacob is repeatedly described
as clumsy yet elegant, awkward yet distinguished: ' "That young man,
Jacob Flanders," they would say, "so distinguished looking – and yet so
awkward." ' (p. 531–2) Like a provocative pair of mismatched shoes the
narrator and character are deliberately out of step. For the most part
Jacob stands superbly aloof, silent as a statue, beautifully and contemptuously out of reach.

It is in these shoes that Jacob has made his imprint, not in any
gesture of momentary heroism. *Jacob's Room* shows us what history
books cannot, the tactile and idiosyncratic nature of individual humans,
as: 'It's not catastrophes, murders, deaths, diseases, that age and kill us;
it's the way people look and laugh, and run up the steps of omnibuses'
(p. 478). Woolf confronts the reader, via the tangibility of the empty
shoes, with the intangible and at times inexpressible vagaries of loss,
longing and desire. This final unforgettable image remains with us
long after we have put the book down. 'Hear the shuffle of shoes left
behind,' Moses Schulstein counsels (op. cit., footnote 11). We hear the
spectral shuffle of Jacob's shoes in our ears, their mutilated music
continuing to lament, having taken that step that is a 'not', a void.

Names, Rooms and Objects

Edward Bishop, in his study of the subject in *Jacob's Room*, posits that 'the name "Jacob" means "usurper" but in fact he usurps nothing' (p. 159). Jacob is a patriarch in the Bible, whereas in the novel Jacob has no descendents. One wonders why his mother Betty – and Woolf – chose this name; a comment perhaps on not only the loss of a generation of men but also the preclusion of unborn descendants that could have shaped their lives to come.

'The loss of Jacob is the loss of *our* self, and thus we mourn even though we do not know him' (Bishop, p. 159). Yet even death is not a privileged moment of authority. It is part of the play between the momentary experience of plenitude and the recognition that in the next moment what was so tangible was nothing other than a fleeting moment, never fully grasped. The value of life is heightened by its transience; life is perpetually threatened, a fragile gift. Opportunities lost, words not spoken, doors not entered, roads not taken, lives not lived, nevertheless resonate beneath the chosen narrative route. It is all captured in the power of suggestion and we, as readers, will continue to be invited to make connections, observe repetitions and to gain and articulate a sense of being in the world. Jacob cannot convey himself to others, not least because he is uncertain of his own desires. Woolf insists on both the ordinariness of the figure she has chosen as the protagonist and the arbitrariness of his fate. There is a haunting knowledge latent in the novel's title: the future it foresees, fears and reaches towards is empty; there is no place in it for Jacob. Indeed, as Melba Cuddy Keane has said: 'Jacob's shoes recast the novel as prologue to a movement that *might* have been' (p. 106). What is visible stands as a cipher for all which cannot be known so explicitly; much is invisibly present. However, despite its unmitigated sadness and pathos the novel celebrates the rich fullness of every moment; moments when Mrs Flanders might 'let her fancy play upon the gold tint of the sea at sunset' and think 'how it lapped in coins of gold upon the shingle. [...] The whole city was pink and gold; domed; mist-wreathed; resonant; strident' (p. 429). Woolf movingly evokes the desolation of death through a corresponding intensity of life and feeling.

In *Jacob's Room* we do not have a luminous drift of thoughts wrapping each object in a stream of phenomenological perceptions, but rather, as David Lodge states: '*Jacob's Room* belongs in the metonymic category. Its experimentalism is all performed on the chain of combination – the chain of contiguous events that is Jacob's life – and consists mainly of

cutting away huge sections of this chain and viewing the remainder
from odd angles and perspectives' (p. 183). The narrative progresses
through a series of impressionistic episodes, seemingly loosely connected. It is no accident that Woolf has Sandra Wentworth Williams
lend Jacob a volume of Chekov's stories because, as Beverly Ann
Schlack observes: 'Woolf and Chekhov share two convictions: that life
is essentially an unknowable mystery, and that human communication
is extremely difficult, if not impossible' (p. 29).

Woolf's comments on Chekhov's 'Gusev' could also be written concerning *Jacob's Room*:

> We are given a few scraps of their talk and some of their thoughts;
> then one of them dies [...] The emphasis is laid upon such unexpected
> places that at first it seems as if there were no emphasis at all; and then,
> as the eyes accustom themselves to twilight and discover *the shapes of
> things in a room*, we see how complete the story is, how profound, and
> how truly in obedience to his vision Chekhov has chosen this, that,
> and the other, and placed them together to compose something new.
> ('Modern Fiction', in *First Common Reader*, pp. 152–3, italics added)

Hence, *Jacob's Room* is composed of scraps of talk, unexpected
emphases, and the shapes of things in a room. Places are stained with
death; the splitting tree, or the rock on which Jacob's existence will
founder, recur in various guises in the novel, from the nanny turned
into a rock on the childhood beach, to the sacrificial rock passed by the
young man, or to the hymn he sings: 'Rock of Ages, cleft for me,/ Let
me hide myself in thee' (p. 46). As Kate Flint notes, 'The figurative
rock of security towards which Jacob hurries proves [...] to be a sinister
emanation of the world existing outside his household sphere: a world
against which, in both its material and social forms, we are to see him
tentatively testing and asserting his identity until he is finally swallowed
up by the War' (pp. 361–2). Litholatry – the worship of stones or
rocks – in the Christian faith is furnished by allusions to the *rock of
refuge*, the *rock* upon which the church of Christ was to be founded,
the *corner stone* which the builders rejected, Jacob's *stony pillow* which
he set up and anointed with oil, the *sling stone* of David, the *rock
Moriah* upon which the altar of King Solomon's Temple was erected,
the *white stone* of Revelation and the *Rock of Ages*. Jacob's stone is of
particular interest as, according to the Old Testament, his namesake,
who later changed his name to Israel and thus became the first
Israelite, laid his head on a stone 'pillow' at Bethel, fell asleep, and had
a dream of 'Jacob's Ladder' upon which he saw angels ascending and

descending.[15] Woolf's Jacob, along with countless young men like him, will be reduced to a name carved into a stone. Prefiguring this, Jacob becomes 'statuesque' and 'eyeless' (p. 543), 'monolithic [...] like a British Admiral' (p. 540) in Bonamy's mind and, in Fanny's vision, akin to a statue in the British Museum (pp. 543–4). Indeed, this institution's stone is likened to the mind:

> Stone lies solid over the British Museum, as bone lies cool over the visions and heat of the brain. Only here the brain is Plato's brain and Shakespeare's; the brain has made pots and statues, great bulls and little jewels, and crossed the river of death this way and that incessantly, seeking some landing, now wrapping the body well for its long sleep; now laying a penny piece on the eyes; now turning the toes scrupulously to the East. Meanwhile, Plato continues his dialogue; in spite of the rain; in spite of the cab whistles; in spite of the woman in the mews behind Great Ormond Street who has come home drunk and cries all night long, 'Let me in! Let me in!'
>
> [p. 497]

Inanimate objects such as stones thus become personified, while the voice of the underprivileged woman crying 'Let me in!' remains for ever excluded. One is reminded of Blake's great poem 'London' where 'the hapless Soldier's sigh/Runs in blood down Palace walls' (p. 150). The cries of both the woman and the hapless soldier are ignored, providing a powerful critique of the ideology of Empire in which minds and hearts have turned to stone.

Objects in *Jacob's Room* become omens pointedly connected with the war, as 'the lamps of London uphold the dark as upon the points of burning bayonets' (p. 488). Apart from Jacob's shoes the most significant objects in the novel are the rooms themselves. Rooms carry complex meanings as the spaces we occupy and shape around ourselves, metaphorically as well as literally, and, like physical appearances, they may be used to characterise their owner; indeed, the room is 'Woolf's

15 Woolf capitalises on the biblical association of Jacob's ladder (Genesis 28:12) in the following incident: '"There's another bunch higher up", murmured Clara Durrant, mounting another step of the ladder. Jacob held the ladder as she stretched out to reach the grapes high up on the vine' (p. 462). The scene has an ironic resonance related to its biblical dimension – Jacob is no patriarch capable of founding a nation, no tragic hero capable of ascending to extraordinary heights: he is not even the one climbing the ladder and picking the grapes.

favourite symbol of personality or state of mind'.[16] Rooms, like our
bodies or our lives, express us yet are only partly ours, carrying the
marks of our predecessors as well as our own histories. Woolf offsets
private rooms with public spaces and the 'opening out' implied by
streets, theatres, restaurants and colleges. Emptiness is associated with
Jacob's room at Cambridge University, described during his temporary
absence in the following passage, where we have a foretaste of Jacob's
silent empty room at the end of the novel: 'Listless is the air in an empty
room, just swelling the curtain; the flowers in the jar shift. One fibre in
the wicker armchair creaks, though no one sits there' (p. 445).

Things moulded by a presence have a secret language of their own; a
breath of air and a familiar chair still speak of the one who has left.
Movement and sound evoke Jacob's absence by implying a presence;
the still life of the room enters time through its evocation of the creaking
of the wicker. The repetition of the quotation above, at the close of the
novel, when Mrs Flanders and Bonamy are in Jacob's room at Lamb's
Conduit Street (p. 548), suggests a timelessness to the scene and an
absence of change. The context, however, changes the meaning: Mrs
Flanders and Bonamy sorrowfully sort through Jacob's effects; the
images reveal that everything has changed. These images represent that
which is beyond representation; that which is no longer there to be
represented.

> Words move, music moves
> Only in time; but that which is only living
> Can only die. Words, after speech, reach
> Into the silence. Only by the form, the pattern,
> Can words or music reach
> The stillness, as a Chinese jar still
> Moves perpetually in its stillness.[17]

Despite the sameness of Jacob's room, the fact of change registers
psychologically, betraying the signs of an existence that will never again
be the same. ' "He left everything just as it was," Bonamy marvelled.
"Nothing arranged. All his letters strewn about for anyone to read.
What did he expect? Did he think he would come back?" ' (p. 548). A
letter is 'this phantom of ourselves' (p. 485), another symbol of the
unseizable self, evidence of 'the power of the mind to quit the body'

---

16 See Harvena Richter, p. 213.
17 T. S. Eliot, 'Burnt Norton', p. 194, v. ll. 1–7

(p. 485). The letters are not even Jacob's – they are addressed *to* him and therefore unable to reveal his psyche. They provide enough to encourage the reader to persist in trying to define him, but not enough to fathom his character. Each person's past is 'shut in him like the leaves of a book known to him by heart; and his friends could only read the title' (p. 464). The covers of the books are shut; the blinds at the window have been drawn down. In the closing stages of the novel these blinds are lifted, turning private grief into a public outpouring, and allowing the shock of war to remain a shock, rather than assimilating it into the codes of sentimentality. The nocturnal women are beating great carpets and, by extension, beating themselves in lamentation over the death of a generation of young men.

Implicit in Woolf's writing is the belief that looking at death as an event, as a moment, as merely 'the end', belies the place of death in life. There is an important sense in Woolf's writing in which death, as an aspect of change and renewal, is ever present throughout life: each passing moment 'dies' as it becomes past experience; each newly experienced moment is immediately 'born' as the future becomes the present. From moment to moment, beginnings and endings perpetually coincide. *Jacob's Room*, then, is not concerned with the finitude of life so much as with death's infinite life, with the possibilities of life at death's end, and with the infinitude of death as it lives on in the historical, social and philosophical, as well as the private, circumstances of those bound to life.

Dorinda Guest

Bibliography

Mikhail Bakhtin, *The Dialogic Imagination*, University of Texas Press, Austin, 1981

Clive Bell, *Art*, Chatto & Windus, London, 1931

Quentin Bell, *Virginia Woolf*, 2 vols, Harcourt Brace Jovanovich, New York, 1972

Shari Benstock and Suzanne Ferriss (eds), *Footnotes: On Shoes*, Rutgers University Press, New Brunswick, 2001

Edward, L. Bishop, 'The Subject in *Jacob's Room*', in *Modern Fiction Studies*, Vol. 38, pp. 147–75

William Blake, *Songs of Innocence and Experience*, Oxford University Press, Oxford, 1992

David Bradshaw, 'Winking, Buzzing, Carpet-Beating: Reading *Jacob's Room*', 4th Annual Birthday Lecture, Virginia Woolf Society of Great Britain, 2003

Julia Briggs, *Virginia Woolf: An Inner Life*, Penguin, London, 2005

T. S. Eliot, *Collected Poems 1909–1962*, Faber & Faber, London, 1974

Kate Flint, 'Revising *Jacob's Room*: Virginia Woolf, Women and Language', in *The Review of English Studies*, Vol. 42/167, pp. 361–79

Christine Froula, *Virginia Woolf and the Bloomsbury Avant-Garde: War, Civilization, Modernity*, Columbia University Press, New York, 2005

Paul Fussell, *The Great War and Modern Memory*, Oxford University Press, Oxford, 1977

Ruth Gruber, *Virginia Woolf: The Will to Create as a Woman*, Carroll & Graf, New York, 1935; republished 2005

Clare Hanson (ed.), *The Critical Writings of Katherine Mansfield*, Macmillan, Basingstoke, 1987

Clare Hanson, *Virginia Woolf*, Macmillan, London, 1994

Judith Hattaway, 'Virginia Woolf's *Jacob's Room*: History and Memory', in *Women and World War I: The Written Response*, Dorothy Goldman, Agnes Cardinal, Judith Hattaway (eds), St Martin's Press, New York, 1993

David Lodge, *The Modes of Modern Writing*, Edward Arnold, London, 1977

Robin Majumdar and Allen McLaurin (eds), *Virginia Woolf: The Critical Heritage*, Routledge, London, 1997

John McCrae, *In Flanders Fields and Other Poems*, Hayes Barton Press, 1919

Wilfred Owen, *The Poems of Wilfred Owen*, John Stallworthy (ed.), Norton, New York, 1986

Harvena Richter, *Virginia Woolf: The Inward Voyage*, Princeton University Press, Princeton, 1970

Michael Rosenthal, *Virginia Woolf*, Routledge & Kegan Paul, London, 1979

Beverly Ann Schlack, *Continuing Presences*, Pennsylvania State University Press, University Park, 1979

Virginia Woolf, *The Complete Shorter Fiction*, Susan Dick (ed.), Hogarth Press, London, 1985

Virginia Woolf, *The Diary of Virginia Woolf*, 5 volumes, edited by Anne Olivier Bell, Hogarth Press, London, 1977

Virginia Woolf, *The Letters of Virginia Woolf*, 6 volumes, edited by Nigel Nicholson and Joanne Trautmann, Hogarth Press, London, 1975–80

Alex Zwerdling, 'Jacob's Room: Woolf's Satiric Elegy', in *English Literary History*, Vol. 48/4, pp. 894–913

JACOB'S ROOM

Chapter 1

'So of course,' wrote Betty Flanders, pressing her heels rather deeper in the sand, 'there was nothing for it but to leave.'

Slowly welling from the point of her gold nib, pale blue ink dissolved the full stop; for there her pen stuck; her eyes fixed, and tears slowly filled them. The entire bay quivered; the lighthouse wobbled; and she had the illusion that the mast of Mr Connor's little yacht was bending like a wax candle in the sun. She winked quickly. Accidents were awful things. She winked again. The mast was straight; the waves were regular; the lighthouse was upright; but the blot had spread.

'. . . nothing for it but to leave,' she read.

'Well, if Jacob doesn't want to play' (the shadow of Archer, her eldest son, fell across the notepaper and looked blue on the sand, and she felt chilly – it was the third of September already), 'if Jacob doesn't want to play' – what a horrid blot! It must be getting late.

'Where *is* that tiresome little boy?' she said. 'I don't see him. Run and find him. Tell him to come at once.' '. . . but mercifully,' she scribbled, ignoring the full stop, 'everything seems satisfactorily arranged, packed though we are like herrings in a barrel, and forced to stand the perambulator which the landlady quite naturally won't allow . . . '

Such were Betty Flanders's letters to Captain Barfoot – many-paged, tear-stained. Scarborough is seven hundred miles from Cornwall:[1] Captain Barfoot is in Scarborough: Seabrook is dead. Tears made all the dahlias in her garden undulate in red waves and flashed the glass-house in her eyes, and spangled the kitchen with bright knives, and made Mrs Jarvis, the rector's wife, think at church, while the hymn-tune played and Mrs Flanders bent low over her little boys' heads, that marriage is a fortress and widows stray solitary in the open fields, picking up stones, gleaning a few golden straws, lonely, unprotected, poor creatures. Mrs Flanders had been a widow for these two years.

'Ja–cob! Ja–cob!' Archer shouted.

'Scarborough,' Mrs Flanders wrote on the envelope, and dashed a bold line beneath; it was her native town; the hub of the universe. But a stamp? She ferreted in her bag; then held it up mouth downwards; then fumbled in her lap, all so vigorously that Charles Steele in the panama hat suspended his paintbrush.

Like the antennae of some irritable insect it positively trembled. Here was that woman moving – actually going to get up – confound her! He struck the canvas a hasty violet-black dab. For the landscape needed it. It was too pale – greys flowing into lavenders, and one star or a white gull suspended just so – too pale as usual. The critics would say it was too pale, for he was an unknown man exhibiting obscurely, a favourite with his landladies' children, wearing a cross on his watch-chain, and much gratified if his landladies liked his pictures – which they often did.

'Ja–cob! Ja–cob!' Archer shouted.

Exasperated by the noise, yet loving children, Steele picked nervously at the dark little coils on his palette.

'I saw your brother – I saw your brother,' he said, nodding his head, as Archer lagged past him, trailing his spade, and scowling at the old gentleman in spectacles.

'Over there – by the rock,' Steele muttered, with his brush between his teeth, squeezing out raw sienna, and keeping his eyes fixed on Betty Flanders's back.

'Ja–cob! Ja–cob!' shouted Archer, lagging on after a second.

The voice had an extraordinary sadness. Pure from all body, pure from all passion, going out into the world, solitary, unanswered, breaking against rocks – so it sounded.

Steele frowned; but was pleased by the effect of the black – it was just *that* note which brought the rest together.[2] 'Ah, one may learn to paint at fifty! There's Titian.[3] . . . ' and so, having found the right tint, up he looked and saw to his horror a cloud over the bay.

Mrs Flanders rose, slapped her coat this side and that to get the sand off, and picked up her black parasol.

The rock was one of those tremendously solid brown, or rather black, rocks which emerge from the sand like something primitive. Rough with crinkled limpet shells and sparsely strewn with locks of dry sea-weed, a small boy has to stretch his legs far apart, and indeed to feel rather heroic, before he gets to the top.

But there, on the very top, is a hollow full of water, with a sandy bottom; with a blob of jelly stuck to the side, and some mussels. A fish darts across. The fringe of yellow-brown seaweed flutters, and out pushes an opal-shelled crab – 'Oh, a huge crab,' Jacob murmured – and begins his journey on weakly legs on the sandy bottom. Now! Jacob plunged his hand. The crab was cool and very light. But the water was thick with sand, and so, scrambling down, Jacob was about to jump, holding his bucket in front of him, when he saw, stretched entirely rigid, side by side, their faces very red, an enormous man and woman.

An enormous man and woman (it was early-closing day) were stretched motionless, with their heads on pocket-handkerchiefs, side by side, within a few feet of the sea, while two or three gulls gracefully skirted the incoming waves and settled near their boots.

The large red faces lying on the bandanna handkerchiefs stared up at Jacob. Jacob stared down at them. Holding his bucket very carefully, Jacob then jumped deliberately and trotted away very nonchalantly at first, but faster and faster as the waves came creaming up to him and he had to swerve to avoid them, and the gulls rose in front of him and floated out and settled again a little farther on. A large black woman was sitting on the sand. He ran towards her.

'Nanny! Nanny!' he cried, sobbing the words out on the crest of each gasping breath.

The waves came round her. She was a rock. She was covered with the seaweed which pops when it is pressed. He was lost.

There he stood. His face composed itself. He was about to roar when, lying among the black sticks and straw under the cliff, he saw a whole skull – perhaps a cow's skull, a skull, perhaps, with the teeth in it.[4] Sobbing, but absent-mindedly, he ran farther and farther away until he held the skull in his arms.

'There he is!' cried Mrs Flanders, coming round the rock and covering the whole space of the beach in a few seconds. 'What has he got hold of? Put it down, Jacob! Drop it this moment! Something horrid, I know. Why didn't you stay with us? Naughty little boy! Now put it down. Now come along both of you,' and she swept round, holding Archer by one hand and fumbling for Jacob's arm with the other. But he ducked down and picked up the sheep's jaw, which was loose.

Swinging her bag, clutching her parasol, holding Archer's hand, and telling the story of the gunpowder explosion in which poor Mr Curnow had lost his eye, Mrs Flanders hurried up the steep lane, aware all the time in the depths of her mind of some buried discomfort.

There on the sand not far from the lovers lay the old sheep's skull

without its jaw. Clean, white, wind-swept, sand-rubbed, a more un-
polluted piece of bone existed nowhere on the coast of Cornwall. The
sea holly would grow through the eye-sockets; it would turn to powder;
or some golfer, hitting his ball one fine day, would disperse a little
dust – No, but not in lodgings, thought Mrs Flanders. It's a great
experiment coming so far with young children. There's no man to help
with the perambulator. And Jacob is such a handful; so obstinate already.

'Throw it away, dear, do,' she said, as they got into the road; but
Jacob squirmed away from her; and the wind rising, she took out her
bonnet-pin, looked at the sea, and stuck it in afresh. The wind was
rising. The waves showed that uneasiness, like something alive, restive,
expecting the whip, of waves before a storm. The fishing-boats were
leaning to the water's brim. A pale yellow light shot across the purple
sea; and shut. The lighthouse was lit. 'Come along,' said Betty Flanders.
The sun blazed in their faces and gilded the great blackberries trembling
out from the hedge which Archer tried to strip as they passed.

'Don't lag, boys. You've got nothing to change into,' said Betty,
pulling them along, and looking with uneasy emotion at the earth
displayed so luridly, with sudden sparks of light from greenhouses in
gardens, with a sort of yellow and black mutability, against this blazing
sunset, this astonishing agitation and vitality of colour, which stirred
Betty Flanders and made her think of responsibility and danger. She
gripped Archer's hand. On she plodded up the hill.

'What did I ask you to remember?' she said.

'I don't know,' said Archer.

'Well, I don't know either,' said Betty, humorously and simply,
and who shall deny that this blankness of mind, when combined with
profusion, mother wit, old wives' tales, haphazard ways, moments of
astonishing daring, humour and sentimentality – who shall deny that in
these respects every woman is nicer than any man?

Well, Betty Flanders, to begin with.

She had her hand upon the garden gate.

'The meat!' she exclaimed, striking the latch down.

She had forgotten the meat.

There was Rebecca at the window.

The bareness of Mrs Pearce's front room was fully displayed at ten
o'clock at night when a powerful oil lamp stood on the middle of the
table. The harsh light fell on the garden; cut straight across the lawn; lit
up a child's bucket and a purple aster and reached the hedge. Mrs
Flanders had left her sewing on the table. There were her large reels of

white cotton and her steel spectacles; her needle-case; her brown wool wound round an old postcard. There were the bulrushes and the *Strand* magazines;[5] and the linoleum sandy from the boys' boots. A daddy-long-legs shot from corner to corner and hit the lamp globe. The wind blew straight dashes of rain across the window, which flashed silver as they passed through the light. A single leaf tapped hurriedly, persistently, upon the glass. There was a hurricane out at sea.

Archer could not sleep.

Mrs Flanders stooped over him. 'Think of the fairies,' said Betty Flanders. 'Think of the lovely, lovely birds settling down on their nests. Now shut your eyes and see the old mother bird with a worm in her beak. Now turn and shut your eyes,' she murmured, 'and shut your eyes.'

The lodging-house seemed full of gurgling and rushing; the cistern overflowing; water bubbling and squeaking and running along the pipes and streaming down the windows.

'What's all that water rushing in?' murmured Archer.

'It's only the bathwater running away,' said Mrs Flanders.

Something snapped out of doors.

'I say, won't that steamer sink?' said Archer, opening his eyes.

'Of course it won't,' said Mrs Flanders. 'The Captain's in bed long ago. Shut your eyes, and think of the fairies, fast asleep, under the flowers.'

'I thought he'd never get off – such a hurricane,' she whispered to Rebecca, who was bending over a spirit-lamp in the small room next door. The wind rushed outside, but the small flame of the spirit-lamp burnt quietly, shaded from the cot by a book stood on edge.

'Did he take his bottle well?' Mrs Flanders whispered, and Rebecca nodded and went to the cot and turned down the quilt, and Mrs Flanders bent over and looked anxiously at the baby, asleep, but frowning. The window shook, and Rebecca stole like a cat and wedged it.

The two women murmured over the spirit-lamp, plotting the eternal conspiracy of hush and clean bottles while the wind raged and gave a sudden wrench at the cheap fastenings.

Both looked round at the cot. Their lips were pursed. Mrs Flanders crossed over to the cot.

'Asleep?' whispered Rebecca, looking at the cot.

Mrs Flanders nodded.

'Good-night, Rebecca,' Mrs Flanders murmured, and Rebecca called her ma'm, though they were conspirators plotting the eternal conspiracy of hush and clean bottles.

Mrs Flanders had left the lamp burning in the front room. There were her spectacles, her sewing; and a letter with the Scarborough postmark. She had not drawn the curtains either.

The light blazed out across the patch of grass; fell on the child's green bucket with the gold line round it, and upon the aster which trembled violently beside it. For the wind was tearing across the coast, hurling itself at the hills, and leaping, in sudden gusts, on top of its own back. How it spread over the town in the hollow! How the lights seemed to wink and quiver in its fury, lights in the harbour, lights in bedroom windows high up! And rolling dark waves before it, it raced over the Atlantic, jerking the stars above the ships this way and that.

There was a click in the front sitting-room. Mr Pearce had extinguished the lamp. The garden went out. It was but a dark patch. Every inch was rained upon. Every blade of grass was bent by rain. Eyelids would have been fastened down by the rain. Lying on one's back one would have seen nothing but muddle and confusion – clouds turning and turning, and something yellow-tinted and sulphurous in the darkness.

The little boys in the front bedroom had thrown off their blankets and lay under the sheets. It was hot; rather sticky and steamy. Archer lay spread out, with one arm striking across the pillow. He was flushed; and when the heavy curtain blew out a little he turned and half-opened his eyes. The wind actually stirred the cloth on the chest of drawers, and let in a little light, so that the sharp edge of the chest of drawers was visible, running straight up, until a white shape bulged out; and a silver streak showed in the looking-glass.

In the other bed by the door Jacob lay asleep, fast asleep, profoundly unconscious. The sheep's jaw with the big yellow teeth in it lay at his feet. He had kicked it against the iron bed-rail.

Outside the rain poured down more directly and powerfully as the wind fell in the early hours of the morning. The aster was beaten to the earth. The child's bucket was half-full of rainwater; and the opal-shelled crab slowly circled round the bottom, trying with its weakly legs to climb the steep side; trying again and falling back, and trying again and again.

Chapter 2

'Mrs Flanders' – 'Poor Betty Flanders' – 'Dear Betty' – 'She's very attractive still' – 'Odd she don't marry again!' 'There's Captain Barfoot to be sure – calls every Wednesday as regular as clockwork, and never brings his wife.'

'But that's Ellen Barfoot's fault,' the ladies of Scarborough said. 'She don't put herself out for no one.'

'A man likes to have a son – that we know.'

'Some tumours have to be cut; but the sort my mother had you bear with for years and years, and never even have a cup of tea brought up to you in bed.'

(Mrs Barfoot was an invalid.)

Elizabeth Flanders, of whom this and much more than this had been said and would be said, was, of course, a widow in her prime. She was halfway between forty and fifty. Years and sorrow between them; the death of Seabrook, her husband; three boys; poverty; a house on the outskirts of Scarborough; her brother, poor Morty's, downfall and possible demise – for where was he? what was he? Shading her eyes, she looked along the road for Captain Barfoot – yes, there he was, punctual as ever; the attentions of the Captain – all ripened Betty Flanders, enlarged her figure, tinged her face with jollity, and flooded her eyes for no reason that anyone could see perhaps three times a day.

True, there's no harm in crying for one's husband, and the tombstone, though plain, was a solid piece of work, and on summer's days when the widow brought her boys to stand there one felt kindly towards her. Hats were raised higher than usual; wives tugged their husbands' arms. Seabrook lay six foot beneath, dead these many years; enclosed in three shells,[6] the crevices sealed with lead; so that, had earth and wood been glass, doubtless his very face lay visible beneath, the face of a young man, whiskered, shapely, who had gone out duck-shooting and refused to change his boots.

'Merchant of this city', the tombstone said; though why Betty Flanders had chosen so to call him when, as many still remembered, he had only sat behind an office window for three months, and before that had broken horses, ridden to hounds, farmed a few fields, and run a little wild – well, she had to call him something.[7] An example for the boys.

Had he, then, been nothing? An unanswerable question, since even if it weren't the habit of the undertaker to close the eyes, the light so soon goes out of them. At first, part of herself; now one of a company, he had merged in the grass, the sloping hillside, the thousand white stones,[8] some slanting, others upright, the decayed wreaths, the crosses of green tin, the narrow yellow paths and the lilacs that drooped in April,[9] with a scent like that of an invalid's bedroom, over the churchyard wall. Seabrook was now all that; and when, with her skirt hitched up, feeding the chickens, she heard the bell for service or funeral, that was Seabrook's voice – the voice of the dead.

The rooster had been known to fly on her shoulder and peck her neck, so that now she carried a stick or took one of the children with her when she went to feed the fowls.

'Wouldn't you like my knife, mother?' said Archer.

Sounding at the same moment as the bell, her son's voice mixed life and death inextricably, exhilaratingly.

'What a big knife for a small boy!' she said. She took it to please him. Then the rooster flew out of the hen-house, and, shouting to Archer to shut the door into the kitchen garden, Mrs Flanders set her meal down, clucked for the hens, went bustling about the orchard, and was seen from over the way by Mrs Cranch, who, beating her mat against the wall, held it for a moment suspended while she observed to Mrs Page next door that Mrs Flanders was in the orchard with the chickens.

Mrs Page, Mrs Cranch and Mrs Garfit could see Mrs Flanders in the orchard because the orchard was a piece of Dods Hill[10] enclosed; and Dods Hill dominated the village. No words can exaggerate the importance of Dods Hill. It was the earth; the world against the sky; the horizon of how many glances can best be computed by those who have lived all their lives in the same village, only leaving it once to fight in the Crimea,[11] like old George Garfit, leaning over his garden gate smoking his pipe. The progress of the sun was measured by it; the tint of the day laid against it to be judged.

'Now she's going up the hill with little John,' said Mrs Cranch to Mrs Garfit, shaking her mat for the last time, and bustling indoors. Opening the orchard gate, Mrs Flanders walked to the top of Dods Hill, holding John by the hand. Archer and Jacob ran in front or lagged behind; but they were in the Roman fortress when she came there, and shouting out what ships were to be seen in the bay. For there was a magnificent view – moors behind, sea in front, and the whole of Scarborough[12] from one end to the other laid out flat like a puzzle. Mrs Flanders, who was growing stout, sat down in the fortress and looked about her.

The entire gamut of the view's changes should have been known to her: its winter aspect, spring, summer and autumn; how storms came up from the sea; how the moors shuddered and brightened as the clouds went over; she should have noted the red spot where the villas were building; and the criss-cross of lines where the allotments were cut; and the diamond flash of little glasshouses in the sun. Or, if details like these escaped her, she might have let her fancy play upon the gold tint of the sea at sunset, and thought how it lapped in coins of gold upon the shingle. Little pleasure boats shoved out into it; the black arm of the pier hoarded it up. The whole city was pink and gold; domed; mist-wreathed; resonant; strident. Banjoes strummed; the parade smelt of tar which stuck to the heels; goats suddenly cantered their carriages through crowds. It was observed how well the corporation had laid out the flower-beds. Sometimes a straw hat was blown away. Tulips burnt in the sun.[13] Numbers of sponge-bag trousers[14] were stretched in rows. Purple bonnets fringed soft, pink, querulous faces on pillows in bath chairs. Triangular hoardings were wheeled along by men in white coats. Captain George Boase had caught a monster shark. One side of the triangular hoarding said so in red, blue and yellow letters; and each line ended with three differently coloured notes of exclamation.[15]

So that was a reason for going down into the Aquarium, where the sallow blinds, the stale smell of spirits of salt, the bamboo chairs, the tables with ashtrays, the revolving fish, the attendant knitting behind six or seven chocolate boxes (often she was quite alone with the fish for hours at a time) remained in the mind as part of the monster shark, he himself being only a flabby yellow receptacle, like an empty Gladstone bag, in a tank. No one had ever been cheered by the Aquarium; but the faces of those emerging quickly lost their dim, chilled expression when they perceived that it was only by standing in a queue that one could be admitted to the pier. Once through the turnstiles, everyone walked for a yard or two very briskly; some flagged at this stall; others at that. But it was the band that drew them all to it finally; even the fishermen on the lower pier taking up their pitch within its range.

The band played in the Moorish kiosk. Number nine went up on the board. It was a waltz tune. The pale girls, the old widow lady, the three Jews lodging in the same boarding-house, the dandy, the major, the horse-dealer and the gentleman of independent means, all wore the same blurred, drugged expression, and through the chinks in the planks at their feet they could see the green summer waves, peacefully, amiably, swaying round the iron pillars of the pier.

But there was a time when none of this had any existence (thought the young man leaning against the railings). Fix your eyes upon the lady's skirt:[16] the grey one will do – above the pink silk stockings. It changes: drapes her ankles – the nineties; then it amplifies – the seventies; now it's burnished red and stretched above a crinoline – the sixties; a tiny black foot wearing a white cotton stocking peeps out. Still sitting there? Yes – she's still on the pier. The silk now is sprigged with roses, but somehow one no longer sees so clearly. There's no pier beneath us. The heavy chariot may swing along the turnpike road, but there's no pier for it to stop at, and how grey and turbulent the sea is in the seventeenth century! Let's to the museum. Cannon-balls; arrow-heads; Roman glass and a forceps green with verdigris. The Reverend Jaspar Floyd dug them up at his own expense early in the forties in the Roman camp on Dods Hill – see the little ticket with the faded writing on it.

And now, what's the next thing to see in Scarborough?

Mrs Flanders sat on the raised circle of the Roman camp, patching Jacob's breeches; only looking up as she sucked the end of her cotton, or when some insect dashed at her, boomed in her ear, and was gone.

John kept trotting up and slapping down in her lap grass or dead leaves which he called 'tea', and she arranged them methodically but absent-mindedly, laying the flowery heads of the grasses together, thinking how Archer had been awake again last night; the church clock was ten or thirteen minutes fast; she wished she could buy Garfit's acre.

'That's an orchid leaf, Johnny. Look at the little brown spots. Come, my dear. We must go home. Ar–cher! Ja–cob!'

'Ar–cher! Ja–cob!' Johnny piped after her, pivoting round on his heel, and strewing the grass and leaves in his hands as if he were sowing seed. Archer and Jacob jumped up from behind the mound where they had been crouching with the intention of springing upon their mother unexpectedly, and they all began to walk slowly home.

'Who is that?' said Mrs Flanders, shading her eyes.

'That old man in the road?' said Archer, looking below.

'He's not an old man,' said Mrs Flanders. 'He's – no, he's not – I thought it was the Captain, but it's Mr Floyd. Come along, boys.'

'Oh, bother Mr Floyd!' said Jacob, switching off a thistle's head, for he knew already that Mr Floyd was going to teach them Latin, as indeed he did for three years in his spare time, out of kindness, for there was no other gentleman in the neighbourhood whom Mrs Flanders could have asked to do such a thing, and the elder boys were getting beyond her, and must be got ready for school, and it was more than most clergymen would have done, coming round after tea, or having them in his own room – as he could fit it in – for the parish was a very large one, and Mr Floyd, like his father before him, visited cottages miles away on the moors, and, like old Mr Floyd, was a great scholar, which made it so unlikely – she had never dreamt of such a thing. Ought she to have guessed? But let alone being a scholar he was eight years younger than she was. She knew his mother – old Mrs Floyd. She had tea there. And it was that very evening when she came back from having tea with old Mrs Floyd that she found the note in the hall and took it into the kitchen with her when she went to give Rebecca the fish, thinking it must be something about the boys.

'Mr Floyd brought it himself, did he? – I think the cheese must be in the parcel in the hall – oh, in the hall – ' for she was reading. No, it was not about the boys.

'Yes, enough for fish-cakes tomorrow certainly – Perhaps Captain Barfoot – ' she had come to the word 'love'. She went into the garden and read, leaning against the walnut tree to steady herself. Up and down went her breast. Seabrook came so vividly before her. She shook her head and was looking through her tears at the little shifting leaves against the yellow sky when three geese, half-running, half-flying, scuttled across the lawn with Johnny behind them, brandishing a stick.

Mrs Flanders flushed with anger.

'How many times have I told you?' she cried, and seized him and snatched his stick away from him.

'But they'd escaped!' he cried, struggling to get free.

'You're a very naughty boy. If I've told you once, I've told you a thousand times. I won't have you chasing the geese!' she said, and crumpling Mr Floyd's letter in her hand, she held Johnny fast and herded the geese back into the orchard.

'How could I think of marriage!' she said to herself bitterly, as she fastened the gate with a piece of wire. She had always disliked red hair in men, she thought, thinking of Mr Floyd's appearance, that night when the boys had gone to bed. And pushing her work-box away, she drew the blotting-paper towards her, and read Mr Floyd's letter again, and her breast went up and down when she came to the word 'love', but not so fast this time, for she saw Johnny chasing the geese, and knew that it was impossible for her to marry anyone – let alone Mr Floyd, who was so much younger than she was, but what a nice man – and such a scholar too.

'Dear Mr Floyd,' she wrote – 'Did I forget about the cheese?' she wondered, laying down her pen. No, she had told Rebecca that the cheese was in the hall. 'I am much surprised . . . ' she wrote.

But the letter which Mr Floyd found on the table when he got up early next morning did not begin 'I am much surprised', and it was such a motherly, respectful, inconsequent, regretful letter that he kept it for many years; long after his marriage with Miss Wimbush, of Andover; long after he had left the village. For he asked for a parish in Sheffield, which was given him; and, sending for Archer, Jacob and John to say goodbye, he told them to choose whatever they liked in his study to remember him by. Archer chose a paper-knife, because he did not like to choose anything too good; Jacob chose the works of Byron in one volume; John, who was still too young to make a proper choice, chose Mr Floyd's kitten, which his brothers thought an absurd choice, but Mr Floyd upheld him when he said: 'It has fur like you.' Then Mr Floyd spoke about the King's Navy (to which Archer was going); and about Rugby[17] (to which Jacob was going); and next day he received a silver salver and went – first to Sheffield, where he met Miss Wimbush, who was on a visit to her uncle – then to Hackney – then to Maresfield House, of which he became the principal – and finally, becoming editor of a well-known series of ecclesiastical biographies,[18] he retired to Hampstead with his wife and daughter, and is often to be seen feeding the ducks on Leg of Mutton Pond.[19] As for Mrs Flanders's letter – when he looked for it the other day he could not find it, and did not like to ask his wife whether she had put it away. Meeting Jacob in Piccadilly lately, he recognised him after three seconds. But Jacob had grown such a fine young man that Mr Floyd did not like to stop him in the street.

'Dear me,' said Mrs Flanders, when she read in the *Scarborough and Harrogate Courier*[20] that the Revd Andrew Floyd, etc., etc., had been made Principal of Maresfield House, 'that must be our Mr Floyd.'

A slight gloom fell upon the table. Jacob was helping himself to jam; the postman was talking to Rebecca in the kitchen; there was a bee humming at the yellow flower which nodded at the open window. They were all alive, that is to say, while poor Mr Floyd was becoming Principal of Maresfield House.

Mrs Flanders got up and went over to the fender and stroked Topaz on the neck behind the ears.

'Poor Topaz,' she said (for Mr Floyd's kitten was now a very old cat, a little mangy behind the ears, and one of these days would have to be killed).

'Poor old Topaz,' said Mrs Flanders, as he stretched himself out in the sun, and she smiled, thinking how she had had him gelded, and how she did not like red hair in men. Smiling, she went into the kitchen.

Jacob drew rather a dirty pocket-handkerchief across his face. He went upstairs to his room.

The stag-beetle dies slowly (it was John who collected the beetles). Even on the second day its legs were supple. But the butterflies were dead. A whiff of rotten eggs had vanquished the pale clouded yellows which came pelting across the orchard and up Dods Hill and away on to the moor, now lost behind a furze bush, then off again helter-skelter in a broiling sun. A fritillary basked on a white stone in the Roman camp. From the valley came the sound of church bells. They were all eating roast beef in Scarborough; for it was Sunday when Jacob caught the pale clouded yellows in the clover field, eight miles from home.

Rebecca had caught the death's-head moth in the kitchen.

A strong smell of camphor came from the butterfly boxes.

Mixed with the smell of camphor was the unmistakable smell of seaweed. Tawny ribbons hung on the door. The sun beat straight upon them.

The upper wings of the moth which Jacob held were undoubtedly marked with kidney-shaped spots of a fulvous hue. But there was no crescent upon the underwing. The tree had fallen the night he caught it. There had been a volley of pistol-shots suddenly in the depths of the wood. And his mother had taken him for a burglar when he came home late. The only one of her sons who never obeyed her, she said.

Morris[21] called it 'an extremely local insect found in damp or marshy places'. But Morris is sometimes wrong. Sometimes Jacob, choosing a very fine pen, made a correction in the margin.

The tree had fallen, though it was a windless night, and the lantern, stood upon the ground, had lit up the still green leaves and the dead beech leaves. It was a dry place. A toad was there. And the red underwing had circled round the light and flashed and gone. The red underwing had never come back, though Jacob had waited. It was after twelve when he crossed the lawn and saw his mother in the bright room, playing patience, sitting up.

'How you frightened me!' she had cried. She thought something dreadful had happened. And he woke Rebecca, who had to be up so early.

There he stood pale, come out of the depths of darkness, in the hot room, blinking at the light.

No, it could not be a straw-bordered underwing.

The mowing-machine always wanted oiling. Barnet turned it under Jacob's window, and it creaked – creaked, and rattled across the lawn and creaked again.

Now it was clouding over.

Back came the sun, dazzlingly.

It fell like an eye upon the stirrups, and then suddenly and yet very gently rested upon the bed, upon the alarm clock, and upon the butterfly box stood open. The pale clouded yellows had pelted over the moor; they had zigzagged across the purple clover. The fritillaries flaunted along the hedgerows. The blues settled on little bones lying on the turf with the sun beating on them, and the painted ladies and the peacocks feasted upon bloody entrails dropped by a hawk. Miles away from home, in a hollow among teasles beneath a ruin, he had found the commas. He had seen a white admiral circling higher and higher round an oak tree, but he had never caught it. An old cottage woman living alone, high up, had told him of a purple butterfly which came every summer to her garden. The fox cubs played in the gorse in the early morning, she told him. And if you looked out at dawn you could always see two badgers. Sometimes they knocked each other over like two boys fighting, she said.

'You won't go far this afternoon, Jacob,' said his mother, popping her head in at the door, 'for the Captain's coming to say goodbye.' It was the last day of the Easter holidays.

Wednesday was Captain Barfoot's day. He dressed himself very neatly in blue serge, took his rubber-shod stick – for he was lame and wanted two fingers on the left hand, having served his country – and set out from the house with the flagstaff precisely at four o'clock in the afternoon.

At three Mr Dickens, the bath-chair man, had called for Mrs Barfoot.

'Move me,' she would say to Mr Dickens, after sitting on the esplanade for fifteen minutes. And again, 'That'll do, thank you, Mr Dickens.' At the first command he would seek the sun; at the second he would stay the chair there in the bright strip.

An old inhabitant himself, he had much in common with Mrs Barfoot – James Coppard's daughter. The drinking-fountain, where West Street joins Broad Street, is the gift of James Coppard, who was mayor at the time of Queen Victoria's jubilee, and Coppard is painted upon municipal watering-carts and over shop windows, and upon the

zinc blinds of solicitors' consulting-room windows. But Ellen Barfoot
never visited the Aquarium (though she had known Captain Boase
who had caught the shark quite well), and when the men came by with
the posters she eyed them superciliously, for she knew that she would
never see the Pierrots, or the Brothers Zeno, or Daisy Budd and her
troupe of performing seals. For Ellen Barfoot in her bath-chair on the
esplanade was a prisoner – civilisation's prisoner – all the bars of her
cage falling across the esplanade on sunny days when the town hall,
the drapery stores, the swimming-bath and the memorial hall striped
the ground with shadow.

An old inhabitant himself, Mr Dickens would stand a little behind
her, smoking his pipe. She would ask him questions – who people
were – who now kept Mr Jones's shop – then about the season – and
had Mrs Dickens tried, whatever it might be – the words issuing from
her lips like crumbs of dry biscuit.

She closed her eyes. Mr Dickens took a turn. The feelings of a man
had not altogether deserted him, though as you saw him coming towards
you, you noticed how one knobbed black boot swung tremulously in
front of the other; how there was a shadow between his waistcoat and
his trousers; how he leant forward unsteadily, like an old horse who
finds himself suddenly out of the shafts drawing no cart. But as Mr
Dickens sucked in the smoke and puffed it out again, the feelings of a
man were perceptible in his eyes. He was thinking how Captain Barfoot
was now on his way to Mount Pleasant; Captain Barfoot, his master.
For at home in the little sitting-room above the mews, with the canary
in the window, and the girls at the sewing-machine, and Mrs Dickens
huddled up with the rheumatics – at home where he was made little of,
the thought of being in the employ of Captain Barfoot supported him.
He liked to think that while he chatted with Mrs Barfoot on the front,
he helped the Captain on his way to Mrs Flanders. He, a man, was in
charge of Mrs Barfoot, a woman.

Turning, he saw that she was chatting with Mrs Rogers. Turning
again, he saw that Mrs Rogers had moved on. So he came back to the
bath-chair, and Mrs Barfoot asked him the time, and he took out his
great silver watch and told her the time very obligingly, as if he knew a
great deal more about the time and everything than she did. But Mrs
Barfoot knew that Captain Barfoot was on his way to Mrs Flanders.

Indeed he was well on his way there, having left the tram, and seeing
Dods Hill to the south-east, green against a blue sky that was suffused
with dust colour on the horizon. He was marching up the hill. In spite

of his lameness there was something military in his approach. Mrs Jarvis, as she came out of the Rectory gate, saw him coming, and her Newfoundland dog, Nero, slowly swept his tail from side to side.

'Oh, Captain Barfoot!' Mrs Jarvis exclaimed.

'Good-day, Mrs Jarvis,' said the Captain.

They walked on together, and when they reached Mrs Flanders's gate Captain Barfoot took off his tweed cap, and said, bowing very courteously, 'Good-day to you, Mrs Jarvis.'

And Mrs Jarvis walked on alone.

She was going to walk on the moor. Had she again been pacing her lawn late at night? Had she again tapped on the study window and cried: 'Look at the moon, look at the moon, Herbert!'

And Herbert looked at the moon.

Mrs Jarvis walked on the moor when she was unhappy, going as far as a certain saucer-shaped hollow, though she always meant to go to a more distant ridge; and there she sat down, and took out the little book hidden beneath her cloak and read a few lines of poetry, and looked about her. She was not very unhappy, and, seeing that she was forty-five, never perhaps would be very unhappy, desperately unhappy that is, and leave her husband, and ruin a good man's career, as she sometimes threatened.

Still there is no need to say what risks a clergyman's wife runs when she walks on the moor. Short, dark, with kindling eyes, a pheasant's feather in her hat, Mrs Jarvis was just the sort of woman to lose her faith upon the moors – to confound her God with the universal that is – but she did not lose her faith, did not leave her husband, never read her poem through, and went on walking the moors, looking at the moon behind the elm trees, and feeling as she sat on the grass high above Scarborough . . . Yes, yes, when the lark soars; when the sheep, moving a step or two onwards, crop the turf, and at the same time set their bells tinkling; when the breeze first blows, then dies down, leaving the cheek kissed; when the ships on the sea below seem to cross each other and pass on as if drawn by an invisible hand; when there are distant concussions in the air and phantom horsemen galloping, ceasing; when the horizon swims blue, green, emotional – then Mrs Jarvis, heaving a sigh, thinks to herself, 'If only someone could give me . . . if I could give someone . . . ' But she does not know what she wants to give, nor who could give it her.

'Mrs Flanders stepped out only five minutes ago, Captain,' said Rebecca. Captain Barfoot sat him down in the armchair to wait. Resting his elbows on the arms, putting one hand over the other, sticking his lame leg straight out, and placing the stick with the rubber ferrule beside it, he sat perfectly still. There was something rigid about him. Did he think? Probably the same thoughts again and again. But were they 'nice' thoughts, interesting thoughts? He was a man with a temper; tenacious, faithful. Women would have felt, 'Here is law. Here is order. Therefore we must cherish this man. He is on the bridge at night,' and, handing him his cup, or whatever it might be, would run on to visions of shipwreck and disaster, in which all the passengers come tumbling from their cabins, and there is the Captain, buttoned in his pea-jacket, matched with the storm, vanquished by it but by none other. 'Yet I have a soul,' Mrs Jarvis would bethink her, as Captain Barfoot suddenly blew his nose in a great red bandanna handkerchief, 'and it's the man's stupidity that's the cause of this, and the storm's my storm as well as his' . . . so Mrs Jarvis would bethink her when the Captain dropped in to see them and found Herbert out, and spent two or three hours, almost silent, sitting in the armchair. But Betty Flanders thought nothing of the kind.

'Oh, Captain,' said Mrs Flanders, bursting into the drawing-room, 'I had to run after Barker's man . . . I hope Rebecca . . . I hope Jacob . . .'

She was very much out of breath, yet not at all upset, and as she put down the hearth-brush which she had bought from the oil-man, she said it was hot, flung the window farther open, straightened a cover, picked up a book, as if she were very confident, very fond of the Captain, and a great many years younger than he was. Indeed, in her blue apron she did not look more than thirty-five. He was well over fifty.

She moved her hands about the table; the Captain moved his head from side to side, and made little sounds, as Betty went on chattering, completely at his ease – after twenty years.

'Well,' he said at length, 'I've heard from Mr Polegate.'

He had heard from Mr Polegate that he could advise nothing better than to send a boy to one of the universities.

'Mr Floyd was at Cambridge . . . no, at Oxford . . . well, at one or the other,' said Mrs Flanders.

She looked out of the window. Little windows, and the lilac and green of the garden were reflected in her eyes.

'Archer is doing very well,' she said. 'I have a very nice report from Captain Maxwell.'

'I will leave you the letter to show Jacob,' said the Captain, putting it clumsily back in its envelope.

'Jacob is after his butterflies as usual,' said Mrs Flanders irritably, but was surprised by a sudden afterthought, 'Cricket begins this week, of course.'

'Edward Jenkinson has handed in his resignation,' said Captain Barfoot.

'Then you will stand for the council?' Mrs Flanders exclaimed, looking the Captain full in the face.

'Well, about that – ' Captain Barfoot began, settling himself rather deeper in his chair.

Jacob Flanders, therefore, went up to Cambridge in October, 1906.[22]

Chapter 3

'This is not a smoking-carriage,' Mrs Norman protested, nervously but very feebly, as the door swung open and a powerfully built young man jumped in. He seemed not to hear her. The train did not stop before it reached Cambridge, and here she was shut up alone, in a railway carriage, with a young man.

She touched the spring of her dressing-case and ascertained that the scent-bottle and a novel from Mudie's[23] were both handy (the young man was standing up with his back to her, putting his bag in the rack). She would throw the scent-bottle with her right hand, she decided, and tug the communication cord with her left. She was fifty years of age, and had a son at college. Nevertheless, it is a fact that men are dangerous. She read half a column of her newspaper; then stealthily looked over the edge to decide the question of safety by the infallible test of appearance . . . She would like to offer him her paper. But do young men read the *Morning Post*? She looked to see what he was reading – the *Daily Telegraph*.[24]

Taking note of socks (loose), of tie (shabby), she once more reached his face. She dwelt upon his mouth. The lips were shut. The eyes bent down, since he was reading. All was firm, yet youthful, indifferent, unconscious – as for knocking one down! No, no, no! She looked out of the window, smiling slightly now, and then came back again, for he didn't notice her. Grave, unconscious . . . now he looked up, past her . . . he seemed so out of place, somehow, alone with an elderly lady . . . then he fixed his eyes – which were blue – on the landscape. He had not realised her presence, she thought. Yet it was none of *her* fault that this was not a smoking-carriage – if that was what he meant.

Nobody sees anyone as he is, let alone an elderly lady sitting opposite a strange young man in a railway carriage. They see a whole – they see all sorts of things – they see themselves . . . Mrs Norman now read three pages of one of Mr Norris's novels.[25] Should she say to the young man (and after all he was just the same age as her own boy): 'If you want to smoke, don't mind me'? No: he seemed absolutely indifferent to her presence . . . she did not wish to interrupt.

But since, even at her age, she noted his indifference, presumably he was in some way or other – to her at least – nice, handsome, interesting, distinguished, well built, like her own boy? One must do the best one can with her report. Anyhow, this was Jacob Flanders, aged nineteen. It is no use trying to sum people up. One must follow hints, not exactly what is said, nor yet entirely what is done – for instance, when the train drew into the station, Mr Flanders burst open the door, and put the lady's dressing-case out for her, saying, or rather mumbling: 'Let me,' very shyly; indeed he was rather clumsy about it.

'Who . . . ' said the lady, meeting her son; but as there was a great crowd on the platform and Jacob had already gone, she did not finish her sentence. As this was Cambridge, as she was staying there for the weekend, as she saw nothing but young men all day long, in streets and round tables, this sight of her fellow-traveller was completely lost in her mind, as the crooked pin dropped by a child into the wishing-well twirls in the water and disappears for ever.

They say the sky is the same everywhere. Travellers, the shipwrecked, exiles and the dying draw comfort from the thought, and no doubt if you are of a mystical tendency, consolation, and even explanation, shower down from the unbroken surface. But above Cambridge – anyhow above the roof of King's College Chapel[26] – there is a difference. Out at sea a great city will cast a brightness into the night. Is it fanciful to suppose the sky, washed into the crevices of King's College Chapel, lighter, thinner, more sparkling than the sky elsewhere? Does Cambridge burn not only into the night, but into the day?

Look, as they pass into service, how airily the gowns blow out, as though nothing dense and corporeal were within. What sculptured faces, what certainty, authority controlled by piety, although great boots march under the gowns. In what orderly procession they advance. Thick wax candles stand upright; young men rise in white gowns; while the subservient eagle bears up for inspection the great white book.[27]

An inclined plane of light comes accurately through each window, purple and yellow even in its most diffused dust, while, where it breaks upon stone, that stone is softly chalked red, yellow and purple. Neither snow nor greenery, winter nor summer, has power over the old stained glass. As the sides of a lantern protect the flame so that it burns steady even in the wildest night – burns steady and gravely illumines the tree-trunks – so inside the Chapel all was orderly. Gravely sounded the voices; wisely the organ replied, as if buttressing human faith with the assent of the elements. The white-robed figures crossed from side to side; now mounted steps, now descended, all very orderly.

. . . If you stand a lantern under a tree every insect in the forest creeps up to it – a curious assembly, since though they scramble and swing and knock their heads against the glass, they seem to have no purpose – something senseless inspires them. One gets tired of watching them, as they amble round the lantern and blindly tap as if for admittance, one large toad being the most besotted of any and shouldering his way through the rest. Ah, but what's that? A terrifying volley of pistol-shots rings out – cracks sharply; ripples spread – silence laps smooth over sound. A tree – a tree has fallen, a sort of death in the forest. After that, the wind in the trees sounds melancholy.

But this service in King's College Chapel – why allow women to take part in it? Surely, if the mind wanders (and Jacob looked extraordinarily vacant, his head thrown back, his hymn-book open at the wrong place), if the mind wanders it is because several hat shops and cupboards upon cupboards of coloured dresses are displayed upon rush-bottomed chairs. Though heads and bodies may be devout enough, one has a sense of individuals – some like blue, others brown; some feathers, others pansies and forget-me-nots. No one would think of bringing a dog into church. For though a dog is all very well on a gravel path, and shows no disrespect to flowers, the way he wanders down an aisle, looking, lifting a paw, and approaching a pillar with a purpose that makes the blood run cold with horror (should you be one of a congregation – alone, shyness is out of the question), a dog destroys the service completely. So do these women – though separately devout, distinguished, and vouched for by the theology, mathematics, Latin and Greek of their husbands. Heaven knows why it is. For one thing, thought Jacob, they're as ugly as sin.

Now there was a scraping and murmuring. He caught Timmy Durrant's eye; looked very sternly at him; and then, very solemnly, winked.

'Waverley',[28] the villa on the road to Girton was called, not that Mr Plumer admired Scott or would have chosen any name at all, but names are useful when you have to entertain undergraduates, and as they sat waiting for the fourth undergraduate, on Sunday at lunchtime, there was talk of names upon gates.

'How tiresome,' Mrs Plumer interrupted impulsively. 'Does anybody know Mr Flanders?'

Mr Durrant knew him; and therefore blushed slightly, and said, awkwardly, something about being sure – looking at Mr Plumer and hitching the right leg of his trousers as he spoke. Mr Plumer got up and stood in front of the fireplace. Mrs Plumer laughed like a straightforward friendly fellow. In short, anything more horrible than the scene, the setting, the prospect, even the May garden being afflicted with chill sterility and a cloud choosing that moment to cross the sun, cannot be imagined. There was the garden, of course. Everyone at the same moment looked at it. Owing to the cloud, the leaves ruffled grey, and the sparrows – there were two sparrows.

'I think – ' said Mrs Plumer, taking advantage of the momentary respite, while the young men stared at the garden, to look at her husband, and he, not accepting full responsibility for the act, nevertheless touched the bell.

There can be no excuse for this outrage upon one hour of human life, save the reflection which occurred to Mr Plumer as he carved the mutton, that if no don ever gave a luncheon party, if Sunday after Sunday passed, if men went down,[29] became lawyers, doctors, Members of Parliament, businessmen – if no don ever gave a luncheon party –

'Now, does lamb make the mint sauce, or mint sauce make the lamb?' he asked the young man next him, to break a silence which had already lasted five minutes and a half.

'I don't know, sir,' said the young man, blushing very vividly.

At this moment in came Mr Flanders. He had mistaken the time.

Now, though they had finished their meat, Mrs Plumer took a second helping of cabbage. Jacob determined, of course, that he would eat his meat in the time it took her to finish her cabbage, looking once or twice to measure his speed – only he was infernally hungry. Seeing this, Mrs Plumer said that she was sure Mr Flanders would not mind – and the tart was brought in. Nodding in a peculiar way, she directed the maid to give Mr Flanders a second helping of mutton. She glanced at the mutton. Not much of the leg would be left for luncheon.

It was none of her fault – since how could she control her father begetting her forty years ago in the suburbs of Manchester?[30] and once begotten, how could she do other than grow up cheese-paring, ambitious, with an instinctively accurate notion of the rungs of the ladder and an ant-like assiduity in pushing George Plumer ahead of her to the top of the ladder? What was at the top of the ladder? A sense that all the rungs were beneath one apparently; since by the time that George Plumer became Professor of Physics, or whatever it might be, Mrs Plumer could only be in a condition to cling tight to her eminence, peer down at the ground, and goad her two plain daughters to climb the rungs of the ladder.

'I was down at the races yesterday,' she said, 'with my two little girls.'

It was none of *their* fault either. In they came to the drawing-room, in white frocks and blue sashes. They handed the cigarettes. Rhoda had inherited her father's cold grey eyes. Cold grey eyes George Plumer had, but in them was an abstract light. He could talk about Persia and the trade winds, the Reform Bill[31] and the cycle of the harvests. Books were on his shelves by Wells and Shaw;[32] on the table serious sixpenny weeklies written by pale men in muddy boots – the weekly creak and screech of brains rinsed in cold water and wrung dry – melancholy papers.

'I don't feel that I know the truth about anything till I've read them both!' said Mrs Plumer brightly, tapping the table of contents with her bare red hand, upon which the ring looked so incongruous.

'Oh God, oh God, oh God!' exclaimed Jacob, as the four under-graduates left the house. 'Oh, my God!'

'Bloody beastly!' he said, scanning the street for lilac or bicycle – anything to restore his sense of freedom.

'Bloody beastly,' he said to Timmy Durrant, summing up his discomfort at the world shown him at lunchtime, a world capable of existing – there was no doubt about that – but so unnecessary, such a thing to believe in – Shaw and Wells and the serious sixpenny weeklies! What were they after, scrubbing and demolishing, these elderly people? Had they never read Homer, Shakespeare, the Elizabethans? He saw it clearly outlined against the feelings he drew from youth and natural inclination. The poor devils had rigged up this meagre object. Yet something of pity was in him. Those wretched little girls –

The extent to which he was disturbed proves that he was already agog. Insolent he was and inexperienced, but sure enough the cities which the elderly of the race have built upon the skyline showed like brick suburbs, barracks and places of discipline against a red and yellow flame. He was impressionable; but the word is contradicted by the composure with which he hollowed his hand to screen a match. He was a young man of substance.

Anyhow, whether undergraduate or shop boy, man or woman, it must come as a shock about the age of twenty – the world of the elderly – thrown up in such black outline upon what we are; upon the reality; the moors and Byron;[33] the sea and the lighthouse; the sheep's jaw with the yellow teeth in it; upon the obstinate irrepressible conviction which makes youth so intolerably disagreeable – 'I am what I am, and intend to be it,' for which there will be no form in the world unless Jacob makes one for himself. The Plumers will try to prevent him from making it. Wells and Shaw and the serious sixpenny weeklies will sit on its head. Every time he lunches out on Sunday – at dinner parties and tea parties – there will be this same shock – horror – discomfort – then pleasure, for he draws into him at every step as he walks by the river such steady certainty, such reassurance from all sides, the trees bowing, the grey spires soft in the blue, voices blowing and seeming suspended in the air, the springy air of May, the elastic air with its particles – chestnut bloom, pollen, whatever it is that gives the May air its potency, blurring the trees, gumming the buds, daubing the green. And the river too runs past, not at flood, nor swiftly, but cloying the oar that dips in it and drops white drops from the blade, swimming green and deep over the bowed rushes, as if lavishly caressing them.

Where they moored their boat the trees showered down, so that their topmost leaves trailed in the ripples and the green wedge that lay in the water being made of leaves shifted in leaf-breadths as the real leaves shifted. Now there was a shiver of wind – instantly an edge of sky; and as Durrant ate cherries he dropped the stunted yellow cherries through the green wedge of leaves, their stalks twinkling as they wriggled in and out, and sometimes one half-bitten cherry would go down red into the green. The meadow was on a level with Jacob's eyes as he lay back; gilt with buttercups, but the grass did not run like the thin green water of the graveyard grass about to overflow the tombstones but stood juicy and thick. Looking up, backwards, he saw the legs of children deep in the grass, and the legs of cows. Munch, munch, he heard; then a short step through the grass; then again munch, munch, munch, as they tore the grass short at the roots. In front of him two white butterflies circled higher and higher round the elm tree.

'Jacob's off,' thought Durrant, looking up from his novel. He kept reading a few pages and then looking up in a curiously methodical manner, and each time he looked up he took a few cherries out of the bag and ate them abstractedly. Other boats passed them, crossing the backwater from side to side to avoid each other, for many were now moored, and there were now white dresses and a flaw in the column of air between two trees, round which curled a thread of blue – Lady Miller's picnic party. Still more boats kept coming, and Durrant, without getting up, shoved their boat closer to the bank.

'Oh–h–h–h,' groaned Jacob, as the boat rocked, and the trees rocked, and the white dresses and the white flannel trousers drew out long and wavering up the bank.

'Oh–h–h–h!' He sat up, and felt as if a piece of elastic had snapped in his face.

'They're friends of my mother's,' said Durrant. 'So old Bow took no end of trouble about the boat.'

And this boat had gone from Falmouth to St Ives Bay, all round the coast. A larger boat, a ten-ton yacht, about the twentieth of June, properly fitted out, Durrant said . . .

'There's the cash difficulty,' said Jacob.

'My people'll see to that,' said Durrant (the son of a banker, deceased).

'I intend to preserve my economic independence,' said Jacob stiffly. (He was getting excited.)

'My mother said something about going to Harrogate,' he said with a little annoyance, feeling the pocket where he kept his letters.

'Was that true about your uncle becoming a Mohammedan?' asked Timmy Durrant.

Jacob had told the story of his Uncle Morty in Durrant's room the night before.

'I expect he's feeding the sharks, if the truth were known,' said Jacob. 'I say, Durrant, there's none left!' he exclaimed, crumpling the bag which had held the cherries, and throwing it into the river. He saw Lady Miller's picnic party on the island as he threw the bag into the river.

A sort of awkwardness, grumpiness, gloom came into his eyes.

'Shall we move on . . . this beastly crowd . . . ' he said.

So up they went, past the island.

The feathery white moon never let the sky grow dark; all night the chestnut blossoms were white in the green; dim was the cow-parsley in the meadows.

The waiters at Trinity[34] must have been shuffling china plates like cards, from the clatter that could be heard in the Great Court. Jacob's rooms, however, were in Neville's Court;[35] at the top; so that reaching his door one went in a little out of breath; but he wasn't there. Dining in Hall, presumably. It will be quite dark in Neville's Court long before midnight, only the pillars opposite will always be white, and the fountains. A curious effect the gate has, like lace upon pale green. Even in the window you hear the plates; a hum of talk, too, from the diners; the Hall lit up, and the swing-doors opening and shutting with a soft thud. Some are late.

Jacob's room had a round table and two low chairs. There were yellow flags in a jar on the mantelpiece; a photograph of his mother; cards from societies with little raised crescents, coats of arms and initials; notes and pipes; on the table lay paper ruled with a red margin – an essay, no doubt – 'Does History Consist of the Biographies of Great Men?'[36] There were books enough; very few French books; but then anyone who's worth anything reads just what he likes, as the mood takes him, with extravagant enthusiasm. Lives of the Duke of Wellington, for example; Spinoza; the works of Dickens; *The Faerie Queene*; a Greek dictionary with the petals of poppies pressed to silk between the pages; all the Elizabethans. His slippers were incredibly shabby, like boats burnt to the water's rim. Then there were photographs from the Greeks, and a mezzotint from Sir Joshua[37] – all very English. The works of Jane Austen, too, in deference, perhaps, to someone else's standard. Carlyle was a prize. There were books upon the Italian painters of the Renaissance, a *Manual of the Diseases of the Horse*,[38] and all the usual textbooks. Listless is the air in an empty room, just swelling the curtain; the flowers in the jar shift. One fibre in the wicker armchair creaks, though no one sits there.

Coming down the steps a little sideways (Jacob sat on the window-seat talking to Durrant; he smoked, and Durrant looked at the map), the old man, with his hands locked behind him, his gown floating black, lurched, unsteadily, near the wall; then, upstairs he went into his room. Then another, who raised his hand and praised the columns, the gate, the sky; another, tripping and smug. Each went up a staircase; three lights were lit in the dark windows.

If any light burns above Cambridge, it must be from three such rooms; Greek burns here; science there; philosophy on the ground floor. Poor old Huxtable can't walk straight; Sopwith, too, has praised the sky any night these twenty years; and Cowan[39] still chuckles at the same stories. It is not simple, or pure, or wholly splendid, the lamp of learning, since if you see them there under its light (whether Rossetti's on the wall, or Van Gogh reproduced,[40] whether there are lilacs in the bowl or rusty pipes), how priestly they look! How like a suburb where you go to see a view and eat a special cake! 'We are the sole purveyors of this cake.' Back you go to London; for the treat is over.

Old Professor Huxtable, performing with the method of a clock his change of dress, let himself down into his chair; filled his pipe; chose his paper; crossed his feet; and extracted his glasses. The whole flesh of his face then fell into folds as if props were removed. Yet strip a whole seat of an underground railway carriage of its heads and old Huxtable's head will hold them all. Now, as his eye goes down the print, what a procession tramps through the corridors of his brain, orderly, quick-stepping, and reinforced, as the march goes on, by fresh runnels, till the whole hall, dome, whatever one calls it, is populous with ideas. Such a muster takes place in no other brain. Yet sometimes there he'll sit for hours together, gripping the arm of the chair, like a man holding fast because stranded, and then, just because his corn twinges, or it may be the gout, what execrations, and, dear me, to hear him talk of money, taking out his leather purse and grudging even the smallest silver coin, secretive and suspicious as an old peasant woman with all her lies. Strange paralysis and constriction – marvellous illumination. Serene over it all rides the great full brow, and sometimes asleep or in the quiet spaces of the night you might fancy that on a pillow of stone he lay triumphant.

Sopwith, meanwhile, advancing with a curious trip from the fireplace, cut the chocolate cake into segments. Until midnight or later there would be undergraduates in his room, sometimes as many as twelve, sometimes three or four; but nobody got up when they went or when they came; Sopwith went on talking. Talking, talking, talking – as if everything could be talked – the soul itself slipped through the lips in thin silver disks which dissolve in young men's minds like silver, like moonlight. Oh, far away they'd remember it, and deep in dullness gaze back on it, and come to refresh themselves again.

'Well, I never. That's old Chucky. My dear boy, how's the world treating you?' And in came poor little Chucky, the unsuccessful provincial, Stenhouse his real name, but of course Sopwith brought back by using the other everything, everything, 'all I could never be' – yes, though next day, buying his newspaper and catching the early train, it all seemed to him childish, absurd; the chocolate cake, the young men; Sopwith summing things up; no, not all; he would send his son there. He would save every penny to send his son there.

Sopwith went on talking; twining stiff fibres of awkward speech – things young men blurted out – plaiting them round his own smooth garland, making the bright side show, the vivid greens, the sharp thorns, manliness. He loved it. Indeed to Sopwith a man could say anything, until perhaps he'd grown old, or gone under, gone deep, when the silver disks would tinkle hollow, and the inscription read a little too simple, and the old stamp look too pure, and the impress always the same – a Greek boy's head. But he would respect still. A woman, divining the priest, would, involuntarily, despise.

Cowan, Erasmus Cowan, sipped his port alone, or with one rosy little man, whose memory held precisely the same span of time; sipped his port, and told his stories, and without book before him intoned Latin, Virgil and Catullus, as if language were wine upon his lips. Only – sometimes it will come over one – what if the poet strode in? 'This my image?' he might ask, pointing to the chubby man, whose brain is, after all, Virgil's representative among us, though the body gluttonise, and as for arms, bees, or even the plough,[41] Cowan takes his trips abroad with a French novel in his pocket, a rug about his knees, and is thankful to be home again in his place, in his line, holding up in his snug little mirror the image of Virgil, all rayed round with good stories of the dons of Trinity and red beams of port. But language is wine upon his lips. Nowhere else would Virgil hear the like. And though, as she goes sauntering along the Backs, old Miss Umphelby sings him melodiously enough, accurately too, she is always brought up by this question as she reaches Clare Bridge: 'But if I met him, what should I wear?' – and then, taking her way up the avenue towards Newnham, she lets her fancy play upon other details of men's meeting with women which have never got into print. Her lectures, therefore, are not half so well attended as those of Cowan, and the thing she might have said in elucidation of the text is for ever left out.[42] In short, face a teacher with the image of the taught and the mirror breaks. But Cowan sipped his port, his exaltation over, no longer the representative of Virgil. No, the builder, assessor, surveyor, rather; ruling lines between names, hanging lists above doors. Such is the fabric through which the light must shine, if shine it can – the light of all these languages, Chinese and Russian, Persian and Arabic, of symbols and figures, of history, of things that are known and things that are about to be known. So that if at night, far out at sea over the tumbling waves, one saw a haze on the waters, a city illuminated, a whiteness even in the sky, such as that now over the Hall of Trinity where they're still dining, or washing up plates, that would be the light burning there – the light of Cambridge.

'Let's go round to Simeon's room,' said Jacob, and they rolled up the map, having got the whole thing settled.

*

All the lights were coming out round the court, and falling on the cobbles, picking out dark patches of grass and single daisies. The young men were now back in their rooms. Heaven knows what they were doing. What was it that could *drop* like that? And leaning down over a foaming window-box, one stopped another hurrying past, and upstairs they went and down they went, until a sort of fullness settled on the court, the hive full of bees, the bees home thick with gold, drowsy, humming, suddenly vocal; the Moonlight Sonata[43] answered by a waltz.

The Moonlight Sonata tinkled away; the waltz crashed. Although young men still went in and out, they walked as if keeping engagements. Now and then there was a thud, as if some heavy piece of furniture had fallen, unexpectedly, of its own accord, not in the general stir of life after dinner. One supposed that young men raised their eyes from their books as the furniture fell. Were they reading? Certainly there was a sense of concentration in the air. Behind the grey walls sat so many young men, some undoubtedly reading magazines, shilling shockers,[44] no doubt; legs, perhaps, over the arms of chairs; smoking; sprawling over tables, and writing while their heads went round in a circle as the pen moved – simple young men, these, who would – but there is no need to think of them grown old; others eating sweets; here they boxed; and, well, Mr Hawkins must have been mad suddenly to throw up his window and bawl: 'Jo–seph! Jo–seph!' and then he ran as hard as ever he could across the court, while an elderly man, in a green apron, carrying an immense pile of tin covers, hesitated, balanced, and then went on. But this was a diversion. There were young men who read, lying in shallow armchairs, holding their books as if they had hold in their hands of something that would see them through; they being all in a torment, coming from midland towns, clergymen's sons. Others read Keats. And those long histories in many volumes – surely someone was now beginning at the beginning in order to understand the Holy Roman Empire, as one must. That was part of the concentration, though it would be dangerous on a hot spring night – dangerous, perhaps, to concentrate too much upon single books, actual chapters, when at any moment the door opened and Jacob appeared; or Richard Bonamy, reading Keats no longer, began making long pink spills from an old newspaper, bending forward, and looking eager and contented no more, but almost fierce. Why? Only perhaps that Keats died young – one wants to write poetry too and to love – oh, the brutes! It's damnably difficult. But, after all, not so difficult if on the next staircase, in the large room, there are two, three, five young men all convinced of this –

of brutality, that is, and the clear division between right and wrong. There was a sofa, chairs, a square table, and the window being open, one could see how they sat – legs issuing here, one there crumpled in a corner of the sofa; and, presumably, for you could not see him, some-body stood by the fender, talking. Anyhow, Jacob, who sat astride a chair and ate dates from a long box, burst out laughing. The answer came from the sofa corner; for his pipe was held in the air, then replaced. Jacob wheeled round. He had something to say to *that*, though the sturdy red-haired boy at the table seemed to deny it, wagging his head slowly from side to side; and then, taking out his penknife, he dug the point of it again and again into a knot in the table, as if affirming that the voice from the fender spoke the truth – which Jacob could not deny. Possibly, when he had done arranging the date-stones, he might find something to say to it – indeed his lips opened – only then there broke out a roar of laughter.

The laughter died in the air. The sound of it could scarcely have reached anyone standing by the Chapel, which stretched along the opposite side of the court. The laughter died out, and only gestures of arms, movements of bodies, could be seen shaping something in the room. Was it an argument? A bet on the boat races? Was it nothing of the sort? What was shaped by the arms and bodies moving in the twilight room?

A step or two beyond the window there was nothing at all, except the enclosing buildings – chimneys upright, roofs horizontal; too much brick and building for a May night, perhaps. And then before one's eyes would come the bare hills of Turkey – sharp lines, dry earth, coloured flowers, and colour on the shoulders of the women, standing naked-legged in the stream to beat linen on the stones. The stream made loops of water round their ankles. But none of that could show clearly through the swaddlings and blanketings of the Cambridge night. The stroke of the clock even was muffled; as if intoned by somebody reverent from a pulpit; as if generations of learned men heard the last hour go rolling through their ranks and issued it, already smooth and time-worn, with their blessing, for the use of the living.

Was it to receive this gift from the past that the young man came to the window and stood there, looking out across the court? It was Jacob. He stood smoking his pipe while the last stroke of the clock purred softly round him. Perhaps there had been an argument. He looked satisfied; indeed masterly; which expression changed slightly as he stood there, the sound of the clock conveying to him (it may be) a sense of old buildings and time; and himself the inheritor; and then tomorrow; and friends; at the thought of whom, in sheer confidence and pleasure, it seemed, he yawned and stretched himself.

Meanwhile behind him the shape they had made, whether by argument or not, the spiritual shape, hard yet ephemeral, as of glass compared with the dark stone of the Chapel, was dashed to splinters, young men rising from chairs and sofa corners, buzzing and barging about the room, one driving another against the bedroom door, which giving way, in they fell. Then Jacob was left there, in the shallow armchair, alone with Masham? Anderson? Simeon? Oh, it was Simeon. The others had all gone.

' . . . Julian the Apostate[45] . . . ' Which of them said that and the other words murmured round it? But about midnight there sometimes rises, like a veiled figure suddenly woken, a heavy wind; and this now flapping through Trinity lifted unseen leaves and blurred everything. 'Julian the Apostate' – and then the wind. Up go the elm branches, out blow the sails, the old schooners rear and plunge, the grey waves in the hot Indian Ocean tumble sultrily, and then all falls flat again.

So, if the veiled lady stepped through the courts of Trinity, she now drowsed once more, all her draperies about her, her head against a pillar.

'Somehow it seems to matter.'

The low voice was Simeon's.

The voice was even lower that answered him. The sharp tap of a pipe on the mantelpiece cancelled the words. And perhaps Jacob only said 'hum', or said nothing at all. True, the words were inaudible. It was the intimacy, a sort of spiritual suppleness, when mind prints upon mind indelibly.

'Well, you seem to have studied the subject,' said Jacob, rising and standing over Simeon's chair. He balanced himself; he swayed a little. He appeared extraordinarily happy, as if his pleasure would brim and spill down the sides if Simeon spoke.

Simeon said nothing. Jacob remained standing. But intimacy – the room was full of it, still, deep, like a pool. Without need of movement or speech it rose softly and washed over everything, mollifying, kindling, and coating the mind with the lustre of pearl, so that if you talk of a light, of Cambridge burning, it's not languages only. It's Julian the Apostate.

But Jacob moved. He murmured good-night. He went out into the court. He buttoned his jacket across his chest. He went back to his rooms, and being the only man who walked at that moment back to his rooms, his footsteps rang out, his figure loomed large. Back from the Chapel, back from the Hall, back from the Library, came the sound of his footsteps, as if the old stone echoed with magisterial authority: 'The young man – the young men – the young man – back to his rooms.'

Chapter 4

What's the use of trying to read Shakespeare, especially in one of those little thin paper editions whose pages get ruffled, or stuck together with sea-water? Although the plays of Shakespeare[46] had frequently been praised, even quoted, and placed higher than the Greek, never since they started had Jacob managed to read one through. Yet what an opportunity!

For the Scilly Isles had been sighted by Timmy Durrant lying like mountain-tops almost awash in precisely the right place. His calculations had worked perfectly, and really the sight of him sitting there, with his hand on the tiller, rosy gilled, with a sprout of beard, looking sternly at the stars, then at a compass, spelling out quite correctly his page of the eternal lesson-book, would have moved a woman. Jacob, of course, was not a woman. The sight of Timmy Durrant was no sight for him, nothing to set against the sky and worship; far from it. They had quarrelled. Why the right way to open a tin of beef, with Shakespeare on board, under conditions of such splendour, should have turned them to sulky schoolboys, none can tell. Tinned beef is cold eating, though; and salt water spoils biscuits; and the waves tumble and lollop much the same hour after hour – tumble and lollop all across the horizon. Now a spray of seaweed floats past – now a log of wood. Ships have been wrecked here. One or two go past, keeping their own side of the road. Timmy knew where they were bound, what their cargoes were, and, by looking through his glass, could tell the name of the line, and even guess what dividends it paid its shareholders. Yet that was no reason for Jacob to turn sulky.

The Scilly Isles had the look of mountain-tops almost awash . . . Unfortunately, Jacob broke the pin of the Primus stove.

The Scilly Isles might well be obliterated by a roller sweeping straight across.

But one must give young men the credit of admitting that, though breakfast eaten under these circumstances is grim, it is sincere enough. No need to make conversation. They got out their pipes.

Timmy wrote up some scientific observations; and – what was the question that broke the silence – the exact time or the day of the month? anyhow, it was spoken without the least awkwardness; in the most matter-of-fact way in the world; and then Jacob began to unbutton his clothes and sat naked, save for his shirt, intending, apparently, to bathe.

The Scilly Isles were turning bluish; and suddenly blue, purple and green flushed the sea; left it grey; struck a stripe which vanished; but when Jacob had got his shirt over his head the whole floor of the waves was blue and white, rippling and crisp, though now and again a broad purple mark appeared, like a bruise; or there floated an entire emerald tinged with yellow. He plunged. He gulped in water, spat it out, struck with his right arm, struck with his left, was towed by a rope, gasped, splashed, and was hauled on board.

The seat in the boat was positively hot, and the sun warmed his back as he sat naked with a towel in his hand, looking at the Scilly Isles which – confound it! the sail flapped. Shakespeare was knocked overboard. There you could see him floating merrily away, with all his pages ruffling innumerably; and then he went under.

Strangely enough, you could smell violets, or if violets were impossible in July, they must grow something very pungent on the mainland then. The mainland, not so very far off – you could see clefts in the cliffs, white cottages, smoke going up – wore an extraordinary look of calm, of sunny peace, as if wisdom and piety had descended upon the dwellers there. Now a cry sounded, as of a man calling pilchards in a main street. It wore an extraordinary look of piety and peace, as if old men smoked by the door, and girls stood, hands on hips, at the well, and horses stood; as if the end of the world had come, and cabbage fields and stone walls and coastguard stations and, above all, the white-sand bays with the waves breaking unseen by anyone rose to heaven in a kind of ecstasy.

But imperceptibly the cottage smoke droops, has the look of a mourning emblem, a flag floating its caress over a grave. The gulls, making their broad flight and then riding at peace, seem to mark the grave.

No doubt if this were Italy, Greece, or even the shores of Spain, sadness would be routed by strangeness and excitement and the nudge of a classical education. But the Cornish hills have stark chimneys standing on them; and, somehow or other, loveliness is infernally sad. Yes, the chimneys and the coastguard stations and the little bays with the waves breaking unseen by anyone make one remember the overpowering sorrow. And what can this sorrow be?

*

It is brewed by the earth itself. It comes from the houses on the coast. We start transparent, and then the cloud thickens. All history backs our pane of glass. To escape is vain.

But whether this is the right interpretation of Jacob's gloom as he sat naked, in the sun, looking at the Land's End, it is impossible to say; for he never spoke a word. Timmy sometimes wondered (only for a second) whether his people bothered him . . . No matter. There are things that can't be said. Let's shake it off. Let's dry ourselves, and take up the first thing that comes handy . . . Timmy Durrant's notebook of scientific observations.

'Now . . . ' said Jacob.

It is a tremendous argument.

Some people can follow every step of the way, and even take a little one, six inches long, by themselves at the end; others remain observant of the external signs.

The eyes fix themselves upon the poker; the right hand takes the poker and lifts it; turns it slowly round, and then, very accurately, replaces it. The left hand, which lies on the knee, plays some stately but intermittent piece of march music. A deep breath is taken; but allowed to evaporate unused. The cat marches across the hearth-rug. No one observes her.

'That's about as near as I can get to it,' Durrant wound up.

The next minute is quiet as the grave.

'It follows . . . ' said Jacob.

Only half a sentence followed; but these half-sentences are like flags set on tops of buildings to the observer of external sights down below. What was the coast of Cornwall, with its violet scents, and mourning emblems, and tranquil piety, but a screen happening to hang straight behind as his mind marched up?

'It follows . . . ' said Jacob.

'Yes,' said Timmy, after reflection. 'That is so.'

Now Jacob began plunging about, half to stretch himself, half in a kind of jollity, no doubt, for the strangest sound issued from his lips as he furled the sail, rubbed the plates – gruff, tuneless – a sort of paean, for having grasped the argument, for being master of the situation, sunburnt, unshaven, capable into the bargain of sailing round the world in a ten-ton yacht, which, very likely, he would do one of these days instead of settling down in a lawyer's office, and wearing spats.[47]

'Our friend Masham,' said Timmy Durrant, 'would rather not be seen in our company as we are now.' His buttons had come off.

'D'you know Masham's aunt?' said Jacob.

'Never knew he had one,' said Timmy.

'Masham has millions of aunts,' said Jacob.

'Masham is mentioned in Domesday Book,' said Timmy.

'So are his aunts,' said Jacob.

'His sister,' said Timmy, 'is a very pretty girl.'

'That's what'll happen to you, Timmy,' said Jacob.

'It'll happen to you first,' said Timmy.

'But this woman I was telling you about – Masham's aunt – '

'Oh, do get on,' said Timmy, for Jacob was laughing so much that he could not speak.

'Masham's aunt . . . '

Timmy laughed so much that he could not speak.

'Masham's aunt . . . '

'What is there about Masham that makes one laugh?' said Timmy.

'Hang it all – a man who swallows his tie-pin,' said Jacob.

'Lord Chancellor before he's fifty,' said Timmy.

'He's a gentleman,' said Jacob.

'The Duke of Wellington[48] was a gentleman,' said Timmy.

'Keats wasn't.'

'Lord Salisbury was.'

'And what about God?' said Jacob.

The Scilly Isles now appeared as if directly pointed at by a golden finger issuing from a cloud; and everybody knows how portentous that sight is, and how these broad rays, whether they light upon the Scilly Isles or upon the tombs of crusaders in cathedrals, always shake the very foundations of scepticism and lead to jokes about God.

> 'Abide with me:
> Fast falls the eventide;
> The shadows deepen;
> Lord, with me abide,'[49]

sang Timmy Durrant.

'At my place we used to have a hymn which began:

> Great God, what do I see and hear?'[50]

said Jacob.

Gulls rode gently swaying in little companies of two or three quite near the boat; the cormorant, as if following his long strained neck in eternal pursuit, skimmed an inch above the water to the next rock; and the drone of the tide in the caves came across the water, low, monotonous, like the voice of someone talking to himself.

'Rock of Ages, cleft for me,
Let me hide myself in thee,'[51]

sang Jacob.

Like the blunt tooth of some monster, a rock broke the surface; brown; overflown with perpetual waterfalls.

'Rock of Ages,'

Jacob sang, lying on his back, looking up into the sky at midday, from which every shred of cloud had been withdrawn, so that it was like something permanently displayed with the cover off.

By six o'clock a breeze blew in off an icefield; and by seven the water was more purple than blue; and by half-past seven there was a patch of rough gold-beater's skin round the Scilly Isles, and Durrant's face, as he sat steering, was of the colour of a red lacquer box polished for generations. By nine all the fire and confusion had gone out of the sky, leaving wedges of apple-green and plates of pale yellow; and by ten the lanterns on the boat were making twisted colours upon the waves, elongated or squab, as the waves stretched or humped themselves. The beam from the lighthouse strode rapidly across the water. Infinite millions of miles away powdered stars twinkled; but the waves slapped the boat, and crashed, with regular and appalling solemnity, against the rocks.

Although it would be possible to knock at the cottage door and ask for a glass of milk, it is only thirst that would compel the intrusion. Yet perhaps Mrs Pascoe[52] would welcome it. The summer's day may be wearing heavy. Washing in her little scullery, she may hear the cheap clock on the mantelpiece tick, tick, tick . . . tick, tick, tick. She is alone in the house. Her husband is out helping Farmer Hosken; her daughter married and gone to America. Her elder son is married too, but she does not agree with his wife. The Wesleyan minister came along and took the younger boy. She is alone in the house. A steamer, probably bound for Cardiff, now crosses the horizon, while near at hand one bell of a foxglove swings to and fro with a bumble-bee for clapper. These white Cornish cottages are built on the edge of the cliff; the garden grows gorse more readily than cabbages; and for hedge, some primeval man has piled granite boulders. In one of these, to hold, a historian conjectures, the victim's blood, a basin has been hollowed, but in our time it serves more tamely to seat those tourists

who wish for an uninterrupted view of the Gurnard's Head.[53] Not that
anyone objects to a blue print dress and a white apron in a cottage
garden.

'Look – she has to draw her water from a well in the garden.'

'Very lonely it must be in winter, with the wind sweeping over those
hills, and the waves dashing on the rocks.'

Even on a summer's day you hear them murmuring.

Having drawn her water, Mrs Pascoe went in. The tourists regretted
that they had brought no glasses, so that they might have read the
name of the tramp steamer.[54] Indeed, it was such a fine day that there
was no saying what a pair of field-glasses might not have fetched into
view. Two fishing luggers, presumably from St Ives Bay, were now
sailing in an opposite direction from the steamer, and the floor of the
sea became alternately clear and opaque. As for the bee, having sucked
its fill of honey, it visited the teasle and thence made a straight line to
Mrs Pascoe's patch, once more directing the tourists' gaze to the old
woman's print dress and white apron, for she had come to the door of
the cottage and was standing there.

There she stood, shading her eyes and looking out to sea.

For the millionth time, perhaps, she looked at the sea. A peacock
butterfly now spread himself upon the teasle, fresh and newly emerged,
as the blue and chocolate down on his wings testified. Mrs Pascoe
went indoors, fetched a cream pan, came out and stood scouring it.
Her face was assuredly not soft, sensual or lecherous, but hard, wise,
wholesome rather, signifying in a room full of sophisticated people
the flesh and blood of life. She would tell a lie, though, as soon as the
truth. Behind her on the wall hung a large dried skate. Shut up in the
parlour she prized mats, china mugs and photographs, though the
mouldy little room was saved from the salt breeze only by the depth of
a brick, and between lace curtains you saw the gannet drop like a
stone, and on stormy days the gulls came shuddering through the air,
and the steamers' lights were now high, now deep. Melancholy were
the sounds on a winter's night.

The picture papers were delivered punctually on Sunday, and she
pored long over Lady Cynthia's wedding at the Abbey.[55] She, too,
would have liked to ride in a carriage with springs. The soft, swift
syllables of educated speech often shamed her few rude ones. And then
all night to hear the grinding of the Atlantic upon the rocks instead of
hansom cabs and footmen whistling for motor cars . . . So she may have
dreamed, scouring her cream pan. But the talkative, nimble-witted
people have taken themselves to towns. Like a miser, she has hoarded

her feelings within her own breast. Not a penny piece has she changed all these years, and, watching her enviously, it seems as if all within must be pure gold.

The wise old woman, having fixed her eyes upon the sea, once more withdrew. The tourists decided that it was time to move on to the Gurnard's Head.

Three seconds later Mrs Durrant rapped upon the door.

'Mrs Pascoe?' she said.

Rather haughtily, she watched the tourists cross the field path. She came of a Highland race, famous for its chieftains.

Mrs Pascoe appeared.

'I envy you that bush, Mrs Pascoe,' said Mrs Durrant, pointing the parasol with which she had rapped on the door at the fine clump of St John's wort that grew beside it.

Mrs Pascoe looked at the bush deprecatingly.

'I expect my son in a day or two,' said Mrs Durrant. 'Sailing from Falmouth with a friend in a little boat . . . Any news of Lizzie yet, Mrs Pascoe?'

Her long-tailed ponies stood twitching their ears on the road twenty yards away. The boy, Curnow, flicked flies off them occasionally. He saw his mistress go into the cottage; come out again; and pass, talking energetically to judge by the movements of her hands, round the vegetable plot in front of the cottage. Mrs Pascoe was his aunt. Both women surveyed a bush. Mrs Durrant stooped and picked a sprig from it. Next she pointed (her movements were peremptory; she held herself very upright) at the potatoes. They had the blight. All potatoes that year had the blight. Mrs Durrant showed Mrs Pascoe how bad the blight was on her potatoes. Mrs Durrant talked energetically; Mrs Pascoe listened submissively. The boy Curnow knew that Mrs Durrant was saying that it is perfectly simple: you mix the powder in a gallon of water; 'I have done it with my own hands in my own garden,' Mrs Durrant was saying.

'You won't have a potato left – you won't have a potato left,' Mrs Durrant was saying in her emphatic voice as they reached the gate. The boy Curnow became as immobile as stone.

Mrs Durrant took the reins in her hands and settled herself on the driver's seat.

'Take care of that leg, or I shall send the doctor to you,' she called back over her shoulder; touched the ponies; and the carriage started forward. The boy Curnow had only just time to swing himself up by the toe of his boot. The boy Curnow, sitting in the middle of the back seat, looked at his aunt.

Mrs Pascoe stood at the gate looking after them; stood at the gate till the trap was round the corner; stood at the gate, looking now to the right, now to the left; then went back to her cottage.

Soon the ponies attacked the swelling moor road with striving forelegs. Mrs Durrant let the reins fall slackly, and leant backwards. Her vivacity had left her. Her hawk nose was thin as a bleached bone through which you almost see the light. Her hands, lying on the reins in her lap, were firm even in repose. The upper lip was cut so short that it raised itself almost in a sneer from the front teeth. Her mind skimmed leagues where Mrs Pascoe's mind adhered to its solitary patch. Her mind skimmed leagues as the ponies climbed the hill road. Forwards and backwards she cast her mind, as if the roofless cottages, mounds of slag, and cottage gardens overgrown with foxglove and bramble cast shade upon her mind. Arrived at the summit, she stopped the carriage. The pale hills were round her, each scattered with ancient stones; beneath was the sea, variable as a southern sea; she herself sat there looking from hill to sea, upright, aquiline, equally poised between gloom and laughter. Suddenly she flicked the ponies so that the boy Curnow had to swing himself up by the toe of his boot.

The rooks settled; the rooks rose. The trees which they touched so capriciously seemed insufficient to lodge their numbers. The tree-tops sang with the breeze in them; the branches creaked audibly and dropped now and then, though the season was midsummer, husks or twigs. Up went the rooks and down again, rising in lesser numbers each time as the sager birds made ready to settle, for the evening was already spent enough to make the air inside the wood almost dark. The moss was soft; the tree-trunks spectral. Beyond them lay a silvery meadow. The pampas grass raised its feathery spears from mounds of green at the end of the meadow. A breadth of water gleamed. Already the convolvulus moth was spinning over the flowers. Orange and purple, nasturtium and cherry pie, were washed into the twilight, but the tobacco plant and the passion flower, over which the great moth spun, were white as china. The rooks creaked their wings together on the tree-tops, and were settling down for sleep when, far off, a familiar sound shook and trembled – increased – fairly dinned in their ears – scared sleepy wings into the air again – the dinner bell at the house.

After six days of salt wind, rain and sun, Jacob Flanders had put on a dinner jacket. The discreet black object had made its appearance now and then in the boat among tins, pickles, preserved meats, and as the voyage went on had become more and more irrelevant, hardly to be believed in. And now, the world being stable, lit by candlelight, the dinner jacket alone preserved him. He could not be sufficiently thankful. Even so his neck, wrists and face were exposed without cover, and his whole person, whether exposed or not, tingled and glowed so as to make even black cloth an imperfect screen. He drew back the great red hand that lay on the tablecloth. Surreptitiously it closed upon slim glasses and curved silver forks. The bones of the cutlets were decorated with pink frills – and yesterday he had gnawn ham from the bone! Opposite him were hazy, semi-transparent shapes of yellow and blue. Behind them, again, was the grey-green garden, and among the pear-shaped leaves of the escallonia fishing-boats seemed caught and suspended. A sailing ship slowly drew past the women's backs. Two or three figures crossed the terrace hastily in the dusk. The door opened and shut. Nothing settled or stayed unbroken. Like oars rowing now this side, now that, were the sentences that came now here, now there, from either side of the table.

'Oh, Clara, Clara!' exclaimed Mrs Durrant, and Timothy Durrant adding, 'Clara, Clara,' Jacob named the shape in yellow gauze Timothy's sister, Clara. The girl sat smiling and flushed. With her brother's dark eyes, she was vaguer and softer than he was. When the laugh died down she said: 'But, mother, it was true. He said so, didn't he? Miss Eliot agreed with us . . . '

But Miss Eliot, tall, grey-headed, was making room beside her for the old man who had come in from the terrace. The dinner would never end, Jacob thought, and he did not wish it to end, though the ship had sailed from one corner of the window-frame to the other, and a light marked the end of the pier. He saw Mrs Durrant gaze at the light. She turned to him.

'Did you take command, or Timothy?' she said. 'Forgive me if I call you Jacob. I've heard so much of you.' Then her eyes went back to the sea. Her eyes glazed as she looked at the view.

'A little village once,' she said, 'and now grown . . . ' She rose, taking her napkin with her, and stood by the window.

'Did you quarrel with Timothy?' Clara asked shyly. 'I should have.' Mrs Durrant came back from the window.

'It gets later and later,' she said, sitting upright, and looking down the table. 'You ought to be ashamed – all of you. Mr Clutterbuck,[56] you ought to be ashamed.' She raised her voice, for Mr Clutterbuck was deaf.

'We *are* ashamed,' said a girl. But the old man with the beard went on eating plum tart. Mrs Durrant laughed and leant back in her chair, as if indulging him.

'We put it to you, Mrs Durrant,' said a young man with thick spectacles and a fiery moustache. 'I say the conditions were fulfilled. She owes me a sovereign.'

'Not *before* the fish – *with* it, Mrs Durrant,' said Charlotte Wilding.

'That was the bet; with the fish,' said Clara seriously. 'Begonias, mother. To eat them with his fish.'

'Oh dear,' said Mrs Durrant.

'Charlotte won't pay you,' said Timothy.

'How dare you . . . ' said Charlotte.

'That privilege will be mine,' said the courtly Mr Wortley, producing a silver case primed with sovereigns and slipping one coin on to the table. Then Mrs Durrant got up and passed down the room, holding herself very straight, and the girls in yellow and blue and silver gauze followed her, and elderly Miss Eliot in her velvet; and a little rosy woman, hesitating at the door, clean, scrupulous, probably a governess. All passed out at the open door.

'When you are as old as I am, Charlotte,' said Mrs Durrant, drawing the girl's arm within hers as they paced up and down the terrace.

'Why are you so sad?' Charlotte asked impulsively.

'Do I seem to you sad? I hope not,' said Mrs Durrant.

'Well, just now. You're *not* old.'

'Old enough to be Timothy's mother.' They stopped.

Miss Eliot was looking through Mr Clutterbuck's telescope at the edge of the terrace. The deaf old man stood beside her, fondling his beard, and reciting the names of the constellations: 'Andromeda, Bootes, Sidonia, Cassiopeia . . . '

'Andromeda,' murmured Miss Eliot, shifting the telescope slightly.

Mrs Durrant and Charlotte looked along the barrel of the instrument pointed at the skies.

'There are *millions* of stars,' said Charlotte with conviction. Miss Eliot turned away from the telescope. The young men laughed suddenly in the dining-room.

'Let *me* look,' said Charlotte eagerly.

'The stars bore me,' said Mrs Durrant, walking down the terrace with Julia Eliot. 'I read a book once about the stars . . . What are they saying?' She stopped in front of the dining-room window. 'Timothy,' she noted.

'The silent young man,' said Miss Eliot.

'Yes, Jacob Flanders,' said Mrs Durrant.

'Oh, mother! I didn't recognise you!' exclaimed Clara Durrant, coming from the opposite direction with Elsbeth. 'How delicious,' she breathed, crushing a verbena leaf.

Mrs Durrant turned and walked away by herself.

'Clara!' she called. Clara went to her.

'How unlike they are!' said Miss Eliot.

Mr Wortley passed them, smoking a cigar.

'Every day I live I find myself agreeing . . .' he said as he passed them.

'It's so interesting to guess . . .' murmured Julia Eliot.

'When first we came out we could see the flowers in that bed,' said Elsbeth.

'We see very little now,' said Miss Eliot.

'She must have been so beautiful, and everybody loved her, of course,' said Charlotte. 'I suppose Mr Wortley . . .' she paused.

'Edward's death was a tragedy,' said Miss Eliot decidedly.

Here Mr Erskine joined them.

'There's no such thing as silence,' he said positively. 'I can hear twenty different sounds on a night like this without counting your voices.'

'Make a bet of it?' said Charlotte.

'Done,' said Mr Erskine. 'One, the sea; two, the wind; three, a dog; four . . .'

The others passed on.

'Poor Timothy,' said Elsbeth.

'A very fine night,' shouted Miss Eliot into Mr Clutterbuck's ear.

'Like to look at the stars?' said the old man, turning the telescope towards Elsbeth.

'Doesn't it make you melancholy – looking at the stars?' shouted Miss Eliot.

'Dear me no, dear me no,' Mr Clutterbuck chuckled when he understood her. 'Why should it make me melancholy? Not for a moment – dear me no.'

'Thank you, Timothy, but I'm coming in,' said Miss Eliot. 'Elsbeth, here's a shawl.'

'I'm coming in,' Elsbeth murmured with her eye to the telescope. 'Cassiopeia,' she murmured. 'Where are you all?' she asked, taking her eye away from the telescope. 'How dark it is!'

Mrs Durrant sat in the drawing-room by a lamp winding a ball of wool.

Mr Clutterbuck read *The Times*. In the distance stood a second lamp, and round it sat the young ladies, flashing scissors over silver-spangled stuff for private theatricals. Mr Wortley read a book.

'Yes; he is perfectly right,' said Mrs Durrant, drawing herself up and ceasing to wind her wool. And while Mr Clutterbuck read the rest of Lord Lansdowne's[57] speech she sat upright, without touching her ball.

'Ah, Mr Flanders,' she said, speaking proudly, as if to Lord Lansdowne himself. Then she sighed and began to wind her wool again.

'Sit *there*,' she said.

Jacob came out from the dark place by the window where he had hovered. The light poured over him, illuminating every cranny of his skin; but not a muscle of his face moved as he sat looking out into the garden.

'I want to hear about your voyage,' said Mrs Durrant.

'Yes,' he said.

'Twenty years ago we did the same thing.'

'Yes,' he said.

She looked at him sharply.

'He is extraordinarily awkward,' she thought, noticing how he fingered his socks. 'Yet so distinguished-looking.'

'In those days . . . ' she resumed, and told him how they had sailed . . . 'my husband, who knew a good deal about sailing, for he kept a yacht before we married' . . . and then how rashly they had defied the fishermen, 'almost paid for it with our lives, but so proud of ourselves!' She flung the hand out that held the ball of wool.

'Shall I hold your wool?' Jacob asked stiffly.

'You do that for your mother,' said Mrs Durrant, looking at him again keenly, as she transferred the skein. 'Yes, it goes much better.'

He smiled; but said nothing.

Elsbeth Siddons hovered behind them with something silver on her arm.

'We want,' she said . . . 'I've come . . . ' she paused.

'Poor Jacob,' said Mrs Durrant, quietly, as if she had known him all his life. 'They're going to make you act in their play.'

'How I love you!' said Elsbeth, kneeling beside Mrs Durrant's chair.

'Give me the wool,' said Mrs Durrant.

'He's come – he's come!' cried Charlotte Wilding. 'I've won my bet!'

'There's another bunch higher up,' murmured Clara Durrant, mounting another step of the ladder. Jacob held the ladder[58] as she stretched out to reach the grapes high up on the vine.

'There!' she said, cutting through the stalk. She looked semi-transparent, pale, wonderfully beautiful up there among the vine leaves and the yellow and purple bunches, the lights swimming over her in coloured islands. Geraniums and begonias stood in pots along planks; tomatoes climbed the walls.

'The leaves really want thinning,' she considered, and one green one, spread like the palm of a hand, circled down past Jacob's head.

'I have more than I can eat already,' he said, looking up.

'It does seem absurd . . . ' Clara began, 'going back to London . . . '

'Ridiculous,' said Jacob, firmly.

'Then . . . ' said Clara, 'you must come next year, properly,' she said, snipping another vine leaf, rather at random.

'If . . . if . . . '

A child ran past the greenhouse shouting. Clara slowly descended the ladder with her basket of grapes.

'One bunch of white, and two of purple,' she said, and she placed two great leaves over them where they lay curled warm in the basket.

'I have enjoyed myself,' said Jacob, looking down the greenhouse.

'Yes, it's been delightful,' she said vaguely.

'Oh, Miss Durrant,' he said, taking the basket of grapes; but she walked past him towards the door of the greenhouse.

'You're too good – too good,' she thought, thinking of Jacob, thinking that he must not say that he loved her. No, no, no.

The children were whirling past the door, throwing things high into the air.

'Little demons!' she cried. 'What have they got?' she asked Jacob.

'Onions, I think,' said Jacob. He looked at them without moving.

'Next August, remember, Jacob,' said Mrs Durrant, shaking hands with him on the terrace where the fuchsia hung, like a scarlet ear-ring, behind her head. Mr Wortley came out of the window in yellow slippers, trailing *The Times* and holding out his hand very cordially.

'Goodbye,' said Jacob. 'Goodbye,' he repeated. 'Goodbye,' he said once more.

Charlotte Wilding flung up her bedroom window and cried out: 'Goodbye, Mr Jacob!'

'Mr Flanders!' cried Mr Clutterbuck, trying to extricate himself from his beehive chair. 'Jacob Flanders!'

'Too late, Joseph,' said Mrs Durrant.

'Not to sit for me,' said Miss Eliot, planting her tripod upon the lawn.

Chapter 5

'I rather think,' said Jacob, taking his pipe from his mouth, 'it's in Virgil,' and pushing back his chair, he went to the window.

The rashest drivers in the world are, certainly, the drivers of post-office vans. Swinging down Lamb's Conduit Street, the scarlet van rounded the corner by the pillar box in such a way as to graze the kerb and make the little girl who was standing on tiptoe to post a letter look up, half frightened, half curious. She paused with her hand in the mouth of the box; then dropped her letter and ran away. It is seldom only that we see a child on tiptoe with pity – more often a dim discomfort, a grain of sand in the shoe which it's scarcely worthwhile to remove – that's our feeling, and so – Jacob turned to the bookcase.

Long ago great people lived here, and coming back from Court past midnight stood, huddling their satin skirts, under the carved door-posts while the footman roused himself from his mattress on the floor, hurriedly fastened the lower buttons of his waistcoat, and let them in. The bitter eighteenth-century rain rushed down the kennel. South-ampton Row, however, is chiefly remarkable nowadays for the fact that you will always find a man there trying to sell a tortoise to a tailor. 'Showing off the tweed, sir; what the gentry wants is something singular to catch the eye, sir – and clean in their habits, sir!' So they display their tortoises.

At Mudie's corner in Oxford Street all the red and blue beads had run together on the string. The motor omnibuses were locked. Mr Spalding going to the City looked at Mr Charles Budgeon bound for Shepherd's Bush. The proximity of the omnibuses gave the outside passengers an opportunity to stare into each other's faces. Yet few took advantage of it. Each had his own business to think of. Each had his past shut in him like the leaves of a book known to him by heart; and his friends could only read the title, James Spalding or Charles Budgeon, and the passengers going the opposite way could read nothing at all – save 'a man with a red moustache', 'a young man in grey smoking a pipe'. The October sunlight rested upon all these men and women sitting immobile; and little Johnnie Sturgeon took the chance to swing down the staircase, carrying his large mysterious parcel, and so dodging a zigzag course between the wheels he reached the pavement, started to whistle a tune and was soon out of sight – for ever. The omnibuses jerked on, and every single person felt relief at being a little nearer to his journey's end, though some cajoled themselves past the immediate engagement by promise of indulgence beyond – steak and kidney pudding, drink or a game of dominoes in the smoky corner of a City restaurant. Oh yes, human life is very tolerable on the top of an omnibus in Holborn, when the policeman holds up his arm and the sun beats on your back, and if there is such a thing as a shell secreted by man to fit man himself[59] here we find it, on the banks of the Thames, where the great streets join and St Paul's Cathedral,[60] like the volute on the top of the snail shell, finishes it off. Jacob, getting off his omnibus, loitered up the steps, consulted his watch, and finally made up his mind to go in . . . Does it need an effort? Yes. These changes of mood wear us out.

Dim it is, haunted by ghosts of white marble, to whom the organ for ever chaunts. If a boot creaks, it's awful; then the order; the discipline. The verger with his rod has life ironed out beneath him. Sweet and holy are the angelic choristers. And for ever round the marble shoulders, in and out of the folded fingers, go the thin high sounds of voice and organ. For ever requiem – repose. Tired with scrubbing the steps of the Prudential Society's office, which she did year in year out, Mrs Lidgett took her seat beneath the great Duke's tomb,[61] folded her hands and half closed her eyes. A magnificent place for an old woman to rest in, by the very side of the great Duke's bones, whose victories mean nothing to her, whose name she knows not, though she never fails to greet the little angels opposite, as she passes out, wishing the like on her own tomb, for the leathern curtain of the heart has flapped wide, and out steal on tiptoe thoughts of rest, sweet melodies . . . Old Spicer, jute[62] merchant, thought nothing of the kind though. Strangely enough he'd never been in St Paul's these fifty years, though his office windows looked on the churchyard. 'So that's all? Well, a gloomy old place . . . Where's Nelson's tomb?[63] No time now – come again – a coin to leave in the box . . . Rain or fine is it? Well, if it would only make up its mind!' Idly the children stray in – the verger dissuades them – and another and another . . . man, woman, man, woman, boy . . . casting their eyes up, pursing their lips, the same shadow brushing the same faces; the leathern curtain of the heart flaps wide.

Nothing could appear more certain from the steps of St Paul's than that each person is miraculously provided with coat, skirt and boots; an income; an object. Only Jacob, carrying in his hand Finlay's *Byzantine Empire*,[64] which he had bought in Ludgate Hill, looked a little different; for in his hand he carried a book, which book he would at nine-thirty precisely, by his own fireside, open and study, as no one else of all these

multitudes would do. They have no houses. The streets belong to
them; the shops; the churches; theirs the innumerable desks; the
stretched office lights; the vans are theirs, and the railway slung high
above the street. If you look closer you will see that three elderly men
at a little distance from each other run spiders along the pavement as if
the street were their parlour, and here, against the wall, a woman
stares at nothing, boot-laces extended, which she does not ask you to
buy. The posters are theirs too; and the news on them. A town
destroyed; a race won. A homeless people, circling beneath the sky
whose blue or white is held off by a ceiling cloth of steel filings and
horse dung shredded to dust.

There, under the green shade, with his head bent over white paper,
Mr Sibley transferred figures to folios, and upon each desk you
observe, like provender, a bunch of papers, the day's nutriment, slowly
consumed by the industrious pen. Innumerable overcoats of the quality
prescribed hung empty all day in the corridors, but as the clock struck
six each was exactly filled, and the little figures, split apart into trousers
or moulded into a single thickness, jerked rapidly with angular forward
motion along the pavement; then dropped into darkness. Beneath the
pavement, sunk in the earth, hollow drains lined with yellow light
forever conveyed them this way and that, and large letters upon enamel
plates represented in the underworld the parks, squares and circuses of
the upper. 'Marble Arch – Shepherd's Bush' – to the majority the
Arch and the Bush are eternally white letters upon a blue ground.
Only at one point – it may be Acton, Holloway, Kensal Rise, Cale-
donian Road – does the name mean shops where you buy things, and
houses, in one of which, down to the right, where the pollard trees
grow out of the paving stones, there is a square curtained window, and
a bedroom.

Long past sunset an old blind woman sat on a camp-stool with her
back to the stone wall of the Union of London and Smith's Bank,[65]
clasping a brown mongrel tight in her arms and singing out loud, not
for coppers, no, from the depths of her gay wild heart – her sinful,
tanned heart – for the child who fetches her is the fruit of sin, and
should have been in bed, curtained, asleep, instead of hearing in the
lamplight her mother's wild song, where she sits against the bank,
singing not for coppers, with her dog against her breast.

Home they went. The grey church spires received them; the hoary
city, old, sinful and majestic. One behind another, round or pointed,
piercing the sky or massing themselves, like sailing ships, like granite
cliffs, spires and offices, wharves and factories crowd the bank; eternally

the pilgrims trudge; barges rest in midstream heavy laden; as some believe, the city loves her prostitutes.

But few, it seems, are admitted to that degree. Of all the carriages that leave the arch of the Opera House,[66] not one turns eastward, and when the little thief is caught in the empty market-place no one in black-and-white or rose-coloured evening dress blocks the way by pausing with a hand upon the carriage door to help or condemn – though Lady Charles, to do her justice, sighs sadly as she ascends her staircase, takes down Thomas à Kempis,[67] and does not sleep till her mind has lost itself tunnelling into the complexity of things. 'Why? Why? Why?' she sighs. On the whole it's best to walk back from the Opera House. Fatigue is the safest sleeping draught.

The autumn season was in full swing. Tristan was twitching his rug up under his armpits twice a week; Isolde[68] waved her scarf in miraculous sympathy with the conductor's baton. In all parts of the house were to be found pink faces and glittering breasts. When a royal hand attached to an invisible body slipped out and withdrew the red and white bouquet reposing on the scarlet ledge, the Queen of England seemed a name worth dying for. Beauty, in its hothouse variety (which is none of the worst), flowered in box after box; and though nothing was said of profound importance, and though it is generally agreed that wit deserted beautiful lips about the time that Walpole died – at any rate when Victoria in her nightgown descended to meet her ministers, the lips (through an opera glass) remained red, adorable. Bald distinguished men with gold-headed canes strolled down the crimson avenues between the stalls, and only broke from intercourse with the boxes when the lights went down, and the conductor, first bowing to the Queen, next to the bald-headed men, swept round on his feet and raised his wand.

Then two thousand hearts in the semi-darkness remembered, anticipated, travelled dark labyrinths; and Clara Durrant said farewell to Jacob Flanders, and tasted the sweetness of death in effigy; and Mrs Durrant, sitting behind her in the dark of the box, sighed her sharp sigh; and Mr Wortley, shifting his position behind the Italian ambassador's wife, thought that Brangaena[69] was a trifle hoarse; and suspended in the gallery many feet above their heads, Edward Whittaker surreptitiously held a torch to his miniature score; and . . . and . . .

In short, the observer is choked with observations. Only to prevent us from being submerged by chaos, nature and society between them have arranged a system of classification which is simplicity itself: stalls, boxes, amphitheatre, gallery. The moulds are filled nightly. There is no need to distinguish details. But the difficulty remains – one has to choose.

For though I have no wish to be Queen of England – or only for a moment – I would willingly sit beside her; I would hear the Prime Minister's gossip; the countess whisper, and share her memories of halls and gardens; the massive fronts of the respectable conceal after all their secret code; or why so impermeable? And then, doffing one's own headpiece, how strange to assume for a moment someone's – anyone's – to be a man of valour who has ruled the Empire; to refer while Brangaena sings to the fragments of Sophocles, or see in a flash, as the shepherd pipes his tune, bridges and aqueducts. But no – we must choose. Never was there a harsher necessity! or one which entails greater pain, more certain disaster; for wherever I seat myself, I die in exile: Whittaker in his lodging-house; Lady Charles at the manor.

A young man with a Wellington nose, who had occupied a seven-and-sixpenny seat, made his way down the stone stairs when the opera ended, as if he were still set a little apart from his fellows by the influence of the music.

At midnight Jacob Flanders heard a rap on his door.

'By Jove!' he exclaimed. 'You're the very man I want!' and without more ado they discovered the lines which he had been seeking all day; only they come not in Virgil, but in Lucretius.[70]

'Yes; that should make him sit up,' said Bonamy,[71] as Jacob stopped reading. Jacob was excited. It was the first time he had read his essay aloud.

'Damned swine!' he said, rather too extravagantly; but the praise had gone to his head. Professor Bulteel, of Leeds, had issued an edition of Wycherley[72] without stating that he had left out, disembowelled, or indicated only by asterisks, several indecent words and some indecent phrases. An outrage, Jacob said; a breach of faith; sheer prudery; token of a lewd mind and a disgusting nature. Aristophanes and Shakespeare were cited. Modern life was repudiated. Great play was made with the professional title, and Leeds as a seat of learning was laughed to scorn. And the extraordinary thing was that these young men were perfectly right – extraordinary, because, even as Jacob copied his pages, he knew that no one would ever print them; and sure enough back they came from the *Fortnightly*, the *Contemporary*, the *Nineteenth Century*[73] – when Jacob threw them into the black wooden box where he kept his mother's letters, his old flannel trousers, and a note or two with the Cornish postmark. The lid shut upon the truth.

This black wooden box, upon which his name was still legible in white paint, stood between the long windows of the sitting-room. The street ran beneath. No doubt the bedroom was behind. The furniture – three wicker chairs and a gate-legged table – came from Cambridge. These houses (Mrs Garfit's daughter, Mrs Whitehorn, was the landlady of this one) were built, say, a hundred and fifty years ago. The rooms are shapely, the ceilings high; over the doorway a rose, or a ram's skull, is carved in the wood. The eighteenth century has its distinction. Even the panels, painted in raspberry-coloured paint, have their distinction . . .

'Distinction' – Mrs Durrant said that Jacob Flanders was 'distinguished-looking'. 'Extremely awkward,' she said, 'but so distinguished-looking.' Seeing him for the first time that no doubt is the word for him. Lying back in his chair, taking his pipe from his lips, and saying to Bonamy: 'About this opera now' (for they had done with indecency). 'This fellow Wagner' . . . distinction was one of the words to use naturally, though, from looking at him, one would have found it difficult to say which seat in the opera house was his – stalls, gallery or dress circle. A writer? He lacked self-consciousness. A painter? There was something in the shape of his hands (he was descended on his mother's side from a family of the greatest antiquity and deepest obscurity) which indicated taste. Then his mouth – but surely, of all futile occupations this of cataloguing features is the worst. One word is sufficient. But if one cannot find it?

'I like Jacob Flanders,' wrote Clara Durrant in her diary. 'He is so unworldly. He gives himself no airs, and one can say what one likes to him, though he's frightening because . . . ' But Mr Letts[74] allows little space in his shilling diaries. Clara was not the one to encroach upon Wednesday. Humblest, most candid of women! 'No, no, no,' she sighed, standing at the greenhouse door, 'don't break – don't spoil' – what? Something infinitely wonderful.

But then, this is only a young woman's language, one, too, who loves, or refrains from loving. She wished the moment to continue for ever precisely as it was that July morning. And moments don't. Now, for instance, Jacob was telling a story about some walking tour he'd taken, and the inn was called the Foaming Pot, which, considering the landlady's name . . . They shouted with laughter. The joke was indecent.

Then Julia Eliot said 'the silent young man', and as she dined with prime ministers, no doubt she meant: 'If he is going to get on in the world, he will have to find his tongue.'

Timothy Durrant never made any comment at all.

The housemaid found herself very liberally rewarded.

Mr Sopwith's opinion was as sentimental as Clara's, though far more skilfully expressed.

Betty Flanders was romantic about Archer and tender about John; she was unreasonably irritated by Jacob's clumsiness in the house.

Captain Barfoot liked him best of the boys; but as for saying why . . .

It seems then that men and women are equally at fault. It seems that a profound, impartial and absolutely just opinion of our fellow-creatures is utterly unknown. Either we are men, or we are women. Either we are cold, or we are sentimental. Either we are young, or growing old. In any case life is but a procession of shadows, and God knows why it is that we embrace them so eagerly, and see them depart with such anguish, being shadows. And why, if this – and much more than this – is true, why are we yet surprised in the window corner by a sudden vision that the young man in the chair is of all things in the world the most real, the most solid, the best known to us – why indeed? For the moment after we know nothing about him.

Such is the manner of our seeing. Such the conditions of our love.

('I'm twenty-two. It's nearly the end of October. Life is thoroughly pleasant, although unfortunately there are a great number of fools about. One must apply oneself to something or other – God knows what. Everything is really very jolly – except getting up in the morning and wearing a tail coat.')

'I say, Bonamy, what about Beethoven?'

('Bonamy is an amazing fellow. He knows practically everything – not more about English literature than I do – but then he's read all those Frenchmen.')

'I rather suspect you're talking rot, Bonamy. In spite of what you say, poor old Tennyson . . . '

('The truth is one ought to have been taught French. Now, I suppose, old Barfoot is talking to my mother. That's an odd affair to be sure. But I can't see Bonamy down there. Damn London!') for the market carts were lumbering down the street.

'What about a walk on Saturday?'

('What's happening on Saturday?')

Then, taking out his pocket-book, he assured himself that the night of the Durrants' party came next week.

But though all this may very well be true – so Jacob thought and spoke – so he crossed his legs – filled his pipe – sipped his whisky, and once looked at his pocket-book, rumpling his hair as he did so, there remains over something which can never be conveyed to a second person save by Jacob himself. Moreover, part of this is not Jacob but Richard Bonamy – the room; the market carts; the hour; the very moment of history. Then consider the effect of sex – how between man and woman it hangs wavy, tremulous, so that here's a valley, there's a peak, when in truth, perhaps, all's as flat as my hand. Even the exact words get the wrong accent on them. But something is always impelling one to hum vibrating, like the hawk moth, at the mouth of the cavern of mystery, endowing Jacob Flanders with all sorts of qualities he had not at all – for though, certainly, he sat talking to Bonamy, half of what he said was too dull to repeat; much unintelligible (about unknown people and Parliament); what remains is mostly a matter of guesswork. Yet over him we hang vibrating.

'Yes,' said Captain Barfoot, knocking out his pipe on Betty Flanders's hob, and buttoning his coat. 'It doubles the work, but I don't mind that.'

He was now town councillor. They looked at the night, which was the same as the London night, only a good deal more transparent. Church bells down in the town were striking eleven o'clock. The wind was off the sea. And all the bedroom windows were dark – the Pages were asleep; the Garfits were asleep; the Cranches were asleep – whereas in London at this hour they were burning Guy Fawkes on Parliament Hill.[75]

Chapter 6

The flames had fairly caught.

'There's St Paul's!' someone cried.

As the wood caught the City of London was lit up for a second; on other sides of the fire there were trees. Of the faces which came out fresh and vivid as though painted in yellow and red, the most prominent was a girl's face. By a trick of the firelight she seemed to have no body. The oval of the face and hair hung beside the fire with a dark vacuum for background. As if dazed by the glare, her green-blue eyes stared at the flames. Every muscle of her face was taut. There was something tragic in her thus staring – her age between twenty and twenty-five.

A hand descending from the chequered darkness thrust on her head the conical white hat of a pierrot. Shaking her head, she still stared. A whiskered face appeared above her. They dropped two legs of a table upon the fire and a scattering of twigs and leaves. All this blazed up and showed faces far back, round, pale, smooth, bearded, some with billycock hats[76] on; all intent; showed too St Paul's floating on the uneven white mist, and two or three narrow, paper-white, extinguisher-shaped spires.

The flames were struggling through the wood and roaring up when, goodness knows where from, pails flung water in beautiful hollow shapes, as of polished tortoiseshell; flung again and again; until the hiss was like a swarm of bees; and all the faces went out.

'Oh Jacob,' said the girl, as they pounded up the hill in the dark, 'I'm so frightfully unhappy!'

Shouts of laughter came from the others – high, low; some before, others after.

The hotel dining-room was brightly lit. A stag's head in plaster was at one end of the table; at the other some Roman bust blackened and reddened to represent Guy Fawkes, whose night it was. The diners were linked together by lengths of paper roses, so that when it came to singing 'Auld Lang Syne'[77] with their hands crossed, a pink and yellow line rose and fell the entire length of the table. There was an enormous tapping of green wine-glasses. A young man stood up, and Florinda, taking one of the purplish globes that lay on the table, flung it straight at his head. It crushed to powder.

'I'm so frightfully unhappy!' she said, turning to Jacob, who sat beside her.

The table ran, as if on invisible legs, to the side of the room, and a barrel-organ[78] decorated with a red cloth and two pots of paper flowers reeled out waltz music.

Jacob could not dance. He stood against the wall smoking a pipe.

'We think,' said two of the dancers, breaking off from the rest, and bowing profoundly before him, 'that you are the most beautiful man we have ever seen.'

So they wreathed his head with paper flowers.[79] Then somebody brought out a white and gilt chair and made him sit on it. As they passed, people hung glass grapes on his shoulders, until he looked like the figure-head of a wrecked ship. Then Florinda got upon his knee and hid her face in his waistcoat. With one hand he held her; with the other, his pipe.

'Now let us talk,' said Jacob, as he walked down Haverstock Hill between four and five o'clock in the morning of November the sixth arm in arm with Timmy Durrant, 'about something sensible.'

*

The Greeks – yes, that was what they talked about – how when all's said and done, when one's rinsed one's mouth with every literature in the world, including Chinese and Russian (but these Slavs aren't civilised), it's the flavour of Greek that remains. Durrant quoted Aeschylus – Jacob Sophocles. It is true that no Greek could have understood or professor refrained from pointing out – Never mind; what is Greek for if not to be shouted on Haverstock Hill in the dawn? Moreover, Durrant never listened to Sophocles, nor Jacob to Aeschylus. They were boastful, triumphant; it seemed to both that they had read every book in the world; known every sin, passion and joy. Civilisations stood round them like flowers ready for picking. Ages lapped at their feet like waves fit for sailing. And surveying all this, looming through the fog, the lamplight, the shades of London, the two young men decided in favour of Greece.

'Probably,' said Jacob, 'we are the only people in the world who know what the Greeks meant.'

They drank coffee at a stall where the urns were burnished and little lamps burnt along the counter.

Taking Jacob for a military gentleman, the stall-keeper told him about his boy at Gibraltar, and Jacob cursed the British army and praised the Duke of Wellington. So on again they went down the hill talking about the Greeks.

A strange thing – when you come to think of it – this love of Greek, flourishing in such obscurity, distorted, discouraged, yet leaping out, all of a sudden, especially on leaving crowded rooms, or after a surfeit of print, or when the moon floats among the waves of the hills, or in hollow, sallow, fruitless London days, like a specific; a clean blade; always a miracle. Jacob knew no more Greek than served him to stumble through a play. Of ancient history he knew nothing. However, as he tramped into London it seemed to him that they were making the flagstones ring on the road to the Acropolis, and that if Socrates saw them coming he would bestir himself and say 'my fine fellows', for the whole sentiment of Athens was entirely after his heart; free, venturesome, high-spirited . . . She had called him Jacob without asking his leave. She had sat upon his knee. Thus did all good women in the days of the Greeks.

At this moment there shook out into the air a wavering, quavering, doleful lamentation which seemed to lack strength to unfold itself, and yet flagged on; at the sound of which doors in back streets burst sullenly open; workmen stumped forth.

*

Florinda was sick.

Mrs Durrant, sleepless as usual, scored a mark by the side of certain lines in the *Inferno*.

Clara slept buried in her pillows; on her dressing-table dishevelled roses and a pair of long white gloves.

Still wearing the conical white hat of a pierrot, Florinda was sick.

The bedroom seemed fit for these catastrophes – cheap, mustard-coloured, half-attic, half-studio, curiously ornamented with silver-paper stars, Welshwomen's hats, and rosaries pendent from the gas brackets. As for Florinda's story, her name had been bestowed upon her by a painter who had wished it to signify that the flower of her maidenhood was still unplucked. Be that as it may, she was without a surname,[80] and for parents had only the photograph of a tombstone beneath which, she said, her father lay buried. Sometimes she would dwell upon the size of it, and rumour had it that Florinda's father had died from the growth of his bones which nothing could stop; just as her mother enjoyed the confidence of a royal master, and now and again Florinda herself was a princess, but chiefly when drunk. Thus deserted, pretty into the bargain, with tragic eyes and the lips of a child, she talked more about virginity than women mostly do; and had lost it only the night before, or cherished it beyond the heart in her breast, according to the man she talked to. But did she always talk to men? No, she had her confidante: Mother Stuart. Stuart, as the lady would point out, is the name of a royal house; but what that signified, and what her business was, no one knew; only that Mrs Stuart got postal orders every Monday morning, kept a parrot, believed in the transmigration of souls, and could read the future in tea leaves. Dirty lodging-house wallpaper she was behind the chastity of Florinda.

Now Florinda wept, and spent the day wandering the streets; stood at Chelsea watching the river swim past; trailed along the shopping streets; opened her bag and powdered her cheeks in omnibuses; read love letters, propping them against the milk pot in the ABC shop;[81] detected glass in the sugar bowl; accused the waitress of wishing to poison her; declared that young men stared at her; and found herself towards evening slowly sauntering down Jacob's street, when it struck her that she liked that man Jacob better than dirty Jews, and sitting at his table (he was copying his essay upon the Ethics of Indecency),[82] drew off her gloves and told him how Mother Stuart had banged her on the head with the tea-cosy.

Jacob took her word for it that she was chaste. She prattled, sitting by the fireside, of famous painters. The tomb of her father was mentioned. Wild and frail and beautiful she looked, and thus the women of the Greeks were, Jacob thought; and this was life; and himself a man and Florinda chaste.

She left with one of Shelley's poems beneath her arm. Mrs Stuart, she said, often talked of him.

Marvellous are the innocent. To believe that the girl herself transcends all lies (for Jacob was not such a fool as to believe implicitly), to wonder enviously at the unanchored life – his own seeming petted and even cloistered in comparison – to have at hand as sovereign specifics for all disorders of the soul Adonais[83] and the plays of Shakespeare; to figure out a comradeship all spirited on her side, protective on his, yet equal on both, for women, thought Jacob, are just the same as men – innocence such as this is marvellous enough, and perhaps not so foolish after all.

For when Florinda got home that night she first washed her head; then ate chocolate creams; then opened Shelley. True, she was horribly bored. What on earth was it *about*? She had to wager with herself that she would turn the page before she ate another. In fact she slept. But then her day had been a long one, Mother Stuart had thrown the tea-cosy; there are formidable sights in the streets, and though Florinda was ignorant as an owl, and would never learn to read even her love letters correctly, still she had her feelings, liked some men better than others, and was entirely at the beck and call of life. Whether or not she was a virgin seems a matter of no importance whatever. Unless, indeed, it is the only thing of any importance at all.

Jacob was restless when she left him.

All night men and women seethed up and down the well-known beats. Late home-comers could see shadows against the blinds even in the most respectable suburbs. Not a square in snow or fog lacked its amorous couple. All plays turned on the same subject.[84] Bullets went through heads in hotel bedrooms almost nightly on that account. When the body escaped mutilation, seldom did the heart go to the grave unscarred. Little else was talked of in theatres and popular novels. Yet we say it is a matter of no importance at all.

What with Shakespeare and Adonais, Mozart and Bishop Berkeley – choose whom you like – the fact is concealed and the evenings for most of us pass reputably, or with only the sort of tremor that a snake makes sliding through the grass.[85] But then concealment by itself distracts the mind from the print and the sound. If Florinda had had a mind, she might have read with clearer eyes than we can. She and her sort have solved the question by turning it to a trifle of washing the hands nightly before going to bed, the only difficulty being whether you prefer your water hot or cold, which being settled, the mind can go about its business unassailed.

But it did occur to Jacob, halfway through dinner, to wonder whether she had a mind.

They sat at a little table in the restaurant.

Florinda leant the points of her elbows on the table and held her chin in the cup of her hands. Her cloak had slipped behind her. Gold and white with bright beads on her she emerged, her face flowering from her body, innocent, scarcely tinted, the eyes gazing frankly about her, or slowly settling on Jacob and resting there. She talked.

'You know that big black box the Australian left in my room ever so long ago? . . . I do think furs make a woman look old . . . That's Bechstein[86] come in now . . . I was wondering what you looked like when you were a little boy, Jacob.' She nibbled her roll and looked at him.

'Jacob. You're like one of those statues . . . I think there are lovely things in the British Museum, don't you? Lots of lovely things . . . ' she spoke dreamily. The room was filling; the heat increasing. Talk in a restaurant is dazed sleep-walkers' talk, so many things to look at – so much noise – other people talking. Can one overhear? Oh, but they mustn't overhear *us*.

'That's like Ellen Nagle – that girl . . . ' and so on. 'I'm awfully happy since I've known you, Jacob. You're such a *good* man.'

The room got fuller and fuller; talk louder; knives more clattering.

'Well, you see what makes her say things like that is . . . '

She stopped. So did everyone.

'Tomorrow . . . Sunday . . . a beastly . . . you tell me . . . go then!' Crash! And out she swept.

It was at the table next them that the voice spun higher and higher. Suddenly the woman dashed the plates to the floor. The man was left there. Everybody stared. Then – 'Well, poor chap, we mustn't sit staring. What a go! Did you hear what she said? By God, he looks a fool! Didn't come up to the scratch, I suppose. All the mustard on the tablecloth. The waiters laughing.'

Jacob observed Florinda. In her face there seemed to him something horribly brainless – as she sat staring.

*

Out she swept, the black woman with the dancing feather in her hat.

Yet she had to go somewhere. The night is not a tumultuous black ocean in which you sink or sail as a star. As a matter of fact it was a wet November night. The lamps of Soho made large greasy spots of light upon the pavement. The by-streets were dark enough to shelter man or woman leaning against the doorways. One detached herself as Jacob and Florinda approached.

'She's dropped her glove,'[87] said Florinda.

Jacob, pressing forward, gave it her.

Effusively she thanked him; retraced her steps; dropped her glove again. But why? For whom?

Meanwhile, where had the other woman got to? And the man?

The street lamps do not carry far enough to tell us. The voices, angry, lustful, despairing, passionate, were scarcely more than the voices of caged beasts at night. Only they are not caged, nor beasts. Stop a man; ask him the way; he'll tell it you; but one's afraid to ask him the way. What does one fear? – the human eye. At once the pavement narrows, the chasm deepens. There! They've melted into it – both man and woman. Farther on, blatantly advertising its meritorious solidity, a boarding-house exhibits behind uncurtained windows its testimony to the soundness of London. There they sit, plainly illuminated, dressed like ladies and gentlemen, in bamboo chairs. The widows of business-men prove laboriously that they are related to judges. The wives of coal merchants instantly retort that their fathers kept coachmen. A servant brings coffee, and the crochet basket has to be moved. And so on again into the dark, passing a girl here for sale, or there an old woman with only matches to offer, passing the crowd from the Tube station, the women with veiled hair, passing at length no one but shut doors, carved door-posts and a solitary policeman, Jacob, with Florinda on his arm, reached his room and, lighting the lamp, said nothing at all.

'I don't like you when you look like that,' said Florinda.

The problem is insoluble. The body is harnessed to a brain.[88] Beauty goes hand in hand with stupidity. There she sat staring at the fire as she had stared at the broken mustard-pot. In spite of defending indecency, Jacob doubted whether he liked it in the raw. He had a violent reversion towards male society, cloistered rooms, and the works of the classics; and was ready to turn with wrath upon whoever it was who had fashioned life thus.

Then Florinda laid her hand upon his knee.

After all, it was none of her fault. But the thought saddened him. It's not catastrophes, murders, deaths, diseases, that age and kill us; it's the way people look and laugh, and run up the steps of omnibuses.

Any excuse, though, serves a stupid woman. He told her his head ached.

But when she looked at him, dumbly, half-guessing, half-under-standing, apologising perhaps, anyhow saying as he had said, 'It's none of my fault,' straight and beautiful in body, her face like a shell within its cap, then he knew that cloisters and classics are no use whatever. The problem is insoluble.

Chapter 7

About this time a firm of merchants having dealings with the East put on the market little paper flowers which opened on touching water. As it was the custom also to use finger-bowls at the end of dinner, the new discovery was found of excellent service. In these sheltered lakes the little coloured flowers swam and slid; surmounted smooth slippery waves, and sometimes foundered and lay like pebbles on the glass floor. Their fortunes were watched by eyes intent and lovely. It is surely a great discovery that leads to the union of hearts and foundation of homes. The paper flowers did no less.

It must not be thought, though, that they ousted the flowers of nature. Roses, lilies, carnations in particular, looked over the rims of vases and surveyed the bright lives and swift dooms of their artificial relations. Mr Stuart Ormond made this very observation; and charming it was thought; and Kitty Craster married him on the strength of it six months later. But real flowers can never be dispensed with. If they could, human life would be a different affair altogether. For flowers fade; chrysanthemums are the worst; perfect overnight; yellow and jaded next morning – not fit to be seen. On the whole, though the price is sinful, carnations pay best; it's a question, however, whether it's wise to have them wired. Some shops advise it. Certainly it's the only way to keep them at a dance; but whether it is necessary at dinner parties, unless the rooms are very hot, remains in dispute. Old Mrs Temple used to recommend an ivy leaf – just one – dropped into the bowl. She said it kept the water pure for days and days. But there is some reason to think that old Mrs Temple was mistaken.

The little cards, however, with names engraved on them, are a more serious problem than the flowers. More horses' legs have been worn out, more coachmen's lives consumed, more hours of sound afternoon time vainly lavished than served to win us the battle of Waterloo, and pay for it into the bargain. The little demons are the source of as many reprieves, calamities and anxieties as the battle itself. Sometimes Mrs Bonham has just gone out; at others she is at home. But, even if the cards should be superseded, which seems unlikely, there are unruly powers blowing life into storms, disordering sedulous mornings and uprooting the stability of the afternoon – dressmakers, that is to say, and confectioners' shops. Six yards of silk will cover one body; but if you have to devise six hundred shapes for it, and twice as many colours? – in the middle of which there is the urgent question of the pudding with tufts of green cream and battlements of almond paste. It has not arrived.

The flamingo hours fluttered softly through the sky. But regularly they dipped their wings in pitch black; Notting Hill, for instance, or the purlieus of Clerkenwell.[89] No wonder that Italian remained a hidden art, and the piano always played the same sonata.[90] In order to buy one pair of elastic stockings for Mrs Page, widow, aged sixty-three, in receipt of five shillings outdoor relief,[91] and help from her only son employed in Messrs Mackie's dye-works, suffering in winter with his chest, letters must be written, columns filled up in the same round, simple hand that wrote in Mr Letts's diary how the weather was fine, the children demons, and Jacob Flanders unworldly. Clara Durrant procured the stockings, played the sonata, filled the vases, fetched the pudding, left the cards, and when the great invention of paper flowers to swim in finger-bowls was discovered, was one of those who most marvelled at their brief lives.

Nor were there wanting poets to celebrate the theme. Edwin Mallett, for example, wrote his verses ending: 'And read their doom in Chloe's eyes', which caused Clara to blush at the first reading, and to laugh at the second, saying that it was just like him to call her Chloe when her name was Clara. Ridiculous young man! But when, between ten and eleven on a rainy morning, Edwin Mallett laid his life at her feet she ran out of the room and hid herself in her bedroom, and Timothy below could not get on with his work all that morning on account of her sobs.

'Which is the result of enjoying yourself,' said Mrs Durrant severely, surveying the dance programme all scored with the same initials, or rather they were different ones this time – R. B. instead of E. M.; Richard Bonamy it was now, the young man with the Wellington nose.

'But I could never marry a man with a nose like that,' said Clara.

'Nonsense,' said Mrs Durrant.

'But I am too severe,' she thought to herself. For Clara, losing all vivacity, tore up her dance programme and threw it in the fender.

Such were the very serious consequences of the invention of paper flowers to swim in bowls.

'Please,' said Julia Eliot, taking up her position by the curtain almost opposite the door, 'don't introduce me. I like to look on. The amusing thing,' she went on, addressing Mr Salvin, who, owing to his lameness, was accommodated with a chair, 'the amusing thing about a party is to watch the people – coming and going, coming and going.'

'Last time we met,' said Mr Salvin, 'was at the Farquhars. Poor lady! She has much to put up with.'

'Doesn't she look charming?' exclaimed Miss Eliot, as Clara Durrant passed them.

'And which of them . . . ?' asked Mr Salvin, dropping his voice and speaking in quizzical tones.

'There are so many . . . ' Miss Eliot replied. Three young men stood at the doorway looking about for their hostess.

'You don't remember Elizabeth as I do,' said Mr Salvin, 'dancing Highland reels at Banchorie. Clara lacks her mother's spirit. Clara is a little pale.'

'What different people one sees here!' said Miss Eliot.

'Happily we are not governed by the evening papers,' said Mr Salvin.

'I never read them,' said Miss Eliot. 'I know nothing about politics,' she added.

'The piano is in tune,' said Clara, passing them, 'but we may have to ask someone to move it for us.'

'Are they going to dance?' asked Mr Salvin.

'Nobody shall disturb you,' said Mrs Durrant peremptorily as she passed.

'Julia Eliot. It *is* Julia Eliot!' said old Lady Hibbert, holding out both her hands. 'And Mr Salvin. What is going to happen to us, Mr Salvin? With all my experience of English politics . . . My dear, I was thinking of your father last night – one of my oldest friends, Mr Salvin. Never tell me that girls of ten are incapable of love! I had all Shakespeare by heart before I was in my teens, Mr Salvin!'

'You don't say so,' said Mr Salvin.

'But I do,' said Lady Hibbert.

*

'Oh, Mr Salvin, I'm so sorry . . .'

'I will remove myself if you'll kindly lend me a hand,' said Mr Salvin.

'You shall sit by my mother,' said Clara. 'Everybody seems to come in here . . . Mr Calthorp, let me introduce you to Miss Edwards.'

'Are you going away for Christmas?' said Mr Calthorp.

'If my brother gets his leave,' said Miss Edwards.

'What regiment is he in?' said Mr Calthorp.

'The Twentieth Hussars,' said Miss Edwards.

'Perhaps he knows my brother?' said Mr Calthorp.

'I am afraid I did not catch your name,' said Miss Edwards.

'Calthorp,' said Mr Calthorp.

'But what proof was there that the marriage service was actually performed?' said Mr Crosby.

'There is no reason to doubt that Charles James Fox . . .' Mr Burley began; but here Mrs Stretton told him that she knew his sister well; had stayed with her not six weeks ago; and thought the house charming, but bleak in winter.

'Going about as girls do nowadays – ' said Mrs Forster.

Mr Bowley looked round him, and catching sight of Rose Shaw moved towards her, threw out his hands, and exclaimed: 'Well!'

'Nothing!' she replied. 'Nothing at all – though I left them alone the entire afternoon on purpose.'

'Dear me, dear me,' said Mr Bowley. 'I will ask Jimmy to breakfast.'

'But who could resist her?' cried Rose Shaw. 'Dearest Clara – I know we mustn't try to stop you . . .'

'You and Mr Bowley are talking dreadful gossip, I know,' said Clara.

'Life is wicked – life is detestable!' cried Rose Shaw.

'There's not much to be said for this sort of thing, is there?' said Timothy Durrant to Jacob.

'Women like it.'

'Like what?' said Charlotte Wilding, coming up to them.

'Where have you come from?' said Timothy. 'Dining somewhere, I suppose.'

'I don't see why not,' said Charlotte.

'People must go downstairs,' said Clara, passing. 'Take Charlotte, Timothy. How d'you do, Mr Flanders.'

'How d'you do, Mr Flanders,' said Julia Eliot, holding out her hand. 'What's been happening to you?'

> 'Who is Silvia? what is she?
> That all our swains commend her?'[92]

sang Elsbeth Siddons.

Everyone stood where they were, or sat down if a chair was empty. 'Ah,' sighed Clara, who stood beside Jacob, halfway through.

> 'Then to Silvia let us sing,
>   That Silvia is excelling;
> She excels each mortal thing
>   Upon the dull earth dwelling.
> To her let us garlands bring,'

sang Elsbeth Siddons.

'Ah!' Clara exclaimed out loud, and clapped her gloved hands; and Jacob clapped his bare ones; and then she moved forward and directed people to come in from the doorway.

'You are living in London?' asked Miss Julia Eliot.

'Yes,' said Jacob.

'In rooms?'

'Yes.'

'There is Mr Clutterbuck. You always see Mr Clutterbuck here. He is not very happy at home, I am afraid. They say that Mrs Clutterbuck . . .' she dropped her voice. 'That's why he stays with the Durrants. Were you there when they acted Mr Wortley's play? Oh, no, of course not – at the last moment, did you hear – you had to go to join your mother, I remember, at Harrogate – At the last moment, as I was saying, just as everything was ready, the clothes finished and everything – Now Elsbeth is going to sing again. Clara is playing her accompaniment or turning over for Mr Carter, I think. No, Mr Carter is playing by himself – This is *Bach*,' she whispered, as Mr Carter played the first bars.

'Are you fond of music?' said Mrs Durrant.

'Yes. I like hearing it,' said Jacob. 'I know nothing about it.'

'Very few people do that,' said Mrs Durrant. 'I dare say you were never taught. Why is that, Sir Jasper? – Sir Jasper Bigham – Mr Flanders. Why is nobody taught anything that they ought to know, Sir Jasper?' She left them standing against the wall.

Neither of the gentlemen said anything for three minutes, though

Jacob shifted perhaps five inches to the left, and then as many to the right. Then Jacob grunted, and suddenly crossed the room.

'Will you come and have something to eat?' he said to Clara Durrant.

'Yes, an ice. Quickly. Now,' she said.

Downstairs they went.

But halfway down they met Mr and Mrs Gresham, Herbert Turner, Sylvia Rashleigh, and a friend, whom they had dared to bring, from America, 'knowing that Mrs Durrant – wishing to show Mr Pilcher. Mr Pilcher from New York – This is Miss Durrant.'

'Whom I have heard so much of,' said Mr Pilcher, bowing low.

So Clara left him.

Chapter 8

About half-past nine Jacob left the house, his door slamming, other doors slamming, buying his paper, mounting his omnibus, or, weather permitting, walking his road as other people do. Head bent down, a desk, a telephone, books bound in green leather, electric light . . . 'Fresh coals, sir?' . . . 'Your tea, sir.' . . . Talk about football, the Hotspurs, the Harlequins;[93] six-thirty *Star*[94] brought in by the office boy; the rooks of Gray's Inn[95] passing overhead; branches in the fog thin and brittle; and through the roar of traffic now and again a voice shouting: 'Verdict – verdict – winner – winner,' while letters accumulate in a basket, Jacob signs them, and each evening finds him, as he takes his coat down, with some muscle of the brain new stretched.

Then, sometimes a game of chess;[96] or pictures in Bond Street;[97] or a long way home to take the air with Bonamy on his arm, meditatively marching, head thrown back, the world a spectacle, the early moon above the steeples coming in for praise, the seagulls flying high, Nelson on his column[98] surveying the horizon, and the world our ship.

Meanwhile, poor Betty Flanders's letter, having caught the second post, lay on the hall table – poor Betty Flanders writing her son's name, Jacob Alan Flanders, Esq., as mothers do, and the ink pale, profuse, suggesting how mothers down at Scarborough scribble over the fire with their feet on the fender, when tea's cleared away, and can never, never say, whatever it may be – probably this – Don't go with bad women, do be a good boy; wear your thick shirts; and come back, come back, come back to me.

But she said nothing of the kind. 'Do you remember old Miss War-grave, who used to be so kind when you had the whooping-cough?' she wrote; 'she's dead at last, poor thing. They would like it if you wrote. Ellen came over and we spent a nice day shopping. Old Mouse gets very stiff, and we have to walk him up the smallest hill. Rebecca, at last, after I don't know how long, went into Mr Adamson's. Three teeth, he says, must come out. Such mild weather for the time of year, the little buds actually on the pear trees. And Mrs Jarvis tells me – ' Mrs Flanders liked Mrs Jarvis, always said of her that she was too good for such a quiet place, and, though she never listened to her discontent and told her at the end of it (looking up, sucking her thread or taking off her spectacles) that a little peat wrapped round the iris roots keeps them from the frost, and Parrot's great white sale[99] is Tuesday next, 'do remember' – Mrs Flanders knew precisely how Mrs Jarvis felt; and how interesting her letters were, about Mrs Jarvis, could one read them year in, year out – the unpublished works of women, written by the fireside in pale pro-fusion, dried by the flame, for the blotting-paper's worn to holes and the nib cleft and clotted. Then Captain Barfoot. Him she called 'the Captain', spoke of frankly, yet never without reserve. The Captain was enquiring for her about Garfit's acre; advised chickens; could promise profit; or had the sciatica; or Mrs Barfoot had been indoors for weeks; or the Captain says things look bad, politics that is, for as Jacob knew, the Captain would sometimes talk, as the evening waned, about Ireland or India;[100] and then Mrs Flanders would fall musing about Morty, her brother, lost all these years – had the natives got him, was his ship sunk – would the Admiralty tell her? – the Captain knocking his pipe out, as Jacob knew, rising to go, stiffly stretching to pick up Mrs Flanders's wool which had rolled beneath the chair. Talk of the chicken farm came back and back, the woman, even at fifty, impulsive at heart, sketching on the cloudy future flocks of Leghorns, Cochin Chinas, Orpingtons;[101] like Jacob in the blur of her outline; but powerful as he was; fresh and vigorous, running about the house, scolding Rebecca.

The letter lay upon the hall table; Florinda coming in that night took it up with her, put it on the table as she kissed Jacob, and Jacob seeing the hand, left it there under the lamp, between the biscuit-tin and the tobacco-box. They shut the bedroom door behind them.

The sitting-room neither knew nor cared. The door was shut; and to suppose that wood, when it creaks, transmits anything save that rats are busy and wood dry is childish. These old houses are only brick and wood, soaked in human sweat, grained with human dirt. But if the pale blue envelope lying by the biscuit-box had the feelings of a mother, the heart was torn by the little creak, the sudden stir. Behind the door was the obscene thing, the alarming presence, and terror would come over her as at death or the birth of a child. Better, perhaps, burst in and face it than sit in the antechamber listening to the little creak, the sudden stir, for her heart was swollen, and pain threaded it. My son, my son – such would be her cry, uttered to hide her vision of him stretched with Florinda, inexcusable, irrational, in a woman with three children living at Scarborough. And the fault lay with Florinda. Indeed, when the door opened and the couple came out, Mrs Flanders would have flounced upon her – only it was Jacob who came first, in his dressing-gown, amiable, authoritative, beautifully healthy, like a baby after an airing, with an eye clear as running water. Florinda followed, lazily stretching; yawning a little; arranging her hair at the looking-glass – while Jacob read his mother's letter.

Let us consider letters – how they come at breakfast, and at night, with their yellow stamps and their green stamps, immortalised by the post-mark – for to see one's own envelope on another's table is to realise how soon deeds sever and become alien. Then at last the power of the mind to quit the body is manifest, and perhaps we fear or hate or wish annihilated this phantom of ourselves, lying on the table. Still, there are letters that merely say how dinner's at seven; others ordering coal; making appointments. The hand in them is scarcely perceptible, let alone the voice or the scowl. Ah, but when the post knocks and the letter comes always the miracle seems repeated – speech attempted. Venerable are letters, infinitely brave, forlorn, and lost.

Life would split asunder without them. 'Come to tea, come to dinner, what's the truth of the story? have you heard the news? life in the capital is gay; the Russian dancers.[102] . . . ' These are our stays and props. These lace our days together and make of life a perfect globe. And yet, and yet . . . when we go to dinner, when pressing fingertips we hope to meet somewhere soon, a doubt insinuates itself: is this the way to spend our days? the rare, the limited, so soon dealt out to us – drinking tea? dining out? And the notes accumulate. And the telephones ring. And everywhere we go wires and tubes surround us to carry the voices that try to penetrate before the last card is dealt and the days are over. 'Try to penetrate', for as we lift the cup, shake the hand, express the hope, something whispers, Is this all? Can I never know, share, be certain? Am I doomed all my days to write letters, send voices, which fall upon the tea-table, fade upon the passage, making appointments, while life dwindles, to come and dine? Yet letters are venerable; and the

telephone valiant, for the journey is a lonely one, and if bound together
by notes and telephones we went in company, perhaps – who knows? –
we might talk by the way.

Well, people have tried. Byron wrote letters. So did Cowper. For
centuries the writing-desk has contained sheets fit precisely for the
communications of friends. Masters of language, poets of long ages,
have turned from the sheet that endures to the sheet that perishes,
pushing aside the tea-tray, drawing close to the fire (for letters are
written when the dark presses round a bright red cave), and addressed
themselves to the task of reaching, touching, penetrating the individual
heart. Were it possible! But words have been used too often; touched
and turned, and left exposed to the dust of the street. The words we
seek hang close to the tree. We come at dawn and find them sweet
beneath the leaf.

Mrs Flanders wrote letters; Mrs Jarvis wrote them; Mrs Durrant too;
Mother Stuart actually scented her pages, thereby adding a flavour
which the English language fails to provide; Jacob had written in his
day long letters about art, morality and politics to young men at college.
Clara Durrant's letters were those of a child. Florinda – the impediment
between Florinda and her pen was something impassable. Fancy a
butterfly, gnat or other winged insect attached to a twig which, clogged
with mud, it rolls across a page. Her spelling was abominable. Her
sentiments infantile. And for some reason when she wrote she declared
her belief in God. Then there were crosses – tear stains; and the hand
itself rambling and redeemed only by the fact – which always did redeem
Florinda – by the fact that she cared. Yes, whether it was for chocolate
creams, hot baths, the shape of her face in the looking-glass, Florinda
could no more pretend a feeling than swallow whisky. Incontinent was
her rejection. Great men are truthful, and these little prostitutes, staring
in the fire, taking out a powder-puff, decorating lips at an inch of
looking-glass, have (so Jacob thought) an inviolable fidelity.

Then he saw her turning up Greek Street[103] upon another man's arm.

The light from the arc lamp drenched him from head to toe. He stood
for a minute motionless beneath it. Shadows chequered the street. Other
figures, single and together, poured out, wavered across, and obliterated
Florinda and the man.

The light drenched Jacob from head to toe. You could see the pattern
on his trousers; the old thorns on his stick; his shoelaces; bare hands;
and face.

It was as if a stone were ground to dust; as if white sparks flew from a livid whetstone, which was his spine; as if the switchback railway, having swooped to the depths, fell, fell, fell. This was in his face.

Whether we know what was in his mind is another question. Granted ten years' seniority and a difference of sex, fear of him comes first; this is swallowed up by a desire to help – overwhelming sense, reason, and the time of night; anger would follow close on that – with Florinda, with destiny; and then up would bubble an irresponsible optimism. 'Surely there's enough light in the street at this moment to drown all our cares in gold!' Ah, what's the use of saying it? Even while you speak and look over your shoulder towards Shaftesbury Avenue, destiny is chipping a dent in him. He has turned to go. As for following him back to his rooms, no – that we won't do.

Yet that, of course, is precisely what one does. He let himself in and shut the door, though it was only striking ten on one of the City clocks. No one can go to bed at ten. Nobody was thinking of going to bed. It was January and dismal, but Mrs Wagg stood on her doorstep, as if expecting something to happen. A barrel-organ played like an obscene nightingale beneath wet leaves. Children ran across the road. Here and there one could see brown panelling inside the hall door . . . The march that the mind keeps beneath the windows of others is queer enough. Now distracted by brown panelling; now by a fern in a pot; here improvising a few phrases to dance with the barrel-organ; again snatching a detached gaiety from a drunken man; then altogether absorbed by words the poor shout across the street at each other (so outright, so lusty) – yet all the while having for centre, for magnet, a young man alone in his room.

'Life is wicked – life is detestable,' cried Rose Shaw.

The strange thing about life is that though the nature of it must have been apparent to everyone for hundreds of years, no one has left any adequate account of it. The streets of London have their map; but our passions are uncharted. What are you going to meet if you turn this corner?

'Holborn straight ahead of you,' says the policeman. Ah, but where are you going if instead of brushing past the old man with the white beard, the silver medal and the cheap violin you let him go on with his story, which ends in an invitation to step somewhere, to his room, presumably, off Queen Square, and there he shows you a collection of birds' eggs and a letter from the Prince of Wales's secretary, and this (skipping the intermediate stages) brings you one winter's day to the Essex coast, where the little boat makes off to the ship, and the ship sails

and you behold on the skyline the Azores; and the flamingos rise; and
there you sit on the verge of the marsh drinking rum-punch, an outcast
from civilisation, for you have committed a crime, are infected with
yellow fever as likely as not, and – fill in the sketch as you like. As
frequent as street corners in Holborn are these chasms in the continuity
of our ways. Yet we keep straight on.

Rose Shaw, talking in rather an emotional manner to Mr Bowley at
Mrs Durrant's evening party a few nights back, said that life was wicked
because a man called Jimmy refused to marry a woman called (if
memory serves) Helen Aitken.

Both were beautiful. Both were inanimate. The oval tea-table
invariably separated them, and the plate of biscuits was all he ever gave
her. He bowed; she inclined her head. They danced. He danced
divinely. They sat in the alcove; never a word was said. Her pillow was
wet with tears. Kind Mr Bowley and dear Rose Shaw marvelled and
deplored. Bowley had rooms in Albany.[104] Rose was reborn every
evening precisely as the clock struck eight. All four were civilisation's
triumphs, and if you persist that a command of the English language is
part of our inheritance, one can only reply that beauty is almost always
dumb. Male beauty in association with female beauty breeds in the
onlooker a sense of fear. Often have I seen them – Helen and Jimmy –
and likened them to ships adrift, and feared for my own little craft. Or
again, have you ever watched fine collie dogs couchant at twenty
yards' distance? As she passed him his cup there was that quiver in her
flanks. Bowley saw what was up – asked Jimmy to breakfast. Helen
must have confided in Rose. For my own part, I find it exceedingly
difficult to interpret songs without words. And now Jimmy feeds crows
in Flanders and Helen visits hospitals. Oh, life is damnable, life is
wicked, as Rose Shaw said.

The lamps of London uphold the dark as upon the points of burning
bayonets. The yellow canopy sinks and swells[105] over the great four-
poster. Passengers in the mail-coaches running into London in the
eighteenth century looked through leafless branches and saw it flaring
beneath them. The light burns behind yellow blinds and pink blinds,
and above fanlights, and down in basement windows. The street market
in Soho is fierce with light. Raw meat, china mugs and silk stockings
blaze in it. Raw voices wrap themselves round the flaring gas-jets. Arms
akimbo, they stand on the pavement bawling – Messrs Kettle and
Wilkinson; their wives sit in the shop, furs wrapped round their necks,

arms folded, eyes contemptuous. Such faces as one sees. The little man fingering the meat must have squatted before the fire in innumerable lodging-houses, and heard and seen and known so much that it seems to utter itself even volubly from dark eyes, loose lips, as he fingers the meat silently, his face sad as a poet's, and never a song sung. Shawled women carry babies with purple eyelids; boys stand at street corners; girls look across the road – rude illustrations, pictures in a book whose pages we turn over and over as if we should at last find what we look for. Every face, every shop, bedroom window, public-house and dark square is a picture feverishly turned – in search of what? It is the same with books. What do we seek through millions of pages? Still hopefully turning the pages – oh, here is Jacob's room.

He sat at the table reading the *Globe*. The pinkish sheet was spread flat before him. He propped his face in his hand, so that the skin of his cheek was wrinkled in deep folds. Terribly severe he looked, set and defiant. (What people go through in half an hour! But nothing could save him. These events are features of our landscape. A foreigner coming to London could scarcely miss seeing St Paul's.) He judged life. These pinkish and greenish newspapers are thin sheets of gelatine pressed nightly over the brain and heart of the world. They take the impression of the whole. Jacob cast his eye over it. A strike, a murder, football, bodies found; vociferation from all parts of England simultaneously. How miserable it is that the *Globe* newspaper offers nothing better to Jacob Flanders! When a child begins to read history one marvels, sorrowfully, to hear him spell out in his new voice the ancient words.

The Prime Minister's speech was reported in something over five columns. Feeling in his pocket, Jacob took out a pipe and proceeded to fill it. Five minutes, ten minutes, fifteen minutes passed. Jacob took the paper over to the fire. The Prime Minister proposed a measure for giving Home Rule to Ireland. Jacob knocked out his pipe. He was certainly thinking about Home Rule in Ireland – a very difficult matter. A very cold night.

The snow, which had been falling all night, lay at three o'clock in the afternoon over the fields and the hill. Clumps of withered grass stood out upon the hill-top; the furze bushes were black, and now and then a black shiver crossed the snow as the wind drove flurries of frozen particles before it. The sound was that of a broom sweeping – sweeping.

The stream crept along by the road unseen by anyone. Sticks and leaves caught in the frozen grass. The sky was sullen grey and the trees of black iron. Uncompromising was the severity of the country. At four o'clock the snow was again falling. The day had gone out.

A window tinged yellow about two feet across alone combated the white fields and the black trees . . . At six o'clock a man's figure carrying a lantern crossed the field . . . A raft of twig stayed upon a stone suddenly detached itself and floated towards the culvert . . . A load of snow slipped and fell from a fir branch . . . Later there was a mournful cry . . . A motor car came along the road shoving the dark before it . . . The dark shut down behind it . . .

Spaces of complete immobility separated each of these movements. The land seemed to lie dead . . . Then the old shepherd returned stiffly across the field. Stiffly and painfully the frozen earth was trodden under and gave beneath pressure like a treadmill. The worn voices of clocks repeated the fact of the hour all night long.

Jacob, too, heard them, and raked out the fire. He rose. He stretched himself. He went to bed.

Chapter 9

The Countess of Rocksbier sat at the head of the table alone with Jacob. Fed upon champagne and spices for at least two centuries (four, if you count the female line), the Countess Lucy looked well fed. A discriminating nose she had for scents, prolonged, as if in quest of them; her underlip protruded a narrow red shelf; her eyes were small, with sandy tufts for eyebrows, and her jowl was heavy. Behind her (the window looked on Grosvenor Square) stood Moll Pratt on the pavement, offering violets for sale; and Mrs Hilda Thomas, lifting her skirts, preparing to cross the road. One was from Walworth; the other from Putney. Both wore black stockings, but Mrs Thomas was coiled in furs. The comparison was much in Lady Rocksbier's[106] favour. Moll had more humour, but was violent; stupid too. Hilda Thomas was mealy-mouthed, all her silver frames aslant; egg-cups in the drawing-room; and the windows shrouded. Lady Rocksbier, whatever the deficiencies of her profile, had been a great rider to hounds. She used her knife with authority, tore her chicken bones, asking Jacob's pardon, with her own hands.

'Who is that driving by?' she asked Boxall, the butler.

'Lady Firtlemere's carriage, my lady,' which reminded her to send a card to ask after his lordship's health. A rude old lady, Jacob thought. The wine was excellent. She called herself 'an old woman' – 'so kind to lunch with an old woman' – which flattered him. She talked of Joseph Chamberlain,[107] whom she had known. She said that Jacob must come and meet – one of our celebrities. And the Lady Alice came in with three dogs on a leash, and Jackie, who ran to kiss his grandmother, while Boxall brought in a telegram, and Jacob was given a good cigar.

A few moments before a horse jumps it slows, sidles, gathers itself together, goes up like a monster wave, and pitches down on the farther side. Hedges and sky swoop in a semicircle. Then as if your own body ran into the horse's body and it was your own forelegs grown with his that sprang, rushing through the air you go, the ground resilient, bodies a mass of muscles, yet you have command too, upright stillness, eyes accurately judging. Then the curves cease, changing to downright hammer strokes, which jar; and you draw up with a jolt; sitting back a little, sparkling, tingling, glazed with ice over pounding arteries, gasping: 'Ah! ho! Hah!' the steam going up from the horses as they jostle together at the crossroads, where the signpost is, and the woman in the apron stands and stares at the doorway. The man raises himself from the cabbages to stare too.

So Jacob galloped over the fields of Essex, flopped in the mud, lost the hunt, and rode by himself eating sandwiches, looking over the hedges, noticing the colours as if new scraped, cursing his luck.

He had tea at the inn; and there they all were, slapping, stamping, saying, 'After you,' clipped, curt, jocose, red as the wattles of turkeys, using free speech until Mrs Horsefield and her friend Miss Dudding appeared at the doorway with their skirts hitched up, and hair looping down. Then Tom Dudding rapped at the window with his whip. A motor car throbbed in the courtyard. Gentlemen, feeling for matches, moved out, and Jacob went into the bar with Brandy Jones to smoke with the rustics. There was old Jevons with one eye gone, and his clothes the colour of mud, his bag over his back, and his brains laid feet down in earth among the violet roots and the nettle roots; Mary Sanders with her box of wood; and Tom sent for beer, the half-witted son of the sexton – all this within thirty miles of London.

Mrs Papworth, of Endell Street, Covent Garden, did for[108] Mr Bonamy in New Square, Lincoln's Inn, and as she washed up the dinner things in the scullery she heard the young gentlemen talking in the room next door. Mr Sanders was there again; Flanders she meant; and where an inquisitive old woman gets a name wrong, what chance is there that she will faithfully report an argument? As she held the plates under water and then dealt them on the pile beneath the hissing gas, she listened: heard Sanders speaking in a loud rather overbearing tone of voice: 'good', he said, and 'absolute' and 'justice' and 'punishment' and 'the will of the majority'. Then her gentleman piped up; she backed him for argument against Sanders. Yet Sanders was a fine young fellow (here all the scraps went swirling round the sink, scoured after by her purple, almost nailless hands). 'Women' – she thought, and wondered what Sanders and her gentleman did in *that* line, one eyelid sinking perceptibly as she mused, for she was the mother of nine – three still-born and one deaf and dumb from birth. Putting the plates in the rack she heard once more Sanders at it again ('He don't give Bonamy a chance,' she thought). 'Objective something,' said Bonamy; and 'common ground' and something else – all very long words, she noted. 'Book learning does it,' she thought to herself, and, as she thrust her arms into her jacket, heard something – might be the little table by the fire – fall; and then stamp, stamp, stamp – as if they were having at each other – round the room, making the plates dance.

'Tomorrow's breakfast, sir,' she said, opening the door; and there were Sanders and Bonamy like two bulls of Bashan[109] driving each other up and down, making such a racket, and all them chairs in the way. They never noticed her. She felt motherly towards them. 'Your breakfast, sir,' she said, as they came near. And Bonamy, all his hair tousled and his tie flying, broke off, and pushed Sanders into the armchair, and said Mr Sanders had smashed the coffee-pot and he was teaching Mr Sanders –

Sure enough, the coffee-pot lay broken on the hearth-rug.

'Any day this week except Thursday,' wrote Miss Perry, and this was not the first invitation by any means. Were all Miss Perry's weeks blank with the exception of Thursday, and was her only desire to see her old friend's son? Time is issued to spinster ladies of wealth in long white ribbons. These they wind round and round, round and round, assisted by five female servants, a butler, a fine Mexican parrot, regular meals, Mudie's library, and friends dropping in. A little hurt she was already that Jacob had not called.

'Your mother,' she said, 'is one of my oldest friends.'

Miss Rosseter, who was sitting by the fire, holding the *Spectator* between her cheek and the blaze, refused to have a fire-screen, but finally accepted one. The weather was then discussed, for in deference to Parkes, who was opening little tables, graver matters were postponed. Miss Rosseter drew Jacob's attention to the beauty of the cabinet.

'So wonderfully clever in picking things up,' she said. Miss Perry had found it in Yorkshire. The North of England was discussed. When Jacob spoke they both listened. Miss Perry was bethinking her of something suitable and manly to say when the door opened and Mr Benson was announced. Now there were four people sitting in that room. Miss Perry aged 66; Miss Rosseter 42; Mr Benson 38; and Jacob 25.

'My old friend looks as well as ever,' said Mr Benson, tapping the bars of the parrot's cage; Miss Rosseter simultaneously praised the tea; Jacob handed the wrong plates; and Miss Perry signified her desire to approach more closely. 'Your brothers,' she began vaguely.

'Archer and John,' Jacob supplied her. Then to her pleasure she recovered Rebecca's name; and how one day 'when you were all little boys, playing in the drawing-room – '

'But Miss Perry has the kettle-holder,' said Miss Rosseter, and indeed Miss Perry was clasping it to her breast. (Had she, then, loved Jacob's father?)

'So clever' – 'not so good as usual' – 'I thought it most unfair,' said Mr Benson and Miss Rosseter, discussing the Saturday *Westminster*.[110] Did they not compete regularly for prizes? Had not Mr Benson three times won a guinea, and Miss Rosseter once ten and sixpence? Of course Everard Benson had a weak heart, but still, to win prizes, remember parrots, toady Miss Perry, despise Miss Rosseter, give tea-parties in his rooms (which were in the style of Whistler,[111] with pretty books on tables), all this, so Jacob felt without knowing him, made him a contemptible ass. As for Miss Rosseter, she had nursed cancer, and now painted watercolours.

'Running away so soon?' said Miss Perry vaguely. 'At home every afternoon, if you've nothing better to do – except Thursdays.'

'I've never known you desert your old ladies once,' Miss Rosseter was saying, and Mr Benson was stooping over the parrot's cage, and Miss Perry was moving towards the bell . . .

The fire burnt clear between two pillars of greenish marble, and on the mantelpiece there was a green clock guarded by Britannia leaning on her spear. As for pictures – a maiden in a large hat offered roses over the garden gate to a gentleman in eighteenth-century costume. A mastiff lay extended against a battered door. The lower panes of the windows were of ground glass, and the curtains, accurately looped, were of plush and green too.

Laurette and Jacob sat with their toes in the fender side by side, in two large chairs covered in green plush. Laurette's skirts were short, her legs long, thin, and transparently covered. Her fingers stroked her ankles.

'It's not exactly that I don't understand them,' she was saying thoughtfully. 'I must go and try again.'

'What time will you be there?' said Jacob.

She shrugged her shoulders.

'Tomorrow?'

No, not tomorrow.

'This weather makes me long for the country,' she said, looking over her shoulder at the back view of tall houses through the window.

'I wish you'd been with me on Saturday,' said Jacob.

'I used to ride,' she said. She got up gracefully, calmly. Jacob got up. She smiled at him. As she shut the door he put so many shillings on the mantelpiece.

Altogether a most reasonable conversation; a most respectable room; an intelligent girl. Only Madame herself seeing Jacob out had about her that leer, that lewdness, that quake of the surface (visible in the eyes chiefly), which threatens to spill the whole bag of ordure, with difficulty held together, over the pavement. In short, something was wrong.

Not so very long ago the workmen had gilt the final 'y' in Lord Macaulay's name, and the names stretched in unbroken file round the dome of the British Museum. At a considerable depth beneath, many hundreds of the living sat at the spokes of a cartwheel copying from printed books into manuscript books; now and then rising to consult the catalogue; regaining their places stealthily, while from time to time a silent man replenished their compartments.

There was a little catastrophe. Miss Marchmont's pile overbalanced and fell into Jacob's compartment. Such things happened to Miss Marchmont. What was she seeking through millions of pages, in her old plush dress, and her wig of claret-coloured hair, with her gems and her chilblains? Sometimes one thing, sometimes another, to confirm her philosophy that colour is sound – or, perhaps, it has something to do with music. She could never quite say, though it was not for lack of trying. And she could not ask you back to her room, for it was 'not very clean, I'm afraid', so she must catch you in the passage, or take a chair in Hyde Park to explain her philosophy. The rhythm of the soul depends on it – ('How rude the little boys are!' she would say), and Mr Asquith's Irish policy,[112] and Shakespeare comes in, 'and Queen Alexandra[113] most graciously once acknowledged a copy of my pamphlet,' she would say, waving the little boys magnificently away. But she needs funds to publish her book, for 'publishers are capitalists – publishers are cowards'. And so, digging her elbow into her pile of books she caused it to fall over.

Jacob remained quite unmoved.

But Fraser, the atheist, on the other side, detesting plush, more than once accosted with leaflets, shifted irritably. He abhorred vagueness – the Christian religion, for example, and old Dean Parker's pronounce-ments. Dean Parker wrote books and Fraser utterly destroyed them by force of logic and left his children unbaptised – his wife did it secretly in the washing basin – but Fraser ignored her, and went on supporting blasphemers, distributing leaflets, getting up his facts in the British Museum, always in the same check suit and fiery tie, but pale, spotted, irritable. Indeed, what a work – to destroy religion!

Jacob transcribed a whole passage from Marlowe.

Miss Julia Hedge, the feminist, waited for her books. They did not come. She wetted her pen. She looked about her. Her eye was caught by the final letters in Lord Macaulay's name. And she read them all round the dome – the names of great men which remind us – 'Oh damn,' said Julia Hedge, 'why didn't they leave room for an Eliot or a Brontë?'

Unfortunate Julia! wetting her pen in bitterness, and leaving her shoe-laces untied. When her books came she applied herself to her gigantic labours, but perceived through one of the nerves of her exasperated sensibility how composedly, unconcernedly and with every consideration the male readers applied themselves to theirs. That young man for example. What had he got to do except copy out poetry? And she must study statistics. There are more women than men. Yes; but if you let women work as men work, they'll die off much quicker. They'll become extinct. That was her argument. Death and gall and bitter dust were on her pen-tip; and as the afternoon wore on, red had worked into her cheekbones and a light was in her eyes.

But what brought Jacob Flanders to read Marlowe in the British Museum?

Youth, youth – something savage – something pedantic. For example, there is Mr Masefield, there is Mr Bennett. Stuff them into the flame of Marlowe[114] and burn them to cinders. Let not a shred remain. Don't palter with the second rate. Detest your own age. Build a better one. And to set that on foot read incredibly dull essays upon Marlowe to your friends. For which purpose one most collate editions in the British Museum. One must do the thing oneself. Useless to trust to the

Victorians, who disembowel,[115] or to the living, who are mere publicists. The flesh and blood of the future depends entirely upon six young men. And as Jacob was one of them, no doubt he looked a little regal and pompous as he turned his page, and Julia Hedge disliked him naturally enough.

But then a pudding-faced man pushed a note towards Jacob, and Jacob, leaning back in his chair, began an uneasy murmured conversation, and they went off together (Julia Hedge watched them), and laughed aloud (she thought) directly they were in the hall.

Nobody laughed in the reading-room. There were shiftings, murmurings, apologetic sneezes and sudden unashamed devastating coughs. The lesson hour was almost over. Ushers were collecting exercises. Lazy children wanted to stretch. Good ones scribbled assiduously – ah, another day over and so little done! And now and then was to be heard from the whole collection of human beings a heavy sigh, after which the humiliating old man would cough shamelessly, and Miss Marchmont hinnied like a horse.

Jacob came back only in time to return his books.

The books were now replaced. A few letters of the alphabet were sprinkled round the dome. Closely stood together in a ring round the dome were Plato, Aristotle, Sophocles and Shakespeare;[116] the literature of Rome, Greece, China, India, Persia. One leaf of poetry was pressed flat against another leaf, one burnished letter laid smooth against another in a density of meaning, a conglomeration of loveliness.

'One does want one's tea,' said Miss Marchmont, reclaiming her shabby umbrella.

Miss Marchmont wanted her tea, but could never resist a last look at the Elgin Marbles.[117] She looked at them sideways, waving her hand and muttering a word or two of salutation which made Jacob and the other man turn round. She smiled at them amiably. It all came into her philosophy – that colour is sound, or perhaps it has something to do with music. And having done her service, she hobbled off to tea. It was closing time. The public collected in the hall to receive their umbrellas.

For the most part the students wait their turn very patiently. To stand and wait while someone examines white discs is soothing. The umbrella will certainly be found. But the fact leads you on all day through Macaulay, Hobbes, Gibbon;[118] through octavos, quartos, folios; sinks deeper and deeper through ivory pages and morocco bindings into this density of thought, this conglomeration of knowledge.

Jacob's walking-stick was like all the others; they had muddled the pigeon-holes perhaps.

There is in the British Museum an enormous mind. Consider that Plato is there cheek by jowl with Aristotle; and Shakespeare with Marlowe. This great mind is hoarded beyond the power of any single mind to possess it. Nevertheless (as they take so long finding one's walking-stick) one can't help thinking how one might come with a notebook, sit at a desk, and read it all through. A learned man is the most venerable of all – a man like Huxtable of Trinity, who writes all his letters in Greek,[119] they say, and could have kept his end up with Bentley. And then there is science, pictures, architecture – an enormous mind.

They pushed the walking-stick across the counter. Jacob stood beneath the porch of the British Museum. It was raining. Great Russell Street was glazed and shining – here yellow, here, outside the chemist's, red and pale blue. People scuttled quickly close to the wall; carriages rattled rather helter-skelter down the streets. Well, but a little rain hurts nobody. Jacob walked off much as if he had been in the country; and late that night there he was sitting at his table with his pipe and his book.

The rain poured down. The British Museum stood in one solid immense mound, very pale, very sleek in the rain, not a quarter of a mile from him. The vast mind was sheeted with stone; and each compartment in the depths of it was safe and dry. The night-watchmen, flashing their lanterns over the backs of Plato and Shakespeare, saw that on the twenty-second of February neither flame, rat, nor burglar was going to violate these treasures – poor, highly respectable men, with wives and families at Kentish Town, do their best for twenty years to protect Plato and Shakespeare, and then are buried at Highgate.

Stone lies solid over the British Museum, as bone lies cool over the visions and heat of the brain. Only here the brain is Plato's brain and Shakespeare's; the brain has made pots and statues, great bulls and little jewels, and crossed the river of death this way and that incessantly, seeking some landing, now wrapping the body well for its long sleep; now laying a penny piece on the eyes; now turning the toes scrupulously to the East. Meanwhile, Plato continues his dialogue; in spite of the rain; in spite of the cab whistles; in spite of the woman in the mews behind Great Ormond Street who has come home drunk and cries all night long, 'Let me in! Let me in!'

In the street below Jacob's room voices were raised.

But he read on. For after all Plato continues imperturbably. And Hamlet utters his soliloquy. And there the Elgin Marbles lie, all night

long, old Jones's lantern sometimes recalling Ulysses,[120] or a horse's
head; or sometimes a flash of gold, or a mummy's sunk yellow cheek.
Plato and Shakespeare continue; and Jacob, who was reading the
Phaedrus, heard people vociferating round the lamp-post, and the
woman battering at the door and crying, 'Let me in!' as if a coal had
dropped from the fire, or a fly, falling from the ceiling, had lain on its
back, too weak to turn over.

The *Phaedrus* is very difficult.[121] And so, when at length one reads
straight ahead, falling into step, marching on, becoming (so it seems)
momentarily part of this rolling, imperturbable energy, which has driven
darkness before it since Plato walked the Acropolis, it is impossible to
see to the fire.

The dialogue draws to its close. Plato's argument is done. Plato's
argument is stowed away in Jacob's mind, and for five minutes Jacob's
mind continues alone, onwards, into the darkness. Then, getting up,
he parted the curtains, and saw, with astonishing clearness, how the
Springetts opposite had gone to bed; how it rained; how the Jews and
the foreign woman, at the end of the street, stood by the pillar-box,
arguing.

Every time the door opened and fresh people came in, those already in
the room shifted slightly; those who were standing looked over their
shoulders; those who were sitting stopped in the middle of sentences.
What with the light, the wine, the strumming of a guitar, something
exciting happened each time the door opened. Who was coming in?
'That's Gibson.'
'The painter?'
'But go on with what you were saying.'
They were saying something that was far, far too intimate to be said
outright. But the noise of the voices served like a clapper in little Mrs
Withers's mind, scaring into the air blocks of small birds, and then
they'd settle, and then she'd feel afraid, put one hand to her hair, bind
both round her knees, and look up at Oliver Skelton nervously, and say:
'Promise, *promise*, you'll tell no one.' . . . so considerate he was, so
tender. It was her husband's character that she discussed. He was cold,
she said.

Down upon them came the splendid Magdalen,[122] brown, warm,
voluminous, scarcely brushing the grass with her sandalled feet. Her
hair flew; pins seemed scarcely to attach the flying silks. An actress of
course, a line of light perpetually beneath her. It was only 'My dear'
that she said, but her voice went yodelling between Alpine passes. And

down she tumbled on the floor, and sang, since there was nothing to be said, round ahs and ohs. Mangin, the poet, coming up to her, stood looking down at her, drawing at his pipe. The dancing began.

Grey-haired Mrs Keymer asked Dick Graves to tell her who Mangin was, and said that she had seen too much of this sort of thing in Paris (Magdalen had got upon his knees; now his pipe was in her mouth) to be shocked. 'Who is that?' she said, staying her glasses when they came to Jacob, for indeed he looked quiet, not indifferent, but like someone on a beach, watching.

'Oh, my dear, let me lean on you,' gasped Helen Askew, hopping on one foot, for the silver cord round her ankle had worked loose. Mrs Keymer turned and looked at the picture on the wall.

'Look at Jacob,' said Helen (they were binding his eyes for some game).

And Dick Graves, being a little drunk, very faithful, and very simple-minded, told her that he thought Jacob the greatest man he had ever known. And down they sat cross-legged upon cushions and talked about Jacob, and Helen's voice trembled, for they both seemed heroes to her, and the friendship between them so much more beautiful than women's friendships. Anthony Pollett now asked her to dance, and as she danced she looked at them, over her shoulder, standing at the table, drinking together.

The magnificent world – the live, sane, vigorous world . . . These words refer to the stretch of wood pavement between Hammersmith and Holborn in January between two and three in the morning. That was the ground beneath Jacob's feet. It was healthy and magnificent because one room, above a mews, somewhere near the river, contained fifty excited, talkative, friendly people. And then to stride over the pavement (there was scarcely a cab or policeman in sight) is of itself exhilarating. The long loop of Piccadilly, diamond-stitched, shows to best advantage when it is empty. A young man has nothing to fear. On the contrary, though he may not have said anything brilliant, he feels pretty confident he can hold his own. He was pleased to have met Mangin; he admired the young woman on the floor; he liked them all; he liked that sort of thing. In short, all the drums and trumpets were sounding. The street scavengers were the only people about at the moment. It is scarcely necessary to say how well disposed Jacob felt towards them; how it pleased him to let himself in with his latchkey at his own door; how he seemed to bring back with him into the empty room ten or eleven people whom he had not known when he set out;

how he looked about for something to read, and found it, and never read it, and fell asleep.

Indeed, drums and trumpets is no phrase. Indeed, Piccadilly and Holborn, and the empty sitting-room and the sitting-room with fifty people in it are liable at any moment to blow music into the air. Women perhaps are more excitable than men. It is seldom that anyone says anything about it, and to see the hordes crossing Waterloo Bridge to catch the non-stop to Surbiton one might think that reason impelled them. No, no. It is the drums and trumpets. Only, should you turn aside into one of those little bays on Waterloo Bridge to think the matter over, it will probably seem to you all a muddle – all a mystery.

They cross the bridge incessantly. Sometimes in the midst of carts and omnibuses a lorry will appear with great forest trees chained to it. Then, perhaps, a mason's van with newly lettered tombstones recording how someone loved someone who is buried at Putney. Then the motor car in front jerks forward, and the tombstones pass too quick for you to read more. All the time the stream of people never ceases passing from the Surrey side to the Strand; from the Strand to the Surrey side. It seems as if the poor had gone raiding the town, and now traipsed back to their own quarters, like beetles scurrying to their holes, for that old woman fairly hobbles towards Waterloo, grasping a shiny bag, as if she had been out into the light and now made off with some scraped chicken bones to her hovel underground. On the other hand, though the wind is rough and blowing in their faces, those girls there, striding hand in hand, shouting out a song, seem to feel neither cold nor shame. They are hatless. They triumph.

The wind has blown up the waves. The river races beneath us, and the men standing on the barges have to lean all their weight on the tiller. A black tarpaulin is tied down over a swelling load of gold. Avalanches of coal glitter blackly. As usual, painters are slung on planks across the great riverside hotels, and the hotel windows have already points of light in them. On the other side the City is white as if with age; St Paul's swells white above the fretted, pointed or oblong buildings beside it. The cross alone shines rosy-gilt. But what century have we reached? Has this procession from the Surrey side to the Strand gone on for ever? That old man has been crossing the bridge these six hundred years, with the rabble of little boys at his heels, for he is drunk, or blind with misery, and tied round with old clouts of clothing such as pilgrims might have worn. He shuffles on. No one stands still. It seems as if we marched to the sound of music; perhaps the wind and the river;

perhaps these same drums and trumpets – the ecstasy and hubbub of the soul. Why, even the unhappy laugh, and the policeman, far from judging the drunk man, surveys him humorously, and the little boys scamper back again, and the clerk from Somerset House has nothing but tolerance for him, and the man who is reading half a page of *Lothair*[123] at the bookstall muses charitably, with his eyes off the print, and the girl hesitates at the crossing and turns on him the bright yet vague glance of the young.

Bright yet vague. She is perhaps twenty-two. She is shabby. She crosses the road and looks at the daffodils and the red tulips in the florist's window. She hesitates, and makes off in the direction of Temple Bar. She walks fast, and yet anything distracts her. Now she seems to see, and now to notice nothing.

Chapter 10

Through the disused graveyard in the parish of St Pancras,[124] Fanny Elmer strayed between the white tombs which lean against the wall, crossing the grass to read a name, hurrying on when the grave-keeper approached, hurrying into the street, pausing now by a window with blue china, now quickly making up for lost time, abruptly entering a baker's shop, buying rolls, adding cakes, going on again so that anyone wishing to follow must fairly trot. She was not drably shabby, though. She wore silk stockings and silver-buckled shoes, only the red feather in her hat drooped, and the clasp of her bag was weak, for out fell a copy of Madame Tussaud's[125] programme as she walked. She had the ankles of a stag. Her face was hidden. Of course, in this dusk, rapid movements, quick glances and soaring hopes come naturally enough. She passed right beneath Jacob's window.

The house was flat, dark and silent. Jacob was at home engaged upon a chess problem, the board being on a stool between his knees. One hand was fingering the hair at the back of his head. He slowly brought it forward and raised the white queen from her square; then put her down again on the same spot. He filled his pipe; ruminated; moved two pawns; advanced the white knight; then ruminated with one finger upon the bishop. Now Fanny Elmer passed beneath the window.

She was on her way to sit to Nick Bramham the painter.

*

She sat in a flowered Spanish shawl, holding in her hand a yellow novel.[126]

'A little lower, a little looser, so – better, that's right,' Bramham mumbled, who was drawing her, and smoking at the same time, and was naturally speechless. His head might have been the work of a sculptor who had squared the forehead, stretched the mouth and left marks of his thumbs and streaks from his fingers in the clay. But the eyes had never been shut. They were rather prominent, and rather bloodshot, as if from staring and staring, and when he spoke they looked for a second disturbed, but went on staring. An unshaded electric light hung above her head.

As for the beauty of women, it is like the light on the sea, never constant to a single wave. They all have it; they all lose it. Now she is dull and thick as bacon; now transparent as a hanging glass. The fixed faces are the dull ones. Here comes Lady Venice displayed like a monument for admiration, but carved in alabaster, to be set on the mantelpiece and never dusted. A dapper brunette complete from head to foot serves only as an illustration to lie upon the drawing-room table. The women in the streets have the faces of playing cards;[127] the outlines accurately filled in with pink or yellow, and the line drawn tightly round them. Then, at a top-floor window, leaning out, looking down, you see beauty itself; or in the corner of an omnibus; or squatted in a ditch – beauty glowing, suddenly expressive, withdrawn the moment after. No one can count on it or seize it or have it wrapped in paper. Nothing is to be won from the shops, and heaven knows it would be better to sit at home than haunt the plate-glass windows in the hope of lifting the shining green, the glowing ruby, out of them alive. Sea glass in a saucer loses its lustre no sooner than silks do. Thus if you talk of a beautiful woman you mean only something flying fast which for a second uses the eyes, lips or cheeks of Fanny Elmer, for example, to glow through.

She was not beautiful, as she sat stiffly; her underlip too prominent; her nose too large; her eyes too near together. She was a thin girl, with brilliant cheeks and dark hair, sulky just now, or stiff with sitting. When Bramham snapped his stick of charcoal she started. Bramham was out of temper. He squatted before the gas fire warming his hands. Meanwhile she looked at his drawing. He grunted. Fanny threw on a dressing-gown and boiled a kettle.

'By God, it's bad,' said Bramham.

Fanny dropped on to the floor, clasped her hands round her knees, and looked at him, her beautiful eyes – yes, beauty, flying through the room, shone there for a second. Fanny's eyes seemed to question, to commiserate, to be, for a second, love itself. But she exaggerated. Bramham noticed nothing. And when the kettle boiled, up she scrambled, more like a colt or a puppy than a loving woman.

Now Jacob walked over to the window and stood with his hands in his pockets. Mr Springett opposite came out, looked at his shop window, and went in again. The children drifted past, eyeing the pink sticks of sweetstuff. Pickford's van swung down the street. A small boy twirled from a rope. Jacob turned away. Two minutes later he opened the front door, and walked off in the direction of Holborn.

Fanny Elmer took down her cloak from the hook. Nick Bramham unpinned his drawing and rolled it under his arm. They turned out the lights and set off down the street, holding on their way through all the people, motor cars, omnibuses, carts, until they reached Leicester Square, five minutes before Jacob reached it, for his way was slightly longer, and he had been stopped by a block in Holborn waiting to see the King drive by, so that Nick and Fanny were already leaning over the barrier in the promenade at the Empire[128] when Jacob pushed through the swing doors and took his place beside them.

'Hello, never noticed you,' said Nick, five minutes later.

'Bloody rot,' said Jacob.

'Miss Elmer,' said Nick.

Jacob took his pipe out of his mouth very awkwardly.

Very awkward he was. And when they sat upon a plush sofa and let the smoke go up between them and the stage, and heard far off the high-pitched voices and the jolly orchestra breaking in opportunely, he was still awkward, only Fanny thought: 'What a beautiful voice!' She thought how little he said yet how firm it was. She thought how young men are dignified and aloof, and how unconscious they are, and how quietly one might sit beside Jacob and look at him. And how childlike he would be, come in tired of an evening, she thought, and how majestic; a little overbearing perhaps; 'But I wouldn't give way,' she thought. He got up and leant over the barrier. The smoke hung about him.

And for ever the beauty of young men seems to be set in smoke, however lustily they chase footballs, or drive cricket balls, dance, run or stride along roads. Possibly they are soon to lose it. Possibly they look into the eyes of faraway heroes, and take their station among us half contemptuously, she thought (vibrating like a fiddle-string, to be played on and snapped). Anyhow, they love silence, and speak beautifully, each word falling like a disc new cut, not a hubble-bubble of small smooth coins such as girls use; and they move decidedly, as if they knew how long to stay and when to go – oh, but Mr Flanders was only gone to get a programme.

'The dancers come right at the end,' he said, coming back to them.

And isn't it pleasant, Fanny went on thinking, how young men bring out lots of silver coins from their trouser pockets, and look at them, instead of having just so many in a purse?

Then there she was herself, whirling across the stage in white flounces, and the music was the dance and fling of her own soul, and the whole machinery, rock and gear of the world was spun smoothly into those swift eddies and falls, she felt, as she stood rigid leaning over the barrier two feet from Jacob Flanders.

Her screwed-up black glove dropped to the floor. When Jacob gave it her, she started angrily. For never was there a more irrational passion. And Jacob was afraid of her for a moment – so violent, so dangerous is it when young women stand rigid; grasp the barrier; fall in love.

It was the middle of February. The roofs of Hampstead Garden Suburb[129] lay in a tremulous haze. It was too hot to walk. A dog barked, barked, barked down in the hollow. The liquid shadows went over the plain.

The body after long illness is languid, passive, receptive of sweetness, but too weak to contain it. The tears well and fall as the dog barks in the hollow, the children skim after hoops, the country darkens and brightens. Beyond a veil it seems. Ah, but draw the veil thicker lest I faint with sweetness, Fanny Elmer sighed, as she sat on a bench in Judges Walk looking at Hampstead Garden Suburb. But the dog went on barking. The motor cars hooted on the road. She heard a faraway rush and humming. Agitation was at her heart. Up she got and walked. The grass was freshly green; the sun hot. All round the pond children were stooping to launch little boats; or were drawn back screaming by their nurses.

At midday young women walk out into the air. All the men are busy in the town. They stand by the edge of the blue pond. The fresh wind scatters the children's voices all about. My children, thought Fanny Elmer. The women stand round the pond, beating off great prancing shaggy dogs. Gently the baby is rocked in the perambulator. The eyes of all the nurses, mothers and wandering women are a little glazed,[130] absorbed. They gently nod instead of answering when the little boys tug at their skirts, begging them to move on.

And Fanny moved, hearing some cry – a workman's whistle perhaps – high in mid-air. Now, among the trees, it was the thrush trilling out into the warm air a flutter of jubilation, but fear seemed to spur him, Fanny thought; as if he too were anxious with such joy at his heart – as if he were watched as he sang, and pressed by tumult to sing. There! Restless, he flew to the next tree. She heard his song more faintly. Beyond it was the humming of the wheels and the wind rushing.

She spent tenpence on lunch.

'Dear, miss, she's left her umbrella,' grumbled the mottled woman in the glass box near the door at the Express Dairy Company's shop.[131]

'Perhaps I'll catch her,' answered Milly Edwards, the waitress with the pale plaits of hair; and she dashed through the door.

'No good,' she said, coming back a moment later with Fanny's cheap umbrella. She put her hand to her plaits.

'Oh, that door!' grumbled the cashier.

Her hands were cased in black mittens, and the fingertips that drew in the paper slips were swollen as sausages.

'Pie and greens for one. Large coffee and crumpets. Eggs on toast. Two fruit cakes.'

Thus the sharp voices of the waitresses snapped. The lunchers heard their orders repeated with approval; saw the next table served with anticipation. Their own eggs on toast were at last delivered. Their eyes strayed no more.

Damp cubes of pastry fell into mouths opened like triangular bags.

Nelly Jenkinson, the typist, crumbled her cake indifferently enough. Every time the door opened she looked up. What did she expect to see?

The coal merchant read the *Telegraph* without stopping, missed the saucer, and, feeling abstractedly, put the cup down on the tablecloth.

'Did you ever hear the like of that for impertinence?' Mrs Parsons wound up, brushing the crumbs from her furs.

'Hot milk and scone for one. Pot of tea. Roll and butter,' cried the waitresses.

The door opened and shut.

Such is the life of the elderly.

It is curious, lying in a boat, to watch the waves. Here are three coming regularly one after another, all much of a size. Then, hurrying after them comes a fourth, very large and menacing; it lifts the boat; on it goes; somehow merges without accomplishing anything; flattens itself out with the rest.

What can be more violent than the fling of boughs in a gale, the tree
yielding itself all up the trunk, to the very tip of the branch, streaming
and shuddering the way the wind blows, yet never flying in dishevelment
away? The corn squirms and abases itself as if preparing to tug itself
free from the roots, and yet is tied down.

Why, from the very windows, even in the dusk, you see a swelling
run through the street, an aspiration, as with arms outstretched, eyes
desiring, mouths agape. And then we peaceably subside. For if the
exaltation lasted we should be blown like foam into the air. The stars
would shine through us. We should go down the gale in salt drops – as
sometimes happens. For the impetuous spirits will have none of this
cradling. Never any swaying or aimlessly lolling for them. Never any
making believe, or lying cosily, or genially supposing that one is much
like another, fire warm, wine pleasant, extravagance a sin.

'People are so nice, once you know them.'

'I couldn't think ill of her. One must remember – ' But Nick perhaps,
or Fanny Elmer, believing implicitly in the truth of the moment, fling
off, sting the cheek, are gone like sharp hail.

'Oh,' said Fanny, bursting into the studio three-quarters of an hour
late because she had been hanging about the neighbourhood of the
Foundling Hospital[132] merely for the chance of seeing Jacob walk down
the street, take out his latchkey, and open the door, 'I'm afraid I'm
late'; upon which Nick said nothing and Fanny grew defiant.

'I'll never come again!' she cried at length.

'Don't, then,' Nick replied, and off she ran without so much as good-
night.

How exquisite it was – that dress in Evelina's shop off Shaftesbury
Avenue! It was four o'clock on a fine day early in April, and was Fanny
the one to spend four o'clock on a fine day indoors? Other girls in that
very street sat over ledgers, or drew long threads wearily between silk
and gauze; or, festooned with ribbons in Swan and Edgar's,[133] rapidly
added up pence and farthings on the back of the bill and twisted the
yard and three-quarters in tissue paper and asked, 'Your pleasure?' of
the next comer.

In Evelina's shop off Shaftesbury Avenue the parts of a woman were
shown separate.[134] In the left hand was her skirt. Twining round a pole
in the middle was a feather boa. Ranged like the heads of malefactors
on Temple Bar were hats – emerald and white, lightly wreathed
or drooping beneath deep-dyed feathers. And on the carpet were her

feet – pointed gold, or patent leather slashed with scarlet.

Feasted upon by the eyes of women, the clothes by four o'clock were flyblown like sugar cakes in a baker's window. Fanny eyed them too. But coming along Gerrard Street was a tall man in a shabby coat. A shadow fell across Evelina's window – Jacob's shadow, though it was not Jacob. And Fanny turned and walked along Gerrard Street and wished that she had read books. Nick never read books, never talked of Ireland, or the House of Lords; and as for his fingernails! She would learn Latin and read Virgil. She had been a great reader. She had read Scott; she had read Dumas.[135] At the Slade no one read. But no one knew Fanny at the Slade, or guessed how empty it seemed to her; the passion for ear-rings, for dances, for Tonks and Steer[136] – when it was only the French who could paint, Jacob said. For the moderns were futile; painting the least respectable of the arts; and why read anything but Marlowe and Shakespeare, Jacob said, and Fielding if you must read novels?

'Fielding,' said Fanny, when the man in Charing Cross Road asked her what book she wanted.

She bought *Tom Jones*.[137]

At ten o'clock in the morning, in a room which she shared with a schoolteacher, Fanny Elmer read *Tom Jones* – that mystic book. For this dull stuff (Fanny thought) about people with odd names is what Jacob likes. Good people like it. Dowdy women who don't mind how they cross their legs read *Tom Jones* – a mystic book; for there is something, Fanny thought, about books which if I had been educated I could have liked – much better than ear-rings and flowers, she sighed, thinking of the corridors at the Slade and the fancy-dress dance next week. She had nothing to wear.

They are real, thought Fanny Elmer, setting her feet on the mantelpiece. Some people are. Nick perhaps, only he was so stupid. And women never – except Miss Sargent,[138] but she went off at lunchtime and gave herself airs. There they sat quietly of a night reading, she thought. Not going to music-halls; not looking in at shop windows; not wearing each other's clothes, like Robertson who had worn her shawl, and she had worn his waistcoat, which Jacob could only do very awkwardly; for he liked *Tom Jones*.

There it lay on her lap, in double columns, price three and sixpence; the mystic book in which Henry Fielding ever so many years ago rebuked Fanny Elmer for feasting on scarlet, in perfect prose, Jacob said. For he never read modern novels. He liked *Tom Jones*.

'I do like *Tom Jones*,' said Fanny, at five-thirty that same day early in April when Jacob took out his pipe in the armchair opposite.

Alas, women lie! But not Clara Durrant. A flawless mind; a candid nature; a virgin chained to a rock (somewhere off Lowndes Square) eternally pouring out tea for old men in white waistcoats, blue-eyed, looking you straight in the face, playing Bach. Of all women, Jacob honoured her most. But to sit at a table with bread and butter, with dowagers in velvet, and never say more to Clara Durrant than Benson said to the parrot when old Miss Perry poured out tea, was an insufferable outrage upon the liberties and decencies of human nature – or words to that effect. For Jacob said nothing. Only he glared at the fire. Fanny laid down *Tom Jones*.

She stitched or knitted.

'What's that?' asked Jacob.

'For the dance at the Slade.'

And she fetched her head-dress; her trousers; her shoes with red tassels. What should she wear?

'I shall be in Paris,' said Jacob.

And what is the point of fancy-dress dances? thought Fanny. You meet the same people; you wear the same clothes; Mangin gets drunk; Florinda sits on his knee. She flirts outrageously – with Nick Bramham just now.

'In Paris?' said Fanny.

'On my way to Greece,' he replied.

For, he said, there is nothing so detestable as London in May.

He would forget her.

A sparrow flew past the window trailing a straw – a straw from a stack stood by a barn in a farmyard. The old brown spaniel snuffs at the base for a rat. Already the upper branches of the elm trees are blotted with nests. The chestnuts have flirted their fans. And the butterflies are flaunting across the rides in the forest. Perhaps the purple emperor is feasting, as Morris says, upon a mass of putrid carrion at the base of an oak tree.

Fanny thought it all came from *Tom Jones*. He could go alone with a book in his pocket and watch the badgers. He would take a train at eight-thirty and walk all night. He saw fireflies, and brought back glow-worms in pill-boxes. He would hunt with the New Forest Staghounds. It all came from *Tom Jones*; and he would go to Greece with a book in his pocket and forget her.

She fetched her hand-glass. There was her face. And suppose one wreathed Jacob in a turban? There was his face. She lit the lamp. But as the daylight came through the window only half was lit up by the lamp. And though he looked terrible and magnificent and would chuck the forest, he said, and come to the Slade, and be a Turkish knight or a Roman emperor (and he let her blacken his lips and clenched his teeth and scowled in the glass), still – there lay *Tom Jones*.

Chapter 11

'Archer,' said Mrs Flanders with that tenderness which mothers so often display towards their eldest sons, 'will be at Gibraltar tomorrow.'

The post for which she was waiting (strolling up Dods Hill while the random church bells swung a hymn tune about her head, the clock striking four straight through the circling notes; the grass purpling under a storm-cloud; and the two dozen houses of the village cowering, infinitely humble, in company under a leaf of shadow), the post, with all its variety of messages, envelopes addressed in bold hands, in slanting hands, stamped now with English stamps, again with colonial stamps, or sometimes hastily dabbed with a yellow bar, the post was about to scatter a myriad messages over the world. Whether we gain or not by this habit of profuse communication it is not for us to say. But that letter-writing is practised mendaciously nowadays, particularly by young men travelling in foreign parts, seems likely enough.

For example, take this scene.

Here was Jacob Flanders gone abroad and staying to break his journey in Paris. (Old Miss Birkbeck, his mother's cousin, had died last June and left him a hundred pounds.)

'You needn't repeat the whole damned thing over again, Cruttendon,' said Mallinson, the little bald painter who was sitting at a marble table, splashed with coffee and ringed with wine, talking very fast, and undoubtedly more than a little drunk.

'Well, Flanders, finished writing to your lady?' said Cruttendon, as Jacob came and took his seat beside them, holding in his hand an envelope addressed to Mrs Flanders, near Scarborough, England.

'Do you uphold Velasquez?'[139] said Cruttendon.

'By God, he does,' said Mallinson.

'He always gets like this,' said Cruttendon irritably.

Jacob looked at Mallinson with excessive composure.

'I'll tell you the three greatest things that were ever written in the whole of literature,' Cruttendon burst out. ' "Hang there like fruit my soul",'[140] he began . . .

'Don't listen to a man who don't like Velasquez,' said Mallinson.

'Adolphe, don't give Mr Mallinson any more wine,' said Cruttendon.

'Fair play, fair play,' said Jacob judicially. 'Let a man get drunk if he likes. That's Shakespeare, Cruttendon. I'm with you there. Shakespeare had more guts than all these damned frogs put together. "Hang there like fruit my soul",' he began quoting, in a musical rhetorical voice, flourishing his wine glass. ' "The devil damn you black, you cream-faced loon!" '[141] he exclaimed as the wine washed over the rim.

' "Hang there like fruit my soul",' Cruttendon and Jacob both began again at the same moment, and both burst out laughing.

'Curse these flies,' said Mallinson, flicking at his bald head. 'What do they take me for?'

'Something sweet-smelling,' said Cruttendon.

'Shut up, Cruttendon,' said Jacob. 'The fellow has no manners,' he explained to Mallinson very politely. 'Wants to cut off people's drink. Look here. I want grilled bone. What's the French for grilled bone? Grilled bone, Adolphe. Now, you juggins, don't you understand?'

'And I'll tell you, Flanders, the second most beautiful thing in the whole of literature,' said Cruttendon, bringing his feet down on to the floor, and leaning right across the table, so that his face almost touched Jacob's face.

' "Hey diddle diddle, the cat and the fiddle",' Mallinson interrupted, strumming his fingers on the table. 'The most ex–qui–sitely beautiful thing in the whole of literature . . . Cruttendon is a very good fellow,' he remarked confidentially. 'But he's a bit of a fool.' And he jerked his head forward.

Well, not a word of this was ever told to Mrs Flanders; nor what happened when they paid the bill and left the restaurant and walked along the Boulevard Raspaille.

Then here is another scrap of conversation; the time about eleven in the morning; the scene a studio; and the day Sunday.

'I tell you, Flanders,' said Cruttendon, 'I'd as soon have one of Mallinson's little pictures as a Chardin. And when I say that . . . ' he squeezed the tail of an emaciated tube . . . 'Chardin was a great swell . . . He sells 'em to pay his dinner now. But wait till the dealers get hold of him. A great swell – oh, a very great swell.'

'It's an awfully pleasant life,' said Jacob, 'messing away up here. Still, it's a stupid art, Cruttendon.' He wandered off across the room. 'There's this man, Pierre Louys [142] now.' He took up a book.

'Now, my good sir, are you going to settle down?' said Cruttendon.

'That's a solid piece of work,' said Jacob, standing a canvas on a chair.

'Oh, that I did ages ago,' said Cruttendon, looking over his shoulder.

'You're a pretty competent painter in my opinion,' said Jacob after a time.

'Now if you'd like to see what I'm after at the present moment,' said Cruttendon, putting a canvas before Jacob. 'There. That's it. That's more like it. That's . . . ' he squirmed his thumb in a circle round a lamp globe painted white.

'A pretty solid piece of work,' said Jacob, straddling his legs in front of it. 'But what I wish you'd explain . . . '

Miss Jinny Carslake, pale, freckled, morbid, came into the room.

'Oh Jinny, here's a friend. Flanders. An Englishman. Wealthy. Highly connected. Go on, Flanders . . . '

Jacob said nothing.

'It's *that* – that's not right,' said Jinny Carslake.

'No,' said Cruttendon decidedly. 'Can't be done.'

He took the canvas off the chair and stood it on the floor with its back to them.

'Sit down, ladies and gentlemen. Miss Carslake comes from your part of the world, Flanders. From Devonshire. Oh, I thought you said Devonshire. Very well. She's a daughter of the Church too. The black sheep of the family. Her mother writes her such letters. I say – have you one about you? It's generally Sundays they come. Sort of church-bell effect, you know.'

'Have you met all the painter men?' said Jinny. 'Was Mallinson drunk? If you go to his studio he'll give you one of his pictures. I say, Teddy . . . '

'Half a jiff,' [143] said Cruttendon. 'What's the season of the year?' He looked out of the window. 'We take a day off on Sundays, Flanders.'

'Will he . . . ' said Jinny, looking at Jacob. 'You . . . '

'Yes, he'll come with us,' said Cruttendon.

And then, here is Versailles. Jinny stood on the stone rim and leant over the pond, clasped by Cruttendon's arms or she would have fallen in.

'There! There!' she cried. 'Right up to the top!' Some sluggish, sloping-shouldered fish had floated up from the depths to nip her crumbs. 'You look,' she said, jumping down. And then the dazzling white water, rough and throttled, shot up into the air. The fountain spread itself. Through it came the sound of military music far away. All the water was puckered with drops. A blue air-ball[144] gently bumped the surface. How all the nurses and children and old men and young crowded to the edge, leant over and waved their sticks! The little girl ran stretching her arms towards her air-ball, but it sank beneath the fountain.

Edward Cruttendon, Jinny Carslake and Jacob Flanders walked in a row along the yellow gravel path; got on to the grass; so passed under the trees; and came out at the summer-house where Marie Antoinette used to drink chocolate. In went Edward and Jinny, but Jacob waited outside, sitting on the handle of his walking-stick. Out they came again.

'Well?' said Cruttendon, smiling at Jacob.

Jinny waited; Edward waited; and both looked at Jacob.

'Well?' said Jacob, smiling and pressing both hands on his stick.

'Come along,' he decided; and started off. The others followed him, smiling.

And then they went to the little café in the by-street where people sit drinking coffee, watching the soldiers, meditatively knocking ash into trays.

'But he's quite different,' said Jinny, folding her hands over the top of her glass. 'I don't suppose you know what Ted means when he says a thing like that,' she said, looking at Jacob. 'But I do. Sometimes I could kill myself. Sometimes he lies in bed all day long – just lies there . . . I don't want you right on the table,' she waved her hands. Swollen iridescent pigeons were waddling round their feet.

'Look at that woman's hat,' said Cruttendon. 'How do they come to think of it? . . . No, Flanders, I don't think I could live like you. When one walks down that street opposite the British Museum – what's it called? – that's what I mean. It's all like that. Those fat women – and the man standing in the middle of the road as if he were going to have a fit . . . '

'Everybody feeds them,' said Jinny, waving the pigeons away. 'They're stupid old things.'

'Well, I don't know,' said Jacob, smoking his cigarette. 'There's St Paul's.'

'I mean going to an office,' said Cruttendon.

'Hang it all,' Jacob expostulated.

'But you don't count,' said Jinny, looking at Cruttendon. 'You're mad. I mean, you just think of painting.'

'Yes, I know. I can't help it. I say, will King George give way about the peers?'[145]

'He'll jolly well have to,' said Jacob.

'There!' said Jinny. 'He really knows.'

'You see, I would if I could,' said Cruttendon, 'but I simply can't.'

'I *think* I could,' said Jinny. 'Only, it's all the people one dislikes who do it. At home, I mean. They talk of nothing else. Even people like my mother.'

'Now if I came and lived here – ' said Jacob. 'What's my share, Cruttendon? Oh, very well. Have it your own way. Those silly birds, directly one wants them – they've flown away.'

And finally under the arc lamps in the Gare des Invalides, with one of those queer movements which are so slight yet so definite, which may wound or pass unnoticed but generally inflict a good deal of discomfort, Jinny and Cruttendon drew together; Jacob stood apart. They had to separate. Something must be said. Nothing was said. A man wheeled a trolley past Jacob's legs so near that he almost grazed them. When Jacob recovered his balance the other two were turning away, though Jinny looked over her shoulder, and Cruttendon, waving his hand, disappeared like the very great genius that he was.

No – Mrs Flanders was told none of this, though Jacob felt, it is safe to say, that nothing in the world was of greater importance; and as for Cruttendon and Jinny, he thought them the most remarkable people he had ever met – being of course unable to foresee how it fell out in the course of time that Cruttendon took to painting orchards; had therefore to live in Kent; and must, one would think, see through apple blossom by this time, since his wife, for whose sake he did it, eloped with a novelist; but no; Cruttendon still paints orchards, savagely, in solitude. Then Jinny Carslake, after her affair with Lefanu the American painter, frequented Indian philosophers, and now you find her in pensions in Italy cherishing a little jeweller's box containing ordinary pebbles picked off the road. But if you look at them steadily, she says, multiplicity becomes unity, which is somehow the secret of life, though it does not prevent her from following the macaroni as it goes round the table, and sometimes, on spring nights, she makes the strangest confidences to shy young Englishmen.

Jacob had nothing to hide from his mother. It was only that he could make no sense himself of his extraordinary excitement, and as for writing it down –

'Jacob's letters are so like him,' said Mrs Jarvis, folding the sheet.

'Indeed he seems to be having . . . ' said Mrs Flanders, and paused, for she was cutting out a dress and had to straighten the pattern, ' . . . a very gay time.'

Mrs Jarvis thought of Paris. At her back the window was open, for it was a mild night; a calm night; when the moon seemed muffled and the apple trees stood perfectly still.

'I never pity the dead,' said Mrs Jarvis, shifting the cushion at her back, and clasping her hands behind her head. Betty Flanders did not hear, for her scissors made so much noise on the table.

'They are at rest,' said Mrs Jarvis. 'And we spend our days doing foolish unnecessary things without knowing why.'

Mrs Jarvis was not liked in the village.

'You never walk at this time of night?' she asked Mrs Flanders.

'It is certainly wonderfully mild,' said Mrs Flanders.

Yet it was years since she had opened the orchard gate and gone out on Dods Hill after dinner.

'It is perfectly dry,' said Mrs Jarvis, as they shut the orchard door and stepped on to the turf.

'I shan't go far,' said Betty Flanders. 'Yes, Jacob will leave Paris on Wednesday.'

'Jacob was always my friend of the three,' said Mrs Jarvis.

'Now, my dear, I am going no farther,' said Mrs Flanders. They had climbed the dark hill and reached the Roman camp.

The rampart rose at their feet – the smooth circle surrounding the camp or the grave. How many needles Betty Flanders had lost there; and her garnet brooch.[146]

'It is much clearer than this sometimes,' said Mrs Jarvis, standing upon the ridge. There were no clouds, and yet there was a haze over the sea, and over the moors. The lights of Scarborough flashed, as if a woman wearing a diamond necklace turned her head this way and that.

'How quiet it is!' said Mrs Jarvis.

Mrs Flanders rubbed the turf with her toe, thinking of her garnet brooch.

Mrs Jarvis found it difficult to think of herself tonight. It was so calm. There was no wind; nothing racing, flying, escaping. Black shadows stood still over the silver moors. The furze bushes stood perfectly still.

Neither did Mrs Jarvis think of God. There was a church behind them, of course. The church clock struck ten. Did the strokes reach the furze bush, or did the thorn tree hear them?

Mrs Flanders was stooping down to pick up a pebble. Sometimes people do find things, Mrs Jarvis thought, and yet in this hazy moonlight it was impossible to see anything, except bones, and little pieces of chalk.

'Jacob bought it with his own money, and then I brought Mr Parker up to see the view, and it must have dropped –' Mrs Flanders murmured.

Did the bones stir, or the rusty swords? Was Mrs Flanders's two-penny-halfpenny brooch for ever part of the rich accumulation? and if all the ghosts flocked thick and rubbed shoulders with Mrs Flanders in the circle, would she not have seemed perfectly in her place, a live English matron, growing stout?

The clock struck the quarter.

The frail waves of sound broke among the stiff gorse and the hawthorn twigs as the church clock divided time into quarters.

Motionless and broad-backed the moors received the statement, 'It is fifteen minutes past the hour,' but made no answer, unless a bramble stirred.

Yet even in this light the legends on the tombstones could be read, brief voices saying, 'I am Bertha Ruck,' 'I am Tom Gage.'[147] And they say which day of the year they died, and the New Testament says something for them, very proud, very emphatic, or consoling.

The moors accept all that too.

The moonlight falls like a pale page upon the church wall, and illumines the kneeling family in the niche, and the tablet set up in 1780 to the squire of the parish who relieved the poor, and believed in God – so the measured voice goes on down the marble scroll, as though it could impose itself upon time and the open air.

Now a fox steals out from behind the gorse bushes.

Often, even at night, the church seems full of people. The pews are worn and greasy, and the hassocks in place, and the hymn-books on the ledges. It is a ship with all its crew aboard. The timbers strain to hold the dead and the living, the ploughmen, the carpenters, the fox-hunting gentlemen and the farmers smelling of mud and brandy. Their tongues join together in syllabling the sharp-cut words, which for ever slice asunder time and the broad-backed moors. Plaint and belief and elegy, despair and triumph, but for the most part good sense and jolly indifference, go trampling out of the windows any time these five hundred years.

Still, as Mrs Jarvis said, stepping out on to the moors, 'How quiet it is!' Quiet at midday, except when the hunt scatters across it; quiet in the afternoon, save for the drifting sheep; at night the moor is perfectly quiet.

A garnet brooch has dropped into its grass. A fox pads stealthily. A leaf turns on its edge. Mrs Jarvis, who is fifty years of age, reposes in the camp in the hazy moonlight.

' . . . and,' said Mrs Flanders, straightening her back, 'I never cared for Mr Parker.'

'Neither did I,' said Mrs Jarvis. They began to walk home.

But their voices floated for a little above the camp. The moonlight destroyed nothing. The moor accepted everything. Tom Gage cries aloud so long as his tombstone endures. The Roman skeletons are in safe keeping. Betty Flanders's darning needles are safe too and her garnet brooch. And sometimes at midday, in the sunshine, the moor seems to hoard these little treasures, like a nurse. But at midnight when no one speaks or gallops, and the thorn tree is perfectly still, it would be foolish to vex the moor with questions – what? and why?

The church clock, however, strikes twelve.

Chapter 12

The water fell off a ledge like lead – like a chain with thick white links. The train ran out into a steep green meadow, and Jacob saw striped tulips growing and heard a bird singing, in Italy.

A motor car full of Italian officers ran along the flat road and kept up with the train, raising dust behind it. There were trees laced together with vines – as Virgil said.[148] Here was a station; and a tremendous leave-taking going on, with women in high yellow boots and odd pale boys in ringed socks. Virgil's bees had gone about the plains of Lombardy.[149] It was the custom of the ancients to train vines between elms. Then at Milan there were sharp-winged hawks, of a bright brown, cutting figures over the roofs.

These Italian carriages get damnably hot with the afternoon sun on them, and the chances are that before the engine has pulled to the top of the gorge the clanking chain will have broken. Up, up, up, it goes, like a train on a scenic railway. Every peak is covered with sharp trees, and amazing white villages are crowded on ledges. There is always a white tower on the very summit, flat red-frilled roofs, and a sheer drop

beneath. It is not a country in which one walks after tea. For one thing
there is no grass. A whole hillside will be ruled with olive trees. Already
in April the earth is clotted into dry dust between them. And there are
neither stiles nor footpaths, nor lanes chequered with the shadows of
leaves nor eighteenth-century inns with bow-windows, where one eats
ham and eggs. Oh no, Italy is all fierceness, bareness, exposure and
black priests shuffling along the roads. It is strange, too, how you never
get away from villas.

Still, to be travelling on one's own with a hundred pounds to spend is
a fine affair. And if his money gave out, as it probably would, he would
go on foot. He could live on bread and wine – the wine in straw
bottles – for after doing Greece he was going to knock off Rome. The
Roman civilisation was a very inferior affair, no doubt. But Bonamy
talked a lot of rot, all the same. 'You ought to have been in Athens,' he
would say to Bonamy when he got back. 'Standing on the Parthenon,'
he would say, or, 'The ruins of the Coliseum suggest some fairly sublime
reflections,' which he would write out at length in letters. It might turn
to an essay upon civilisation. A comparison between the ancients and
moderns, with some pretty sharp hits at Mr Asquith – something in the
style of Gibbon.[150]

A stout gentleman laboriously hauled himself in, dusty, baggy, slung
with gold chains, and Jacob, regretting that he did not come of the
Latin race, looked out of the window.

It is a strange reflection that by travelling two days and nights you
are in the heart of Italy. Accidental villas among olive trees appear;
and menservants watering the cactuses. Black victorias[151] drive in
between pompous pillars with plaster shields stuck to them. It is at
once momentary and astonishingly intimate – to be displayed before
the eyes of a foreigner. And there is a lonely hill-top where no one ever
comes, and yet it is seen by me who was lately driving down Piccadilly
on an omnibus. And what I should like would be to get out among the
fields, sit down and hear the grasshoppers, and take up a handful of
earth – Italian earth, as this is Italian dust upon my shoes.

Jacob heard them crying strange names at railway stations through
the night. The train stopped and he heard frogs croaking close by, and
he wrinkled back the blind cautiously and saw a vast strange marsh all
white in the moonlight. The carriage was thick with cigar smoke, which
floated round the globe with the green shade on it. The Italian gentleman lay snoring with his boots off and his waistcoat unbuttoned . . .
And all this business of going to Greece seemed to Jacob an intolerable
weariness – sitting in hotels by oneself and looking at monuments –

he'd have done better to go to Cornwall with Timmy Durrant ... 'O–h,' Jacob protested, as the darkness began breaking in front of him and the light showed through, but the man was reaching across him to get something – the fat Italian man in his dicky, unshaven, crumpled, obese, was opening the door and going off to have a wash.

So Jacob sat up, and saw a lean Italian sportsman with a gun walking down the road in the early-morning light, and the whole idea of the Parthenon came upon him in a clap.

'By Jove!' he thought, 'we must be nearly there!' and he stuck his head out of the window and got the air full in his face.

It is highly exasperating that twenty-five people of your acquaintance should be able to say straight off something very much to the point about being in Greece, while for yourself there is a stopper upon all emotions whatsoever. For after washing at the hotel at Patras, Jacob had followed the tramlines a mile or so out; and followed them a mile or so back; he had met several droves of turkeys; several strings of donkeys; had got lost in back streets; had read advertisements of corsets and of Maggi's consommé; children had trodden on his toes; the place smelt of bad cheese; and he was glad to find himself suddenly come out opposite his hotel. There was an old copy of the *Daily Mail* lying among coffee-cups; which he read. But what could he do after dinner?

No doubt we should be, on the whole, much worse off than we are without our astonishing gift for illusion. At the age of twelve or so, having given up dolls and broken our steam engines, France but much more probably Italy and India almost for a certainty draw the superfluous imagination. One's aunts have been to Rome; and everyone has an uncle who was last heard of – poor man – in Rangoon. He will never come back any more. But it is the governesses who start the Greek myth. Look at that for a head (they say) – nose, you see, straight as a dart, curls, eyebrows – everything appropriate to manly beauty; while his legs and arms have lines on them which indicate a perfect degree of development – the Greeks caring for the body as much as for the face. And the Greeks could paint fruit so that birds pecked at it. First you read Xenophon; then Euripides. One day – that was an occasion, by God – what people have said appears to have sense in it: 'the Greek spirit'; the Greek this, that and the other; though it is absurd, by the way, to say that any Greek comes near Shakespeare. The point is, however, that we have been brought up in an illusion.

Jacob, no doubt, thought something in this fashion, the *Daily Mail* crumpled in his hand; his legs extended; the very picture of boredom.

'But it's the way we're brought up,' he went on.

And it all seemed to him very distasteful. Something ought to be done about it. And from being moderately depressed he became like a man about to be executed. Clara Durrant had left him at a party to talk to an American called Pilchard.[152] And he had come all the way to Greece and left her. They wore evening-dresses, and talked nonsense – what damned nonsense – and he put out his hand for the *Globe Trotter*, an international magazine which is supplied free of charge to the proprietors of hotels.

In spite of its ramshackle condition modern Greece is highly advanced in the electric-tramway system, so that while Jacob sat in the hotel sitting-room the trams clanked, chimed, rang, rang, rang imperiously to get the donkeys out of the way, and one old woman who refused to budge, beneath the windows. The whole of civilisation was being condemned.

The waiter was quite indifferent to that too. Aristotle, a dirty man, carnivorously interested in the body of the only guest now occupying the only armchair, came into the room ostentatiously, put something down, put something straight, and saw that Jacob was still there.

'I shall want to be called early tomorrow,' said Jacob, over his shoulder. 'I am going to Olympia.'

This gloom, this surrender to the dark waters which lap us about, is a modern invention. Perhaps, as Cruttendon said, we do not believe enough. Our fathers at any rate had something to demolish. So have we for the matter of that, thought Jacob, crumpling the *Daily Mail* in his hand. He would go into Parliament and make fine speeches – but what use are fine speeches and Parliament, once you surrender an inch to the black waters? Indeed there has never been any explanation of the ebb and flow in our veins – of happiness and unhappiness. That respectability and evening parties where one has to dress, and wretched slums at the back of Gray's Inn – something solid, immovable and grotesque – is at the back of it, Jacob thought probable. But then there was the British Empire which was beginning to puzzle him; nor was he altogether in favour of giving Home Rule to Ireland. What did the *Daily Mail* say about that?

For he had grown to be a man, and was about to be immersed in things – as indeed the chambermaid, emptying his basin upstairs, fingering keys, studs, pencils and bottles of tabloids strewn on the dressing-table, was aware.

That he had grown to be a man was a fact that Florinda knew, as she knew everything, by instinct.

And Betty Flanders even now suspected it, as she read his letter, posted at Milan, 'Telling me,' she complained to Mrs Jarvis, 'really nothing that I want to know;' but she brooded over it.

Fanny Elmer felt it to desperation. For he would take his stick and his hat and would walk to the window, and look perfectly absent-minded and very stern too, she thought.

'I am going,' he would say, 'to cadge a meal of Bonamy.'

'Anyhow, I can drown myself in the Thames,' Fanny cried, as she hurried past the Foundling Hospital.

'But the *Daily Mail* isn't to be trusted,' Jacob said to himself, looking about for something else to read. And he sighed again, being indeed so profoundly gloomy that gloom must have been lodged in him to cloud him at any moment, which was odd in a man who enjoyed things so, was not much given to analysis, but was horribly romantic, of course, Bonamy thought, in his rooms in Lincoln's Inn.

'He will fall in love,' thought Bonamy. 'Some Greek woman with a straight nose.'

It was to Bonamy that Jacob wrote from Patras – to Bonamy who couldn't love a woman and never read a foolish book.

There are very few good books after all, for we can't count profuse histories, travels in mule carts to discover the sources of the Nile, or the volubility of fiction.

I like books whose virtue is all drawn together in a page or two. I like sentences that don't budge though armies cross them. I like words to be hard – such were Bonamy's views, and they won him the hostility of those whose taste is all for the fresh growths of the morning, who throw up the window, and find the poppies spread in the sun, and can't forbear a shout of jubilation at the astonishing fertility of English literature. That was not Bonamy's way at all. That his taste in literature affected his friendships, and made him silent, secretive, fastidious, and only quite at his ease with one or two young men of his own way of thinking, was the charge against him.

But then Jacob Flanders was not at all of his own way of thinking – far from it, Bonamy sighed, laying the thin sheets of notepaper on the table and falling into thought about Jacob's character, not for the first time.

The trouble was this romantic vein in him. 'But mixed with the stupidity which leads him into these absurd predicaments,' thought Bonamy, 'there is something – something' – he sighed, for he was fonder of Jacob than of anyone in the world.

*

Jacob went to the window and stood with his hands in his pockets. There he saw three Greeks in kilts; the masts of ships; idle or busy people of the lower classes strolling or stepping out briskly, or falling into groups and gesticulating with their hands. Their lack of concern for him was not the cause of his gloom; but some more profound conviction – it was not that he himself happened to be lonely, but that all people are.

Yet next day, as the train slowly rounded a hill on the way to Olympia, the Greek peasant women were out among the vines; the old Greek men were sitting at the stations, sipping sweet wine. And though Jacob remained gloomy he had never suspected how tremendously pleasant it is to be alone; out of England; on one's own; cut off from the whole thing. There are very sharp bare hills on the way to Olympia; and between them blue sea in triangular spaces. A little like the Cornish coast. Well now, to go walking by oneself all day – to get on to that track and follow it up between the bushes – or are they small trees? – to the top of that mountain from which one can see half the nations of antiquity –

'Yes,' said Jacob, for his carriage was empty, 'let's look at the map.'

Blame it or praise it, there is no denying the wild horse in us. To gallop intemperately; fall on the sand tired out; to feel the earth spin; to have – positively – a rush of friendship for stones and grasses, as if humanity were over, and as for men and women, let them go hang – there is no getting over the fact that this desire seizes us pretty often.

The evening air slightly moved the dirty curtains in the hotel window at Olympia.

'I am full of love for everyone,' thought Mrs Wentworth Williams ' – for the poor most of all – for the peasants coming back in the evening with their burdens. And everything is soft and vague and very sad. It is sad, it is sad. But everything has meaning,' thought Sandra Wentworth Williams, raising her head a little and looking very beautiful, tragic and exalted. 'One must love everything.'

She held in her hand a little book convenient for travelling – stories by Chekhov[153] – as she stood, veiled, in white, in the window of the hotel at Olympia. How beautiful the evening was! and her beauty was its beauty. The tragedy of Greece was the tragedy of all high souls. The inevitable compromise. She seemed to have grasped something. She would write it down. And moving to the table where her husband sat reading she leant her chin in her hands and thought of the peasants, of suffering, of her own beauty, of the inevitable compromise, and of how she would write it down. Nor did Evan Williams say anything brutal, banal or foolish when he shut his book and put it away to make room for the plates of soup which were now being placed before them. Only his drooping bloodhound eyes and his heavy sallow cheeks expressed his melancholy tolerance, his conviction that though forced to live with circumspection and deliberation he could never possibly achieve any of those objects which, as he knew, are the only ones worth pursuing. His consideration was flawless; his silence unbroken.

'Everything seems to mean so much,' said Sandra. But with the sound of her own voice the spell was broken. She forgot the peasants. Only there remained with her a sense of her own beauty, and in front, luckily, there was a looking-glass.

'I am very beautiful,' she thought.

She shifted her hat slightly. Her husband saw her looking in the glass; and agreed that beauty is important; it is an inheritance; one cannot ignore it. But it is a barrier; it is in fact rather a bore. So he drank his soup; and kept his eyes fixed upon the window.

'Quails,' said Mrs Wentworth Williams languidly. 'And then goat, I suppose; and then . . . '

'Caramel custard presumably,' said her husband in the same cadence, with his toothpick out already.

She laid her spoon upon her plate, and her soup was taken away half finished. Never did she do anything without dignity; for hers was the English type which is so Greek, save that villagers have touched their hats to it, the vicarage reveres it; and upper-gardeners and under-gardeners respectfully straighten their backs as she comes down the broad terrace on Sunday morning, dallying at the stone urns with the Prime Minister to pick a rose – which, perhaps, she was trying to forget, as her eye wandered round the dining-room of the inn at Olympia, seeking the window where her book lay, where a few minutes ago she had discovered something – something very profound it had been, about love and sadness and the peasants.

But it was Evan who sighed; not in despair nor indeed in rebellion. But, being the most ambitious of men and temperamentally the most sluggish, he had accomplished nothing; had the political history of England at his finger-ends, and living much in company with Chatham, Pitt, Burke and Charles James Fox[154] could not help contrasting himself and his age with them and theirs. 'Yet there never was a time when great men are more needed,' he was in the habit of saying to himself, with a sigh. Here he was picking his teeth in an inn at Olympia. He had done. But Sandra's eyes wandered.

'Those pink melons are sure to be dangerous,' he said gloomily. And as he spoke the door opened and in came a young man in a grey check suit.

'Beautiful but dangerous,' said Sandra, immediately talking to her husband in the presence of a third person. ('Ah, an English boy on tour,' she thought to herself.)

And Evan knew all that too.

Yes, he knew all that; and he admired her. Very pleasant, he thought, to have affairs. But for himself, what with his height (Napoleon was five feet four, he remembered), his bulk, his inability to impose his own personality (and yet great men are needed more than ever now, he sighed), it was useless. He threw away his cigar, went up to Jacob and asked him, with a simple sort of sincerity which Jacob liked, whether he had come straight out from England.

'How very English!' Sandra laughed when the waiter told them next morning that the young gentleman had left at five to climb the mountain. 'I am sure he asked you for a bath?' at which the waiter shook his head, and said that he would ask the manager.

'You do not understand,' laughed Sandra. 'Never mind.'

Stretched on the top of the mountain, quite alone, Jacob enjoyed himself immensely. Probably he had never been so happy in the whole of his life.

But at dinner that night Mr Williams asked him whether he would like to see the paper; then Mrs Williams asked him (as they strolled on the terrace smoking – and how could he refuse that man's cigar?) whether he'd seen the theatre by moonlight; whether he knew Everard Sherborn; whether he read Greek and whether (Evan rose silently and went in) if he had to sacrifice one it would be the French literature or the Russian?

'And now,' wrote Jacob in his letter to Bonamy, 'I shall have to read her cursed book' – her Chekhov, he meant, for she had lent it him.

Though the opinion is unpopular it seems likely enough that bare places, fields too thick with stones to be ploughed, tossing sea-meadows halfway between England and America, suit us better than cities.

There is something absolute in us which despises qualification. It is this which is teased and twisted in society. People come together in a room. 'So delighted,' says somebody, 'to meet you,' and that is a lie. And then: 'I enjoy the spring more than the autumn now. One does, I think, as one gets older.' For women are always, always, always talking about what one feels, and if they say 'as one gets older', they mean you to reply with something quite off the point.

Jacob sat himself down in the quarry where the Greeks had cut marble for the theatre. It is hot work walking up Greek hills at midday. The wild red cyclamen was out; he had seen the little tortoises hobbling from clump to clump; the air smelt strong and suddenly sweet, and the sun, striking on jagged splinters of marble, was very dazzling to the eyes. Composed, commanding, contemptuous, a little melancholy, and bored with an august kind of boredom, there he sat smoking his pipe.

Bonamy would have said that this was the sort of thing that made him uneasy – when Jacob got into the doldrums, looked like a Margate fisherman out of a job, or a British admiral. You couldn't make him understand a thing when he was in a mood like that. One had better leave him alone. He was dull. He was apt to be grumpy.

He was up very early, looking at the statues with his Baedeker.

Sandra Wentworth Williams, ranging the world before breakfast in quest of adventure or a point of view, all in white, not so very tall perhaps, but uncommonly upright – Sandra Williams got Jacob's head exactly on a level with the head of the Hermes of Praxiteles.[155] The comparison was all in his favour. But before she could say a single word he had gone out of the museum and left her.

Still, a lady of fashion travels with more than one dress, and if white suits the morning hour, perhaps sandy yellow with purple spots on it, a black hat, and a volume of Balzac, suit the evening. Thus she was arranged on the terrace when Jacob came in. Very beautiful she looked. With her hands folded she mused, seemed to listen to her husband, seemed to watch the peasants coming down with brushwood on their backs, seemed to notice how the hill changed from blue to black, seemed to discriminate between truth and falsehood, Jacob thought, and crossed his legs suddenly, observing the extreme shabbiness of his trousers.

'But he is very distinguished looking,' Sandra decided.

And Evan Williams, lying back in his chair with the paper on his knees, envied them. The best thing he could do would be to publish, with Macmillans, his monograph upon the foreign policy of Chatham. But confound this tumid, queasy feeling – this restlessness, swelling and heat – it was jealousy! jealousy! jealousy! which he had sworn never to feel again.

'Come with us to Corinth, Flanders,' he said with more than his usual energy, stopping by Jacob's chair. He was relieved by Jacob's reply, or rather by the solid, direct, if shy manner in which he said that he would like very much to come with them to Corinth.

'Here is a fellow,' thought Evan Williams, 'who might do very well in politics.'

'I intend to come to Greece every year so long as I live,' Jacob wrote to Bonamy. 'It is the only chance I can see of protecting oneself from civilisation.'

'Goodness knows what he means by that,' Bonamy sighed. For as he never said a clumsy thing himself, these dark sayings of Jacob's made him feel apprehensive, yet somehow impressed, his own turn being all for the definite, the concrete and the rational.

Nothing could be much simpler than what Sandra said as she descended the Acro-Corinth,[156] keeping to the little path, while Jacob strode over rougher ground by her side. She had been left motherless at the age of four; and the park was vast.

'One never seemed able to get out of it,' she laughed. Of course there was the library, and dear Mr Jones, and notions about things. 'I used to stray into the kitchen and sit upon the butler's knees,' she laughed, sadly though.

Jacob thought that if he had been there he would have saved her; for she had been exposed to great dangers, he felt, and, he thought to himself, 'People wouldn't understand a woman talking as she talks.'

She made little of the roughness of the hill; and wore breeches, he saw, under her short skirts.

'Women like Fanny Elmer don't,' he thought. 'What's-her-name Carslake didn't; yet they pretend . . .'

Mrs Williams said things straight out. He was surprised by his own knowledge of the rules of behaviour; how much more can be said than one thought; how open one can be with a woman; and how little he had known himself before.

Evan joined them on the road; and as they drove along uphill and downhill (for Greece is in a state of effervescence, yet astonishingly clean-cut, a treeless land, where you see the ground between the blades, each hill cut and shaped and outlined as often as not against sparkling deep blue waters, islands white as sand floating on the horizon, occasional groves of palm trees standing in the valleys, which are scattered with black goats, spotted with little olive trees and some-times have white hollows, rayed and criss-crossed, in their flanks), as they drove uphill and down he scowled in the corner of the carriage, with his paw so tightly closed that the skin was stretched between the knuckles and the little hairs stood upright. Sandra rode opposite, dominant, like a Victory[157] prepared to fling into the air.

'Heartless!' thought Evan (which was untrue).

'Brainless!' he suspected (and that was not true either). 'Still . . . !' He envied her.

When bedtime came the difficulty was to write to Bonamy, Jacob found. Yet he had seen Salamis, and Marathon in the distance. Poor old Bonamy! No; there was something queer about it. He could not write to Bonamy.

'I shall go to Athens all the same,' he resolved, looking very set, with this hook dragging in his side.

The Williamses had already been to Athens.

Athens is still quite capable of striking a young man as the oddest combination, the most incongruous assortment. Now it is suburban; now immortal. Now cheap continental jewellery is laid upon plush trays. Now the stately woman stands naked, save for a wave of drapery above the knee. No form can he set on his sensations as he strolls, one blazing afternoon, along the Parisian boulevard and skips out of the way of the royal landau which, looking indescribably ramshackle, rattles along the pitted roadway, saluted by citizens of both sexes cheaply dressed in bowler hats and continental costumes; though a shepherd in kilt, cap and gaiters very nearly drives his herd of goats between the royal wheels; and all the time the Acropolis surges into the air, raises itself above the town, like a large immobile wave with the yellow columns of the Parthenon firmly planted upon it.

The yellow columns of the Parthenon are to be seen at all hours of the day firmly planted upon the Acropolis; though at sunset, when the ships in the Piraeus fire their guns, a bell rings, a man in uniform (the waistcoat unbuttoned) appears; and the women roll up the black stockings which they are knitting in the shadow of the columns, call to the children, and troop off down the hill back to their houses.

There they are again, the pillars, the pediment, the Temple of Victory and the Erechtheum,[158] set on a tawny rock cleft with shadows, directly you unlatch your shutters in the morning and, leaning out, hear the clatter, the clamour, the whip cracking in the street below. There they are.

The extreme definiteness with which they stand, now a brilliant white, again yellow, and in some lights red, imposes ideas of durability, of the emergence through the earth of some spiritual energy elsewhere dissipated in elegant trifles. But this durability exists quite independently of our admiration. Although the beauty is sufficiently humane to weaken us, to stir the deep deposit of mud – memories, abandonments, regrets, sentimental devotions – the Parthenon is separate from all that; and if you consider how it has stood out all night, for centuries, you begin to connect the blaze (at midday the glare is dazzling and the frieze almost invisible) with the idea that perhaps it is beauty alone that is immortal.

Added to this, compared with the blistered stucco, the new love songs rasped out to the strum of guitar and gramophone, and the mobile yet insignificant faces of the street, the Parthenon is really astonishing in its silent composure; which is so vigorous that, far from being decayed, the Parthenon appears, on the contrary, likely to outlast the entire world.

'And the Greeks, like sensible men, never bothered to finish the backs of their statues,' said Jacob, shading his eyes and observing that the side of the figure which is turned away from view is left in the rough.

He noted the slight irregularity in the line of the steps which 'the artistic sense of the Greeks preferred to mathematical accuracy', he read in his guide-book.

He stood on the exact spot where the great statue of Athena used to stand, and identified the more famous landmarks of the scene beneath.

In short he was accurate and diligent; but profoundly morose. Moreover he was pestered by guides. This was on Monday.

But on Wednesday he wrote a telegram to Bonamy, telling him to come at once. And then he crumpled it in his hand and threw it in the gutter.

'For one thing he wouldn't come,' he thought. 'And then I dare say this sort of thing wears off.' 'This sort of thing' being that uneasy, painful feeling, something like selfishness – one wishes almost that the thing would stop – it is getting more and more beyond what is possible – 'If it goes on much longer I shan't be able to cope with it – but if someone else were seeing it at the same time' – Bonamy is stuffed in his room in Lincoln's Inn – 'oh, I say, damn it all, I say' – the sight of Hymettus, Pentelicus, Lycabettus[159] on one side, and the sea on the other, as one stands in the Parthenon at sunset, the sky pink feathered, the plain all colours, the marble tawny in one's eyes, is thus oppressive. Luckily Jacob had little sense of personal association; he seldom thought of Plato or Socrates in the flesh; on the other hand his feeling for architecture was very strong; he preferred statues to pictures; and he was beginning to think a great deal about the problems of civilisation, which were solved, of course, so very remarkably by the ancient Greeks, though their solution is no help to us. Then the hook gave a great tug in his side as he lay in bed on Wednesday night; and he turned over with a desperate sort of tumble, remembering Sandra Wentworth Williams with whom he was in love.

Next day he climbed Pentelicus.

The day after he went up to the Acropolis. The hour was early; the place almost deserted; and possibly there was thunder in the air. But the sun struck full upon the Acropolis.

Jacob's intention was to sit down and read, and, finding a drum of marble conveniently placed, from which Marathon could be seen, and yet it was in the shade, while the Erechtheum blazed white in front of him, there he sat. And after reading a page he put his thumb in his book. Why not rule countries in the way they should be ruled? And he read again.

No doubt his position there overlooking Marathon somehow raised his spirits. Or it may have been that a slow capacious brain has these moments of flowering. Or he had, insensibly, while he was abroad, got into the way of thinking about politics.

And then looking up and seeing the sharp outline, his meditations were given an extraordinary edge; Greece was over; the Parthenon in ruins; yet there he was.

(Ladies with green and white umbrellas passed through the court-yard – French ladies on their way to join their husbands in Constan-tinople.)

Jacob read on again. And laying the book on the ground he began, as if inspired by what he had read, to write a note upon the importance of history – upon democracy – one of those scribbles upon which the work of a lifetime may be based; or again, it falls out of a book twenty years later, and one can't remember a word of it. It is a little painful. It had better be burnt.

Jacob wrote; began to draw a straight nose; when all the French ladies opening and shutting their umbrellas just beneath him exclaimed, looking at the sky, that one did not know what to expect – rain or fine weather?

Jacob got up and strolled across to the Erechtheum. There are still several women standing there holding the roof on their heads. Jacob straightened himself slightly; for stability and balance affect the body first. These statues annulled things so! He stared at them, then turned, and there was Madame Lucien Gravé perched on a block of marble with her Kodak pointed at his head. Of course she jumped down, in spite of her age, her figure and her tight boots – having, now that her daughter was married, lapsed with a luxurious abandonment, grand enough in its way, into the fleshy grotesque; she jumped down, but not before Jacob had seen her.

'Damn these women – damn these women!' he thought. And he went to fetch his book which he had left lying on the ground in the Parthenon.

'How they spoil things,' he murmured, leaning against one of the pillars, pressing his book tight between his arm and his side. (As for the weather, no doubt the storm would break soon; Athens was under cloud.)

'It is those damned women,' said Jacob, without any trace of bitterness, but rather with sadness and disappointment that what might have been should never be.

(This violent disillusionment is generally to be expected in young men in the prime of life, sound of wind and limb, who will soon become fathers of families and directors of banks.)

Then, making sure that the Frenchwomen had gone, and looking cautiously round him, Jacob strolled over to the Erechtheum and looked rather furtively at the goddess on the left-hand side holding the roof on her head. She reminded him of Sandra Wentworth Williams. He looked at her, then looked away. He looked at her, then looked away. He was extraordinarily moved, and with the battered Greek nose in his head, with Sandra in his head, with all sorts of things in his head, off he started to walk right up to the top of Mount Hymettus, alone, in the heat.

That very afternoon Bonamy went expressly to talk about Jacob to tea with Clara Durrant in the square behind Sloane Street where, on hot spring days, there are striped blinds over the front windows, single horses pawing the macadam outside the doors, and elderly gentlemen in yellow waistcoats ringing bells and stepping in very politely when the maid demurely replies that Mrs Durrant is at home.

Bonamy sat with Clara in the sunny front room with the barrel-organ piping sweetly outside; the water-cart going slowly along spraying the pavement; the carriages jingling; and all the silver and chintz, brown and blue rugs and vases filled with green boughs, striped with trembling yellow bars.

The insipidity of what was said needs no illustration – Bonamy kept on gently returning quiet answers and accumulating amazement at an existence squeezed and emasculated within a white satin shoe (Mrs Durrant meanwhile enunciating strident politics with Sir Somebody in the back room) until the virginity of Clara's soul appeared to him candid; the depths unknown; and he would have brought out Jacob's name had he not begun to feel positively certain that Clara loved him – and could do nothing whatever.

'Nothing whatever!' he exclaimed, as the door shut, and, for a man of his temperament, got a very queer feeling, as he walked through the park, of carriages irresistibly driven; of flowerbeds uncompromisingly geometrical; of force rushing round geometrical patterns in the most senseless way in the world. 'Was Clara,' he thought, pausing to watch the boys bathing in the Serpentine, 'the silent woman? – would Jacob marry her?'

But in Athens in the sunshine, in Athens, where it is almost impossible to get afternoon tea, and elderly gentlemen who talk politics talk them all the other way round, in Athens sat Sandra Wentworth Williams, veiled, in white, her legs stretched in front of her, one elbow on the arm of the bamboo chair, blue clouds wavering and drifting from her cigarette.

The orange trees which flourish in the Square of the Constitution, the band, the dragging of feet, the sky, the houses, lemon and rose coloured – all this became so significant to Mrs Wentworth Williams after her second cup of coffee that she began dramatising the story of the noble and impulsive Englishwoman who had offered a seat in her carriage to the old American lady at Mycenae (Mrs Duggan) – not altogether a false story, though it said nothing of Evan, standing first on one foot, then on the other, waiting for the women to stop chattering.

'I am putting the life of Father Damien into verse,'[160] Mrs Duggan had said, for she had lost everything – everything in the world, husband and child and everything – but faith remained.

Sandra, floating from the particular to the universal, lay back in a trance.

The flight of time which hurries us so tragically along; the eternal drudge and drone, now bursting into fiery flame like those brief balls of yellow among green leaves (she was looking at orange trees); kisses on lips that are to die; the world turning, turning in mazes of heat and sound – though to be sure there is the quiet evening with its lovely pallor, 'For I am sensitive to every side of it,' Sandra thought, 'and Mrs Duggan will write to me for ever, and I shall answer her letters.' Now the royal band marching by with the national flag stirred wider rings of emotion, and life became something that the courageous mount and ride out to sea on – the hair blown back (so she envisaged it, and the breeze stirred slightly among the orange trees), and she herself was emerging from silver spray – when she saw Jacob. He was standing in the square with a book under his arm looking vacantly about him. That he was heavily built and might become stout in time was a fact.

But she suspected him of being a mere bumpkin.

'There is that young man,' she said, peevishly, throwing away her cigarette, 'that Mr Flanders.'

'Where?' said Evan. 'I don't see him.'

'Oh, walking away – behind the trees now. No, you can't see him. But we are sure to run into him,' which, of course, they did.

But how far was he a mere bumpkin? How far was Jacob Flanders at the age of twenty-six a stupid fellow? It is no use trying to sum people up. One must follow hints, not exactly what is said, nor yet entirely what is done. Some, it is true, take ineffaceable impressions of character at once. Others dally, loiter, and get blown this way and that. Kind old ladies assure us that cats are often the best judges of character. A cat will always go to a good man, they say; but then, Mrs Whitehorn, Jacob's landlady, loathed cats.

There is also the highly respectable opinion that character-mongering[161] is much overdone nowadays. After all, what does it matter – that Fanny Elmer was all sentiment and sensation, and Mrs Durrant hard as iron? that Clara, owing (so the character-mongers said) largely to her mother's influence, never yet had the chance to do anything off her own bat, and only to very observant eyes displayed deeps of feeling which were positively alarming; and would certainly throw herself away upon someone unworthy of her one of these days unless, so the character-mongers said, she had a spark of her mother's spirit in her – was somehow heroic. But what a term to apply to Clara Durrant! Simple to a degree, others thought her. And that is the very reason, so they said, why she attracts Dick Bonamy – the young man with the Wellington nose.[162] Now *he's* a dark horse if you like. And there these gossips would suddenly pause. Obviously they meant to hint at his peculiar disposition – long rumoured among them.

'But sometimes it is precisely a woman like Clara that men of that temperament need . . . ' Miss Julia Eliot would hint.

'Well,' Mr Bowley would reply, 'it may be so.'

For however long these gossips sit, and however they stuff out their victims' characters till they are swollen and tender as the livers of geese exposed to a hot fire, they never come to a decision.

'That young man, Jacob Flanders,' they would say, 'so distinguished looking – and yet so awkward.' Then they would apply themselves to Jacob and vacillate eternally between the two extremes. He rode to hounds – after a fashion, for he hadn't a penny.

'Did you ever hear who his father was?' asked Julia Eliot.

'His mother, they say, is somehow connected with the Rocksbiers,' replied Mr Bowley.

'He doesn't overwork himself anyhow.'

'His friends are very fond of him.'

'Dick Bonamy, you mean?'

'No, I didn't mean that. It's evidently the other way with Jacob. He is precisely the young man to fall headlong in love and repent it for the rest of his life.'

'Oh, Mr Bowley,' said Mrs Durrant, sweeping down upon them in her imperious manner, 'you remember Mrs Adams? Well, that is her niece.' And Mr Bowley, getting up, bowed politely and fetched strawberries.

So we are driven back to see what the other side means – the men in clubs and cabinets – when they say that character-drawing is a frivolous fireside art, a matter of pins and needles, exquisite outlines enclosing vacancy, flourishes and mere scrawls.

The battleships ray out over the North Sea, keeping their stations accurately apart. At a given signal all the guns are trained on a target which (the master gunner counts the seconds, watch in hand – at the sixth he looks up) flames into splinters. With equal nonchalance a dozen young men in the prime of life descend with composed faces into the depths of the sea; and there impassively (though with perfect mastery of machinery) suffocate uncomplainingly together. Like blocks of tin soldiers the army covers the cornfield, moves up the hillside, stops, reels slightly this way and that, and falls flat, save that, through field glasses, it can be seen that one or two pieces still agitate up and down like fragments of broken matchstick.

These actions, together with the incessant commerce of banks, laboratories, chancellories and houses of business, are the strokes which oar the world forward, they say. And they are dealt by men as smoothly sculptured as the impassive policeman at Ludgate Circus. But you will observe that far from being padded to rotundity his face is stiff from force of will, and lean from the efforts of keeping it so. When his right arm rises, all the force in his veins flows straight from shoulder to finger-tips; not an ounce is diverted into sudden impulses, sentimental regrets, wire-drawn distinctions. The buses punctually stop.

It is thus that we live, they say, driven by an unseizable force. They say that the novelists never catch it; that it goes hurtling through their nets and leaves them torn to ribbons. This, they say, is what we live by – this unseizable force.

'Where are the men?' said old General Gibbons, looking round the drawing-room, full as usual on Sunday afternoons of well-dressed people. 'Where are the guns?'

Mrs Durrant looked too.

Clara, thinking that her mother wanted her, came in; then went out again.

They were talking about Germany at the Durrants, and Jacob (driven by this unseizable force) walked rapidly down Hermes Street and ran straight into the Williamses.

'Oh!' cried Sandra, with a cordiality which she suddenly felt. And Evan added, 'What luck!'

The dinner which they gave him in the hotel which looks on to the Square of the Constitution was excellent. Plaited baskets contained fresh rolls. There was real butter. And the meat scarcely needed the disguise of innumerable little red and green vegetables glazed in sauce.

It was strange, though. There were the little tables set out at intervals on the scarlet floor with the Greek king's monogram wrought in yellow. Sandra dined in her hat, veiled as usual. Evan looked this way and that over his shoulder; imperturbable yet supple; and sometimes sighed. It was strange. For they were English people come together in Athens on a May evening. Jacob, helping himself to this and that, answered intelligently, yet with a ring in his voice.

The Williamses were going to Constantinople early next morning, they said.

'Before you are up,' said Sandra.

They would leave Jacob alone, then. Turning very slightly, Evan ordered something – a bottle of wine – from which he helped Jacob, with a kind of solicitude, with a kind of paternal solicitude, if that were possible. To be left alone – that was good for a young fellow. Never was there a time when the country had more need of men. He sighed.

'And you have been to the Acropolis?' asked Sandra.

'Yes,' said Jacob. And they moved off to the window together, while Evan spoke to the head waiter about calling them early.

'It is astonishing,' said Jacob, in a gruff voice.

Sandra opened her eyes very slightly. Possibly her nostrils expanded a little too.

'At half-past six then,' said Evan, coming towards them, looking as if he faced something in facing his wife and Jacob standing with their backs to the window.

Sandra smiled at him.

And, as he went to the window and had nothing to say, she added, in broken half-sentences: 'Well, but how lovely – wouldn't it be? The Acropolis, Evan – or are you too tired?'

At that Evan looked at them, or, since Jacob was staring ahead of him, at his wife, surlily, sullenly, yet with a kind of distress – not that she would pity him. Nor would the implacable spirit of love, for anything he could do, cease its tortures.

They left him and he sat in the smoking-room, which looks out on to the Square of the Constitution.

'Evan is happier alone,' said Sandra. 'We have been separated from the newspapers. Well, it is better that people should have what they want . . . You have seen all these wonderful things since we met . . . What impression . . . I think that you are changed.'

'You want to go to the Acropolis,' said Jacob. 'Up here then.'

'One will remember it all one's life,' said Sandra.

'Yes,' said Jacob. 'I wish you could have come in the daytime.'

'This is more wonderful,' said Sandra, waving her hand.

Jacob looked vaguely.

'But you should see the Parthenon in the daytime,' he said. 'You couldn't come tomorrow – it would be too early?'

'You have sat there for hours and hours by yourself?'

'There were some awful women this morning,' said Jacob.

'Awful women?' Sandra echoed.

'Frenchwomen.'

'But something very wonderful has happened,' said Sandra. Ten minutes, fifteen minutes, half an hour – that was all the time before her.

'Yes,' he said.

'When one is your age – when one is young. What will you do? You will fall in love – oh yes! But don't be in too great a hurry. I am so much older.'

She was brushed off the pavement by parading men.

'Shall we go on?' Jacob asked.

'Let us go on,' she insisted.

For she could not stop until she had told him – or heard him say – or was it some action on his part that she required? Far away on the horizon she discerned it and could not rest.

'You'd never get English people to sit out like this,' he said.

'Never – no. When you get back to England you won't forget this – or come with us to Constantinople!' she cried suddenly. 'But then . . . '

Sandra sighed.

'You must go to Delphi, of course,' she said. 'But,' she asked herself, 'what do I want from him? Perhaps it is something that I have missed . . . '

'You will get there about six in the evening,' she said. 'You will see the eagles.'

Jacob looked set and even desperate by the light at the street corner and yet composed. He was suffering, perhaps. He was credulous. Yet there was something caustic about him. He had in him the seeds of extreme disillusionment, which would come to him from women in middle life. Perhaps if one strove hard enough to reach the top of the hill it need not come to him – this disillusionment from women in middle life.

'The hotel is awful,' she said. 'The last visitors had left their basins full of dirty water. There is always that,' she laughed.

'The people one meets *are* beastly,' Jacob said.

His excitement was clear enough.

'Write and tell me about it,' she said. 'And tell me what you feel and what you think. Tell me everything.'

The night was dark. The Acropolis was a jagged mound.

'I should like to, awfully,' he said.

'When we get back to London, we shall meet . . . '

'Yes.'

'I suppose they leave the gates open?' he asked.

'We could climb them!' she answered wildly.

Obscuring the moon and altogether darkening the Acropolis the clouds passed from east to west. The clouds solidified; the vapours thickened; the trailing veils stayed and accumulated.

It was dark now over Athens, except for gauzy red streaks where the streets ran; and the front of the palace was cadaverous from electric light. At sea the piers stood out, marked by separate dots, the waves being invisible, and promontories and islands dark humps with a few lights.

'I'd love to bring my brother, if I may,' Jacob murmured.

'And then when your mother comes to London – ' said Sandra.

The mainland of Greece was dark; and somewhere off Euboea[163] a cloud must have touched the waves and spattered them – the dolphins circling deeper and deeper into the sea. Violent was the wind now rushing down the Sea of Marmara between Greece and the plains of Troy.

In Greece and the uplands of Albania and Turkey, the wind scours the sand and the dust, and sows itself thick with dry particles. And then it pelts the smooth domes of the mosques, and makes the cypresses, standing stiff by the turbaned tombstones of Mohammedans, creak and bristle.

Sandra's veils were swirled about her.

'I will give you my copy,' said Jacob. 'Here. Will you keep it?'

(The book was the poems of Donne.[164])

Now the agitation of the air uncovered a racing star. Now it was dark. Now one after another lights were extinguished.[165] Now great towns – Paris – Constantinople – London – were black as strewn rocks. Waterways might be distinguished. In England the trees were heavy in leaf. Here perhaps in some southern wood an old man lit dry ferns and the birds were startled. The sheep coughed; one flower bent slightly towards another. The English sky is softer, milkier than the Eastern. Something gentle has passed into it from the grass-rounded hills, something damp. The salt gale blew in at Betty Flanders's bedroom window, and the widow lady, raising herself slightly on her elbow, sighed like one who realises, but would fain ward off a little longer – oh, a little longer! – the oppression of eternity.

But to return to Jacob and Sandra.

They had vanished. There was the Acropolis; but had they reached it? The columns and the temple remain; the emotion of the living breaks fresh on them year after year; and of that what remains?

As for reaching the Acropolis who shall say that we ever do it, or that when Jacob woke next morning he found anything hard and durable to keep for ever? Still, he went with them to Constantinople.

Sandra Wentworth Williams certainly woke to find a copy of Donne's poems upon her dressing-table. And the book would be stood on the shelf in the English country house where Sally Duggan's *Life of Father Damien* in verse would join it one of these days. There were ten or twelve little volumes already. Strolling in at dusk, Sandra would open the books and her eyes would brighten (but not at the print), and subsiding into the armchair she would suck back again the soul of the moment; or, for sometimes she was restless, would pull out book after book and swing across the whole space of her life like an acrobat from bar to bar. She had had her moments. Meanwhile, the great clock on the landing ticked and Sandra would hear time accumulating, and ask herself, 'What for? What for?'

'What for? What for?' Sandra would say, putting the book back, and strolling to the looking-glass and pressing her hair. And Miss Edwards would be startled at dinner, as she opened her mouth to admit roast mutton, by Sandra's sudden solicitude: 'Are you happy, Miss Edwards?' – a thing Cissy Edwards hadn't thought of for years.

'What for? What for?' Jacob never asked himself any such questions, to judge by the way he laced his boots; shaved himself; to judge by the depth of his sleep that night, with the wind fidgeting at the shutters and half a dozen mosquitoes singing in his ears. He was young – a man. And then Sandra was right when she judged him to be credulous as yet. At forty it might be a different matter. Already he had marked the things he liked in Donne, and they were savage enough. However, you might place beside them passages of the purest poetry in Shakespeare.

But the wind was rolling the darkness through the streets of Athens, rolling it, one might suppose, with a sort of trampling energy of mood which forbids too close an analysis of the feelings of any single person, or inspection of features. All faces – Greek, Levantine, Turkish, English – would have looked much the same in that darkness. At length the columns and the temples whiten, yellow, turn rose; and the Pyramids and St Peter's arise, and at last sluggish St Paul's looms up.

The Christians have the right to rouse most cities with their interpretation of the day's meaning. Then, less melodiously, dissenters of different sects issue a cantankerous emendation. The steamers, resounding like gigantic tuning-forks, state the old old fact – how there is a sea coldly, greenly, swaying outside. But nowadays it is the thin voice of duty, piping in a white thread from the top of a funnel, that collects the largest multitudes, and night is nothing but a long-drawn sigh between hammer-strokes, a deep breath – you can hear it from an open window even in the heart of London.

But who, save the nerve-worn and sleepless, or thinkers standing with hands to the eyes on some crag above the multitude, see things thus in skeleton outline, bare of flesh? In Surbiton[166] the skeleton is wrapped in flesh.

'The kettle never boils so well on a sunny morning,' says Mrs Grandage, glancing at the clock on the mantelpiece. Then the grey Persian cat stretches itself on the window-seat, and buffets a moth with soft round paws. And before breakfast is half over (they were late today), a baby is deposited in her lap, and she must guard the sugar basin while Tom Grandage reads the golfing article in *The Times*, sips his coffee, wipes his moustaches, and is off to the office, where he is the greatest authority upon the foreign exchanges and marked for promotion. The skeleton is well wrapped in flesh. Even this dark night when the wind rolls the darkness through Lombard Street and Fetter Lane[167] and Bedford Square it stirs (since it is summertime and the height of the season) plane trees spangled with electric light and curtains still preserving the room from the dawn. People still murmur over the last word said on the staircase, or strain, all through their dreams, for the voice of the alarm clock. So when the wind roams through a forest innumerable twigs stir; hives are brushed; insects sway on grass blades; the spider runs rapidly up a crease in the bark; and the whole air is tremulous with breathing; elastic with filaments.

Only here – in Lombard Street and Fetter Lane and Bedford Square – each insect carries a globe of the world in his head, and the webs of the forest are schemes evolved for the smooth conduct of business; and honey is treasure of one sort and another; and the stir in the air is the indescribable agitation of life.

But colour returns; runs up the stalks of the grass; blows out into tulips and crocuses; solidly stripes the tree trunks; and fills the gauze of the air and the grasses and pools.

The Bank of England emerges; and the Monument with its bristling head of golden hair; the dray horses crossing London Bridge show grey and strawberry and iron-coloured. There is a whir of wings as the suburban trains rush into the terminus. And the light mounts over the faces of all the tall blind houses, slides through a chink and paints the lustrous bellying crimson curtains; the green wine-glasses; the coffee-cups; and the chairs standing askew.

Sunlight strikes in upon shaving-glasses; and gleaming brass cans; upon all the jolly trappings of the day; the bright, inquisitive, armoured, resplendent, summer's day, which has long since vanquished chaos; which has dried the melancholy medieval mists; drained the swamp and stood glass and stone upon it; and equipped our brains and bodies with such an armoury of weapons that merely to see the flash and thrust of limbs engaged in the conduct of daily life is better than the old pageant of armies drawn out in battle array upon the plain.

Chapter 13

'The height of the season,' said Bonamy.

The sun had already blistered the paint on the backs of the green chairs in Hyde Park; peeled the bark off the plane trees; and turned the earth to powder and to smooth yellow pebbles. Hyde Park was circled, incessantly, by turning wheels.

'The height of the season,' said Bonamy sarcastically.

He was sarcastic because of Clara Durrant; because Jacob had come back from Greece very brown and lean, with his pockets full of Greek notes, which he pulled out when the chair man came for pence; because Jacob was silent.

'He has not said a word to show that he is glad to see me,' thought Bonamy bitterly.

The motor cars passed incessantly over the bridge of the Serpentine; the upper classes walked upright, or bent themselves gracefully over the palings; the lower classes lay with their knees cocked up, flat on their backs; the sheep grazed on pointed wooden legs; small children ran down the sloping grass, stretched their arms, and fell.

'Very urbane,' Jacob brought out.

'Urbane' on the lips of Jacob had mysteriously all the shapeliness of a character which Bonamy thought daily more sublime, devastating, terrific than ever, though he was still, and perhaps would be for ever, barbaric, obscure.

What superlatives! What adjectives! How acquit Bonamy of sentimentality of the grossest sort; of being tossed like a cork on the waves; of having no steady insight into character; of being unsupported by reason, and of drawing no comfort whatever from the works of the classics?

'The height of civilisation,' said Jacob.

He was fond of using Latin words.

Magnanimity, virtue – such words when Jacob used them in talk with Bonamy meant that he took control of the situation; that Bonamy would play round him like an affectionate spaniel; and that (as likely as not) they would end by rolling on the floor.

'And Greece?' said Bonamy. 'The Parthenon and all that?'

'There's none of this European mysticism,'[168] said Jacob.

'It's the atmosphere, I suppose,' said Bonamy. 'And you went to Constantinople?'

'Yes,' said Jacob.

Bonamy paused, moved a pebble; then darted in with the rapidity and certainty of a lizard's tongue.

'You are in love!' he exclaimed.

Jacob blushed.

The sharpest of knives never cut so deep.

As for responding, or taking the least account of it, Jacob stared straight ahead of him, fixed, monolithic – oh, very beautiful! – like a British admiral, exclaimed Bonamy in a rage, rising from his seat and walking off; waiting for some sound; none came; too proud to look back; walking quicker and quicker until he found himself gazing into motor cars and cursing women. Where was the pretty woman's face? Clara's – Fanny's – Florinda's? Who was the pretty little creature?

Not Clara Durrant.

The Aberdeen terrier must be exercised, and as Mr Bowley was going that very moment – would like nothing better than a walk – they went together, Clara and kind little Bowley – Bowley who had rooms in Albany, Bowley who wrote letters to *The Times* in a jocular vein about foreign hotels and the aurora borealis – Bowley who liked young people and walked down Piccadilly with his right arm resting on the boss of his back.

'Little demon!' cried Clara, and attached Troy[169] to his chain.

Bowley anticipated – hoped for – a confidence. Devoted to her mother, Clara sometimes felt her a little, well, her mother was so sure of herself that she could not understand other people being – being – 'as ludicrous as I am,' Clara jerked out (the dog tugging her forwards). And Bowley thought she looked like a huntress and turned over in his mind which it should be – some pale virgin with a slip of the moon in her hair, which was a flight for Bowley.

The colour was in her cheeks. To have spoken outright about her mother – still, it was only to Mr Bowley, who loved her, as everybody must; but to speak was unnatural to her, yet it was awful to feel, as she had done all day, that she *must* tell someone.

'Wait till we cross the road,' she said to the dog, bending down.

Happily she had recovered by that time.

'She thinks so much about England,' she said. 'She is so anxious – '

Bowley was defrauded as usual. Clara never confided in anyone.

'Why don't the young people settle it, eh?' he wanted to ask. 'What's all this about England?' – a question poor Clara could not have answered, since, as Mrs Durrant discussed with Sir Edgar the policy of

Sir Edward Grey,[170] Clara only wondered why the cabinet looked dusty, and Jacob had never come. Oh, here was Mrs Cowley Johnson . . .

And Clara would hand the pretty china teacups, and smile at the compliment – that no one in London made tea so well as she did.

'We get it at Brocklebank's,' she said, 'in Cursitor Street.'

Ought she not to be grateful? Ought she not to be happy?

Especially since her mother looked so well and enjoyed so much talking to Sir Edgar about Morocco, Venezuela, or some such place.

'Jacob! Jacob!' thought Clara; and kind Mr Bowley, who was ever so good with old ladies, looked; stopped; wondered whether Elizabeth wasn't too harsh with her daughter; wondered about Bonamy, Jacob – which young fellow was it? – and jumped up directly Clara said she must exercise Troy.

They had reached the site of the old Exhibition.[171] They looked at the tulips. Stiff and curled, the little rods of waxy smoothness rose from the earth, nourished yet contained, suffused with scarlet and coral pink. Each had its shadow; each grew trimly in the diamond-shaped wedge as the gardener had planned it.

'Barnes never gets them to grow like that,' Clara mused; she sighed.

'You are neglecting your friends,' said Bowley, as someone, going the other way, lifted his hat. She started; acknowledged Mr Lionel Parry's bow; wasted on him what had sprung for Jacob.

('Jacob! Jacob!' she thought.)

'But you'll get run over if I let you go,' she said to the dog.

'England seems all right,' said Mr Bowley.

The loop of the railing beneath the statue of Achilles[172] was full of parasols and waistcoats; chains and bangles; of ladies and gentlemen, lounging elegantly, lightly observant.

' "This statue was erected by the women of England . . . " ' Clara read out with a foolish little laugh. 'Oh, Mr Bowley! Oh!' Gallop – gallop – gallop – a horse galloped past without a rider. The stirrups swung; the pebbles spurted.

'Oh, stop! Stop it, Mr Bowley!' she cried, white, trembling, gripping his arm, utterly unconscious, the tears coming.

'Tut-tut!' said Mr Bowley in his dressing-room an hour later. 'Tut-tut!' – a comment that was profound enough, though inarticulately expressed, since his valet was handing his shirt studs.

Julia Eliot, too, had seen the horse run away, and had risen from her seat to watch the end of the incident, which, since she came of a sporting family, seemed to her slightly ridiculous. Sure enough the little man came pounding behind with his breeches dusty; looked thoroughly annoyed; and was being helped to mount by a policeman when Julia Eliot, with a sardonic smile, turned towards the Marble Arch on her errand of mercy. It was only to visit a sick old lady who had known her mother and perhaps the Duke of Wellington; for Julia shared the love of her sex for the distressed; liked to visit death-beds;[173] threw slippers at weddings; received confidences by the dozen; knew more pedigrees than a scholar knows dates, and was one of the kindliest, most generous, least continent of women.

Yet five minutes after she had passed the statue of Achilles she had the rapt look of one brushing through crowds on a summer's afternoon, when the trees are rustling, the wheels churning yellow, and the tumult of the present seems like an elegy for past youth and past summers, and there rose in her mind a curious sadness, as if time and eternity showed through skirts and waistcoats, and she saw people passing tragically to destruction. Yet, heaven knows, Julia was no fool. A sharper woman at a bargain did not exist. She was always punctual. The watch on her wrist gave her twelve minutes and a half in which to reach Bruton Street. Lady Congreve expected her at five.

The gilt clock at Verrey's was striking five.

Florinda looked at it with a dull expression, like an animal. She looked at the clock; looked at the door; looked at the long glass opposite; disposed her cloak; drew closer to the table, for she was pregnant – no doubt about it, Mother Stuart said, recommending remedies, consulting friends; sunk, caught by the heel, as she tripped so lightly over the surface.

Her tumbler of pinkish sweet stuff was set down by the waiter; and she sucked, through a straw, her eyes on the looking-glass, on the door, now soothed by the sweet taste. When Nick Bramham came in it was plain, even to the young Swiss waiter, that there was a bargain between them. Nick hitched his clothes together clumsily; ran his fingers through his hair; sat down, to an ordeal, nervously. She looked at him; and set off laughing; laughed – laughed – laughed. The young Swiss waiter, standing with crossed legs by the pillar, laughed too.

The door opened; in came the roar of Regent Street, the roar of traffic, impersonal, unpitying; and sunshine grained with dirt. The Swiss waiter must see to the newcomers. Bramham lifted his glass.

'He's like Jacob,' said Florinda, looking at the newcomer.

'The way he stares.' She stopped laughing.

Jacob, leaning forward, drew a plan of the Parthenon in the dust in Hyde Park, a network of strokes at least, which may have been the Parthenon, or again a mathematical diagram. And why was the pebble so emphatically ground in at the corner? It was not to count his notes that he took out a wad of papers and read a long flowing letter which Sandra had written two days ago at Milton Dower House with his book before her and in her mind the memory of something said or attempted, some moment in the dark on the road to the Acropolis which (such was her creed) mattered for ever.

'He is,' she mused, 'like that man in Molière.'

She meant Alceste.[174] She meant that he was severe. She meant that she could deceive him.

'Or could I not?' she thought, putting the poems of Donne back in the bookcase. 'Jacob,' she went on, going to the window and looking over the spotted flower-beds across the grass where the piebald cows grazed under beech trees, 'Jacob would be shocked.'

The perambulator was going through the little gate in the railing. She kissed her hand; directed by the nurse, Jimmy waved his.

'*He's* a small boy,' she said, thinking of Jacob.

And yet – Alceste?

'What a nuisance you are!' Jacob grumbled, stretching out first one leg and then the other and feeling in each trouser-pocket for his chair ticket.

'I expect the sheep have eaten it,' he said. 'Why do you keep sheep?'

'Sorry to disturb you, sir,' said the ticket-collector, his hand deep in the enormous pouch of pence.

'Well, I hope they pay you for it,' said Jacob. 'There you are. No. You can stick to it. Go and get drunk.'

He had parted with half a crown, tolerantly, compassionately, with considerable contempt for his species.

Even now poor Fanny Elmer was dealing, as she walked along the Strand, in her incompetent way with this very careless, indifferent, sublime manner he had of talking to railway guards or porters; or Mrs Whitehorn, when she consulted him about her little boy who was beaten by the schoolmaster.

Sustained entirely upon picture postcards for the past two months, Fanny's idea of Jacob was more statuesque, noble and eyeless than ever.

To reinforce her vision she had taken to visiting the British Museum, where, keeping her eyes downcast until she was alongside of the battered Ulysses, she opened them and got a fresh shock of Jacob's presence, enough to last her half a day. But this was wearing thin. And she wrote now – poems, letters that were never posted – saw his face in advertisements on hoardings, and would cross the road to let the barrel-organ turn her musings to rhapsody. But at breakfast (she shared rooms with a teacher), when the butter was smeared about the plate, and the prongs of the forks were clotted with old egg yolk, she revised these visions violently; was, in truth, very cross; was losing her complexion, as Margery Jackson told her, bringing the whole thing down (as she laced her stout boots) to a level of mother-wit, vulgarity and sentiment, for she had loved too; and been a fool.

'One's godmothers ought to have told one,' said Fanny, looking in at the window of Bacon, the map-seller, in the Strand – told one that it is no use making a fuss; this is life, they should have said, as Fanny said it now, looking at the large yellow globe marked with steamship lines.

'This is life. This is life,' said Fanny.

'A very hard face,' thought Miss Barrett, on the other side of the glass, buying maps of the Syrian desert [175] and waiting impatiently to be served. 'Girls look old so soon nowadays.'

The equator swam behind tears.

'Piccadilly?' Fanny asked the conductor of the omnibus, and climbed to the top. After all, he would, he must, come back to her.

But Jacob might have been thinking of Rome; of architecture; of jurisprudence; as he sat under the plane tree in Hyde Park.

The omnibus stopped outside Charing Cross; and behind it were clogged omnibuses, vans, motor cars, for a procession with banners was passing down Whitehall, and elderly people were stiffly descending from between the paws of the slippery lions,[176] where they had been testifying to their faith, singing lustily, raising their eyes from their music to look into the sky, and still their eyes were on the sky as they marched behind the gold letters of their creed.

The traffic stopped, and the sun, no longer sprayed out by the breeze, became almost too hot. But the procession passed; the banners glittered far away down Whitehall; the traffic was released; lurched on; spun to a smooth continuous uproar; swerving round the curve of Cockspur Street and sweeping past government offices and equestrian statues down Whitehall to the prickly spires, the tethered grey fleet of masonry, and the large white clock of Westminster.

Five strokes Big Ben intoned; Nelson received the salute. The wires of the Admiralty shivered with some far-away communication. A voice kept remarking that Prime Ministers and Viceroys spoke in the Reichstag;[177] entered Lahore; said that the Emperor travelled; in Milan they rioted; said there were rumours in Vienna; said that the Ambassador at Constantinople had audience with the Sultan; the fleet was at Gibraltar. The voice continued, imprinting on the faces of the clerks in Whitehall (Timothy Durrant was one of them) something of its own inexorable gravity, as they listened, deciphered, wrote down. Papers accumulated, inscribed with the utterances of Kaisers, the statistics of ricefields, the growling of hundreds of work-people, plotting sedition in back streets, or gathering in the Calcutta bazaars, or mustering their forces in the uplands of Albania, where the hills are sand-coloured and bones lie unburied.

The voice spoke plainly in the square quiet room with heavy tables, where one elderly man made notes on the margin of typewritten sheets, his silver-topped umbrella leaning against the bookcase.

His head – bald, red-veined, hollow-looking – represented all the heads in the building. His head, with the amiable pale eyes, carried the burden of knowledge across the street; laid it before his colleagues, who came equally burdened; and then the sixteen gentlemen, lifting their pens or turning perhaps rather wearily in their chairs, decreed that the course of history should shape itself this way or that way, being manfully determined, as their faces showed, to impose some coherency upon Rajahs and Kaisers and the muttering in bazaars, the secret gatherings, plainly visible in Whitehall, of kilted peasants in Albanian uplands; to control the course of events.

Pitt and Chatham, Burke and Gladstone[178] looked from side to side with fixed marble eyes and an air of immortal quiescence which perhaps the living may have envied, the air being full of whistling and concussions, as the procession with its banners passed down Whitehall. Moreover, some were troubled with dyspepsia; one had at that very moment cracked the glass of his spectacles; another spoke in Glasgow tomorrow; altogether they looked too red, fat, pale or lean, to be dealing, as the marble heads had dealt, with the course of history.

Timmy Durrant in his little room in the Admiralty, going to consult a Blue Book,[179] stopped for a moment by the window and observed the placard tied round the lamp-post.

Miss Thomas, one of the typists, said to her friend that if the cabinet was going to sit much longer she should miss her boy outside the Gaiety.[180]

Timmy Durrant, returning with his Blue Book under his arm, noticed a little knot of people at the street corner; conglomerated as though one of them knew something; and the others, pressing round him, looked up, looked down, looked along the street. What was it that he knew?

Timothy, placing the Blue Book before him, studied a paper sent round by the Treasury for information. Mr Crawley, his fellow-clerk, impaled a letter on a skewer.

Jacob rose from his chair in Hyde Park, tore his ticket to pieces, and walked away.

'Such a sunset,' wrote Mrs Flanders in her letter to Archer at Singapore. 'One couldn't make up one's mind to come indoors,' she wrote. 'It seemed wicked to waste even a moment.'

The long windows of Kensington Palace[181] flushed fiery rose as Jacob walked away; a flock of wild duck flew over the Serpentine; and the trees were stood against the sky, blackly, magnificently.

'Jacob,' wrote Mrs Flanders, with the red light on her page, 'is hard at work after his delightful journey . . . '

'The Kaiser,' the far-away voice remarked in Whitehall, 'received me in audience.'

'Now I know that face – ' said the Reverend Andrew Floyd, coming out of Carter's shop in Piccadilly, 'but who the dickens – ?' and he watched Jacob, turned round to look at him, but could not be sure –

'Oh, Jacob Flanders!' he remembered in a flash.

But he was so tall; so unconscious; such a fine young fellow.

'I gave him Byron's works,' Andrew Floyd mused, and started forward, as Jacob crossed the road; but hesitated, and let the moment pass, and lost the opportunity.

Another procession, without banners, was blocking Long Acre. Carriages, with dowagers in amethyst and gentlemen spotted with carnations, intercepted cabs and motor cars turned in the opposite direction, in which jaded men in white waistcoats lolled, on their way home to shrubberies and billiard-rooms in Putney and Wimbledon.

Two barrel-organs played by the kerb, and horses coming out of Aldridge's[182] with white labels on their buttocks straddled across the road and were smartly jerked back.

Mrs Durrant, sitting with Mr Wortley in a motor car, was impatient lest they should miss the overture.

But Mr Wortley, always urbane, always in time for the overture, buttoned his gloves, and admired Miss Clara.

'A shame to spend such a night in the theatre!' said Mrs Durrant, seeing all the windows of the coachmakers in Long Acre ablaze.

'Think of your moors!' said Mr Wortley to Clara.

'Ah! but Clara likes this better,' Mrs Durrant laughed.

'I don't know – really,' said Clara, looking at the blazing windows. She started. She saw Jacob.

'Who?' asked Mrs Durrant sharply, leaning forward.

But she saw no one.

Under the arch of the Opera House large faces and lean ones, the powdered and the hairy, all alike were red in the sunset; and, quickened by the great hanging lamps with their repressed primrose lights, by the tramp, and the scarlet, and the pompous ceremony, some ladies looked for a moment into steaming bedrooms near by, where women with loose hair leaned out of windows, where girls – where children – (the long mirrors held the ladies suspended) but one must follow; one must not block the way.

Clara's moors were fine enough. The Phoenicians[183] slept under their piled grey rocks; the chimneys of the old mines pointed starkly; early moths blurred the heather-bells; cartwheels could be heard grinding on the road far beneath; and the suck and sighing of the waves sounded gently, persistently, forever.

Shading her eyes with her hand Mrs Pascoe stood in her cabbage-garden looking out to sea. Two steamers and a sailing-ship crossed each other; passed each other; and in the bay the gulls kept alighting on a log, rising high, returning again to the log, while some rode in upon the waves and stood on the rim of the water until the moon blanched all to whiteness.

Mrs Pascoe had gone indoors long ago.

But the red light was on the columns of the Parthenon, and the Greek women who were knitting their stockings and sometimes crying to a child to come and have the insects picked from its head were as jolly as sand-martins in the heat, quarrelling, scolding, suckling their babies, until the ships in the Piraeus fired their guns.[184]

The sound spread itself flat, and then went tunnelling its way with fitful explosions among the channels of the islands.

Darkness drops like a knife over Greece.

'The guns?' said Betty Flanders, half asleep, getting out of bed and going to the window, which was decorated with a fringe of dark leaves.

'Not at this distance,' she thought. 'It is the sea.'

Again, far away, she heard the dull sound, as if nocturnal women were beating great carpets. There was Morty lost, and Seabrook dead; her sons fighting for their country. But were the chickens safe? Was that someone moving downstairs? Rebecca with the toothache? No. The nocturnal women were beating great carpets. Her hens shifted slightly on their perches.

Chapter 14

'He left everything just as it was,' Bonamy marvelled. 'Nothing arranged. All his letters strewn about for anyone to read. What did he expect? Did he think he would come back?' he mused, standing in the middle of Jacob's room.

The eighteenth century has its distinction. These houses were built, say, a hundred and fifty years ago. The rooms are shapely, the ceilings high; over the doorways a rose or a ram's skull is carved in the wood. Even the panels, painted in raspberry-coloured paint, have their distinction.

Bonamy took up a bill for a hunting-crop.

'That seems to be paid,' he said.

There were Sandra's letters.

Mrs Durrant was taking a party to Greenwich.

Lady Rocksbier hoped for the pleasure . . .

Listless is the air in an empty room, just swelling the curtain; the flowers in the jar shift. One fibre in the wicker armchair creaks, though no one sits there.

Bonamy crossed to the window. Pickford's van swung down the street. The omnibuses were locked together at Mudie's corner.[185] Engines throbbed, and carters, jamming the brakes down, pulled their horses sharp up. A harsh and unhappy voice cried something unintelligible. And then suddenly all the leaves seemed to raise themselves.

'Jacob! Jacob!'[186] cried Bonamy, standing by the window. The leaves sank down again.

'Such confusion everywhere!' exclaimed Betty Flanders, bursting open the bedroom door.

Bonamy turned away from the window.

'What am I to do with these, Mr Bonamy?'

She held out a pair of Jacob's old shoes.

NOTES

Chapter 1

1 (p. 421) *Scarborough is seven hundred miles from Cornwall*
Scarborough is approximately 440 miles from St Ives, but Betty
Flanders may feel farther from home than she is, or she may not
have a good grasp of facts.

2 (p. 422) *it was just that note which brought the rest together* Roger
Fry's 'An Essay on Aesthetics' argues: 'In a picture . . . unity is due
to a balancing of the attractions of the eye about the central line of
the picture.' (See *Twentieth-Century Theories of Art*, James Matheson
Thompson (ed), Carleton University Press, Ontario, 1994, p. 68.)

3 (p. 422) *Titian* Tiziano Vecellio (*c.*1487–1576) was acknowledged
as *the* master painter in Venice during the period we now call the
High Renaissance. Known as Titian, he became the official painter
to the Republic in 1516, but greater fame arose in the 1530s when
Emperor Charles V commissioned a series of portraits. It may be
the latter to which Charles Steele is referring, although his facts
may simply be as unreliable as Betty Flanders's.

4 (p. 423) *a skull, perhaps, with the teeth in it* Note also the carving of
the ram's skull over the doorway of Jacob's lodging in Lamb's
Conduit Street. James Ramsay, in *To the Lighthouse*, has a boar's
skull nailed to the bedroom wall.

5 (p. 425) *the Strand magazines* The *Strand*, named after a fashionable London street, was founded by George Newnes in 1891. Aiming
at a large middle-class audience for both fiction and non-fiction, its
success was assured when it contracted with Arthur Conan Doyle
for a series of Sherlock Holmes stories.

Chapter 2

6 (p. 427) *enclosed in three shells, the crevices sealed with lead* Graves at
this time were at the mercy of grave robbers, so those who could
afford it often had double or triple coffins. Seabrook is imaginatively
apprehended through windows in his coffin. Jacob's own room is a
figurative coffin with windows.

7 (p. 427) *'Merchant of this City' . . . well, she had to call him something*
Betty is creating her own enduring fiction about her husband.

Woolf is mocking the conventions of the Edwardian novel, where a man's title would have summarised him.

8 (p. 428) *the thousand white stones* The problem of overcrowded graveyards was not new. St Cuthbert had first added churchyards to churches in 752 when it was decided to provide consecrated ground in which to bury the dead. In 1267 all churchyards were enclosed thereby limiting their size.

9 (p. 428) *lilacs that drooped in April* This is not the case. Woolf admitted her error here in a letter to C. P. Sanger (*Letters*, II, pp. 577–8).

10 (p. 428) *Dods Hill* This is fictitious. Castle Hill is in Scarborough, while Dodd Hill is a summit in south-western Scotland.

11 (p. 428) *the Crimea* the Crimean War, 1854–6

12 (p. 428) *the whole of Scarborough . . . laid out flat* In the novel Scarborough is a mixture of fact and fiction as the street plan of the town is far from flat.

13 (p. 429) *Tulips burned in the sun* another mistake Woolf identified for C. P. Sanger.

14 (p. 429) *Sponge-bag trousers* Formal trousers, either in check or stripes; they also feature in *The Voyage Out* (1915) and *Orlando* (1928).

15 (p. 429) *Triangular boardings . . . exclamation* The hoardings were used for advertising.

16 (p. 430) *Fix your eyes upon the lady's skirt* That history may be marked in the changing styles of women's dress is a prominent theme in *Orlando*.

17 (p. 432) *Rugby* one of the oldest public schools (founded in 1567), immortalised in Thomas Hughes' *Tom Brown's Schooldays* (1857)

18 (p. 432) *a well-known series of ecclesiastical biographies* Mr Floyd is a traditionalist.

19 (p. 432) *Leg of Mutton Pond* Situated on the western edge of Hampstead Heath, this pond is part of the Longford River, an artificial river channel commissioned by Charles I to provide a water supply for Hampton Court.

20 (p. 432) *the Scarborough and Harrogate Courier* an invention by Woolf

21 (p. 433) *Morris* Francis Orpen Morris (1810–93) was a Victorian ornithologist and entomologist, born near Cork, Ireland. He wrote popular books on natural history.

22 (p. 438) *1906*   Woolf's brother Thoby Stephen died of typhoid fever on 20 November 1906.

Chapter 3

23 (p. 438) *a novel from Mudie's*   Mudie's circulating library was founded in 1842. Between 1842 and 1894 Charles Edward Mudie's lending library influenced Victorian literature in two important ways: by making sure that almost all novels appeared in three volumes, it had important effects on the structure, plot, style and even imaginative worlds of the Victorian novel; and by acting as a censor, demanding fiction suited to the middle-class family, it influenced the subject, scope and morality of the novel.

24 (p. 438) *the Morning Post . . . the Daily Telegraph*   This was the era of the rise of the newspaper.

25 (p. 439) *one of Mr Norris's novels*   William Edward Norris (1847–1925) was a novelist whose works Woolf reviewed regularly and disliked. In her 1905 review of *Barham of Beltana*, Woolf noted that it lacked probability and innovation (*Essays*, I, p. 37).

26 (p. 439) *the roof of King's College Chapel*   King's College Chapel's master mason John Wastell built the famous vaulted roof between 1512 and 1515.

27 (p. 439) *the subservient eagle bears up for inspection the great white book*   There is no lectern in the form of an eagle in King's College Chapel. The eagle, symbol of war and imperial power, is here fused with the gospel in subservience to the rule book.

28 (p. 440) *Waverley*   after Sir Walter Scott's (1771–1832) Waverley Novels

29 (p. 441) *went down*   graduated from university

30 (p. 441) *the suburbs of Manchester*   a place of intellectual barrenness for Woolf who visited there in 1921 (cf. Chapter 1 of *Night and Day*)

31 (p. 442) *the Reform Bill*   An Act of Parliament in 1832 introducing wide-ranging changes to the electoral system of the United Kingdom. The Act granted seats in the House of Commons to large cities that had sprung up during the Industrial Revolution, and took away seats from the 'rotten boroughs'. The Act also increased the number of individuals entitled to vote.

32 (p. 442) *Wells and Shaw*   Herbert George Wells (1866–1946) and George Bernard Shaw (1856–1950) were among those who, for Woolf, were the epitome of Edwardian materialism.

33 (p. 443) *Byron*   Lord George Byron (1788–1824), one of the English
    Romantic poets. His major works include *Childe Harold's Pilgrimage*
    (1812–18) and *Don Juan* (1819–24).

34 (p. 444) *Trinity*   Trinity College Cambridge, which Woolf's
    brother Thoby first attended in 1899. It was here that he met Lytton
    Strachey, Clive Bell, Saxon Sydney-Turner and Leonard Woolf.

35 (p. 444) *Neville's Court*   the courtyard at Trinity College

36 (p. 445) *Does History Consist of the Biographies of Great Men?*   A
    question that invokes Thomas Carlyle's *Hero and Hero-Worship*,
    Lecture I, in which he states: 'The history of the world is but the
    biography of great men.' It is a question laden with irony in the
    context of a novel preoccupied both with the difficulty of knowing
    individuals and with the *sameness*, rather than the exceptionality, of
    male 'greatness'.

37 (p. 445) *Sir Joshua*   Sir Joshua Reynolds (1723–92), famous portrait
    painter and founder member and first president of the Royal
    Academy of Art (1768). The following year he was knighted and
    in 1784 he was appointed painter to George III.

38 (p. 445) *a Manual of the Diseases of the Horse*   A remnant of rural
    gentlemanliness; the motor car was still a relatively new invention.

39 (p. 445) *Huxtable . . . Sopwith . . . Cowan*   These are all fictitious
    dons at Cambridge.

40 (p. 445) *Van Gogh reproduced*   Vincent Van Gogh (1853–90) painted
    several pairs of shoes or boots during his lifetime. To this day,
    philosophers and art historians look at his painting of a pair of shoes
    (1886) and argue over the function of art, the value of interpretation
    and the nature of existence. The debate ignited in 1936 when
    Martin Heidegger saw the painting in Amsterdam and wrote an
    essay entitled 'The Origin of the Artwork'. Over the following
    years scholars and thinkers, including Meyer Schapiro and Jacques
    Derrida, have expressed their views on Van Gogh's shoes.

41 (p. 447) *Virgil's . . . arms, bees, or even the plough*   from Virgil's
    Georgics, Book 2

42 (p. 447) *the thing she might have said . . . for ever left out*   The
    censorship of women's language is something Woolf explores further
    in *A Room of One's Own*.

43 (p. 448) *the Moonlight Sonata*   the Piano Sonata No. 14 in C-sharp
    minor, Op. 27, No. 2, by Ludwig van Beethoven (1801), popularly
    known as the Moonlight Sonata

44 (p. 448) *shilling shockers* These were the early-twentieth-century equivalent of 'penny dreadfuls'. Shilling shockers were usually characterised by sensational incidents and lurid writing.

45 (p. 450) *Julian the Apostate* This Roman emperor (*c.*331–363) endeavoured to destroy Christianity by persecuting Christians and promoting paganism. Julian's life inspired Henrik Ibsen's play *Emperor and Galilean* (1873).

Chapter 4

46 (p. 451) *Although the plays of Shakespeare . . . placed higher than the Greek* Thoby Stephen placed Shakespeare higher than the Greeks (*Moments of Being*, pp. 138–9).

47 (p. 453) *spats* a type of shoe accessory, made of short cloth or leather

48 (p. 454) *The Duke of Wellington . . . Keats . . . Lord Salisbury* Arthur Wellesley, first Duke of Wellington (1769–1852), hero of the Battle of Waterloo and Prime Minister 1828–30; in *Jacob's Room* he typifies the values of the British Empire. John Keats (1795–1821) was a key Romantic poet who died young from tuberculosis; an apposite figure to invoke here as the tone of the novel changes subtly. Lord Salisbury (1830–1903) became Foreign Secretary in 1878 and leader of the Conservative Party in 1881.

49 (p. 454) *Abide with me* a popular hymn, composed by Henry Francis Lyte (1793–1847) in 1847

50 (p. 454) *Great God, what do I see and hear?* a hymn by an anonymous composer (1802), subsequently revised by W. B. Colyer (1812) and T. Cotterill (1819), among others

51 (p. 455) *Rock of Ages* a hymn by Augustus Montague Toplady (1740–78). The biblical reference is 1 Corinthians 10:1–4, ' . . . that Rock was Christ.'

52 (p. 455) *Mrs Pascoe* Mrs Pascoe is based on a real person: she appears in Woolf's 1905 Cornwall journal.

53 (p. 456) *the Gurnard's Head* a rocky promontory on the north coast of Cornwall and in walking distance of St Ives

54 (p. 456) *tramp steamer* a commercial vessel with no fixed schedule that takes on and discharges cargo whenever hired to do so

55 (p. 456) *Lady Cynthia's wedding at the Abbey* Lady Cynthia Charteris married the Prime Minister's son (by his first wife), Herbert Asquith, in Westminster Abbey in 1910. John Singer Sargeant painted her portrait in 1909.

56 (p. 459) *Mr Clutterbuck*   Arthur Clutton Brock (1869–1924),
essayist, art critic and journalist who wrote for the *Times Literary
Supplement*

57 (p. 462) *Lord Lansdowne*   Henry Petty Fitzmaurice (1845–1927). A
Liberal politician, Lansdowne resigned from Gladstone's government over Irish land reform in 1880. After serving as Governor
General of Canada and Viceroy of India, he joined Salisbury's 1895
cabinet. As leader of the Unionist peers from 1903 to 1916, he was
much criticised for his conduct in opposition to Asquith's Liberal
government.

58 (p. 465) *Jacob held the ladder*   An allusion is made here to Jacob's
biblical namesake, who saw a ladder leading from earth to heaven in
a dream (Genesis 28:11–19)

Chapter 5

59 (p. 465) *a shell secreted by man to fit man himself*   The same image
features prominently in *The Waves* (1931).

60 (p. 465) *St Paul's Cathedral*   designed by Sir Christopher Wren
and built between 1675 and 1710 after its predecessor was destroyed
in the Great Fire of London (1666)

61 (p. 465) *the great Duke's tomb*   The Duke of Wellington's tomb lies
in the crypt of St Paul's Cathedral.

62 (p. 465) *jute*   a plant fibre used in the construction of canvas,
sacking and cordage

63 (p. 465) *Where's Nelson's tomb?*   It is in the crypt along with the
Duke of Wellington's.

64 (p. 465) *Finlay's Byzantine Empire*   George Finlay's *History of the
Byzantine Empire from 716 to 1057* (London, 1906), originally
published as two volumes in 1854

65 (p. 466) *the Union of London and Smith's Bank*   Smith's Bank merged
with the Union Bank of London in 1902.

66 (p. 467) *the arch of the Opera House*   The Covent Garden Royal
Opera House, Bow Street, opened in 1732.

67 (p. 467) *Thomas à Kempis*   Thomas Haemmerlein or Thomas
Haemmerken (1380–1471), an Augustinian monk and author of
Christian mystical works, the most famous of which is *De Imitatione
Christi* , or *On the Imitation of Christ*

68 (p. 467) *Tristan was twitching his rug . . . Isolde*   *Tristan und Isolde*, an
opera in three acts by Richard Wagner, first performed in Munich
in 1865

69 (p. 467) *Brangaene* Isolde's attendant and companion in *Tristan und Isolde*

70 (p. 468) *Virgil . . . Lucretius* Publius Vergilius Maro Virgil (70–19 BC), whose poetry was generally considered to rival the Greeks; his works included the *Aeneid, Eclogues* and *Georgics*. Titus Lucretius Carus (c. 99–55), Roman author of *De Rerum Natura*; the line in Book I: 'There's place intangible, a void and room', is fitting for Jacob.

71 (p. 468) *Bonamy* Jacob's fondest friend, just as Lytton Strachey had been to Woolf's brother, Thoby Stephen

72 (p. 468) *an edition of Wycherley* William Wycherley (1641–1715), whose plays, mostly satirical and sometimes savagely so, include *Love in a Wood*, or *St James's Park* (1672), *The Gentleman Dancing Master* (1673), *The Plain Dealer* (1674) and *The Country Wife* (1675). His plays were condemned by Macaulay as licentious.

73 (p. 468) *the Fortnightly, the Contemporary, the Nineteenth Century* respectable literary periodicals of the time

74 (p. 469) *Mr Letts* Mr Letts is Woolf's personification of a printer of pocket-sized diaries.

75 (p. 471) *Parliament Hill* Formerly known as Traitor's Hill, Parliament Hill is the gateway to London's Hampstead Heath. In 1605 the Gunpowder Plot conspirators are alleged to have waited and watched on Parliament Hill to see Parliament blow up.

Chapter 6

76 (p. 472) *billycock hats* A hat, circa 1850, thought to be named after William Coke, nephew of the Earl of Leicester of Holkham, who commissioned James Lock to design a close-fitting, low-crowned hat. Lock named it the coke hat after his customer, and it soon became known as the billy coke or billycock. In later years the hat was more generally known as the bowler after the Bowler brothers who went on to manufacture it.

77 (p. 472) *Auld Lang Syne* 'For old times' sake' in Scottish vernacular, from a poem by Robert Burns, and set to music. Traditionally it is sung on the stroke of midnight each New Year's Eve, but in Scotland, where it originates, it is also sung on Burns Night, 25 January, to celebrate the poet's life.

78 (p. 472) *barrel-organ* a musical instrument in which air from a bellows is admitted to a set of pipes by means of pins inserted into a revolving barrel

79 (p. 472) *they wreathed his head with paper flowers*   Jacob's beauty is
    acknowledged when he is garlanded and honoured as a Greek god.
    Woolf may have in mind Shelley's *Hellas* (1822), in which a chorus
    of Greek captive women 'strew these opiate flowers/On thy restless
    pillow'.

80 (p. 474) *she was without a surname*   Florinda's lack of surname is
    suggestive of her slender means of identification.

81 (p. 474) *the ABC shop*   See Note 95 to *Night and Day*, page 396.

82 (p. 474) *his essay upon the Ethics of Indecency*   Jacob's essay continues
    the earlier discussion of the bowdlerisation of the Wycherley
    edition.

83 (p. 475) *Adonais*   Percy Bysshe Shelley wrote his 'Adonais' elegy
    immediately after hearing of John Keats's death. It was composed
    during the spring of 1821 and first published in July 1821. 'Adonais'
    was composed as a pastoral elegy, specifically in the tradition of
    Milton's *Lycidas*.

84 (p. 475) *All plays turned on the same subject*   With the impact of
    Ibsen, the subject of marital discord was a popular theme in drama.

85 (p. 475) *a snake . . . sliding through the grass*   a reference to concealed
    sexual motives

86 (p. 476) *Bechstein*   a generic name for one of the Jews referred to
    by Florinda

87 (p. 477) *She's dropped her glove*   a prostitute would drop her glove
    to indicate her availability. A character named Florinda appears in
    Aphra Behn's *The Rover* (1677), and Thomas Killigrew's (1612–
    83) *Thomaso* (1664). There is a clear distinction between virgin
    and whore in *Thomaso*, whereas Behn's *Rover* presents a parallel
    between the two.

88 (p. 477) *The problem is insoluble. The body is harnessed to a brain*   The
    mind/body duality is fundamental to most Western philosophy.

Chapter 7

89 (p. 479) *Notting Hill . . . or the purlieus of Clerkenwell*   slum areas at
    the time

90 (p. 479) *Italian remained a hidden art, and the piano always played
    the same sonata*   Clara, like many upper-middle-class girls, is engaged
    in good work among the poor which keeps her too busy for other
    pursuits.

91 (p. 479) *outdoor relief*   organised relief for the poor, the alternative
    being the workhouse or the hospital

92 (p. 482) *Who is Silvia . . . commend her?* lines from Shakespeare's *The Two Gentleman of Verona*, Act IV, Scene 2, put to music by Franz Schubert (1797–1828)

Chapter 8

93 (p. 483) *the Hotspurs, the Harlequins* The Hotspurs football club was founded in 1882; the Harlequin was founded in 1866.

94 (p. 483) *Star* a popular newspaper founded (1887) and edited by Thomas Power O'Connor (1848–1929), Irish journalist, politician and author. His most important works were *The Parnell Movement* (1886) and *Memoirs of an Old Parliamentarian* (1929).

95 (p. 483) *Gray's Inn* one of four Inns of Court in London

96 (p. 483) *Then, sometimes a game of chess* echoes of T. S. Eliot's *The Waste Land, Part II* (1922)

97 (p. 483) *pictures in Bond Street* Bond Street is home to many art galleries.

98 (p. 483) *Nelson on his column* on the south side of Trafalgar Square

99 (p. 483) *Parrot's great white sale* biannual stocktaking sales held in department stores

100 (p. 483) *Ireland or India* Self-government was a major political issue at this time, with Gladstone in favour of Home Rule for Ireland, and the Indian Councils Act or Morely–Minto Reforms (1909), named after Secretary of State for India, John Morley, and Lord Minto, Governor General of India. This was an important landmark in the history of constitutional development towards self-government for India.

101 (p. 483) *Leghorns, Cochin Chinas, Orpingtons* breeds of chicken

102 (p. 485) *the Russian dancers* Serge Diaghilev's (1872–1929) Ballets Russes staged more than 50 new works between 1909 and 1929.

103 (p. 486) *Greek Street* a street in London's Soho

104 (p. 488) *rooms in Albany* Albany, off Piccadilly, is a London building with bachelor chambers and a list of famous former occupants, including Byron, Lytton and Macaulay.

105 (p. 488) *the yellow canopy sinks and swells* the London smog. It is these incalculable evanescent things that propel events forward as much as the 'unseizable force' of history. The sinister use of poison gas in WWI may also be alluded to here; a gas which would descend as a yellow-green cloud, rendered so powerfully in Wilfred Owen's 'Dulce et Decorum Est', written in 1917 and published posthumously in 1920: 'And floundering like a man in

fire or lime./Dim, through the misty panes and thick green light/ As under a green sea, I saw him drowning.'

Chapter 9

106 (p. 490) *Mol Pratt . . . Mrs Hilda Thomas . . . Lady Rocksbier*   Three aspects of London life are represented here: the flower-seller from the slums; the respectable middle-class woman from the suburbs; and the aristocrat.

107 (p. 491) *Joseph Chamberlain* (1836–1914) When Gladstone produced his Home Rule Bill in 1885, to create an Irish parliament, Joseph Chamberlain opposed it on the grounds that it diluted the powers of the national Parliament. He resigned from the cabinet, and very much through his efforts the Home Rule Bill was defeated; the Liberal Party split, and in 1886 the Conservative Party returned to power.

108 (p. 491) *did for*   cleaned for him

109 (p. 492) *like two bulls of Bashan*   The fierce enemies of the righteous man in the Psalms: 'They surround him like strong bulls of Bashan. Their mouths opened like a raging and roaring lion' (Psalm 22:12–13).

110 (p. 493) *the Saturday Westminster*   A literary weekly newspaper, the *Saturday Westminster* was an offshoot of the *Westminster Gazette*.

111 (p. 493) *Whistler*   James Abbott McNeill Whistler (1834–1903), an American artist, noted for his paintings of nocturnal London, for his striking full-length portraits and for his etchings and lithographs.

112 (p. 494) *Mr Asquith's Irish policy*   Herbert Henry Asquith (1852–1928) became Prime Minster in 1908 and served until 1916.

113 (p. 494) *Queen Alexandra*   Danish wife of Edward VII

114 (p. 495) *Mr Masefield . . . Mr Bennett . . . Marlowe*   John Edward Masefield (1878–1967), English writer and poet laureate; Arnold Bennett (1867–1931), novelist, playwright, essayist, critic and journalist; Christopher Marlowe (1564–93), dramatist; they are all included in the accepted male literary canon.

115 (p. 496) *the Victorians, who disembowel*   an attempt to rescue the Elizabethan writers from the bowdlerising butchery of nineteenth-century editors

116 (p. 496) *Plato, Aristotle, Sophocles and Shakespeare*   Another example of the extent and range of the male canon. Plato, Greek philosopher

(c.428/7–348/7 BC); Aristotle (348–22 BC), Greek philosopher and student of Plato; Sophocles (496–46 BC), Attic tragedian; and Shakespeare (c.1564–1616), whose work was influenced by them.

117 (p. 496) *the Elgin Marbles* A term used to refer to sculptures, inscriptions and architectural features Lord Elgin acquired in Athens between 1801 and 1805. These objects were purchased by the British Parliament and presented to the British Museum in 1816.

118 (p. 496) *Macauley, Hobbes, Gibbon* Thomas Babbington Macaulay (1800–59), author of *History of England* (1849–55); Thomas Hobbes (1588–1679), renowned philosopher and political theorist and author of *Leviathan* (1651); Edward Gibbon (1737–94), author of *The Decline and Fall of the Roman Empire* (1776–88). Three further examples of 'great men' of whose biographies history is held to consist.

119 (p. 497) *writes all his letters in Greek* perhaps an allusion to Saxon Sidney-Turner (1880–1962), a friend of Woolf's brother Thoby Stephen, a Cambridge apostle who gained a double first in classics and could read Greek fluently

120 (p. 498) *Ulysses* the hero of Homer's epic poem. James Joyce's *Ulysses* (1922) is more explicit in reference to Homer's original than *Jacob's Room*, but nevertheless parallels can be drawn. Both Stephen Dedalus and Jacob Flanders are from poor families with a missing parent, both have a romantic interest in art and culture and both journey to Paris to round off their education. But while Jacob is comfortable, even complacent in his environment, Stephen is isolated. Though a sense of entrapment is present in both worlds, Stephen is a victim of the past while Jacob is its unconscious beneficiary. While Jacob can muse on the proposed Home Rule Bill, he does not feel the effects in the same way Stephen and his fellow countrymen do.

121 (p. 498) *The Phaedrus is very difficult* Plato's dialogue – between Socrates and Phaedrus – on love. The dialogue begins with a playful discussion of erotic passion, then extends the theme to consider the nature of inspiration, love and knowledge. The centrepiece is the myth of the charioteer – the famous and moving account of the vision, fall and incarnation of the soul.

122 (p. 498) *The splendid Magdalen* a name, with biblical origins, given to a type of impure 'fallen woman', as opposed to the pure woman, the Madonna

123 (p. 501) *Lothair*   Benjamin Disraeli's (1804–81) novel, published
in 1870 when Disraeli was Leader of the Opposition in Parliament.
Lothair follows its eponymous hero, rich and aristocratic but
orphaned, as he attempts to find his place in the world. Taking in
England, Italy, Malta and the Holy Land and moving among the
highest society of Europe, the novel follows its hero as he agonises
over his faith and is bewildered by love.

Chapter 10

124 (p. 501) *the disused graveyard in the parish of St Pancras*   Many
London parish graveyards were closed after the passing of the
burial act of 1852 and large cemeteries were opened much farther
out. Over the next few years some grounds were built on, while
the remainder were (supposedly) protected from any further
development by the Disused Burials Act of 1884.

125 (p. 501) *Madame Tussaud's*   famous waxworks exhibition

126 (p. 502) *a yellow novel*   a cheap edition

127 (p. 502) *The women in the street have the faces of playing cards*
Cosmetics, previously frowned upon in society as the mark of a
prostitute, increased in use in the new pre-war fashions.

128 (p. 503) *the promenade at the Empire*   one of the most popular
features of the Empire music-hall in Leicester Square, allegedly a
favourite haunt of prostitutes

129 (p. 504) *Hamstead Garden Suburb*   situated north of Hampstead,
to the west of Highgate and east of Golders Green. Founded in
1907 by Dame Henrietta Barnett, the Suburb was designed to be a
model community with people of all classes living together in
beautiful houses set in a verdant landscape. Laid out by Raymond
Unwin, with Edwin Lutyens, the houses and flats represent the
best of English domestic architecture of the early twentieth century.

130 (p. 504) *The eyes of all the . . . women are a little glazed*   They are
preoccupied with their children. Woolf's final novel, *Between
the Acts* (1941), portrays women similarly preoccupied, trundling
perambulators up and down the terrace.

131 (p. 505) *the Express Diary Company's shop*   another tea-shop,
popular with 'respectable' members of the working and lower
middle classes

132 (p. 506) *the Foundling Hospital*   Located in Guildford Street, WC1,
the Foundling Hospital was established by Royal Charter in 1739.
It was the first purpose-built home for abandoned children in Britain.

133 (p. 506) *Swan and Edgar's*   One of London's first department stores, located in Regent Street. The shop-front was one of the West End businesses targeted by the suffragettes in their window-breaking spree on 21 November 1911. The premises were rebuilt and integrated in 1910–20 to a design by Sir Reginald Blomfield and became a popular place of assignation for Londoners for many generations. The store was hit by the last Zeppelin raid on London in 1917.

134 (p. 506) *In Evelina's shop . . . the parts of a woman were shown separate*   The novel gradually taxonomises the adult fascination with objects.

135 (p. 507) *Dumas*   either Alexandre Dumas *père* (1802–70) or his son Alexandre Dumas *fils* (1824–95), French playwrights

136 (p. 507) *the Slade . . . Tonks and Steer*   The Slade School of Fine Art established in 1871, part of University College London, is named after Felix Slade who founded chairs in fine art at Oxford, Cambridge and London. It was the first English art school to offer female students equal opportunities to study from the life model. Henry Tonks (1862–1937), English painter and Slade Professor of Fine Art 1918–30; Philip Wilson Steer (1860–1942), English landscape painter, the son of portrait painter Philip Steer (1810–71).

137 (p. 507) *Tom Jones*   Henry Fielding's (1707–54) novel is both one of the great comic masterpieces of English literature and a major force in the development of the novel form.

138 (p. 507) *Miss Sargent*   a joke on Woolf's part. The portrait painter John Singer Sargent taught at the Slade School and had a following of women students. It may also allude to Mary Sargent Florence who studied at the Slade School under Legros and whose daughter Alix married James Strachey (brother of Lytton Strachey).

Chapter 11

139 (p. 509) *Velasquez*   Diego Rodriguez de Silva y Velázquez (1599–1660), Spanish painter and leading artist at the court of King Philip IV

140 (p. 510) *Hang there like fruit my soul*   a line from Shakespeare's *Cymbeline*, Act V, Scene 5, l. 263

141 (p. 510) *The devil damn you black, you cream-faced loon!*   from Shakespeare's *Macbeth*, Act V, Scene 3, l. 11

142 (p. 511) *Pierre Louÿs* (1870–1925)   French erotic poet and novelist

143 (p. 511) *Half a jiff*   Wait just a moment.

144 (p. 512) *air-ball*   balloon

145 (p. 513) *will King George give way about the peers?*   King George V
     ascended the throne in the midst of a constitutional crisis: the
     budget controversy of 1910. Tories in the House of Lords were at
     odds with Liberals in the Commons pushing for social reforms.
     When George agreed to create enough Liberal peers to pass the
     measure the Lords capitulated and gave up the power of absolute
     veto, resolving the problem officially with passage of the
     Parliament Bill in 1911.

146 (p. 514) *garnet brooch*   In *To the Lighthouse* (1927) Minta Doyle's
     brooch, a weeping willow set in pearls and left to her by her
     grandmother, is similarly lost. Woolf lost her own brooch while in
     the process of composing *Jacob's Room* (*Diary*, II, 10 March 1921,
     p. 98).

147 (p. 515) *'I am Bertha Ruck', 'I am Tom Gage'*   The figures of art
     and reality become inextricably mixed when Woolf brings in pieces
     of existence from life, sometimes unintentionally. Berta Ruck was
     in fact a prominent novelist who objected to this premature burial
     and threatened litigation, although the incident ended amicably
     (see Quentin Bell's biography of Woolf, Vol. II, pp. 91–2 for an
     account of the incident). Tom Gage presumably never existed, but
     it did not prevent Lytton Strachey and Dora Carrington from
     writing a bogus letter purportedly from Gage, complaining about
     the loss of his job because of Woolf's appropriation of his name
     (*Letters*, II, p. 597).

Chapter 12

148 (p. 516) *There were trees laced together with vines – as Virgil said*
     Virgil, *Georgics*, Book I, l. 2: ' . . . it is well to turn the soil, and
     wed vines to elms.' Trees were used as props for vines, and the
     relationship between the two is often described in terms of a
     marriage. See, for example, in Horace's *Ode* 4.5: 'Condit quisque
     diem collibus in suis/et uitem uiduas ducit ad arbores.' Each [farmer]
     spends the day in his own hills / and joins the vine to unwed trees.

149 (p. 516) *Virgil's bees had gone about the plains of Lombardy*   Virgil
     was born in Mantua in the district of Lombardy, northern Italy.

150 (p. 517) *something in the style of Gibbon*   Edward Gibbon (1737–
     94) is regarded as the master of the 'male sentence'.

151 (p. 517) *Black victorias*   A victoria is a type of horse-drawn carriage.

152 (p. 519) *an American called Pilchard*   The American's name is of
     course Pilcher.

153 (p. 521) *Chekhov* Anton Pavlovich Chekhov (1860–1904), much admired in the early twentieth century for both his short stories and his plays. Woolf refers to him in her essay 'Modern Fiction'.

154 (p. 522) *Chatham, Pitt, Burke, and Charles James Fox* eighteenth-century statesmen and politicians

155 (p. 524) *The Hermes of Praxiteles* The statue, at the Temple of Hera, dates from 343 BC and is made from Parian marble. It is the only original work of Praxiteles known to have survived. The sculpture, representing Hermes holding the small Dionysius, was discovered in AD 1877.

156 (p. 525) *the Acro-Corinth* a high mountain dominating the landscape at Corinth. On the higher of the twin peaks of the Acro-Corinth are the remnants of the Temple of Aphrodite.

157 (p. 526) *like a Victory* the famous Winged Victory of Samothrace (*c.* 200 BC), a statue found in a sanctuary on the Greek island of Samothrace in 1863

158 (p. 526) *the Erechtheum* Six caryatids (columns carved in the shape of females) supported the roof of the Erechtheum, built between 421 and 395 BC on the Acropolis of Athens. A caryatid came to the British Museum in 1816 with Lord Elgin's Marbles.

159 (p. 527) *Hymettus, Pentelicus, Lycabettus* mountains near Athens

160 (p. 530) *putting the life of Father Damien into verse* Father Joseph Damien (1841–89) was a Belgian priest who worked at a leper colony. When Woolf visited Florence in April 1909, she met a woman poet who had written his life in verse (see *A Passionate Apprentice* pp. 400–1).

161 (p. 531) *character-mongering* In Woolf's essay 'Phases of Fiction' (1929), she settles on five phases cutting across history and genre: 'Truth-Tellers'; 'Romantics'; 'Character-Mongers and Comedians'; 'Psychologists'; and 'Poets'. She cites Charles Dickens as an example of a character-monger (*Essays*, V, p. 55).

162 (p. 531) *Wellington nose* The Duke of Wellington was nicknamed 'old nosey'.

163 (p. 535) *Euboea* the second largest Greek island, located north-west of Athens

164 (p. 536) *the poems of Donne* John Donne (1572–1631) was a metaphysical poet and preacher, born to a Catholic family in London in 1572.

165 (p. 536) *one after another lights were extinguished*   This foreshadows European statesman Sir Edward Grey's famous words in August 1914: 'The lamps are going out all over Europe; we shall not see them lit again in our lifetime.'

166 (p. 537) *Surbiton*   a suburban area of London in the Royal Borough of Kingston-upon-Thames

167 (p. 538) *Lombard Street and Fetter Lane*   two streets in the City's financial district

Chapter 13

168 (p. 539) *European mysticism*   Christianity and its trappings. Jacob prefers the Greek pagan rites.

169 (p. 540) *Troy*   An oblique hint that Jacob is reaching the end of his odyssey.

170 (p. 541) *the policy of Sir Edward Grey*   Sir Edward Grey (1862–1933) became Foreign Secretary in December 1905 and advocated a policy of peaceful negotiation. However, it is argued that had Grey clearly stated in late July 1914 that Britain either would or would not support France in the event of war, the conflict could have been avoided. With Lloyd George's ascent to power as Prime Minister in December 1916, Grey was replaced by Balfour as Foreign Secretary.

171 (p. 541) *the site of the old Exhibition*   the Great Exhibition of 1851 held in the Crystal Palace

172 (p. 541) *the statue of Achilles*   This statue by Sir Richard West-macott, erected in 1822 in honour of the Duke of Wellington, stands near Hyde Park Corner on the edge of Hyde Park.

173 (p. 542) *for Julia . . . liked to visit death-beds*   Virginia Woolf's mother, Julia Prinsep Stephen, was often occupied in the service of others less favourably circumstanced. She produced a privately printed booklet *Notes from Sick-Rooms* in 1883.

174 (p. 543) *Alceste*   from Molière's *Le Misanthrope* (1666)

175 (p. 544) *the Syrian desert*   Syria was part of the Turkish Empire until the end of the First World War.

176 (p. 544) *the paws of the slippery lions*   Four lions sit at the four corners of the base of Nelson's Column in Trafalgar Square; they were cast in bronze and designed by Edwin Landseer.

177 (p. 545) *the Reichstag*   the seat of the German parliament in Berlin

178 (p. 545) *Pitt and Chatham, Burke and Gladstone* statesmen: William Pitt, first Earl of Chatham (1708–78), his second son William Pitt (1759–1806), Edmund Burke (1729–97) and William Ewart Gladstone (1809–98)

179 (p. 545) *Blue Book* an official publication of the British Parliament, commonly known as such because of the blue cover traditionally used for its binding

180 (p. 545) *the Gaiety* popular music-hall in the Strand

181 (p. 546) *Kensington Palace* a Jacobean house, first adapted as a royal residence in 1689 by Sir Christopher Wren

182 (p. 546) *Aldridge's* The horse bazaar, or 'repository for horses and carriages', in Upper St Martin's Lane, WC2, was a well-known mart for horses at the time.

183 (p. 547) *The Phoenicians* Phoenicians traded for tin with the inhabitants of the southern coast of Britain.

184 (p. 547) *Greek women . . . until the ships in the Piraeus fired their guns* See *A Passionate Apprentice*, pp. 325, 328.

Chapter 14

185 (p. 548) *locked together at Mudie's corner* the location of the famous Circulating Library

186 (p. 548) *Jacob! Jacob!* Bonamy's anguished cry recalls the voice of Archer searching for his brother on the beach in the novel's opening pages.